ORDER OF THE DRAGON

ALLISON A. ANDREWS

ALSO BY ALLISON A ANDREWS

<u>The Order of the Dragon Trilogy (Paranormal Romance)</u>

Illusions – Order of the Dragon Book I

Blood Memories – Order of the Dragon Book II

Phoenix Rising – Order of the Dragon Book III

<u>Circle Of Friends (Contemporary Romance)</u>

The Winning Ticket

Chasing Horizons

Dance With Me

Pieces of Us

<u>Calgary Mounties (Hockey Romance)</u>

On Thin Ice

CONTENTS

ILLUSIONS

Song List   5
Prologue   7
Chapter 1   9
Chapter 2   15
Chapter 3   23
Chapter 4   33
Chapter 5   41
Chapter 6   51
Chapter 7   59
Chapter 8   69
Chapter 9   79
Chapter 10   91
Chapter 11   101
Chapter 12   117
Chapter 13   127
Chapter 14   141
Chapter 15   149
Chapter 16   161
Chapter 17   171
Chapter 18   185
Chapter 19   199
Chapter 20   207
Chapter 21   215
Chapter 22   225
Chapter 23   237
Chapter 24   245
Epilogue   257

BLOOD MEMORIES

Song List	265
Prologue	267
Chapter 1	269
Chapter 2	277
Chapter 3	285
Chapter 4	295
Chapter 5	305
Chapter 6	315
Chapter 7	329
Chapter 8	337
Chapter 9	347
Chapter 10	357
Chapter 11	363
Chapter 12	369
Chapter 13	375
Chapter 14	383
Chapter 15	393
Chapter 16	399
Chapter 17	407
Chapter 18	417
Chapter 19	427
Chapter 20	433
Chapter 21	439
Chapter 22	447
Chapter 23	453
Chapter 24	461
Chapter 25	467
Chapter 26	477
Chapter 27	487
Chapter 28	491
Epilogue	501

PHOENIX RISING

Song List   507
Prologue   509
Chapter 1   511
Chapter 2   517
Chapter 3   525
Chapter 4   533
Chapter 5   539
Chapter 6   545
Chapter 7   549
Chapter 8   555
Chapter 9   563
Chapter 10   571
Chapter 11   581
Chapter 12   587
Chapter 13   593
Chapter 14   597
Chapter 15   603
Chapter 16   611
Chapter 17   623
Chapter 18   629
Chapter 19   635
Chapter 20   643
Chapter 21   649
Chapter 22   655
Chapter 23   663
Chapter 24   671
Chapter 25   679
Chapter 26   685
Chapter 27   691
Chapter 28   697
Chapter 29   705
Chapter 30   711
Chapter 31   719
Chapter 32   723
Chapter 33   733

Chapter 34   741
Chapter 35   747
Chapter 36   753
Chapter 37   759
Chapter 38   765
Chapter 39   771
Chapter 40   777
Chapter 41   783
Chapter 42   791
Epilogue   797
If you have a moment   805
Acknowledgments   807

ILLUSIONS

BOOK ONE

SONG LIST

Hold On - Chord Overstreet
Without You - Ursine Vulpinr, Annaca
Ghost Town - Benson Boone
Take On The World - You and Me at Six
On The Rise - Generdyn, Bellsaint
Unsteady - X Ambassadors
Sanctuary - Welshly Arms
Not Your Baby - Cadmium, Jex
I Guess I'm in Love - Clinton Kane
Warriors - League of Legends, 2WEI, Edda Hayes
Survivor - 2 WEI, Edda Hayes
Everybody Wants To Rule The World - Lorde

PROLOGUE

I sat in my car, staring ahead momentarily, my mind racing and my heart beating a hundred miles an hour. These things just did not exist in real life. Yet, here I sat, staring at the scene before me. They moved so quickly, almost as if they were dancing with each other. Yet the end of the dance would culminate in one of their deaths. One protected me from the other, yet I still did not understand why. Why me? Why had I been chosen? Why was I the one who had to discover that the reality that so many others lived with was an illusion? To find out that the actual truth was so terrifying that it made me wish that my ignorance still protected me?

And most importantly... Why was I still sitting in this car when I could be gone by now? Surely normal, sane people did not wait to see who was about to win in a battle to the death when their own death would surely follow...

I guess I should start from the beginning...

CHAPTER ONE

"Happy Birthday Isolde," My identical twin sister, Aurora, said as she walked into my bedroom, and I woke groggily with a groan. Being reminded that I had just turned a quarter of a century old was not my ideal way to be woken up. I had once vowed that I would refuse to tell people how old I was after I turned twenty-one, and well... Twenty-five felt like a death sentence.

"Hey. Thanks. And happy birthday to you too," I managed to respond through the haze of the hangover that was currently holding me hostage. My head felt as though it had been invaded by a hive of bees, and I looked around, half expecting to see the bus that I was certain had hit me in the middle of the night.

"Big night?" Aurora grinned evilly at me, and I threw a cushion at her from where I had swept it onto the floor next to my bed the night before.

"Maybe just a little. A girl only turns twenty-five once, right?" I reached for the bottle of water that I had remembered putting next to my bed, wishing I had thought to take Panadol before falling asleep. I had long ago learned that alcohol and I were not a good mix, but my best friend Ainslie Wilson had insisted on taking me out for a girl's night before I turned twenty-five, and it had somehow turned into an alcohol-binging session. I was struggling to remember the activities of the night before, but all I could remember were random images that didn't make much sense to me.

Swearing never to drink again, I crept slowly out of bed, attempting to avoid the rush of blood to my head, and headed for the bathroom. One glimpse at myself in the mirror and I knew I resembled the Bride of Frankenstein. Or maybe the monster himself. Usually, my reflection was one that I was happy with. With green eyes, long dark reddish-brown hair, tanned skin, and a curvy figure, I knew I was attractive, and I normally took great pride in my appearance. However, I appeared to have forgotten to remove my make-up the night before, and my face looked more like the Joker from Batman than my usual clear-skinned, bright-eyed self.

"Wow... babe, you're a mess!" My boyfriend, Will Blake, entered the bathroom behind me and caught a look at my reflection as I gasped at it in horror. He seemed to realise it was the wrong thing to say as I glared at him through eyes that were ringed with smudged mascara.

"You think?! Remind me not to go out with Ainslie for a girl's night ever again," I grumbled as I turned the hot water on and stripped my pyjamas off. Will just shook his head, laughing, as he closed the door behind him, and I stepped under the steaming hot water.

As I washed the makeup off my face, I again struggled to make sense of the images from last night that flashed through my mind. I remembered having dinner with Ainslie, Will, and Ainslie's boyfriend, Alex. Then the rest of the night consisted of flashes of light, dancing, singing into a microphone drunkenly (I seriously hoped that was a nightmare and not something that I had actually done), then being in an alley with a man who seemed familiar to me, before being in the back of a taxi.

It was the image of the man that had me worried the most. What on earth had I been doing in an alley with a guy who wasn't Will?

The man's incredibly handsome face was not one that I recognised, yet there was something familiar about him. Like I was meant to know him. And that he knew me very well.

After an eternity in the shower, I stepped out, feeling marginally better, and dried myself off. I wrapped the towel around myself securely and returned to the bedroom I shared with Will. My clothes from the night before were strewn across the room, something that was usually unheard of. Both Aurora and Will constantly joked about my almost manic cleanliness.

"Oh, so you are going to work today?" Will asked, walking up behind me as I reached for the hideous uniform I was forced to wear to my job as a duty manager of Opalescence, a bar in the city. The uniform was for day shifts when the bar was respectable. Night shifts were less formal, and I could wear jeans and a singlet top. Showing the appropriate amount of cleavage, of course. By day, we served alcohol and pub meals to business people attending meetings, and by night, we served alcohol to those same business people, but they were different kinds of meetings they were attending then. Many a clandestine affair had both started and ended at Opalescence.

"Of course I'm going to work... Unless you have a better offer?" I smiled coyly as Will wrapped his arm around my bare waist.

"Oh, I have a better offer." He nuzzled my neck. "Happy birthday, by the way." I allowed myself to briefly close my eyes and lean back into him as he slowly kissed his way down my neck. A brief flicker of déjà vu that was gone too soon made me wish that I could stay standing there for longer. However, I knew I couldn't afford to miss work, and my boss wouldn't accept a hangover as a good enough excuse to call in sick, especially on my birthday.

"How about we pick this up tonight? I'm working until seven, and then I'm all yours." I gently pulled away from him and he sighed, knowing that there was no use. He was used to spending half of every weekend keeping himself amused. It was part of the reason we had moved in together in the first place.

"Sounds good. Want me to pick you up?" Will went to sit on the edge of the bed as I continued getting ready.

"No, I'll catch the ferry. You can cook dinner, though." I grinned at him, knowing that I would come home to pizza but not caring much. The idea of working with this hangover was scary enough without the thought of coming home to cook dinner.

I eventually made it out the door and drove to the City Cat ferry terminal. Grabbing my handbag, I headed to wait for the ferry, scrolling mindlessly through all my various social media apps while I stood behind several other commuters waiting on the gangway.

Suddenly, out of nowhere, a rush of images hit me, and I must have looked crazy as I struggled to stay upright. I had never experienced anything like this before, almost like psychic visions that you see people having in movies. I thought I must have been losing my mind. Or my imagination was running away with me, which was more than likely.

I was remembering more from my time in the alley with the mystery man, but the images I saw could not be right... He was whispering in my ear, trying to tell me something important. I could hear his voice in my ear, low and urgent, but it was as though the sound was down very low, and his words were nothing more than a low murmur... I could not for the life of me remember anything he said.

I had led what you would call a fairly normal, even boring, existence up until now. My mother swore that I was born mature and grew even wiser than her every day. My father said I had an old soul, that I had lived before. My sisters just thought I was boring and never had any fun. Of the opinions expressed, I was inclined to believe the latter above all the others. I had always done exactly what was expected of me. I had graduated high school with good grades, went to university, had a good job, and was in a relationship with the perfect guy... The only rebellious thing I ever did was to drop out of uni to travel to the UK and work. And that only ended up lasting four months because I missed Will too much, so I'd come back home and worked for a few years before going back to uni to finish my degree. So, that didn't explain the bizarre images in my mind right now.

I shook my head to clear it as I looked around to find myself already sitting on the City Cat, halfway to the city, the river winding away in front of me...

How on earth did that happen?

My apparent sleepwalking puzzled me as my mobile buzzed in my handbag. I pulled it out absentmindedly and read the text message from Ainslie, wishing me a happy birthday. I hadn't even thought about the fact that it was my birthday since I'd left home, and I suddenly realised that I had not received any presents yet. I was instantly ashamed that the thought had entered my mind. That was not what birthdays were about... Well, it shouldn't be what birthdays were about, at the very least.

But something had to make up for the fact that I was ageing, without my consent, I might add. Presents were just compensation for the ageing process once you turned twenty, and the next milestone birthday was thirty... Or even worse... Fifty. I shuddered at that thought.

I was pulled from my musings when a nearby tour guide started pointing out places of interest around us, and I found myself listening in with a small smile.

"So, welcome to Brisbane, Queensland's thriving capital city. It's the third biggest city in Australia, and it was built on either side of the river we are now on, the very originally named Brisbane River, which winds from beautiful Moreton Bay behind us, right up into the mountains you can see over there." She pointed with her little stick topped with a flag, and all the tourists nodded and smiled. "This river is a big part of the lives of all who live here, and we even have a festival once a year that is all about the river called the River Festival. We do love coming up with original-sounding names here, as you can tell." She tittered, and the tourists all laughed politely. I covered my snort with a cough.

"Brisbane's inhabitants are split between north-siders and south-siders, depending on which side of the river you hail from. We just got on at Bulimba, which is one of our inner city suburbs on the south side." I popped my headphones on to sit back and enjoy the ride along the river.

I always loved seeing people visit Brisbane and had heard the spiel given many times by different tour guides when they brought their groups on the ferry. Although I'd travelled some, I still loved my hometown. After heading to London when I was twenty, I knew how lucky I was to live in Australia, with our fantastic weather and laid-back attitude to life. I still enjoyed my time away, but I'd never been so happy to return to the sunshine state and the country of 'She'll be right, mate'. Even on a mid-winter day, all that was required was a singlet top and a warm jacket. Sure, we complained of being cold, but we really had nothing to complain about. And with how hot it was today, in the height of summer, I would have happily taken the winter chill over the heat that had me sweating whilst I sat at the back of the ferry.

Moving to slide my phone back into my handbag, I saw a flash of something on the inside of my wrist, something golden, and I turned my arm over to look, but there was nothing there.

Vowing never to drink again, as it now seemed to mean I was seeing things, I closed my eyes and attempted to clear my mind of visions and other weird occurrences before I had to start an eight-hour shift, helping other people become intoxicated instead.

CHAPTER TWO

I arrived home that night, pulled my car into the visitor space next to our townhouse and climbed out of the car, digging around in my handbag to find my house key. As I unlocked the front door, I was surprised to find all the lights out, as Will's car was still in the driveway.

Moving through the house, turning on lights as I went, I called out to Will without any response. I knew that Aurora wasn't at home, as she and her boyfriend, Jacob, were out celebrating Aurora's birthday together, but Will had messaged me ten minutes ago to see how much later I would be, so his absence now was strange. Coming to the top of the stairs, I could see a flickering light shining through the crack at the bottom of our bedroom door, and I moved to open it a little uncertainly, apprehensive of what I might find on the other side. My hand was still on the door handle, and it took me a moment to register what I was seeing before I let out a gasp at the scene before me.

The room was lit entirely by tea-light candles placed all around the room, with rose petals scattered all over the place. And there, lying on the bed on his side, propped up on one elbow, was Will, nervously playing with what looked like a ring box.

The look on my face must have been priceless as I gaped at him in shock. I raised a shaking hand to my mouth, watching as he rose to his feet and moved to stand in front of me, silently dropping to one knee and holding the ring box open in front of me.

"Isolde Smith... I love you more than I ever thought it was possible to love someone. Would you do me the honour of becoming my wife?" His voice was thick with emotion that he struggled to hide, and I was momentarily struck by how handsome he was, with his brown hair cut short and his perfect sun-kissed skin. Wearing a fitted t-shirt and jeans, I could appreciate the effect that regular hours in the gym and running had on his body.

Swaying in place for a moment, my heart swelled, and I had to remind myself to breathe. After another stunned moment of silence, I dropped my handbag and flung myself at him as he rose to meet me. I kissed him hard, unable to think straight. We had talked about getting married for a while, but I had no idea he had been planning this. I felt as though the breath had been knocked out of me.

"Is that a yes?" He asked with a grin as he stepped back to look at me. I smiled at him, rapidly blinking to keep the happy tears from escaping my eyes, and simply nodded, unable to speak. I couldn't imagine marrying anyone else. With a small laugh, he lifted me off the ground and swung me around for a moment before setting me back down and kissing me softly. We looked down together as he slid the most perfect ring onto my finger.

"I had this designed months ago. I hope you like it?" He asked nervously as I stared at the elegant ring that now sat on my left ring finger. Vintage inspired, with a large square diamond set in a white gold band, it was surrounded by multiple little diamonds and garnets, my birthstone.

"It's gorgeous! I couldn't have chosen better if I tried." I held my hand out before me, transfixed, as I turned my hand this way and that, the diamonds catching the light of the candles nearest to me. I could stare at it all night.

"That's fantastic... Now go get ready 'cause we're going to your parents for dinner." He smacked me playfully on the butt, and I was momentarily knocked out of my happy place, looking up into Will's smirking face in surprise.

"What? You propose to me, then drag me off to my parent's house to have dinner... What's so romantic about that?" I asked, attempting to keep the disappointment out of my voice. I thought a romantic dinner at home followed by a mind-blowing love-making session was in order, not a forced visit to my parent's house.

"Sorry, babe, but they rang today to confirm that we were going there for dinner for your birthday. Did you maybe forget to mention something about that after you last spoke to your mother?" I wracked my brain, trying to remember the details of my previous conversation with my mother last week. She may have mentioned something, but I couldn't remember saying yes. Knowing my mother, that didn't matter.

"Surely, when you told them you were proposing, Mum would have understood?" Even saying the words, I knew that wasn't likely, and Will laughed as he shook his head.

"Have you met your mother? I'm surprised she didn't insist that she was sitting in the room as it happened. This was the compromise, propose first on my own, then hand you over to them all." Will's eyes twinkled as he grinned with a shrug, and I sighed, knowing full well that there was no point in trying to get out of it.

"Fine." I pouted, and after a few more kisses of joy, I headed into the bathroom to get ready for a visit to my family.

As I stood in the shower, I paused to think about what had just happened. I was now engaged. I had a fiance... Perhaps even harder to grasp was that *I* was someone's fiancee. I remembered the first time Will had ever called me his girlfriend, back when we were nineteen, and I felt the same tingle of excitement run up my spine at the thought. At the time, I had already been referring to him as my boyfriend to my friends, but we had never actually used those words in front of one another, and I was so excited when he was the first one to say it. I was sure I would feel the same excitement when I heard him use the word fiancee for the first time. I tried hard not to even think about what my reaction would be the first time he used the word wife... It was all a lot for a girl to take in on her twenty-fifth birthday... However, it was something I could get used to.

We arrived at my parent's house, and I knew instantly that Mum had told my sisters. Aurora and I were the youngest and second set of twins in the family. My five other sisters, Briseis, Dido, Guinevere, and fraternal twins, Selena and Aphrodite were all gathered in the lounge room of my parent's house as Will and I walked through the front door. My mother had a thing for mythological names, probably to compensate for our rather standard last name. There was a look of bittersweet happiness on my twin's face, which I assumed was because this was just another step towards adulthood that we had to take together.

Everyone held their collective breaths, and my sisters all sat on the edges of their seats, each trying to get a glimpse of my left hand. With a grin, I held my hand up and was immediately set upon by six screeching women who ranged in age from twenty-five to thirty-two. The chaos was interrupted as my mother and father entered the room, followed closely by five children, my nieces and nephew, who had been in the kitchen hounding my mother about dinner. My sisters' collective partners were already out on the back patio, and Will quickly made his escape to join them, closely followed by my father after he gave me a congratulatory hug.

"So, how long has everyone known about this?" I eventually got the chance to ask as they all sat back down again, and I joined Aurora on the floor.

As the women of my family all answered at once, I marvelled at my luck to have such a close family. My parents had both come from big families and had wanted a tribe of their own. My mother was the youngest of ten, with three older brothers and six older sisters, and my father was the youngest of twelve, with six older brothers and five older sisters. When they started their own family, they continued to try for a boy but eventually gave up with the arrival of a second set of twin girls. My dad had to settle for seven tomboys instead. We had all enjoyed camping and fishing as children, and we had still maintained our strong family bond. We were all just lucky that the partners we had each found were happy to be with women whose family was their world.

I listened absently as Aurora began telling us about Will's plan to have her out of the house so he could propose tonight, as my youngest and favourite niece, Annelise, crawled into my lap. She was Briseis' daughter, and I had recently been named her godmother, something that I was immensely proud of. I played with her curls, seeing another flash of gold on the inside of my wrist. However, as soon as I looked down at my wrist properly, it was gone again. Refusing to give any more brain space to strange occurrences, I put it down to a trick of the light. I sighed contentedly. I hoped my life would always be this way, surrounded by family and loved by a man who would never leave me...

As I lay asleep in Will's arms later that night, I was pulled into a vivid dream.

"Isolde, you have to be careful. It's starting." I ran to keep up with the man in front of me as he signalled for me to follow him. He was at least a head taller than me, and I raced to try and keep up with him through the fog swirling around us.

"What's starting? Why do I need to be careful?" I had to yell as he was getting further and further ahead of me, slowly melting away into the fog with each step until all I could make out was a shadow.

I could hear the faintest laugh that slowly began to get louder behind me. I turned in a half circle as the laugh took on a sinister tone, filling the space all around me. My heart started to race with fear, and I clapped my hands over my ears and fell to my knees as the laughter began to echo inside my head, making my ears ring.

It ended abruptly, and now the sound of my breathing echoed through the fog.

"Get up! We need to get out of here!" As I tried to get back on my feet, the man appeared at my side and took hold of my arm. I kept a close eye on him as he surveyed our surroundings with a great deal of anxiety. I was struck by his intensely handsome features; his dark brown hair, chiselled jawline, and sun-kissed skin left me in awe. He stood tall and had a well-defined physique, with his muscles showing through his shirt sleeves. However, what truly caught my attention were his eyes; they were a striking shade of blue that seemed almost unreal.

A shadow crept closer behind him, bringing my focus back to the situation we were in, and I let out a piercing scream as the laughter resumed, even louder than before. Squinting through the thick fog, I could only make out the silhouette of a man, but his piercing blue eyes shone through.

"Isolde." It was almost as though the shadows sang my name, and a chill ran through me. "We will find you, Isolde. He can't keep you from us forever, Isolde." Never had the sound of my name been so terrifying. The voice that spoke sounded ancient and sinister, and I began to shake.

The man in front of me whirled to face the shadowy figure behind him, just as it was joined by another with the same eyes, another laugh joining the one that was already deafening me. I couldn't make out if this figure was a male or female.

My companion urged me to run, yelling the word as he charged into the fog to face the shadowy figures. I strained to see through the haze, but all I could discern were muffled sounds of battle. Suddenly, a woman's voice whispered urgently in my ear. "It's not time yet, Isolde. You need to wake up!"

I sat up with a start, my breathing ragged, as the darkness of my bedroom replaced the images from my dream.

"Babe? What's wrong?" Will's voice cut through the darkness, groggy, and I could tell that I'd woken him up.

"Sorry baby... Just a weird dream... Go back to sleep." His breathing evened out again, and I envied his ability to fall asleep so quickly. I gently pushed back the covers and climbed out of bed, going into the adjoining bathroom to get a drink of water.

After a quick glance at myself in the mirror, I refused to look at my reflection, not wanting to see the paleness of my skin and dark circles under my eyes. That dream had done a number on me, and my hand shook slightly as I turned on the tap to fill my glass.

As my grasp on reality slowly returned, I was puzzled at what I'd just seen. The man who had been protecting me in the dream was the same man from my sketchy memories from the night before. There was something eerily familiar about him. But it was the two shadowy figures that concerned me the most. Even now, I could hear that laugh ringing in my ears, and another shiver ran through me. There was something very sinister about that laugh. And what did that voice mean about finding me? Whatever it was, I was certain I didn't want the owner of that laugh to ever find me.

But it was just a dream, right?

CHAPTER THREE

Our engagement party was the weekend before I returned to university for my final semester. My parents had offered to host it for us, as our townhouse wasn't big enough for all of our family and friends to gather.

After Will proposed, the weeks had flown by in a flurry of engagement invitations and wedding preparations. We agreed that a spring wedding in September would be perfect, but we had limited time to organise everything. Thankfully, my bridesmaids, Ainslie and Aurora, were incredibly supportive and enthusiastic about the dress designs and colours I had chosen. Throughout the entire process, Will was an amazing fiance. He made sure to be involved in every step of the planning, and we ultimately decided on a garden wedding at his grandparents' property in the Gold Coast Hinterland. The location was not only breathtakingly beautiful but also cost-effective. I kept waiting for something to go wrong, but everything was turning out perfectly.

We spent the day rushing around madly with my sisters and parents, making all the final arrangements, and when the first of the guests arrived, I was still upstairs in my old bedroom, putting the finishing touches on my outfit. Will entered the room behind me and stood looking at me as I turned to face him and struck a pose.

"How do I look?" I asked as he walked forward, wrapping me in his arms, the love in his eyes threatening to make me cry and ruin my makeup.

"Like the woman that I can't wait to marry in eight months," he said huskily, kissing me on the forehead. I hugged him tightly, wishing that I didn't have to go down and play hostess. I rose onto my tip toes to kiss him softly, and he wove his fingers through my hair in the way he knew I loved. I deepened the kiss, pressing my body closer, and his other hand slid down my back before coming to rest on my hip. I felt his grip tighten as I wrapped a leg around him, and I could feel him begin to harden against my abdomen as he started kissing down my neck. I did nothing to stop the moan escaping my lips as I arched my back and ground myself against him, causing him to emit a low groan.

"Damn, Isolde, whatever is going on with your libido lately, I'm loving it." His words were muffled against my neck as he reached between us.

Just as he was about to slide his fingers beneath the band of my underwear, my father called my name from downstairs, announcing the arrival of our first guest. Will sighed as I reluctantly pulled away, and we shared a look confirming that we would pick this up later. I had long since discovered that the members of my family were fantastic at killing the mood.

Hours later, the party was in full swing, and I entered the kitchen to organise another platter of food, happy to have a second to myself. I hadn't slept well for weeks, and it was beginning to take its toll on me. There was nothing I wanted more right now than to curl up beside Will and fall into a dreamless sleep.

I took a moment to close my eyes and leaned against the pantry door, allowing myself to think of the nightmares that had been plaguing me since my birthday. Always the same, and yet they made no sense to me at all. Images of violence and creatures that were human in appearance, but their faces were cruel, their eye teeth replaced by fangs.

Will told me that I had taken to talking in my sleep, something that I had never done before, and the lack of sleep was affecting him too. Two mornings ago, I had awoken to discover that he had moved to the couch in the middle of the night to sleep without being awoken by my cries of "No, please don't!" He was concerned that it was because of all the stress of the wedding and returning to uni, but I could only hope it was that simple. Something about the dreams made me think that the stress of my everyday life had nothing to do with it at all. I was still seeing flashes of something gold on the inside of my right wrist. It was like when you see a movement in the corner of your eye, but it's gone when you look right at it. Maybe I was just losing the plot.

"Babe, you okay?" Ainslie interrupted my musings as she came in search of me, looking to help with the food.

"Yeah, I'm okay. Just tired." I gave my best friend of fifteen years a quick hug before busying myself with the food platters. Ainslie hesitated as she looked at me for a moment, before starting to cut up more cheese and cabana. I could see her looking at me every few minutes as we chatted about superficial things, the concern on her face obvious.

The doorbell rang and I left Ainslie with the food to see who it was. I opened the front door and smiled at my fathers' brother, James, and his wife, Sophia, my favourite uncle and aunt.

"Hey guys, we were wondering where you were! Now the party can really get started." I kissed them both on the cheek and took their jackets.

As I turned to close the door behind them, the hairs on the back of my neck suddenly stood on end, and I froze, looking out into the darkness. Although I could see no reason for my sudden anxiousness, something kept me from moving. I knew, without a doubt, that something was watching me from the darkness. Something with ice blue eyes.

"Isolde? What's wrong, honey? Is someone else coming in?" Sophia came to stand beside me for a moment, looking outside as well. I forced myself to smile and shut the door firmly, locking the deadbolt.

"No, no one's there. I just saw the neighbour's dog, that's all." I sucked at lying, and my aunt and uncle looked at me with a fleeting look of concern before I hurried them out to the backyard. We had strung fairy lights through the trees and along the fence to make it more inviting for people to sit outside, as the house was just too hot with this many people to be inside. My aunt commented how beautiful it all looked, and I answered automatically, my mind still on the presence that I had felt outside.

I wished that I could talk to someone about it, but something was stopping me. I had no idea why I felt that I couldn't tell anyone, but nothing about the situation made any sense to me at all. I looked over to where Will and Aurora stood away from the others. From the look on Will's face, Aurora was saying something that was concerning to him, and he looked up, noticing me watching them. After a beat, he smiled at me, and Aurora followed his gaze. She hesitated briefly before smiling as well. I couldn't help wondering if they were talking about me, as neither of their smiles seemed to meet their eyes. Probably discussing what the hell was going on with me...

Somehow, I managed to make it through the rest of the engagement party without any more incidents. I was even game enough to bravely say goodbye to each of the guests, walking them to their cars with

Will at my side. I no longer felt the presence that I had felt before, though I could sense that someone was still out in the darkness, watching me. I didn't know whether that was more or less alarming. Not only was someone watching me in the dark, but there appeared to be more than one person out there.

After all the guests had left, we got to work tidying everything up with the help of both our families. This was the worst part about having a party at home... the dreaded cleanup.

"Isolde, is everything alright? You've been spaced out all night." Aurora came up beside me, shaking me out of my reverie, as I stood with a garbage bag in my hand, staring off into space.

"Yeah, just tired." I went back to collecting rubbish, though my twin continued to look worried.

"Will said you've been having nightmares. Are you sure nothing's worrying you?" I could see that Aurora wasn't going to let it go, but there wasn't anything that I could think of to tell her. Everything in me wanted to tell her what I had been feeling. I desperately wanted to share the details of my weird dreams about the blue-eyed men, but from the time that this all started, the instinct not to share the horrors with anyone else had stopped me from saying anything to my loved ones. People would think that I was going insane... And who was to say that I wasn't?

I looked at my twin and smiled. "I guess I'm just stressed, consumed with wedding plans and so on."

I resumed collecting rubbish, hoping that my words were enough to stop her from asking any more questions. Soon after, Aurora wandered away to busy herself with stacking chairs.

Why was it so important for me not to tell anyone? I never kept secrets from my sister or Will, yet now, here I was, lying to both of them, pretending to be fine when my head felt like it was running around in circles trying to work out this mystery. Who were the two terrifying men in my dreams? Why was my mystery man protecting me from them? All of these questions were constantly plaguing me, and I had no answers.

I had a strong feeling that something had shifted within me, and I couldn't shake the sense that something bad was on the horizon.... That particular thought was not helping me sleep at night, even without the nightmares.

The following Monday, I caught the City Cat to university, ready to begin the final semester of my degree. I didn't have any idea what I would end up doing, but I had always had a keen interest in the lives of those in the past, so had majored in European History. It was probably a good thing that Will earned good money as a property developer, as I wasn't likely to be rolling in money any time soon.

I stared out the window as the City Cat flew along the river. I enjoyed people watching, observing as the tourists snapped photos of the massive houses along the river, gazed up at the Story Bridge and pointed to the various landmarks along the way. This sure beat catching the train or the bus, and I smiled, letting the wind whip my hair around my face as we sped along the river. Leaning my head back against the headrest, I closed my eyes and finally experienced the much-needed sense of peace and tranquillity that I had been yearning for over the past few weeks.

My first lecture for the day was Witchcraft and Demonology, a subject that I had been looking forward to studying ever since I had started my degree. I'd deliberately left it to my last semester so that I had at least one subject that didn't stress me out to the point of crying, as had been the case with one of my third-year subjects the semester before.

I took my laptop out and turned it on, looking around to see if anyone I knew was in this class as well. I spotted a few familiar faces and smiled at acquaintances that I had made over the past few years. I had just started to return my attention to my computer when I recognised someone, and I froze, as it was someone that could not possibly be there.

It can't be him, surely.

I had been seeing this mystery man in my dreams for weeks now. The only face that was clear amongst all the madness. However, I still had no idea who he was, and now he had appeared in the flesh. Gorgeous as ever, he walked up the stairs to the back of the lecture theatre and looked completely at ease.

I must be hallucinating. Or am I still dreaming?

It would be a nice change to my nightmares of late, but I knew, even as I pinched myself, that this was not a dream. I stared in wonder, shocked to discover that this man existed and was no longer a figment of my imagination. Maybe I had noticed him at some point over the past couple of years, and my subconscious was putting his face on my mystery man. However, if that was the case, I was certain I would have remembered this guy before now. He looked like someone I would normally only see in a magazine. Because people this stunning did not exist without airbrushing and makeup. While Will was attractive, this man was on a whole different level.

He took a seat at the very back of the room, and it wasn't until he gazed directly at me that I realised that I was completely turned around in my seat, staring at him. I wanted to turn away, but his eyes held me, transfixed. We gazed at each other for what could have been an eternity.

Everything about him pulled me in, and although we were separated by several rows of other people, it felt like we were the only ones in the room. He felt dangerous, yet I knew, without a doubt, that I would be completely safe with him.

It wasn't until the lecturer started speaking that I turned back to face the front of the room, embarrassed at how long I had been staring. I shook my head to attempt to remove all distractions from my mind, wanting to take everything in. When I looked down at my keyboard, I saw a hint of gold on the inside of my wrist once again. But this time, it didn't disappear straight away, and I got a proper glimpse of what had been slowly driving me a little mad. If someone had asked me what it was, I wouldn't have been able to describe it, but it was as though a golden tattoo of something was there, just beneath my skin.

The person beside me cleared their throat loudly, and I jumped, having momentarily forgotten where I was. When I glanced back down, my wrist was bare once again.

I managed to take lecture notes, but knowing that the person who could potentially answer all of my questions was sitting only a few rows behind me was enough to distract even the most dedicated of students. I had to fight the urge to turn around on more than one occasion, especially as I could feel his eyes on me. It was at that moment that something occurred to me.

His eyes.

In my dreams, his eyes were blue. But now they were brown... The eyes of my mystery man were so distinct that there was no way I could have imagined them. They were the most piercing blue I'd ever seen before; there was just something about them. Those same eyes were on the other two figures in my dreams, and yet the mystery man's eyes had a quality to them. I did not fear his eyes as I did the eyes of the other two. Although he sat a few rows behind me, I would have been able to see those eyes from a mile away. It couldn't be him... and yet, everything else about him was the same...

As the lecture ended, I gathered my belongings as quickly as I could, but I didn't see him leave, even though I had kept my eyes on the door the whole time. One of my friends came over to talk to me, but I craned my neck to look around her, trying to work out where he'd gone. It was as if he had vanished. One more thing to add to the mystery.

Just what I need, another thing to obsess over.

I spent the rest of the day looking for him in my other class and all over the campus, but I never saw him again. I wished that I could call Aurora or even Ainslie and talk to them about this, but they would wonder why I was obsessing over some guy when I was getting married to the perfect man.

Maybe that was the key to all of this!

Perhaps I was subconsciously scared to get married, and I was making up all these crazy things as a way to let my fears out. I was sure that was what a psychologist would say, like the words of the one I saw briefly when I was young. I hadn't thought about that period of my life in such a long time, but I realised now with a start that the reason I had been taken to see a psychologist at the time was that I was having weird dreams... I was told by my family that I had woken them on several occasions, screaming in terror, but I was never able to remember them when I awoke.

They had started not long after a childhood friend of both mine and Aurora's, Bianca, had mysteriously disappeared one day when we were six. No one had ever found her, but Aurora and I were the last people to see her. I shivered at this memory, and I realised then that I needed to stop thinking about all of these things and just let them go, but I didn't know how to. It was consuming me, and it was starting to worry the people that I loved.

As I sat on the City Cat on the way home that evening, I made the decision that I was going to let it go. I was going to stop imagining that someone was watching me in the dark, and I would find some way to help stop the nightmares. I had no idea how I was going to accomplish these things, but I needed to try. Otherwise, my life would begin to unravel, and I could not have that happen.

CHAPTER FOUR

After making that decision to push my issues aside, I was able to make a conscious effort to return to normal. Although I did still have the nightmares, they were not as constant, and after almost six weeks, they occurred only once or twice a week. I avoided seeking faces in a crowd for fear that I would start seeing the face of my mystery man everywhere. I had managed to get day shifts at work for a few weeks, and I used assignments as excuses not to go out, avoiding leaving the house after dark... And for now, I was breathing again...

I finally started to resemble my former self again. Will's sleeping patterns had now returned to normal, as I no longer kept him awake every night because of my nightmares. I still had not been able to rid myself of the constant sensation of being watched. It wasn't always a sinister feeling, but even when I felt protected, there was still the knowledge that someone was watching me from the darkness at night. And I was still seeing flashes of gold on the inside of my wrist occasionally when I moved my arm.

It was our sixth anniversary, and Will was determined to take me out to dinner to celebrate. I had just completed my final mid-semester exams with flying colours and was able to take a brief reprieve from my hectic study schedule.

As I dressed to go out, I ignored the anxiety I was feeling about leaving the house at night, and I allowed myself to daydream, recalling that night six years ago when our relationship had finally changed. I'd had a crush on him for years, all through high school, and on that fateful April day, a group of us had gone out for an evening of fun. We'd somehow separated from the others and ended up wandering through South Bank Parklands. Stopping to admire the view of the city, I'd turned to say something to him as we found a bench to sit on. Something in the way he was looking at me caused me to stop and take a breath. It was as if he'd just suddenly realised that I was no longer the little girl in pigtails that I'd been all those years ago.

He had cupped my face gently in one hand, looked at me for a moment, and then kissed me softly. After what felt like an eternity, he looked at me again and said, 'I just wanted to know what it would be like to kiss you."

"And what was it like?" I'd managed to whisper, unable to believe that this was happening.

"Like something that I could get used to," he'd whispered back, and we had continued to kiss until our group of friends happened upon us again.

They'd all been taking bets as to how long it would be before Will finally woke up to the fact that I was there, and none of them was even the slightest bit surprised.

We started dating after that, even though I had plans to head to the UK in six months. Will was adamant that I shouldn't give up those plans for him. We did take a break from our relationship while I was away, but we kept in touch, and neither of us dated anyone else in the months I was gone. We knew we had something special, and I was more than happy to step into his waiting arms when I got off the plane.

We had been together ever since, and I thanked my lucky stars every day that Will had finally seen me.

Will had the night all planned out. He'd told me to wear something comfortable but dressy, so I wore my favourite dress, which happened to be one of Will's favourites as well. I was reminded of this when he looked at me appreciatively as I walked out of the bathroom, commenting that maybe we should just stay in instead. I smiled at him coyly, and it took quite a lot of effort on both our parts to walk out the door instead of stripping that dress off right then and there.

The night was young, and I climbed into Will's new work car, curious about where he was taking me, as he had been adamant about keeping it a surprise. He drove into Fortitude Valley, holding my hand the whole time, looking at me every chance he got.

As soon as Will pulled into the car park, I knew exactly where he was taking me. It was a restaurant that relied solely on word of mouth for advertising and was tucked away in an unnamed building. I had been there several years ago for a friend's birthday and had fallen madly in love with it. There were no chairs, just pillows on the floor on either side of a low table, and each group of diners were curtained off to give the illusion of privacy, although you could hear everything that happened around you. It was dimly lit and intimate, and it was exactly how I wanted to celebrate our anniversary.

I turned to Will as we waited to be seated, kissing him softly in the hallway that resembled a rainforest.

"Thank you for being so good to me. I don't think I could have ever asked for anyone more perfect to fall in love with."

"And here I was thinking that I was the one who'd won the prize. I have never been happier in my whole life than when I'm with you."

He took my hand and squeezed it as the waitress led us to our curtained-off area, tucked away in the back corner. We sat side by side, our fingers entwined as we talked. Still waiting for the waitress to return, I excused myself to go to the ladies and made my way through the maze of curtains.

After washing my hands, I redid my lipstick, and I caught yet another glimpse of the mark on my wrist. I ignored it, choosing to forget about visions and weird marks. I knew that my state of bliss was evident on my face, and I was happy it was there for the entire world to see. This was exactly how a woman in love was supposed to look.

I returned to the table, and Will pulled me back down to sit close beside him, putting an arm around me and running his fingers down my arm slowly.

"I ordered you a Pina Colada." He leaned in and nuzzled my neck. I felt a shiver run through me at the feeling of his breath on my skin, and he let out a low chuckle.

"I've been thinking about this for weeks, especially with how easy it's been to make you come lately," he whispered in my ear as he ran a hand up my leg, slowly slipping it under my dress. He trailed light kisses slowly down my neck before returning to claim my mouth as his hand began working its way under the lace band of my under-wear, causing me to gasp against his lips.

"I do love the privacy in this place. Almost as much as I love the sight of you in that dress." I was too turned on to utter a response, and I reached my hand up to tangle my fingers in his hair, pulling him closer and kissing him back hungrily. Being so sensitive to his touch came in handy, and within minutes, I was moaning against his mouth, coming as he worked his hand expertly between my legs.

Will moved back a fraction and smirked. "I knew I'd love that. Watching you come undone and knowing anyone could walk in at any moment." I looked at him with a smile, trying to regain my breath. The excitement of what we had just done swirled within me, and I was more than aware of how flushed I was. I went to respond to him, but at that moment, the waitress appeared with our drinks.

"Ready to order?" She handed us our drinks, and Will grinned at me before glancing up at her as I worked to get myself under control. I noticed that I was holding the menu upside down, and I felt Will fighting not to laugh beside me as he answered her.

"We'll just need another few minutes."

After a few hours that flew by too quickly, Will asked for our bill and we left the restaurant. As we walked back to the car, the unsettling feeling of being watched overwhelmed me and I stopped for a moment to look behind us. I'd had a few cocktails and the world had taken on the slightly fuzzy look that it got after consuming a few too many alcoholic beverages. There was no one else around, and I didn't know if this should relieve or scare me. Will turned to look as well, before looking down at me, concerned.

"What's wrong?" There was an edge to his voice, and I forced myself to look up at him with a smile.

"Nothing. I just thought I heard something. Guess I was just imagining it." But as I breathed these words of comfort, Will was knocked off his feet with such force that his hand was ripped from mine.

I screamed as a dark shape landed on top of him, moving with such speed that all I could make out was a blur of motion, as Will cried out in pain. I rushed forward to rip him free but froze as the thing that was holding him down turned and snarled at me. It was a man, of that much I could see, but he looked feral. His face was twisted in rage, but what scared me most were his eyes. They were piercing blue.

I didn't know what to do other than continue to scream, trying to pull him away, wanting to help Will but unable to rip the creature from him. It continued to attack Will in a frenzy, and his screams mingled with my own.

The creature (surely it couldn't be a man) moved with such frightening speed that I could barely make out its movements as it slashed at Will, and not just with its hands, but with teeth that almost looked like fangs. He threw me off him and I landed on the ground with a thud.

Rising to my feet, I rushed forward again, finally managing to shove the creature from Will's now silent form lying on the ground. As it wheeled to turn its fury on me, another blur of motion knocked it to the ground, and I fell to my knees beside Will, lifting his head into my lap. Blood gushed from the wounds all over his face, neck and chest.

So much blood.

I was completely ignorant of the fight that was happening behind me until the noise stopped. I looked up and locked eyes with my rescuer, only to realise that I already knew who it would be. The eyes of my mystery man, the same piercing blue from my dreams, were looking at me with utter devastation as I continued to rock Will in my arms, begging him to open his eyes.

"Please, baby, come on! Don't you dare leave me!" I begged him with everything in me, and still, he did not move. I turned to look up at my rescuer again, as he stood motionless, staring down at Will's still form.

"Please, help me! I don't know what to do!" I sobbed imploringly, and he hesitantly took a step forward. As he did so, two police officers tore around the corner, having been alerted by my screams. With a fleeting glance at me once more, the mystery man disappeared so quickly it was as if he had never been there.

The officers arrived at my side and began asking me questions, but all I could do was ask them for help repeatedly, unable to comprehend anything beyond the fact that Will still had not opened his eyes. One officer managed to lead me away, but I refused to look away from where her co-worker attempted to revive Will.

An ambulance arrived moments later, and the two paramedics set to work on my fiance as the police officers again attempted to question me. I managed to tell them vaguely what had happened, that a crazed man had attacked us, but that another man had arrived and fought him off. I couldn't tell them if a weapon had been used because I had no memory of seeing one. I was sure that the man had used his bare hands. And possibly his teeth. It was all a blur of screams and snarls.

They loaded Will into the ambulance, and we raced to the hospital with the siren wailing...

At 9:43pm, he was pronounced dead on arrival.

CHAPTER FIVE

I couldn't breathe. This could not be happening. I must be in one of my nightmares again. I felt as though I was floating, and I wished that I could wake up. I sat motionless on the hospital bed, being treated for shock, unable to take in anything that was happening around me.

I did manage to look up when my parents flew into the room, anguish and grief written all over their faces as my mother took me in her arms, crying and rocking me. It was then that it hit me, and I began to shake uncontrollably. I realised that I was not just shaking, as I started heaving with great, racking sobs. My father hugged both my mother and me, unable to handle my grief, wanting to take my pain away as all fathers are supposed to. But how do you save your child from the pain of losing the love of their life?

Sunlight streamed through the window, and I awoke slowly, reaching for Will as I did every morning. Only the bed was empty beside me. I opened my eyes slowly and was confused to find myself in my bedroom at my parent's house.

What am I doing here? And where is Will?

Slowly, my mind drifted back to the events of the night before, and I lay in agony, feeling as though my heart had been ripped from my chest. I lay like this for what may have been minutes or hours until my mother came into the room to check on me.

"Honey? Are you awake?" I couldn't answer as my throat was raw from crying, and I just stared at the ceiling. Aurora entered the room after my mother, her face tear-stained. I didn't react as she lay down beside me, but once she wrapped her arms around me, the tears began to flow again, and I buried my face into her chest as she rocked me, crying just as hard as I was.

My mother sat on the edge of the bed, smoothing my hair in a way that only a mother can, unsure of what else she could do for me. Our family had never been touched by a tragedy such as this, and none of us knew how to get through it. But eventually, my sobs died down, and I fell asleep again, welcoming the deep, black void of nothingness because there was nothing left for me when I was awake.

The following days were a blur. Will's family and mine gathered in silence. No one could find the words to express how we were feeling, least of all me. I hadn't spoken since the hospital, not even to Aurora. Will's sister handled the funeral arrangements, as I was no use to anyone, and Will's mother was in a similar state. Will's father just sat stiffly with his arm around his wife, his eyes staring into a far-off place, no doubt a place where his son still lived and where there was no talk of muggings and death.

The police had arrived the day after the attack to get my statement, but my mother had asked them to wait for when I was ready, explaining that I could barely speak, let alone think, about the events of that night.

However, all I did was think about that night. I played the scene over and over in my head, day and night, trying to work out what I could have done. My sisters were taking turns sitting with Aurora and me, as I could barely handle having her out of my sight for longer than it took for either of us to go to the bathroom. I wished that it had been me that the creature had gone for. But then, Will would be here, experiencing the pain that I was in, and I couldn't wish that on him. Surely, death would be easier than the thought of a future in which the love of your life no longer existed?

If only I had been able to pull the thing off of him. If only I had not paused to look back, we would have seen what was in front of us. If only my mystery rescuer had arrived earlier, he could have stopped the creature before it even crossed our path.

If only, if only, if only…

The day of the funeral dawned bright and sunny, and I lay in bed cursing the world. Had I led too blessed a life up until now? Had the Fates decided that I needed to have a bucket full of trauma to make up for years of unknown bliss? If that was the case, couldn't they have given me some sort of warning so that I could have appreciated everything more? I looked back over the years with Will and felt so much agony at all the moments that I took for granted. No one expects the love of their life to die. It was just too much to deal with.

"Isolde? Are you awake?" Aurora entered the darkened room, two steaming mugs in her hands, letting the sunlight from the hallway spill in behind her. As far as I was concerned, the sunlight was taunting me. Just reminding me that I had been living a carefree life, and now I was paying for it.

Putting the cups on the bedside table, Aurora crawled into the bed next to me and put her arms around me. We had both been staying at our parents' house since Will had died, with Jacob dropping into the townhouse to get us anything we needed. I just couldn't face the house yet. It was too painful. I felt as though I had no more tears left to cry, and I was sure that everyone around me was worried about my numbness. I was just too exhausted from the lack of sleep, the constant thinking and worrying.

"Are you going to be okay today?" Aurora was still pushing me to talk, whereas everyone else had given up. I was grateful not to have to answer questions with the others, but Aurora had been persistent. I turned to face her and studied her face for a moment.

"Aura, I don't think I'm ever going to be okay again." My voice was croaky from lack of use, but Aurora just looked relieved that my silence seemed to have been broken finally.

The funeral was moving, as funerals are meant to be, but I had little memory of it by that evening. The night of the funeral felt as though the end of my life with Will was now finalised. He was buried now, so I was meant to start moving forward again. Of course, no one was going to say that to me, and maybe they didn't even feel that way. Perhaps it was just me projecting my own feelings onto the situation, but I couldn't help the way I was feeling. Aurora kept hovering, and my parents never let me out of their sight, but I was starting to feel claustrophobic in my old bedroom. It was time to return to my home. To begin to pick up the pieces of my former self.

It was late in the night when I pulled up in front of the house, which no longer felt as welcoming as it used to. Now it was just a painful reminder of what would no longer be. I would have to sell it. There was no way I could afford to live here without Will's income to pay the mortgage, and the memories that it held were too painful to endure.

I sat in my car, staring at the front door for what felt like hours, when a movement in my rear-view mirror jerked me from my reverie. Before I had a chance to do anything more than squint at the reflection in the mirror, the driver's side door was flung open, and I was pulled roughly from the car.

"You shouldn't be here. It isn't safe." A body pressed me firmly against the rear passenger door, and I gasped as I looked up into the face of the man who had jerked me from the car. With a faint trace of an Irish accent, all I could do was stare into the eyes of my mystery man. I hadn't been this close to him in our previous physical interactions, but I remembered now just how tall he was, as I had to crane my neck to look up at him when we stood this close together. Eventually, I found my voice as he looked around, obviously searching for the danger he was talking about.

"Well, I would say that's obvious, seeing as you've just taken it upon yourself to rip me out of my otherwise safe car." He looked back at me briefly as I spoke before continuing to scan the area, barely acknowledging my words. I was starting to get annoyed, a feeling that I should be grateful for, as it was the first emotion I'd felt since Will's death that had managed to make its way through my mind-numbing grief.

"I want some answers right now. Who the hell are you?" I pushed him away from me and glared at him. He still refused to look at me for longer than a second, constantly watching for the apparent danger that had led him to drag me from my car. After another moment of silence, I couldn't take the frustration anymore, and I pushed past him, pulling my house keys from my handbag.

"Fine, if you want to continue this whole mystery man routine, I'm going inside." A split second after the words were out of my mouth, I was promptly knocked to the ground, the wind knocked out of me, and a body lay heavily across me, holding me down. At first, I thought it was *mystery man*, as I had started referring to him in my head until I realised that my attacker had come from beside me, not from behind.

In the time it took me to come to this realisation, the weight on top of me was gone, and the sound of fighting broke out behind me. I scrambled to my feet and plastered myself to the side of my car once again, transfixed by what was happening in front of me. It couldn't possibly be true.

The person who had knocked me to the ground was Will.

"Stop it!" I found my voice as the two of them traded kicks and blows so fluidly it was as if they were dancing. Will had always been active, but I had no idea where he had developed these skills from. Momentarily distracted by the sound of my voice, Will stopped for a moment, and I took a step towards him. But one powerful kick from my mystery man sent Will flying across the front lawn. The force with which he had kicked Will had lifted him off his feet and sent him flying at least twenty feet, something that no normal human being could do.

I gaped in shock at the scene before me as the man spun on the spot and shoved me into the back seat of my car, taking my keys from me before diving into the driver's seat and tearing out of my drive-way, hitting the central locking at the same time. All of this occurred in a split second, and we were already halfway down the street before I realised what was happening. I slammed my hand against the door, knowing it was useless, and I was not suicidal enough to leap from a car that was tearing along suburban streets at such a terrifying speed.

"What the hell is going on?! We have to go back. That was Will!" I knew I had finally reached hysteria.

"I'll explain everything once you are safe!" A glance at me in the rear-view mirror was all I got. I was still unable to process what I had just witnessed. How could my dead fiance be in my front yard, performing these fantastic martial arts moves that he could only have fantasised about doing when he was alive? Why was a stranger rescuing me from him? I had far too many questions, and I was not prepared to wait until I was 'safe' - a situation which I doubted that I would agree with - as I had no idea who this man was, and both times I'd been alone with him in the past week had been at the scene of some violent attack.

"Start talking right now, or I will ring for help faster than you can drive, so help me God. I am beyond my limit right now!" I said through clenched teeth, with my fists balled into tight fists at my side, though whether this was from anger or fear, I couldn't tell; the adrenaline felt the same. The car began to slow to a more agreeable speed, and for the first time, he looked me directly in the eye, though it was via the rear-view mirror.

"My name is Liam."

Finally!

"Alright, Liam. What the fuck is going on?" My voice was thick, and I had reached the point where my usual filter on swearing was lifted. I would have preferred to have had this conversation face to face, as I felt myself starting to tear up. I hated that my body reacted to sadness and anger in the same way by causing me to cry.

Almost as if he could read my mind, Liam pulled the car to a stop next to a playground. He unlocked my door and took my hand to help me out of the car, which struck me as very courteous, especially for someone who had just, in effect, kidnapped me and stolen my car. He led me to a picnic table and sat facing me. He was still not entirely relaxed, but at least he was now able to look me in the eye, something he hadn't done before.

"Okay, here's the truth. Your fiance was killed by a vampire." He stated this so seriously that I may have believed him if it wasn't so ridiculous.

"Aha... A vampire... Right... And what are you, some sort of vampire slayer? I've seen that show too... What else have you got?" My disbelief was more than evident in my sarcastic response, but he just continued speaking as though I hadn't interrupted.

"Will is now a vampire himself. A vampire that is intent on turning you into one as well. And it is my job to keep that from happening. He was never meant to be turned; that wouldn't have been Adam's plan, but unfortunately, he had not fed in a while, and he got sloppy. He should have decapitated Will to keep him from turning, but you stopped that from happening." He went to continue, but this was enough for me.

"*Excuse me*? He *should* have decapitated my fiance?! He killed him. He didn't need to pull his fucking body apart!" Disgusted, I started to rise to my feet, intent on storming off, but Liam reached up and pulled me back down.

"I know this all sounds crazy. I remember my reaction when I was first told of all of this, but I cannot sugarcoat this for you." His gaze held mine, and I found it impossible to look away. "Your life has changed now in more ways than you know. Adam had a goal that night. He was meant to get you instead, to turn you into a vampire like him. He failed, but in turning Will, he has recruited the perfect foot soldier to do it for him. Will still retains his love for you, but his love is now an obsession, and he will stop at nothing until he has you." He was so serious. Whether real or imagined, he believed everything he was telling me.

In my mind, I went over everything he had just told me. Could this all have been some massive practical joke that they had cooked up together? If I hadn't known Will so well and known he would never put me through this sort of grief, I might have believed that over this crazy story, I was being told. However, there was something about Liam that made me think that he was telling me the truth.

"Wait... why did this... Adam... Why did he want to turn me into a vampire?" I couldn't believe I was talking about vampires in all seriousness.

Liam took a deep breath.

"Because of the prophecy. You're the one that is meant to bring peace and stop them. He was trying to stop that from happening." I couldn't help but gape at him now. He had truly lost his mind somewhere along the way. Vampires, prophecies... It was as if I had stepped straight onto the set of some seriously lame horror movie. This guy was one of those people who wrote fan fiction in their spare time, convinced that the dark was out to get him. And here I was, all alone in the dark with him.

He must have realised that my mood had changed and shook his head.

"I know this is all hard to believe. However, some part of you knows that I am telling the truth. I know that you have begun to see things. It all started the night we first met. The night before your twenty-fifth birthday." In all the craziness of the past week, I had forgotten about the alley in my flashes, instead focusing only on Liam's involvement in Will's death.

"I know you don't remember anything from that night, but I told you then that the danger was coming. And I know you have been sensing a presence in the dark. I know you've been having the nightmares." How the hell did this guy know all of this? Was he a stalker, on top of being seriously delusional?

"Did you drug me that night? Is that why I can't remember anything except blurred images?" I went with the only logical explanation for this weirdness, but he just shook his head.

"No. You cannot remember anything because the first day or so when the change sets in is incredibly disorientating. Throw in the amount of alcohol you'd had that night, and I'm surprised you remember anything at all, to be perfectly honest." That last part was said with underlying judgement, and I raised an eyebrow at him, but he didn't look away. It felt eerily like I was being told off by my father. Although admittedly, he was much closer to my age than my father, and I found him disturbingly attractive, even with everything that had been going on lately.

"The change? What change?" He'd made it sound like I was starting menopause.

"Your psychic ability." Right, that was it. This guy was insane.

"My psychic ability? Okay, seriously, Liam, if that's even your real name, you're fucking nuts." Again, I went to get up, but this time when he pulled me back down, he held me in place. The strength in just one hand was enough to render me motionless, even without losing myself to his unblinking gaze.

"I know that you think this is all crazy. If we had time to waste on trying to ease you into this, then I would be happy to do so, but there is not enough time for that. You need to understand the danger that you are in. I have been placed in your life to keep you from being turned into one of them, and I need you to be aware of what is going on." He moved his hand away, perhaps sensing that I wasn't going to run off yet again. "You cannot be making stupid mistakes like the one you made tonight." I glared at him, offended. He continued talking, not looking the slightest bit concerned. "You cannot go back to that house at night. It was the home you shared with Will, and he can get in there without an invitation. Your sister cannot return there either. Jacob has been safe up until now because Will only awakened tonight. You can return during the daylight to pack up your things. You will be safe with your parents because you never shared a home with Will there." None of this made sense. I was struggling to take everything he was saying in, and I shook my head.

"Liam, you haven't told me how you know anything about any of this. Who are you?" He looked at me for the longest time. Eventually, he took my right hand and turned it over, palm facing upwards. He traced a finger over my wrist before looking up at me again.

"You're not ready to know that yet."

CHAPTER SIX

I woke the next morning, convinced that the night before had just been another one of my dreams. Until I saw the bruise on my arm from where I had fallen when Will knocked me to the ground. Liam had driven me back to my parents' house in silence and had no doubt maintained his vigil outside in the dark somewhere. I couldn't take any of it in. I didn't want to accept what I had seen. Will, the love of my life, had attacked me, intent on killing me. It just could not have happened. I had to have made it all up as a way of dealing with my grief. Right?

Wrong... I could feel Liam's eyes on me all day. Finally having confirmation that someone was always watching me didn't make me feel any better, and when a real estate agent just happened to call me to discuss selling the house, I wondered at the timing, the convenience of the phone call. I noticed my knuckles turning white as I gripped the phone, as the woman prattled on, her voice echoing through my bedroom as I stared down at the phone in my hand.

"Can we meet at the house tomorrow?" I had barely heard her speaking, but I found myself saying yes, without really understanding what I was agreeing to.

"You're going to organise to sell the Townhouse already?" Aurora had been listening in from the bedroom door, having heard the phone ring, and looked taken aback. She sat down on my bed, pulling her legs up and wrapping her arms around them to hug them close. "Are you sure about this? It doesn't seem like the right time to be making such huge decisions, Is." I shook my head.

"It's just a conversation... I don't have to decide straight away, I guess. But we can't afford to stay there without Will's income; you know that." I swallowed hard, my eyes welling up. I could feel the panic beginning to rise, as once again, the idea of trying to navigate through life without Will overwhelmed me. Never mind the fact that I'd seen him walking around the night before. My hands started shaking, and Aurora got to her feet, moving to stand in front of me as she took my hands in her own. She held my gaze as she squeezed my fingers.

"Hey, we'll figure this out, okay? You're not alone in this. Just breathe." She guided me through some deep breaths, and I squeezed her fingers back.

"I'm okay. Thanks." She pulled me into a hug, and I relaxed into her arms for a moment before stepping back. "I think I need a bit more sleep."

Aurora nodded, although she hesitated at the door, turning back to watch me as I climbed back under the covers, suddenly so very, very tired.

The next morning, I drove back to the townhouse earlier than the others, determined to face it on my own, before I was joined by my parents and sister to meet with the real estate agent. I parked in the driveway and made my way to the front door, head down as I dug through my bag to find my house keys. But once I reached the front door, I came to an abrupt halt, noticing that the door was already open a crack. Surely Jacob hadn't forgotten to lock up when he'd last been here?

I hadn't gotten close enough to the door the night I'd last been here to notice if the door was open then, but I was remembering Liam's words of caution. That a vampire could enter a house they used to reside in without invitation. I stepped forward cautiously and pushed the door open, not yet crossing the threshold. I could feel my heart thumping loudly in my chest, the adrenaline beginning to kick in, as I slowly eased my way into the house, scanning the downstairs area. I could see the whole first floor from here, and nothing appeared to be out of place. Moving as silently as I could, I slowly made my way upstairs, and by the time I reached the top of the staircase, the sound of my heart beating rapidly was deafening in my ears. Aurora's bedroom door was open, as was Will's office and the main bathroom, and I could see that all were empty. That just left our bedroom, across the landing, with the door closed.

I swallowed hard as I stood in front of the closed door, trying not to think about the last time I'd come home to a seemingly empty house to find a surprise proposal behind this door. Now was not the time to crumple into a heap. I slowly turned the door handle and let the door swing open. The room was empty, and I could see that our bathroom was also empty through the walk-in robe. I let out the breath I'd been holding, feeling the tension leave my body. I surveyed the room, and for a moment, I felt relieved until my eyes fell on the bed, and I noticed the bunch of flowers lying there, next to a note. I stood staring at it for a moment, positive that I did not want to read it.

A few thunderous heartbeats later, I finally moved closer, walking around the bed and gingerly lifted the letter with a shaking hand.

Roses are Red,

Violets are Blue.
We're meant to be forever,
I'm coming for you.

I could feel tears beginning to sting my eyes as I read the words written in Will's distinctive handwriting. My hand shook uncontrollably, and I let the letter fall to the ground as I stepped back and slid down the wall on my side of the bed, staring at the flowers. They were an elaborate arrangement with two large white lilies at the centre. Will had been buying me white lilies for six years.

I had no idea how long I sat there, but I was jerked out of my living nightmare by the sound of my parents and sister entering the front door, calling out to me. I shot to my feet, snatching the letter off the ground and shoving it into my handbag. I couldn't bring myself to touch the flowers as I fled back downstairs. I would never be able to feel safe in that room again.

That afternoon, my family and I set about the task of packing up the house and making it ready for the real estate agents to show people through. The woman that had contacted me the day before had wandered through the house with dollar signs in her eyes. She gleefully informed me that a townhouse in the heart of Bulimba would have no problems at all selling for the asking price, not even noticing as I had gripped my father's arm.

"It really would be best to pack up the house and get it staged. It makes it easier for the buyers who come through for the inspections to imagine themselves here and the lives they want to lead. We'd target young couples starting out. This is the perfect starter home in this suburb. I've got a few interested parties looking already that a home like this would appeal to. It will sell quickly; I can almost promise you that."

But what about the life I had meant to start in my home?

Aurora had had a word with the woman after this, asking if she could kindly curb her enthusiasm in light of the terrible circumstances that caused me to sell my home in the first place. She'd had the sense to look ashamed after that but still advised us to stay with our parents so that we would not be constantly cleaning.

As I battled the overwhelming prospect of packing up the life that Will and I had been building together so soon after his death, I wondered if Liam had had anything to do with the real estate agent's last request. It did seem a little odd, as most people remained living in their homes whilst they were on the market. It just seemed too neat and tidy. I brushed the thought aside, as there was no way Liam could have influenced some random woman before I even knew I was going to be putting the house on the market.

Although who knew? I knew nothing about 'mystery man', as I was still in the habit of calling him. Maybe he had some mind control powers. I mean, I had just discovered that vampires were real, so why not people with supernatural powers as well?

My family had noticed the change in my mood over the few days that it took to pack up the house. I was no longer silent, no longer the walking zombie that I had become in the days that followed Will's death. Yet there was something manic in my turn of personality, according to my ever-perceptive twin sister. Aside from several breakdowns when packing up our belongings, I kept looking over my shoulder as though expecting someone to be there. Of course, only I knew that this was with good reason. They couldn't understand why I refused to allow anyone in the house after the sun went down, forcing everyone to leave as soon as I noticed the sunlight fading away, no matter if they were in the middle of packing a box. No one was game enough to argue with me, though, putting it down to post-traumatic stress after the attack.

I was more than willing to let them believe this, as the letters that awaited my arrival each morning were hard to ignore, each one more ominous than the last, and accompanied by increasingly creepier gifts. The letter today had been in the form of yet another poem.

Roses are Red,
Violets are Blue.
You can't live without me,
You know that it's true.

It had been placed on the kitchen bench next to a dead bird, the neck twisted at a sickening angle that was almost certainly broken. It had taken all my resolve not to throw up. I had managed to dump the bird in the wheelie bin before Aurora and Jacob had come inside, the letter joining the others, each one a crumpled ball inside my handbag. Painful reminders of what Will had become and that I was no longer safe within the walls of the home we had shared together.

"Alright, that's it. What's going on?!" Aurora demanded as she dumped the last load of boxes onto the back of Jacob's ute. I had been once again scanning the front yard. I was ever watchful, and it was driving my sister crazy. Jacob had the sense to busy himself with doing one final sweep of the house, leaving me to come up with a reason for my actions. Thankfully, I had a pretty good one, even though it was not the main reason.

'Well, let's think about this for a moment. A week and a half ago, I watched as my fiance was attacked by some psycho who ripped him apart in a dark alley... Don't you think that's enough of a reason for me to be just the slightest bit freaked out?!" Although I knew Aurora didn't deserve it, all my frustration and confusion from the past few weeks was now focused on her. A part of me was angry that she didn't just guess what was going on so that she could know what I was going through, frustrated that she had not worked it out. I knew

I was being stupid, that there was no way any normal, sane person could guess what I was going through, even my identical twin. However, they always say you hurt the ones you love... and my secret had gotten Will killed; the one person I loved more than anything, and anyone in the world was gone, and now I knew that it was because of me.

Without realising it, I found myself curled up on the ground beside the ute, shaking with silent sobs, as my sister held me in her arms, unable to fix my problems or understand what was going on. And I could never let her know.

Jacob and Aurora eventually drove back to our parent's house, leaving me to follow behind in my car. But I didn't immediately leave. I let myself back inside one last time, moving silently around the house. My steps echoed through the empty rooms, once so full of life and love. We had lived here for three years, and it was full of so many memories. We had planned to start a family here one day when we were ready, and to see the rooms now empty was yet another painful reminder that our life together was now over.

The hardest part of these last few days, aside from the very unwelcome poems and gifts, had been packing up Will's belongings. After an unsuccessful attempt to pack up his clothes and his office that led to one of my worst breakdowns, I eventually asked one of my sisters to do it, and those boxes had been taken to his parent's house the day before, to sit in the garage until we were all ready to go through them. I had no idea if I would ever be ready for that moment.

CHAPTER SEVEN

That night I sat staring out my bedroom window at my parents' house, unwilling to unpack the boxes that were scattered around the room. I refused to get settled here, as I knew I could only handle a few weeks in my parents' house. They had said that they wanted Aurora and me to stay, but we had both agreed that we needed to find our own place to rent as soon as possible. I refused to be one of those boomerang children, coming home every time something went wrong. Granted, usually, the things that were wrong were trivial things, like running out of money or having issues with roommates, nothing quite as drastic as a dead fiance, but still, I did not want to fall into that category.

I was so lost in thought that I didn't notice someone staring back at me through the window until they moved. I jumped, startled out of my dark thoughts, and caught my breath as Liam tapped on the window. I moved to open it, wondering why he did not just come to the front door rather than climb up to a second-story window.

"Hello." His voice was quiet as he sat on the outer side of the windowsill, resting his feet on one of the large branches of the tree he had just climbed up.

"Do you want t-" Liam cut me off before I could finish inviting him in, raising his hands in protest, almost in fear.

"Don't invite anyone you don't know in... Or anyone that you have not seen in a while. I will just stay out here for now. It's better this way, trust me." I raised my eyebrows.

"Trust you? Why should I do that? You've got me jumping at shadows and fearing the dark!" It felt good to have someone to blame for all the crap going on in my life. Liam just shrugged, which infuriated me more.

"You know what's in the dark now; you should be afraid." His simple response caused me to growl under my breath, knowing he was right but liking nothing about it. He ignored my obvious hostility and continued like there had not been days between our last talk and this one.

"Are you ready to hear the truth now?" Why was he asking me this? He was the one who told me I wasn't ready!

I said as much, but he waved it aside.

"There are still a lot of things you're not ready to know about yet. I meant about what's out there in the dark." I paused to think about this for a moment.

"I guess even if I'm not ready, I still need to know what's out there. Especially since the dark seems fixated on me for some reason." I shuddered involuntarily at the memory of Will's unwelcome gifts.

"It's a long story." Liam settled himself more comfortably, leaning back against the window frame so that I could see him side-on, and crossed his arms.

"If it starts with once upon a time, I'm pushing you off the roof," I said as I sat back down on my bed, pulling my pillow to me and hugging it to my chest like a security blanket. Liam huffed a laugh that didn't reach his eyes as he turned to look at me.

"Well, it certainly doesn't end in - and they all lived happily ever after." I shivered at that; I did *not* need reminding that the world was no longer a happy place.

"Five hundred years ago, there were two brothers. Their father was the master of a small estate in Ireland, and the eldest brother was set to inherit the estate upon their father's death, leaving the youngest with no inheritance, as was the case in those days. The youngest brother had joined the priesthood, and both were happy with their lot in life." Liam no longer looked at me as he told the story, instead staring off into the dark as if watching the story unfold before his eyes.

"However, one day, the eldest brother went missing. After a year of searching, their father lost hope, and upon his death, the estate fell to the youngest brother. He didn't want the position, as he was happy in the cloisters of the church and did not much like the idea of leaving to take a wife." He flashed a look at me before turning away, continuing to speak with his arms still crossed firmly over his chest.

"But he did his duty and went to his father's home. When he took up his role, he also inherited the secrets that his father had kept from him. His father had died several days short of his twenty-fifth birthday, and that was when the nightmares started. The younger brother did not know what they meant and believed it was just the grief of losing his father and his brother so close together." He turned to look at me properly again and held my gaze as he continued. I stared at him, giving him my full attention, unable to pull myself away from the haunted look in his blue eyes.

"However, his mother came to him and told him of his true birthright. She'd had five sons before the births of his brother and himself, though none had survived infancy. This made him the seventh son, like his father before him, who had lost six older brothers before becoming the master of the estate. This made the young man the seventh son of a seventh son.

"Upon his birth, his parents had been approached by a stranger, a woman. She had told them that he was destined to be part of an order of men and women, each destined to protect humanity from the realm of the supernatural. They called themselves The Order of the Dragon." I felt my eyebrows raise at this but didn't dare interrupt as Liam went on.

"The young man was thrown by this, unable to understand what this meant. But on the night that his mother told him of his supposed destiny, his brother reappeared in the company of a stranger. At first, the younger brother was overjoyed that his brother had returned, but as the night wore on, he noticed differences between the person his brother used to be and the man before him. Upon closer inspection, he noted, with fear, that there was cruelty about him. He would not tell them where he had been, but he watched his younger brother and mother hungrily, as though waiting to pounce." Liam cleared his throat now, emotion beginning to show.

"And then he did. He allowed the stranger to attack their mother, holding his younger brother down and forcing him to watch as the stranger drained the life from her, an unwilling witness to the murder of the last remaining member of their family. Once he'd finished, the stranger turned to him, moving to bite him as he had done their mother after putting him through the trauma of watching him remove her head from her body.

"However, before he could bite him, the house was suddenly under siege as the tenants of the estate attacked. The servants of the home had recognised what the older brother and his companion were and sounded the alarm. Vampires." He stared at his hands as he took a breath, steadying himself before he continued. I remained still, processing everything as best I could.

"The younger brother managed to flee separately, as he feared the mob would come after him as well, as he was covered in his mother's blood. Eventually, he found an abandoned church. It was within those crumbling walls that he crossed the path of another vampire. He managed to escape the clutches of two vampires, only to meet another and succumb to their bite. For seven days, he remained, until he awoke the final night, and the change was complete." A long pause followed as Liam gathered his thoughts some more. The story was taking its toll on him, but he continued.

"However, he was something different to his brother. Though

he, too, had become a vampire, his personality was unchanged. He was still the man that he had been before. Although, he now had a strength that he did not previously have. While he now craved blood, he was able to quench his intense thirst with the blood of animals.

"As he remained in the church, he began to sense the presence of others nearby, and he eventually came out of his hiding place. And that was when they found him, the members of the Order that his mother had been telling him about." Liam looked at me once again that piercing gaze holding me transfixed once more.

"They had come in search of him, each using their unique gifts to seek him out. Although they knew what he had become, they also knew that there was something different about him. He had both the powers of a vampire as well as the gifts that he was born to, making him more powerful than either side. As he learned more about his powers, along with those of his brother, he realised that his brother appeared to have powers that were unheard of in other nightwalkers. Because of this, the brothers were evenly matched and battled against each other for centuries.

"Although the members of the Order aged slower than normal humans, they are not immortal, and soon there were only a handful of people who remained as families grew smaller and less likely to have as many children. The Order held some hope, however, in a prophecy of a young woman who would have powers even greater than both the brothers, a young woman who would defeat the darkness finally. She was the seventh daughter of both a seventh daughter and a seventh son, and her powers would have no bounds." He fell silent finally, his story now finished.

I looked down at my lap, noting that I had almost ripped my pillow in half as I had pulled and scrunched at it throughout his long tale. Realisation dawned on me. Something I'd never really thought about before. My mother was the seventh daughter in her family, and my father was the seventh son in his. And I was their seventh daughter.

How had I never put this together before?

"Are you trying to tell me that this... this prophecy... it's supposed to be about me?" I whispered, unable to speak any louder. I think my voice had run away, and I wished the rest of me could have done the same. This was all too much to take in.

"It's not supposed to be about you, Isolde; it is about you. You are the one we have been waiting for, knowing that you would finally end this war." Liam watched me closely as I took this in.

"And this is why you've been following me? Why you were at my university that day?" For once, it was Liam's turn to look confused.

"What do you mean? You've only ever seen me the night before your birthday... and then, when Will..." He didn't finish his sentence, but the memory of that night came flooding back, and I let it go for the time being.

"Does this mean that you are one of them? The Order?" I had guessed this much anyway but wanted to hear it said aloud. Liam nodded.

"And so are you. Even if the prophecy had not been about you, you would have been one of us. You still would have had gifts, but the powers you have are so much more than gifts. Eventually, you will see a tattoo show up on the inside of your right wrist. A golden dragon. It's a symbol to show that you will remove the darkness from the world." I started, looking down at my wrist, which presently was bare, with no sign of the gold I had still noticed from time to time.

"When you say powers, what exactly am I meant to be able to do? So, I can sense a presence in the dark? Most women can do that." Aside from the nightmares, I could think of nothing else. And the nightmares didn't feel like power, more like a curse.

"The reason you aren't aware of them is because you haven't been introduced into this world yet. That is why Adam was trying to get to you first.

"You see, depending on which of the bloodlines a vampire belongs to, if a person is turned by them, they will either be evil or... well, not good, but on the side of good..."

I must have looked confused because Liam suddenly shook his head.

"Sorry, I hadn't told you about that part yet. There are two different vampire bloodlines. When the youngest brother came to hide in the church, another vampire was already there. The blood memories that flooded through him as he lay there for seven days were not those of an evil race but of those who fought against them, who did not need to feed on the blood of men. The two bloodlines began before Christ. We do not know if those who began the war are even still walking this earth." He rubbed his neck as though he felt the bite at his own throat.

"So, when a human is changing, they are flooded with the blood memories of those who turned them?" I was trying to put it all together, and Liam nodded.

"It is through those memories that they become either a night-walker or one who can walk in the light, what we call daywalkers. Although they do not usually fight with the Protectors, they are usually always there somewhere. It is how our side has managed to hold out for this long. But with our numbers now dwindling so low, it's only a matter of time before there are no Protectors left, just the two bloodlines once more."

"What is a Protector?" I was confused, trying to keep track of all these different names being thrown around.

"The Members of the Order call themselves the Protectors. Protecting humanity from the realm of the supernatural."

Good lord... this is crazy! I must have spoken the words out loud, as Liam laughed softly, though there was no humour behind it.

"That was along my line of thinking when this was all told to me. The night that I was told about the Order, I thought that the world had gone mad."

"So, there are two different breeds of vampires? And the good ones can walk in the daylight?" I still couldn't grasp all of this.

"The nightwalkers are the ones we fight against; they can only feed off the blood of humans and can't consume human food. They retain only the worst of their human personalities, although they seem to be able to continue to love. Still, it is obsessive love, as I explained to you that night about Will." Liam's eyes flicked over my face as tears welled in my eyes. I swallowed and nodded, motioning for him to continue, as the memory of the notes from Will made it hard to breathe.

"The daywalkers are a little different. They still require blood to survive, but they can survive on animal blood, and they still consume food. They aren't entirely good, as they can be cruel and less in touch with their feelings than humans. They often appear devoid of emotion, but it's more that they don't feel the same way about things that humans do, as they find most human problems trivial. But they are at war with the nightwalkers and have been since before anyone that I know can remember. We'll be able to explain more tomorrow when you meet the others." I shook my head at these last words.

"No, tomorrow I go back to uni and work. Tomorrow, I start going back to normal again. This is all some sort of crazy nightmare that I'm now going to wake up from." Liam looked at me sympathetically.

"Isolde... this is the real world... the rest of it is the dream..." I felt a tear roll down my face. No, I stubbornly thought to myself, I would not be brought into this. I needed normal right now.

There was a knock on my door, and I turned as Aurora entered the room backwards, her arms laden with boxes. I jumped up to block the window, but Liam was already gone, so fast that I thought he had fallen. There was no thud or groan, and if Aurora noticed anything unusual, she didn't show it as she placed the boxes under the very window where Liam had just sat. She didn't notice that my entire world was completely different now. After she left again, I sat down on the bed and stared intently at my wrist, willing myself to see the flash of gold that I had seen so many times. Nothing appeared.

Thoughts swirled in my head. He had to be wrong. Surely, the stories weren't about me. I was too normal. Boring even! Until now, everything had been stock standard in my life. Leave school, go to university, get a job, meet a guy, travel, and get engaged. Nowhere in my plan had there ever been the words "save the world"! I was not an activist. I never took any interest in world peace; I ran away from all the different activist groups that set up shop around campus at uni... There had to have been some mistake.

However, as these thoughts were going through my head, something happened. Faintly at first, a symbol began to appear on my wrist. It started as a flash of gold, nothing more. Then it grew brighter. Eventually, it was as though someone had come along with a pen and drawn a symbol in gold ink and then turned a light on. It was so bright.

But it was not the dragon that Liam said members of the Order had on their wrists. It was a rising sun.

A symbol to show that you will remove the darkness from the world. Sunlight eliminates the darkness.

I had no idea where that thought had come from, and the appearance of the tattoo did not make me feel any better. In fact, it scared the crap out of me!

CHAPTER EIGHT

After breakfast the next morning, I resolutely placed my laptop in my backpack and packed my uniform into a separate bag. I pulled on a jumper, ensuring that the tattoo was covered by the sleeve, as it was now fully formed and hadn't faded since last night. At least it had stopped glowing, though. I was adamant I was going to uni first, then straight to work. That was until I went out to my car to discover Liam already sitting in the driver's seat.

"No," I said firmly, refusing to accept that this was how it was. Liam ignored me and reached across, opening the passenger door and waiting for me to get in. He looked ahead as though he were a parent waiting for a belligerent teenager to do as they were told. I went around and threw myself in the car, tears of anger and frustration rolling down my face, once again feeling as though I had no control over my own life. I didn't even realise that I hadn't shut the door until it slammed shut on its own, and I stared at it in shock.

"Yes, that was you," Liam said as he started the engine and began to drive. He headed towards the city, and I wondered, with a curiosity that I refused to show, where we were going.

Twenty minutes later, when he pulled up in front of a very old and run-down home in New Farm, I began to wonder again if this wasn't all some sort of joke until I stepped through the front door and realised that the outside was all just an illusion.

"It's a glamour," Liam explained, seeing my look of shock as I took in my surroundings. On the outside, the house looked to be a simple three-bedroom old Queenslander, which was in a complete state of disrepair. Once through the doors, though, I entered a... Grand Manor. There must have been over twenty rooms, and I was guessing that the other homes around this one were all one glamour to hide this same building.

"Why didn't you guys just get office space?" I couldn't understand why they needed to go to this sort of trouble just for their headquarters.

"We not only work here; this is also our home as well. As long as we call it home, no nightwalker can cross this threshold. And because of the glamour, if one of us is turned, we can't find it again. It's part of the magic." More surprises.

"Magic is real too?!" *When would the craziness stop?*

A soft laugh from above made me jump, and I looked to see a breathtakingly beautiful woman peering down at me from the landing on the second floor. Her long black hair rippled behind her as she descended the grand staircase with agile grace. I took in her simple jeans and singlet top, her casual attire seeming out of place with her stunning features. She would have looked more at home in a ball gown. If I were to try to guess her age, I'd say somewhere in her mid-thirties, but she seemed almost ageless.

"Welcome, Isolde. We have been expecting you. I see that Liam still has not divulged everything yet." She shot Liam a look over my shoulder, her green eyes filled with understanding, before continuing. "It is all a bit much to take in at once. I wish someone had told me in stages." She came forward and took my hand gently, giving it a squeeze.

"I'm Patrice. Before long, you will learn everything, and it will all stop being such a shock." I seriously doubted this part but allowed myself to be towed through several rooms, each filled with fancy antiques, reminding me of the palaces I had visited in Europe. We came to a stop finally, coming to a room that seemed completely out of place in this grand old building. It looked like it belonged in a James Bond movie, filled with computer monitors and gadgets as far as the eye could see. In the centre of the room stood a massive round table with several people sitting around it of various ages. As we entered the room, a sudden silence descended, and I found myself feeling uneasy due to the various looks I was getting. These looks ranged from mild curiosity to full-blown admiration, but one woman around my age seemed to be strongly disapproving. Someone in this room did *not* want me there, but Lord only knew why.

"Everyone, as you all know, this is Isolde. Isolde, meet... well... everyone." Patrice waved her hand toward those seated at the table as Liam walked around the other side. He took a seat beside the woman who did not so much as look at me now, busying herself with scanning the screen of the laptop in front of her. I nodded at the group and allowed Patrice to lead me to an empty chair directly across the opulent table from Liam. The silence continued for a moment until a middle-aged man on my left reached out to shake my hand.

"It's nice to see you again, Isolde. I'm Gerard." I looked at him closely, trying to place where I knew him from.

"Wait a minute... Mr O'Connell? You look the same!" Realising that the man beside me was, in fact, the same man who had taught me in grade two, I looked around the table once more, looking at the others properly for the first time. I recognised more familiar faces, noting people who had been scattered throughout my past, and not a single one of them appeared to have aged a day since I had last seen them. They all smiled back.

"We've been protecting you since you were first born, Isolde."

The last sentence was spoken in a familiar Spanish accent, and I looked over to see Katyana, from my brief stay in London, smiling at me from where she sat at a computer across the room.

"But... you're the same age as me..." I was confused at the sight of Katyana, with whom I had shared a bedroom in a share house in London. We had spent many a drunken night at the Walkabout Pub near our house as I drowned my homesick sorrows. Seeing her here, now, was very surreal.

"I'm forty-five, actually."

I remembered now about what Liam had said, that they aged differently to normal people, and I wondered briefly how old Liam was. I also found myself scanning the people around me, wondering if one of them was the vampire, the younger brother from Liam's story last night. A few men here could have fit the description, so I was left wondering.

Everyone looks so human.

We had come in during the middle of a meeting, and they all continued the discussion we had walked into, deferring to Patrice now that she had joined them. I tried to follow along with what was being discussed, but I found myself just looking around at the people at the table. I didn't know how to feel about all of these revelations, and I almost felt violated by how much they all knew about me. It was like finding out I was on some sort of reality TV show that I hadn't auditioned for. Some of them treated me as though I was the Messiah, the second coming, which I found very uncomfortable, whereas others, like Patrice, Katyana and Liam, treated me as though I was one of them, on the same level as them. The woman next to Liam seemed to perceive me as a threat to whatever was happening between them as she moved closer to him without even glancing at me. Her name, as she was introduced to me, was Alana, and she was from the US, somewhere in the south, judging by her accent. I realised I'd have to set the record straight with her, as I had no intention of having anything romantic happen between Liam and myself. Will wasn't even cold in his grave yet! Then I realised with a jolt that he never would be either.

After the meeting, Patrice took me on a tour through the lower levels of the Manor and gave me more details about the Order.

"This location is one of about a hundred others like it around the world. This one was set up around the time of your birth." She threw me a sad smile over her shoulder as she lead me into the kitchen. "Vampire activity in Brisbane wasn't much of a problem until then."

Fantastic, more deaths on my hands.

Liam joined me as I sat on a seat at the bench and watched Patrice move around the kitchen, making lunch for us both. He remained silent as Patrice handed me a sandwich, moving to sit on my other side as she ate her own. I wasn't quite sure what to make of all of this, simply taking a bite of the sandwich and looking around the room quietly, although I could feel Liam watching me closely.

Afterwards, Patrice led me upstairs, and I realised that I had misjudged the size of the Manor. It was far bigger than I first thought. There were at least thirty bedrooms, branching off several hallways, each one with its own bathroom and designed to be inhabited by a member of the Order. Most appeared to be filled with personal items, although I was unsure how many members of the worldwide order resided here full-time.

"This is your room... should you wish to stay here," Patrice said, showing me a room at the end of one of the many halls. She smiled as I opened my mouth to protest.

"It will be yours no matter what, even if you do not choose to live here." Liam had followed behind us, and Patrice left us alone to see to other affairs. During the meeting, I learned that she was one of the elders and the leader of this particular chapter of the Order. As I stood in the middle of 'my' room, an overwhelming sensation threatened to take hold of me again, and I swayed on my feet.

"Here, sit down." Liam guided me to a soft armchair, which I gratefully sank into.

"I keep waiting for someone to yell cut or something, to discover that I've walked onto the set of a movie..." I looked around in wonder, trying not to fall in love with the room that I was in.

"Where do you think people got the ideas for those sorts of movies from? Our presence is not as secret as we would like to believe it is, although it does have its advantages. Your reaction mirrors exactly how the rest of the world would be if they found out it was all real." Liam sat on the bed, facing me. He was, quite possibly, the most beautiful man I had ever seen. I blushed a little at that thought, unable to hold his gaze for long as he smiled a slow, easy smile.

Suddenly I was overwhelmed with the need to sleep; the weight of it all was just too much for my brain to deal with. Liam saw the shift in my energy, possibly noting the fact that I was about to pass out because within seconds, I was curled up on the bed and Liam was quietly letting himself out of the room, having placed a blanket over me. I felt myself being pulled into a deep sleep, everything that I had learned in the past week flooding through my mind, making its way into my dreams.

When I awoke, I couldn't remember anything from those dreams, but I realised, with an empty feeling in the pit of my stomach, that I wasn't going to be able to run away from this. I felt a single tear slide down my cheek, and I rolled over, wiping it away, to discover Patrice sitting in the armchair that I had vacated earlier, a steaming mug sitting next to her as she read from an incredibly old-looking book.

"Hi." I yawned as I sat up, and Patrice looked up with a smile, closing her book and handing me the mug, which turned out to be filled with chamomile tea.

"Liam said you'd probably need someone to talk to once you'd woken up." She said this as she moved to sit on the edge of the bed. I felt a connection with Patrice, almost as if she was another mother whom I had known all my life. I pulled my legs up underneath me, giving her more space.

"So, is Liam my very own guardian angel or something? He keeps showing up at exactly the right moment to save me." I left out that he couldn't save my fiance. A bit too bitter, and it was not Liam's fault.

"It's one of Liam's gifts. He can tune into any one of us, and he can also see into our thoughts if he wishes." I must have looked taken aback at this because Patrice patted my legs reassuringly. "Don't worry; it's not something that he enjoys doing often, and he tends to be able to switch it off, only using it when necessary. Unfortunately, with your circumstances lately, it's been necessary for him to see your whereabouts quite a lot." This did not make me feel much better, remembering the thought I'd had about how attractive he was when we were talking earlier, but it brought me to the subject that had been bothering me since last night.

"What gifts or powers am I meant to have? Because I don't think I'm going to be shooting laser beams out of my eyes any time soon." Patrice smiled at this, seeing through my bravado.

"We don't know. They will present themselves in time. However, Liam told me about the car door this morning, so we can assume that you have some telekinetic abilities." She gave my leg another reassuring pat. "We will work on those in time. But the prophecy does say that your powers will know no bounds, so I know we can expect great things from you." As she leaned forward to push a strand of my hair behind my ear, I closed my eyes for a moment, trying not to wallow in self-pity. I wasn't sure how I would cope with the weight of all these expectations on me.

"I know it feels like a lot now, but you're surrounded by people who know exactly what you're going through. Who have all experienced something similar. If you need to talk, any one of us will be here for you." As she left the room, I bit back on the words that I wanted to say. How many of these people had mysterious prophecies about them? How many of them were expected to be the answer to ending a war they knew nothing about?

That afternoon, I walked through the ground floor rooms of the Manor, talking to some of the others and watching as they went about their tasks. I didn't feel as though I was a part of this... couldn't feel like I belonged. Or, more accurately, wouldn't allow myself to feel like I belonged. This was not my world. I just wanted normalcy again. I just wanted to finish my university degree and start piecing my life back together. I did not want to belong to a secret world that I could not even tell my loved ones about.

Then I found the training room. I watched as Alana and Liam sparred with one another, trading punches and amazing kicks, and realised that this was something that I did want to learn. Something to channel my anger and frustration through. As I stood watching, Liam stepped up his attack on Alana, who had previously had the upper hand. She threw all her weight into her next punch, which Liam blocked with his right forearm, before ducking low and sweeping her feet out from underneath her with his foot, stopping to kneel on one knee beside her as she lay winded on her back. Leaning a forearm on his knee, he looked over at me as I stood at the door. Noticing that Liam's attention was elsewhere, Alana arched her neck and looked up over her head. Even across the room, I could see her eyes roll before she sprung to her feet in a move that I could have only dreamed of doing one day.

"I should have guessed." She spat the words over her shoulder as she walked out through the door on the opposite side of the room. I tried not to take her attitude personally, but as I could see no reason for it, this was incredibly hard to do. Liam could see how her rudeness threw me, shrugging with an exasperated look.

"Sorry about Alana. She is jealous for several different reasons, which I will tell you about another time. She is a nice person, though." Liam began putting away the weights that lay scattered around the room.

"Yeah... I guess I'll just have to take your word for it, Liam." I leaned against the frame of the door, hesitant to enter the room, even though I was itching to get my hands on the punching bag that was hanging in the corner.

"How was your sleep? Feel better?"

"Not even remotely. Until I wake up from this nightmare, I don't think sleep is going to be much of a relief." I tried to hide the resentment I felt from him, but he sensed it, nonetheless. I remembered what Patrice said about him being able to hear our thoughts, and I heard him sigh as he came to stand in front of me before lifting my chin so that I was forced to look directly into his eyes. I knew I should be uncomfortable at the familiarity he had with me, but something about it just felt normal. The only normal thing about my life right now.

"Isolde. I know that right now, this all seems crazy. That your world is shattering apart, and there doesn't seem to be any way to fix it. However, eventually, the hurt fades. The memories that you and Will shared will always be there. But you are going to be around for a very long time. And the destiny ahead of you is so much more than this. All of this." I looked up at Liam with tears of anger in my eyes.

"You have no idea what this feels like, Liam! I lost the love of my life only two weeks ago, and since then, I've discovered that he is a vampire who is on a mission to turn me into a vampire as well, all because of some crazy ass destiny that I am supposed to have. Not to mention the fact that I have been keeping secrets and lying to my twin sister, the one person in the whole world who knows everything about me!" I was getting angrier with every word that I spoke, and Liam seized me by the shoulders, turned me around and marched me over to the punching bag.

"All that anger you're feeling? That's good. Anger is the first step to take in dealing with all of this; it is about time you got past denial. Now take your anger out on that." He pointed at the punching bag as he handed me a pair of boxing gloves. I couldn't believe the nerve of this guy. It was him that I felt like punching, not the bag, but after seeing his skills before, I knew I was no match for him.

So, I punched the bag. I punched with such force that it caused the bag to fly back. Thankfully, Liam caught it before it could swing back and hit me. I gaped at it for a second before hitting it again... and again... I felt the past three months' worth of fear, confusion, grief and anger flowing through me into the bag as I pounded with all my might. I even threw in a few kicks for good measure. I didn't know when the tears started to flow, but suddenly I was shaking uncontrollably as fat tears rolled down my cheeks by the bucket load. I stopped punching and slowly melted to the ground, no longer able to stand under the force of the emotions that had slammed into me.

I felt Liam's arms come around me, and he rocked me gently as I sobbed my heart out. I rested my head against his shoulder as my sobs quietened, and I continued to cry silently now, no longer mad at him but unable to look at him either.

"Believe me, Isolde. I understand your pain more than you know."

CHAPTER NINE

"$\mathcal{I}$solde? Did you hear me?" I looked over at my mother, noticing her concerned face, as we sat across from each other the next morning, eating breakfast.

"Sorry, Mum. What'd you say?" She continued to look at me for a few more moments before speaking again.

"I said, what time is your meeting with the solicitor?" I chewed my mouthful of cereal slowly, swallowing before responding.

"In an hour and a half." I was dreading this meeting, knowing it was one more step closer to the end of my life with Will. I was due to be meeting with the solicitor who was in charge of his estate, along with his parents and sister. After yesterday's events, and knowing everything I did now about what was really out in the world, the last thing I wanted was to be sitting in a room with Will's family and having to lie to them.

"Dad said he'll be back in time to take you." My mother watched as I got up and put my empty bowl in the dishwasher. I nodded silently and headed up to my room to get ready. I'd asked my father to come along, as I honestly wasn't sure how much I would take in, and I figured someone had better be there who could make sense of it all for me.

After a shower and putting on make-up for the first time in weeks, I stood in front of the mirror on my bedroom door and stared at my reflection. I barely even recognised the woman staring back at me. My face was pale, even with makeup on, and my hair hung limply down my back. I couldn't even remember the last time I'd washed it, and I wound it into a bun on top of my head to hide the oiliness.

Get it together, Isolde.

I pulled on a pair of jeans and a singlet top, before throwing a cardigan on over the top.

This is as good as it's going to get.

I went and sat in the armchair next to my window, staring outside. Yesterday, I'd been able to function, but today was a different story. All I wanted to do was crawl back between my sheets and sleep until the grief and darkness had lifted, and I could breathe once more. Was this what my life would be like from now on? A constant, aching black hole that consumed my waking hours, and nightmares about the monster that Will had become when I slept?

"Peanut? You ready to go?" My father stood at my door, and I felt my heart break a little at the sadness on his face. I wondered how long he'd been standing there, but I could tell it had been long enough to see his youngest daughter lost in a world of despair. I tried to smile, but I knew it wasn't doing much to relieve him, as he squeezed my arm when I walked past him, leading the way out to his car. This was going to be a long day.

Several hours later, I was back at home, still reeling from the meeting with the solicitor. Will's family had been just as depressed as I was about being there, but his parents were aware of the information that was shared prior to the meeting, so it was just a formality for them. Will had gone with them only six months ago to get all of his affairs in order, around the time that he'd picked up the ring. Ready to start our lives together.

It turned out, even at the age of twenty-five, Will had begun to amass a large investment portfolio, including properties and shares. Worth several million already. His parents were pretty well off, but I had never known just how much money they all had. And now, everything that had been Will's belonged to me, his sole beneficiary. He'd left some personal items for his parents and sister, but everything else was to be left for me and any children we may have. Since we hadn't managed to get to the baby-making part of Will's life plan, the reality that I was now a multi-millionaire at the age of twenty-five whilst still a university student was a lot to process.

"Will had planned to tell you all of this on your wedding night. A bit of a wedding gift, I guess. He was so excited about the life he was building for you both, Isolde." His father's voice was shaking with emotion as he'd given me a tight hug at the end of the meeting. I'd just stared at him in shock. Finding out that Will owned the town-house outright, having paid off the mortgage last year, had been the biggest shock though. When we'd arrived home and Aurora overheard my father telling my mother everything, the first thing she'd done was come running upstairs to find me.

"So, you won't be selling anymore, right?" It took me a moment to work out what my twin was referring to. Then I felt fear grip my belly and I shook my head frantically.

"No, Aura, I'm still selling the Townhouse." I couldn't tell her the main reason why, but I honestly didn't know that I wanted to keep it, even without the issue of Will being able to get in and murder us all in our sleep. "There are too many memories in that house. I can't bear being there anymore."

Aurora studied my face briefly. "But, you might change your mind. We shouldn't rush into anything."

"There's no we in this decision, Aurora. It's my choice, and I'm selling it." I didn't mean to sound as harsh as I did, but I was tired and it had been a very emotional day. Aurora looked stunned for a moment before her face closed off. I knew that look well. My sister had always been the more dominant of the two of us, and she didn't like it when I stood up to her.

"Sorry Aurora. I just... I won't change my mind about it, okay?" She nodded stiffly at me after a moment, and I could tell this wasn't going to be the last I heard of it.

"We'll talk about it later, I guess. When you're ready to decide what we should do." The tone in her voice indicated that once I was no longer considered to be in a delicate state, my sister was going to tell me exactly how she felt about the fact that all the decisions were up to me right now. I could only hope that my parents could talk her out of whatever mood she ended up in later tonight, cause I was tapped out. And, I had somewhere to be.

"Can't I just burn the house down?" Liam looked at me thoughtfully, as I ranted later that evening, sitting across the table from him in the study that was off his room at the Manor. We were meant to be going through mind-clearing techniques in an attempt to unlock my abilities, but I could tell that shutting my brain off was going to be difficult when I had so many problems rolling around inside my head. One would think that becoming a multi-millionaire in one day was a good thing, but it was just giving me one more thing to stress about now.

"I think we should avoid committing arson just to keep your sister from arguing with you about selling the house, Isolde." He smirked a little, as I flopped back in my chair and sighed. It was the first time I'd seen him out of black clothes, and I found myself taking note of the fit of his white long-sleeve shirt that clung to his impressive biceps. He cleared his throat, and I shook myself out of my distracted state.

"It would be so much easier than dealing with Aurora when she gets like this. She does not do well with being told no." He laughed a little, and I raised an eyebrow.

"I'm very aware of how strong-willed your sister is." That was true. As he'd been tasked with guarding me for my entire life up until now, I had no doubt that he had witnessed many of the moments in our lives where Aurora had tried to get me to do what she wanted.

"Then you know I'm right." Liam just shook his head, still smirking.

"Be that as it may, I think burning the house down is a bit extreme. In our experience with the nightwalkers, once the target of their obsession has moved out of the home that they were in together, they don't tend to return. There shouldn't be any need to burn it down, no matter how much easier it would be for you when it comes to Aurora." His statement made me think of a question that had been burning in the back of my mind.

"So, does the Order just rock up to people's houses when their loved ones are turned into nightwalkers and just say 'FYI, ya gotta move cause your husband is a vampire now, oh, and truth bomb, he's gonna murder you now unless you get outta this house?'." My words were glib, but I did want to know how that all worked, as they'd told me they also had to keep the Order a secret from the rest of the world. Liam laughed a little before answering.

"It's not quite like that, but we do influence the family to move in our own way. Magic is obviously used to help persuade them that it's suddenly a really good time to sell up and move far away, start a new life and so on. We are also fortunate that, as more people are getting cremated these days, we don't have quite as many people turning as we used to. Nightwalkers tend to also be quite brutal in their feeding habits, so they don't turn as many people as you'd think." Well, that all made sense, and was also slightly terrifying. I regarded Liam for a moment, as I processed what he'd just said.

"Well, I guess that works. It's still amazing that no one has worked out that vampires are real and are shouting about it all over the internet."

"Modern technology has brought with it a lot of challenges for us, that's true. But, the few who have learned the truth and started broadcasting it everywhere have mostly been written off as crazy. The tin foil hat wearers, for instance." That was easy to believe. I was suddenly forced to question everything I'd believed about the crazy people yelling about conspiracies on the internet. I was now part of an organisation that was a conspiracy-theorists wet dream.

"So, what do I do about Aurora then?"

"You could just tell her no." He stated it so simply, and now it was my turn to laugh, though it didn't have much humour behind it.

"Sure. You make that sound so easy."

"In my experience, it becomes easier when you stop trying to keep everyone else happy and just start to focus on what you need instead." I regarded him thoughtfully for a moment.

"You're right, I guess. But, when does that ability kick in? Cause that's not something that too many people my age have been successful at, in my experience." I was hoping he'd reveal how old he was, but he just shook his head with a smile.

"When you realise that the only person in the world who can make you happy is yourself, Isolde." I stared at him, as his words struck down deep within me. And the meaning behind it.

After the longest time, I cleared my throat, needing to get this training session back on track.

"So, what do I need to do to clear my mind?" He nodded over to the corner behind me, and I turned to look. I'd not noticed when I first came into the room, but he had a little meditation corner set up. There were cushions on the floor, on either side of a low table, with 3 candles on it.

"Take a seat over there." He got up and went to switch off the lights as I took a seat on the cushion closest to the wall. The room fell into darkness, lit only by the flickering candles, and I was suddenly struck by the intimacy of the situation. Liam hesitated for a moment, before coming closer.

"I find it easiest to switch off from all the chaos in this house when I come to this spot and focus on the flame. I've been using these techniques for a while now, whenever things get too noisy in my head, to try and bring myself some peace." He sat down with surprising grace for someone so tall. But then, this man could make fighting look like a dance, so I shouldn't be surprised by anything he did.

"So, do I close my eyes, or..."

"Focus all your concentration on the centre candle." I followed his direction, lowering my eyes from his face to gaze at the tallest candle in the middle, noticing how everything else around me became darker as I stared into the bright flame. "I have always found staring into a flame to be calming. I believe it has the same effect on you, from my observations over the years."

There was truth to his words. I had always found myself drawn to flames when given the opportunity. When camping, I always gravitated towards the campfire and had spent many an evening staring into the flickering flames, entranced. Moments when I thought I had been alone and unnoticed.

"Now focus on your breathing. Narrow your consciousness down to only the flame and your breaths." His voice had taken on a calming tone, and I focused on willing my thoughts to drift away, slowing my breathing. I continued, losing count of how many breaths I'd taken, forgetting where I was, and everything going on in the world around me, and just gazed into the flame. I felt a calm descend upon me, and everything else ceased to exist, there was only my breathing and the flame, which seemed to be growing bigger the longer I stared at it. I was no longer aware of where Liam was in the room, where I was, or even who I was at that exact moment.

The sound of a door slamming startled me, and I jumped as the flame leapt up in a ball into the air, the candle falling with a thud. Liam jumped to his feet as the flame hung suspended in the air, my gaze seemingly holding it there. I could feel his shock without looking at him, knowing that my face must have a similar expression. Slowly, he reached down to pick up the candle, raising it so that the small ball of fire attached to the wick once more. I let out the breath I had been holding as he lowered it back to the table, grateful that I hadn't managed to set fire to the Manor on my first night of working on my powers. He watched me intently, as I continued to stare at the candle in shock.

"Well... that was interesting."

I'll say...

An hour later, I let myself out of Liam's suite, having fallen back into my mind-clearing exercise with no more incidents. Liam said he needed a bit of sleep before I left and he was on guard duty again, so I decided to find Patrice to discuss when we would start my magic lessons. As I shut the door behind me, I turned to find Alana standing a few feet away, the expression on her face showing her surprise at seeing me there. Her eyes narrowed as if she'd just realised whose room I had come out of. Before I could say anything, she turned on her heel and stormed back around the corner. I shook my head. I had a strange feeling that this woman and I were never going to be friends, especially if she thought I was moving in on the man that she clearly had feelings for. I had no idea what the relationship between herself and Liam was, but I had no intention of getting caught in the middle of it all and feeding into the little melodrama that they had going on. I had far more important things to worry about.

Finding Patrice in the kitchen yet again, I accepted the bowl of noodles that she handed me, as she seemed determined to keep feeding me any time she saw me.

"How was your session with Liam?"

"Interesting." I wasn't quite sure how to describe to her what had happened with the flame, so I thought I'd leave it up to Liam to tell her. He probably understood what had happened far better than I did anyway. "When should we start working on my magic lessons? You mentioned yesterday that I'd need to start working on a few things?" I was realising now that I was eager to throw myself into anything to distract me from the grief I was still dealing with. Patrice smiled sadly, and I knew she'd worked that out too.

"How about we just get you through your last exams, first? Don't you have an assignment due next week?"

Honestly, was there anything about my life that these people didn't know?

"Yeah. I was going to ask for an extension though. I haven't opened a book in three weeks." Because that's how long it had been since my fiance had been brutally murdered before my eyes and turned into a vampire. Surely, that would be enough to get my lecturer and tutor to give me a compassionate extension... I just needed like a few months... I didn't think I'd get quite that long though.

"How about we go into the library now for a few hours, and Katyana and I can help?" With the exception of Alana, everyone had made me feel so welcome, and I felt my throat constrict with emotion a little. Maybe they didn't quite understand the pressure they were putting on me with this whole prophecy deal, but they were at least attempting to help me feel like I belonged here. I nodded, and once we finished eating, I followed Patrice into the library and we got down to the task of getting me through the final few weeks of my academic life.

I returned to my parent's home in the early hours of the morning, allowing Liam to drive me home so that he could take up his vigil outside. It had felt strange knowing that I was going to sleep while he just sat out in the dark, but he assured me that he was more than used to it. I knew that was true, given that he'd had more than twenty-five years of experience now. I still hadn't learned who the daywalker was amongst the Order, but I felt like standing guard in the dark for hours and hours was more of a job for him, rather than Liam.

After several fitful hours of sleep where my dreams were once again plagued by mysterious figures with blue eyes and sinister laughs that made my ears feel like they were bleeding, I dragged myself out of bed and went in search of my sister. As it was a weekend, I knew I'd find her in bed still. Jacob was at work, so I knew she'd be alone, and I let myself in, sneaking into bed beside her. Although our interaction the day before had been strained, I didn't like fighting with my sister, and I just needed to get things sorted with her.

Aurora rolled over and looked at me, slowly waking up.

"Hey." I pushed a strand of hair out of her face, and she blinked at me slowly.

"Hey. You okay?" Lately, it had been her climbing into my bed, not the other way around.

"Sort of. Are we okay?" I sounded so needy, but with my sister, I didn't care. It was the one relationship where I had always felt completely honest. At least, until this year, when everything started to turn to shit. I couldn't shake the feeling that my dishonesty was a large part of why everything had turned awful. But it wasn't like I could tell her. The Order had been very firm about that, and really, I wasn't sure that she would believe me anyway. She'd definitely be marching me off to the mental health ward, thinking that I'd finally lost it.

"Of course we're okay. I'm just worried about you, babe. You're making so many snap decisions lately, and I'm worried that one day you're going to wake up after the grief has lessened, and suddenly you regret all these changes." She reached over and pulled me to her, and I snuggled into her arms, grateful for the contact.

"I know... I guess I just need you to trust that I know what I'm doing. Can you try and understand that?"

"Okay... But what are we going to do about finding somewhere to live? Because as much as I love Mum and Dad, I can't take much more of the constant parental interaction." I could relate. Our parents had been hovering a lot since we moved back in, and the attention was starting to become grating.

"How about we start looking for somewhere to rent together? We don't need to buy this time. You and Jacob will want your own place one day, I'm sure?" Aurora hesitated for a moment, and for a split second, I wondered if everything was okay with their relationship. She eventually nodded though.

"Yeah, you're right. That's a good idea. Let's start looking today, okay?" And just like that, we had a plan, and I hadn't had to get into an argument with my sister. Or burn my old house down.

CHAPTER TEN

The following fortnight, I finally got around to speaking to my boss.

"We'll miss you around here, Isolde. I'm so sorry about everything that happened. Will was a good man." Danielle gave me a hug as I stood up after having dropped the bomb that I wasn't going to be coming back. I fought to keep the tears at bay. I had always known this was a temporary job, but we had been like a little family here, and they had all known Will. I hadn't seen any of them since the funeral, but they had all been texting constantly. I really needed to start to do a better job of keeping in contact with everyone, but had been struggling to respond to messages ever since Will's death.

"Thanks, Danielle. I'm going to miss you all too. But with everything that has happened, I just need a fresh start." She nodded in understanding.

"Do you know what you're going to do?"

"Yeah, I've got a job lined up. I'll be starting once I finish my exams in two weeks. It's a research assistant position. Might as well put that university degree to use." I figured this was the closest I'd get to telling people the truth, and I wasn't technically lying. The Order did pay their members, and quite well, I might add. And I was researching... I was just leaving out the ass-kicking aspect of my new position.

Aurora was growing increasingly suspicious and regularly questioned my whereabouts over the following weeks. With my time constantly taken up by the Order in the months since Will's death, I wasn't actively searching for a new home, causing frustration for Aurora. Adjusting to more change was something I wasn't ready to handle yet. I hadn't told her that I wasn't returning to work, so I was able to use that as an excuse for the most part. However, that didn't explain my change in attitude and the fact that I was slimming down rapidly due to my daily workouts with Liam. Both my twin and I had curvy builds, but all the exercise combined with forgetting to eat a lot had meant I'd become quite thin at an alarming rate.

Though others seemed hesitant to comment, it was something that had concerned Patrice greatly, as she informed me when she pulled me aside one Saturday morning as I walked through the front door.

"Isolde, I'm worried about you," she stated simply as she lead me by the hand into the kitchen.

"Why?" I had thought I'd been doing well, not falling into a grieving heap every hour, as I had been doing up until around a month earlier. I had been burying myself in my studies, training with Liam and taking tentative steps towards learning about my, as yet elusive, powers... I thought I'd been doing a great job of pretending.

But apparently not. This was made quite clear as Patrice put a plate full of bacon, eggs and hash browns down in an empty spot at the large bench. Liam was already there, having headed straight to the kitchen when we arrived together. He was sitting at the long table with Alana, Katyana and another man by the name of Sam, whom I had only met for the first time the week before. Sam was English and looked to be around thirty, though I was fast learning that looks meant nothing when it came to age with these people. I had found out that Patrice was two hundred years old the week before, something I was still reeling from. The idea that I was now going to live such a long life was incredibly overwhelming.

"You are becoming far too thin, and I rarely see you eat." Patrice served herself the same food, glancing at my plate with a look that told me to sit my butt in the chair and eat my breakfast. I wondered briefly if I would be allowed to leave the table if I left so much as a piece of rind on my plate. Alana was watching this exchange with a smirk, and I felt something in me snap.

"What is your problem, Alana?!" My words were harsh, and she looked shocked for a moment before her eyes narrowed. I had so far just avoided her and not reacted to any of her little snippy comments, but I was tired. She opened her mouth to retort now, but Liam cut her off.

"Leave it." She closed her mouth again, still glaring at me, which I found even more frustrating. I could see that whatever the problem was, I was not going to find out any time soon, so I ate my breakfast in a quiet rage, seething at everyone, including Sam and Katyana, who had sat with their heads down through the entire non-conversation, obviously knowing more than they were willing to admit.

After I begrudgingly finished my breakfast, I went into the library and started studying where I had left off the night before. I'd sat my last exam two weeks ago, and now that I was finished with uni, I was going through the histories of the Protectors, trying to learn all I could about what exactly their part was in this war. I had started from the beginning, as I figured it would be best to know everything. I read back over my notes from the night before, figuring my half-asleep brain needed a refresher.

The history of the Order goes back as far as Ancient Greece, but the written histories only started from around the first century AD. The Order of the Dragon didn't exist as we know it until that time.

Before then, each of the seventh sons or daughters simply fought against the dark as individuals. As the Roman Empire expanded its borders, the Order slowly formed. With members coming from different civilisations to band together in secret, they were united in their intent to keep the presence of vampires a secret from the rest of humanity. This allowed them the ability to live under the illusion that they were the superior race on Earth.

When the Roman Empire began to fall, and society became more superstitious, it had been harder to keep the war contained, and that was when the Order formed in the way it was now known, with elders and the use of magic.

I had somehow managed to condense over two thousand years of history into three paragraphs. I wasn't entirely sure if that was a positive thing or just showed how much more I had left to read. I pulled out the book that I'd been reading last night and opened it up to where I'd left my place marker. After half an hour of study, I felt someone's eyes boring into the back of my head, and I didn't need to turn around to know that I wasn't the only one still pissed about the hostility in the kitchen.

"Fuck off, Alana." I knew that she would hear me, but I found I just didn't care. For the past two months, all that she had done was treat me with disdain, as if my presence was an insult to her personally.

"Whatever, Isolde. You want to know what my problem is with you?" I turned as her voice rang out across the quiet room, ready for the fight that had been brewing for weeks.

"Sure. Enlighten me. Why are you such a bitch?" She glared at me, still leaning against the door frame.

"You have no idea, do you? You haven't got a clue."

"No, I bloody well don't. All I know is that since I first met you, you have been nothing but a snooty bitch to me when I've done nothing to deserve it." She scoffed at this. I resisted the urge to throw the incredibly heavy – and ancient - text that I was holding at her. I figured that the others would probably see this as an insult to the book, though.

"You've had it so easy. Your life has been so blessed. Do you have any idea what it has been like having to keep you safe these past twenty-five years? You've just had everything handed to you." I had no idea what this woman was babbling about, but I was not going to listen to another moment of this crap as Alana came further into the room, her hands balled into fists at her side.

"Excuse me?!" I was on my feet now, turning to face her as my own hands clenched into fists at my sides. "Blessed?! Not even eight weeks ago, I witnessed the love of my life get ripped apart by a vampire and then found out that he is now one himself. Not to mention the fact that it is on me to stop some vampire war that I know nothing about. So, you can stick your blessed life comment up-"

"Oh, poor you, you watched your fiance die? I watched my entire fucking family die. I didn't have anyone to protect me. I didn't get treated like cotton wool when I turned twenty-five and had all of this thrust upon me." I was beginning to see that nothing I said to this woman would make her happy as she came to stand right in front of me. Now I was becoming royally pissed off.

"So, your life sucked? That is *not* my fault. Nor did I ask to be treated like cotton wool, as you so nicely put it. You clearly have some issues that you need to deal with on your own, and you can quit taking them out on me because I didn't fucking ask for any of this to happen to me, in case you forgot." Once I started swearing, I often had an issue with stopping, but at this moment, I didn't feel like being polite.

"That, right there." She pointed a finger in my face, and I smacked it away, seething. "That is your problem. You keep whining about how you didn't ask for this. Toughen up, princess, and get over it-" Alana's tirade was cut off by the sound of Liam clearing his throat as he leaned against the door frame, just as she had done moments ago.

"We can hear the pair of you from upstairs," Liam said quietly, looking at Alana meaningfully. She just shrugged and spun on one heel, pushing past him as she marched out of the room in a way that clearly said this was not over. As far as I was concerned, it was. She was just a bitch, plain and simple.

"It's not as simple as that," Liam commented, and at first, I thought I must have spoken aloud, but I remembered what Patrice had said about his powers.

"I thought you didn't like to use your mind-reading abilities." I flopped back down, wanting to just be left alone. For his part, Liam ignored this last thought and came over to sit across from me at the desk.

"I didn't particularly need to use them; it was written all over your face. And yes, Alana does have issues, which she shouldn't be taking out on you." I realised he was dressed for sleep in a pair of grey sweatpants and a white long-sleeve shirt. Our argument must have brought him from his bed. I knew he tended to sleep during the day for a few hours, having spent his nights ensuring my safety.

"Look, she told me about her family. And I get it, her life sucked, but I don't see how that has got anything to do with me." Liam sighed, rubbing his face as I glowered at him.

"It's not just that. Her family was killed when she was a child in a house fire, and she was the sole survivor. Her extended family was fractured, and she spent her childhood going from foster home to foster home, and it was not the most pleasant childhood, as you can well imagine." I nodded, though I still saw no reason why her childhood gave her any right to be such a bitch to me. Liam continued on, his expression showing that he'd heard my train of thought.

"When she first showed up on our radar, she was twenty, and the elders had originally thought, incorrectly, that it was her that the prophecy was about, as her mother had been a seventh daughter, and we believed her father had been a seventh son. For the few years after she turned twenty-five, she was trained much as you are being trained now.

"Then you were born. And we realised that we'd got it wrong. When the elders looked back over her family history, it turned out there had been a stillborn older brother before her father, the birth was never registered, though, and her father hadn't known of him. Therefore, for a few short years, Alana had gone from feeling like nothing to believing that she had this destiny. To be told that the same destiny was not hers but was the birthright of this young woman who had everything in life that she'd never had... Can you see where this is going?" I could, and although I pitied her, which I was sure she would be thrilled about, I found that I was angry as well.

"She wants this destiny? She can have it for all I care!" I was beginning to feel like a petulant child, but I was beyond caring.

"Unfortunately, it doesn't work that way, as you know." The way that he spoke to me, like a parent, was beginning to grate on me, but I gritted my teeth, as there was still another question that I felt needed answering.

"There is more to it than that, though, isn't there? She seems to think that I'm out to steal you away from her or something to that effect... Doesn't she?" I looked him directly in the eye and was amused to see him squirm a little uncomfortably at the question.

"She is jealous of the fact that we spend so much time together, as she has made it clear to me, on several occasions over the years, that she wished to have a relationship with me. She is under the impression that you and I have developed feelings for each other." I rolled my eyes, though I ignored the fact that I was pleased that he didn't appear to return her feelings, telling myself it was because I believed that he was too good for her.

"Does the fact that I was engaged to be married until three months ago even factor into her way of looking at things?" Liam smiled a little.

"No, unfortunately, it doesn't. Anyway, that is why Alana is, rightly or wrongly, treating you the way that she is. Now, why don't we head to the gym to work off some of that anger you've still got stored up? Seeing as I'm clearly not going to be able to get any sleep while you're this angry and screaming every thought in your head." He got to his feet, putting a hand out towards me. I took it and stood, looking up at him.

"I thought you could block out our thoughts?"

"I usually can. But with your thoughts, Isolde... I seem to have trouble tuning you out." He held my gaze for a moment before turning and leading the way out of the room. I could see that the conversation was now over, but I didn't feel any better for it and just wished that Alana would get over her issues and realise that if it were up to me, I would give up my destiny in a heartbeat if it meant that I could go back in time and still be a happily engaged woman, preparing to marry the love of my life. I didn't understand why she would think something was happening between Liam and I, anyway. I treated him no differently than I did anyone else in the house, and I couldn't see anything different in how Liam treated me compared to the others... I mean, sure, he looked out for me, but that was his job, right? I guess we all had a few issues to deal with...

That afternoon, Aurora and I went to have a look at a few houses together, finally taking a step up from scrolling through the rental listings online. After looking at the first three houses, I was starting to feel a little disheartened, as the homes that were in our price range weren't what we had hoped. We stopped into the real estate agent who had handled the sale of the townhouse, thinking that they may have apartments for us to at least look at.

"Hello, girls. I heard you're house hunting?" It was the same shameless woman who had sold the townhouse for me. I'd hoped never to have to deal with her again after the settlement went through a few weeks ago, and I was almost tempted to ask for another estate agent, but she had already started talking.

Don't they usually have different people who handled the rental side to the sales side of the business?

"I have the perfect place for you. It's just a few streets away…" She continued prattling off info about the house, and Aurora and I wrote down the address, saying we would meet her there in ten minutes, as it was currently empty.

"I doubt this place is going to be any good, Is. I mean, is a house in Bulimba really going to be in our price range? It's probably just an old shack." I nodded in agreement as Aurora tried to find the house listing on her phone while sitting in the passenger seat.

I followed the directions the GPS lady gave me in her prim and proper voice, and moments later, Aurora and I got out of the car, gaping at the house in front of us. This couldn't be it, surely? The address we wrote down must have been wrong…

On the outside, the house ticked all of our boxes. It had a small front yard with a simple garden and a beautiful big frangipani tree that was still in flower, unheard of in late June.

We stepped through the gate and met the estate agent at the door.

"Megan, are you sure we can afford this place?" I was certain she had made a mistake. She probably hadn't been listening properly. I looked around the wide verandah, wishing that I could afford an old Queenslander like this. It had been renovated to pristine condition. Through the window, I could see polished floorboards.

"It's under the amount you told me." Aurora and I must have had identical looks of disbelief on our faces as Megan nodded vehemently as she continued. "Yeah, the landlord was adamant about how much to list it for. Only just went on the market today. Come on. We'll have a look inside." Aurora and I exchanged excited looks and clung to each other, both trying not to get our hopes up.

But upon stepping through the door, I knew immediately that we'd found our new home. With its polished wooden floors and high ceilings, the four-bedroom house was exactly what I had always imagined living in. The location was perfect, only three streets away from the river. I could easily walk to and from the ferry if I wanted to. Two of the large bedrooms had adjoining bathrooms, which meant I wouldn't have to share with Aurora and Jacob... I forced aside the tightening feeling in my chest and tried not to imagine growing old here with Will and instead pictured the home that Aurora and I could make for ourselves... It was bittersweet, but I knew we had to make this place ours. The twinkle in my sister's eye confirmed my feelings, and we did our best not to do a happy dance right in the middle of the lounge room.

After having dragged both of our parents all over the house and signing all the paperwork at the real estate agents to get the ball rolling Aurora and I could do nothing else but talk excitedly about our new home. My father was convinced that at that price, there must be something wrong with it, but I refused to let myself be concerned. It was the first time since Will's murder that I had felt any kind of excitement. It felt good to feel something other than grief, anger, frustration or the debilitating numbness that I was so familiar with.

I made myself a simple dinner that night, enjoying having the house to myself for the first time since we'd moved back in, as everyone else was out for various reasons. After indulging in a lovely, relaxing bath, I entered my bedroom that evening and immediately brought Ainslie's number up on the messages app on my phone. I was excited to share some great news with her, having dropped off the radar with her lately. I hadn't been in touch with any of my friends much since Will's death, and I knew I needed to start to reach out more.

A movement out of the corner of my eye made me look up and promptly stopped texting. Sitting on my window ledge, just as Liam had done several weeks earlier, was Will.

CHAPTER ELEVEN

I dropped the phone and stood motionless, staring at Will, who leaned casually against the window frame, as though sneaking up the sides of houses and terrorising women in their bedrooms was something that he did every day... Which, for all I knew, could be true these days.

It had been seven weeks since I had seen him, although I had felt his presence in the dark outside of the house, a constant reminder of what he had become. But the creature sitting on my window looked exactly like my Will, the man that I had loved for the greater part of my life.

He smiled his breathtakingly beautiful smile that had always been able to make me melt at the knees.

"Hey, beautiful." God, his voice. I hadn't heard it since that fateful night, which felt like a lifetime ago, but was only three short months.

Every part of me wanted to run into his arms and hold him so tight that he could never disappear again. Every part except the pit of my stomach, which was screaming at me to run back out the door.

"What... No hug? Is that any way to greet your dead fiance?" I backed up a step, although I knew he could not come into the room.

"What are you doing here?" I finally found my voice, though it sounded alien to me, robotic even.

"I came to see you. I miss you." This was near impossible. Although I knew what he was, what he'd become, he didn't look like the demonic creature that had attacked me in my front yard. Why did he have to be so beautiful, so perfect... so Will? I took a deep breath and stepped back again, now standing in the doorway of my bedroom, still staring at the man at my window.

"Leave now. I know what you are, and you are not welcome here." As I said this, I sent a silent plea to Liam, hoping against all hope that he was listening from somewhere nearby. I hadn't spoken to anyone from the Order since this morning, but I knew Liam was usually the one on the nighttime watch when I wasn't at the Manor.

"Now, now. Someone has been telling you stories, haven't they? Telling you that I'm one of the bad guys." Will shook his head, the condescension in his voice making me want to throw something at him, but I was still frozen where I stood. "Did you ever stop to think that maybe your precious Protectors are the bad guys? What sort of person spends their entire lives stalking someone?" I raised an eyebrow at this last question.

"Yes, who would spend their entire lives stalking someone? Tell me, Will, what is it you have been doing every single night since you woke up? Leaving me threatening notes and dead animals? Staring up at my bedroom window, by any chance? Or hiding in the shadows, waiting for me to be alone? I've felt your presence, Will, so don't try to deny you've been the one doing the stalking."

"I won't deny that I've been watching you, Isolde. You're the love of my life, and it breaks my heart to see you with him." Will spat out the word 'him' as though it was a bad taste in his mouth. For a moment, I wondered who he was talking about, but then I realised he must be referring to Liam. I didn't know how to respond to this and just stared at Will, praying that Liam would appear soon and this torture would be over.

"You know what he is, don't you?" Will continued to taunt me, but this question threw me.

"He's one of the Protectors. Like me." I shrugged as though this statement meant nothing.

"He's nothing like you or any of the others." Will was enjoying this; I could see it in his ice-blue eyes. Eyes that were so similar to Liam's, now that I thought about it.

I refused to let him get to me, although I knew where he was going with his goading remarks, and I didn't like it.

"Don't you want to know what I'm talking about? The Isolde that I knew would have been bursting at the seams with curiosity." Something in me flickered, a memory, though it was gone before I could recall it.

"The Isolde that you knew is gone. She disappeared the night you died." Although I said this with a hardness that I truly wished I felt, inside, I was falling apart.

As I struggled to pull myself together, Will continued to grin at me cruelly. It was a smile that I would never have thought possible on his face. He truly had become a stranger to me.

"You can't fool me, Isolde. You forget I know you better than anyone, probably even better than you know yourself." How true this statement once was.

As I struggled for a comeback to this last remark, Will suddenly disappeared from the window. I heard a loud crash and the sounds of struggle, though I was too afraid to go near the still-open window. I could hear the sounds of fists hitting flesh, and every part of me wished that I could see what was going on, that I could see who had come to my rescue. My instincts, however, told me that it was Liam. With the racket they were making, for the first time, since I'd learned the truth, I was grateful that my family was out after dark.

After what felt like an eternity, the sounds of fighting disappeared, and I stood motionless in my bedroom doorway, preparing to flee the room if necessary. When Liam appeared soundlessly at my window, I let out the breath that I had been holding and moved to sit down on the bed, my legs unable to hold me up anymore.

"Are you alright?" Liam made no move to come through the window, taking Will's place on the window ledge, and my suspicions of his true nature were doubled. Seeing him sitting where Will had sat only moments ago did not help my feelings of unease, and he watched me warily.

"Not even the smallest bit. He's going to keep coming back, isn't he? I'm never going to feel safe again." I wrapped my arms around myself, feeling as though I needed to protect myself from some unseen danger. I missed the feeling of protective arms around me, of someone else shielding me from the world's dangers. The realisation that I was now alone in a cold and dangerous world was crashing down on me. I didn't realise I was hyperventilating until I looked in the mirror and saw my reflection. Liam could do nothing from his vigil at my window, and I realised that he was the one who would be there to protect me, no matter who or what he was.

"Come in." I managed to breathe these words out in between my gasps for air, and after a moment's hesitation, Liam climbed through the window and was at my side, his arms enfolding me as I continued to sob silently.

"You're not alone, Isolde." Liam held me close, stroking my hair in a way that made me feel safe, something that Will had done only a few short months ago when I awoke in terror. Something that my mother used to do when I awoke from my nightmares as a child. Nightmares about creatures in the dark, with piercing blue eyes, terrorising my dreams. As I rested my head against his shoulder, tears streaming down my face, the memories of all my nightmares over the years came flooding back to me. With startling realisation, I understood now that Liam had been in the dark, watching me my whole life, and entering my dreams, almost as though his presence in my mind drove out the terrifying creatures that lurked in the dark.

I pulled away and looked up at him through my tear-filled eyes. He reached to wipe a tear away, and I clasped his hand in my own.

"You've been in my dreams all my life, haven't you?" Liam touched my face again with his free hand, wiping away another tear that slid slowly down my face.

"I've been watching over you since you were born, Isolde. I have protected you from your nightmares as much as I could over the years, though I could not do it after you turned twenty-five. Those nightmares are part of the process that you need to go through to deal with what your life now involves. The ones you had as a child, though, I could protect you from those." We sat so close that I felt as though I was falling into his eyes. I had known that part of his mind-reading abilities meant he was able to communicate telepathically to a degree, but I had never put the connection together. Something had changed between us in that instant of realisation, and I was petrified of what I was feeling.

"You're the younger brother, aren't you? The daywalker?" I had to know, though I didn't know what I would do with this information once it was confirmed. It was probably better for me not to know, but I couldn't bear being treated so delicately anymore. I needed to know everything. Liam just looked at me sadly for a moment before nodding. I let out another long breath, feeling as though I was deflating.

"Why didn't anyone tell me?" I was tired of all the secrets and lies, of being treated as though there were things I wasn't allowed to be told. Liam let go of me and stood up. I thought he was going to leave, but he just moved to the door, closing it so that the light that had previously flooded into the room from the hall was reduced to a sliver under the door. I should have been afraid, but I had come to trust Liam so much with my safety that it did not occur to me to be scared. I just wanted answers.

"In life, I was Liam O'Brien. These days, my last name has disappeared, as has the love I once held for my brother. I am simply Liam. However, yes, I am the younger brother. When I said I understood more than you could know, I meant it. I know how it feels to have my whole life ripped apart and have all of this thrust upon me. " The sadness in his eyes was heartbreaking. "And the reason that no one told you was that I asked them not to. I wasn't ready to have you look at me with the same fear that you hold for Will and Adam." Liam didn't return to sit on the bed, instead sitting on the window frame again, as though waiting for me to tell him to leave.

"Liam, the number of times that you've come to my aid in the past three months alone, and yet you still thought I'd view you as a monster?" I tried not to be offended at this thought, and Liam smiled, relaxing a little. I moved to his side, peering out the window to reassure myself that Will had truly left, before leaning against the window, my arm lightly touching his.

"I guess I keep forgetting how incredibly well-adjusted you are. Although you thought that we were all mad and that this was some nightmare, you've accepted it, taken it all in, and just got on with it." I thought he might have been thinking of someone else; there was no way anyone could have believed that I was well-adjusted. I had certainly declared that all of them were insane and needed to visit the mental ward on several occasions. Liam smiled, and I knew he must have heard my train of thought, which raised another question.

"Patrice told me you hate to use your mind-reading ability... Yet you always seem to know what I am thinking, and you said that you had trouble blocking me out... Why is that?" Liam looked at me for a moment before answering.

"I guess because I've been so attuned to you for so long that when it comes to your thoughts, I have a lot of trouble blocking them out... Does it bother you?" Now it was my turn to be silent for a moment, gathering my thoughts.

"I don't think it bothers me... It certainly comes in handy, like tonight, having you be able to hear me... I guess it's just a little scary having someone else up here beside me." I tapped my temple, and Liam smiled again. I enjoyed seeing him smile, something that felt so rare with the life we both lived. Looking into his eyes, I realised I should have put the connection together before now with his incredibly distinct eyes.

"How come when I saw you at Uni that day, your eyes were brown? It was only that one time; every other time, your eyes have been the colour they are now." That really should have been the give-away for me. His eyes, the startling, amazing blue that on Will, terrified me, but on Liam, it looked right. Liam looked at me in confusion.

"That's the second time you've mentioned seeing me at your university, yet I swear, you have only ever seen me twice in your life, prior to the night outside the townhouse."

"But... I saw you; we were looking straight at each other?!" Why was he not admitting it? For his part, Liam looked alarmed, though still confused, and it made me wonder if I'd just imagined him that day. Maybe that was why he had disappeared so quickly...

After a long moment, I noticed that I was leaning close to him, closer than was necessary. Both our hands at our sides on the window ledge, our fingers lightly brushed against each other's, and I felt a thrill run up my spine, which took me by surprise. He noticed at the same time, and I stepped back, pushing my hair back from my face in a way I hoped looked natural.

"Oh, I have good news, Aurora and I found a house. We signed the lease this afternoon."

It felt strange to be discussing something from my normal life with Liam, the centre of my very not-normal life, but I needed normal right now.

Liam smiled at me, and I marvelled that I had managed to get three smiles from him in the space of ten minutes.

"I know... It's one of our safe houses." And just like that, my news didn't feel so exciting anymore. I felt myself deflate once again, and I moved to flop down on the bed.

"Of course it is! I guess I shouldn't be surprised. I knew it was too good to be true... Why exactly did everyone bother with the charade?" Staring up at the ceiling, I was annoyed, and Liam knew it.

"Because they knew how important it was for you to retain some semblance of your former life."

"Then why tell me the truth now?" I was confused as to why he was giving up the truth so easily.

"Two reasons... One, I won't lie. I see no point to it, and two, I believe that you need to face up to reality and accept that this is your destiny, and I refuse to play games." I was momentarily stunned before the anger set in. Liam could tell that the warm fuzzy feelings I'd had moments earlier had fled the room as I pulled my knees into my chest and crossed my arms over them.

"I think I want to be alone now." Liam simply nodded and was out the window in one fluid movement, which annoyed me even more. These people had been in my life in one way or another since I was born, and it aggravated me that, though they had all watched me grow up, they still treated me as though I was a petulant child who needed to be coddled... All of them except for Liam, who was the only one who successfully made me feel like one...

The next morning, I arrived at the Manor in the same mood that I had been in when I went to sleep. Cranky.

"Good morning, Isolde. I heard about your late-night visitor." Patrice sat down next to me as I stared at the pile of books before me, struggling to remember where I was up to.

"Who? Liam?" I wasn't paying attention, but Patrice looked surprised.

"Will." She said with raised eyebrows.

"Right, him. Sorry, I'm just a little distracted, I guess." Patrice was at a momentary loss for words. I had just brushed aside the fact that I had seen my dead fiance appear at my window and taunt me for pleasure. I was crankier than I thought.

"Liam also told me you now know the truth of who he is..."

Patrice was not going to leave me alone, even though it was clear I was not the best communicator at the moment.

"Yeah." I shrugged, not sure what I was expected to say about it.

"Do you want to talk about it?"

"Not really. I'm in a bad mood right now. I'm probably best left alone." I knew I was being rude, but I just didn't have it in me to care at the moment.

"Okay. I'll leave you to it then." Patrice nodded at me, and I had the sense to hope that she was not offended by my attitude. She left the room, and I found myself staring at the page, reading the same words repeatedly.

After twenty minutes of this, I gave up, shoving the books away from me. I left them piled on the table and headed for the training room, figuring I could put all of my stored-up anger to good use and pummel the crap out of the punching bag. I stopped at the door as I saw Liam doing exactly what I had planned to do. I turned to leave again.

"We might as well do some training while you're this worked up," Liam didn't stop what he was doing as he spoke, and I briefly pictured myself punching him, no doubt amusing him even further.

"Fine." I headed to the changing rooms and changed into my workout clothes, the whole time seething at him.

I came out to find him doing push-ups, continuing to ignore me until I was ready. I took a few practice swings at one of the punching bags to warm up. When we started practising together, I found myself channelling everything I had been feeling, about Will, Liam and everyone else, into my attempts to kick Liam's ass. I wasn't even thinking about what moves to make or when to block, I simply acted on instinct. I threw a punch with my right fist, which he blocked expertly, but failed to see the kick that I followed it with. I connected with his head for a brief second, but he was gone in an instant, appearing behind me. He pulled my other hand up behind me in a vice-like grip, letting me know I had lost that round.

He let me go, and I turned to face him again, not even pausing between attacks. Liam could tell I meant business, and we each threw more energy into sparring than we had ever done together before. It seemed I wasn't the only one with issues right now.

Moments later, he had me pinned against the wall, both of my hands held over my head with one of his own. We were both breathing heavily at this point, and our faces were so close that I could look nowhere but into his eyes, which were boring into mine with a fierceness that I knew was reflected in my own. I didn't know what to make of it all, but I found my gaze drifting down to his lips, which threw me off balance.

What the hell is going on?

We stood staring at each other for what felt like an eternity, the tension palpable between us. Even as our breathing started to steady, neither of us moved, each waiting for the other to make the first move. Eventually, he released my hands and moved away, grabbing a bottle of water from the fridge and tossing me another. He left the room without a look back, leaving me standing alone, wondering what had just happened.

Over the next few weeks, I found myself surrounded by moving boxes yet again. I'd avoided being at the Manor as much as I could, still fuming at Liam and also incredibly confused by whatever had been happening between us.

Early on the day of the move, I shuffled into the kitchen as my mother was boiling the kettle, six mugs sitting on the breakfast bar with coffee in them.

"Who else is coming over?" For a brief moment, I worried that she was accidentally making one for Will out of habit, as she had done the day Aurora and I finished moving back in.

"Your friend Liam got here about twenty minutes ago. I must say, I'm relieved we've got another strong, young back to help out. I was worried that your father would be trying to do too much to help

Jacob." I was too stunned by what she said to be insulted that she felt that Aurora and I needed men to help us.

"I'm sorry, who's here?" I was convinced I had heard her wrong. There was no way Liam would be here to help me with my sad attempt to grasp some semblance of my past. I was still a little bitter.

"Your friend from uni... I'm sure he said his name was Liam, but maybe I was wrong. He said he was here to help you move..." Mum looked uncertain for a moment, but I quickly nodded like I knew exactly what she was talking about.

"No, that's right, I just wasn't expecting him so early..." I went outside, still convinced that she had made a mistake. But there he was, sitting on our back patio, eating toast with my father, Jacob and Aurora, looking like he belonged there. I stopped in my tracks and stared at him.

"What are you doing here?" I asked, not realising how rude I sounded until my father looked at me with raised eyebrows. For his part, Liam just smiled his heart-melting smile, the one that I saw so rarely...

Wait, where had that thought come from?

Thankfully, he gave no indication that he had heard me, and it seemed to be one of those rare moments when Liam was able to tune me out while I continued to stare at him.

"I know I'm here early, but I was up, so I figured I might as well get over here to help out as soon as I could." He was a far better actor than I would have expected. Given that, I knew he'd been outside all night.

"Right..." I went back inside to help my mother with the coffee and to escape the weirdness, Aurora following closely behind me.

"So, who is Liam?" I could hear in her tone that she wasn't happy. I figured there could be any number of reasons why, namely that she had never heard mention of this guy who had just shown up out of the blue to help us move. But I didn't have the energy to think about it. I was already exhausted, and I hadn't lifted a single piece of furniture yet.

"Just a friend from uni. I was complaining about moving, and he offered to help, no big deal. I didn't think he'd show up, to be honest, which was why I was surprised to see him here." I thought I did pretty well, though I was becoming concerned at the ease with which I was lying to my sister.

"I didn't realise you were in touch with any uni friends still." She wasn't going to let this go.

"A few... but Liam and I work together now, too, at my research job." And the lies just kept easily rolling off my tongue.

For her part, Aurora continued to look suspicious but, thankfully, let it drop. Although we had never lied to each other, Aurora was usually one to push you to tell her something even if you didn't want to, so I was both relieved and a little sad that she didn't push me further.

Everything in me wanted to tell her about the craziness that was now my life, but I couldn't, and it was killing me. I was tired of lying. Tired of grieving. Tired of my life spiralling out of control... However, there was nothing I could do about it. So, I just ate my cereal in silence and watched as Liam got on way too well with my family.

Once all of the boxes and furniture were loaded into the cars, I slid into the passenger seat of my car as Liam got behind the wheel, assuming the role of the driver yet again. I hadn't driven the car once when we'd been together, something that I had let happen far easier than I would have expected.

We hadn't had a moment alone together since breakfast, and I wanted some answers. My jaw was sore from clenching it all morning as he chatted easily with my father and made plans to fill an extra slot in Jacob's social soccer team next weekend whilst one of his team-mates were out of town.

"Right, spill. What's going on? Is there danger looming? Some new, unforeseen evil I'm being protected from?" I should not have been so snappy with him, but moving never brought out the best in me, and I was still smarting from his comments about dealing with my destiny. We had not talked much since the weirdness that had occurred at the Manor, and I had gotten the impression he had been avoiding being alone with me. Not that I'd been going out of my way to spend time with him either, as I sorted through my mixed feelings that were developing and that I refused to fully acknowledge.

"Nope, no evil, just helping a friend move." Liam pulled out of the driveway, and I looked at him closely as he kept his eyes on the road.

"I didn't know we were friends. I just figured I was someone you had to keep safe." I was being brutal now, and Liam sighed, looking over at me finally.

"Of course we're friends. What else would we be?" I wasn't quite sure how to respond to that question, so I just turned to stare out the window, pondering why on earth Liam was here, in my car, helping me move.

"Because I felt bad about what I said." I started, realising that Liam was in my head again.

"Why do you care?" I knew I sounded like a bitch, but I didn't care.

"Because although I said you need to deal with your destiny, I also forgot that I didn't deal with all of this so well in the beginning, either. I had it thrust upon me. The night I was told about the Order was also the night I became a vampire, and I didn't get a chance to deal with it like everyone else, as a human." I kept forgetting about his vampire side, having always seen him as a human with the same limitations as myself. But there was more to him than I realised.

"I guess I am pushing it all aside, but I had my future taken away from me, the future that I dreamt of for myself my whole life, to be married to Will, to have his children... All of that was within my grasp, and I had it all stolen from me in such a brutal way. It's going to take me a long time to deal with it. This life to me feels like a punishment," I whispered the final sentence, not wanting to admit to Liam that every moment I was around him reminded me that Will was no longer alive, at least not in the capacity he was meant to be. Liam took my hand in his as he continued to drive without really looking at the road.

"I do understand. Although I may not be able to relate to that particular part, I do understand all of it. I also know how much it kills you not to be able to talk to Aurora about all of this. My brother and I have been at war for so long that I sometimes forget that he is my brother." His jaw clenched, and he looked back at the road for a moment as if looking at me made it harder to acknowledge. He returned his gaze to me as he spoke again.

"Then I come face to face with him, and it starts all over again. The pain, the guilt that I could not have saved him... Missing the once unbreakable bond... Believe me; I understand that." Liam looked intently into my eyes, which should have scared me, given that he was driving my car, and yet we somehow arrived at the house in one piece. We remained in the car, continuing to look at each other for a few heartbeats more than necessary. I watched him breathe for a moment when something occurred to me.

"You breathe..." I looked at him curiously, and he nodded.

"Daywalkers are basically living vampires. We can eat food, although we still need blood. Our hearts still beat as well." I was surprised by this, and without thinking, I raised my hand to his chest to feel his heart beating against the thin shirt he wore beneath his hooded jumper. I stared at his chest for a few beats first before looking up and finding his gaze on my face as he moved to cover my hand gently with his own, holding it in place.

In the space of one five-minute car drive, everything between us had shifted, and I knew he felt it too. I felt my breath hitch as his eyes lowered to my lips.

We were shaken from our reverie as a car door shut outside, and I looked up to see Katyana and Sam walking over from where they'd parked one of the Order's cars across the road. I looked back at Liam in surprise as he moved his hand away.

"We figured the more, the merrier." He shrugged with a half smile before climbing out of the car. I did the same, and we were joined by the others as Liam opened the boot.

"Put us to work, lady." Katyana smiled at me, and I wondered if either she or Sam had noticed what had just happened between myself and Liam in the car. It didn't appear so, as they started helping Liam unpack boxes. I shook my head and went to join them.

CHAPTER TWELVE

The next morning, I awoke abruptly, ripped from sleep by the sound of the doorbell ringing. Disorientated, I groaned and rolled out of bed. I winced as my feet hit the cold floorboards and slipped into my fluffy bunny slippers before leaving the room. Grumbling about how early it was, having been up until the early hours unpacking, I opened the front door and was surprised to see Liam, Katyana and Celeste standing there. I was awake enough to take note that Liam was holding a tray of coffee cups.

"What are you guys doing here?" I realised too late how rude that sounded as I stepped aside and let them walk through.

"Well, we figured we'd help you get settled," Celeste said, handing me a bunch of flowers with a big smile. Surprised, I watched as Liam walked into the kitchen and set the tray of coffees down. I noted that there were six as Aurora and Jacob came out of their room, looking as exhausted as I felt. Knowing that the others had bought coffee for everyone made me think my sister might be more welcoming than she had been yesterday with Liam.

"Hi, I'm Celeste." Celeste put her hand out towards my sister, who looked at her briefly before throwing me a look over her shoulder.

"Let me guess, more uni friends that you've never mentioned before?"

Guess I was wrong about the being more welcoming part.

I wondered when my sister had become so prickly towards strangers, but at least she shook Celeste's hand. Celeste, for her part, ignored my sister's rudeness and introduced herself to Jacob, who was much more polite and gladly accepted the coffee that Liam handed him.

"We know how much moving sucks, so we figured we'd come help unpack. Anything to help you guys out after the past few months." Celeste deftly avoided the mention of uni, which I was grateful for, as I didn't want to tell any more outright lies to my sister if I could avoid it.

I watched everyone chat for a bit before heading into my room to get changed out of my pyjamas, suddenly aware that I was still dressed in my fuzzy pink pants and singlet top sans bra.

When I came back out, Celeste and Katyana were joking around with Liam in the kitchen as the three of them set about unpacking all the glasses and plates. I noticed that Aurora was on board with accepting the help that was offered after all, as she'd obviously assigned them the task before she and Jacob headed back into their room.

I found myself watching them for a while, smiling at how they all interacted together, a brother with his two younger sisters.

"Seriously, Liam, why would you put the dinner plates in the same cupboard as the saucepans?" Celeste asked with mock disgust, and Liam threw his hands up in surrender.

"In his defence, he had servants the last time he had to deal with such mundane tasks." Katyana teased, and Liam scowled.

"Hey, that's not true. I've helped with plenty of the Orders relocations."

"Yeah, but when was the last time you were in the kitchen

without Patrice?" I spoke up, and he turned to give me an incredulous look as the others laughed, loving that I'd involved myself in the teasing.

"Traitors, both of you." He pointed at the others, and Katyana threw a tea towel at him.

It was at that moment that I realised that these people were now my family too. The past few months, I had kept to myself most of the time when around the others, so wrapped up in my grief that I hadn't once noticed how often they all tried to reach out. The only person who had so far been able to get past my wall had been Liam, and I felt bad about that now. These were good people.

At lunchtime, we were joined by Sam and Celeste's husband, Daniel, another member of the Order, and before long, I was joking along with them as we ate the pizza that the men had brought with them, determined to let them all see how appreciative I was for the unspoken offer of friendship. They all smiled back at me with ease. To them, I had always been a part of the family.

When they were all ready to leave later that afternoon, I walked them to the door. Liam let the others go on ahead before turning back to me as I stood waiting to wave them off.

"I'll come pick you up tonight, okay?" He was standing so close, and it felt so natural when he pushed a strand of hair back over my ear. I was due to start magic lessons in earnest tonight with Katyana and Patrice, and they'd explained that it could be quite physically and mentally draining. Aware that I wasn't ready to stay in the Manor yet, Liam had offered to collect me when Katyana had mentioned it again earlier, and I was grateful once again that he could read my mind, saving me from having to admit out loud that I wasn't ready to give up my freedom and stay in the room that had been set aside for me at the Manor. Even if it was the most beautiful room I'd ever been in, and had been laid out especially for me.

I only noticed the intimacy of how we stood as I heard Aurora clear her throat, having come to stand just behind me. I wasn't sure what look she had given Liam, but I noticed a flash of annoyance in his eyes as he stepped away, walking to where Sam and Katyana stood waiting by the car he'd driven over earlier. I turned to face my sister as I closed the door once they'd all driven off. Aurora shot me a judgemental look before she walked away again, and I sighed as I headed into my bedroom to continue unpacking, alone once again.

I avoided my sister for the rest of the day as I set my room up how I wanted it. It felt so strange to have a room that was entirely my own once again. Aside from the brief time back at my parent's house these past four months, I had shared a bedroom with either Aurora or Will. Even during my brief time in London, I had shared with Katyana and another German student. To have a space that was only filled with my things felt weird to me. And lonely.

When I knew Liam was on his way to come and get me, I had a quick shower and made sure I was waiting outside to avoid having another awkward exchange with Aurora, and I knew that Liam took note of this as he pulled up beside me.

"Thanks for picking me up." I buckled myself in as he pulled away from the curb and turned the car around to head back to the Manor.

"No problem. It gives me a chance to catch up on some sleep anyway while you're with the others." He kept his eyes on the road this time as he drove, and I tried not to think about that too much, although I couldn't help wondering if he was distancing himself a little after the stand-off with Aurora earlier. I wasn't sure if I should be concerned that I was hoping that wasn't the case, having grown used to the moments between us when he reached out to touch me. And I enjoyed them. Best to just push those thoughts out of my mind entirely when I knew he could hear what I was thinking.

I was grateful that he didn't comment at all, but he did reach over and take my hand, squeezing my fingers briefly without looking over. That was comforting at least. I squeezed back and turned to look out the window, continuing to hold his hand. I'd just ignore that too. I was good at ignoring the things that were hard to accept, and I wasn't ready to acknowledge the feelings swirling around inside me yet.

Once we arrived at the Manor, Liam left me to head off in search of Patrice and Katyana while he had a few hours of sleep. The benefit of being a daywalker was that he didn't need as much sleep as a human did, but with the odd hours he had to keep when guarding me, he was using any chance he was able to get what few hours of sleep that he could. I tried not to think about how much easier it would be for him if I just caved and moved in here.

I found Patrice in her office, sitting across from Damon, one of the other elders who had recently arrived from London. So far, I wasn't quite sure what to make of him. He was quite standoffish and barely spoke to anyone except Patrice and occasionally Liam. But I had found him watching me with keen interest several times now, and something about it made me feel uncomfortable. It was different to how the others watched me when they were ready to offer me support and reach out a hand of friendship, except for Alana, who I just tried to avoid completely.

When I'd noticed Damon had been watching me, it had been as though he was assessing me. And had so far been unimpressed with what he'd seen. It was quite disconcerting, and I didn't like it. I hadn't signed up to be scrutinised by a grumpy old man. Although he looked like he was maybe in his mid-forties, being an elder, I had to assume he was at least two hundred or so years old.

Patrice and Damon both looked up at me quickly as I knocked on the open door frame.

"Patrice? Sorry to interrupt. Katyana mentioned today that you wanted to start my magic lessons properly tonight. Something about the moon phase?" Patrice looked briefly at Damon as she nodded.

"Yes, it's a full moon tonight." I wasn't sure if that was directed at me or Damon, but as I had no idea what that meant, I left it to Damon to respond.

"Ah, of course."

Well, that was useless to me.

Patrice smiled when she noted the blank look on my face and rose to her feet as she waved Damon out of the room, dismissing him.

"A full moon is when magic is at its strongest, Isolde. So we should be able to perform a few spells with you tonight. And we may be able to get a read on how strong your power truly is." Right, well, no pressure then. I wasn't feeling particularly confident in these abilities that everyone kept expecting from me, as aside from the fire incident with Liam and the occasional floating object, my powers had been pretty elusive.

I followed Patrice as she led the way out of her office and into the room across the hall that I hadn't yet entered, knowing that it was one of her private areas in the house. The interior of the room was devoid of windows and modern technology, situated in the heart of the Manor. To compensate for the lack of light, an array of unlit candles of different hues and sizes were placed on every surface. The only furnishings present were a low table similar to the one in Liam's study and a collection of large cushions for seating. The room had a ledge running around it, with evenly-spaced candles placed along it. Patrice summoned Katyana from the kitchen, and the three of us took our seats on the cushions.

"So, I'm going to show you how to channel the power of the full moon through you. Essentially, your body will become a conduit for that power, and it will allow you to tap into your inner strength." I blinked at Patrice's bold statement.

"Ooookay..." I wasn't confident about this.

"Just follow my lead and repeat what I say." She began a slow chant, using a language I didn't recognise, and Katyana nodded at me enthusiastically, encouraging me to repeat the words. I closed my eyes, the same as Patrice and began to chant the words along with her. I lost track of anything else in the room, and it wasn't until a few minutes later that I realised that Patrice was no longer chanting with me. I opened my eyes, not sure what I was going to see, but nothing appeared to have changed. Katyana and Patrice exchanged a confused look.

"What exactly were you expecting to happen?" I was disappointed that nothing had happened, but I also wasn't entirely sure that I trusted Patrice at this moment when it seemed like she had no idea what to expect.

"It was a spell to light the candles." That would have been really nice to know beforehand. Given our location in the centre of the manor, I didn't know how I felt about setting fire to this many candles without having any real idea how to control the power.

We continued trying for another hour, and by the end, all that happened was that I had broken out in a sweat and had a headache from straining so hard. Patrice looked quite disheartened as she returned to her office to do some more research, and I tried not to feel like I'd disappointed her.

"Hey, don't worry about it, Isolde. You've had a lot going on. We'll work out what the source of your power is eventually." Katyana gave me a quick squeeze before she left as well, as Sam was waiting for her to go on patrol with him. Trying to push aside how dejected I was feeling, I trudged up to the room that I so rarely entered. My bedroom.

Someone had set up a space in the corner for me, similar to the one that Liam had in his study for mind-clearing. I sat on one of the cushions and used the lighter on the table to light the candles, beginning to take myself through the process that Liam had taught me. Of everything I'd learned so far, this was something I had found the most beneficial, and I used it regularly whenever I had begun to feel overwhelmed by this life I now led.

After a long time, perhaps hours even, my mind began to clear out all the thoughts swirling around, and I felt calmer as I continued to stare at the middle flame. I was startled by a knock on the door. Just like the first time, the flame from the middle candle leapt into the air, this time joined by the flames from the other two, and they hung in the air before me as Liam came into the room. He stayed where he was in the doorway, realising he'd interrupted me, and watched as I gazed intently at the three balls of light. I had no idea what I was doing, but the flames seemed to be growing bigger now, and I concentrated on the one in the middle. I willed it to begin moving around the other two in a small circle, and I felt a smile break out on my face as it worked. Becoming more confident now, I then split my focus and encouraged the second and third balls of light to follow the first, and eventually, we both watched as the three flames whirled in a slow circle in front of me.

"Try and see if you can guide them back to the candle wicks one at a time," Liam suggested quietly, and I did as he said. I concentrated on keeping the other two circling while I led the first back down to the candle successfully. Once I did the first one, the other two followed suit easily, and I grinned up at Liam proudly.

"Was that what Patrice was teaching you tonight?" Liam asked, coming further into the room now, taking a seat in the armchair near the window. I shook my head.

"No. She was trying to teach me to do a spell to light candles, not control flame."

"Did it work?" Liam watched me curiously as my disappointment from earlier returned, and I shook my head again.

"No. I couldn't get it to work, although we tried for over an hour. She seemed really disappointed." Liam looked thoughtful now and looked at the candles burning in front of me for a moment. He stood up from the chair and came closer, taking a seat on the cushion opposite from where I sat. He leaned forward and blew out the candles, and the room was engulfed in darkness.

"Try again now." I could make out his face in the moonlight from the window as my eyes adjusted to the lower light. I didn't particularly want him to witness my failure, but something about the earnest expression on his face made me try again. I closed my eyes as I began chanting once more. Nothing happened.

I looked at Liam, expecting to see the same disappointment I'd witnessed earlier from Patrice, but he was just studying the candle closely.

"Try it without the chant."

"What, just think about it lighting up?" That seemed like a crazy idea. If I couldn't make it work with the chant, I seriously doubted I could get it to work without it.

"Just humour me, Isolde."

"Get out of my head, Liam," I grumbled, and he chuckled.

"Stop pouting and just try it." I huffed, and after pouting for another moment, I looked down at the outline of the candle from where I could see it in the moonlight. Taking a deep breath, I began staring at it intently.

Light.

Not only did the candle light up, but every single other candle in the room followed suit until the room was aglow. I hadn't realised how many candles were in the room until that moment, and I gaped around in shock before bringing my gaze back to Liam.

"You don't need spells."

Later, as we drove back to my house in silence, I pondered over the events of the evening. When we saw Patrice again before we left, Liam didn't mention a thing to her about what I had just done, and I wondered at the reasoning behind it. I hadn't noticed that we'd pulled to a stop outside my home until Liam cleared his throat.

"You doing okay over there? You haven't said a word out loud since you lit the candles." The fact that he said the words "out loud" confirmed that he had been able to hear my thoughts for the past half an hour and was leaving me to sort through them all in peace.

"Can I trust the Order, Liam?" I figured I'd just ask the question outright, seeing as he already knew what I'd been thinking. To his credit, he didn't answer me straight away. It gave me some relief that he didn't immediately jump to their defence and assure me that my misgivings were unfounded.

"I think we've been waiting so long for the end of this war that some people are rushing into things too quickly, not having any real idea of what to expect from you and your powers. At least, that's what I got from what little I heard before I came and found you."

That was a very diplomatic answer.

"It was, wasn't it?" Liam responded to my thought out loud with a smile, perhaps to remind me that he was always listening. I gave him a small smile back and placed my hand on the door handle.

"Thank you for dropping me home. I'll see you tomorrow." I opened the door, and Liam reached to take my hand before I could climb out of the car.

"Regardless of what happened tonight, Isolde, I can promise you one thing. You can always trust me, okay? I will always be truthful with you." I scanned his face, seeing the sincerity there, and nodded slowly.

"Thanks, Liam." He held my hand for a beat longer before letting it go, and I swear my skin tingled from where we'd touched. I held his gaze for another few breaths before he nodded, and I headed inside, comforted to know that he would be watching over me.

CHAPTER THIRTEEN

Several days later, having finally finished unpacking, Liam took me out for dinner to celebrate.

Since he had helped me move, something in our relationship had changed. It wasn't just about the crazy world we lived in anymore; we had begun to form a friendship. It felt good to have male company again. To have someone open my door for me and pull out my chair. Even just having that guiding hand on my lower back as he let me go first. All the little things that I hadn't realised that I craved jumbled in with all the numerous other things that I missed about Will.

I let Liam order the wine as I looked over the menu. He had brought me to an Italian restaurant that was well known for having some of the best pizzas in Brisbane, and there were so many options to choose from.

"I think I'll get the Margherita pizza. Why not go with the classic, right?" I handed the menu to the waiter, and Liam ordered the same. Once the waiter left, I turned back to Liam.

"So why'd you pick this place?" I was interested to get to know Liam outside of all the madness that was our lives in the Order.

"I've just always enjoyed watching the people here. It's always so busy, and people come to celebrate so many different occasions." I could understand that, having always enjoyed the chance to people-watch myself.

Once the waiter returned with our wine, the conversation moved on to Liam's long life, and I was fascinated to hear him talk about all the centuries he had lived through. All the moments in history that he'd witnessed. He had been present at the beheading of Anne Boleyn, watched Elizabeth I's coronation, witnessed the massacre at Culloden, the beheadings of Luis XVI and Marie Antoinette, and watched as numerous plagues tore through Europe. It was all a history student's dream come true to speak to someone who had been there and seen it all.

I found myself leaning closer and closer to him as he told me all the amazing stories, fascinated at the life he had lived. To anyone else around us, we must have looked like young lovers on a romantic date.

When we arrived back at my house, Liam walked me to the door, and for a brief, awkward pause, we looked at each other. We seemed to have finally run out of things to say. Once again, there was tension between the two of us that both excited and scared me at the same time. After a beat too long, he kissed me quickly on the forehead and stepped back as I unlocked the door and waved goodbye, knowing that he would be watching out for me in the dark once more.

"So, where did you guys go tonight?" Aurora asked as I walked into the lounge room, where she and Jacob were unpacking the last of the boxes. There had been an underlying sense of hostility coming off her all week as members of the Order had joined me each day, helping me unpack and bringing me coffee. Even Patrice had come by, the first time I'd seen her leave the manor since I'd met her. Fostering friendships that I had previously been keeping at arm's length.

"He took me out for pizza in Milton. Best pizza I've had away from Italy. I've got to take you there." I pushed my stomach out slightly to show off my food-baby, and Jacob laughed. Aurora shot him a sharp look, and he went back to unpacking with his head down. I loved Jacob, but he really needed to learn to stand up to my very strong-willed sister.

"Was it a date?" She asked bluntly, and I bristled at her tone.

"No. It's not like that with Liam. We're just friends." I tried to keep the hurt from my voice, but I was also annoyed that Aurora seemed unhappy that I was making friends. Then again, Liam had been around a fair bit since we had moved, helping unpack and make the house feel like a home, and no doubt, the tension between us was evident, especially to my hyper-aware twin sister.

"As long as he's on the same page as you. I don't know many guys who would help a girl move all day without expecting something in return." Jacob made a lame excuse about needing a drink and pretty much fled to the kitchen, obviously expecting a fight. However, I wasn't interested in getting into it with Aurora.

"You don't know many decent guys then, Aura." I shook my head at her, refusing to give her the fight she was so clearly pushing for. "I'm off to bed. Good night." I headed to my room and shut the door, leaning back against it. After a moment of staring at the ceiling, I kicked off my shoes and flopped down on my bed, looking around the room. It still felt wrong to be surrounded by things that were only mine. A stab of grief hit me again, and a tear rolled down my face as I wondered if it would ever stop hurting.

A knock on my window made me jump, and I looked up to see Liam standing outside. I opened the window, and he climbed through.

"Is everything okay?" I wiped away the tears that were still in my eyes, not bothering to hide them as I spoke. It's not like Liam couldn't tell what was wrong with me anyway.

"I heard what happened between you and Aurora… just thought I'd see if you were alright." I smiled at him sadly.

"To be honest, no. I hate not being able to tell her what is going on. It would be safer all around if she did know. What's to stop Will going after her?" I sat back down on my bed as Liam moved to take a seat in my favourite armchair, which sat in the corner.

"You know why. I know it's hard to accept, but a large part of our role in the Order is to ensure the general population remains unaware of the existence of vampires. You've read through the histories; you know what happens when people find out." Remembering the stories of mass hysteria and violence, I knew he was right, but that didn't make it any easier to accept. He could sense my frustration. "We do keep an eye on Aurora. Because she is so close to you and lives in the same home, we do watch out for her to make sure that they do not try to get to you through her. So, she is safe."

"But if something happens to her or Jacob, it would be my fault." Liam could see that I wasn't going to feel any better no matter what he said, so he simply moved to sit beside me, putting his arm around me, and I rested my head on his shoulder. After a few minutes, I looked up at him to find him looking down at me, his look of concern mixed with something else. Purely instinctively, I found myself moving closer. Our lips met, and we kissed softly. As the kiss grew, he drew me to him with the arm that had been around me, bringing his other hand up to stroke my cheek. Softly, he brushed a lock of hair away from my face and wove his fingers through the hair at the nape of my neck, drawing me closer until I practically sat in his lap. We continued to kiss for what felt like an eternity until I reluctantly pulled away, and my brain suddenly kicked in.

"I'm sorry. I don't know what I was thinking." His words were shaky as he sat back, putting distance between us as he rubbed his hand over his face, though he didn't move the one that had slid down to my lower back.

"It wasn't just you. We both let it happen." I knew Liam well enough by now to know he would be blaming himself, thinking himself responsible for what had just happened, but I had been just as much a willing participant as he had been. Liam smiled, and I knew he was in my head again.

"It's something we've been dancing around for weeks. But we shouldn't. You're still grieving. And with the lives we lead..." Our legs were still touching, and I found it difficult to concentrate. Because the memory of his lips on mine was far more powerful than I had imagined. He was the first person I had kissed aside from Will my entire life, and to have it seem so normal, so right, confused me more than anything else. Liam was still in my thoughts as he reached over to stroke my cheek again, our eyes locked. We both knew we should say no, but our actions appeared to be out of our control. Before I knew what was happening, we were kissing again. But this time, it was Liam who pulled away, jumping to his feet so quickly it was just a blur of movement, and I almost toppled off the bed.

"I'm sorry." He glanced back briefly before jumping out the window in one swift, fluid motion. For a tiny moment, he looked back at me with sadness in his eyes before disappearing into the darkness. I sat stunned for a few seconds before falling back to lie on the bed again.

"This can't be happening," I muttered to myself, though I knew without a doubt that Liam would have still been within earshot. Neither of us had planned for this complication.

Late the next morning, I arrived at 'mission control', as I had come to dub the Manor, worried about the reception I would receive from Liam after our encounter the night before. I shouldn't have been surprised that he wasn't there, but I felt myself deflate as I realised that I had wanted to see him. Patrice must have noticed my reaction as she told me he was off on another task, having been sent out when he returned at dawn, which I thought was odd, but I figured my safety wasn't Liam's only responsibility. She gave me a knowing, sad smile as I took my seat at the breakfast table across from Alana, who did not even look up, though I could feel the resentment coming off her in waves. No doubt, by the end of the morning, we would have one of our now weekly face-offs. Unfortunately, our relationship had not seen any of the changes that I'd had with the others.

"So, you're finished with your degree and your move finally?"

Patrice asked as she handed me a plate full of bacon and eggs. She was still concerned about my lack of appetite, although lately, that hadn't been as much of an issue.

"Yes, thank goodness. Not that I'm ever going to get to use my degree now." I shrugged as I made this comment, and Alana snorted derisively across from me before pushing away from the table, letting her chair scrape loudly across the floor before she stomped out of the room. Everyone else acted as though nothing had happened. The conversations around me continued, although Sam shot me a grin across the table. He had a prickly relationship with Alana as well.

"I was hoping to talk to you sometime today about what you were going to be doing now. Come to my rooms later on today, and we can have a chat." Patrice excused herself then, and I was left wondering what else in my life was about to change.

A few hours later, I found myself sitting across from Patrice and Damon. I was suddenly nervous. The meeting felt very official, with them both sitting side by side.

"Now that you've finished your degree and worked out your living arrangements, it has been discussed, and I think you should start to actively take part in the group. A large part of being a member of our family is protecting humanity from vampires. You have been doing your research, so you know this has been a fight we have been waging for centuries, but so far, you've been shielded from what is ultimately your birthright.

"Now that the last of your previous life commitments are done with, we see no reason why you cannot be out there, fighting the fight with the rest of us. You are still a target, but the prophecy does say that you will be the one to turn the fight back in our favour, so although we will still be protecting you, we're going to stop shielding you as we have been." This was the most I'd ever heard Damon speak, and I could hear

Liam's words come back to haunt me; *I'm of the belief that you need to face up to reality and accept that this is your destiny, and I refuse to play games.* I felt like I was being told off, yet I had never asked anyone to protect me. I just didn't want to live this life they had all forced upon me.

Patrice could see that this approach was not the way to go. She placed a hand gently on Damon's arm, and after a moment of hesitation, he excused himself.

"I know that Damon is rather blunt, and I know that you didn't ask to be coddled, but we thought, now that you were no longer attending classes and preoccupied with your living arrangements, that you would like to finally get out there in the field and experience the real deal. You and Liam have been training hard, and we think you are more than ready for it." I took this all in and realised that I had not actually said a word since I sat down.

"So, where will I be going?" Although I had read all the histories and I had been training with Liam, I didn't have the confidence in my abilities that the others seemed to have. However, I also knew that they would not be letting me do this if there was any danger that I might not come back in one piece. I was too valuable to them. At least, that's what I told myself.

"You, Liam and Alana will be checking out a nest of vampires that Alana found last night when she was... when she was out." There was something that Patrice was leaving out, but I let it go, as there was something else that she had said that I was more concerned with.

"Alana? On my first night out? Who came up with that idea?" I was not impressed, and Patrice could tell.

"It was my idea. I thought it was time for the pair of you to get over your differences and learn that you are on the same team." She said this pointedly, and I opened my mouth to state that it was not me with the problem, but it was Liam who spoke up behind me from the open doorway.

"I honestly don't know if that's such a good idea, Patrice." I wasn't sure which part of the grouping he had a problem with, but I didn't want to get into it with Patrice around.

"Well, it's been decided now, so you'll all just have to make the best of a bad situation." I could tell from her tone that Patrice was done with the conversation, so I let myself out, careful not to brush against Liam as I stepped around him while he remained standing in the doorway. Clearly, he was not done with the conversation. He shut the door behind me, but I lingered in the hallway, waiting to see if he could persuade her not to put Alana and me together. It was Patrice who spoke first, though.

"Do you want to explain to me exactly what happened last night?" There was an edge to Patrice's voice that made it clear that she knew what had happened between Liam and me the night before.

Seriously, is there anything these people don't know?!

"It was a slip-up. It won't happen again." Liam knew I was still there, and I could just imagine how uncomfortable this all was for him.

"I know it won't. You know what that young woman has been through and what she means to our cause. And for Alana to be the one to witness it all. You've certainly gotten yourself into a bit of a mess, Liam." Patrice had gone into mum mode again, and I had a mental image of Liam with his head bowed, possibly even scuffing his feet like a little boy who was being told off. I heard Liam cover a small laugh with a cough and knew he had seen my mental image as well. Whilst he was older than Patrice, she was like a mother to all of us, and I knew she worried about the impact a relationship between myself and Liam would have, not just on us but on the rest of the Order as well.

I decided to leave them to it, not wanting to hear anything further and went off to do some practice in the gym. Not long afterwards, Liam joined me. Neither of us brought up the night before or his conversation with Patrice but settled into our workouts in companionable silence.

But now everything was different. I caught him shooting me an appreciative look as I started punching and kicking the punching bag in front of me, attempting to make my transitions as smooth as possible. Realising I had seen him, he turned back to his own workout, rolling his head from side to side, trying to shake it off. Something unsaid hung over both of us, and I had to force myself not to be distracted by the sight of Liam as he shed his shirt and started doing chin-ups. The smirk on his face let me know he could hear my thoughts, and I started to think about mundane things to try and keep the sexual tension under control.

But it wasn't easy to control your thoughts when the object of your lust was nearby without a shirt on. As he'd only ever worn long sleeve shirts around me, even when I'd seen him in his sleeping clothes, I was surprised at the presence of a large tattoo that covered his left arm from the elbow up to his shoulder and onto his chest. It was an intricate tattoo featuring elaborate Celtic knotwork, a sundial of some kind with glyphs that I didn't recognise, flowing into a dragon's head, stopping just over his heart. I had never cared for tattoos in the past, but the one adorning Liam's body instantly quickened my pulse. I had to turn my back on him then, for both our sakes, and I didn't envy Alana for having to deal with the pair of us tonight. I knew it would be hard for her, knowing her feelings for Liam and her dislike of me. It was going to be an interesting night.

Just before dusk, armed with only the stakes that were strapped to my thighs and in my pockets, I found myself alone in a car with Liam and Alana. I had an earpiece in one ear and was wearing a tiny, hi-tech camera attached to the puffy vest I wore. I felt like I was on some sort of SWAT team. Which, I guess, was close to the truth. The tension in the air was so thick I could almost see the knife that was stuck in it, a mental image that again had Liam smothering a laugh with a cough. None of us had uttered a word since we had left the Manor, and we had been driving for twenty minutes. I recognised the streets we were winding through and realised that this nest was definitely an issue, as it was only moments from my new place, as well as my parents and a few of my sisters. I also had an unsettling feeling that it might be the nest where Will was living now. I had not expected to come face-to-face with him on my first night out, and I found myself shaking at the thought.

I noticed Liam watching me and shaking his head, reassuring me that this was not the nest that Will now called home. Alana saw this exchange from the back seat, and I could tell that this all just made her even angrier. We really needed to stop pissing her off, or one of us was going to end up dead tonight. Liam rolled the car to a stop, and my heart began to race. I started to realise I wasn't ready for this. Liam turned to me, just looking me in the eyes, letting me know I could do this. From the backseat, Alana cleared her throat loudly.

"Sorry to interrupt yet another lover's moment, but would the pair of you kindly tear yourselves away from each other for one moment so that we can discuss strategy?" The venom in her voice was so evident that I was convinced that one of us would be going home injured, at the very least. This was not a good start.

Five minutes later, I stood at the back of the house, Liam a few feet behind me, his attention split between watching the house and monitoring how I was faring. Alana had taken point and moved into the house as the sun was setting. Nervously, I watched as the first vampire burst from the house and hung back as Liam quickly dispatched her as another raced past them. I moved forward, prepared to take him on. The adrenaline had kicked at the moment I had stepped from the car, and it felt good to unleash the first punch. My opponent was momentarily knocked back, stunned. He righted himself, getting a good look at my face, and I could tell he recognised me as his lips curled up into a sneer.

"So, they've finally let her out of her gilded cage." His eyes flicked towards where Liam was fighting a third vampire, though I knew he was aware of my every move. "But her knight in shining armour is ever-present."

"You talk too much." I stepped forward and punched him in the face, frustrated that he seemed to know all about me. I heard something crunch, and he reeled back, clutching his nose. I didn't allow him to speak any further, going after him and pummelling him in the chest with both fists, driving him further back until he was pressed back against the wall of the house. I pinned him there with my left forearm and yanked out the stake that was in my right pocket, plunging it hard into his heart. I knew I'd hit my mark as he twitched and the glow of his blue eyes faded out.

As his body slid down the wall, I stepped back. I had lost track of what was going on behind me and was startled as an arm wrapped around my chest. My attacker pulled me hard against his chest and attempted to yank my head to the side to get at my neck. I brought my right foot down sharply to crush his foot, and he let out a grunt of pain, momentarily distracted from trying to bite me. I used that split second to my advantage and grabbed the arm across my chest, leaning forward and pulling down at the same time, propelling him over my head. He crashed forward and landed on his back, staring up at me in shock. I didn't give him a chance to get his bearings as I held him down with my knee and used my stake once again, driving it deep into his heart with both hands.

"Isolde!" I jumped up and spun around as Liam called out, seeing another vampire running towards me. Liam was squaring off with another of their coven, and I was grateful he'd allowed himself that brief moment of distraction to alert me. These two appeared to be the last, as Alana had appeared behind them in the doorway and watched as I spun on the spot and connected with the woman's face as she rushed at me. Her head snapped back as she flew through the air, and I tried not to allow myself to be distracted by the strength that I had used in order to make a fully-grown vampire fly.

Distantly, I was aware that Liam had dispatched the vampire he'd been fighting, and both he and Alana were holding back to watch as I fought the last of them. My opponent was back on her feet, and her face twisted with rage as she charged towards me again. I took on a fighter's stance, my left foot forward and both fists raised as if preparing to punch her. But as she reached me, I feinted left, spinning myself as she lost her balance, passing the space I'd previously stood. Now behind her, as she tipped forward slightly, I unleashed a flying kick that sent her sprawling forward onto the ground. As she attempted to flip herself over, I was beside her in an instant, and as she rolled onto her back, I brought my stake down and slammed it into her chest. She let out a scream, but it cut out, and I watched with satisfaction as the glow of her eyes faded.

The silence around me was deafening, and I raised my head slowly to find both Liam and Alana watching me closely. Liam's face shone with both pride and awe, as though I'd surprised him with my abilities. Alana looked surprised at first before something else flashed across her face. I wasn't entirely sure, but I got the distinct impression that she was angry. Had she wanted me to fail?

We encountered no further nightwalkers, and by around 2 am, I sat on the large, four-poster bed in my room at the Manor, listening as Liam and Patrice talked outside my door. I had my legs curled up beneath me, a mug of hot chocolate clutched between both my hands. I was staring ahead of myself, unable to believe what had taken place earlier.

"There was no touching her. It was as if she was the most experienced fighter there. I've been training with her for months, and I knew she was good, but I had no idea she was going to be that good." I could hear Liam pacing backwards and forwards in the hall. "No other Protector has been that confident on their first time out, Patrice. It was like.." He trailed off.

"It was like watching you fight, Liam." Alana's voice sounded from further away, and I realised she must have come from her own room, further down the other end of the hall. She had practically fled away from us once we returned to the Manor, unable to handle spending any further time in our presence.

"It must be one of her abilities coming out. The prophecy did say that she would have powers we'd never come across before." There was an edge to Patrice's voice, and I wondered if her mind was racing as fast as mine was. Well, if this was an ability that no one understood, I liked this one, but I was still going to need to adjust to suddenly possessing skills that even a ninja would envy.

Whilst Liam and Patrice continued to talk in the hall, I stared off into space, not realising at first what I was doing, until I noticed that the vase of fake flowers on the chest of drawers across the room from me was trembling. I had been staring directly at it intently.

Am I doing that?

I rolled my head from side to side, the residual adrenaline from the night's events still rolling off me in waves, and I was finding it hard to stay still. I focused on the vase, attempting to channel my nervous energy into getting it to move.

"I don't think even I could take her, Patrice. This changes everything." I was distracted from my musings as I realised that Liam was thinking that I may not need the round-the-clock protection detail anymore. I agreed with him, but I worried this meant I wouldn't see him as much anymore. I had become so used to having him close by that the thought of being alone again scared me more than I was willing to admit.

"I don't know. I certainly don't feel like testing her new abilities too much. We will just continue on the way we have been going for now. Let her adjust to her newfound strength." I tuned them out now, focusing on taking deep, calming breaths. I needed to find some way to work off all this leftover energy.

Patrice checked in on me again before heading downstairs, and Liam entered the room to sit beside me on the bed.

"How are you doing?" He asked needlessly, as he could no doubt hear the freaked-out thoughts going through my head.

"Um... yeah... I'll have to get back to you on that." I tried to laugh off my fear, but he simply looked at me. He knew me well, and not just because he could read my thoughts. I felt myself being drawn closer to him, but I jumped up suddenly, stepping away from the bed. Being on a bed with him was not a good idea right now.

"I'm going to have a shower." I nodded towards the bathroom connected to my room. He stood as well, nodding.

"I'll leave you to it." He moved quickly towards the door as I headed for the bathroom, closing the door behind me and leaning against it, staring up at the ceiling. Jumping his bones probably wasn't the best way to burn off these feelings, but that knowledge didn't make it any less appealing.

CHAPTER FOURTEEN

After the longest shower of my life, I dressed in loose black pants and a white cropped shirt that left my stomach exposed. I stood in front of the bedroom mirror and breathed in deeply. With my eyes closed, I focused on each breath, my chest rising and falling rhythmically as I did so. I was trying to use the mind-clearing techniques that Liam had taught me, but without the flame to focus on, I was struggling. When I reached twenty, I gave up and opened my eyes. The shower had done nothing to ease the adrenaline of the night I'd had, along with the tension that had been rolling off the pair of us in waves.

Ever since my birthday, I'd had a high libido, something that Will had commented on enthusiastically and used to his advantage. At the time, I had put this down to the excitement of being an engaged woman. After Will's death, I'd been too numb to everything except grief and anger, but as the fog of grief had begun to lift, I'd been noticing my sex drive kicking in once again. The past few days had not been helping either.

I looked in the mirror now, taking in my reflection. Through the thin material of my clothes, I took note of the changes that had slowly been occurring in my body since I'd started training with Liam daily. Muscles I had never noticed before were now defined, and I wasn't unhappy to see how strong I had become.

Remembering the sexually charged intensity between myself and Liam in the gym earlier in the day, I shut my eyes and counted again, continuing to focus on my breathing as I attempted to get my feelings under control. I was very aware that Liam would no doubt be able to hear my thoughts, and I struggled to shut down my train of thought. Without realising it, Will's role in my fantasies had slowly been replaced by someone else, and I had always had a very vivid imagination.

I imagined the feel of his hands on my body, of his mouth on mine. I could practically feel the sensation now as his fingers ran through my hair before wrapping it around his fist as he pulled my head back.

Lost in my overactive imagination of how he would make my body sing in ways it hadn't done in months, it took a moment for me to note the sound of heavy breathing other than my own.

Liam's heavy breathing.

I slowly opened my eyes and met his gaze in the mirror as he stood at the door to my bedroom. He must have left the door partially open when he had left, causing the door to swing silently open when he knocked. His hands grasped the top of the door frame as he stretched up, surveying every inch of my body like he could see through the very thin clothing I wore. He was wearing only his grey sweatpants, having just finished in the shower himself.

From the heated look he gave me, he'd heard every thought going through my mind in the last twenty minutes. I couldn't keep myself from admiring him. The fact that he was the most beautiful man I'd ever seen was sending my overactive libido into overdrive. I felt my gaze drift to the tattoo on his left arm and chest once more, eyeing it hungrily in the mirror as he continued watching the reflection of my face. He cleared his throat.

"I thought I'd try and help you with the mind-clearing again."

He nodded towards the low table where we had sat days earlier when I had played with the flames. I felt like I was playing with a different kind of fire now, in this moment.

I nodded at him, unable to speak, and turned to face him finally. He hesitated for a moment, almost as though he was afraid to step into the room. That was understandable, given the thoughts I was struggling to keep a grip on. It was a dangerous line we were walking right now, one that, if crossed, may have repercussions we weren't yet ready to face. He finally crossed the threshold, but instead of going over to the table, he came towards where I still stood, watching his every movement. Until now, I'd never really appreciated how gracefully he walked. His movements were so fluid, no doubt from the centuries of martial arts training that had honed that beautiful physique.

He came to a stop in front of me, looking down as he studied my face closely, as though trying to work out the answer to a puzzle. Whenever we stood this close to each other, I was afraid I would get lost in those eyes. I forced myself to look away, still trying to get a lock on the swirling emotions inside of me. Instead, I focused on the details of his tattoo, which was now at my eye level. Mesmerised, I traced a finger around the swirls on the dragon's head and neck, noticing as he tensed beneath my touch, but he didn't move, holding himself perfectly still as I traced every swirl over his heart. I noticed the goosebumps that appeared on his skin.

"This is beautiful," I whispered, still refusing to look up at him. He brought his hand up to cover mine, forcing me to stop moving my finger over his skin.

"Perhaps some Tai Chi would be better than mind-clearing right now. Probably shouldn't be playing with any flames at the moment." He had a point there. The last time I'd attempted mind-clearing when my emotions were this heightened, two nights ago, I'd nearly set fire to the table. The ball of fire had grown so large while I stared at it that it had been like a miniature sun, and I'd struggled to control it. Liam had been shaken then, and if something managed to rattle Liam, I didn't want to be messing around with it.

He lowered my hand slowly before placing both of his on my shoulders and turned me back around to face the mirror. I still couldn't bring myself to look at him, even if it was only in the mirror, and I could feel my heart racing as he stood close behind me. For someone who was meant to be trying to help me clear my mind, he was doing a terrible job with all this close contact.

I had thought that he would step back then, hearing the dangerous train of thought that was plaguing me, imagining all the ways he could use those hands on my skin to help me find the release that I so desperately craved. Instead, he moved even closer until his body was pressed up against my back, and I was unable to hide the gasp that escaped me.

"You are so beautiful, Isolde.' His voice was low and husky, and something told me that I wasn't the only one having trouble concentrating on clearing their mind. My gaze met his in the mirror finally, and his eyes remained locked on mine with every movement. Neither of us seemed capable of looking away.

'You think I'm beautiful?" My voice was barely louder than a whisper.

"You know I do." His hands were still on my shoulders, and I watched his face as he began massaging my neck and shoulders. I sighed as he worked each knot out slowly, continuing to watch my face in the mirror, gauging my reactions. Eventually, I let my head fall back against his chest. This is what I wanted. Not mind-clearing. Not Tai Chi. What I needed was his hands on my body. He pressed himself harder against my back, bringing his mouth to my ear, and I shivered at the feel of his breath on my skin.

"What do you need, Isolde? I need to hear the words out loud," he whispered in my ear.

Slowly, I reached down and took his hand, guiding it to my right breast. I let out a sigh as he squeezed it gently.

"I want your hands on me," I whispered, and his breath hitched slightly as he moved his hand to slide slowly under my loose top. He cupped my breast briefly before moving to roll my nipple between his fingers. A low moan escaped my lips as I watched him. His touch was firm and warm, and I could feel the strength in his hands, the kind of hands that could crush you if they wanted to. Or provide the lightest touch. I shivered as he ran his other hand along my ribs before moving it up to cover my other breast.

"Like this?" He whispered, cupping my breasts gently in his hands. I nodded, my eyes closing, enjoying the feeling of his hands on my body.

"No, don't close your eyes. Look at me." I opened my eyes, my gaze finding his once again in the mirror. Both of us tracked the path of his hand that slid slowly down my stomach. I shivered as he began tracing a circle around my belly button.

His other hand moved to the opposite breast, massaging it as he used his arm to hold me tightly to him. His gaze returned to my face, drawing my eyes to his once more, and I felt his hand move lower, pushing below the band of my pants that hung loosely on my hips, tracing a path down my lower abdomen until he finally found that bundle of nerves. I drew in a sharp breath as he drew circles around it with his forefinger, and I moaned softly, my hips moving against him, as I bit down on my lip.

"Just like that? Is that helping?" He asked, his voice still low and husky, as we continued to hold eye contact in the mirror. I spread my legs even wider, inviting him to explore further. He did just that as he slowly slipped a finger between my folds. I was so turned on, and he could tell from how wet I was as he worked his finger inside of me. His thumb replaced his finger on the most sensitive part of my body and began to stroke firmly.

"Yes." I breathed out huskily as I watched him. I felt the warmth exuding from my body, the goosebumps all over my skin. "Please don't stop." Slowly, he used his body against my back to gently urge me to ride his hand, rocking me back and forth in a slow rhythm.

"That's it. Just like that, Isolde." I felt myself becoming more and more aroused as he whispered the words in my ear, working his finger in and out in a steady rhythm as his thumb continued stroking. I tried to control my breathing, trying not to come too quickly.

I reached my hand up and gripped the back of his head as he pressed light kisses to my neck before gently taking my ear lobe between his teeth, never taking his eyes from mine in the mirror. My hips were moving on their own now, and I continued riding his hand as he worked a second finger inside me. I could feel the pressure building inside me, knowing I was moments from coming. I attempted to slow my breathing, trying to control my body as I could feel my orgasm building. I needed this to last after weeks of the build-up. Liam began working his hand faster, and I whimpered. I felt my body tighten as my breaths started to come faster. I could feel how hard he was against my back, and he continued to hold me tightly against him, pinching my nipple with the hand that had continued teasing my breast.

"Oh, God, I'm coming, I'm coming," I chanted in a whisper, and my hips took off against his hand, bucking and twitching in time with my gasping breaths. The building pleasure finally exploded, sending shock waves of euphoria through my body. I felt every single one of those waves crashing over me, one after another, my breathing remaining heavy as I collapsed against his chest. He held me tightly as I rode out the orgasm, his fingers still buried inside of me. As I worked to get my breath back under control, he slowly removed his hand and moved to step back. I grabbed his hand.

"I want you. Right here, right now," I said, my voice cracking. His eyes gleamed with lust as we stared at each other in the mirror. I turned to face him, and he cleared his throat. I could tell he was battling an internal war between what he *should* do and what he *wanted* to do. His hand shook slightly as he raised my hand to his lips, turning it over to kiss my palm.

"You should get some sleep. It's been a long night." His voice wavered as he spoke quietly.

Without thinking, I leaned into him, and he put his arms around me tightly, holding me close as I processed everything. He was right; it had been a long night. However, that didn't stop me from wanting Liam, and I knew he felt it as well, especially after what we had just done.

I leaned back to look up at him and found him already looking down at me. Rising onto my toes, I kissed him hungrily, trying to get as close to him as I could. He held me close, and our bodies pressed together. Stepping forwards, he pushed me back against the mirror, and I gasped as my back met the cold glass, and we continued to kiss with growing intensity, months of frustration flowing through us both. He had his hand under my top, his fingers digging into my back. I wrapped my leg around him, urging him to keep exploring. A knock sounded at the door, and we stopped suddenly, both looking over to see the door handle moving.

"Isolde?" Patrice's voice called through the door, and it started to open slowly. Liam was away from me in an instant, and by the time Patrice had the door fully open, he was seated on the other side of the room, looking as casual as ever. Patrice took in his shirtless appearance and my flushed face as she surveyed the scene before her.

"Are you sure you're okay to go home tonight? You still look a little..." She couldn't think of what to say, but I nodded.

"Yes, I'll be fine. I think I'll head off now." I looked at Liam, who nodded. There were so many reasons why we shouldn't do what we had nearly done, and I knew I needed to get home and be away from him.

I had a cold shower when I got home, hoping that would help, as they always talked about those in the movies. However, it only made me shiver uncontrollably, and I tossed and turned for the remainder of the night, unable to forget the feeling of Liam's body pressed against mine, his fingers moving inside of me. Of his intense gaze in the mirror as he made my body sing. And no matter how much I knew we shouldn't have crossed that line, I wished like crazy that Patrice had not come to check on me.

CHAPTER FIFTEEN

Early the next morning, after only a couple of hours of fitful sleep, I arrived at the Manor to find everyone rushing around frantically. Patrice noticed my arrival and rushed towards me.

"What's going on?" I questioned Patrice. I tried not to react as Liam appeared at my side.

"Alana and a few others went out last night on another hunting mission, but not one we knew about." Patrice's face was tear-stained, and I knew instantly that this was not going to end well.

"Who's missing?" Although I didn't like Alana, I still didn't want anything to happen to her.

"Alana is missing... The others... There were no other survivors." Liam answered from beside me, his voice almost wooden, and I could feel him blaming himself. He had been too distracted by everything that had happened with me.

"Who was with her?" I asked, scared to hear the response. Liam looked as though he was struggling to answer, so I looked to Patrice, who swallowed hard before responding.

"Omari, Kazeem..." She began listing names of some of the newer Protectors that were close to Alana and had kept their distance from me, but my blood went cold as she stumbled over the last two names. "Sam... and Katyana." I felt myself starting to tear up as she named the two Order members that I had started to become closest to. Beside me, Liam had balled his hands into fists, and I could see him struggling to keep his emotions in check. With tears rolling down my cheeks, I placed a hand on his arm, bringing his gaze to me. His eyes were shining with unshed tears.

"This isn't your fault, Liam. You couldn't have done anything." Though he may have been able to hear what they were planning, it was not his responsibility to police the actions of the others.

"Isolde is right, Liam. This wasn't your fault." Patrice stated as she handed Liam a set of car keys.

"We still don't know why they went there. You need to go back and see what you can find out." With a nod, Liam turned to walk back out the door, but Patrice stopped him with a hand on his arm.

"Take Isolde with you." It was a simple command, but I couldn't understand why it was being given. Why should I go with him? Surely, it would be better to have a more experienced member of the Order partner with him. Without saying a word, Liam nodded and took me by the hand, towing me along behind him. I looked back at Patrice, who nodded at me with a knowing look.

"Why did she ask you to bring me along?" I asked Liam's back as he led me into the elevator that led down to the basement car park. The car that we climbed into was a tank. The majority of the Orders cars were bulletproof, but this one looked like it could withstand anything, including a bomb going off underneath it.

"Patrice thought it would be good for you to come along and see if you can pick anything up that I can't." This line of thought confused me.

"I don't understand. What do you mean by 'pick anything up'?"

"We're still yet to fully test your abilities. Patrice wants to explore if you may have any psychic abilities. A few of the others have them, and as your powers are meant to be the strongest, the elders are eager to explore what else you can do." Liam had still been refusing to make eye contact with me. I had come to know Liam pretty well over the past few months, and I knew that he was blaming himself, no doubt believing that if we hadn't been together last night, he would have been able to prevent what had happened.

I touched the hand that he rested on the gearshift, giving it a squeeze.

"Hey. Don't do this. I know that you are blaming yourself for what Alana did, but she obviously kept you out of it for a reason. You saw how she was after what happened when we were all together last night." I had been so focused on my newfound ninja skills and crazy sexual tension that I was only just realising that Alana had been acting strangely when we returned to the Manor. No doubt jealous of my abilities and the attention that others had been giving me.

"That doesn't excuse the fact that I was so distracted that I didn't know what was going on."

"You can't save everyone, Liam. Especially when they don't want to be saved." Liam remained silent, and I finally gave up, staring out the window. Now that I was no longer trying to convince Liam that he wasn't responsible, I struggled with the realisation that Katyana and Sam were now gone. I tried to push away the grief that was threatening to overwhelm me, knowing that I couldn't afford to fall apart just yet.

We arrived at the address that Patrice gave us, an unused warehouse in the northern suburbs on the outskirts of the city limits. It had all the signs of having fallen into disrepair, with broken windows and graffiti on the walls. It also had a strong sense of foreboding around it.

"That feeling that you're having right now is exactly the sort of thing Patrice is hoping for," Liam said as we climbed out of the car, and I looked over at him apprehensively as I shut the door.

"I still don't know how I feel about everyone just waiting for me to develop magical powers." I stopped as Liam handed me a stake, still not really looking at me as he scanned the area. "What exactly are you expecting to find here? Wouldn't the vampires that attacked them all be gone by now?"

"We cleared the area earlier, but we still need to be careful." Liam led the way as we did an entire loop of the building, and I followed behind as he looked through the broken windows, checking to ensure that we were indeed alone. I followed behind, checking doors for any way inside. I was overwhelmed by the strong sense that something bad had happened here.

"How did everyone know what happened if no one knew about this mission?" Liam turned to look at me properly finally.

"We have a team of seers in our London location, and one of them contacted Patrice about 5 hours ago. Unfortunately, the team had already left, and by the time I got here with Daniel and Celeste, it was too late." Although he delivered the information very matter-of-factly, I could see the emotion in his eyes, the guilt he harboured for not knowing about what was happening beforehand. I realised that the team must have been gathering whilst he and I were preoccupied last night. I swallowed hard, nodding at him, and he continued moving on.

When we returned to the back of the building, I placed my hand on the door handle, as I had done with all the others. This time, however, a flash of images hit me, and I was nearly knocked off my feet.

I wrenched the door open, and we raced inside, expecting to have the element of surprise. But, we were met by a small army of vampires, and they moved tightly around the five of us, sealing off our escape. We hadn't expected so many. It was unheard of to have this many night-walkers gathered in one place.

To my right, I saw Adam step forward and grasp Sam by the neck with one hand, lifting him off the ground. His toes scraped the ground as Adam held him there for a moment, choking the life out of him before snapping his neck with a flick of his wrist. I felt terror build up inside me as Katyana cried out, struggling against the nightwalker who had grabbed her from behind. He bit into her neck and fed off her with such aggression that he eventually ripped her head from her shoulders. To my left, Omari and Kazeem managed to hold their own for a little longer, but I was held in place by several nightwalkers, forced to watch as everyone that I had led here was ripped apart.

I was forced to kneel before Adam, who stepped forward and wrenched my head to the side. As his teeth bit into my neck, I knew at that moment that my death would be different to the others, and I felt fear I had never felt before as I realised that my fate was sealed.

"Isolde?" Liam shook me back to reality, and I looked up, realising that the force of the vision had knocked me to the ground. "Are you okay?" He had been watching me with concern, and that had distracted him from being able to see into my mind properly. I slowly climbed to my feet.

"No..." I was struggling to piece my words together, reeling from everything I had just seen, watching people I had come to consider friends die in such brutal ways. I didn't even bother trying to stop the tears that rolled down my face. And experiencing what had happened to Alana... I felt nausea rolling through me, and I bent forward, retching. Liam moved forward to hold my hair back while I emptied the contents of my stomach. I eventually stood up straight again, still feeling hot and clammy.

"I just saw... I was inside Alana's head as... They turned her, Liam. The entire group of vampires that were here drained, Alana. They took her with them and left everyone else. Why?" Liam could see the confusion in my eyes, the sadness. I hadn't liked Alana, but after seeing her death flash before my eyes, I felt her loss keenly.

"I don't know. I don't even know why they came here. This wasn't a nest." Liam returned to the car to grab me a towel to wipe my mouth with. I followed close behind him as he moved back to the door. I let him open the door this time and lead the way inside, hesitant to touch the door again in case the vision reappeared. I led Liam to the spot where I had seen Alana killed. He knelt and touched the ground, brushing the blood-stained concrete with his fingertips, his eyes briefly taking on a far-away look before he looked back up at me.

"How much did you see?" I reluctantly replayed the vision in my mind again, allowing Liam to see everything I had seen. Revisiting it all was like ripping a wound open over and over again. Once I had finished, I opened my eyes to find he was looking at me with surprise. His gaze returned to the blood on the concrete.

"Your visions are the same as the ones I see when I'm..." He trailed off, almost as though he realised he had said too much.

"What do you mean, the same as yours? You have psychic abilities as well?" I don't know why I was surprised. With his mind-reading abilities, it made sense.

"My visions are the same as yours, experienced from the perspective of the person involved. The others that have some psychic ability just get fragments or, in some cases, just an impression of what occurred." He looked thoughtful for a moment.

"Liam?"

"Hm?" He looked at me after a brief moment, his mind elsewhere.

"How do you get visions?" Something about the way he'd looked down at the blood had me intrigued.

"What do you mean?" He was stalling now, and he could tell that I knew that.

"What triggers them for you? For me, it must be touching something that they did, like the door handle that Alana touched. What triggers them for you?" He looked at me for a moment, clearly wondering how much to tell me. After a moment, he nodded, resigning himself to the truth.

"I get my visions from blood."

I recalled how he had just brushed the blood-stain with his fingertips, his eyes losing focus briefly.

"So, when you touch blood?"

"Not just touching." This was the first time we'd ever come close to speaking about his... eating habits. He usually avoided any discussion with me about his vampiric side.

"So... when you're..."

"Feeding. Yes." He looked uncomfortable, but I pushed on.

"You told me once that daywalkers only fed off the blood of animals." I found myself wrapping my arms around myself unconsciously, and I stopped, not wanting to appear apprehensive. Liam was watching me, clearly hearing my racing thoughts.

"What I said was we could survive off the blood of animals. That they could quench our thirst."

"But you also drink human blood?" I didn't know why I wanted to know... Then again, maybe I did.

"Sometimes, yes."

"When?" Liam was growing more and more uncomfortable. He ran a hand over his face.

"Isolde, do we really need to..." He looked at me, almost pleading with me to drop it. Unfortunately, I had reached the point where I needed to know.

"When do you feed from humans, Liam?" He sighed, shoving his hands in his pockets.

"When they let me." He looked straight at me, deciding to just go with brutal honesty.

"What do you mean when they let you? Who has let you?" I tried to keep the dismay from my voice, but it was there. I couldn't fathom the appeal of having someone bite me after seeing the brutality when the nightwalkers fed. Liam continued looking into my eyes before answering.

"Alana has before. And there have been others over the centuries." I felt myself draw back, away from him.

"Alana?" I was shocked at this turn in the conversation. I couldn't take it all in. However, Liam had clearly decided that I was going to hear it all now that I had pushed it this far.

"Yes. About thirty years ago, Alana and I had a brief dalliance. I have been around for centuries, Isolde. There have been women in my life along the way."

"But you said that you'd made it clear to Alana that you weren't interested in her that way." I was trying not to be hurt by this, to appreciate the honesty. But I was losing.

"No, I was never in love with her, not in a way that meant anything at least, and when I'd realised the depth of her feelings for me, I ended the sexual side of our relationship."

"So, what's been going on with us? Am I just the next one to come along in a long line of women that you've cast aside once they fall in love with you?" I didn't care if he knew how I was feeling anymore. I was hurt, unable to believe I'd almost allowed myself to be used in such a way. Liam moved towards me, shaking his head, but I stepped back, refusing to allow him to touch me. He let the hand he'd raised to touch my cheek fall to his side.

"No. I could never have done that to you."

"Because I'm the chosen one? Because everyone treats me like I'm about to break?" I was angry now, tired of being treated with such fragility, ready to break at the slightest movement.

"Because I have been with you every day of your life since you were born. I have been protecting you, watching over you. When Will died, I felt that grief with you. Although you only met me five months ago, I have known you your entire life. And lately." His words trailed off for a moment. "How I feel about you now... I've never felt that for anyone before." His words were angry like he didn't want to admit to either himself or to me that he had developed feelings for me.

"So, my entire life, you've watched me?" I'd known this, yet discussing it now, I didn't know how to feel about it. I hadn't truly allowed myself to think of him standing in the dark each night for twenty-five years, watching over me from the time I was a baby until now.

"Not in the creepy way you make it sound. I needed to keep you safe."

"So, I'm just a job to you?" He groaned, shaking his head in frustration as he turned away.

"Now you're just trying to pick a fight with me." He led the way to the car, and I trailed behind him, unsure of what to make of everything we had just discussed.

"No, I really want to know." I reached for the passenger door. He was behind me in an instant, moving at the uncanny speed that I'd seen him do so many times now, turning me to face him. He moved closer, pressing me back against the car.

"As I've come to know you properly, to develop a connection with you..." His voice trailed off as he gazed into my eyes. He cleared his throat, gathering his thoughts. "I have never wanted to keep anyone alive more in my entire existence. It is the hardest thing I have ever done. You are not a job to me, Isolde. You have become my reason for existing. I need to keep you safe because the idea of anything happening to you terrifies the shit out of me. And it's got nothing to do with prophecies or your destiny or what you mean to the fucking Order." He gripped my chin, forcing me to hold his gaze. "For twenty-five years, keeping you safe has been my sole purpose. And these past few months..." His eyes stared intently into my own, and his body pressed hard against mine. I could feel his heart beating against my chest. I knew my own was beating fast, processing everything he was confessing. "If anything happened to you, I would burn the world to the ground." He held me in his gaze for what felt like an eternity before stepping back and going around to the other side of the car.

I stood still for a moment, attempting to pull myself back together, trying to take in every word he had just said and the three words that he had left unsaid. Silently, I climbed into the car. Neither of us said a word as we drove back to the Manor.

✳

Once we returned, everyone gathered in the communications room to discuss what had been discovered so far.

"The seers contacted us at 3 am. They had only just seen what was happening, and there was not enough time for us to save anyone. We arrived at the warehouse to find a bloodbath. We found no night-walkers, though, just bodies." Celeste started going through everything that they had seen when they arrived at the warehouse earlier that morning. Celeste and Daniel were the head of most missions, in charge of the teams who went out each night. Celeste normally remained at command, running point, but not this morning. They had grabbed Liam as he was getting ready to head to my house to take up his usual guarding duty. It was decided that he would be needed more on this mission. Their sole purpose on the initial mission had been to clear the area before anyone else, such as the police, arrived. But when they came across the scene, that mission changed to returning with the bodies of our fallen team members. Once the sun was up, the elders sent Liam back to get the full story of what had occurred, aware of his psychic abilities. I was just thrown in as a training exercise.

"Does anyone know why they were there?" Patrice looked around the table, but everyone shook their heads.

"Isolde did have a vision while we were there. It appears that Alana has been turned." Liam filled everyone in on what we had both seen.

"And you say that Adam was there?" Patrice looked over at me. I nodded in the affirmative.

"Yeah, I didn't recognise any of the others, though. Will wasn't there, from what I could tell." Patrice nodded, looking stressed.

"If Adam is involved, then it can't have been a coincidence that many vampires were together. No doubt Connor has something brewing," Liam stated, and I looked over at him, wondering who Connor was.

"Agreed. We are going to have to step up our patrols. Something is coming. I can feel it." I shivered at Patrice's words, not liking the sound of what she said but sensing the same foreboding that she did.

CHAPTER SIXTEEN

The following days were spent attempting to determine why the team had left that night and where they may have taken Alana's body while she transitioned. From what we could tell, Alana had been jealous of the attention I received on my first mission out and had decided to take on Adam to win favour with the elders.

Liam avoided being alone with me, and I couldn't tell if this was because he was still punishing himself for being distracted or if he didn't want to explore what had been developing between us. For my part, I was trying to deal with the grief of losing yet more people who meant something to me. Katyana had been such a massive presence in the Manor, and I felt her absence every time I walked through the door. Sam had been the closest in age to me amongst the Order, and I missed the way we both joked about the older generation around us. Hell, I even missed the daily arguments with Alana.

I wished I'd been given the chance to get to know Kazeem and Omari. There were so few Order members these days that to lose even one was tragic. Losing five at once was devastating, and I could see its impact on the others. Celeste had lost her best friend when Katyana died, and she was struggling to focus, torn between needing to find Alana's body and wanting to break down and mourn the loss of her friend. Due to how long they all lived and the fact that our jobs were so dangerous, I somehow believed that they were immune to grief. It was only through watching them all now that I realised how very wrong I had been. When they'd said that they understood my grief when Will died, I had been so wrapped up in my depression that I'd failed to put that connection together. Something I was deeply ashamed of now. When you lived for centuries, death was more brutal to bear.

Time was ticking by, and we knew that Alana would be awakening in two days if we didn't find her beforehand to halt the transition. Every waking hour was consumed by our attempts to find answers, but we were coming up short and now relying on the seers in London to try and find her location. I needed to get away from the stress for a few hours, and after letting Patrice know where I was going, I climbed into my car and headed home.

I drove in a dream state, and I marvelled at the fact that I had not killed others, or myself, in a car accident, as I rarely remembered getting to destinations in my car these days, just arriving wherever I was headed in one piece. At least, on the rare occasions I was alone in my car. I had become so used to Liam's presence that I struggled to remember the last time I had driven without him. However, tonight I made a conscious effort to pay attention to getting home. For some reason, I felt something in the air, like something was about to happen, and it was with a sense of foreboding that I realised this something couldn't be good, given all that I had learnt since Will's death. Well, apparent death... Could you consider someone dead if their body was still walking around, determined to bring about your demise?

Failing to pay attention on the drive home, I found myself sitting in front of my house, the engine ticking as it cooled down... How long had I been sitting here? I needed to start paying attention to what was happening around me. The park across the road stood empty and foreboding like each tree hid an invisible enemy.

Suddenly, I was knocked from my internal musings by the sudden movement of my car. I jumped in my seat and looked around to see what had forced my car to rock violently. Maybe I had just imagined it. It was possible but seemed unlikely. My senses were suddenly on high alert, and I could feel my heart begin to race. Everything was still for a moment, and I was grateful that I now always drove with all my car doors locked. Too many stories about women being carjacked scared me into the habit. That and my first face-to-face encounter with Will as a vampire when Liam had yanked me from the car.

But it was no crazed carjacker that was attempting to rip me from my car two seconds later. I screamed as I saw the face of the man I once loved appear next to my window, twisted in fury as he attempted to rip the driver's door off the car. From what Liam had told me of vampire strength, he should have succeeded, and yet my door held fast. I didn't allow myself time to think about why as I used the extra time to crawl over to the passenger seat. I wasn't sure what good I thought this would do me, but thankfully, I didn't have the chance to find out. There was a blur of movement outside. Then Will was knocked to the ground. I couldn't see where he had gone, which scared me even more. Two blurred figures appeared in front of the car, and I watched with terrified fascination as they danced around each other. I realised that Liam had once again come to my aid. Will had the strength of a new vampire on his side, but Liam had the advantage of years of training on his... Well, centuries.

I wanted to hide behind my hands until it was over like I used to while watching horror movies. A fast-forward button would be handy right now. But unfortunately, neither of these things was an option. I could not hide because if Liam lost, Will would come after me next. And there was no way I wanted to fast-forward to that. Despite my newly developed vampire-fighting skills, I was still uncertain that I had the mental strength to kill the man I had loved for over a decade. I held my breath as the two lunged at each other in mid-air. Liam kicked Will in the head, and they both landed hard. I leaned forward to see better and dug my nails into the dash as Will jumped to his feet and took on a fighter's stance, ready for the next round, but Liam was already moving again.

I didn't see what happened next as they moved at lightning speed, but the next thing I knew, Will was gone, and Liam was leaning heavily against the side of my car. With trembling hands, I unlocked my door and climbed out, shaking so hard I could barely walk. Liam was by my side instantly, all signs of fatigue gone as he raced me to the front door. I had my keys gripped in my hand, and he took them from me as I was shaking too hard to unlock the door. Once through the door, I was so grateful that Aurora wasn't home, yet at the same time, I was terrified because she wasn't. I couldn't guarantee her safety if she wasn't within these walls.

I realised after a moment that I was sobbing uncontrollably, and this was causing the shaking. Liam held me tightly as I struggled to get myself under control. After the past few days, it was all a bit too much for me to handle, although I could pull myself together much quicker than I had after my past freakouts.

'Are you okay?' I asked Liam hoarsely after a moment, my forehead pressed against his shoulder, working to get my emotions back under control.

'Fine.' He answered shortly, and I looked up at him. He was looking at me with concern. 'I think I should be the one asking you that.'

I took a deep breath and then let it out again. "How did he find me? I thought the Order had the house cloaked from nightwalkers?"

"He saw you drive through an intersection near here and followed you. He can't get in and won't be able to find this place again on his own." Liam looked at me, still concerned, as I was swaying slightly. "You're safe, Isolde."

'I'll be okay. I just need to sit down for a minute.' I allowed him to guide me to the couch, and we sat down. I couldn't let go of him, and he held me in his lap as I took deep breaths. He held me tightly, and as I gained more control over myself, I realised how close we were to each other. I shifted to look up at him, and we gazed at each other momentarily.

"I thought it had been decided that you didn't need to guard me anymore?" I whispered, moving so that our foreheads met. He let out a ragged breath and closed his eyes.

"I couldn't stay away." He spoke so softly that I could barely hear him.

I sat back slightly, and he opened his eyes. I reached up and ran a hand through his hair before bringing my lips to press gently against his. He kissed me back softly as he wove his fingers through my hair with one hand whilst pulling me closer to him with the other. I moved so that I was straddling his lap, and he ran his hands down to my hips, deepening the kiss, as he pulled me forward so that my chest was pressed against his. He gripped my hips and rocked my pelvis against him as he trailed kisses down my neck. I moaned and continued rocking my hips as he lifted my sweater and shirt over my head, and I undid my bra, sliding it down both arms and tossing it onto the floor behind me as he moved his lips to my right breast and began sucking hard. I gasped as his hand returned to my hip and continued rocking me against him, and I felt how hard he was already rubbing against the seam of my jeans. He moaned along with me as I rocked faster, moving his mouth to my other breast. I arched into him, urging him to suck harder.

"Fuck, Isolde." He lifted me off him and looked up at me as he began slowly undoing the button on my jeans, then dragged the fly down one agonising tooth at a time, smirking up at me as I panted with need. Sliding my jeans down my legs and moving to sit on the edge of the couch, he pressed a kiss against my abdomen, and I ran my fingers through his hair as he trailed kisses along the lace edge of my underwear before sliding them down. Pausing, he looked up at me with questioning eyes. Asking for consent. I nodded, my hair spilling over my shoulder and breast.

Taking his time, Liam ran his hand up the inside of my leg, and I tipped my head back with a sigh as he used a finger to start circling the bundle of nerves at the apex of my thighs with a feather-light touch, surrendering myself to his caress. He worked me up gently, and I moaned softly, then gasped as his tongue replaced his finger. Feeling myself sway a little, I was grateful when he pulled me closer and held me in place with one hand as he moved the other between my legs, sliding a finger inside me, and his tongue and finger began to work in tandem to bring me to the edge. My breathing became ragged as I moaned and writhed against him, riding his tongue and finger together.

"Oh God, Liam, I'm coming." I cried out, and he sucked harder as he sped his hand up, and I came hard, my legs giving out from under my body, and he caught me, keeping me from falling to the floor. He lowered me to sit across him before gently guiding me to lay back on the couch, continuing to work me up slowly to a second, intense orgasm with his hand as I writhed in his lap. My vision blurred as I came again with a hoarse cry.

"I could watch that all night." He breathed, slowly taking my hand and pressing a kiss to my palm, his eyes on mine as I breathed heavily, waiting for the stars to clear from my vision. I took my hand from his lips and ran my fingers through his hair as I sat up and kissed him. He palmed my breast with one hand as he used the other to tangle his fingers through my hair.

"I want you, Liam," I whispered against his lips before rising to my feet, pulling him up and leading him into my room. There would be no one to interrupt us tonight, as Aurora and Jacob were away for the weekend, staying down the Gold Coast to attend a wedding. Liam closed the door behind him, and I leaned into him as he stood with his back against the door. I wound my arms around his neck, kissing him hard before I stepped back to pull his shirt over his head.

"You have far too many clothes on. Let me help you fix that." He watched as I stepped back slightly to admire him, and he gave me an amused smirk as I ran my hand down his chest and over his toned abs. Centuries of kicking ass had caused him to develop muscles in all the right places. With a single finger, I traced each detail of his tattoo, and he shivered when I reached the head of the dragon, coming to a stop at the edge of its nose, right over his heart. I looked into his eyes then, as my hands moved slowly down to the buckle on his belt, and his breath became uneven.

He made no move to help me, allowing me to take my time and set the pace. It took all my self-restraint not to jump on him and devour him right there. I moved forward and planted a kiss over his heart, and he let out a long breath as I moved slowly down his body, planting soft kisses as I went, finally managing to undo his belt. I knelt to remove his jeans and boxers until he stood before me, as naked as I was. I looked up at him from where I knelt before him and watched as he let his head fall back against the door as I ran my hand over his erection. He moaned and closed his eyes as I took him in my mouth and ran my tongue over the tip, working my hands and mouth together. He tangled his hand in my hair, looking down at me and slowly rocking his hips in time with my head bobs, his gaze full of lust.

Growing impatient, it wasn't long before he pulled me off him and raised me to my feet before hoisting me up. Grabbing my thighs and urging me to wrap my legs around his waist as he kissed me hard, his hands gripped my butt as he carried me slowly towards the bed. He turned so that he sat on the edge, and I straddled his lap again. I raised myself onto my knees, watching his face as I lowered myself down onto him. We both moaned together as I took him inside slowly, inch by glorious inch.

He framed my cheeks with his hands and pulled my face gently down to his, our foreheads touching as I began to rock slowly, my arms wrapped around his neck and back. Moving his hands away from my face, he slid one behind my neck and wrapped my hair around his fist gently whilst the other gripped my hip, guiding me up and down.

"God, Isolde, you're so perfect," He whispered, trailing kisses down my neck as he pulled my hair gently back so that he could gain better access to my breasts. He took my right nipple in his mouth and sucked hard as I continued rocking harder and harder against him. I could feel another orgasm growing, and he let go of my hip, reaching between us to help me along with his fingers.

"Fuck, Liam. Oh, God!" I cried out as I came, his mouth still at my breast and his hand rubbing furiously, causing yet another orgasm to follow immediately after. My legs started to give out, and I slowed down, the pleasure running through me, making it difficult to move.

He lifted me off him, turning to lay me down on my back and pressed a kiss to my belly before sliding up my body and bringing his lips to mine. Easing back inside, our eyes locked as he started to rock his hips slowly. We moved together like this for what could have been minutes or hours, the chorus of our moans and sighs filling the room until I began to feel another orgasm building. He picked up his pace as my inner walls tightened around him, and pleasure shot through me once again as I cried out. He kissed me gently, and I struggled to breathe as the aftershocks rippled through me.

Slowing his pace once again, he allowed me the chance to get my breath back but continued to keep me on edge, little shock waves continuing to cause me to shudder. Once I gained control of myself again, I wrapped my legs around his hips as he pulled himself upright. As he rocked his hips back and forth at increasing speed, he ran his hands up and down the front of my thighs. I could feel him getting closer to coming himself as he reached down and rubbed my most sensitive spot once again.

"Come with me, Isolde," he said, and my back arched off the bed with his words as we came together in one last powerful thrust. He lowered himself on top of me as I kept my legs wrapped around him, holding him close in my arms as we breathed heavily together.

Not long after, I lay wrapped in Liam's arms; his chest pressed to my back as I fought off the sleep I knew would inevitably come. I was afraid to fall asleep, knowing that everything would have changed when I woke, and I worried about the consequences of crossing the line we had just set ablaze. Because although I knew that his feelings were as intense as my own, I was very aware that he didn't need much sleep. This gave him plenty of time to think about this change in our relationship. Now, we had gone way past complicated. I turned in his arms to face him and traced a finger across his lips, and he kissed it softly.

"You should get some sleep," he said quietly, raising his hand to push my hair behind my ear before running it gently down my back.

"I'm scared to fall asleep," I whispered, and he looked at me thoughtfully for a moment before nodding.

"You think I won't be here when you wake up?" He continued moving his hand up and down my back as he spoke, and I snuggled closer into him.

"You are notorious for overthinking things," I mumbled, resting my forehead against his. He kissed me softly for a moment and then pulled me in tighter.

"How about if I promise to be here when you open your eyes? Will that help?"

"That depends. Are you planning to talk yourself out of this while I'm sleeping?" I struggled to fight off sleep, but I was slowly losing the battle.

"I can't fight this anymore. Now go to sleep." Comforted by his words, I snuggled into him and allowed sleep to take over finally.

CHAPTER SEVENTEEN

A beam of sunlight lay across my face, and my first thought was that I had forgotten to shut the curtains. My second, panicked thought was of Liam, and I turned my head so quickly that I wrenched my neck. I let out a yelp before finally noticing the arm that was wrapped around my waist and the body pressed up against my back. Liam raised himself up on his elbow and looked down at me with a smirk before moving his hand to massage my sore neck.

"I gave you my word, and you still didn't trust me to be here in the morning?" I blushed a little, but he laughed, a laugh that was so relaxed and normal. I loved seeing this side of him. I rolled to face him, and he rearranged us so that I lay on top of him. He guided my face to his and kissed me softly.

"Good morning." I gazed down at him as he ran his fingers through my hair and lightly down my back, which sent a shiver down my spine. I loved it when he played with my hair.

"Good morning." He smiled at me with a knowing smile. I kissed him again, harder this time and let myself get lost in this perfect moment.

Hours later, I emerged from my room, unsure of the reception I would be receiving from Aurora, as I'd heard her and Jacob come home earlier. Liam was in my shower, and Aurora entered the kitchen, stopping when she saw me, surprised.

"Oh, I thought you were in the shower. Who's in there?" From the look on her face, she already knew the answer to that question.

"Liam." I didn't bother explaining, knowing Aurora was a big enough girl to work it out on her own. Jacob came in behind her and was equally surprised to see me.

"Liam's in the shower," Aurora told Jacob, who raised an eyebrow before snagging an apple from the fruit bowl.

"I'm gonna leave you two ladies to it. No doubt you're both about to start yelling." He backed out of the room, hands in the air, before all but fleeing back to their room. Smart man.

"Well, go on, let it out. I know you're dying to give me your opinion." I continued to make breakfast for myself and Liam, my back to my sister, knowing the look that she was giving me was no doubt full of judgement.

"So much for 'we're just friends' then, huh?"

"Looks like it." I was purposely being aloof, and I could tell it was pissing Aurora off.

"So, you're a couple now, is that it? I can't believe you got over Will so quickly." I turned toward her, doing nothing to hide the anger that I knew was written all over my face. As I did so, something caught Aurora's eye, and I saw her look at my wrist as I pushed my hair back. Too late, I realised that I was not wearing a jumper, which I had taken to wearing to hide my tattoo. "And when the hell did you get a tattoo?!" I disregarded the question, still focused on her last statement.

"You know nothing about how I grieved him or what I've been through. I will always love Will, he was my first love, and if he were still alive, I would be marrying him soon. I have forgotten nothing." I spat the words at her, and she recoiled, stunned by my anger. I never spoke to her like this. "But I have to move on with my life, and I have chosen to do so with Liam, who is a kind and caring man. You should be happy for me instead of expecting me to wallow in self-pity for the rest of my life." I was fuming, and Aurora finally saw how she was hurting me, backing down slightly.

"I'm sorry. I guess I was just thrown by the fact that you found someone else so quickly. You loved him so much... I guess I just expected you to take years to get over him..." She had run out of things to say. I angrily wiped away a tear, annoyed that I had started to cry. This conversation was ruining the great mood I had woken up in.

"Well, I have found someone, and you're just going to have to deal with that." I took the two plates of toast and brushed past her as she remained leaning against the bench before heading back into my room. Liam was sitting on my bed, a towel wrapped around his waist, with one eyebrow raised.

"Don't ask." I could not help but admire him, eyes drawn once again to his amazing chest and the tattoo. I felt the corners of my mouth raise as my eyes drifted over his abs, and he smirked at me.

"Stop that. You'll make me blush." I knew he was in my head, and I put the plates down on the bedside table. I headed towards my open bathroom door, slowly unbuttoning my pyjama top. As I reached the door, I looked back over my shoulder.

"Well, aren't you coming?" I giggled as he came after me in one fluid movement, lifting me so I could wrap my legs around his waist, and he walked us into the bathroom, kissing me as we went.

As the morning grew later, I knew that we should head for the Manor, but I could not bring myself to leave the comfort of my bed and Liam's arms. I lay on my stomach, propped up on my elbows, as

I looked down at Liam, who was playing with a few strands of my hair.

"Are you happy?" I asked quietly. He let the strands of my hair fall through his fingers as he reached up to stroke my face gently.

"In all my existence, I don't think I've ever been happier... With you, it is as if I forget about all of the supernatural parts of the world and can just feel human for a while. I'm back to being the twenty-five-year-old man I was all those years ago." I smiled and kissed him softly before fixing him with a playful grin.

"So, all of those women who came before me... You never felt this way for any of them?" Although I tried to sound casual, he knew it was something I was genuinely concerned about. He looked up at me thoughtfully. "Okay, you're taking way too long to answer. Now I'm worried." Liam put a finger to my lips and smiled reassuringly.

"I'm just trying to think of what I can say that will make you see that those women were nothing more than passing phases without making me sound like a complete cad."

"A cad? I keep forgetting how old you are until you use terms like that... That's something that I've only ever heard my grandfather say." I grinned, and Liam rolled his eyes.

"Ha ha." He said drily. "In all seriousness though... Remember when I told you that I had to give up my role in the Church once my brother disappeared? And that the idea of taking a wife, of tying myself to someone, was not something I had ever wanted for myself? I meant that. Until you entered my life, I'd never met anyone that I could imagine wanting to spend a lifetime with. Many lifetimes." I was speechless for a moment, trying to work out how to respond to this. After a moment, I sat up, trying to gather my thoughts.

"Why me? What's so special about me?" I couldn't fathom how someone who had been alive for so long, who had experienced so many lives and seen so much, could feel so strongly for someone like me, who had experienced nothing of life in comparison. It was like comparing a toddler to a great-great-grandfather. Liam sat up beside me, gently bringing his hand to my chin and urging me to bring my gaze to his.

"Why not you?" He asked, looking me in the eye. "Although you believe you're so young, look at all you have been through. You are an old soul, wise beyond your years." He pushed my hair back behind my ear and leaned in close. "You're beautiful." He gently kissed my forehead. "Sexy." Kissed my nose. "And never before in my life have I ever met someone so determined and self-aware. You intoxicate me." He kissed my lips softly. "I have protected a lot of people in my life, but never before have I wanted to keep someone safe as badly as I do you." He kissed me again, and I kissed him back hungrily but pulled back after a moment to look at him again.

"So, you think I need to be kept safe? Is that why I appeal to you so much, because I play the damsel in distress so well?" Liam groaned and flopped back into the pillows, pulling me on top of him.

"Believe me, Isolde, I know you are more than capable of holding your own. Everything I do is driven by a need to protect you. To keep you safe and shield you from further heartbreak. However, at the same time, the things that you have been through... They've made you who you are." He stated this so simply, and yet I felt as though he had just given a rousing speech, much like you see in the movies. I searched his face, knowing that he would truly do anything to keep me safe.

"Thank you." I kissed him softly again. His hands began stroking up and down my back as the kiss grew, and he grabbed my hips, starting to rock them against his. Just as I started to trail kisses down his chest, we were interrupted by the sound of Liam's mobile ringing. He groaned as I reluctantly rolled off him, and he grabbed it from the bedside table.

"Hello?" I headed for the bathroom as he took the call, figuring that I would have to leave the safety of my room now. Sure enough, when I emerged a few moments later, it was to find Liam sitting on the bed, already wearing his jeans.

"They need us at the Manor," he said, looking up at me as I stood in front of him and absently ran my fingers through his hair.

"Of course they do." I sighed, pushing my hair out of my face to pull it back into a messy bun on top of my head.

"So..."

"So, what?" I asked, leaning into him as he wrapped his arms around my waist.

"So, I'm going to need my shirt back." He tugged at the hem of the shirt I was wearing. His shirt. Which I had pulled on as I headed to the bathroom. It was all that I was wearing.

"Really? Are you sure? I think you look great without it." I smirked, and he laughed.

"I'm just going to have to take it off you; you realise that, don't you?"

"You can try." I darted out of his arms and attempted to run for the door, but he caught me in his arms, turned me to face him and kissed me. Within a second, I was naked once again, and he was fully clothed, his lips pressed to mine as he held me close to him. He pulled away with a cheeky grin, and I loved seeing him this relaxed... So free.

"That's playing dirty." He sat back down, watching me appreciatively as I walked to my dresser and started digging through it to find something to wear.

"I know, but it was fun." I threw a shirt at his head.

Half an hour later, we entered the Manor hand in hand, figuring there was no point in being secretive. Gerard was the first person to see us as we walked through the door, and he raised an eyebrow but refrained from commenting. Patrice, however, was not so stoic.

"Is there something the two of you would like to share?" She asked, an edge to her voice, but Liam simply shrugged, letting me take this one as he went off in search of Celeste. But not before giving me a brief kiss on the lips and exchanging a look with Patrice.

"Not really. I'm not sure why we need to keep everyone informed of our relationship status." I followed Patrice into the kitchen, in desperate need of coffee.

"I know that you are new to this life, Isolde, but there are certain ways of going about things. You're being in a relationship with Liam was not part of your destiny." I hadn't noticed Damon as he followed us in as well, and I rolled my eyes. All Damon ever did was lecture me about my destiny and my duty. I had had enough, and Patrice could see I had reached the end of my tether.

"I've already had a similar conversation to this one this morning, so I'll make it quick. What I do and whom I do those things with is not a topic of discussion amongst the elders. I did not ask for this life, and I am more than happy to walk away from it the first chance I get, so just keep trying to control me, Damon, and you will see how serious I am about that." I put a hand up as he opened his mouth to protest, stopping him in his tracks. After a look from Patrice, he stopped himself from commenting, leaning back against the bench and crossing his arms as I continued. "Now, I understand your concern, and while I appreciate it, my relationship with Liam is our business alone," I swear I saw a glimmer of respect in Patrice's eye as I gave my little speech.

For his part, Damon continued to look pissed, but he must have realised that I truly had no issues with walking away from this life. As it was, I had no qualms about walking away from this conversation. I moved to leave the room before turning back to say one final thing. "And not a word to Liam about this. I don't want to hear that you've been lecturing him about how I need to be protected and how we shouldn't be together. We are two consenting adults, and if we want to be together, then you are all just going to have to deal with it."

I found Liam in the Intel room with Celeste and Daniel. They didn't seem to care about the fact that Liam and I were now an item, and I figured that they had had to deal with their fair share of crap from the elders regarding their relationship. If it were up to the elders, we would all be celibate. Liam stifled a laugh as I leaned against the table beside him, no doubt having heard my rant at Damon.

"What have I missed?"

"Celeste was just going through what they found last night."

"Catch me up?" I looked at Celeste expectantly. She looked briefly taken aback by my take-charge approach before getting down to business.

"We managed to track the vampires that took Alana." She nodded towards the map on the large TV screens on the walls. A red beacon was blipping away in the middle of what appeared to be a satellite image.

"Where is that?" I was no good with maps if they didn't have suburbs and street names written on them. I saw a look exchanged between the other three and began to realise that I probably didn't want to know. Liam was the one to answer me.

"It's your old house." Yep, I was right. I didn't want to know.

"You mean the townhouse? The one that you convinced me not to burn to the ground?" I crossed my arms over my chest, leaning my hip against the desk next to me as I surveyed the three of them.

"Yes. We know that Will had full access to the house while you were living there, but when it was sold to the new owners, we figured he would no longer have any interest in it. That has usually been the case in the past." As Celeste spoke, I could feel Liam watching me, waiting for my reaction.

"So now he's killed off the new owners, and they are using it as a base." Celeste and Daniel exchanged a thoughtful look as I summed up what they were avoiding saying out loud.

"That certainly looks like what's happened," Daniel said to Celeste, who nodded.

"We'll look into this further. Looks like you guys might be off on a mission tonight." They both turned back to the monitors, pretty much dismissing us. This was their department, planning the missions while we were the muscle. Liam led the way out of the room and down the hall to the training room.

"I don't think you should come tonight." I turned to face Liam in surprise, from where I'd started to wrap my hands to prepare to start taking my frustration out on one of the many punching bags.

"What? Why?"

"Because when it comes to Will, you freeze. Any other vampire nest, I would not have any hesitation to have you at my side, especially with your abilities. However, one where he might be... Not to mention that these vampires are the ones gunning for you." What he said made sense, and yet, I was still fuming at the amount of people trying to tell me what to do today.

Liam was clearly in my head and ready for my argument as he came towards me and wrapped his arms around my waist, pulling me to him. "How about this, you stay here, logged into the comms, and that way, it's like you being there?" I felt like I was a child, being placated with a lollipop. Liam smiled down at me. "Your mental images are some of the most imaginative and entertaining I've ever seen." I smacked his shoulder.

"Shut up!" I think I just successfully disproved his theory this morning of having an old soul with that one little outburst. However, he contented himself to know he had won this round for the time being as he pulled me back in for a kiss. Sighing, I had to admit that he was right. When it came to Will, I did freeze. And we could not afford that sort of mistake.

I helped the others prepare, watching as Daniel, Dylan, Yumi, Edward, Colin and Zuri strapped themselves with various weapons. As usual, Liam was armed only with a stake that he had strapped to his thigh. I briefly kissed Liam goodbye and watched them leave, ignoring the pang of discomfort at being the one left behind.

Once they had departed, I headed back into the intelligence room where Celeste sat, watching as the GPS trackers on the cars allowed us to track their route to my old home. Patrice sat cross-legged on a table in the corner of the room, surrounded by candles. I sat down at the computer that Celeste had assigned me, attaching a communications device to my ear. On the monitor in front of me, I could see the back of the first car as I watched the world through Liam's eyes, or rather, through the camera attached to his black, padded vest. Each of the team wore one, and the images were filtered onto one massive screen on the wall.

Celeste had assigned me to Liam whilst she and a few others monitored everyone else. I gratefully took the coffee that Barbara handed me as she walked past on her way to her monitor. I had already decided that I did not enjoy being on this side of an operation. Although I could see everything, I was powerless to do anything.

"Can you hear me?" I said into my headset.

"Loud and clear." Liam's voice came back to me.

"Well, at least for once, you can only hear what I'm saying." I mused. I stayed silent for the remainder of their drive as the team discussed tactics amongst themselves. Whilst everyone else was to deal with any vampires they came across, it was Liam's job to find Alana. As the cars rounded the corner into my old street, my heart rate increased. I wasn't sure what to expect once they entered the property, and I was not looking forward to seeing my old home being used as a vampire nest.

Once they arrived, the team fanned out around the property, intending to enter simultaneously through the back and front doors, as well as through the windows at both sides of the house. Across the room from me, I saw Patrice begin to perform a cloaking spell to prevent civilians from witnessing the breaking and entering that was about to occur. The last thing we needed was for the police to show up.

I had watched Patrice perform several spells over the past few months and admired the fluid and graceful movements as she used her entire body, the chants almost sounding like a song as she uttered the words to bring a cloak of silence and invisibility over the exterior of the house, coming down behind the team. As soon as Patrice completed the spell, she nodded at Celeste, who simply said, "Go!" into her headset.

Then all hell broke loose. As one, the entire unit moved into the house. It was like watching some cop movie on mute, as not a single sound was made. I watched as Liam entered the home, proof enough that there were no living residents remaining. I had provided everyone with a detailed description of the layout of the house, advising Liam that the master bedroom was upstairs, at the back of the house. I had surmised that it would be the most likely place that they had left Alana. Not only was it the largest room, but it also got the least amount of sunlight. Liam followed my directions towards the stairs at the back of the house. Ahead of him, I saw Daniel take down the first vampire that they had come across.

Liam continued through the house, yet to come across any resistance. It didn't look like there were many vampires there, which was good but surprising. It didn't make Liam's ultimate job any easier, though. He came to the top of the stairs, throwing a small female vampire down the stairs when she attempted to attack him. I couldn't see what became of her, but I imagined one of the others downstairs dealt with her after that. A larger vampire stood in front of the bedroom door, guarding it. In life, he could have been a rugby player and built like a small mountain. I watched, not realising I was holding my breath, as Liam took him out with ease, staking him in the heart before the vampire had so much as moved.

Then he opened the door, and I fought back a wave of guilt. The new owners lay dead in a heap in the corner of the room, their necks twisted at an odd angle, their eyes staring vacantly at a world they could no longer see. I attempted to swallow the lump in my throat, knowing now was not the time.

"We should have burned it to the ground," I said bitterly.

"Don't blame yourself, Isolde. We had no way of knowing this would happen," Liam said, as beside me, Celeste put her hand over mine. Her eyes were still focused on the progress of the rest of the team, who were spread throughout the house, most of them taking out at least one vampire each.

I returned my gaze to the screen in front of me to see that Liam knelt next to the bed, where Alana's body lay. She certainly looked dead, and it was hard to believe, as we looked down at her, that she was being bombarded with the blood memories of the entire coven. Including the same blood memories that had coursed through Will all those months ago, turning him into the soulless being he had become.

I watched as Liam's hand gently brushed a strand of hair away from Alana's face, and I felt a wave of sadness for him. I knew that although Liam had no romantic feelings for Alana, he still cared for her deeply, and what he was about to do was going to be incredibly hard for him. I had tears in my eyes as I watched Liam's hand raise the stake above Alana's chest before plunging it deep into her heart.

I jumped back as Alana's eyes flew open, no longer brown, having already turned to the tell-tale piercing blue. They were glazed over, unseeing. Then, slowly, her body disintegrated into dust, which took me by surprise. I looked at Celeste with a raised eyebrow.

"That's normal. When they are in the process of turning, it's like the body doesn't know what to do, so it simply disintegrates into nothing," she said, and I swallowed hard as Liam took Alana's necklace from the dust and placed it into his pocket. All that remained of her.

The team arrived back an hour later, having disposed of the bodies of all of the vampires. They were subdued, sadness coming off each of them in waves, pained by the task that they had to perform. I realised that although Alana had not been nice to me, she had been a much-loved member of the Order. Now that they were no longer preoccupied with the task of finding her before she turned, I was a witness to their mourning.

They were now able to grieve the deaths of all the Protectors that had been killed on the ill-fated raid. It scared me how the deaths had diminished the ranks of the Order. I wasn't sure how much more death and loss I could handle, and it made me fear becoming too close to anyone else. Because letting people close to my heart made it easier to lose another piece of it when they were ultimately ripped from me. And yet, I found myself clinging tighter to Liam as he walked through the door, and we drew strength from each other as we held one another amongst the heavy cloud of grief.

CHAPTER EIGHTEEN

Several days later, I sat beside Liam, holding his hand as we went through the process of saying goodbye to our fallen friends. I was surprised to discover that a small section of the Toowong Cemetery was cloaked to hide a burial plot for the Order. I had come across dates going back to the settlement of Brisbane in the early nineteenth century, though most were recent, from when the official branch had taken up residence here when I was born.

Liam squeezed my hand, and I returned my thoughts to the present to see that Sam's was the latest coffin being lowered into the ground, and I immediately felt my stomach clench. A tear began to form in the corner of my eye, and I swallowed hard. I had already watched the Priestess perform the death rites for Omari and Kazeem, and I felt as though I was engulfed in a cloud of grief. Mostly, though, I felt like an intruder. I did not feel as though I should be here. Some of those buried had been as old as one hundred, but I had only known them for a few months.

Liam let go of my hand and put his arm around me, pulling me closer, and I realised he had heard my thoughts. I knew he was also drawing his own comfort from my presence, and I gripped his hand as Katyana's coffin was lowered next, blinking back the tears that were starting to sting my eyes.

The final coffin was for Alana. Without a body to bury, they had instead placed a small urn inside that contained her necklace. I felt my throat constrict with emotion, and the tears finally started to track down my face. I had witnessed too much death over the past few months and was unsure how much more I could take.

As the group slowly dispersed, I stood before the headstone erected in Katyana's memory, a single rose in my hand. I couldn't bring myself to leave, and Liam stood speaking to Patrice for a while before coming to stand beside me. Neither of us spoke as we stood looking at the headstone. This was not how it was meant to end for her. To end a life like ours, alone and interred in the ground. To eventually be forgotten... Liam put his arm around me again as tears slid down my cheek.

"I feel as though all I've done these past six months is cry," I said sadly as Liam kissed the top of my head and pulled me close to his side.

"I've buried a lot of people in my time... And it never gets any easier. However, you were wrong about one thing. They are never forgotten." And I realised he was right. With the slow ageing and having Liam around, they weren't forgotten. It was a small glimmer of happiness in an otherwise bleak moment.

Liam stepped away from me, going to talk to the Priestess who had presided over the ceremonies. I walked amongst the headstones, reading the names of the fallen. As I read the name "Isabel King 25.10.1870 – 28.11.1994", which was relatively young for a member of the Order, a movement out of the corner of my eye caused me to look up. I froze, sure that I must be seeing things.

Alana stood a few feet from me, her eyes wide as she stared intently at me, her hand raised, as she beckoned me towards her. I looked around, hoping that someone else could see her as well. However, no one was looking in her direction other than me.

I must be going insane.

Her lips moved, but I heard nothing.

"I can't hear you..." I strained for any trace of a sound as her lips stopped moving, and she lowered her hand.

"Liam?" I said his name quietly, looking back at where he stood a few feet away. He excused himself from the conversation with the Priestess and came to join me. I looked back to where I had seen Alana, but she was gone.

"Are you okay? You look like you've seen a ghost."

"I think I may have," I said, staring at the spot Alana had stood moments ago.

"What do you mean?" Liam looked confused.

"I just saw Alana standing right there. She was reaching out to me, and I think she was trying to tell me something, but I couldn't hear her." Now Liam's expression turned to one of concern.

"You saw her?"

"Yes... Is that something unusual? I'm never sure what's weird and what's normal anymore." Liam scanned the group as I spoke, looking for someone. He spotted Patrice and signalled her over.

"Is everything okay?" Patrice came to join us, looking down at the headstone of Isabel King, assuming it must be something to do with our location.

"Isolde just saw Alana," Liam said, and Patrice looked up at me sharply.

"What did she say?" This line of enquiry took me aback. There was no question of my sanity nor any doubt of what I had seen.

"Um... Her lips were moving, but I couldn't hear her," I said, and Patrice looked crestfallen. "I don't understand; why am I seeing her ghost?" I figured if she were going to appear to anyone, it certainly would not be me.

"Ghosts generally appear to people they have a message for."

"Why would she have a message for me?" I asked, confused. Patrice looked at Liam, who shrugged, shaking his head.

"I don't know." It was puzzling, and we headed for the cars when it looked like Alana would not reappear. I kept looking back over my shoulder at the spot where I had seen her, all the while wondering why on earth Alana would have a message for me.

A few nights later, I sat on my bed. It was the first time I had been truly alone in months, having forced Liam to stay at the Manor and Aurora and Jacob were away for the weekend. With the magical wards over the house, the elders had agreed that there was no point in having someone watching over me when no vampire could cross the transom. I told him that I just wanted some me time. Which was true, but I did not intend to stay home to do it.

There was something that I needed to do. And I needed to do it alone. My phone had been blowing up with unread messages from friends and family, each reaching out in their own way. I had become so distant from everyone that I doubted anyone would be surprised by my silence on today, of all days.

It was meant to be my wedding day.

I sat on that bed for hours, going through photo albums that had been packed in a box since we had moved from the townhouse. Before all the craziness had happened in my life, I was known for taking photos to document every occasion, and as a result, I had thousands of happy snaps. Most of them were photos of myself and Will over the years. It was the first time I had been able to bring myself to look at them since Will had died, and going through them all now brought tears to my eyes. Things had been simple back then.

I saw a photo of the two of us at a friend's wedding eighteen months ago. There was a twinkle in Will's eye, and I knew now, looking at this photo, that it was at this time that he had decided it was time to propose to me. In the picture, I stared at him as he looked at the photographer, toasting the camera. The look of devotion on my face sent a shiver down my spine. My world, indeed, had revolved around him.

Why had no one told me I was almost unnaturally devoted to him? For someone who claimed to be an independent woman, my entire life had been about him. I had been in love with him from age ten when I stopped seeing him as someone with boy germs. I had even come home early from the trip of my dreams because I couldn't bear to be away from him. Yet, when he was no longer in my life, I had moved on quicker than anyone had believed possible, including myself, if I was honest. I had never doubted anything in my relationship with Will and could never fault his devotion to me.

But on meeting Liam, it was as if I was seeing everything more clearly. My life with Will had been an illusion—a fairy tale. With Liam, he indeed saw me. He saw the good, the bad... everything. He didn't just expect me to be in love with him; he questioned it daily, even though he could read my mind. Will had just taken my devotion to him for granted. And why wouldn't he have? I followed him around for more than half of our lives. However, he had never followed me.

I tucked the photo away in my pocket and closed the last of the photo albums. I was finished with them and knew I would never look at them again. I couldn't bring myself to destroy them, though. Some part of me needed to keep that part of my life alive. I didn't want to lose touch with the people who remained around me. However, I was moving on.

After midnight, I left my house and headed towards my former home with Will. I drove through the streets of Bulimba, which lay silent in the darkness. Pulling up across the road from the complex where we once lived, I took out a book I had smuggled out amongst my belongings that morning when I left the Manor. Having witnessed Patrice perform the cloaking spell several times, I was confident I could do it, even if only for a few minutes. A few minutes was all that I needed.

Now that I'd worked out that I didn't need chants to harness my power, I wondered if I even needed the book, but I couldn't risk anyone seeing what I was about to do until I was ready. After familiarising myself with what I needed to understand about the spell in order to cloak the house against prying eyes and ears, I fearlessly stepped out of the car. I didn't envy any vampire who tried to cross me tonight.

Coming to a standstill in my old driveway, I surveyed the remains of the crime scene tape hanging from the door frame, fluttering in the breeze. After the team had removed all the vampires from the house, we had put in an anonymous call to the police to let them know of the fate of the new owners. There was an ongoing investigation, but no solid leads. There were now whispers of gang activity, and the police were searching for a connection between Will's death and the current occupants' grizzly demise. The theory was that I had been the target. Our connections inside the police force were working on drug-related theories, keeping the truth firmly hidden, as usual.

I entered the house and shut the door softly behind me. After checking for any remaining vampires and ensuring that I was alone, I took out the candles from my backpack and set them up in a circle before stepping inside. I sat on the ground with my legs crossed.

The concept of the spell was simple. Chant the words, and a cloak would come down over the area I envisioned in my head, creating an illusion that any passers-by would see nothing but an empty house, and no noise would be detected outside the barrier. But, because I was doing it without the chanting or the actual spell, I hoped that envisioning the barrier would be enough. I took a deep breath and focused on the candle directly before me.

Light.

I smiled as all the candles lit at once. At least I knew I could still do that little bit of magic. Now to work out the barrier... I closed my eyes and tried to imagine a barrier encircling the house, and I felt a calm fall over me that I'd not felt in a long time. I focused on my breathing and ignored any other sounds, bringing all my senses down to the rhythmic inhale and exhale.

Barrier.

Nothing happened. I tried not to let the disappointment cause me to lose focus, but I opened my eyes to stare at the flame again. As much as it seemed incredible to be able to do magic without spells or chants, it was rather inconvenient not knowing what to say to get the larger magical enchantments to work.

I first focused on the magic that I had perfected with the flames and spent a few minutes spinning the balls of light in the air. I'd been practising this daily since I'd done it the first night with Liam. I could now make them all go in multiple directions simultaneously before coming together to form a giant ball of light, like a miniature sun hanging in the air. Once I'd reminded myself that I was competent at something, at least, I returned each flame to the candles and closed my eyes again.

Hide and protect me.

Instantly, I felt a power run through me as the air around me began to pop and crackle. I knew without a doubt that it had worked, as I looked out the window to see that a shimmering haze now surrounded the house, my car just a blur on the driveway. I probably should have included my car in that thought...

I stepped out of the circle and went to where I had left my backpack by the door. Kneeling to unzip it, I pulled out two fuel cans. I was about to do something that I never thought I would do in my life. And something I should have done months ago.

As I walked through the vacant rooms, I approached our old bedroom. Before entering, I took a deep breath and attempted to suppress the disturbing memories of the previous occupants' tragic fate. Upon entering, I took a moment to survey the space and deliberately concentrated on the happy memories it held. Every laugh we'd shared while lying in bed. Every kiss and touch. I tried not to tear up at the memory of the room lit up and covered in flower petals.

At last, I took a deep breath and slowly poured the fuel out in a line until I found myself at the front door again. The smell of petrol was strong now, and after gathering my belongings, I opened the door to stand on the front step. Making sure I had no petrol on myself, I held a single candle and willed it to light again. I focused on the flame and took a deep breath, working up the courage to do what needed to be done.

I raised the flame and stared at it briefly before slowly lowering it to the ground before me. And watched as the line of petrol lit up. Watching as the fire ran the length of the hall and up the stairs, I took the photo of Will and me out of my pocket, placing it into the fire. Then I turned and walked away.

As I sat in my car, I watched as the house was engulfed in flames. Once the deafening roar of the fire reached me, I lifted the cloaking enchantment from the property. I applied it to my car, ensuring that the containment enchantment remained intact to avoid any harm to nearby homes. Onlookers emerged from their houses as the blaze grew, stunned by the spectacle. I called the fire department using a prepaid phone I had purchased earlier in the day, and soon after, I heard the sound of a siren in the distance. With my car still shielded by the second cloaking spell, I drove away unnoticed.

As I was too wired to return home or to the Manor, I drove the streets for a while, not comprehending where I was going until I found myself at the top of Bartley's Hill in Ascot. Although it was across the river from Bulimba, I could see the smoke from my arson attack, and I let what I had done truly sink in. In setting my former home ablaze, I had let go of the past. I hoped I could now face Will without being bombarded by memories of what we'd shared. The

Will I knew was dead, and I had to stop allowing myself to see him in the creature that he had become.

I watched the sunrise from the lookout, but exhaustion soon set in. Unsure of how my return would be received, I quietly returned to the Manor. The rest of the Order were asleep when I let myself in through the front door and headed to Liam's room. He was sleeping peacefully, and I slipped out of my jeans before snuggling beside him. Resting my head on the pillow, I closed my eyes and drifted off to sleep, feeling content and happy to be there.

When I awoke hours later, I rolled over to find Liam watching me, a small smile playing on his lips. He had been up for a while and was fully clothed, sitting in the armchair next to my side of the bed.

He reached over and pushed aside the lock of my hair that lay across my cheek.

"Anything you want to tell me about last night?" I could tell he already knew everything I'd done in the early morning hours.

"It was just something I had to do," I said, my voice thick with sleep. He lifted the covers and slid into bed beside me, pulling me close, and we lay facing each other, our noses almost touching.

"I know." He kissed me then, and I lost myself in the moment with him, allowing everything else to fall away.

No one else seemed to know what I'd done, and when Liam didn't say anything to Patrice, I wondered, not for the first time, why there were things that he didn't share with the elders.

"Do you not trust the Order, Liam?" I asked later that afternoon as I wrapped my hands, preparing for another sparring session. Liam moved to help me, his hands gently cradling mine as he secured the wraps. Once he was done, he pulled me close and rested his chin on my head. I clung to him, unsure whether I should be concerned or not.

"I just have this feeling that there is more going on than what we're being told. It's not that I don't trust the Order, but I definitely don't trust Damon. From the few conversations I've seen between them, he's been putting a lot of pressure on Patrice. There is something slightly erratic about Damon's behaviour when it comes to your powers, and I don't think we should be giving away too much about your abilities until we know more." I pulled back slightly to look up at him. Although I'd asked, I hadn't expected him to share that he had doubts about the group he had been a part of for over five hundred years. But I also had suspicions about Damon, and it made me feel better to know that they weren't entirely unfounded. After a few more moments of scanning his face, I nodded.

"Okay. I'll follow your lead then. We're a team, right?" He lowered his lips to mine, kissing me softly. I felt my heart skip a beat as he rested his forehead against mine, the tenderness evident on his face.

"It's you and me, Isolde. Always."

The next few days were uneventful. Almost scarily so.

After yet another quiet night, I returned to the Manor along with Daniel. We had checked out a few places in Fortitude Valley which were common feeding grounds for nightwalkers, but had come across nothing more than a few drunks stumbling home after a big night. It was making me edgy.

I dropped my stuff in my bedroom and changed into a sweater dress before searching for Liam, who'd been out with Gerard and a few others in the city. According to the chatter through my earpiece, their night had been as quiet as mine. I found him sitting behind his large desk, a massive pile of books before him.

"Hey," I said, sitting on the bed behind him. He swivelled his chair around to face me.

"Hey. You had a slow night as well, I gather?" He already knew the answer, although I nodded anyway.

"Yeah. It's starting to freak me out a little."

"It's not a good sign, especially because they were active only a week ago. Something is coming." I was not comforted by this line of conversation. I indicated towards the pile of books, eager to change the subject before the troublesome thoughts consumed me.

"Just catching up on some light reading?" I asked, and Liam laughed.

"Hardly. I'm reading through the histories to see if there is anything in here that could tell us what we might be about to come up against."

"How would the histories help you? Wouldn't it be better to read books from the prophecy section?" I raised an eyebrow, and he shrugged.

"I've never been all that good with prophecies. The thing with the prophecy section is that all the books there seem to be written in tongues."

"Huh?"

"They're incredibly hard to understand." He translated.

"Even for you, who's been around forever?" I had assumed that Liam knew everything, and this conversation confused me.

"Usually, the only person who can understand the prophecy is the person who made it, to be perfectly honest." Liam didn't acknowledge the jibe about his age, though he did smirk slightly. I got to my feet with a sigh.

"Well, it can't hurt to look, right?" I had never looked at any prophecy books and realised, with a jolt, that I'd never even read the prophecy about myself. Liam raised an eyebrow.

"Be my guest. I'll stick with these." He tapped the nearest book. His attitude was not giving me any confidence that I would find anything useful, but I figured doing something was better than sitting back and waiting.

I went down to the library, wondering where to start. After perusing the shelves for a while, I came across the section I sought. Selecting a few books at random seemed to be the way to go. However, as I started to pull books from the shelves, I came across one that caught my eye. THE GEMINI PROPHECY.

Being a twin, I was immediately drawn to the title of the slender book. It looked much newer than the ones around it and was tucked away, almost as though it wasn't meant to be seen. I set aside my other books and brought them to the closest armchair to read.

In the dark of night, when the moon is high,
Two sets of twins, born of different time.
One set of boys, one set of girls,
Destined to face off in a battle that twirls.
The long-running war, ancient and dark,
In a struggle for power, a vicious shark.
Two twins were chosen, one from each set,
To lead their side and never forget.
The last of the girls will be the missing piece,
Of a puzzle that will not cease.
Their fates are sealed, and their tasks defined,
To fight to the end, and never mind.
One twin from each set will stand strong,
For good or evil, right or wrong.
The balance of power rests in their hands,
To bring peace to the land, regardless of the order's demands.
With strength and courage, they'll face their fear,
The fate of all mankind on their shoulders to bear.
But with unwavering will and steadfast hearts,
They'll win the war and never depart.
Rivers will rise, and rain will fall,

The earth will become a danger to all.
And at that time,
The horsemen will begin their ride.
Thus the prophecy foretells,
Of the twins who rose, as on a spell.
Heroes of a vampire war,
It shall come to pass at New Years Dawn.

"What?" I spoke the words out loud, even though no one was around to answer the burning questions that this raised. I could now understand what Liam meant about them not making sense, but I knew without a doubt that there was something about this prophecy I should know about.

This couldn't be the prophecy that everyone had been talking about. And the horsemen will begin their ride? As in, the horsemen of the Apocalypse? I didn't know much about the Bible, having been raised without any real dedication to any religion. Still, I knew enough about the last book of the Bible, Revelations, to remember that it mentioned the four horsemen who would see the beginning of the Apocalypse... No one had said anything to me about the end of the world. With shaking hands, I put the book aside, not wanting to read anymore. The idea of the end of the world was not something I could deal with at the moment... or ever...

When sleep finally claimed me that night, images of fire and a river of blood plagued my dreams. I decided I didn't like prophecies...

CHAPTER NINETEEN

The next day I invited Celeste to join me for coffee. I was hoping to take a break from the vampire world and have some female bonding time, having realised how much I missed my close friendships before joining the Order. But my life had drastically changed, which made it harder to maintain the friendships that had previously meant the world to me. I found it challenging to discuss my current life and evade the truth, despite Aurora's constant – and judgmental - reminders. Thus, avoiding them all together seemed like the easiest option.

We bought drinks from a local cafe and wandered from the Manor down to New Farm Park, finding a spot on the grass near the rose garden under a large tree. We contented ourselves with a spot of people watching while we sat in companionable silence at first, just soaking up the fresh air and the chance not to have to think too much.

"How are you holding up?" Celeste finally broke the silence, sipping her coffee as she turned to look at me.

"I think I'm handling everything a lot better now. I don't think I've thought about how insane we must be for at least a week now, so that's an improvement." I smiled at her, and she laughed.

"Honestly, I've been in this life for nearly sixty years now, and it still strikes me as strange now and again. Thank goodness for Daniel." She smiled as she mentioned her husband's name, and it was nice to see her take a moment to appreciate having someone to share the insanity with.

"How long have you two been married?" Although we had been making small steps towards a friendship, I still didn't know much about her life before meeting her, and I thought it was time I started to change that. Her smile grew, appreciating the hand of friendship that I was extending.

"We've been married for fifty-four years. Daniel was already in the Order when I turned twenty-five. At first, it was just flirting, but one day, he saved me from a nightwalker attack, and after that, it just all fell into place for us. No one talks about it much, but it is rare for Order members to marry. So what we have is something we work hard not to take for granted." I nodded, having observed that most of the other Order members avoided developing romantic entanglements with others.

"Is there a reason why others tend to avoid becoming involved? I would have thought it would be easier than developing relationships outside of the Order. Especially with our longer life spans and all the secrets we keep?" It was the first time I'd had a chance to ask someone these questions, and I wondered if Celeste had ever discussed her relationship with Katyana through their many years of friendship. I tried not to focus on the tightness in my chest at the memory of our friend, the pain of her loss still raw.

"Honestly, I think it's because they are scared that if the relationship ends, it's a long time to live alongside that person. And with our heightened sex drives, quite a few prefer not to form attachments and focus on the physical aspect." She shrugged, but something she said caught my attention as I nodded.

"When you say we have heightened sex drives..." I had never really been one to discuss my sex life in depth with friends, but her words had touched on a subject that had been in the back of my mind for months.

"Ah, so you've noticed that, huh?" She said with a bit of a smirk, and I blushed. She reached over and squeezed my knee. "I didn't understand what was happening at first, but in my first few years within the Order, my sex drive rocketed, and Daniel and I were at it like rabbits. Even now, after fifty-plus years of marriage, I still can't get enough of that man."

"Why is that? The high sex drive, I mean?" She took another sip of coffee before answering my tentative question.

"The theory is that it's because of the magic that runs through each of us in different ways and our connection to it. Sex, at its basic level, is all about furthering the human race, and our role in the Order is to protect humanity. But honestly, I think it's because sex is all about pleasure, and the magic in our blood heightens so many of our senses, so why not that as well?" I let her words sink in. It made sense, and it felt good to have some answers as to why I couldn't get enough when I was with Liam.

"So, is that why I seem so much more... receptive..." I didn't know how to talk about this easily, and Celeste laughed now, seeing my discomfort.

"You mean, is that why you can have so many orgasms in one session that you feel like you might combust?" She had no such issue with putting into words how my body was put through the wringer each time I was with Liam. I nodded, taking a quick mouthful of coffee to hide my embarrassment. "Well, Liam's exquisite looks and amazing body aside, yes, that is why you're able to orgasm at the lightest touch. Sometimes, I'm convinced all it would take is a certain look from Daniel, and I'll explode. It also helps that Liam has had so many years to truly hone his craft." She grinned, and I huffed a little. I didn't need to be reminded how many women he had undoubtedly been with over the centuries. She gave my knee another squeeze.

Even without the ability to read my mind, I sensed that she understood my feelings on the matter.

"You've known Liam a long time. Has he ever…" I wasn't sure what I wanted to ask, and it felt like I was betraying Liam just having this conversation. Celeste noted my hesitation and cocked her head to the side.

"I've known Liam for a long time. Almost an entire lifetime, really. And in that time, I have *never* seen him like this. Even when he had that brief dalliance with Alana, he has always been all about the job. He has friendships with us all, but since you've become a part of the family, it's like it's awakened something inside him. And I love that he has found that with you. You both deserve happiness after the grief you've both experienced." I felt something inside of me uncoil at her words, as though I'd been holding on to a fear that what was developing between myself and Liam was just a passing phase for him. I blinked back a tear and smiled at Celeste.

"Thank you… I hadn't realised how much I needed to hear that." She reached over and gave me a one-armed hug.

"You've been through a lot in your short life, Isolde. And we have no idea what this life has in store for any of us. You have a lot of responsibility that has been put on your shoulders, but don't forget to allow yourself to have moments of joy. It's those moments that make the hard times worth it. It's all we can try to strive for. Hold on to those beautiful moments. It's what will get you through the tough ones." Her words hit hard, and without thinking, I turned to her and wrapped her in a tight hug.

"Thank you," I whispered, and she squeezed me back.

"Any time, Isolde. We are all here for you, don't forget that. You just need to let us in."

We passed another hour chatting about everything and nothing all at once, and I felt lighter than I had in months when I returned to the Manor. Almost as though I was finding myself once again. And I liked that feeling very much.

That night, I sat in my meditation corner and began clearing my mind, staring at the flame once more. I'd decided to step up the exploration of my abilities, and Liam sat quietly in the armchair near the bed, reading a book, although I wasn't sure how much he was taking in, as I could feel his eyes on me constantly. I'd told him I wanted to attempt to connect with the blossoming telekinetic abilities I'd noticed in brief moments where my emotions were heightened. This had sparked his own interest as well, but now I was finding that interest distracting.

"It's tough to concentrate when you keep staring at me all the time." I continued to stare at the flame as I spoke, and he closed the book, getting to his feet.

"Do you want me to go?"

"No. I want you to come closer." I didn't know what made me say that, but I smiled as he walked over, sitting behind me. He reached forward and lifted me into his lap, and I laughed as he nuzzled my neck.

"Is this close enough, Isolde?" His breath tickled my neck as he whispered in my ear, and I pushed aside the wave of arousal that threatened to overwhelm me. Any time we were close like this, I found it difficult to resist him.

"Perfect. Now be quiet." I tried to speak authoritatively, and he kissed my neck softly before running his hands down my sides, circling my waist, and holding me close. When I was confident that he would behave himself, I returned my concentration to the flame before me, and eventually, our breathing settled into an identical rhythm. I willed every candle in the room to light up and worked on bringing the flames together, practising the magic that I had perfected now before willing them back to their respective candles.

Liam remained still, allowing me to play with my power without distraction, offering me the support of his presence and nothing more. Taking a deep breath, I turned my focus now to the book that Liam had left on the chair across the room. At first, nothing happened. But I was learning that I needed to find the correct commands within myself to give direction to the magic that flowed through me.

Perhaps reading my thoughts and intentions, Liam gently ran his hand down my arm, taking my hand and raising it. He held both our arms outstretched, reaching towards the book, which began to move in place a little. I felt power begin to tingle through me, almost as though it flowed from his body into mine. Closing my eyes, I followed his silent direction, keeping my arm outstretched towards the chair.

Rise.

I felt Liam's intake of breath, his chest pressed hard against my back, and I opened my eyes slowly. The magic flowed through both of us as though we were one body and mind, and I could feel it crackling through the air around us. From how Liam was tensing behind me, I could tell that he felt it too. The book had risen in the air and was lazily turning clockwise. Together, almost as though we could anticipate each other's movements, we slowly turned our hands and beckoned the book closer. I watched with fascination as it floated gently towards us before finally lowering into my lap. Liam returned his arm to my waist and squeezed me tightly as I stared at the book in amazement. I could still feel the air humming with the shared power that flowed through us both.

"Is this normal?" I could barely utter the words, as I feared it would shatter the energy that bound us together. He reached around and gently placed his hand on my chin, tilting my head, and I twisted slowly in his lap until I could look into his eyes.

"That was the first time I've been able to tap into any physical power. I've never felt an energy like this before," he whispered, his words filled with awe. I leaned into him, pressing my lips softly to his.

I was afraid to make sudden movements, not wanting this feeling to end. I could tell that Liam felt the same way, as his actions remained slow and gentle, sliding his other hand up my back and tangling his fingers in my hair, holding my head there as we continued the kiss. This wasn't about sex, I realised. It was about the feelings that had been building for months, and I allowed myself to get lost in this perfect moment, simply enjoying the closeness and the power that swirled around us. I'd never felt so connected to another person; it was like a drug. I could get used to this.

Moving at a snail's pace, I turned myself until I straddled his lap, my dress riding up my thighs. Slowly, he ran his hands down my back until both rested on my hips, and I allowed him to pull me closer. I expected the magic to disappear entirely as clothes were shed and we brought our bodies together. Instead, the magic flowed back and forth between us, shattering through our bodies over and over as we moved against each other. It was a long time before either of us was able to move afterwards, our bodies depleted by both the magic and the pleasure that had rippled through us so intensely.

Eventually, we gathered our strengths and dressed once more, but I felt more aware of him than ever, and I could tell he felt the same. It was like he had become my other half, and I was aware of every breath and heartbeat that flowed through him. It was hours before the sensation dissipated, and I wondered what it all meant.

CHAPTER TWENTY

A few weeks passed, and before I'd realised, it was a week from Christmas. Time had begun to move so quickly that I hadn't even known it was the holiday season. Christmas in my family was usually a huge family gathering, generally at New Farm Park, as none of our homes were big enough to accommodate a family of our size. When I had mentioned the holiday to Liam, he'd looked surprised, evidently having forgotten about it himself.

"What do you normally do?" I asked him as I settled on my bed at home, surrounded by the presents I had just bought on my frantic shopping trip. He stood in the doorway, staring at the mountain of gifts in amazement.

"Um... it's not usually a big thing amongst the Order. We might have lunch or something, but it's just another day for us." He shrugged, and I looked at him in surprise.

"We don't celebrate Christmas?!" I was alarmed. Coming from a big family with children around all the time, Christmas was my favourite time of the year. Discovering that I was expected to spend the next few centuries amongst people who barely acknowledged it was pretty disheartening.

"I guess when you see as many Christmases as we do, you just get over it after a while." He said it so flippantly, and I felt my heart sink momentarily before shaking my head firmly.

"Well, this year, we are celebrating Christmas. God knows we need some cheer with all the crap we've been through lately." I went back to my task of wrapping the gifts before me. Liam sat down in my overstuffed armchair, shaking his head, obviously thinking I would have no luck getting everyone to join in.

But I proved him wrong. The following day, I approached Patrice with my plan for a giant Christmas feast, and her face lit up with excitement as she agreed it was just what we needed.

"I'll organise everything! Leave it to me." I was relieved to hear her say that. After my initial announcement, I hadn't been entirely sure of how I would pull off arranging something at such short notice. I had come to the realisation that I would need to make an appearance at four separate Christmas celebrations. Between my immediate and extended family, seeing Will's parents, and now gathering with the Order, that was a lot of Christmas Cheer to spread around.

I roped Liam into staying at my parents' house on Christmas Eve, figuring it was time for him to meet the rest of my family. I hadn't seen most of my sisters in months, which was something I'd realised with disbelief. Since finding out about my apparent destiny, I hadn't had much opportunity to spend time with them, something that they had all started to notice.

As I walked through the front door with Liam in tow, I was set upon by a gang of over-excited children, all under the age of six. Liam looked a little panicked at seeing this many children, but I gathered as many of them to me as possible in a giant group hug, overjoyed to see them all again. As the night wore on, I noticed how uncomfortable Liam was. I was so used to seeing him around the other members of the Order that I hadn't stopped to think about what it would be like to be surrounded by people he didn't know. As most of my family had never met him, and some did not even know of his existence, they were all a little taken aback by him, and Liam could no doubt hear the confusion in their thoughts. No one had expected me to move on from Will so quickly, and although they all tried to talk to and include him, it was a relief for both of us when we retired to my old room.

"I'm sorry," I said as he wrapped me in his arms once the door was closed. We leaned into the embrace, drawing comfort from each other.

"It's okay. I understand where they are all coming from." Liam rested his cheek against the top of my head. It was the first time in my whole life that I felt disconnected from my family, and I realised with a jolt that this was how it would be for the rest of my life. At least whilst my family was still around. It was something I had avoided thinking about until now. I would outlive the rest of my family... Unless I were killed in some violent way first, I would watch as my family grew old without me... It was not a very comforting thought.

By the time Christmas Day drew to a close, I felt emotionally drained. Breakfast with my family had been just as strained as the night before. So much so that I let Liam off the hook with the extended family in the afternoon, and he returned to the Manor with relief.

Lunch with Will's family only lasted an hour and a half as an air of despair hung over everyone. We all felt Will's absence, and I hated that I knew what he had become whilst they believed he was buried in the ground. His parents and sister didn't mention my new boyfriend once, but I could feel the judgement, and it was a relief to leave. Something else to feel guilty about, even though I knew I had done nothing wrong.

The family BBQ, which I usually looked forward to, made me feel like a stranger amongst people I had known my entire life. I realised everything was different now. No one else had changed; it was just me. I felt as though I was acting out a part in a play. I knew all the lines by heart, but there was no feeling behind it anymore.

I pulled my car into the underground garage of the Manor and sat for a moment, listening as the engine ticked away, cooling down. After the day's strain, the last thing I felt like was another gathering of people, and I wish I hadn't thought to suggest it. I dragged my feet as I stepped into the elevator, but when the doors opened, I gaped in shock at the scene before me. It looked as though Christmas had blown up in the front foyer. It was covered in decorations that put Santa and his elves to shame. A tree stood from floor to ceiling, and the lights twinkled prettily from amongst its branches.

I stood staring at it all in wonder as Liam appeared at my side, a broad grin on his face as he took in my expression.

"Did Patrice do all of this?" I found I was unable to tear my eyes away from the decorations.

"We all did. After everything last night and this morning, I thought you could use a bit of Christmas cheer, and Patrice was already organising a 'feast to die for', as she describes it, so we thought we would get into the Christmas Spirit. Hence the snow." He pointed upwards, and my mouth fell open to see snow falling, though it disappeared before it reached us. I looked at Liam in stunned silence, unable to take it all in.

"Most of us come from the northern hemisphere. We prefer a white Christmas to the searing heat," Celeste remarked as she came down the stairs. She was dressed in a beautiful red and white dress, and I looked down at my shorts and t-shirt, suddenly very aware of how under-dressed I was.

"If you go to your room, you'll find something that will make you feel less conspicuous." Celeste smiled warmly, and I grinned back in appreciation. I was so grateful for the friendship that had developed between us, and I hugged her quickly. I headed to my room and gaped at the beautiful dress and matching shoes that were laid out on the bed. Liam came into the room behind me and wrapped his arms around my waist. I turned in his arms and hugged him hard as tears welled in my eyes.

"Thank you so much for all of this," I whispered into his chest, overwhelmed.

"You're welcome," he whispered back, kissing the top of my head. He left me to get ready, and I sat on the bed, staring at the dress. It was an ice blue and white, one-shoulder number in a shimmery material. The lengths that had been taken to ensure that I had at least one happy moment at Christmas made me realise something. Although I felt disconnected from the family I had been born to, I had a new family now. One that I didn't have to lie to or keep secrets from. It made me realise that I was truly home.

After a quick shower and slipping into the dress, I entered the dining room downstairs. The lights had been switched off, and candles illuminated the room. The table was laid out beautifully, and I felt a lump form in my throat as I looked around the room, taking it all in. I slid into the chair next to Liam, and he sat back in his seat, slinging his arm casually along the back of mine. There was an air of excitement in the room as everyone gathered around, and it was so lovely to share this moment with them all.

That night, after several hours of laughter and great food, I slept in Liam's arms in my bed at the Manor for the first time. The dinner had been perfect, and it had had the effect that Patrice had desired, a much-needed tender moment amongst all the grief we'd been feeling lately.

Initially, my sleep was dreamless, a first for a long time.

Then Alana appeared. Looking around, I realised we were back in the abandoned warehouse. This time, when her lips moved, I could hear her.

"Isolde, I have to tell you something," she said urgently, and I searched her face for any of the hate that used to be there. All I could see was fear.

"Alana, what is it? Why did you come here that day?" I motioned to our setting. In the back of my mind, I knew it was a dream, but it seemed so real. Alana's skin was deathly pale, with dark rings around her sunken eyes.

"Something is coming. And it's not good. You will not be safe. No one will be."

"Alana, you're not making any sense. What do you know?" Alana looked frustrated.

"You're not listening! Something is coming!" She snapped, and I saw a flash of the Alana that I used to know. "It is not just you that they want. And you won't be able to save your sister." She started to fade before me.

"Wait! Which sister?! Why do they want one of my sisters?!" I rushed towards her as if grabbing her would make her stay solid, to keep her from fading away further. My hand went straight through her as I grabbed for her wrist. Before she disappeared completely, her lips moved again, and I strained to hear her whisper... And then I woke up, sitting bolt upright in bed.

"Hey, hey. Isolde, it's okay!" I realised I had yelled Alana's name as I had woken abruptly, and Liam sat up next to me as I tried to stop myself from hyperventilating.

"Did you see her?!" I asked stupidly before remembering that

Alana had been in my dream, not reality. Liam surprised me, however, when he nodded. "Were you in my dream too?" I didn't remember seeing him there.

"No, I could see it in your mind, the same as your thoughts."

"What do you think she meant?" I asked, already on my feet. We both threw our clothes on haphazardly.

"I'm not sure. I wish she hadn't been so cryptic." Liam followed me downstairs to the communications room, where, as usual, Patrice was in discussions with some of the Elders in various locations worldwide via the computer.

"Isolde? Liam?" Patrice jumped as she turned off the monitor abruptly, which struck me as odd, but I had more important matters to consider.

We filled Patrice in on Alana's message, and she looked at me with great concern.

"Do you know why she knew where to find Adam?" Patrice asked, and both Liam and I shook our heads.

"I asked her, but she just said something was coming." I could feel myself becoming more and more frustrated by the whole situation. Liam touched my shoulder and squeezed it reassuringly from behind me.

"It will be okay. We'll work it out, won't we?" He looked at Patrice pointedly, and she nodded distractedly.

"Of course... Of course, we will! We've already got people watching your family, keeping them safe."

Patrice hugged me, no doubt attempting to offer some reassurance. However, something felt wrong. Why did it feel like more was happening here than what I was being told?

CHAPTER TWENTY-ONE

Over the next several days, I went through the motions of what had become my life. By day, I continued privately working on my abilities and training with Liam. In the evenings, I was a part of the various teams dispatched to keep order in the supernatural world. Sleep was often a last priority when I fell into bed, tangled in the sheets with Liam, either at home or in one of our rooms at the Manor.

However, things had changed over the past few months. Since my fighting abilities had become so much more advanced than all the others, I was no longer just one of the team. I was the main fighter. For the first time, my abilities were being utilised, and sometimes I was separated from Liam, each being sent off on different missions where our abilities were more helpful. I found it disconcerting on the missions where we were separated, as I had grown so used to his constant presence, and I missed him, even though we were only apart for a few hours.

On New Year's Eve, I was sent out with one of the teams tasked with monitoring the crowds at South Bank. Because it was expected to be so busy, our numbers had been doubled, and for the first time, I learnt that not all members of the Order of the Dragon were seventh sons and daughters. Because numbers in the recent decades had started to dwindle, they had decided to start using outsiders as well; those who, due to their encounters with the supernatural, chose to fight alongside us. I discovered that Megan, the real estate agent that Aurora and I had dealt with, was one of these people. I had been surprised when she had come forward and sheepishly shook my hand again, apologising for her part in the deception at the time. Although these people were aware of our dangerous world, they did not live as we did, usually living relatively everyday lives, helping only when necessary. It felt strange to be discussing the realm of the supernatural with people who had not been forced into it as I had been. I envied their freedom to choose. Even though I had accepted this life for myself finally, I still envied others for their freedom to live under the illusion of normalcy.

I mingled with the crowds at South Bank as the time drew closer to midnight. The worst year of my life was ending, and I was happy to see the back of it. Liam was also stationed somewhere else in the crowd, and I wished he was nearby. So far, there had been no sightings of any vampires, and I hoped it would be an uneventful evening. Moving along with the flow of the crowd, I eventually found myself on the spot where Will and I had shared our first kiss. It had taken me a little while to understand why I had a strange sense of déjà vu, and once I had put the connection together, I wished I hadn't. In my mind, I was swept back to that night. It had been a much quieter night, and it had been just the two of us, sitting on the garden wall, watching as the City Cats came and went from the ferry terminal. Everything about that night had been perfect, as most of our relationship had appeared to be, and being forced to remember it was painful. As I was lost in my memories, I didn't realise the countdown to midnight had started. The next thing I knew, the people around me were joyfully exchanging New Year's greetings as the fireworks began. With tears in my eyes, I watched the impressive display above me as couples all around shared their first kisses of the new year. I tried to imagine that Liam was standing beside me, wrapping his arms around me in his usual way, keeping me safe. A tap on my shoulder brought a smile to my lips, and I turned, expecting to see Liam.

"Happy New Year, Isolde." Will looked so much like his former self that, for a moment, I was speechless. He made no goading comments or nasty remarks. He just stood before me, his crooked half-smile playing over his lips.

Then he kissed me. At first, I kissed him back out of habit and a longing for the past. But then reality set in. I used my extra strength and shoved him away, and he groaned as I glared at him.

"Get the hell away from me," I hissed, trying to sound like I was not being torn apart inside.

"And here I thought we were sharing a moment. It's not nice to lead boys on, Isolde." And there it was, the creature that Will had become, which made it much easier to do what I did next. I brought my knee up sharply between his legs, momentarily stunning him. By this time, Liam had joined me. Not far behind him, I saw Daniel and Megan shoving their way through the crowd.

As Will straightened up again, a few people around us started to notice the commotion and were watching us rather than the fireworks. There was nothing we could do but glare at each other, as Will appeared to be alone, and we couldn't draw attention to ourselves any more than we already had. Will growled and faded back into the crowd, and I felt my legs start to give way under me as Daniel and Megan trailed after him to ensure no harm came to anyone in the crowd.

It was the first time I had come face to face with Will since he had followed me home that night, and although I'd moved on with Liam, it was still heart-wrenching to see the creature he had become. Liam guided me to a nearby bench, which had been recently vacated so that the former occupants could get a better view of the fireworks. I cursed my weakness when it came to Will. I could stake any other vampire without a second glance, but when confronted with Will, I froze.

"Are you okay?" Liam held my face in his hands, inspecting me as though he thought I was about to pass out. I looked up at him for a moment before answering.

"I am now." He breathed out, pulling me into a tight embrace, almost like he feared losing me. And I realised that was precisely what he was feeling. He had heard everything going on in my mind and had no doubt seen the kiss. I knew it would have hurt him. The idea of losing me was one of his deepest fears, and seeing me kissing Will, even if it was just a momentary slip, would have just about killed him.

"I'm so sorry," I whispered into his ear, and he held me tighter. After a moment, he drew back and looked down at me.

"I'm just sorry that he was the one who kissed you at midnight and not me," he said, attempting to push it all aside. I knew it was an act but decided to play along for now.

"I'm sure it's midnight somewhere in the world right now." I leaned into him, and he kissed me hungrily. There was something more intense about this kiss than any we had shared before. Almost as though he was trying to erase any memory of the earlier kiss with Will and compete with the past.

Later that night, as we drove back to the Manor along with the rest of the team, I stared silently out the window, trying not to be affected by the events of the evening. Everything in my head was a mess, and I knew that Liam was trying not to hear what I was thinking, as thrown by his intense reaction as I was. So many times in the past few weeks, things had shifted between us. We were relaxed, at peace with each other. We had enjoyed the quiet times and spent many a morning lying in each other's arms. However, there had been brief moments when things had been so intense that I had almost feared how we hungered for each other, especially after evenings spent hunting for nightwalkers, adrenaline coursing through us. In all my years with Will, we had never had a passion like that, and I was unsure how to handle it. I had never envied those women who seemed almost addicted to their partners, preferring the ease of my relationship with Will. They fought so passionately and often would be sent on massive crying jags that I could not handle watching, believing their relationships to be toxic and unhealthy. But I had come to understand that I had been playing it safe with Will. I had loved him with all my heart, but it was only now that I realised something was missing. Something I didn't even know that I had wanted.

After the teams debriefed, I made my way up to my room alone, hoping that a warm shower would calm the turmoil in my mind.

As I came out of the bathroom wrapped in a towel, I wasn't surprised to find Liam sitting on the edge of the bed, staring at his hands. I stopped a few feet from him, waiting for him to speak first.

"I'm sorry," he said quietly, still not looking up at me. "I don't know what I was thinking."

"I'm sorry that I made you feel that way," I said, knowing that my actions tonight were not blameless. No matter what occurred after, I still allowed Will to kiss me, even if just for a moment. Liam looked up at that quickly, the hurt and even a little anger evident in his eyes.

"Seeing you kissing him... It hurt. And I know you're not over him, and maybe you never will be." He looked down at his hands again, and I moved closer to him now, though still out of his immediate reach.

"A part of me will always belong to him. He was my first love. He was safe, the sort of man most parents dream their daughters will end up with." I watched as Liam tightened his hand reflexively into a fist, still not looking up at me. "However, I never would have had a life with Will. I see that now in a way that I never saw before." I waited for Liam to look up at me again, and he eventually did so, reluctantly. "I'm never going to be safe. The life that I was born for doesn't leave room for safe. No matter what happened to Will, I never would have been able to marry him, to live the life I had believed I wanted. I was always destined for this life of constant chaos and danger. He could never have known me the way that you do." As I said this, I moved to stand immediately in front of Liam, and he began tracing his fingers over the pattern of my towel along my hip.

"I love you." He gripped my hip at those words, and I heard his sharp intake of breath, causing me to repeat them before I continued. "I love you. In a way that is so different to how I loved him that I know this is the reality. The life that I had with him was just an illusion." It was the first time that either of us had said the words to each other, and I felt my heart beat hard in my chest as I waited for his response.

In one swift movement, he pulled me forward so that I straddled his lap and kissed me fiercely, pulling my towel off me in the process. I kissed him back just as hungrily, wanting him more than ever. He began moving me fast against him, and the desire to be closer to each other was overriding everything else. I felt how hard he was against me, and I quickly undid his fly while he worked his fingers inside of me, readying me for him. He hissed as I moved his hand away, lowering myself onto him and rocking my hips, taking him all in.

"I love you too, Isolde." I ground myself against him as he breathed the words, revelling in hearing them said out loud. As he kissed my neck, I found that I craved something more from him. Following the direction of my thoughts, he pulled back, surprised. I moved my hair to the side and almost unconsciously tilted my head.

Yes. The consent that I gave him through my thoughts was all the invitation that he needed, and I gasped with unexpected pain, quickly giving way to pleasure, as he bit into my neck. It was unlike anything I had ever imagined, and I lost myself in the moment, understanding now why others had asked for this. Perhaps even begged for it.

Moving quickly against him, his hands guiding me up and down, with his mouth at my throat, I felt the most explosive orgasm of my life shatter through me, taking him over the edge as well, and we collapsed back on the bed together, completely spent.

Later, as we lay naked beside each other, our legs tangled together, I sensed a sadness in Liam as he stroked his hand gently up and down my back. I raised myself onto my elbow, looking into his eyes as I wondered at the melancholy behind them.

"I had a vision." He brushed my hair back over my shoulder, his fingers tracing lightly over the bite mark on my neck, knowing I had been about to ask what was wrong.

"From my blood?" I hadn't thought about that in the moment, having been so lost in the act of loving him. He nodded. "What did you see?" I wasn't sure I wanted an answer, knowing it likely wasn't good.

"I saw your future." I felt a shudder go down my spine, and he pulled me closer to him. "You were a vampire." I realised that I wasn't surprised by this, almost as though a part of me had expected that, at some stage, I would become a vampire.

"Was I a nightwalker or a daywalker?"

"You were kissing Will, so I'm guessing you were a nightwalker." He couldn't bring himself to look at me, and I knew that, for some reason, he was blaming himself. I placed a hand on the side of his face.

"Hey. Look at me." He did, slowly. "Just because you had a vision, it doesn't mean that it's going to be true. We are forewarned now so that we can stop it." I could sense his disbelief as he surveyed my face.

"That's not how it works." He gazed into my eyes sadly.

"Have all of your visions come true in the past?" I was a little thrown by the resignation in his eyes.

"Most of them have, yes."

"Most, but not all of them, right?" I was clinging to that little glimmer of hope.

"We have managed to change the outcome of a few, but that chance is scarce. And we don't know the circumstances of how you change. I can't guarantee I can save you when I don't know what will happen." I looked down at him, concerned at how he always took the world on his shoulders.

"Liam, I have faith in you. I know that we will stop this. But, if a time ever comes when it looks like that might be my future, I want you to promise me something." He looked almost fearful. As if he knew what I was about to ask, which he probably did. "I want you to promise that if I am bitten, and it looks as though I am going to become a nightwalker, I want you to be the one who makes sure that I come back as a daywalker... or not at all." Liam started shaking his head, but I stilled it with my hand on his chin. "Promise me."

"Isolde, you don't know what you're asking me to do." His voice shook, but I held his gaze.

"Promise me." Holding my gaze for the longest time, clearly wrestling with his thoughts, it was a long time before he breathed.

"I promise." His words were barely a whisper, and I knew that promising either to turn me or end my life was killing him, but I needed to ensure that I would not become a monster. I bent to kiss him softly, and he pulled me on top of him, needing to hold me close, knowing that, at least for the moment, now was not the time to worry about the future.

The next day, I decided to make an appearance at home, if for no other reason than to get some clothes. I hadn't spoken to Aurora properly in weeks and I missed my sister. I hated the way things had become so strained between us. Where once we had told each other everything, now there was silence in our home, when I bothered to be there at all.

I let myself in the front door, before coming to a stop on the threshold, surprised to see a suitcase beside the couch.

"What's going on?" I asked as Aurora came down the hall.

"I've got that conference in Sydney to organise," Aurora replied, and I looked at her questioningly. She laughed bitterly.

"Of course, you wouldn't remember." She rolled her eyes. "I told you about this months ago. Work is sending me to run a conference between our offices here and the ones in the US." I remembered now. Aurora had been so excited when she told me, having been given an opportunity that could very well see her get a promotion at the company where she worked as an events coordinator. I kicked myself mentally for forgetting that it was in January. She was due to get back the day before our birthday. I felt my heart begin to race as panic set in.

"When do you leave?"

"I'm leaving now. So, sorry you forgot. I know how much you would have loved to have come and seen me off on what could be the biggest opportunity of my career," she said sarcastically, and I bit back a retort. There was no use in allowing her to get to me, to let her see how much the deterioration of our relationship was upsetting me.

"Well, have a safe trip." I brushed past her, but she caught my arm, sighing.

"I'm sorry, that was mean and uncalled for." I looked at her momentarily, waiting to see where this was going.

"After Jacob picks me up next week, we should go out. I know Ainslie has been dying for a catch-up, and it would be good to do things like we used to... I've missed you," she said sadly, and I smiled.

"That sounds really good. I've missed you too." I hugged her tightly as a tear slipped down my cheek. I knew she was crying too, and we both laughed.

"So soppy." She kissed me on the cheek. "See you in ten days."

I waved goodbye as Jacob backed out of the driveway, watching Aurora wave back from the passenger seat. As soon as they were out of sight, I rang the Manor and was reassured by Celeste that Colin was already on it. At least they hadn't forgotten that Aurora was leaving town for a few days.

Somehow, my involvement in the fire at my old townhouse had finally been discovered. I knew the balance of power in the Order was shifting, with myself slowly rising to the top. As far as they were aware, though, I had used the spell book that I had taken from the Manor. My use of magic that night had everyone on edge around me —everyone except Liam.

Patrice pulled me aside when I left Liam's room the following day.

"You should not have performed magic without the proper training, Isolde. Don't you realise the danger you put yourself in?" The concern in her eyes was tinged with fear, though I did not know if it was *for* me or *of* me. The powers everyone had expected of me had been slow to arrive, but now that they were starting to present themselves, people were beginning to question whether it was a good thing. I learnt that no one else had been able to use magic as quickly as I had, having gone through years of training to perform simple glamours. To perform cloaking and containment spells with the power I had done and control them was unheard of. And that was without them being aware of my fire abilities.

For his part, Liam just went on as usual. He had known this was coming, had seen it in his visions as he had fed on me several times while we had sex. Neither of us had shared the knowledge of these visions or my growing powers with the rest of the Order, the doubts about their intentions still holding us back. And I had to admit; it felt good to be the one with the knowledge for once.

CHAPTER TWENTY-TWO

The day Aurora was due back, I headed home in the afternoon, expecting to find Aurora and Jacob. I had been waiting to hear from Aurora since she had left, but there had been silence, although Jacob had received text messages sporadically. I had hoped she was just busy and worked hard to convince myself that we would have heard if anything bad had happened.

I unlocked the door and dropped my bag on the floor. Liam remained in the car, having just taken a call from Celeste as we pulled up.

"Aura? Jacob? You guys here?"

"Hey." Jacob walked out of the kitchen, freshly made sandwich in hand.

"Where's Aurora?" I realised it was just the two of us at home. Jacob looked at me in surprise.

"What do you mean? You were meant to pick her up." Jacob looked at me, confused.

"No, she told me you were picking her up," I said slowly, and he shook his head.

"She texted me this morning saying she'd asked you to pick her up. Something about wanting some girl time." He shrugged.

"Jacob... Aurora never texted me. We haven't had girl time in a long time." I was worried now, though I tried not to show it. I grabbed my bag and rummaged around for my mobile as Jacob looked on in confusion.

"Yeah, I thought that was weird too." I started dialling Aurora's number. It went straight to voicemail. "Maybe her flight was delayed, and she's still on the plane?" Jacob was trying to sound optimistic whilst I was starting to lean towards blind panic.

"Yeah, maybe..." I walked back out the front, already dialling the Manor's number. As I raised the phone to my ear, Liam appeared at my side, no doubt alerted by my frantic thoughts. I hit the red button on my phone as I took in the worried look on his face.

"Have they heard anything from Colin?" I asked Liam in a low voice as I heard Jacob leaving a voicemail for Aurora in the other room. Colin was the Protector assigned to follow Aurora on her trip to Sydney.

"No... And they're worried." I could feel panic rising, and Liam placed a steadying hand on my shoulder, squeezing gently.

"Hey... She'll be okay." I wasn't convinced, and he knew it.

"Jacob, I'm going to the airport." I grabbed a copy of Aurora's itinerary from the coffee table. I wrote her flight number on my hand, struggling to ignore the million and one scenarios going through my head, primarily so Liam wouldn't hear. Car keys still in hand, Liam laced his fingers through mine, bringing my hand to his lips as we headed out the door.

"Wait, I'm coming too." Already at the car, we both turned to see Jacob closing the door behind him before jogging down the stairs. I exchanged a worried glance with Liam, but we couldn't think of a good enough reason to tell him why he shouldn't join us without raising suspicion.

As Liam drove, I sat silently in the front passenger seat, every possible scenario going through my head. Liam reached over and squeezed my hand again. No doubt, Jacob thought I was overreacting. And maybe I was. However, if Jacob knew what I knew, he would be freaking out too. Liam put his foot on the brake as the light turned red, just as my phone rang, and I jumped before ripping it out of my pocket. The number was blocked. I prayed it was my twin.

"Aurora?"

"Hey, sorry. My phone died." Relief flooded through me.

"That's okay. Who is meant to be picking you up?" I shot the guys a thumbs up, and Jacob fell back against the back seat with a relieved sigh.

"Well, I was going to text you and ask, but my phone died, and I missed my flight. I figure this is all a sign to stay down here a couple more days. Sarah and Ian broke up, and she desperately needs some girl time." It seemed like a typical Aurora thing to do, but something nagged at me. The light turned green, and Liam started to change direction before we got stuck on the bridge over the river with no way to turn around.

"Are you sure?"

"Yeah, I'll be home Monday. I'll text you my flight details, although Jacob should be able to pick me up." After another few moments of conversation, I passed the phone back to Jacob and breathed out, willing myself to relax. The nagging feeling in the back of my mind was still there. Something wasn't right. Aurora hadn't even mentioned the fact that by delaying her trip, we'd be spending our birthday apart for the first time in our lives.

"She'll be fine, Isolde." Liam looked at me earnestly as Jacob spoke to Aurora. I wondered if Jacob had noticed that Liam had not looked at the road once since she rang.

"I'll feel better once she's home." I stopped talking as Jacob returned my phone to me, and that was all we could say on the topic.

"You had me freaking out, Isolde! Don't do that again," Jacob said angrily from the backseat, and I absently apologised, not even really listening.

"Well, I guess it's just you and Ainslie tonight." Jacob's words drifted through my reverie.

"Huh? Oh, yeah. I guess so. That's okay. I'm sure we can still get up to enough mischief without Aurora." I grinned at Liam, who rolled his eyes. He had yet to meet Ainslie, but he'd seen me the night before my twenty-fifth birthday and knew my intoxicated state was partly due to Ainslie's influence. Mostly her influence, really. She did like to party.

I am going to try Colin again as soon as I get her home. Something isn't right.

Upon hearing this, I looked sharply over at Liam, only to discover that he hadn't spoken. I stared at him, unable to understand what had just happened... Had I imagined those words?

Why is she staring at me like that? Liam looked at me searchingly, and I felt my mouth drop open. The stricken look on my face concerned him even further.

Because I've just heard everything you were thinking! I almost screamed this aloud, though I knew the yelling in my head was enough for Liam. For his part, Liam did well not to drive off the road.

"Jacob, I'm going to head to Liam's for a bit. I'll see you later," I said as calmly as possible as Liam pulled up out the front of the house. I was unable to take my eyes off him, and the calm facade fell away once Jacob was inside.

"How the hell am I hearing your thoughts suddenly?" I knew it was pointless to have this conversation aloud, but I was desperately clinging to normal right now. Well, normal for us. "And hey, you were just telling me everything was fine, but then you were thinking you need to call Colin!" Liam pulled away from the curb.

"I don't know why you're suddenly hearing my thoughts... And you can't get mad at me for agreeing with you!" Liam looked as freaked out as I felt, so I forced myself to wait until we reached the Manor before asking any more questions. It was tough not to respond to the questions Liam was asking himself, and I admired that he got us back to the Manor without crashing, as every thought he had caused him to look sheepishly at me.

"Is this what it's like to be you?" I asked, frustrated. I didn't like having someone else's thoughts in my head. Dealing with my own was hard enough. Although I suppose it could be helpful when I didn't know what he was thinking.

"No poking around up here." Liam tapped his temple.

"Hey! Now you know how it feels."

"I spend most of the time attempting to block out your thoughts to respect your privacy." I shot him a shrewd look.

Yeah, right.

Liam laughed, shaking his head. We pulled into the basement car park and headed into the house. I prepared myself for the onslaught of thoughts as I entered. But it didn't come. The only thoughts in my head, other than my own, were Liam's. I raised an eyebrow at him questioningly, but he looked as confused as I felt, and his thoughts confirmed that he truly had no answer as to what was going on between us.

"Isolde? I thought you headed home for the night?" Patrice came out of the kitchen, her face showing her concern.

"We've got a bit of a problem... Potentially. And it would also seem that another ability has emerged, though it's confusing." Liam trailed off, but I could hear his train of thought continue. *Have we formed a bond?*

It was my turn to look confused. *Bond?*

"Come into the comms room." Patrice led us down the hall.

"Okay. The problem first." Patrice indicated that I should sit down at the large table in the middle of the room, but I was too agitated and started pacing instead.

"Apparently, no one has heard from Colin. Is that true?" Patrice looked concerned, though not surprised.

"Yes, it's true. We sent James to follow him up. Strangely, we haven't heard anything from him yet either, but he only left yesterday."

"Well, Aurora missed her flight. She texted Jacob to say I would pick her up from the airport, but I never spoke to her about it. Then she rang when we were on the way to the airport to say her phone had died." As I said it, I could tell I sounded crazy, but that didn't stop the nagging feeling.

"How did she sound? Did she say anything was wrong?" Patrice asked calmly, her tone of voice shifting to one of comfort.

"No... She said she missed her flight, which is unlike Aurora, and that her friend down there had broken up with her boyfriend and needed some girl time."

"And does that sound like Aurora?" Patrice's voice was kind, and I could tell she thought I was worrying too much.

"I guess... I just have this nagging feeling that something is wrong." I shrugged, unable to explain anything more than that. Put it down to twin intuition.

"I'm sure everything is okay. I will admit that it is strange that we've not heard from Colin, but James will let us know what he finds in Sydney. I promise to let you know if there is anything to worry about." I supposed that was the best I could hope for without sufficient evidence, so I nodded. It wasn't lost on me that they hadn't seen fit to inform me that they had lost contact with Colin in the first place.

"Now, this new ability?" Patrice raised an eyebrow at Liam.

"Well... It would appear that Isolde is now hearing thoughts." Patrice looked surprised.

"That's not the best part... It would seem I'm only hearing one person's thoughts." I looked sideways at Liam as he started thinking about the bond again.

"Yours?" Patrice looked at him again, not sounding the least bit surprised. Both Liam and I looked at her, confused.

"You were expecting this." Liam was clearly in Patrice's head, which I found frustrating.

"Why were you expecting this?" I almost felt like stamping my foot, and Liam grinned, amused by my mental tantrum.

"It's just a theory, but I've noticed how attuned you are to Liam and his abilities. Your fighting abilities, for one. They appeared when you were fighting alongside each other. Your ability to sense vampires is also a stronger form of one of Liam's natural daywalker abilities, not to mention your stronger visions... I don't know why you can only hear Liam's thoughts, though." This took me aback. I had not put this together before. I realised that this also explained so much more about the abilities that we were still yet to share with the Order. I noticed as Liam shifted beside me, prompting me to turn and study his face. He appeared to be focused on Patrice, deliberately avoiding making eye contact with me.

"I think I know why she can only hear me. I have heard of this connection amongst daywalkers. I met a couple about a century ago. They were connected in a way that I never thought possible. They were completely bonded, psychically. They could sense everything with each other, read each other's thoughts, often over great distances and even experience things through each other."

I looked at him searchingly.

"What formed that bond?"

"They had the bond before he turned... They believed they were soulmates..." I noticed absently as Patrice slipped out of the room to give us some privacy while I processed this information.

"Soulmates... Is that even possible?" This threw me. Soulmates were not something I'd given much thought to before now.

"I don't know. But this does explain why I have a harder time tuning you out, unlike with everyone else." Liam leaned back against the table, crossing his arms, and looked at me searchingly.

"I just... Do you believe it now?" I didn't know why this affected me, and I could tell Liam was unsure of how to take my reaction.

"I know I love you. I don't know anything other than how I feel about you," he said, and I realised how my hesitation must look to him. I moved to stand in front of him and touched the side of his face.

"I love you too. I think a part of me always has. You've been in my dreams my whole life." I kissed him softly, and he pulled me closer, wrapping his arms around me as I melted into him, surrendering myself to him and his words in my mind.

I love you, too – more than I ever thought possible.

It's strange hearing your voice in my head while I'm kissing you...

Welcome to my world.

Later that evening, I sat at a table at the restaurant as I waited for Ainslie and played nervously with my water glass.

Okay, so, girl's night with Ainslie. I can't tell her anything about my life these days, and I suck at lying to her. We're going to have heaps to talk about. I shot a sarcastic thumbs up at Liam, who sat at the bar with a book, remaining in my line of sight as I sat waiting for Ainslie to show up. Liam held my gaze for a moment, a small smile playing across his lips.

Well, you know I will be around, so at least that's something...

This is distracting. I still haven't worked out how to get you out of my head.

Do you want to? I thought you enjoyed knowing what I was thinking for a change. I looked towards the door, making a show of waiting for Ainslie to appear. I could hear the teasing in his tone, but I had to admit that he had a point. That still didn't make it any less frustrating. I looked back at Liam, who was smirking, and I rolled my eyes.

"Hey!" I jumped as Ainslie appeared in front of me.

"Hey yourself!" I leapt up to hug her. "It's so good to see you!" I felt tears well in my eyes and blinked quickly, trying to keep my emotions in check. I hadn't seen Ainslie in months, which felt so strange. I used to spend all my time with Ainslie, Alex and Will, but ever since Will died and my world had gone topsy-turvy, I had seen Ainslie only a handful of times. She didn't even know about Liam. I really had become a terrible friend.

"I know. I can't believe how much we haven't seen each other. I was only saying to Alex how much I missed you the other day, and I thought, screw it, make a plan and force you to come! And then you called anyway!" It was such a typical Ainslie statement, and just like that, it was as if no time had passed between us.

We chatted easily over dinner, keeping the topic on Ainslie and her exploits. Then the waitress appeared with the cocktail menu.

"So, what about you?" Ainslie asked after we'd ordered (Pina Colada for me, Cosmo for Ainslie, just like always).

Crap. "What about me?" I drank the last mouthful of my wine, left over from my dinner, and hoped I sounded casual. My palms had started sweating.

"Well, we've talked about me for over an hour now. As much as I enjoy the time in the spotlight, we didn't come here just to talk about my fabulous life. So, spill, what have you been up to that's kept you so busy?"

Fighting vampires, regular battles with my undead fiance, discovering that I'm destined to end a war that has been raging for millennia? I shot a glance at Liam as the answers I couldn't give raced through my mind, and he smiled back sympathetically.

"Um, nothing much. Working a lot?"

"I went into Opalescence about a month ago, and they said you'd quit not long after everything happened last year. Are you working somewhere new now?" Nothing was accusing about the questions, but I could feel my anxiety spike.

"Yeah, I started working as a research assistant at a place in the Valley," I blurted out without thinking, remembering the line I'd fed to my family months ago.

Nice. Liam looked impressed. He hadn't been there when I'd had that conversation with Aurora and my parents, and I hadn't thought about it in a long time.

Thanks, figured I'd stick with the original story.

I mean, it's sort of true... You do research a lot. He smirked, and I resisted the urge to roll my eyes.

"Cool! That sounds awesome! Researching what exactly?" I returned my attention to my friend.

"Just history stuff." I shrugged, hoping Ainslie, who had never been even slightly interested in history, wouldn't ask any further questions.

"So, is that where you met your boyfriend?" Ainslie asked casually, and I must have looked surprised because she grinned as I searched for a response.

"How did you – What boyfriend?" Too late. Ainslie laughed.

"Come on, Is. I know there's a guy. I do still see Aurora at parties, at the very least." I grimaced, and Ainslie patted my hand. "Don't worry; she only said good things."

Huh, that would have been interesting to hear. I had to agree with Liam's cynical comment there.

"Well, Aurora doesn't approve."

"Oh, bully to her. So, who is he?" Ainslie settled back in her seat, fishing for gossip.

"His name is Liam. He's Irish. We met at Uni." Might as well stick with the original lie.

"Cool. What's he like?" I knew we had Liam's full attention now as I saw him sit up straighter in his seat, listening intently for my response.

"Well, obviously, he's a great guy, or I wouldn't be with him." Ainslie nodded.

"And? Come on. I need more details than that, babe. How do I know this guy is good enough for my best friend?" I had forgotten how details-based Ainslie was.

"Like what?"

"Is he hot? Does he give you the warm fuzzies? You gotta give me something, woman." I laughed.

"Well, hot is an understatement. He is probably the hottest guy I have ever laid eyes on." I smiled, purposely not looking at Liam as I continued. "Very caring and protective. He's got the charm going, that's for sure. And definitely an old soul."

"Do you love him?" Ainslie asked quietly, almost sadly.

"Yes. Yes, I do love him. I didn't think I would find someone else after what happened with Will. But it's almost like I have known Liam my whole life. It's hard to explain."

I love you too. I must have looked lost in thought as I smiled at Liam over her shoulder because Ainslie reached across the table, holding my hand.

"I can't wait to meet him. He sounds like a special guy..."

"He is. He is incredibly protective. I feel safe with him."

"I guess with everything that has happened, that is very important." I smiled sadly at her words, struggling to keep my emotions in check once again.

"I never thought about it that way, but you're right." I pushed my chair back and stood up. "I'm just going to duck into the ladies. I'll be back in a second."

"Oh, hon, I'm sorry! I've put my foot in it, haven't I?" Ainslie looked stricken, but I waved her away.

"Don't be silly. Nature calls, that's all." I excused myself and wove through the tables to the hall leading to the bathrooms. I rounded the corner and walked straight into Liam, who folded me into his arms.

"Hi." It was all I needed to help me feel better, although something in the back of my mind caused me to feel slightly off. I pushed it aside, surrendering myself to the hug.

"Hi." I smiled up at him and raised myself onto my toes to kiss him. Alarm bells started going off in my head as he kissed me back.

"Just thought I'd make sure you were okay." As he said this, I heard his voice in my head.

Isolde... who are you talking to?

I gasped sharply as I realised the man before me was not Liam... The man with deep brown, almost black, eyes. I stepped back and his expression turned predatory.

You failed to mention that your brother is your identical twin, Liam.

CHAPTER TWENTY-THREE

I somehow managed to keep my face neutral, as Liam appeared at my side, wrenching me out of his brother's arms.

"Stay the hell away from her, Connor," Liam growled, and I pressed myself against the wall behind him, unsure of who I was more afraid of at this point.

So, this was Connor—Liam's 'older' brother. Older by mere minutes, it would seem.

"Hello, Liam, brother dear. How are you?" Connor asked with a smile, which sent shivers down my spine. The smile was cold and calculating, like a cat playing with a mouse before it swallows it whole.

"What are you doing here?" Liam hissed, keeping me firmly between himself and the wall, shielding me from Connor. I prayed that no unsuspecting patron would round the corner.

"Just checking up on my baby brother. Dear William told me you had finally settled down after all these centuries. And with his fiancee, no less. I had to meet the young woman who has so many of my people worked up." Connor ran his eyes over what little he could see of me from behind Liam as if appraising livestock. I moved closer to Liam's back, feeling a strong urge to get as far away from Connor as possible. "She is beautiful... You've done well. Pity you will have to watch her become one of us, Liam. You know how much it pains me to see you hurting." I could feel Liam's muscles become even more tense, and resisted the urge to shiver again.

"Isolde... Go back to the table. Keep Ainslie safe." I was surprised by this direction. Usually, Liam wouldn't let me out of his sight in such circumstances. Heeding his words, I slipped away from the pair and headed back to Ainslie, my legs barely holding me up.

"Hey, are you okay?" Ainslie asked me, concerned, as I sat down shakily.

"Fine, fine... Just ran into someone that I know in the bathroom." I tried to sound as if nothing was wrong, but as I spoke, I spied a familiar face over Ainslie's shoulder and felt my blood run cold. Will sat directly behind her, waving at me, his face twisted into that now familiar smile that sent tremors through every inch of my body.

Liam... we have a serious problem.

"Isolde? You look like you've seen a ghost. Are you sure you're okay?" Ainslie glanced over her shoulder. At first, she didn't see Will, turning back to face me. Then realisation dawned on her face, and she turned back slowly, freezing as Will smiled at her.

"Hi, Ainslie. It's been a long-time... You look good." I fought the urge to be sick. Instead, I stood up, pulling Ainslie out of her seat and putting myself between them.

"Isolde... What's going on?" Ainslie's voice rose with fear as Will rose to his feet as well.

"Leave. Now." I ignored Ainslie as I spoke to Will. I looked around the restaurant, trying to ignore the panic I could feel rising within me. I needed to protect Ainslie and keep her from being caught in the middle of what was about to turn into an ugly confrontation.

"Isolde... What the hell is going on here?!" Ainslie gripped my hand tightly, her voice shaking. Will moved towards me in a blur before grabbing me roughly by the hair and pulling my face close to his.

"Oh, I'll leave Isolde. But I won't be leaving alone." Will kissed me hard, and I struggled against him, pushing him away with my free hand as I used the other to move Ainslie as I backed away.

"I'm not going anywhere with you, William," I said as Liam appeared at my shoulder and shoved Will away.

Isolde, Connor is still around the corner. We are going to have to fight our way out of here.

What about Ainslie? Will had stopped and was glaring at us angrily, seeing the two of us exchanging looks.

"So, it's true... You're able to read each other's minds." I felt Ainslie grip my hand tighter.

How the hell... I shot Liam a quick questioning look, and he shook his head ever so slightly.

I have no idea, but we will work on that once we are out of here.

"Will, we don't want a scene here." I thought that statement was a stretch on Liam's part, trying to negotiate with a pissed-off vampire. Then again, he was also a pissed-off vampire, so maybe he figured it might work.

"Oh, Liam, brother. I think a scene is exactly what we need." Connor appeared beside Will. Around us, the other diners were starting to rise to their feet, and I realised, with a sinking feeling, that we were in a restaurant full of nightwalkers.

Why couldn't I sense this? I practically screamed this at Liam in my head.

It was Connor. He cloaked their presence. I was too freaked out to unpack that particular piece of information. Until now, I thought nightwalkers weren't able to wield magic.

We have to get Ainslie out of here, Liam...

And then I felt all the air leave the room as the newest member of Adam's coven rounded the corner behind Connor and Liam with casual grace, the trademark cruel smile on her face. My face.

My hand went limp in Ainslie's vice-like grip.

Then my legs started to give way from under me, though Liam caught me before I collapsed.

"Aurora?" I breathed, my eyes welling up. Her new, piercing blue eyes bored into mine, sadistic pleasure written all over her face.

"Hiya, sis."

I felt the world start to spin, and I fought the urge to black out.

Isolde, come on. Get it together. We have to get ourselves out of here first. Then we can fall apart. I wasn't sure if it was Liam's voice or my own, but I followed the advice in my head and reeled myself back together. By this point, we had reached the door. I could see the car from where we stood and shoved Ainslie in that direction.

Unlock the car! As I sent that thought to Liam, I pointed Ainslie to the car, with its lights flashing to show that the central locking was released.

"Get in! Go!" I yelled as one of Connor's minions launched himself at me. Ainslie screamed and ran as Liam, and I started fighting them off. I snapped a kick to the nearest vampire's midsection as I punched another in the face.

Get in the car! I am right behind you! Liam's voice commanded in my head, and I raced for the passenger side as Liam ran along behind me. He dived into the driver seat and locked us in, slamming his foot down on the accelerator as he threw the car into reverse, tearing out of the parking space and narrowly avoiding a collision with another car that slammed to a halt behind us. I struggled to comprehend what had just happened as we fled the scene. I could only see Aurora's face, that cruel smile and piercing blue eyes. It was all too much.

"Isolde... What is going on? Will... Aurora..." Ainslie's voice from the back seat brought me back to reality. I had forgotten she was even there. I looked over at Liam.

I have to tell her something.

Tell her. They can do a memory charm at the Manor. I let out a breath.

"Will didn't die last year... Well... actually, he did, but now he's a vampire. And now, apparently, so is Aurora." I choked out the words as Liam reached over to grip my hand tightly. Ainslie remained silent in the back seat, and I turned to look at her, noting the confusion and disbelief written all over her face.

"What?! Have you completely lost your mind?!" She cried, her voice wavering. I let out a hollow laugh, no doubt adding to Ainslie's belief that my sanity was hanging precariously by a thread.

"I wish! Think about it, Ainslie. Try and find a better explanation for what you've just witnessed. I've tried to come up with thousands, and none of them have come close to the truth." I couldn't deal with this right now. I just wanted to curl up and cry.

"Who are you? Where are we going?" Ainslie moved her attention to Liam as I turned to stare out the window.

"I'm Liam. Sorry we aren't meeting under better circumstances..." Liam glanced at Ainslie in the rear vision mirror and no doubt Ainslie was gaping back at him.

The rest of the short drive was silent, and I dragged myself back to the present as Liam was pulling the car into the basement of the Manor.

"Where are we?" Ainslie looked as though she was about to refuse to get out of the car, but the look on my face when I opened her door must have persuaded her otherwise.

"Mission control." I led the way upstairs and headed straight for the comms room, where a meeting was underway.

"Ah, Isolde, Liam, we were just... Who is this?" Gerard looked stunned as Ainslie trailed into the room behind us.

"A friend. We have a problem." I looked around the room, spying Celeste and Daniel sitting across the table. "Did you find Colin and James?" Celeste only shook her head, perhaps sensing that now was not the time to say too much.

"Figured. Well, you can stop trying to work out what happened to them. They are either dead or nightwalkers because they failed. Aurora is now a nightwalker." I stated angrily before storming out of the room. I headed up to my room and slammed the door behind me before throwing myself onto my bed and beginning to sob uncontrollably. A few moments later, Liam entered the room and sat behind me, unsure what to do. I turned to face him, and he lay down beside me, pulling me close and allowing me to sob into his chest, my tears staining his shirt for what felt like the thousandth time since we first met.

I am so sorry...

I awoke a few hours later after having fallen into a fitful sleep. I went back downstairs and found Liam now in the comms room with Patrice and a few others. He'd left me after I'd fallen asleep, and they were trying to put together a plan, from what I could tell.

"Isolde... You shouldn't be up." Patrice approached, attempting to hug me, but I stepped out of her reach.

"How did this happen? Everyone told me she was being given the highest protection available, yet here she is, a vampire." I was angry, and the others looked at me, unsure what to say. "How the hell do I explain this to my family? To Jacob? My parents shared a home with her; she can kill them anytime." I looked out the window, seeing that it was still dark outside. "She could be killing them right now." I spun on my heel and sprinted from the room. Liam was behind me in a split second, his hand gripping mine, preventing me from leaving.

"Isolde, you can't leave. It's too dangerous now." It was Patrice who spoke, but it was Liam who was looking at me pleadingly.

Isolde... Please...

"My parents are in danger. Do any of you understand that? Aurora has already been killed... I won't let the rest of my family be slaughtered." I tried to shake Liam's hand away, but he wouldn't let go.

"We have people at your parent's house already," Patrice said, and I scoffed.

"Forgive me, but that is not a comfort to me right now!"

Isolde, calm down. Stop attacking everyone. It is not their fault. I looked into Liam's sad eyes as angry tears poured down my face.

No... It's not... It's mine. Liam looked as though his heart was breaking.

"Let me go, Liam," I said aloud. Liam looked down with tears in his eyes. He took a deep breath and slowly removed his hand, letting me go. He let his breath out shakily as I turned and walked away.

Be careful.

I never looked back.

I jumped into one of the bulletproof four-wheel drives and gunned the engine, tearing out of the basement. According to the clock on the dashboard, it was after 3 am, so traffic wasn't an issue, and I arrived at my parents' house within ten minutes, breaking every road rule possible.

The house was shrouded in darkness as I exited the car, unsure of what I would say to my parents. How would I tell them that one of their daughters was a vampire? And that they would now need to move. I took a deep breath and started to walk up the footpath. I didn't get far.

"Isolde! What are you doing here?!" Celeste stepped out of the darkness, with Daniel two steps behind her, like always.

"Telling my parents that their daughter is dead," I said woodenly, angry at their inability to protect my sister, even though I knew logically that the blame did not lie with them.

"They're not here. We told them there was a gas leak, and we had to evacuate them." I took in their appearance for the first time, realising they were both dressed in emergency services uniforms.

"Why are you still here then? And where are they?"

"They are in the guest room of your house." I opened my mouth to protest, but Celeste talked over me. "It's a safe house, Aurora won't be able to find her way back there, and the same magic protects it as the Manor. Daniel and I left Gerard there and returned here in case Aurora did come to pay a visit." As she spoke, a movement out of the corner of my eye caused me to turn away.

When I looked back a split second later, Will stood behind Celeste, a hand on either side of her head. He snapped her neck with a crack, and I screamed as he let her fall to the ground at his feet. Behind him, Daniel struggled against Adam, whose face was contorted into the same feral visage that he had worn the night he turned Will. Daniel cried out as his wife's body lay lifeless on the ground, and this distraction was all that Adam needed to gain the upper hand. He wrenched Daniel's head to the side and savagely bit his neck.

I screamed again, moving to fight Adam off, but was stopped by a hand that snaked around from behind me and clamped itself over my mouth.

"Hello, sister dearest," Aurora hissed in my ear. "We've got some catching up to do." I struggled to free myself, but Aurora's grip on me was like a vice. Connor appeared before me, smiling pleasantly. Adam let Daniel fall to the ground, and I watched helplessly as he tried to drag himself one-handed to Celeste's side, blood pouring from the wound at his neck as he clamped his hand over it.

"I have been looking forward to this for a long time, Isolde." The last thing I saw was Connor reaching towards my forehead before everything went black.

CHAPTER TWENTY-FOUR

As I sat in the bedroom that Will and I used to share, I noticed four small collections of gifts in front of me, all bearing my name as the giver. Each gift had a label indicating its intended recipient - one for Will, one for Aurora, one for Connor and one for Liam.

I reached for the pile labelled Will. The first gift I opened was something I had never seen before. It was a glass sphere with what looked like sunlight glaring at me, blinding me with brilliance. Blinking away the bursts of colour in my vision, I put it aside, reaching for the next gift in the pile. It was an antique watch, like the ones men used to wear attached to their clothes. The hands spun around in a blur before suddenly stopping to show the time 9:43. The time he had been pronounced dead. My hand shook as I put that aside as well and reached for the final gift. The wrapping fell away, and I turned it over in my hands. It appeared to be a sign; its wooden letters looped together to form the word 'acceptance'.

Next, I reached for the pile marked with Aurora's name. The first gift was a snow globe, a photo placed at the bottom. When I shook it, the snowflakes swirled together, forming the word "forgiveness" when they fell back to the bottom. The photo within it was of the two of us, standing face to face, with Aurora kissing me on the forehead. The second was a single vial of blood with my name written on it. I stared at it for a long time, trying to understand its meaning.

When no answers came to me, I set it aside and moved along to the third group of gifts, the one marked for Connor. Curious, I reached for the first gift, able to tell from the shape and feel that it was a book. I pulled it from the wrapping and read the title 'Life is an Illusion'. Once again, I struggled to understand the meaning as I put it aside. The second was a mirror, and I held it up, expecting to see my face reflected back at me. Instead, my features were blurred, and the word 'sacrifices' shimmered over the top.

"Isolde!" Liam appeared behind me as I turned at the sound of his voice. I looked at him, then back at the pile with his name on it.

"Isolde, where are you? Where did they take you?" I ignored him, his words making no sense to me. I reached for the pile of gifts with his name on it.

The first gift was a framed photo of the two of us. Our faces were out of focus as we stood cheek to cheek, our eyes on our hands held before us, our fingers intertwined.

"Isolde, look at me. I need you to focus. Where have they taken you?" Liam came to stand before me and took my face in his hands, forcing me to look at him.

"I... don't know." I still didn't know what he was talking about, and a sinister laugh began echoing around us. Just like in my nightmares, two shadowy figures appeared nearby, moving closer to where we stood. This time, however, I was able to make out their faces and realised, with a jolt, that it was Connor and Aurora. The laughter was growing louder still, and I clamped my hands over my ears once again as the room around us began to change, and we now stood outside, standing in front of a dilapidated old house.

"I know this place. Is this where they've taken you?" The laughter halted abruptly, and I surveyed the house.

"We used to play here. Dad worked for the people who owned it." On the ground, something shiny caught my attention. I knelt to pick it

*up. It was a delicate ID bracelet with the words "Eternally Yours"
engraved into it. I looked up at Liam.*

"I love you. Do you know that? It's you. It was always meant to
be you." *Liam gently touched my face as I spoke, stroking my cheek
before kissing my forehead.*

"I love you too. And I'm coming for you." *He vanished, and
suddenly I was all alone. I felt cold and rubbed my arms, looking up at
the house, which stood cold and empty. A sense of foreboding sent a
shiver up my spine.*

*Before me, words began to drift across the breeze that lifted my
hair gently, the words starting to swirl around me before coming up as
though they were appearing on a giant TV screen.*

In a world blemished by darkness and light,
A young woman shall rise with power and might.
Her destiny was foretold in a prophecy of old,
To bring balance to the turmoil untold.
Of seventh son and seventh daughter born,
Her heart will be set to mourn.
There will be trials that she must endure,
Before she reaches the future so pure.
Her power will be unmatched and rare,
Her soul will be pure, her intentions fair.
But to end the apocalypse, she must pay a cost,
To sacrifice what she loves and lost.
A decision she must make with a heavy heart,
For she knows this is where her journey must start.
With tears in her eyes, she'll rise with grace,
To battle the evil she must face.
The fate of the world will rest upon her hand,
As she brings an end to the chaos of the land.
Her journey will end with a triumph so bright,
As she brings balance between the wrong and the right.

• • •

Something hard struck me across the face, and I reeled back as everything around me tilted slightly. I was struck hard again, and the scene around me faded. One more hard blow and I realised it was all a dream.

"Wake up!" A voice snarled at me. It was a voice I knew well.

Everything around me was turning red, and as I came to, I became aware of a throbbing pain in my head and a burning sensation across my left cheek.

I opened my eyes slowly, looking directly into Aurora's new piercing blue eyes. She smiled at me, her lips curled back to show her new, glistening fangs. I shuddered and leaned back, attempting to distance myself from her as much as possible, which was hard to do as I was sitting on a hard wooden chair, my hands tied to the two centre beams that ran up behind my back.

"Good morning, sleeping beauty." She reached over to ruffle my hair, but I jerked my head away, glaring at her.

"Stay the hell away from me," I spat out, and she laughed.

"Oh, dear. That's not nice at all." She slapped me across the face again, bringing tears to my eyes with the force of the blow.

"Do you recognise where we are? I thought it was the perfect setting for our little reunion." Aurora danced across the room to where Will sat sprawled on a dirty old couch, flicking through an ancient-looking book.

"Why is it perfect?" I asked, looking around, not seeing anything particularly interesting about our current location.

"Don't you remember? This is where we were the first time you started talking about vampires and secret orders..." She spread her arms wide, her smile sickly sweet.

"What are you talking about?" I looked at her, confused.

"Oh... whoops." Aurora giggled and looked over at Will, putting her finger to her lips. "Not supposed to tell." If I didn't know better, I would have thought she was drunk.

"No, you weren't, naughty girl." Will grinned back at her, tossing his book aside and getting to his feet.

"Did you know we'd had magic used on us as children? Bet your precious Protectors never told you about that," Aurora said tauntingly. I tried to look like I knew what she was talking about, but I was failing miserably. Will laughed as Aurora came forward again and straddled my lap, getting as close as she could to my face. She walked her fingers over my forehead.

"It's all locked away in here. A memory charm. Just like the one they no doubt used on poor Ainslie tonight." I tried to lean away from her touch, but Aurora gripped my face with one hand, forcing me to look at her.

"Seeing as you clearly don't remember, how about I enlighten you?" Still gripping my chin, she jerked my head painfully, forcing me to look over to where she pointed at one of the corners of the room. "It was right there. We were six. We were playing with Bianca while Dad worked up at the big house. We weren't supposed to come in here, everyone told us it wasn't safe because it was falling apart, but we snuck in anyway. And we disturbed a vampire while he was sleeping." I tried not to look like I cared about what she was saying. "When he got a good look at us, it was like Christmas had come early... The chosen ones..." My eyes widened. "You know the prophecy? The one that the Protectors told you all about?" Her eyes glistened with excitement, clearly enjoying her story's effect on me. "There are two prophecies. We both have a destiny. It's not all about you, for a change. It's about both of us. And Liam and Connor, of course. The identical twins. One set of men, one set of women... Eventually becoming daywalkers and nightwalkers... But now... You're the only human left..." She grinned evilly as Will came up behind her and nuzzled her neck. I looked away, unable to stomach the sight of them together. Aurora was silent for a while, and I turned back to see them kissing each other hungrily. I felt nauseous.

"So. Back to my story." They had moved away, and Will sat back down on the couch, pulling Aurora into his lap. "When the vampire realised who we were, he got excited. He had us both locked in the room with him, intending to keep us here until the sun went down. Remember how Bianca went missing all those years ago? And we were the last to have seen her, but we didn't know anything? He killed her right in front of us. It was a traumatic experience, especially for two little girls as sheltered as we were... Then He came. Your Knight in Shining Armour," she said with disgust, as though being rescued had been the greatest disaster in the world.

"Liam," I whispered, not intending to speak but forgetting myself. Will growled into Aurora's neck, causing her to giggle. The contents of my stomach were threatening to make a reappearance now.

"Yes, your precious Liam. He busted down that door and took that vampire out without a second glance. He had someone else with him, a woman. She performed the memory charm on us and took Bianca's body away. Protecting us, they said. We weren't meant to know any of this yet. It was not our time. Deciding what we should and shouldn't know, as if they were Gods, making decisions on behalf of others, without regard for what they want or truly need." It wasn't reassuring to hear any of this. Yet unsurprising, with everything that I had seen. The Order took it upon themselves to control the outcome of every situation they encountered, especially within my life.

"Oh, and here's the best part... The destiny they have been telling you about. The one with your magical powers... Well, they left out a part." Aurora smiled cruelly, enjoying every moment as she wielded the knowledge I had not been privy to.

"Let me guess. You and I are meant to be mortal enemies?" I was growing tired of this and willing Liam to hurry up.

"Well, that's a possibility... But it just depends on who gets to you first."

"What are you talking about?" It was Will's turn to laugh cruelly this time.

"God, I can't believe how much they haven't told you! This is awesome. And they think of themselves as being the white hats. All that is pure and good. Yet they haven't told you a single thing. Not what really matters. Guess they aren't as honest as they portray themselves." He laughed again. I was becoming incredibly pissed off as I struggled to release my hands from the ropes that itched at my wrists.

"If you know everything, then spill. What have they left out?" I knew I shouldn't give them the satisfaction of knowing they were getting to me, but I couldn't keep my curiosity to myself. Aurora rolled her eyes.

"Oh, fine, spoil my fun. She has always been good at that..." She crossed her arms, looking put out as she directed this comment to Will.

When did I ever spoil her fun?

"I thought we decided that was in the past?" They had started conversing between themselves, ignoring my obvious attempts to break free from the chair.

"What can I say? I'm tired of pretending that everything between you was this perfect love story when you and I both know there was more to it than that." They had my full attention now.

"What the hell are you talking about now?" I couldn't believe it, but Will actually looked at me with a guilty look on his face.

"Your perfect fiance failed to tell you something when you returned from London. While you were away, the two of us started seeing each other. We both said it was because we missed having you around. But when you came back, and he went running back to you, I realised that it wasn't simply that. I had fallen in love with him. And I have always been in love with him. And he still had feelings for me too. But it was always about you. I had to protect my perfect younger sister. Couldn't hurt Isolde." Aurora was beginning to work herself up into a real tizz, but I looked at Will, wanting answers.

"Is that true?" Yep, the guilt was there, alright. How was this possible? "Well, you got your wish Aurora. He's all yours now." I felt ill again.

"Oh, thanks so much for your permission."

"Oh, get the hell over yourself!" I'd had enough. "For the last few months, all you've done is bitch and whine at me!" It was pointless yelling at her. The woman before me was no longer my sister but a creature who wore her face. And that creature was enjoying all of this just a little too much.

"I still haven't gotten to the punch line of my joke. The joke that is your existence."

"Well, hop to it then. I know you're dying to tell me." All I wanted now was to hear Liam's voice telling me they were about to storm in.

"The Protectors left out the key part of the prophecy. It's not about a human woman." She paused for effect, and I couldn't help but look at her now.

"It's about a vampire. The last of the four twins to be turned. The prophecy says that you'll be the one to end it all. But, if we could get you first, and turn you into a nightwalker, then there's no risk of you winning, is there?" Although I picked up on some of her story, she was rambling, and I didn't fully understand what she was telling me.

"Speak plain English, would you?!"

"Fine! Your destiny is to become a vampire! It was both of our destinies! And the Order of the Dragon knew it all along!" That stopped me in my attempts to get my hands free.

"You're lying..." I said quietly.

"Am I? Think Isolde. Think really hard," she said with a cruel smile, not noticing as Connor entered the room silently behind her and took in the scene before him.

"What, pray tell, is going on?" He asked with a smile, but there was a dangerous look in his eye as he looked at Aurora, who was puffing away, her anger having worked her up too much.

"Aurora couldn't keep her mouth shut," a voice said from behind me, and I turned to see Adam, who must have been standing there all along, keeping a silent vigil.

"I gathered," Connor tsked at her, and I watched in disbelief as she cast her eyes down like a child being scolded. Connor came to stand immediately in front of me and lowered himself to look me right in the eye. I noted the colour of his eyes.

How could his eyes change colour when none of the other night-walkers did? Last night, they were a deep chocolate brown. The same eyes on the man I had seen at Uni all those months ago. It was then that I realised that it must have been Connor that I saw that day, which was why Liam was so confused every time I had ever brought it up. But now, they were the telltale blue that was the same as the other nightwalkers in the room. The same as his brother's.

He winked at me with a cocky grin and straightened up again.

"So, Isolde, now you know the truth that the Order has been keeping from you all this time. Although, my dear little brother was just as clueless as you about the Gemini Prophecy. The elders only told him about the prophecy about you, and there was no mention of you becoming a vampire." I glared at Connor through narrowed eyes.

"You're all lying. Trying to turn me against my people."

"Really? Is that what you really believe?" He asked quietly, walking towards me. "Maybe this will help." He touched my fore-head, just as he had done outside my parents' house hours before.

Instead of passing out this time, an onslaught of memories hit me. I flashed back to an old memory, one that had been hidden from me.

Liam stood over me, and I looked up at him, terrified. Behind him, Bianca's lifeless body lay on the ground, her neck twisted at an awkward angle.

"Isolde. Look at me. It's going to be okay. It is not time for you to know any of this yet. It is too soon. You deserve to have a normal child-hood. It's the least we can give you." He crouched before me, a grown man looking into the eyes of a terrified six-year-old. I looked at my

sister, who sat crying in Patrice's lap in the corner. Patrice was hugging her closely with tears in her eyes as she performed the memory charm, whispering the words as she rocked her back and forth.

"Who are you?" I asked Liam, still afraid.

"I'm someone who will protect you."

Then the night in the alley, the eve of my twenty-fifth birthday.

"It's you… I remember you." I told Liam, who had appeared before me on the dance floor in the nightclub. He had simply looked at me before turning and walking away. And I had followed him drunkenly outside and into the alley between it and the hotel beside it.

"Wait. How do I know you?" Liam stopped and turned back to me.

"We've met before. In your dreams." I snorted, thinking it was some line. Except, I knew his face. I had seen it in my nightmares on and off over the years.

"How…"

"Everything in your life is about to change."

"What do you mean?" I had leaned back against the wall, struggling to keep the world from spinning in my drunken state.

"I can't tell you yet. You need to start remembering on your own. But know this. Things are about to get very bad. And I can't protect you anymore." With that, he turned and walked away. I stumbled back into the club and told Ainslie it was time to go home and that it wasn't safe.

Every time I'd come across Patrice and Damon conversing, and they'd immediately gone silent, flashed through my mind as Connor took his hand away, and I returned to the present, feeling sick to my stomach.

"So now you know the truth," Connor said as I struggled to keep myself from falling apart. How had I not noticed all of this before? How could I have believed that they had told me everything? How could I have trusted them all so completely?

My mind was reeling, but suddenly, we were all drawn to the sound of someone kicking the front door in, and we all looked towards the door.

The sound of wood splintering and snapping was followed by complete chaos as the outer room filled with voices and the sounds of fighting. In my head, Liam was screaming at me to hold on, but I blocked him out.

This was how it was meant to be. It was always going to come down to this. Ever since Adam had turned Will and this nightmare had begun, it was always going to come down to all of us here in this room. I was ready to end this, finally.

Aurora and Connor had both turned their backs on me as the door to the room was flung open, not seeing me as a threat while I was still tied to the chair. Unaware of the abilities that I had been developing.

I concentrated all my energy on the ropes wrapped tightly around my wrists, imagining them coming undone, and eventually, I felt them slither off and hit the ground. Slowly, I rose to my feet and tapped Aurora on the shoulder. She turned, almost bemused, not expecting to see my fist flying into her face. Nor did Connor expect the roundhouse kick to the head. Unfortunately, this did not knock either of them out, but it allowed me to see what was happening in front of them.

Liam and Will circled each other whilst Patrice, David, and someone I didn't recognise had Adam pinned against the wall across the room. Gerard and another vampire were dancing around each other, trading blows. This still left me to deal with the other two alone. I could hear the sounds of fighting from the adjoining room and knew that the other Protectors were momentarily preoccupied. Realising this, Connor and Aurora turned to me at the same time. In the space of a heartbeat, they both had me pinned against the wall, and I gasped as the breath was knocked out of me.

"That wasn't very nice, sis. Sneaking up from behind, that's playing dirty." Aurora's words were a low whisper in my ear, and Connor grabbed her as she went to lean in to bite me.

"We do this together, little one." I couldn't believe they were arguing about who got to turn me into a vampire. I saw my opportunity and struggled to free myself, but Connor just looked amused, his grip tightening on my shoulder. Aurora nodded.

"Of course." And with the briefest of exchanged looks, they both turned on me, moving as one. I cried out in pain as they bit into either side of my neck. I tried to free myself, but that made them bite down harder, causing me to scream louder. Finally, Liam saw what was happening, and I heard him yell out from far away. I could hear the sounds of the fighting now as though it were in a far-off place, an annoying sound in the distance. I heard, more than felt, as both Aurora and Connor were pulled off me. I had no way of knowing who had won and who had lost. I just felt myself slipping into the darkness.

I kept wavering in and out, feeling myself being lifted from the ground and moving fast. What felt like hours later, I distantly felt the motion of a car being driven at high speed. I could hear arguing and Liam saying, "No, I won't do it." And Patrice yelled the words, "She's almost completely drained. I can't stop the bleeding. You've got to!"

I couldn't weigh in on this argument, did not even know what they were arguing about. I just wished they would all go away and let me sleep. I was seeing faces, so many faces. They were calling me to them. They had stories to tell me. I longed to hear those stories.

Then suddenly, Liam's voice was in my ear. The last thing I heard was his beautiful voice, whispering the words, "I'm sorry. Please forgive me."

Then there was another bite on my neck, though not as painful this time...

Eventually, darkness took over, and as I felt my last breath leave my body, I heard the sound of screeching tyres and crunching metal... Then the world went black.

EPILOGUE

LIAM

I opened my eyes, briefly aware of the pounding in my head, before the pain dissipated, and I took in the room around me. I sat slumped in a chair in the corner of a vaguely familiar room. But I only cared about the body lying on the bed across from me. Isolde lay utterly still, her head propped up on a pillow with her eyes closed.

I leapt to my feet and crossed the room in two strides before stopping at the side of the bed, looking down at her. Remembering everything that had happened until someone crashed into us, I knew the transition had begun. I could hear my heart pounding in my ears, and I leaned down to push a lock of hair off her face, kissing her gently on the forehead. I could only pray now that I had gotten to her in time. We would have to wait for another seven days until we knew the truth.

Working to push my anxiety aside, I looked around the room again, trying to figure out where I was. Though the room itself was unfamiliar, the furniture I knew well, and I realised with anger who must have been responsible for the car accident that had knocked me out. I felt my fury growing, and I stalked over to the door. Glancing back over my shoulder to look at Isolde briefly, I wrenched the door open and let it slam against the wall as I entered the hallway. A door further down the hall opened, and a familiar figure stepped out, assessing me coolly.

"Where the fuck is she?" Ronson raised an eyebrow at me. A man of few words, he gestured towards the stairs, and I glared at him for a moment before going off in search of the one I knew would have all the answers—the source of centuries' worth of frustration.

"I see you've woken up." She stood in the centre of an elaborate library to the left of the bottom of the staircase. Her long black hair was hanging down her back, and she was wearing barely any clothes, as usual. She had always been aware of her beauty and wielded it like a weapon. I'd seen many men fall to their feet before her, though it had never had that effect on me, much to her annoyance.

"What the fuck, Eve?" I demanded of her, not even attempting to hide my anger at seeing her standing before me. Although she was small, barely coming to my shoulder, she exuded power.

"Careful, Liam. Your feelings are showing," she said with a smirk, her blue eyes holding my own as she stepped closer. I stayed perfectly still, watching her every move tensely. "Aren't you happy to see your family again?" She ran a hand down my left arm, and I gritted my teeth, refusing to play her games.

"Why are we here, Eve?" I glared at the woman who had changed my life five hundred years ago and noted the gleam in her eyes. Her lips curled into a delighted smile.

"Waiting for your young lover to wake up and for the madness to end finally, of course." She spread her arms wide as though I should know what the fuck she was talking about. I moved closer, raising my hands to grip her shoulders tightly, ignoring the fact that she most likely enjoyed this. She'd always enjoyed pain.

"Explain."

"All in good time, Liam dear." She patted one of my hands before stepping out of my grasp and moving to sit in one of the overstuffed armchairs. She waved at the one across from her.

"Take a seat, Liam." She was enjoying this far too much. Her lips curled into a smirk as her eyes danced with barely concealed glee. She knew how I felt about her and the world she'd dragged me into in 1510. When I was a man who had just turned twenty-five and thought I was accepting comforting words from a stranger within the walls of a darkened church. Instead, the stranger had taken my life from me and dragged me into this world without my consent, tying me to her for eternity. I hadn't seen her in twenty-six years, but I'd felt her presence over the years and knew she hadn't been far away. Her blood memories coursed through my veins, and blood called to blood, always. I grudgingly moved to sit across from her and crossed my arms over my chest.

"What now?" I asked my sire angrily, and she shrugged.

"Now we wait. Get comfortable, my love. It's all starting now." She gestured towards the television in the corner, and I noted for the first time that it showed images of the Wivenhoe Dam, the city's main water source. Its floodgates were open, and the banner down below announced that it had burst open without warning. The city was about to be covered in water with no way of stopping it.

Seven more days. And then we would know if I managed to keep my promise to Isolde or if I would be forced to kill the only woman I had ever loved.

I closed my eyes and leaned back to stare up at the ceiling as I let out a frustrated breath. The wait was going to be excruciating.

BLOOD MEMORIES

BOOK TWO

*To the BookTok and Bookstagram communities
for supporting Indie Authors and making reading
cool again!*

SONG LIST

Dynasty – MIIA
How Villains Are Made – Madalen Duke
Raise Up The Lights – League of Legends, The Seige
White Flag – Bishop Briggs
Human – Rag'n'Bone Man
...Ready for It? – Taylor Swift
I Didn't Ask For This – Beth Crowley
Redemption – Besomorph, Coopex, RIELL
In A Perfect World – Dean Lewis, Julia Michaels
I Wish You Cheated – Alexander Stewart
Six Feet Under – Oshins, Leslie Powell
Born To Die – Euphoria, Bolshiee
Up In Flames – Ruelle
I Don't Want To Watch The World End With Someone Else –
Clinton Kane

PROLOGUE

Until a year ago, I had led what you would call a normal life. Boring even. I'd always done everything that was expected of me - getting good grades at school, attending a good University, and finding a man who loved and wanted to marry me.

All of that changed when my fiance, Will, was murdered in front of me.

By a vampire.

I discovered that I was part of a secret organisation, the Order of the Dragon, which had been formed to keep the reality of the world's darkness from the human race.

Will returned from the dead, hell-bent on also turning me into a vampire.

I was informed that it was my destiny to end a war waged for centuries between two different races of vampires, daywalkers and nightwalkers.

Oh, and I fell in love with a daywalker who was closer to six hundred than my own ripe age of twenty-five.

But none of that compared to what happened last week.

My lover's identical twin brother, along with my own identical twin sister, had taken it upon themselves to attempt to turn me into one of them—a nightwalker.

And because of a promise I had extracted from Liam, the love of my life, was forced to take matters into his own hands, hoping that when I woke up, I wouldn't be on the wrong side of this war.

I've begun to realise that the world's reality is not as simple as discerning good from evil.

Sleeping Beauty had it easy. After True Love's kiss, she woke to the sight of Prince Charming and happily ever after.

I woke up to find my prince charming was keeping secrets, and the world sucked.

Welcome to reality.

CHAPTER ONE

The smell surrounded me and blocked out all my other senses. Once I could get past the assault that smelled of rotting fruit, sewerage and a mixture of men's and women's cologne, I opened my eyes to take in my surroundings. I felt like I was pushing through a dense fog, cloying at every part of my body as if holding me back in the dark.

My brain was a jumbled mess of thoughts, and I had no idea where I was. Or even who I was, for that matter. All I could do was look around me in wonder, noticing the spider's web in the corner in great detail. I was able to make out the tiny hairs on the legs of the spider that spun its web with ease.

The room I was in was lavishly furnished. I lay on a giant four-poster bed with rich burgundy hangings. Two antique oil lamps made of a mosaic of ornate-coloured glass on both bedside tables burned brightly in the darkness.

The window was open, allowing a breeze to enter the room, laced with the faintest trace of the ocean and the other scents that continued to lay siege upon my senses.

I sat up quickly and walked to the window, looking outside as I attempted to make sense of my current situation.

Where am I?

The view was breathtaking. Although the moon was high in the sky, I could make out every single detail. The stars twinkled in a way I had never seen before. I could see a river that ran fast and strong, with debris strewn through it, items that appeared to be pontoons with... I looked closer... Yep, that was a jetski on top of that pontoon.

What was going on? I couldn't recognise anything about my surroundings. Who am I? My thoughts were all over the place, and none made sense. I couldn't even remember my name, let alone how I got here, or where *here* even was...

"You're safe," a voice said from behind me. I turned quickly, backing up against the wall next to the window, staring at the man standing in the doorway. In one hand, he held a ceramic jug, in the other an empty glass, and he wore an expression that was a mixture of concern and relief.

I stared at him, taking in everything about him. He was familiar, yet I had no idea who he was. He was incredibly handsome, with a well-built, lean body and thick, brown hair that was so dark it was almost black. His piercing blue eyes were intense while he ran his gaze over every inch of me.

"I know you're confused at the moment. It will all come back to you soon. But you're safe here. You're with me. Liam..." His words trailed off, and somewhere within my mind, I knew that the name meant something to me. That *he* meant something to me.

He cautiously entered the room fully, placing the jug and glass on the bedside table. He moved towards me slowly, keeping his hands where I could see them. I watched him from where I remained pressed against the wall, still uncertain of everything.

"Isolde... I'm not going to hurt you."

Isolde... the name rang in my ears. A whisper of a memory pushed at my mind, pressing to be let in amongst all the other thoughts bouncing around inside my brain. He stopped in front of me, so close that I was forced to lift my face to look up at him.

He touched the side of my face softly, and the familiarity of his touch quickly squashed the urge to pull away, and a memory rushed to the surface. A memory of us standing exactly how we were now, my back against a wall, his face close to mine. With his fingers tangled in my hair and the need to be close to him. To be kissing him.

I gave in to that need now, wrapping my arms around his neck and pulling him closer while I reached to kiss him. He resisted briefly before relaxing into it, pulling me tight against him while he deepened the kiss, a hand tangled in my hair. His other hand moved across the small of my back, his fingers running lightly along the waistband of my jeans with such familiarity that I knew we'd perfected this.

The need to be closer to him grew more urgent, and I pulled him closer. His mouth moved away from mine to begin kissing my neck. As his lips pressed into my neck, another memory surfaced of his teeth sinking into my skin and the ecstasy of his bite. I moaned his name, gripping his shoulders as my memories came flooding back.

Liam pulled away and looked me in the eye.

"What do you remember?" He asked, and I could feel tears starting to form in the corners of my eyes.

"Everything," I whispered, my voice shaking.

He began firing off questions rapidly, gripping my shoulders tightly.

"Who are you?"

"Isolde Smith."

"Where are you from?"

"Brisbane... Australia."

"Who am I?"

"You're Liam—my boyfriend. Well, I guess you're my boyfriend. Boyfriend seems like a weird word for a five-hundred-year-old," I said with a small smile, but he wasn't ready to joke around yet.

"What else do you remember?"

I paused to gather my thoughts, looking at a spot on the wall as I worked through the fog as memories clicked into place.

"You have a twin brother, Connor, who is a nightwalker and one of the people responsible for my sister being turned," I said, pushing aside the pain that this memory caused.

Liam's jaw clenched before he slowly nodded.

"And they both tried to turn me into a nightwalker... But you saved me... Right?"

Liam froze then, and I knew I was missing something vital.

"Liam, what happened? Where are we? What am I?" My voice wavered, and I looked into his eyes again. "You didn't save me, did you? Or you tried... The last thing I remember is you saying you were sorry, more pain and then the sound of a car crash..."

The sadness in his eyes confirmed this, and I began to shake.

"I... I couldn't stop the change... You were already so far gone... I didn't know what you would be like when you woke up...." His voice was unsteady, and he brought his hand to my cheek.

Something else occurred to me.

"Can't you hear my thoughts?" I asked.

One of Liam's abilities was to read the thoughts of those around him. He often tried not to, in attempts to avoid invading the privacy of others, but he had always been in tune with me. The day before my abduction, I had begun to be able to hear his thoughts within my mind, having formed a spiritual bond with him.

My stomach dropped when I noticed I could no longer hear him either.

"I'm sure it'll come back...." His tone didn't give me much confidence that he genuinely believed that.

I pushed aside a burning sensation at the back of my throat.

"So that means...."

"You're a vampire, Isolde," a voice said, and Liam scowled, spinning to face the woman who entered the room behind him. She was petite, at least a foot shorter than myself, with long black hair and the striking blue eyes that each vampire had. She was beautiful, and her voice had a slight accent that I couldn't place.

"Eve," I whispered.

Although Liam had never spoken of her to me, I already knew who she was, though I didn't remember ever having met her. My emotions were swirling, and I could feel myself growing more on edge with each step that brought her closer to me. Liam stood before me, perhaps to keep the distance between us.

"You know who I am, don't you, Isolde?" Her voice was sultry, and there was something incredibly sexy about her. I'd never been attracted to women before, but something about her drew me in. Although there was nothing particularly threatening in her appearance, I could feel the magic surrounding her, and everything inside me screamed that she was incredibly powerful.

"How... How do I know you?" I attempted to step around Liam, but he put his arm out in front of me, forcing me to stay behind him while looking at her over his shoulder.

"Your mind will eventually begin to clear." She said with a shrug, not giving anything away.

I was growing frustrated by her nonchalance and Liam's defensive stance in front of me. I pushed against him, expecting some resistance, but was surprised when he moved aside, giving in quicker than he had ever done in the past. It was a moment before I remembered I had increased strength now, and he had moved more out of necessity than having given up.

I stood beside him as a fourth person entered the room. He was around the same height as Liam, though he was stockier. He had blonde hair and appeared a little rough around the edges, although I was more than sure that Liam could hold his own against this man should it come down to it.

That he was also a vampire was obvious, given the company he kept, but I felt the same familiarity with him as I did with Eve.

"Ronson," I said his name quietly, and the look Liam gave me out of the corner of my eye confirmed that I was correct.

"OK, seeing as no one appears to want to tell me how I know you two, can someone please explain where I am and what is going on?" I demanded, becoming aware of the change in my voice for the first time. I had always had a reasonably low voice, but now it sounded deeper, throatier.

"You are in my home," Eve replied, opening her arms wide while watching me intently. There didn't appear to be anything inviting about how she was looking at me. It was almost like being a bird in a cage with the family cat sitting across the room, flicking its tail from side to side as it worked out how best to get the bird out of the cage and into its mouth. Ronson's face held the same look, and I felt Liam tense up beside me, his hand reaching out to pull me behind him again. Despite the power I could feel surrounding Eve, I refused to allow myself to be intimidated by either of them, seeing as I had no idea what they believed I would do. I wrapped my hand around Liam's wrist and shook my head at him.

"And where exactly might that be? Are we still in Brisbane?" I directed this question at Liam, who nodded but never took his eyes off the others, his jaw clenched.

"A lot has happened whilst you were sleeping, Isolde." Eve gestured towards the window beside me, and I looked outside once more at the raging river.

"That's the Brisbane River? But I don't understand... I have never seen the River flow like that, and it is so high...." I watched a huge tree float past, the current forcing it to move quicker than I ever thought possible.

"The day that you were turned, the floods started," Ronson stated, speaking for the first time. He struck me as the silent type, speaking only when necessary.

"Everything has started now," Eve added.

I had no idea what she meant by that statement, and the way that Liam clenched his jaw next to me made it clear that he wasn't impressed with how this little meet and greet was going.

"I think you should leave now. Give Isolde time to adjust." Liam stepped forward and stared them both down. Eve watched me for a moment more before finally turning and indicating for Ronson to follow her. He shut the door behind him, and Liam turned to face me again.

"I don't understand anything that just happened," I said. The mess in my mind was starting to become beyond frustrating. I felt like I needed to shake my head to get the chaotic thoughts back into some order, but I knew that would be a useless effort.

I turned to the window, leaning against the frame, and stared into the darkness again. Liam came to stand beside me and pressed his hand lightly on the small of my back. I sensed he needed to touch me to ensure I was truly there.

"Where are we, Liam? I know we are in Eve's house, but where exactly is that? Nothing looks familiar," I said quietly. The fact that the river appeared to be taking over the city I loved probably wasn't helping me recognise any landmarks.

"We're in West End. Eve and Ronson set up residence here shortly after the Order did." I knew he meant that they moved here when I was born, and everything started to change. I turned to face him, leaning my hip against the window ledge. His hand moved, resting gently against my opposite hip.

"So they know about the prophecy? And what exactly is their part in all of this? What happened when I blacked out? I remember hearing a car crash." Liam reached up to push my hair off my face with his free hand, his eyes glistening a little as he took a deep breath.

"When I held you in my arms, all I could hear was your voice begging me not to let you become a nightwalker. To drain the blood out of you - what was left of it - was the hardest thing I've ever done, but you were going to die, and I couldn't let that happen. I couldn't let you become one of them. I couldn't lose you." He let out a ragged breath, and I slid my hand up to rest over his heart. "And then we were hit, and someone knocked me out and tore you from my arms. When I woke up, we were here, and Eve told me that it was her and Ronson that took us, that took you from my arms, and I didn't know if I'd succeeded in keeping you from the darkness. I've spent the past week watching over you, not knowing if you would wake up with evil inside you. To have you standing here in front of me like this, to know that I was able to save you, you have no idea of the relief I feel right now." His voice was thick as he pulled me to him and hugged me close.

I pressed my face into his chest, letting my tears stay hidden.

Because I didn't think he had saved me. Not really. I never wanted to be a vampire. Good or bad, this wasn't what I had ever wanted for myself. Although everything else within me was a confused mess, I was sure of that much. Feeling Liam's relief while he held me tightly filled me with guilt.

He pulled away slightly, lifting my chin and lowering his lips to mine. I let myself become lost in the sensation, the familiarity giving me a brief sense of comfort.

I felt myself sinking into his arms, but a memory that had been pushing at the back of my mind finally made its way through the chaos, and I was swept away to a place that I had never been before and yet knew so well...

CHAPTER TWO

I gazed into the firelight, attempting to process the information my mother had imparted earlier, when the sound of a booming knock on the front door caused me to jump. Who could be visiting at this time of night?

I followed Callum to the door, standing back while the servant unbolted the lock and pulled the heavy oak doors open.

I was struck dumb momentarily, unable to take in the vision before me.

It couldn't be. It just wasn't possible. After all these months?

"Connor?" I asked quietly, staring as my twin brother stepped across the threshold. He was accompanied by another man, both dressed in travelling clothes and wrapped in cloaks to protect themselves from the bitter cold.

"Hello, brother." Connor smiled, and I rushed forward to hug him fiercely, relief flooding through my veins. Pulling away from me, Connor continued to smile, turning to look back at his companion, who was still lingering on the stone steps.

"Liam, why don't you invite my companion in, out of the cold?" While the request was odd, I knew it would be bad manners to expect

anyone, even a stranger, to remain outside on such a bitterly cold evening.

"Of course, of course. Please come in. Any friend of Connor's is welcome here." I said, indicating to Callum to take their coats. Callum stood frozen, the door handle still gripped in his hand. I clapped my hands while Connor's companion stepped through the doorway, causing Callum to jump to attention.

"Callum, take their coats," I commanded, embarrassed, but Connor waved Callum's misstep aside.

"Callum, old man. It is so good to see you," Connor said. Callum stared at him open-mouthed, only answering once I'd cleared my throat.

"And you too, Master Connor." Callum's voice trembled slightly, and I knew I would need to speak with him about his strange behaviour later. I led the way back into the sitting room while Callum hurried off to fetch our mother, along with some tea to warm our guests.

Once seated before the fire, I gazed at my brother in wonder.

"Connor. Where have you been all these months? Father sent men out everywhere searching for you." I found something about the smile on my brother's face unnerving, although I could not put a finger on it. His companion continued to sit silently. His presence was off-putting while he looked around the room with a sneer.

"I apologise for the worry my absence has caused everyone. I've been off on a remarkable adventure," Connor said, his voice taking on an almost dream-like quality. I didn't know what to make of him. He appeared the same, but everything about his demeanour had changed... Although, upon closer inspection, I realised not everything about his appearance was the same. His eyes, once the same green-blue as mine, were now a piercing, almost glowing, blue. Not only that, there was something else in them that I could not identify.

I began to feel nervous while Connor continued to avoid answering my questions about his whereabouts, instead making polite conversation whilst looking around the room, clearly noting the changes I had made since our father's passing. He never asked about our father, leading me to believe he knew he had passed and did not care for specifics. His gaze fell on the stand in the corner where my Bible lay open, and he seemed to be resisting the urge to say something about its presence, which I found odd. He had always respected my devotion to the Lord. Like I had overlooked his dalliances with whichever woman he was courting at the time.

I shook myself from my musings, looking up to see our mother run into the room in a most unladylike manner. She came to an abrupt halt just inside the door, staring at Connor. Unlike the joy I had expected, something else was written on her face.

"Connor, is it really you?" She whispered, her brown hair escaping from under her nightcap in wisps, making her appear dishevelled.

"Hello, Mother." Connor rose to his feet and moved towards her, his arms outstretched. She stepped back, and I noted her expression was the same one that had appeared on Callum's face. I could not see Connor's face, but I assumed he still wore his eerily pleasant smile.

"Stay back. I know what you are." Mother's voice was forceful and took me by surprise.

"What am I? Mother, it is me, your son. I am Connor." Though he still had his back to me, his voice became mocking, and I raised an eyebrow.

"Connor is dead. You are a demon!" She screamed, backing out of the room before fleeing down the long hallway. I stared after her.

"Demon? What is she talking about, Connor?" I demanded.

Connor turned around abruptly, but it was to his companion that he directed his following words.

"Keep him here!" He commanded, and the man grabbed me so quickly it was as if he had been standing right behind me instead of across the room.

"What are you doing?! Unhand me this instant!" I struggled to free myself, but the man, who appeared to have brute strength on his side, was far stronger than myself, a man who had dedicated his life to books. Connor had left the room in pursuit of our mother. The man

held me in his vice-like grip, and I heard her scream. I pictured her cowering while Connor stalked her through the house.

Eventually, he reappeared, dragging our mother behind him, his arm clasped around her chest and shoulders while she struggled against him.

"What are you doing?!" I exclaimed. My assailant released his hold, tossing me roughly aside and moving back to Connor's side. My head hit the wall hard, and pain shot through my body. Connor threw our mother down on the chaise in the corner, and his companion moved forward to pin our mother in place. I was amazed at his strength, watching him while he held her still with only one hand. Connor's face remained twisted into the strange smile that sent chills down my spine as he leaned closer to her.

"Mother, that is no way to greet your long-lost son," he said, admonishing our mother, and despite myself, I gasped when she spat in his face.

"You are no son of mine! I know what you are!" She yelled, continuing in her attempt to break free. Connor casually wiped her spittle off his face with a handkerchief.

"Connor! I demand you tell me at once what is going on here! Why are you doing this?!" I hoped my voice sounded more commanding than I felt.

His smile was now fixed upon me, and I shuddered involuntarily. Mother's words from the night before came flooding back to me.

"You're a vampire?" I whispered, the fear beginning to rise within me.

How could this be true?

I struggled to get to my feet, but nausea rolled through me, dizziness overpowering me from the knock I'd taken to my head.

"Ah, so she's finally told you about your birthright." Connor grinned at our mother, watching her struggle to push his companion off. "It's about time, woman. Although I admit his ignorance and disbelief made all of this go according to plan, thank you for standing by your misguided loyalty to the precious Order. It's been most helpful."

Connor paused in his escape, staring back at me from the doorway. I could hear the yells of the mob, and some part of me knew that they would turn on me next. With a final, almost sad look, Connor turned and fled, and I stumbled out of the room through the opposite door, exiting the house through the servant's quarters. The mob had not yet reached the back of the manor, and I started running towards the woods bordering our property.

I ran for as long as possible, losing track of where I was and feeling lightheaded from the pain radiating from my head. Eventually, I came across what looked like an old, abandoned church. I had no memory of any church in the area, though I was grateful for its presence now as I collapsed on what was left of the altar. Exhausted and dizzy, I closed my eyes to keep the world from spinning above me.

A noise caused me to open my eyes, and I realised I was not alone. I looked up to find a woman standing over me. In my confused state, I couldn't quite understand what her expression meant, the pain in my head becoming more intense.

"You're injured." It wasn't a question, though I couldn't have answered her anyway, as I was too exhausted and weak. I could feel sleep taking me, and I closed my eyes.

I felt a sharp pain in my neck, and the world slowly turned black.

CHAPTER THREE

*T*he fog in my brain lifted, and I was back in Liam's embrace.

"You just saw one of my memories, didn't you? What was it?" His eyes searched mine while I struggled to comprehend what I had just seen. I shook my head slightly, and he tightened his grip briefly before stepping back.

"Well... Now I know why Eve looks so familiar... she was your sire...." I whispered, and Liam's eyes widened, hesitating before nodding slowly. I let out a long exhale, piecing myself back together.

"What was the memory?" He asked again. I tried not to read anything into the wariness that was evident in his voice. As though there were things in his past that he was concerned about me seeing...

"It was the night Connor and Adam showed up at your door," I said, returning to the bed to sit down.

Liam stayed where he was, looking down at me as I stared at my hands, trying to shake off the memory and return to reality, to myself, rather than seeing the world through his eyes. It was surreal to have someone else's memories running through your mind like they were your own. I was not fond of it. Would I eventually lose myself while I blended more with Liam? After all, I'd only been alive for twenty-five years, which was much less to remember than five hundred!

"You might have to be a bit more specific, seeing as, unfortunately, those two have shown up on my doorstep several times over the centuries, although all had similar outcomes...." His voice trailed off, and I saw that his face had taken on a distant expression while he became lost in the past.

"This was the first time. The night Adam killed your mother. The night you met Eve." Tears pricked at the corner of my eyes at the memory of watching my - well, Liam's - mother die. As if I was still there, and it had happened to me.

Liam sat beside me now, and I rested my head on his shoulder while he wrapped his arm around me, pulling me closer and kissing the top of my head.

"Is this what it's going to be like from now on? Remembering things from your past as if they happened to me?" The tears that slid silently down my cheeks were no longer for a long-dead woman but for the loss of yet another part of my world, the last vestiges of humanity that had now been ripped away from me.

"It eventually gets easier..." His voice was thick with emotion, and I knew that "eventually" would be a very long time.

"How do I stop myself from losing who I am... Or who I was?" I wanted to crawl into his lap so that he could wrap his arms around me and I could feel safe. But I stayed where I was, knowing that no matter where I was, safety would never be an option again.

"It's hard at first. But I'm going to help you. You're not alone, Isolde." He said, and I turned my face toward him and buried it in his chest, finally giving in to the sobs fighting to be released. He lifted me as easily as he would a child, and I ended up right where I'd wanted, in his lap, his arms around me, while I mourned everything I had lost.

I cried for what could have been minutes or hours. What was the point of keeping track of time when you suddenly had eternity ahead of you?

My sobs eventually lessened, and Liam held me close, running his hand up and down my back. His nearness still had the same effect on me that it had always had, and I was grateful for that small semblance of normalcy. I twisted slightly so that I was looking up into his eyes. There were so many emotions in his eyes, and I knew he was right there with me, ready to help where he could.

It was comforting to know that I would at least have someone who understood what I was going through, even if it had been centuries since he'd had to adjust to this life.

"I love you," he whispered against my lips, kissing me softly.

"I love you too." I deepened the kiss, reaching up to wrap my arms around his neck and pull him closer. It was like an emotional switch had been flipped within me. Where seconds ago I was filled with sorrow, I was now consumed with a burning desire to get as close as possible to Liam, to push aside everything else and concentrate on nothing but being able to touch him and have him touch me.

His hands gripped my hips when I straddled his lap, trying to ignore the burning at the back of my throat, which had grown steadily more insistent since I opened my eyes.

Liam began moving his lips along my jaw, and I tilted my head back to allow him access to my throat, closing my eyes and attempting to focus only on his lips. On his hands and the effect they were having on my body. But the burning wouldn't cease. My gaze drifted over his shoulder to the jug and glass that he had placed on the bedside table when he'd first entered the room.

Sensing the shift in my focus, Liam pulled back to look at my face, then turned over his shoulder towards where I was looking, cursing softly under his breath.

"You need to feed." He said, but I shook my head quickly.

"No, I don't want to stop. Just keep kissing me, please?" I begged softly, not ready to deal with it all. Liam hesitated momentarily, nodding slowly before pulling me to him again. I tried desperately to lose myself once more to the sensation of his lips pressing to my skin just below my earlobe, and his hands continued holding my hips, pulling me further onto his lap. I drew his lips back to mine and kissed him fiercely while fighting the urge to surrender to the burning. But Liam slowly pulled back to look me in the eye. I was breathing heavily and trying with all my might not to look at the jug.

"Isolde, the more you try to fight it, the worse it will be. We need to get some blood into you. Now," he said, and I finally allowed him to slide me off his lap and get to his feet.

Although I still shook my head, I knew that he was right. I couldn't think of anything else while my throat burned like this.

He walked around the bed and began pouring the contents of the jug into the glass. The hunger kicked up another notch while I watched the thick, red liquid slide slowly down the side of the glass. I clenched my hands into fists to keep myself from launching off the bed and ripping the glass from his hands.

Once the glass was full, Liam brought it back to where I continued to sit, breathing heavily while I fought to maintain control. He handed me the glass, and although I was beyond hungry, I stared at the contents, fighting an internal war within myself. I knew that I needed to drink it to rid myself of the uncontrollable hunger, but the knowledge that I was about to ingest blood voluntarily was something I couldn't get past.

"Who's blood is this?" I stared at the glass while Liam watched me closely.

"It's animal blood," he replied. That didn't make me feel any better, and I imagined Eve killing a poor, defenceless animal to drain it of all its blood. I don't know why I assumed Eve had provided the blood - I guess I didn't want to think of Liam killing animals. Let alone the idea of him drinking from a human, even if that person willingly allowed it, as I had occasionally done for him.

I gave myself a mental shake and slowly brought the glass to my lips, resisting the urge to gag as I took my first mouthful. It still tasted like blood, but instead of being repulsed by it, it was the most fantastic thing I had ever tasted. I knew that it was still blood and the fact that I needed to drink it was wrong, but that didn't stop me from draining the glass before handing it back to Liam and requesting another.

Once my hunger had been appeased, the realisation of what I had just done hit me, and I found I wasn't in the mood to return to our previous activities. Liam lay down on the bed and pulled me to him. I curled up in a ball and cried silently while outside, people went about their lives, and I mourned the life I had lost.

Hours later, I pulled myself together enough to ask questions that hadn't occurred earlier.

"Where are my parents? Are they safe?" Because they had once shared a home with Aurora and me, their house was no longer safe because Aurora didn't need an invitation. And neither did I. Vampires required an invitation before they could enter the threshold of any new dwelling that housed humans, but they could still enter any home they had previously resided in.

This same strange magic was the reason why I'd had to sell the townhouse that Will and I had bought together (I'd eventually burned it to the ground after the next occupants were murdered and a nest of nightwalkers took up residence), and Aurora and I had rented our dream home, which had turned out to be a safe house for the Order of the Dragon.

"Yes. However, your house and theirs have a few feet of water through them. So they are staying with Briseis."

"And what do they know? About Aurora and I, I mean."

"You've been exchanging messages with them, and they think Aurora is still in Sydney," Liam said, and I studied his face for a moment, the meaning behind his words slowly sinking in.

"You mean someone from the Order has been impersonating me on the phone?" I wasn't sure how to feel about that, though I knew there wasn't any other way to keep my parents from freaking out and taking out a missing person's report on us. Liam nodded, and I cursed under my breath.

"What about Jacob? Where is he?" Aurora's boyfriend had also been living with us, and I suddenly wondered how exactly I would keep Aurora's death and current undead status from everyone we loved. And my own, for that matter. Although seeing that I wouldn't attempt to murder everyone, I figured my secret would be easier to keep.

"Jacob received a text message from Aurora's phone, breaking up with him, telling him that she was planning on staying in Sydney indefinitely."

"That's a bit harsh," I said with raised eyebrows.

"Harsh, but at least he'll be safe now. I spoke to him on the phone when he called, looking for you. He's pretty torn up. He packed up his stuff the day after everything happened and moved in with a friend for the time being, but he was talking about moving back to Townsville to get away from here." That's where Jacob had grown up and his family remained. I was saddened by the knowledge that I wouldn't see him anymore. He had been a good friend and a great boyfriend for Aurora. However, I had learned in the hours before my untimely demise that Aurora had been in love with Will. So, the knowledge that Jacob had escaped without learning the truth was a small comfort.

"What about Ainslie? Last time I saw her, the Order was going to perform a memory charm so that she didn't remember any of the stuff from the restaurant?" I asked. When she had seen my "dead" fiance sitting just inches from her, my best friend of fifteen years had slightly freaked out, and Liam and I had been forced to tell her the truth, something that the Order tended to frown upon. But, given that I'd just seen my twin sister and realised she was now a nightwalker, I had lost all ability to give a crap what the Order wanted.

"Ainslie still knows everything we told her. Once she calmed down, Patrice talked with her, and Ainslie decided she wanted to join the Order." Liam said, and I raised an eyebrow. Although the Order had been made up of seventh daughters of seventh daughters and seventh sons of seventh sons, in recent years, with the size of families getting smaller, the Order had been forced to begin to allow civilians to join. Though they were kept in the dark about a large part of the organisation, they were called upon to help when more significant numbers were needed. They tended to be kept on a need-to-know basis, and none of them were told anything more than 'vampires are bad'. Although daywalkers tended not to be a threat to the general human population, Liam was the only one I knew of who worked side by side with the Order, and that was due to his history with them—from what I knew of his past, his time spent with the Order had caused others of his kind to steer clear. That is why he was the only daywalker I had met, although now I guess I could add Eve and Ronson to that list. If they were anything to go off, though, I wasn't sure I was ready to meet others. The idea that I was now one of them wasn't sitting well.

"I'm not sure I like the idea of Ainslie being involved with anything to do with the Order." I frowned, and Liam nodded.

"I know, I said as much to Patrice before everything turned to shit, but she pointed out that it was Ainslie's choice. She doesn't know about what has happened to you, though. The Order has been keeping tight-lipped about that." He ran a hand through his hair, and I noticed how exhausted he looked. This past week couldn't have been easy on him. He didn't require much sleep, but I sensed what little sleep he should have had eluded him while he struggled to keep my death from my family while anxiously waiting to see if I would wake up as an evil monster. I touched his face while he stared at the roof, forcing him to look at me while he continued lying on his back.

"Thank you for watching over me and caring for my friends and family." I kissed him softly before lying back down and allowing him to pull me close to his side again.

"I'd do it again in a heartbeat. I haven't seen anyone. It's all been over the phone. Although Eve and Ronson haven't technically been keeping me a prisoner here, there was no way in hell I was leaving you alone with them for even a second. I couldn't risk them disappearing with you to keep you away from the Order. I asked Gerard to leave a car nearby if I needed it." He gripped me tightly, and I could feel the tension in his body. I propped myself up on my elbow so that I could look at him once again.

"I'm here now. I'm not going anywhere. We'll sort out what we can - we always do. I love you. I'm realising now just how much I love you." I ran my fingers through his hair, and he closed his eyes briefly before pulling me down so that he could kiss me once more. I could feel his tension easing, and there was some desperation behind this kiss. His arms tightened around me, and I pushed every other thought aside, allowing myself to get lost in this moment with him, sighing while I sunk further into the kiss, and he wound his fingers through my hair. His other hand ran up and down my back under my shirt, his fingers lightly trailing a path along my spine, and I arched into his touch while he ran kisses down my throat.

"God, I missed you so much this last week. I don't know what I would have done if you had woken up as a nightwalker." His words were desperate, and I could hear the raw emotion in his whispered "I love you" when he rolled me onto my back and hovered over me, looking me over again. I saw the need in his eyes and raised my hand to his cheek. He leaned into my touch, closing his eyes, before turning to place a kiss on my palm. I moved to sit up, and he sat back, watching while I began peeling my clothes off frantically. He followed suit, and we were pressed together, skin to skin, holding each other close. I needed to feel every part of him against me. I needed him inside of me.

He moved down my body and used his tongue to trace a circle around my nipple while his hand worked its way between my legs. My back arched off the bed, his mouth and hand working in tandem. The sensation was like nothing I'd felt before when we were together, and I moaned, one hand clutching the sheet beside me while the other dug into his shoulder. My senses were heightened, and I could feel the orgasm building within seconds.

"God, Liam, please."

He moved faster, plunging two fingers inside me, rubbing my most sensitive spot firmly with his thumb and continued sucking hard on my breast until I exploded, crying out his name again.

Before I could breathe, he moved over and slid inside me with one fluid movement. I arched my back again and wrapped my legs around him tightly, drawing him in fully. I began rocking against him, urging him on while he hissed his approval and started moving with me.

"Tell me you love me," he growled, thrusting steadily, his eyes locked on mine.

"I love you." I moved my hips in time with his, and he groaned. I used that moment to flip us, rolling him onto his back and beginning to ride him, moving my hips while I ground down on him.

"Tell me you belong to me," I said, placing a hand on his throat, hips rolling faster until another orgasm began to build, even more powerful than before. He wrapped a hand around my wrist, using the other to guide my hips even faster, his gaze boring into mine.

"I'm yours, eternally fucking yours, Isolde. Now come apart for me." He moved his hand from my hip, and a single press with his finger just above where we were joined made me see stars again. He sat up to meet me when I collapsed into his arms. Gathering myself again, my forehead pressed to his shoulder while he guided my body to move up and down on him at a slower, more leisurely pace. I moaned, every movement overwhelming my senses.

Energy returning, I sat back up to look him in the eyes while I began rolling my hips again, and my gaze drifted to his throat. I wondered what it would be like to bite him like he had done with me in the past.

Taking one hand off my hip, he gripped my head, tangling his fingers in my hair, kissing me hard, stroking my tongue with his. I continued rolling my hips and gripped his face, needing to feel him against me.

He used his grip on my hair to pull my head back, and the protest

I was about to utter died on my lips when he tilted his head. I hesitated, and he tightened his grip on my head, pushing me towards his exposed throat. I ran my tongue along my teeth, feeling how sharp my canines suddenly were, before placing my mouth on his skin. I bit down, and he moaned, gripping my hips and rocking me faster while I continued to feed as we worked closer and closer to orgasm.

"Fuck, Isolde."

I felt him tightening and began to move faster than I'd ever moved before, rocketing us both over the edge.

Our movements finally slowed, and we collapsed onto the bed together, arms wrapped firmly around one another. I pulled my mouth away and brought my lips to his before pressing our foreheads together while we fought to steady our breaths.

"I could get used to that." I smiled at his words and opened my mouth to answer him, but a rush of memories hit me, and I felt myself collapse down on him.

CHAPTER FOUR

I watched her move slowly from room to room, checking to make sure there was no one in the house with her. I had silently guarded this woman from the shadows ever since she was born, yet it was like seeing her for the first time tonight. She had grown into a truly stunning woman, and the confidence in every action showed that she was sure of herself. It saddened me to know that within weeks, that would all disappear once the nightmares kicked in, the visions and the knowledge that all was not right with the world.

It had been so long since I had experienced the awakening, and I had only had a day of it. Isolde had months of it ahead of her until the Order could be sure she was ready. She had no idea that her entire world was about to change.

Will pulled up in his car and went inside. I witnessed their embrace at the front door and fought back the anger that was beginning to stir within me. I knew that Will had been seeing Aurora behind her back, attempting to experience the best of both worlds. I wished I could let Isolde know that the man she loved had, on occasion, spent time in another woman's arms. Her twin sister's arms.

But she didn't even know I existed. And so I remained silent, *standing alone night after night, always in the dark, always on the edge of her life looking in.*

The Order had so much invested in this woman that they had stopped viewing her as a person and saw only a being who needed to be prepared for the life they believed she was destined for.

I wanted to protect her from that so badly, yet I was powerless. My vampiric side stopped me from reaching the higher ranks of the Order. They were all trained to be wary of me, and I knew I was not truly one of them in the eyes of many outside my Manor. I was tolerated for my connections to the other daywalkers, but they, too, had become wary of me, believing me to be a turncoat.

I existed yet did not truly belong anywhere. But when I looked at Isolde, I felt like I had found my home.

"Isolde?" Liam was shaking me, rolling me off him and onto the bed. I shook off the remnants of the memory.

"You knew? About Will and Aurora? Why didn't you tell me?!" I demanded. Liam paused for a moment before answering.

"I didn't tell you because I didn't want to do anything that would sour your memories with Will. I know he did love you very much. As did Aurora."

I fought back the urge to take my anger out on him. I looked away from him for a moment and felt a strange sensation in my eyes. Almost like they flashed. Once I took a few deep breaths, I looked back at him again.

He watched me closely, and I nodded at him.

His response didn't make me feel even slightly better about the fact that my fiance and twin had been sneaking around behind my back, but I knew Liam wasn't responsible for either of their actions.

He kissed my forehead, and I allowed him to pull me close, drawing my back to his chest to spoon me. I forced myself to focus on those first traces of his feelings towards me that had stirred in that memory. The love that was buried beneath the protectiveness.

Sleep eventually claimed us both, but he kept his tight grip on me, even in slumber.

I awoke a few hours later, with Liam still asleep beside me, and finally allowed myself to remember the events of the last night of my human life. I recalled the moment when Liam's twin brother, Connor, had touched my forehead and unlocked memories that had been taken from me by the Order. I knew it had apparently been done for my own good, but the knowledge that my memories had been manipulated so that I would end up exactly how I was now . That wasn't okay with me. I was doing my best to ignore Liam's part in the web of lies, but I knew I would eventually have to ask him the tough questions. I had spent the past eight months doing everything I could to keep my family safe, only to discover that my sister becoming a nightwalker was all a part of the Order's end game. Their goal was for me to become a vampire, no matter that I didn't want that for myself, that I had begun to develop abilities without becoming the very thing I feared most.

I remembered the anger I felt when Connor had revealed the truth, the sudden loss of trust in the people I believed to be loyal to me, including Liam. The man with his arms around me had become my most trusted confidant in the past eight months, and in one moment, I learned that he may have been involved in keeping numerous secrets from me. About who I was and what I was apparently destined to become.

Although I loved him with all my heart, I struggled to accept that the lies had been for my own good. And my feelings towards the Order members who had been involved in this were doubly mixed, especially towards Patrice. The woman had become like a second mother to me, and to find out that not only had she known about the secrets and lies, but had been behind some of them... Let's just say I wasn't entirely sure if I was ready to face her yet.

My thoughts swirling in my head must have triggered something while another memory emerged.

"The prophecy must be wrong... Her powers were growing every day. I'm almost convinced she could take on Adam himself." I paced backwards and forwards in front of Patrice, where she sat behind her desk, shaking her head. I had been frantically attempting to get into Isolde's head ever since the team had called in that they had found the car that Isolde at her parent's house, along with Daniel, who was clinging to life while he gripped Celeste's body to him. I couldn't bring myself to mourn her death yet, the fear for Isolde overpowering everything else.

"The prophets have always held that her powers will be unbidden once she has become a vampire. But she must be the final twin to turn. It had to be after Aurora was finally turned, or it would have all been for nothing." I glared at Patrice, disgusted at the truths that had started to come out since Isolde left hours ago.

"The Order has been lying to her! Lying to me!" That my fate was tied to a prophecy I knew nothing about was just the latest occurrence to have me questioning everything I knew to be true about the Order.

"You knew there would be consequences when you started your relationship with her, Liam. You knew that there was an ultimate plan of the Order," Damon said from where he sat in the corner, and I fought the urge to throttle him. I had known this man for years but barely knew anything about him. Right now, I would happily beat him senseless.

"I didn't know anything about this, though! She is one of us! I can't accept that you were all sitting back, waiting for Aurora to be turned into a vampire before kicking this plan into motion!"

"If you do your part, Liam, she will be a daywalker like you. Then you can spend an eternity together once this war is won," Damon said with a smirk.

I couldn't believe he'd played that card. Patrice had the sense to look concerned when I continued to shoot murderous looks Damon's way.

"If I turn her, I doubt Isolde will ever want anything to do with me again. You know how the blood memories work. She will know everything, including all of the scheming the Order has been doing now. And that they sacrificed her and her twin sister to reach their ultimate goal." I couldn't stomach the idea of Isolde turning away from me.

"Well, who else would turn her, Liam? From what I understand, your contacts amongst the daywalkers are slowly drawing away from you. They don't trust you due to your connection to the Order," Patrice said, and I grimaced as I finally turned away from Damon to answer her.

"Eve would do it," I said.

Patrice raised an eyebrow.

"I highly doubt that the vampire who turned you would be the best one to turn Isolde. With the history between the pair of you? Doesn't Eve still hold out hope of you one day returning to her side? She turned you to become her lover, did she not?"

I felt uncomfortable having this conversation with Patrice. Few knew the truth behind my relationship with my sire, and I preferred not to think of it at the best times.

"If she knew the reasoning behind it, Eve would do it."

"I didn't realise you were still in contact with Eve. We need someone here now to do it." Patrice said, and I could hear her suspicions running through her thoughts.

"I don't know where Eve is now, but we can contact each other. If I needed her, she would come." That was a lie. I knew where Eve was. I knew Eve had always been nearby, keeping tabs on me. She generally left me alone, but I always knew she wasn't far.

"Have you told Isolde of Eve? How does she feel about her?"

I shifted uncomfortably, and Patrice didn't need me to respond.

"Ah, you haven't told her about your relationship with your sire. Tell me, Liam, what exactly do you and Isolde talk about, seeing that you haven't told her much about yourself?"

It was a question that Patrice didn't need me to answer. She was well-practised at lying.

Especially to Isolde.

I lay silently for hours, stewing on the memory of the woman I had come to trust so much, just casually discussing my transition like it was nothing. When the darkness outside gave way to the first signs of dawn, Liam finally awoke, and I could feel his eyes on me without even looking at him.

"Hey... You OK?" He rubbed a hand over his face before propping himself up on his elbow to look down at me while I turned to face him.

"Not really... Life just became beyond screwed up, and I've been lying here for hours mulling it all over in my head."

He exhaled, taking my hand in his and running his thumb in circular motions over the back of it.

"Anything I can do to help?"

"Take me home?"

An hour later, I stood in front of my house and felt as though my stomach was in knots. I had fallen in love with this house the minute I first saw it, and part of its appeal had been its proximity to the river... The same river that now lapped around my ankles, and this was apparently after the water had receded... The dirty marks on the outside walls were above the windows, indicating that the entire house had been close to being completely underwater. While the house was close to the river, it had been slightly uphill, so the fact that there was still water at my ankles meant that other places further down the street were still completely covered. And no one had gotten any of my stuff out, which meant all my belongings had been under at least eight feet of dirty, disgusting river water.

This was just too poetic. My life was technically over, so why not have all of my worldly possessions completely destroyed. Yeah, it was all still there, but it was all completely ruined, exactly like me.

Looking around me, I could see that most of our neighbours had had the chance to get most of their valuables to safety, but not us.

Liam stood next to me. He had seen the news reports, so he'd had some idea of what to expect, but it was still a whole different experience seeing it in person. And it was harder when it was happening to someone you knew, or yourself, in my case.

"Couldn't anyone from the Order have come in and saved at least some of my stuff?" I asked.

Liam hesitated before responding.

"Well, I guess they were more concerned with your condition..."

Meaning they weren't sure that it was worth saving my stuff in case I woke up as a nightwalker.

"Good to see they are no longer playing at the whole 'family' thing. Seeing that I know the truth now and all." I couldn't hide the bitterness in my voice, and the look on Liam's face told me that my comment had hit home. Usually, the idea of hurting Liam would have upset me, but the thoughts I had been suppressing all night, mixed with the sight of my home, was enough to have all my emotions on overload once more.

"Isolde -" Liam started to speak, but I raised my hand to stop him.

"Not now, Liam. Not a good time to start with me." I walked towards the front door, the water rippling around my ankles, leaving Liam beside the four-wheel drive. I unlocked the front door with his key, but the wood of the door was swollen, making it difficult to open. I rammed my shoulder against the door, and it popped open with such force that I had to catch the door with my hand to keep from falling into the house. Another memory kicked in when my hand connected with the door handle, and I felt myself slipping away into someone else's mind once again.

. . .

"You're going to propose to Isolde?" I struggled to process the bomb that Will had just dropped on me, cunningly disguised as a happy announcement. Will hadn't been able to look me in the eye since Jacob and I had sat down. Around us, people were chatting away pleasantly, unaware that my heart was breaking. I had been waiting for this day for years and knew that was where Will and Isolde were headed, but having it confirmed still stung like a slap in the face.

"Yes. I thought it was time," Will said to Jacob from where he sat across from my boyfriend, preferring to look at Jacob instead. Though how that made him feel any less guilty was beyond me. I had trouble looking at Isolde these days, and lying in Jacob's arms at night was like a knife to the heart. I loved my boyfriend, but he wasn't Will Blake. And he never would be. I knew that Will was telling us together so that he wouldn't have to deal with my reaction, aware that I wouldn't cause a scene, the web of lies around us far too tangled.

"Congratulations, man, that's awesome!" Jacob shook Will's hand, then grabbed his wallet off the table, "We need to celebrate. The usual?"

Will and I nodded at him, and Jacob wound his way through the tables towards the bar.

"So you're proposing to my sister out of guilt. Fantastic." My words were flat, and I began ripping up the napkin before me. I needed to keep my hands busy.

"It's not that, Aurora. I love her. You know that."

"I don't think you know what you want, Will. Because last week you were in bed with me, and this week you're proposing to my sister. We can't keep doing this!" I kept my voice low so that the people at the surrounding tables couldn't hear the traitorous conversation taking place in their midst. However, something in the way Will looked at me made me realise that things were different this time. There was pity in his eyes. He felt sorry for me! His following words confirmed it.

"You're right, Aurora... It's always been Isolde."

And there they were. These were the words that I had always known but never admitted to myself. I was the second-best twin. Although I was born first, Isolde always came before me with every-

thing. The brighter twin, the stylish twin. The twin who got everything without even trying. The twin who I loved with all my heart and who owned the heart of the man of my dreams.

"When are you planning to propose?" I tried to keep my voice from shaking, with limited success. I could see Jacob heading back to the table, his hands full of celebratory drinks... I didn't feel much like celebrating right now.

"Next Saturday."

"On my birthday..."

"It's Isolde's birthday, too, Aura."

For the first time since Will had chosen Isolde over me all those years ago, I had to resist the urge to slap him. I would have done, too, if Jacob hadn't chosen that moment to arrive at the table with the drinks.

It all started to come into focus. My feelings meant nothing to Will. For someone who appeared to be such a nice guy, he had no concern about ripping my heart out. It was all an act.

And this was the man who was going to marry my sister. I wanted to protect her from that, but any attempt I made to shield Isolde would ultimately lead to my deceit coming out. And I couldn't lose my sister. As contradictory as it sounded, her love for me was sometimes the only thing stopping me from completely despising myself.

Back in my own mind, I stared at my hand gripping the door handle, reeling at what I'd just experienced.

What the fuck was that?!

"Isolde, what's wrong?" Liam asked. I hadn't even noticed that he had come up behind me. I turned and stared up at him, and I could tell it was driving him mad that he couldn't hear what was going through my mind.

"I... I don't know what just happened..." I looked back down at the door handle and then at him. He narrowed his eyes while he studied my face.

"Did you have a vision?" He asked.

Before my turning, I had been developing psychic abilities and had visions triggered by touch. But the visions were usually linked to the location and the person, and that memory I'd just had from inside Aurora's mind had taken place before Will's death, before we'd ever entered this home.

"I just had a flash of one of Aurora's memories... When Will told her he was going to propose to me...." I was still staring into Liam's eyes, trying to understand everything.

"What? Aurora's memories? But... that's not possible..." Liam eyes drifted down to where my hand still gripped the door handle. I was surprised it hadn't exploded with the force I used to squeeze it. My knuckles had gone white.

"What is going on?" I asked.

Since I'd met him, Liam had always had the answer to everything. The look of utter confusion on his face while I looked to him for answers filled me with dread.

"I don't know... But, I know who might." Even before he said it, I knew what he would suggest and began shaking my head.

"We need to go and see the Order, Isolde."

"Absolutely not."

CHAPTER FIVE

Unfortunately, deep down, I knew Liam was right, and that's how I found myself sitting in front of the manor about twenty minutes later, glaring at the rundown ruin that it was glamoured to look like from the outside. Liam sat silently in the driver's seat beside me, letting me take the lead on how this would play out. Although it had been his idea, I knew he had reservations about being here as well and would only walk through those doors when I asked him to. I tried to focus on that devotion rather than on his acts of deception. He'd been almost as much of a pawn in the Orders schemes as I was—emphasis on the word *almost*.

The fact that we had parked out the front instead of driving into the basement car park was proof enough that Liam had no intention of staying here any longer than necessary to get the answers we needed.

I took a deep breath, opened the passenger-side door, and stepped out, hearing Liam follow suit from the driver's side. I waited for him to join me on the curb. He took my hand, and we both stared at the house together.

"A week ago, this place was my haven. Now I can barely stomach the idea of walking inside and facing those people." I turned to look at Liam, who nodded. For him, the betrayal was almost worse. Yes, the secrets kept from me were harder to stomach, but Liam had lived amongst these people for centuries and had treated most of them like family. With the deaths of Katyana and now Celeste, along with the betrayal from Patrice, I'd lost the last of the people I'd grown closest to, but Liam had long relationships with almost all of them.

"How many of them know the truth?" I asked.

Liam glanced over at me and shrugged.

"I honestly don't know. I've only been discussing logistics with them for the past week. I haven't seen them since Eve and Ronson took us, and I've only spoken to Gerard." The fact that he hadn't spoken to Patrice spoke volumes about how much he intended to turn his back on them all.

Nodding at each other, we headed up the stairs and stepped inside. The entry foyer was empty, but Gerard came out from the training room a moment later and greeted us.

"I was wondering how long you two would stand out the front. Welcome back. I'm so glad you're okay." His genuine smile while he scanned me from head to toe gave me a sense that not everyone was involved in the deception. Liam studied him briefly before looking at me with a subtle nod. I assumed this meant that Gerard didn't appear to be keeping anything from us.

"Thanks, I guess...." I didn't bother to cover the coolness of my tone. I still didn't trust anyone in this building, and Gerard's eyebrows raised while he looked between myself and Liam. Liam shrugged at him.

"Where are Patrice and Damon?" I asked as I fixed my eyes on Gerard, who looked like he was about to step back. He swallowed and continued to look between Liam and me for a moment.

"What's going on?" Barbara entered the foyer from the dining room, followed by one of the newer transfers from Europe, Christian. They both stopped to survey the scene before them. Everyone was suddenly on edge. It was hard to miss the anger rolling off both of us, given that we were both ready to explode.

"I don't know..." Gerard looked over at her before turning back at us.

"I'll ask again. Where are Patrice and Damon?" I asked quietly, and Gerard stood up a little straighter, his features hardening.

"What's with the attitude?" Christian asked, and Barbara elbowed him, silencing him. Liam growled quietly beside me, and I looked over at him.

"They're in the command room."

I could tell Liam had gleaned this knowledge from one of their minds, and I nodded, leading the way. I heard the others rushing to follow us, not willing to stay back in case trouble was about to start.

Patrice turned from where she was standing in front of one of the many monitors, and her eyes widened when she took in my entrance. I felt Liam tense beside me in the fraction of a second before I was across the room, stopping immediately in front of Damon, who stood beside her. My face was so close to his that I could feel his sharp intake of breath before his eyes narrowed and glared into mine.

"You know..." Patrice had the sense to look extremely guilty from where she stood at his side, making no move to help him.

"That the Order sacrificed my sister for your ridiculous prophecy? Yeah, I fucking know." I returned my gaze to Damon, taking note of the flare of his nostrils and the glances he threw over my shoulder toward Gerard, Barbara and Christian. I glanced back at them briefly. I could tell from their faces that this was news to them. None of them had known about Aurora's part in the prophecy, it would seem. Whether they knew I was meant to become a vampire remained unknown. I looked back at Damon, allowing every drop of anger to show in my eyes. For his part, he didn't back down, instead choosing to meet my gaze head-on.

"Let me ask you. What wins wars? Who is considered to be on the side of good? Those who sacrifice the one for the good of many, or the ones who sacrifice the lives of all to save the one?"

I saw red, and before anyone could react, including Liam, I had Damon pinned to the wall, my hand at his throat, and his feet hanging in the air while I inspected him like the bug that he was.

"Save me the self-righteous bullshit." I tightened my grip on Damon's throat, and he gasped for air, his eyes wide while his legs kicked wildly beneath him. "The Order is broken. Have you all forgotten why we are called the Order of the Dragon in the first place? It's because, in all the legends, Dragons were protectors! Has it been so long since you all read why the original order members banded together in the first place?!" A moment passed before I let Damon go, and he sank to the floor before me when I stepped back. I watched with disgust while he rubbed his throat, desperately sucking down air. "I can't believe I followed along when you were so willing to throw innocents to the lions for slaughter."

"Isolde, it's not like that." Patrice looked like she would try to play down their deceit, but she clamped her mouth shut when Liam and I turned as one to glare at her.

"I have questions, and you will be answering them," I said. There would be no arguing from any of them. If they considered telling me more lies, Liam would know, and I would take them down. The look exchanged between Patrice and Damon indicated they were fully aware of this.

"What do you want to know?" Patrice asked, and I looked at Liam for a moment. Although we could no longer read each other's minds, it seemed we were still in sync when he gave me a slight nod.

"Firstly, Liam can no longer hear my thoughts, and I can't hear his anymore either. Why?"

Patrice hesitated for a moment before answering.

"That is something I am not sure of. From my understanding, Liam has always been able to hear everyone's thoughts, correct?" She looked over at Liam, and he nodded.

"Everyone except Adam, Connor and Eve, that is." I wasn't aware of that and looked at him with a raised eyebrow. He shook his head quickly, and I returned my gaze to Patrice. We would be discussing *that* bit of information later.

"Fine, next question. When we were at my house just now, I had a vision. A memory of Aurora's. It occurred when I touched our door handle, but the memory wasn't from the house; it occurred before Will's death. Do you have any idea why my abilities would now be changing?" There was another exchanged look between Damon and Patrice, and I narrowed my eyes, turning to look at Liam while he watched them closely.

"We don't know... This is all unknown now. Now that you've transitioned, we have no idea what you will be capable of. Only that you will be more powerful than all of us combined." Patrice answered me finally.

"You sent me off into a den of vipers, and you had no idea what would happen to me?" I asked, my words coming out with a growl. My patience was wearing dangerously thin, and Liam stepped closer. "Not the smartest thing to do when you all knew how important my family is to me and the fact that I was apparently going to be so powerful."

"We had no idea they would get to you before we had a chance to have someone turn you into a daywalker." Damon had the nerve to speak once more, and I looked down at him to see him shoot a look at Liam, making it obvious who the *someone* he was referring to was. He still hadn't moved from where he had slumped to the floor when I'd let go of him. At least he'd had some sense, I guess. However, speaking now was a big mistake.

"You could have told me the fucking truth before I went to save my parents." My voice continued to be low and dangerous, and Damon recoiled, wisely choosing to remain silent once again, seemingly aware that one more word from his mouth may lead, at the very least, to more pain. I continued staring at him, and Liam reached for my hand, squeezing my fingers, perhaps sensing that my emotions were so heightened that murder seemed like an excellent option.

"You knew what I was walking into. Maybe not everyone." I

looked over at Gerard, Barbara and Christian. Gerard shook his head, his face showing his feelings about being left in the dark about the elders' plans. I looked back at Damon. "But you fucking knew. And you threw Aurora and me to the wolves." I turned and walked towards the door, stopping before I left and fixed a look back at them all. "I'm done being a fucking pawn in your little games. Before this is over, I will bring the Order to its knees." I sent Patrice a look filled with promise before turning and leaving the room, Liam close behind. I saw her shiver and relished it.

Fuck them all.

I entered my room upstairs and looked around, taking stock of what I had left there. Liam followed behind me and shut the door, sitting at my desk while I gathered everything together. There were a few dresses, some underwear and workout clothes. And my laptop. All that I had left.

Glancing over at Liam while I shoved the last of my clothes into a bag, I took in the look on his face—the wariness evident while he watched me move around the room.

"What is it?" I stopped before him, and he looked at my face, his eyes searching mine.

"I just don't know how to process all of this. Everything I knew to be true is a fucking lie..." Liam so seldom swore that I knew he must be reeling inside. I reached to touch his face, stroking his cheek.

"Welcome to my thought process for the last year," I said, and he held my gaze for a moment more before turning his head, kissing my palm, and standing up. He gathered me into his arms and squeezed me quickly before letting go and moving towards the door.

"I'm going to pack up my stuff. Stay here until I get back. The less we interact with everyone, the better, I think."

I nodded at him and took his place at my desk, turning on my laptop to check my messages. I had no idea where my phone had ended up, but my messages were linked to my computer, and I needed to get up to speed with the lies that the Order had been feeding my friends and family for the past week.

I scanned through the unanswered messages from several friends, surprised that anyone was still trying to reach out to me at this point. I had stepped away from so many people once the Order had come into my life. I felt a pang of regret at letting so many lifelong friendships fall to the side due to the Order and their lies. But I had felt safe here. Like I belonged.

I thought I had found a family.

Blinking back tears, I found the message trail between myself and Mum. Discussing the flood that impacted both our homes, the happenings with the family and her offers to have my sisters go to the house to get our stuff before the flood destroyed everything Aurora and I owned. When I saw that my response was that Liam and I were dealing with it, I growled. Not only had the Order fucked me over, but they had actively had my stuff destroyed. Rage boiled within me, along with the burning in my throat, and I wondered if Liam had been thinking of the others when he suggested we limit our interactions with them. I considered ignoring his advice, but then I saw a message from Mum that had come directly to my computer, not my phone, and I paused in my murderous thoughts to open it.

Mum:

Isolde, when you wake up, come and see me. We have things we need to discuss.

undefined

When I wake up? That seemed like an odd request.

The message had been sent this morning. I wondered why she'd sent the message to my computer rather than my phone.

I began tapping on the keyboard.

· · ·

Me:

Mum?
undefined
The little message bubble immediately popped up, almost like she had been staring at her phone, waiting for me to respond.

Mum:

Where are you? Are you with the Order?
undefined
I gasped and stared at my computer in stunned silence.

Was this some sort of trick? Another message from an Order member, continuing to pull strings to manipulate me and my life? I grew even more wary when another bubble popped up.

Mum:

Isolde, if this is really you, you need to come and see me. Your father and I are staying with Breseis and Dean. As soon as you can get away, come here.
undefined
What did she mean by, 'if this is really you'? How did she know that there was a chance it wasn't me when she was messaging my phone?

I didn't know how to reply, and I was still staring at my computer when Liam came back into the room, a duffle bag slung over his shoulder. Seeing the look on my face, he came to stand beside me and looked down at the messages on my computer.

"What the hell?" His words were barely a whisper while I watched him read the messages.

"Does my mother know the truth?" I asked, and he looked at me with raised eyebrows, shaking his head.

"No... At least, not that I'm aware of. This has got to be some kind of trick... We need to be careful, Isolde. I have no idea who we can trust anymore." The concern on Liam's face was evident. I nodded, looking back at the messages before shutting my laptop and putting it into the bag filled with what was left of my belongings.

"Where to now?" I was unsure what to do next, and Liam took my hand, leading me out of my room. I paused briefly, giving it one last look, saying goodbye to the room that had become my haven. I doubted I would see it again. Liam squeezed my hand, and I looked up at him.

"We go home."

CHAPTER SIX

ome was a large house, high on the hill in Ascot, overlooking the river and the city skyline beyond. I gaped at the beautiful home before us as Liam punched a code in on a panel at the gate.

"What is this place?" I asked, watching the gate slowly open in front of the car.

"My house," Liam said, looking over at me sheepishly.

"You have a house."

"I have a house."

"Since when do you have a house?!" I asked, and Liam chuckled as he drove towards a garage off the side of the large three-storey building.

"I bought it a few years ago. I needed somewhere to escape to when the house became too crowded. It all got too loud up here," he said, tapping the side of his head.

"Why didn't we ever come here?"

"Honestly, I rarely come here, even less so once we became involved. I didn't need to be alone as much once you came along." He smiled, and I felt myself melt a little at the sight of it.

"Does anyone else know about this place?" I asked. Liam pulled the car into the garage and pressed the button to close the automatic door behind us.

"No. This was the first place I ever bought for myself, and I just needed..." His words trailed off as we climbed out of the car.

"Something that was just yours?" I asked, looking at him over the bonnet of the car. He nodded with a small smile.

"Something that's ours, now."

I felt my chest tighten a little. *Ours.*

I let Liam lead the way inside from the garage and looked around in wonder. He watched me with a small smile as I took everything in while he gave me the tour.

Everything about this place reminded me of him. It was spacious, yet I noted the bookcases that lined the walls of almost every room except for the kitchen and several bathrooms—so many books. I could picture him sitting in any of the comfortable and mismatched armchairs spread through the house, book in hand, while he relaxed in the silence he so often craved.

The tour ended in the master bedroom that took up the entire third floor of the house. He dumped his bag in the walk-in wardrobe and came to take mine from me, dropping it next to his before returning to gather me in his arms. I breathed in his smell, allowing myself to appreciate this small moment of peace amongst all the chaos surrounding us. We hadn't spoken a word since we entered the room, and I was happy to stay silent a little longer.

"What do you need?" Liam whispered in my ear while he rubbed his hand up and down my back. His other hand rested against the back of my neck with his fingers tangled through my hair. I squeezed him tight, not yet ready to speak. I felt him nod before resting his chin on the top of my head. I appreciated him letting me sort through the mess in my mind. His soothing presence was a reminder of why I had fallen so hard for him, having always had the ability to provide me with an anchor amongst the raging storm around me. No matter what part he'd played in the Order's deception surrounding the truth about my future, he had always been there for me, his love unwavering.

After what could have been an eternity or mere minutes, I took a breath and stepped back to look up at him. The burning in my throat was quickly getting to a point where I could no longer ignore it, and something in my eyes must have given this away because he nodded and led me back down to the kitchen on the floor below.

"I arranged for some provisions to be delivered yesterday. I had no idea what would happen, but I had a feeling we'd end up here sometime in the next few days." He said, and I watched from a stool behind the bench while he returned to the garage again. I heard a fridge opening and closing before he returned carrying a large carton to the kitchen. Bringing it to the bench in front of me, he opened it, and I saw containers of blood inside.

"Who delivers cartons of animal blood?" I was intrigued about this side of his life that I had failed to ask about when I was alive, preferring to ignore that side of his world where possible. How naïve I had been.

"Daywalkers have contacts within the human world. A company arranges these sorts of things for us all over the world. The head of this company is a daywalker, but he does employ humans. They don't realise what the blood is used for, and he pays them well to ensure they don't ask questions."

I knew I had a lot to learn, but at this point, I was just grateful for the glass of blood that Liam had pressed into my hand. I drank it down and was relieved when the burning subsided. It was difficult to focus on anything else when my throat was on fire. When I'd finished, Liam took the glass from me and put it in the dishwasher. I watched while he finished his own glass of blood, the first I'd seen him have. He didn't seem to need it as often as I did. I hoped this meant that, eventually, the need for blood wouldn't be quite so overwhelming.

Our hunger sorted, I let Liam lead me into the lounge room and pull me down beside him on the couch. I snuggled into his side, and he wrapped an arm around me, holding me tightly to him. I let him draw comfort from me while he ran his fingers through the hair that fell down my back and side, something that he had often done over the past few months, and I'd come to take comfort from it myself.

After a few more moments of silence, he finally spoke the words I'd been avoiding thinking about.

"What do we do now?"

The fact that he was deferring to me concerned me. I had only been back for less than a day and had no answers to give.

"I honestly have no idea Liam. I need some time to sort through everything. To see what else is going to pop up in here." I tapped my temple, and he grimaced, understanding that I meant what other memories of his would surface.

He nodded and used his free hand to take mine, bringing it to his mouth to plant a kiss on the back of it, our fingers laced together.

"No matter what happens, what memories surface in there... I love you with all my heart, and I will be at your side," His voice was rough, and I sat back from his embrace to look him in the eye.

"I love you too. But we need to discuss some things, especially if I'm going to see things from your past that you might not want me to see."

Liam nodded after a moment, perhaps resigning himself to the inevitable and preparing himself for the truths he'd avoided for some time.

"Ask me anything. I won't keep anything from you anymore – you have my word," he said. I searched his face and saw the honesty there, the sadness that lay behind his eyes.

"How much of the truth about the Order did you know? About the prophecy? Or prophecies, as it turned out?" I allowed him to continue holding my hand whilst using the other hand to run his fingers through my hair. I sensed that what he would say would hurt and figured I'd let us both continue to draw comfort from those touches while he spoke.

"When I had that vision of you as a nightwalker, I spoke to Patrice. To ask her if that was a possibility. When she was answering me, a glimpse of the truth came through in her thoughts, and I questioned her on it. They had always told me that the prophecy was of a human who would have the power to end the war. I never questioned this, as when it was spoken about before me, no one's thoughts gave away any other versions of the prophecy. It seems as though certain members of the Order had become skilled at guarding their minds in a way I didn't know was possible. But Patrice slipped up. I found out the day after I first fed from you."

So he'd known for a few weeks and hadn't told me.

I felt my body tense up while I sorted through everything he had just said, and his grip on my hand tightened.

"I didn't tell you because I didn't want to believe it. And I only knew about the belief that you would become a vampire. I had no idea about the damn Gemini Prophecy." His voice shook at the mention of the prophecy that affected both of us. And our siblings alongside us. "If I'd known their plans for Aurora, I promise you, not only would I have told you, I would have been right by your side while you laid that place to ruins and told Aurora the truth."

I had felt that emotion when I'd seen his memory of talking to Patrice earlier and knew he was telling the truth. However, some of his other words prompted my next question.

"What other memories are you worried about? You told Patrice I would no longer want to be with you if I had your blood memories."

Liam searched my face for a moment before dropping my hand and getting up, going into the office that was off the room I currently sat in. I waited until he returned moments later, a book in hand. Judging by the worn leather binding, it was a very old book. I opened it up to see pages and pages of his handwriting.

"What's this?" I looked up at him. He stood before me with his arms hanging at his sides, his eyes downcast.

"One of my hundreds of journals. Start with this one. It will probably help trigger the memories. I have kept them all. They are in the study. I'll give you some space to go through them. Come and get me when you're ready." He dropped to his knees suddenly in front of me, knocking the book closed as he took my face in his hands and kissed my lips desperately, drawing my body into his and clinging to me. Almost as if he was attempting to give me something to hold onto before I stepped into the abyss.

Then he was gone, leaving me with the journal and the truths it and the others held.

I was suddenly wary of discovering things I'd rather not know. But I opened the book once more and began reading. Before long, I felt the now familiar sensation of being pulled into memory, and I closed my eyes, surrendering to the inevitable.

I slipped quietly from the bed I shared with Eve and pulled on my trousers. While I laced them up, I looked down at her sleeping form. In slumber, no one would ever know her true nature. Her mind was always one step ahead of everyone else, always thinking of some master plan. She claimed to love me, but it felt more like an obsession. Though deeply connected with her, I had no true love for her. Her memories had coursed through my veins while I lay dead. An eternity of memories now lay in my mind and my own of the last hundred and forty years. To know someone so wholly was something few could imagine. On a physical level, we worked exceptionally well together. But something was missing between us. I believed she'd lost the ability to feel love, and a millennia of walking amongst the human race had turned her heart cold. But I still yearned for what I once thought I didn't need. In life, I had believed that the love of a woman was unnecessary in my pursuit of the divine. After more than two lifetimes of experience, I knew that that wasn't so.

I stepped out into the cool night air, stepping around the drunk who had passed out in the doorway. If only he knew he'd chosen to fall asleep on the threshold of the home of vampires... The knowledge of our existence was still just as prevalent as it was one hundred and forty years ago, but I had left the backward thinking of the Estates long behind me. Eve had homes in many places throughout Europe, though we currently presided in her London base. I also kept a room with the Order in their Headquarters, but being around them too often made me miss my humanity, and I tended to become far too melancholy around them.

I walked past the Tower of London and couldn't help but marvel at its ability to send shivers down my spine. So much death had occurred there. I had only once been within its walls, at the beheading of Anne Boleyn. It had only been a few years after I had been turned. Eve had known Anne and her sister Mary before they became favourites of King Henry VIII and had watched with a morbid fascination while Anne rose far beyond her station in life to become Queen of England. But what goes up must come down. And she had fallen hard. I never knew if the accusations of witchcraft and adultery were true, but Eve had insisted on being there to witness her beheading. Having been close enough to have had some arterial blood splash on me after the axe fell, I felt her terror in the moments leading up to her death. I found my psychic connection with blood to be a rather heady experience. After that particular memory, I found it difficult to be near the Tower and its ominous presence. But it lay between myself and my destination, so on I went, ignoring the ghosts that I knew walked within its walls.

I continued down Eastcheap, finally reaching Pudding Lane. Like every night for the past month, a candle burned on the window ledge of the bakery. I smiled, feeling a warmth I'd now grown used to. After over a century of feeling nothing more than a vague interest in women, I believed that romantic love was only something from fairy tales. Now I knew that it had been because I had yet to meet the woman for whom all time stood still.

It had been three months ago when I first met her. I had been reading a book in a small park near where I now stood. It had been a warm afternoon, and I had looked up to see a young woman sitting on the bench beside me. She had some mending with her, and I could tell from her hands that she was working class, though she held herself like a woman far above her station in life. While I returned to reading Utopia, I found myself distracted when she began humming softly to herself whilst her hands worked away. Eventually giving up on the make-believe world of Sir Thomas More, I struck up a conversation with her. Intrigued by her intelligence, rare in a woman from the lower classes, I had lost myself in the conversation. Her name was Isabel, and she was a maid for the King's Baker, Thomas Farriner. She had lost her father and brother in the Great Plague, and her family had fallen below their station. As she was the only person able to support her mother and remaining siblings, she worked seven days a week, though Thomas gave her Sunday mornings off to attend Church. I had smiled at that, knowing she was meant to be at Church now.

"Oh, but it was just too nice a day to be cooped up in Church. God will forgive me just this once. And I had so much mending to do anyway."

She returned the following Sunday. And the next. I doubted she had set foot in that Church once since the passing of her father and brother, using those mornings off to have some time to herself instead. It was refreshing to meet someone who rebelled against the doctrines of the Church, yet at the same time, the small part of me that still remembered the need to spend Sundays communing with the Almighty thought she was being careless with her immortal soul. I knew my fate was to spend eternity roaming the Earth, never standing before the Gates of Heaven. But she shouldn't have to miss that.

I discussed many things with her - philosophy, art, and religion. Her father had been a scholar, responsible for her education, which was usually overlooked in daughters. Many a day, she had sat at her father's knee while he read to her from the writings of Aristotle and his contemporaries.

I had started to look forward to our Sunday morning discussions, and when the first Sunday came that she did not appear, I found myself seeking her out at the bakery that night. It was her job each evening to ensure the fires were put out, which meant she was the last one there every night. It was that night that I realised what my true feelings were for her. To discover that she, too, felt the same way was beyond comprehension. She had not come that morning, as she feared that her feelings for me were inappropriate and thought it best that she not see me. But when I found her alone that evening, our mutual attraction was something that the two of us could no longer deny.

The first kiss had been like nothing I'd ever experienced, alive or undead, and I knew she, too, felt the connection between us. I had returned every night since, and tonight was no exception.

Isabel was busy with the ovens in the back, and I let myself in, playing absently with the flower I had snatched from a nearby garden along the way.

"Liam, is that you?" Isabel entered the main room, and I smiled at the flour in her hair and all over her clothes. She was still the most beautiful woman I had ever met, even covered in flour. And I had met a lot of women. She had long auburn hair, beautiful green eyes, and a creamy, clear complexion.

She smiled coyly at me then, and I realised I had been staring at her. Wordlessly, I handed her the flower, and she kissed me softly. I pulled her close, kissing her hungrily. She kissed me back with the same fierceness, the kiss growing deeper and hungrier. At that moment, I realised we were about to cross the invisible line we had drawn. We had never kissed like this before, with such abandon, and I wondered if I should stop this before things went too far.

Isabel never stopped, though. She was the sort of person who, once they made a decision, there was no turning back. When we shed our clothes, I was determined to make her first time as memorable as possible, pleasuring her in ways that had her coming apart in my hands and against my lips, eliciting moans she had no idea she was capable of. I revelled in the thoughts that cascaded through her mind while I brought her to orgasm as often as her body would allow.

Afterwards, when we lay beneath the window, our arms wrapped around each other, I wondered if I would ever feel this content again.

But I was only given that one brief moment to ponder this.

"Oh, my dear brother. How touching it is to see you with a woman finally. Aside from Eve, of course, though I don't think she counts." My head snapped up to see Connor lurking in the doorway.

Over the past century and a half, I had often crossed paths with Connor. Always the antagonist, Connor was prone to appear when I least expected it, catching me off guard and proving to me just how much of a monster he had become. I had witnessed the massacre of many people at the hands of himself and his followers and had fought against them so many times in this endless war between our two bloodlines.

I leapt to my feet, placing myself between Isabel and Connor. Isabel attempted to cover herself while Connor leered at her, looking her over with appreciation.

"I must say, Liam, you truly have impeccable taste," Connor said with a laugh, and I growled. Isabel pulled her dress back on and stood slightly behind me, getting her first good look at our intruder. She gasped, looking between us, seeing the identical features. Her thoughts were chaotic while she took in the predatory look in my brother's eyes and sensed that something wasn't right with him.

"Liam. What is going on? Who is this man?" She asked, her voice higher than usual, and Connor smirked.

"I'm hurt. Although, I'm not surprised that he has not mentioned his twin brother. He is so very ashamed of me."

"Liam?" Isabel repeated my name, her eyes still locked on my twin.

"Am I to understand, dear brother, that you haven't told your lover the truth of who you are?" Connor's eyes glinted in the moonlight, though the startling blue glowed, even without the help of light.

I glared at Connor, seeing Isabel swallow hard and begin to back away out of the corner of my eye.

"What are you?" I looked over at her and realised it wasn't my brother causing her to begin to flee, with her gaze now fixed on me.

"Isabel, don't be scared. I swear, you have nothing to fear from me."

She shook her head.

"No. Something is wrong here. Tell me what you are!" She demanded.

"Oh, this is fun! Go on, Liam. Tell her what we are." The sound of Connor laughing again set my teeth on edge.

"You and I are nothing alike, Connor. You are a creature of pure evil." I glowered at him.

"I doubt that will matter to your true love. A vampire is a vampire to the human race. They don't understand the difference. If there truly is any." Connor shrugged, and I wanted to punch him even more than usual.

"Vampire." I heard the word escape Isabel's lips, though she had barely whispered it. I heard the fear and realisation in that one word and saw it pass over her face. I felt my heart tighten as though someone gripped it tightly in their fist.

"Isabel, I can explain." I reached out to her, but she recoiled from me.

Like my touch would burn her.

"No, stay away from me!" The fear was written all over her face now, her eyes searching wildly for a means to escape. She ducked past me and ran up the stairs to the house above, unknowingly fleeing to where I could not follow, having not been invited. Every crashing footfall on the stairs was like a knife thrust into my chest, and I struggled to contain the emotions running through me.

"Oh, dear. That didn't go so well." Connor's words brought me back to myself, and I turned on him in a blind rage. He didn't expect the fury of my attack and fell to the ground in surprise while I punched him with my fists mercilessly. I saw an expression cross his face that I couldn't place before he threw me off and jumped back to his feet, towering over me when I slumped against the wall, my rage giving away to despair.

"Why do you insist on ruining everything!" I wished the words had not escaped my lips, yet the sneer I expected did not come.

He stood, looking at me with the same expression I'd seen moments ago. Was that pity? Remorse? It wasn't possible. Nightwalkers weren't capable of such emotions. Whatever it had been, it was gone instantly, and I knew I must have imagined it.

"Life never goes according to plan, little brother. You should know that. I stopped her from making the biggest mistake of her life."

"Since when do you care about the lives of humans?" I asked, and Connor shrugged, not bothering to answer, before he turned and walked away.

After what felt like an eternity, I got to my feet again. I had been undressed throughout the entire exchange, and I struggled to put my clothes back on before fleeing into the night, wanting to put as much distance between myself and this place as possible.

I spent the next few hours stalking through the shadows, wavering between anger and despair. After a while, I realised that the night's noises were louder than usual, and I pushed myself out of the dark cloud I was in to realise that the noises I heard were not the typical sounds of the dark streets of London. I could hear voices raised in fear and people yelling—the sound of fire crackling. I looked back the way I had come and saw a bright glow in the distance. From where I stood on Tower Hill, I could see a great ball of fire. It spread from building to building at a speed I could not comprehend, and I realised that Isabel was right in the middle of it all. Fear, unlike anything I'd felt since the night my mother was murdered before my eyes, crashed over me, and I began running towards the flames. A crowd of people met me when I drew closer, fleeing from the path of the fire. The crowd was too strong, and I was swept away with them, unable to return. But I knew in my heart that it was too late. If what I was hearing was true, that the fire had begun at the bakery, then this was all my fault. Isabel was most likely dead, destroyed in the fire, when an unattended oven had set the bakery and surrounding buildings alight. I couldn't bear the agony that tore through my heart.

* * *

I felt the journal slipping from my fingers while I came out of the memory. The knowledge that Liam had somehow been responsible for the Great Fire of London rocketed in my head. With a shaky breath, I reached for the journal where it had fallen onto the floor, being pulled into another memory as my fingers brushed the cover.

But the memory was not one of Liam's.

CHAPTER SEVEN

I looked down at my brother's face while he slumped against the wall where I had just thrown him. I had taken every hit from his fists and willed myself to fight back, but I knew I deserved every blow he had rained down upon me. I followed his gaze to where he stared at the stairs that his lover had run up moments ago.

I knew I was supposed to relish the agony I had caused him, but I felt only remorse. Every exchange between myself and Liam this past century and a half had been bittersweet. Seeing my once devout and sheltered brother step into the real world and experience things he would not have done if I hadn't made the choices I had gave me some joy. Still, knowing that he and I were destined to continue to walk for hundreds of years across this wretched planet, mortal enemies instead of allies, was a lot to stomach. Sometimes, I wondered at the decision I had made all those years ago. At the path I had chosen for us both. To begin a chain of painful yet necessary events. Or so that witch had said. I had often replayed the words whispered to me long ago on a night in an abandoned Church. Of a destiny that I was told belonged to me. To me and Liam. To two women yet to be born.

Moments like this made me wish to go back and make different choices. But of all my powers, the ability to change the past was not one of them.

I shook my head. The fog that had descended with the memory that didn't belong to Liam finally lifted, and I stared at the journal in my hand. How had I just seen Connor's memory? And what *was* that? It didn't seem like the sort of memory that belonged to a creature of pure evil like the one I had met—the one who had turned my twin sister against me and fed upon me with delight.

I sat on that couch for hours, surrounded by Liam's journals, immersing myself in his words. I tuned into the memories that each one triggered within me until I had trouble discerning where he ended, and I began.

There was still so much I didn't know, but I had seen enough for the night, and although I felt a deep resentment growing for Eve, I had yet to come across anything that made my feelings for Liam disappear. If anything, watching what he had been through, at how every potential relationship had been destroyed by either Eve or his brother, made me love him more. For his resilience in surviving the last five hundred years, watching members of the Order that he had grown close to grow old and die eventually. My heart broke knowing how alone he felt amongst the daywalkers due to his ties to the Order.

It was all a lot to take in. For him to have continued to be the man I had grown to love, to retain the ability to love so wholeheartedly and allow me into his heart... It wasn't anger that filled me now, only compassion and love.

I was sure I still had yet to see many things, but I craved his closeness now more than the need to learn more about his eternal life.

Rising from the couch, I went looking for the man who held my heart so tightly, finding him brooding while lying on the bed, staring at the ceiling. I came to stand by him, and the look on his face when he looked at me felt like someone had taken my heart in their hand and squeezed it so hard that it might explode. He was so convinced I would turn against him, believing himself to be unloveable because of several lifetimes of choices he had been forced to make.

I reached down and ran my fingers gently through his hair, and he closed his eyes, leaning into my touch.

"Look at me, Liam."

He opened his eyes and looked into mine, both of us able to see each other clearly despite the darkness that had fallen. One of the advantages of being a vampire was that I would no longer need to bother finding a light switch at night. He searched my face while I continued running my fingers through his hair.

I searched for the words to give him some comfort that my feelings hadn't changed.

"Nothing you have seen and done will change my love for you. I see you, Liam, and I do not turn away from everything you are."

He sighed quietly and shook his head.

"You have only been in there for a few hours. There is no possible way you could have seen every bad decision I've made. Every life I've ultimately been responsible for ending. All the people hurt either by me or because of me."

He truly believed that he was not worthy of my love.

I felt my heart break a little at the resignation behind his words and knew that nothing I said could change his mind. So I decided to show him in the only way I knew how.

I moved to lay on top of him, and although his expression didn't change, he reached around to hold me against him, anchoring my body to his. I placed my hand against his cheek, forcing him to continue looking me in the eye while my other hand returned to stroke his hair. I rested my forehead against his, and we both closed our eyes, taking comfort in the closeness. A sense of peace settled over me. The rest of the world ceased to exist, and it was just us.

"You are my world, Liam. Yes, I'm sure there are moments in

your past that you aren't proud of. Choices that you have made that may hurt me. But what we have, what this is between us... It's the truest, most genuine feeling I've ever felt. I choose you, Liam, regardless of any ridiculous prophecy that has been uttered about us. Despite every heartache that we have both experienced. I choose you." I moved my hand from his cheek to touch his chest, covering the place where his heart was still beating by some miracle. Beating for me. "I choose this." With my heightened sense, I could hear his heart beating quickly, and I opened my eyes again, finding him looking at me. The love he felt for me shone through unshed tears. He released a shaky breath, and his lips met mine in a slow, tentative kiss. I deepened the kiss, and we continued like there were no outside pressures.

As though we had all the time in the world. Where earlier, our joining had been filled with need, this was to be slow and full of love.

He rolled me gently onto my back and began moving his lips down my body, reaching down to pull my top up. I sat up to remove it and unhooked my bra, watching him remove his shirt with one swift tug over his head.

His mouth returned to my collarbone, and he eased me back onto the bed, moving his lips slowly down to my right breast, sucking gently while I let out a whisper of a moan and ran my fingers through his hair. His eyes met mine while he ran his tongue over my nipple before moving to the other side and giving the other breast equal attention. I arched into his touch, and he chuckled, sending a shiver through me.

I wondered if I could come just from the attention he gave my breasts. He seemed intent on finding out while spending more time on my breasts than he had ever done before, and I was panting with need by the time he started moving down my body.

He moved between my legs, kneeling on the floor and pulling me gently towards the edge of the bed. He began undoing each button on the opening of my jeans before raising my hips so that he could slide them, along with my underwear, down my legs and leave me bare before him.

I raised myself onto my elbows to watch while he placed both my legs over his shoulders and lowered his mouth to the bundle of nerves between my legs. I gasped at the first contact, my head falling back when he began to work me up with his tongue.

It wasn't long before I was moaning in ecstasy as the first orgasm began rolling through me.

I met his mouth with my own when he stood up and bent over to kiss me from where I half sat up, the shock waves still running through me and causing me to shiver uncontrollably.

He moved his hand to continue where his lips had been only moments before, circling with his thumb and thrusting inside of me with two fingers. At the same time, his mouth returned to my breasts again, moving slowly from one to the other while I writhed beneath him, panting loudly and gasping as another orgasm built within me.

"Come undone, Isolde." His words vibrated against my breast while he continued circling it with his tongue, and I did just that, crying out when I came again. Slowly, the ringing in my ears and stars in my eyes cleared. I met his gaze while he looked down at me, his fingers still inside me to give me something to ride out the wave of ecstasy on.

"You're wearing too many clothes." I sat up and began undoing the fly on his jeans, and he shed them quickly. I ran my hand down his erection slowly and began pumping my hand up and down, intending to take him in my mouth. He shook his head, pushing me back onto the bed and helping me shimmy back up so that he lay on top of me, nudging my entrance when I wrapped my legs around him.

"I just need to be inside you now." He pushed slowly into me, and I arched my back to meet him. He moaned quietly when I used my internal muscles to squeeze gently, but he didn't move, instead stopping to look into my eyes. He lowered his lips to mine and kissed me softly with the first roll of his hips, and I felt my eyes roll back in my head at the feel of him inside of me. At the pleasure that bloomed with every, oh so slow thrust.

"Every part of me, Isolde. Everything. It's all yours." He whispered the words between the gentle kisses he moved down my throat between each thrust. I rolled my hips to meet each one, the two of us in sync.

It was like our souls had melded and become one. I knew every movement he would make before he made it, and my love for him grew stronger with each roll of our hips.

"I love you, Liam. You're mine." I claimed him with those words, and he slowly picked up the pace, almost like my words had broken the last wall within him.

I met him repeatedly until we came together with one final thrust, and our lips met again when we moaned in unison.

We stayed like that for the longest time, and I returned my hand to run my fingers through his hair again, our foreheads pressed together while we remained joined.

"Hold onto this moment, Liam. Keep it in your heart, like I will. This is real. This is us." I kissed his lips, feeling him nod while he kissed me back.

"I love you, Isolde." He pressed a kiss to my forehead before rolling off of me. We showered together in the large bathroom attached to the master bedroom before settling back on the bed together, foreheads touching, with our arms wrapped around each other and legs tangled together. As we fell asleep, I felt the now familiar sensation of slipping into a memory.

"So, you've awakened." Liam stood before me, and I looked around, unsure of where I was or what was happening.

"What do you mean? You've been with me all day."

His laugh was low, the sound familiar, yet not one I'd ever heard from the man I loved.

"Connor." I took a step away from him. He smirked at me before sketching a low bow.

"In the flesh... well, not really, as this is a dream. I believe in the present you are currently lying wrapped around that dear brother of mine, having both exhausted yourselves thoroughly after constantly comforting each other that your love is eternal, and so on." His words were meant to be scornful, and yet I sensed something else behind them. I ignored the curiosity I felt at him knowing what was happening in the real world, and instead studied him closely while he continued to watch me.

"You sound like you might be jealous, Connor." I raised an eyebrow.

"Hardly," he said with a scoff. Although he waved the words away, I could sense the truth and found that interesting. Everything I had come to understand about the man before me led me to the conclusion that nothing of the brother Liam had loved remained. And yet, there was something beneath the surface.

I could tell this interaction wasn't going as he thought it should, and he glowered at me for a moment. I felt my lips curl up, delighting in the knowledge that I had unsettled him in a way he wasn't expecting.

"What can I do for you, Connor?" I noticed that the room we were in was the one we'd been in when he and Aurora had fed on me. My eyes fell on the chair I had been tied to before breaking out of my constraints and then roamed to the wall they had backed me against when they'd fed on me together. I could tell that he had chosen this location to rattle me, and I wasn't going to allow him the satisfaction of knowing he had succeeded. I returned my gaze to him while I moved to sit on the chair, spinning it to sit on it backwards, and I smirked at the look that skittered across his features before the mask of evil fell over his face again.

"Just thought I'd see if this connection was in place, as I'd planned. That my mind had connected with yours."

I raised an eyebrow when he crossed his arms and leaned back so his butt rested against the table behind him while he studied me. It was a *move I had seen his brother do countless times, and I found it very unsettling that even after all this time, their movements and mannerisms were still so similar. And that I seemed to find him just as attractive as Liam.*

"I'm not a nightwalker if that's what you were coming to see." I had no idea what he was doing, so I took a stab in the dark.

He just smirked back, continuing to run his gaze over me.

"Aren't you? It doesn't seem like you're entirely a daywalker, either. I can sense the difference in you that I think you've already started to notice. The hunger for blood is more pronounced for you than for Liam, isn't it? Your anger is just a little bit faster and stronger than his towards those who have kept so many things from you both. You enjoyed pinning that asshole to the wall earlier. Relished the rush of power you felt while you watched him gasp for air and knew you could end his life."

I stared at him, maintaining the mask on my face that gave an air of boredom, but inside, I was shaking.

His smirk grew, and his eyes flashed, no longer blue but the same brown I had noticed previously—one of the many confusing things about this man.

"We're done with this conversation." I got to my feet and willed myself to wake up. Connor chuckled, remaining where he stood and nodded.

"For now. Sweet dreams, Isolde. I'll be seeing you."

The dream around us faded, and I woke suddenly, briefly disorientated, before I burrowed closer to Liam's chest and allowed him to hold me tighter in his sleep. It was a long time before I could close my eyes again, unable to shake the truth of Connor's words and not liking what they meant.

CHAPTER EIGHT

"Ok, we need a plan." Liam stood before me in the kitchen the following day, leaning back against the kitchen bench in a stance that was eerily similar to the one his brother had used in the dream the night before.

"I honestly have no idea what we should do next. Our list of allies has rapidly shrunk to the two people in this room." I said, and Liam grunted in response, nodding.

"I don't trust Eve and Ronson, and I sure as fuck don't trust the Order. But I need to see my family and make sure they are safe from Aurora, at the very least. And get in touch with Ainslie because I don't want her involved with the Order in any way." I needed a drink. Everything was a mess. "I can still drink and eat, right? Something besides blood?"

Liam nodded towards what I assumed was a liquor cabinet. I strode over to open the doors and was pleased to see a wide array of alcohol.

"Bit early, isn't it?" He raised an eyebrow when I poured myself a shot of whiskey.

"It's required right now. I need something to take the edge off." I threw my head back with the glass at my lips, welcoming the burning in my throat from something other than a need for blood.

"OK, so the immediate plan," I said as I clinked the glass back down on the bench, staring at it while I tried to sort through my thoughts. "We go and see my Mum and Dad. After we work out what to say, that will lead to them never setting foot inside that house again so that there is no risk of Aurora getting to them." Thankfully, Aurora had never lived with any of my sisters outside of Mum and Dad's place, so they were all safe at home, at the very least...

"How about the truth?"

I whipped my head up to look at Liam. Since we had met, it had been all about keeping the world of vampires a secret.

"The need to keep vampires a secret is all from the Order. Daywalkers couldn't give a shit if humans knew about them. They go about their lives. The Order's mission has been to keep humans in the dark, to keep order and control the narrative. I've been doing a fair bit of thinking over the past week, and I'm done following the party line. If telling your family the truth is what it takes to keep them safe, then that's what we'll do."

"Thank you." I felt love for him swell inside, and I wrapped my arms around his waist.

"But, we may need to use some of the Orders resources, as much as I hate to admit it," he said, and I growled against his chest. He put his hands on both of my shoulders and squeezed. "I know, but they can make the issues with the house side disappear. They have connections everywhere, and although I am still incredibly angry with Patrice and especially Damon, we need them for some things."

I disagreed with this, but I knew I needed to defer to Liam when it came to this sort of thing. He'd had far more experience than I did, and honestly, I didn't want to be the one making the decisions right now. My mind was still a chaotic mess, and I wasn't ready to deal with the idea of saving the world when I still couldn't even get a handle on this constant need for blood. Liam stepped back and pulled out his phone, and I moved towards the fridge to pour myself a glass of blood from a pitcher.

Liam's eyes tracked my movements while he spoke to Gerard. I wondered if he was concerned about how much blood I seemed to need. I'd already had far more than he had in the past twenty-four hours, but I'd assumed it was because of my newbie vampire status.

What if it wasn't normal?

Connors' words from last night still rattled around in my mind, and I knew deep down that it hadn't been a dream. I was sure he had been talking to me through a psychic connection he'd put in place for us, and I found it deeply unsettling that an evil vampire mastermind had access to my mind whenever he felt like coming for a visit.

Liam ended the call with Gerard and went to grab the car keys.

"I'm going to go and meet Gerard and arrange things to get a plan in motion for your family."

I opened my mouth to protest.

"With minimal input from the Order." He added.

I grimaced before nodding.

"Hang tight here. I'll be gone an hour, tops. And then we can go and see your family."

"You don't want me around any Order members right now, do you?" Maybe I was being paranoid, but I was concerned about being left out of this part of the plan and thought it was strange that Liam was leaving me behind. He let out a breath, his shoulders dropping a little.

"Honestly, no. But not because I'm worried that you might lose it. You're vulnerable right now, and I don't want them getting any further into your head than they already are. Until you've run the gauntlet with all the blood memories going through your mind, it's safest we minimise any contact with them until you've got a handle on your emotions. The first few weeks after the change are like dealing with a mental illness. Some really high highs, and some really low lows." He came close and pulled me tightly against his chest, wrapping his arms around me. I pressed my face against his neck, breathing in his comforting, familiar scent, letting it centre me once again. I knew this would be a regular occurrence and wondered if I would end up allowing this to become a crutch. I relied on his presence to make me feel less of a mess, and I wasn't sure how to feel about that.

"OK. Be safe. Don't let them get inside your head either, alright? This has all been a lot for you as well," I said. Our eyes locked on one another, a slight smile on his lips.

"Don't worry about me, my love. Nothing will take me from your side. Especially not anything that the Order will throw at me." He left with a nod and an all-too-brief kiss, and I was left alone with my thoughts.

I found myself back on the couch, surrounded by Liam's journals. I figured I might as well get back to jogging those blood memories and speed the process up, if possible.

I opened the closest one and discovered it was more recent, from when I was born. I began reading and was soon transported to that time in Liam's life.

I rounded the corner and saw Alana pacing back and forth in the hall outside my room. She saw me walking towards her and immediately rushed to meet me before I could make it further than four steps. I could tell she had just found out what had happened, and heard the rage and sorrow swirling through her thoughts. I could generally shut those thoughts out, but it had been a long day, and I was exhausted.

"Is it true? Did they make a mistake with me?" Her words were frantic, her eyes wild, and I worried, not for the first time today, how she would handle the complete change in her treatment that was about to occur. To go from being the chosen one to being just like the rest of the Order...

"Unfortunately, it seems like it. The child was born two weeks ago in Australia. The seers have just sent word. It appears her presence had been cloaked somehow until now, so they couldn't sense her." I could feel

a tightening in my chest as she pressed a hand to her mouth, her eyes shining with unshed tears.

"How could this be? Why were they so convinced that it was me if there was even a chance they could be wrong? Did no one consider how this would affect me?" The tears started falling, and I reached out to comfort her, but she stepped away. "No. I can't bear your pity. Not after you broke my heart." She fled down the hall towards her room, and I silently cursed my stupidity again.

Five years ago, during a brief dalliance, I discovered that her feelings for me had developed into something far stronger than what I had felt for her and had been forced to end it. It had been nothing more than physical interaction for me, a way to scratch the itch. Although time had passed since then, she still held a place for me in her heart, and I knew I should never have let it happen. I should have sought out someone else instead of this vulnerable young woman whose entire self-worth had been tied to her status in the Order. Hell, I should have just gone and shared a bed with Eve. At least the complications with her didn't cause me any regrets because I cared little for her emotional well-being. She had Ronson for the relationship shit, as much as she wished she could have it with me.

I let myself into my room and sat on the bed before flopping back and staring at the ceiling.

A knock sounded at the door, and I groaned, getting back up to let Patrice in. The benefit of hearing others' thoughts was that no one could ever really sneak up on me, even if it made it near impossible for a moment's peace when I was in this house.

"I see that Alana knows the truth?" Patrice asked, her face pale, and I nodded. "Well, we'll have to deal with that as best we can. But, for now, we need to organise setting up the new headquarters in Australia. Damon is already on a plane and wants you down there ASAP." The joys of being the only daywalker amongst the Order meant that I was forever on protection detail. I had thought this part of my existence was over now that Alana was past her twenty-fifth birthday and had been learning the skills to protect herself. But the birth of this

child explained why her skills hadn't developed any differently from those of other members of the Order before her.

I nodded and took the paperwork she handed me, which included a one-way plane ticket from Los Angeles to Brisbane, Australia. I had to admit, I wouldn't miss the USA, but I wasn't sure if Australia would be much better. I missed Europe and wished, not for the first time, that I wasn't tied so strongly to this group that dictated my eternal life and movements. At least Australia was someplace new. I had been in this country for far longer than I'd expected, and we'd never needed to be in Australia before now, with minimal nightwalker activity. They preferred areas further North, where the nights were longer in winter. Or at least, they had before. In recent years, their movements had become far less predictable.

"You leave tomorrow. There is a photo of the family in that file and as much information as they could gather on short notice. They were completely off the radar. I have no idea how this slipped through the cracks." Patrice's mind was racing, something that very seldom happened, and I wondered at the fact that, for once, the Order seemed to have slipped up. I shouldn't have found that humorous, but watching them all scramble to appear as though this wasn't the biggest fuck up had certainly provided some entertainment today. Amongst the daywalkers, the Order was viewed as humans with a puffed-up sense of importance, but they could prove annoying, so they mostly just gave them a wide berth. Eve had often voiced her disgust at my ties to the group.

Thoughts of Eve made me realise I should tell her and Ronson of this latest development.

With another groan and a longing look at my bed, I left my room again and headed off into the night.

Arriving at the palatial mansion in Orange County, I let myself into Eve's home, having long passed the formality of knocking. She had always preferred large properties and kept an entourage, so there were multiple rooms that other daywalkers resided in occasionally. That daywalkers

CHAPTER NINE

"How did it go?" I found Liam in the kitchen after abandoning my position in the library. He tossed the car keys in a bowl on the bench and pulled my phone out of his pocket.

"Gerard is going to arrange that the insurance assessor that goes out is one with connections to the Order, and they will ensure that the house is a complete knockdown and rebuild." He handed my phone to me.

"So, the home all my sisters and I grew up in will be knocked down... That's going to be a lot to process for everyone." I could only imagine my sisters' reactions, let alone my parents. But I knew it was necessary. As long as that house remained standing, it was a liability to any occupants.

"It was either that or take your approach and burn it to the ground... I didn't think that would be the way to go... Knocking down and rebuilding seemed like the less traumatic choice." He poured himself a glass of blood, which he drank whilst getting a pot of coffee going.

Blood and coffee, the breakfast of champions.

"Fair." I wiggled my phone in my hand. "So, who had this? I've already seen the messages sent to people, and I've gotta admit, I'm not thrilled."

"Gerard handed it to me, but he didn't tell me who had been sending the messages. We didn't meet at the Manor. I think yesterday's exchange has been a bit of an eye-opening experience for a few people. Trust is a little thin on the ground over there right now. He just said he swiped it on his way out the door."

It was nice to hear that we weren't the only ones disillusioned with the Order of the Dragon and its heavy-handed tactics.

"I wonder if getting a whole new phone might be better... I don't trust that they aren't tracking us using our phones. The less they know about our movements now, the better," I said. Liam pulled his phone out and stared at it.

"You're probably right. We'll get that sorted before we go see your parents."

"Do you know where my car has ended up? Is it still in the parking garage?" I hadn't even thought about it until now, but Liam had been using one of the Orders cars, and I knew they were all fitted with trackers.

"No. I traded with Gerard. Yours is now here. I figured it was time to start cutting all the ties that bound us to them. But we should get yours checked out for trackers to be safe."

I heaved a sigh and flopped onto the stool nearest to him.

"I hate this. Having to worry about being tracked, avoiding the people I thought I could trust... This is what the rest of our lives will be like, right?"

Liam came to stand next to me and ran a hand up and down my back while I put my head on my arms on the bench.

"This is all new to me too. I've been working alongside the Order for close to five hundred years... It's going to be an adjustment."

I sat up to look at him while he stared into the distance.

"I guess Eve is going to be happy."

He stiffened slightly before answering. I could tell he was still adjusting to me knowing about Eve and the other daywalkers associated with her.

"I trust them about as much as the Order right now. Everyone has their agendas, and knowing they want something from us is concerning."

I still hadn't told him about my connection to Connor, knowing that would most likely be the news that sent him over the edge. I'd wait to see how those interactions played out before I dropped that bombshell.

My phone alerted me to an incoming message, and I pulled it out of my pocket.

Mum:

Isolde, we need to talk. Call me once you're safe.
undefined

I stared at the message before showing it to Liam.

"Something is going on, Liam. This message, on top of the ones from yesterday... It's like Mum knows something."

He studied the message, his expression unreadable.

"You're right. We should head over there. Maybe she is worried because she hasn't seen you in person...." His words trailed off, but I knew he believed that about as much as I did.

"How could she possibly know anything about the Order?"

He hesitated before shrugging.

"Honestly, I'm realising how little I knew about anything. I wish I had answers for you, Isolde, but at the moment, I'm the last to know in most cases, so it seems."

I could tell this was really worrying him, so I let it drop. His entire existence was in question, and I remembered that feeling all too well. Instead, I got to my feet and wrapped my arms around his waist. His arms came around me, and he sighed, holding me close and resting his chin on my head. We stayed like that for a long time.

After a brief detour for Liam to grab us a new phone each, he pulled my car up outside Briseis and Dean's house an hour later. He had never been here before, and I'd never lived here...

"How do we get inside if Briseis doesn't say the words 'Come in' when she answers the door?" I turned to ask Liam, and he smiled.

"You'd be surprised how often people say something to that effect when you're at their door."

I thought about it for a moment and realised he was right. The first time he had appeared at my window, I had automatically tried to ask him if he wanted to come in, but he'd cut me off.

We walked up the front path together, and Liam knocked while I shifted from one foot to the other. How would my family react to the news I was about to drop on them? On the drive over, we'd agreed that we would have to go with some version of the truth. There was no other way we could think of to keep everyone safe from Aurora.

Briseis came to the door and immediately gathered me in a big hug when she stepped outside. She was the sister closest in age to Aurora and me, and I was godmother to her youngest daughter. We had always been close, and I was glad she was the one I would tell first out of all my sisters.

"Come in, come in." She waved us both on through, and I exchanged a small smile with Liam.

We followed my sister into her large kitchen, where my parents sat at the bench, finishing their breakfast. Briseis was getting her kids set up with cartoons in the lounge room while they ate their breakfast, and I studied Mum's face while she looked at me closely. Dad got to his feet and pulled me tightly into one of his comforting Dad hugs. But it didn't feel comforting now. His scent was causing an overload on my senses, and I took a deep breath, torn between the knowledge that this was my father and the overpowering smell of blood threatening to consume me. Over his shoulder, Mum went rigid, staring into my eyes, her jaw clenching hard while she gripped her coffee cup tightly. A range of emotions crossed her features. Shock. Wonder. Despair. When she finally settled on fear, my suspicions were confirmed, and I forced myself to step back from Dad's arms.

"You know." My tone was flat. It wasn't a question. It was a statement. I knew the truth without her having to utter a word.

Dad looked at me, confused, but I paid no attention. I had no interest in anything but the truth, which seemed to be something Mum possessed. I studied her closely, and she swallowed hard. Her eyes continued to bore into mine as though she hoped she was wrong and was trying to find any sign of my former self. She eventually took her eyes off me and turned to look at Dad, who didn't know who to look at. In a less tense moment, I would have likened him to watching a tennis match. His confusion was beginning to give way to annoyance at not knowing what was happening.

"Know what? What's going on?" Never having been one to take a back seat in any situation, Dad was unaccustomed to being in the dark.

"You might as well give it up, Mum." I had never spoken to Mum the way I was now. My disappointment in her was laced through every word. Besides Aurora, Mum had always been someone I could count on. Never before would I have believed that she kept a secret from me. That she could lie to me. To realise that she had been lying to me for a very long time hurt more than I could ever have imagined. But then again, Aurora had been in love with my fiance and lied to me for years, so maybe I was just naive in believing I could trust anyone in my family.

"Abigail? What is she talking about?" Dad's voice started getting louder, and Mum sighed before taking a deep breath.

Like she was preparing herself for battle.

"Yes. I know."

And there it was. Confirmation that there was no one left in the world that I could trust.

"You know what I am." I crossed my arms, though whether it was to protect myself or to keep my anger in check, I didn't know. I felt Liam step close behind me when Mum glanced at him over my shoulder. I had no doubt the expression that was most likely on his face was making her nervous, but I didn't particularly care.

"What you are?! Would someone please tell me what is going on?" Dad demanded. Honestly, I half expected him to stomp his foot in frustration.

"I know about the Order, yes." Mum continued to ignore him, her tear-rimmed eyes searching mine. A small part of me wanted to tell her it was okay. But nothing about this was okay.

"And the rest?" I wanted to believe that was all she knew, that she didn't know about the prophecy and what I had been destined to become. But I had seen the look in her eyes.

"I know you're a vampire." The words tumbled from her lips. I didn't know who was hurt most by her knowledge as the first tears escaped her eyes. For his part, Dad just stared at her. He turned his incredulous gaze to me, finally noting my changed eyes, his expression demanding answers.

"Has your mother lost her mind?"

So, I was right in assuming that Dad didn't know any of this. It was only Mum who had lied to me.

That didn't make me feel any better.

"How? How do you know about the Order? How do you know what I am?"

Mum hesitated to answer for the longest time.

"Your Grandfather. He was a seventh son of a seventh son."

I felt Liam's hand on my shoulder tighten, and now it was my turn to be silent. Of all the scenarios I had come up with, this was the last thing I had ever imagined.

I watched her deflate before me, having completely given up any attempt to hide the truth any longer. Surprisingly, Dad remained silent, along with myself and Liam, obviously deciding to hear Mum out before writing us both off as crazy.

"My father, when he died, was just shy of two hundred years old. He'd left the Order when he met my mother. Not something that was easily done, as I'm sure you know, Liam." She glanced at Liam over my shoulder before continuing. "When they had only daughters, he was so relieved. He hadn't wanted to bring a son into the same life he'd been forced to live."

I nodded, understanding why my grandfather wouldn't want to pass his curse on to the next generation.

Mum looked down at her hands while she shared this secret she'd kept for so long.

"I knew nothing about this until your father and I learned we were having a second set of twin girls. Seven daughters. Born to his seventh daughter. My father was beside himself. He'd worried when I married your father, not because he didn't like him, but because he was a seventh son." She said, and Dad's eyebrows flew up at this. "Of course, he'd told himself the chances of us having seven children were slim, let alone having seven daughters... He knew about the prophecy, you see..." She let out a ragged breath, barely keeping her emotions in check.

"So that's why Grandad always treated me differently to everyone else..." I had always known I was my grandfather's favourite among his many grandchildren. Now I knew it was because, out of all his offspring and their children, I was the one who would understand him the most. Mum watched me while I processed all of this.

"When he told me all of this, I swore he'd begun to lose his mind to old age. Vampires weren't real, and neither were prophecies. I didn't believe him, as he and my mother had kept the truth of his age and background a secret for my entire life."

"What changed your mind then?" In my desperate need to know the truth, all my questions came out as demands.

"Your change in character after you turned twenty-five. Your sudden fear of the dark and the way you jumped at shadows. And then Will's murder confirmed it all."

"Why didn't you say anything?!" It was the closest I had come to yelling since we entered the room, and I struggled to keep the desperate anger within from boiling over.

"Because I wasn't meant to know!" Mum yelled back, her eyes wide. "I know how the Order works. Your grandfather explained it all. I would have had my memory erased, possibly even lost you for good. They had the power to make us all forget that you ever existed, to believe that we had only six daughters instead of seven. And I couldn't risk that." Her voice was pleading, the tears flowing freely down her face.

"I still don't understand... You said Isolde is a vampire..." Dad said quietly, staring at me.

"Because she is a vampire now," Mum whispered, almost choking on the words.

"Did you... Are you saying it was Isolde who murdered Will?! How could you believe such a thing?!"

She shook her head frantically.

"Of course not! No one who saw the grief she experienced would ever believe that Isolde had anything to do with how Will died."

"Then what are you saying?" Dad threw his hands up.

"You worked it out, didn't you? When you couldn't reach me..." I hadn't realised until that moment just how much Mum had known and how much she had kept from me. "Did you know they believed I had to become a vampire as part of the prophecy?! Did you know about Aurora?! Did you know what would happen to her?!"

She raised her hand to cover her mouth and shook her head vehemently while the words spewed out of me in anger, and Liam's grip tightened again.

"What do you mean? What about Aurora?" Tears had begun to well in her eyes, and I realised, with sickening clarity, that Mum had no idea what had happened to my sister. I felt Liam tense behind me.

"What are you talking about? What happened to Aurora?" Dad

watched us closely while I tried to work out how to answer them both, and I steeled myself to drop the bombshell.

"She's a vampire."

"Like you?"

I shook my head slowly.

"I don't get it..."

Mum began to cry, and some of my anger dissipated.

"There are two different types of vampires. Daywalkers and nightwalkers. Nightwalkers are the creatures we hear about in horror movies and books. Creatures without any sense of right and wrong. Only the selfish need to meet their desires."

"And what's that?" There was a tone in Dad's voice now that I had never heard before. Fear.

"Their need for blood and power. And they kill without remorse to get it." Mum answered him this time, continuing to study me closely.

"And you're both telling me that Aurora is one of *them* now?"

I still wasn't sure if he believed everything we told him, so I nodded. He stared at me for a moment, the silence deafening.

"But... what does that make you?" He half whispered.

"Daywalkers are the opposite of nightwalkers. They are still immortal but maintain who they were before changing. They fight against the nightwalkers." Mum answered him again while he stared at me like I was a stranger.

"And that's what you are?" I could tell he was having trouble comprehending everything that had just been dropped on him, and I nodded slowly. I stared at my parents for a long time, wishing I could make them feel better.

I focussed on Mum. That she had started crying only at the mention of something happening to Aurora irked me, though I knew I was being slightly irrational.

"So, you only care that Aurora is a vampire? Am I expendable? It was only me that you didn't care about." I said flatly.

"I care about you both! I didn't want anything to happen to

either of you! You were my babies. But I couldn't stop what happened to you. I was powerless. I never imagined that Aurora also had a role in this!"

"Did you know that it was foretold that I would become a vampire?! Did Grandad know that part of the prophecy?"

"No!" Mum's hands were clenched into fists at her sides.

At this moment, Briseis entered the room again and stopped short, taking in the sight of us all facing off in her kitchen.

"Okay... What did I miss?"

CHAPTER TEN

I sat on Briseis' back deck, staring out over the backyard. I'd left Liam inside with my family, unable to be around them any longer. Aside from the intense attack on my heightened vampire sense of smell, my anger and frustration consumed me.

Although Mum had told me that she knew, I was so tired of all the lies and feeling like everything I ever believed was bullshit. I'd heard the occasional raised voices from Dad and Briseis, and I was pretty sure more of my sisters had arrived, but still, I stayed where I was.

Liam came out to join me sometime later, and I heard people crying from inside. He sat on the top step beside me and put his arm around me. I automatically leaned into him to draw comfort from his presence once more.

"Are you ok?" He asked, tensing when I let out a low, humourless laugh.

"I don't know that I'll ever be ok again. Everything I've ever believed about myself, my family, the entire world... It's all been complete bullshit." I stared down at my hands, willing the tears in my eyes to disappear.

"Do you want to come inside?"

I shook my head while I wiped away a tear that had escaped. He began running his hand up and down my back slowly.

"What's the point? I'm dead. They might as well grieve me like they are grieving Aurora."

Liam wrapped both arms around me then, and I buried my face into his chest, finally allowing myself to give in to all the rage and sorrow I felt.

We stayed there until nightfall, and Liam convinced me to return inside and face the rest of my family.

But when we got to our feet, a movement from the side of the house caught my eye. I exchanged a look with Liam, who nodded, indicating he'd seen it too. The hairs on the back of my neck raised, and I sensed the presence of a vampire in the dark.

At least that ability had remained.

We both moved silently. Liam handed me a spare stake, as I hadn't brought any. Liam took the lead while we moved as one, now able to work together without words after months of fighting side by side.

"Fancy meeting you here, Isolde."

The words came from the other side of the house, and we spun together. My heart began to race when Aurora stepped out of the shadows. A noise behind us had me looking back over my shoulder, and I saw Will approaching. Both their faces wore identical twisted grins.

"Leave. Now." I stared my sister down, but she just laughed.

"Why should I? You're here. Aren't you just as dangerous to our family as I am?" She was surveying me slowly before meeting my gaze.

"You failed Aurora. Sorry to burst your bubble, but your attempt to turn me failed. I'm nothing like you."

She grinned again, opening her mouth to respond, but a sound from up on the deck made her pause, and we both looked up. My blood ran cold at the sight of two of our older sisters stepping out the door.

"Isolde? Are you out here?"

The feral look on Aurora's face unleashed something in me when Guinevere and Selena looked out over the railing and spotted us. They froze in place, and I moved quicker than they would have known possible, blocking Aurora's access to the stairs before she could reach them.

Will and Liam had begun fighting, but I focussed on my twin while I screamed for my sisters to get back inside. Neither moved, and I groaned when even more of my family joined them instead, alerted by their screams once they'd noticed Will and Aurora. Exasperation and terror mingled inside me while I watched Aurora to see what she'd try to do next. They'd just learned about the presence of vampires, and now they were all hanging out in the dark, watching us fight. If we all survived this, I would do some severe telling-off.

"So, I see they all know?" Aurora said, waving a hand casually towards our family, completely ignoring the fight between Liam and Will right behind her.

"Yes. I thought it best that they know the truth."

Aurora laughed again.

"The truth?! You've been lying to everyone for a year, and now you're all up on your high horse about telling the truth? You're so full of shit, Isolde! Always having to be the good twin. Always the favourite. Well, too bad for you. They all know that's not true anymore." Aurora moved towards me with super speed and attempted to throw me aside. Although she had vampire strength and speed on her side, I had been trained to fight even before my change, and I blocked her fist before bringing my own up into her ribs. She flew back with a grunt, and I heard gasps behind me when she landed in the middle of the yard. I spun to face my family.

"Get. In. Side." I knew my tone was terrifying, which seemed to spur Mum into action. She and Dad began grabbing my sisters and dragging them back into the house. Thankfully, they went without a fuss, and I could return my attention to the scene before me. Undoubtedly, they were all pressed against any windows that overlooked this part of the yard. As long as they were inside, I didn't care.

Liam had also managed to knock Will across the yard and came to join me. We stood side by side, having shifted as one into position, ready for the next attack. Aurora and Will faced off against us when a shrill whistle sounded, and Liam's gaze snapped up to discern where it had come from. Aurora and Will immediately began moving back before turning and disappearing in a flash, leaving us staring after them.

I didn't dare take my eyes off where they had disappeared into the dark, but Liam continued to survey the trees and surrounding fence line. Slowly, the presence I had sensed disappeared, and I allowed myself to relax a bit.

"Any idea who called them off?" I still surveyed the area but saw Liam shake his head out of the corner of my eye.

"No, but my bets are on either Connor or Adam. I'd assume those two wouldn't be far when it comes to Will and Aurora. Especially not if they are tracking us."

I nodded while we backed up towards the stairs before quickly entering the house.

As soon as I closed the door, I was met with hysterical questions from my family.

"I thought you said Aurora was dead?!" Guinevere turned on Liam immediately, and I looked at Mum.

"Didn't you tell them the truth?"

She shook her head.

"No, I did tell them the truth, but Guinevere and Selena refused to believe me. However, I'm guessing that display outside has assisted in my attempts." She eyed my sisters, who at least had the decency to look chastened.

Aphrodite was standing to the side, her gaze roaming over me slowly.

"Does that mean what Mum said about you and Liam is also true?" She sounded scared, and I couldn't blame her, not with what she had just seen. Even without the 'Aurora's back from the dead' act, Will's presence had thrown them all into a chaotic mess.

"Well, I'm not sure what Mum said about Liam, but yes... I am a vampire now," I said, and Selena and Dido visibly recoiled from me. For her part, Briseis remained close, and I was relieved.

"But you're not like them, right?" Guinevere was still eyeing Liam up and down, seeming to hold him responsible for everything, judging by the angry look on her face. Unmoving, Liam just held her gaze. My sister had the sense to look away first.

"No. Liam and I aren't like Aurora and Will. We can walk in daylight, which Briseis, Mum, and Dad have already witnessed. And we don't feed on humans." I figured I'd leave out the part where we *could*. We just didn't *need* to.

"But... Aurora's... She's like the ones on TV..." Aphrodite's voice was so quiet, and her lower lip trembled. It broke my heart to witness my sisters trying to process this all. I nodded.

"Nothing of the Aurora that you all knew and loved remains," Liam answered from behind me, his chest to my back, and I leaned back into him.

"You all need to be wary now. Her coming here tonight proves that she isn't going to leave anyone alone. Please promise me, no matter what, you won't let her in your homes." I begged my sisters, and they all nodded, each processing their grief. I turned to look at Liam.

"We need to get the Order to put cloaking spells on everyone's homes. It's the only way we can at least guarantee everyone's safety when they are at home."

The fear for my family struck me then. Until now, my focus has been on how to talk to my family about Aurora's death. The enormity of what was ahead of me was starting to hit home.

"You all need to come up with a plan moving forward. I don't think I can protect you all at once, and I don't trust the Order to do it anymore, either." I looked at Mum again. "This falls on you now. You couldn't protect me, but you will damn well keep everyone else safe."

I was painfully aware of the tears reappearing in Mum's eyes. Dad looked like he wanted to say something in her defence, but he could see that I was also breaking apart.

"Liam and I will stay here tonight. It's unsafe for you to leave until we can get your houses cloaked. Call anyone you need to and tell them anything to ensure they don't leave the house if they hear anything outside. No matter what they hear." I looked at each of my sisters individually, and slowly, they all started to grasp the enormity of the situation and that their lives were all changed forever.

When everyone began talking at once, I became painfully aware that I was standing in a room full of humans. As my sisters closed in around me, every heartbeat grew louder until it was all I could hear, and the sweet smell of their blood began to wash over me.

I turned and left the room, needing to put myself as far from everyone and their grief as possible. It was all too much, and I was barely keeping it together.

CHAPTER ELEVEN

Sometime after midnight, while I sat on the bench seat in the front room, looking out at the street for any movement, I heard Mum talking to Liam in the kitchen. My family had slowly moved to various rooms to get some sleep, having spoken to their significant others and attempted to ensure their safety. A few of my sisters had tried to leave to ensure their children and partners were safe, but I had again fought them to stay here. Liam had called Gerard, and it was only on the assurance that the Order would send someone to each house that I could convince them to stay.

"Was it you that turned Isolde?" Mum asked Liam.

"I tried to get to Isolde, to save her, but Aurora and my brother had already begun to feed on her... My only choice was that they turn her, and I had to kill her or attempt to turn her into a daywalker. It was something I hoped I'd never have to do." His voice was low, though he knew I could hear him, and I closed my eyes against the latest wave of grief. Silence fell over the kitchen for a few moments, and then Dad spoke up, doing nothing to keep quiet.

"You should have done a better job of protecting her."

"I know. There isn't a single part of me that doesn't feel responsible for what has happened."

I could picture Liam looking at Dad, wishing he had been able to protect his daughter instead of aiding in her descent into the paranormal.

"You said you had no idea about the prophecy about the twins... Did you know about the prophecy about Isolde becoming a vampire?" Mum asked softly.

"No, Abigail. I swear it to you. I had been told that she would be more powerful than anyone could imagine and that she would be responsible for ending this war. It wasn't until after Aurora took her that the elders finally let it slip in front of me. I don't even know how they managed to keep it from me all these years, which has weighed heavily on me."

I heard Mum sigh.

"My father spoke of the Order with fear and anger. He said the elders had kept many things from them, and he'd lost faith in their cause. He feared what they had planned for Isolde but told me that I couldn't do anything to stop them, or we'd lose her to them entirely. I wonder now if we could have hidden her away somewhere instead."

I could tell she was blaming herself, but I knew there was no way of hiding from the Order, not for a regular person. I stared down at the inside of my right wrist, idly tracing the golden tattoo. My thoughts wandered for a moment while I pondered, not for the first time, about its meaning and why my tattoo differed from all the other order members. I was tired of not knowing the answers to what lay before me.

"You couldn't have done that, Abigail. They have eyes everywhere." Liam said, echoing my thoughts. Mum began to cry. I assumed Dad was attempting to comfort her and wasn't surprised when Liam joined me a moment later, leaving them to their grief.

I looked up when he stopped beside me.

"We need to go and see the Order tomorrow. I want answers," I said while he gazed at me, and his jaw clenched. "Particularly, how they managed to keep all this shit from you for centuries when you can read minds."

It had been bugging me since I'd learned the truth, and I knew it was also plaguing him.

"In the morning, we'll go there first thing." He nodded, and we turned our gazes to the street, lost in our thoughts. I exhaled, feeling myself start to slip into another memory.

I finished checking into my hotel and dumped my suitcase in my room before heading off to find food, enjoying being alone for a change. The past few months had been awful, between losing Will and watching Isolde disappear, becoming involved with someone else so quickly. There was just something about Liam. I couldn't put my finger on it, but there seemed to be so much more that he knew than he was letting on. I still suspected Isolde and Liam were involved before Will's death. But maybe that was just my guilty conscience.

I bought myself some sushi and a drink, carrying it while I searched for somewhere comfortable to sit in the Botanical Gardens, overlooking the Opera House and Harbour Bridge. I'd always liked Sydney and had found myself toying with the idea of moving here lately. This conference was a chance to show work my capabilities, and network with the Sydney office and see if a transfer was possible. I didn't know how Jacob would feel about it, but I'd been feeling us drifting apart recently, and I knew that was my fault. Will's death had hit me hard, and I think Jacob had come to suspect the truth. We'd been spending less time together. Maybe a break was what we needed.

I stayed there until the sun was low on the horizon, admiring the sunset behind the bridge and reflecting off the curves of the Opera House. I knew the gardens were due to close and hustled to head back to my hotel before it grew too dark. I wasn't keen to be in the gardens in the dark on my own.

My hotel wasn't far, and I stopped to grab some food for breakfast in the morning. I needed a good night's sleep, and I'd be ready to take on the next week of work ahead of me. I'd worry about my personal life when I got back to Brisbane. I knew I needed to talk to my sister and attempt to fix the fracturing relationship, but I had no idea how to go about that when I still held so much resentment towards her. Most of it wasn't her fault - she had no idea about Will and me, but I was so angry at how easily she had moved on. Even though Liam was hot (even I could see that, no matter how much I didn't trust him), nothing explained how easily she had fallen for him and seemingly left behind all memories of Will.

I was so lost in thought that it took me a moment to notice that my hotel room door was open slightly. I stared at it, my heart racing, unsure whether I should go in or not. I was positive that the door had been locked when I left. I stayed in the hall for a few heartbeats more, but I heard no noise from inside, and I decided that whoever had broken in had already left. With a shaking hand, I pushed the door slowly open, looking around from the hallway. There was no movement, so I eased my way in slowly, wishing I had some sort of weapon with me.

My room was a mess, furniture strewn all over. My suitcase, whilst still closed, had been thrown into a corner and was sitting against the wall. But the stranger slumped in the corner was the most startling thing in the room. He didn't move, and I muffled a scream as I took in the way his head hung at an odd angle. As if it was broken. His eyes were open, and I could tell he was dead when I moved closer.

While I was staring at him, I heard a noise behind me, and I spun around, my heart racing so fast that all I could hear was it pounding in my ears.

The person standing before me couldn't possibly be here. Couldn't possibly be walking around. I backed up against the wall, avoiding the man at my feet.

"Will..." I barely whispered his name and felt the terror grow when he smiled at me, a cruel, twisted smile that I had never seen on his face before. With his new, startling blue eyes and how he carried himself, I sensed that this new version of Will was a skilled predator.

"Hi, Aurora. Have you missed me?"

I had no words. I wasn't even sure that I could speak through the terror. Will stepped aside while another two men came into the room with him. I did a double take when I recognised one of them as Liam.

"What... Liam..." I couldn't complete a coherent sentence, and I looked around the room wildly, searching in vain for some way around them all and out of this god-forsaken hotel room.

"Wrong. I'm the better-looking one." The man who wasn't Liam smiled almost sadly at me while he stood back behind Will and the third man.

"Twin... Liam never said he was a twin...."

Not that we'd ever spoken much, I'd mostly avoided getting to know him... I was starting to regret that now.

"Liam wouldn't have many nice things to say about me. He likes to pretend I don't exist. Easier that way." Not Liam said, and Will growled. "Calm down, William. You'll get your shot at him soon enough."

I stared at them, trying to deal with the fact that I was seeing them side by side. Even if he wasn't Liam, he looked exactly like his brother, and seeing him standing next to Will was unnerving.

I was so focused on the two of them that I hadn't noticed that the third man had moved closer until he stood before me. I could feel myself shaking uncontrollably while I stared into his cold, ice-blue eyes. Eyes that were the same as Will's. The same as Liam and his brother.

"Good girl, Aurora. Don't fight it... This is only going to hurt a little bit." The stranger pinned my shoulders against the wall while he whispered into my ear, and I felt tears start rolling down my face while he trailed his nose down my throat. I cried out when I felt a sudden, sharp pain where his teeth pierced the skin of my neck, and the last thing I saw was Will's gleeful smile and the sad, resigned expression on the face of Liam's twin. And then everything went black.

CHAPTER TWELVE

I came out of the memory and found myself in a ball, rocking back and forth, with tears rolling down my face. Liam was hovering over me, and my parents were behind him, with no idea what was happening. I struggled to gather myself, unable to look at any of them.

"Isolde? Baby, are you ok?" Mum moved tentatively towards me, but Liam flung an arm before her. He crouched before me to look at my eyes, searching my face. Although I couldn't read his thoughts, I could tell he was trying to work out what I'd seen of his memories, and I shook my head subtly.

"In the first weeks after turning, a vampire is exposed to the memories of the vampire who turned them. They already had them go through their minds while they were unconscious. That's what determines their temperament before they wake... But they relive the memories as if they are their own for weeks. In my case, because of how old my sire was, it went on for months. I'm not sure how long it will last for Isolde." Liam explained to my parents, although he never took his eyes off my face, watching while I brought myself back together.

"So, Isolde just experienced one of your memories?" Dad asked. I could tell that he was still unsure how to deal with the idea of speaking to the man who had turned his little girl into a vampire.

I took a deep breath and looked up at my parents, tearing my gaze from Liam's face. I had no idea how to explain that I had just witnessed my sister being turned into a nightwalker. Something I shouldn't be able to see as a daywalker.

"Yes," I said. I hated myself for lying, but something was happening inside me, and I wasn't ready to try and face it.

In the early morning hours, my parents finally retired to the room they had been staying in. We had spoken a little more after my episode, but I hadn't been able to tell them much, and we'd settled for trying to make a plan.

The hardest part had been finding where to go from here. We wanted to mourn the Aurora we knew, the daughter and sister that she had been. But we also couldn't tell people she had died. The genuine fear that she may show up at the homes of loved ones kept us from that reality. All we could agree on was that we needed to tell people that she was dangerous and to keep their distance. At this point, I needed to leave that with my family to deal with. I had too many other burdens to carry on my shoulders right now.

Liam had remained with me, neither of us having needed to sleep, and we watched the sun rise over the houses in the street.

"I spoke to Gerard. We should head to the manor soon. Get this conversation over with." I nodded, leaning into his side from where he sat with his arm around me.

We waited until some of my sisters came downstairs and told them we would inform them once their homes were safe before leaving.

While we drove back to the Manor, I stared out the window, trying to process everything that had happened in the last twenty-four hours.

"You doing okay over there?" Liam asked, pulling me from my musings when he turned the car into a service station.

"Not even remotely. Why are we here?"

He pointed at the fuel light.

"This just came on. I'll be five minutes, at most." He unbuckled his seatbelt and stepped out of the car. I stayed in the car for a moment before doing the same, and he looked at me in surprise over the roof.

"I can go pay." He raised an eyebrow at me and looked like he wanted to protest, but I didn't allow him to speak, turning to head inside. Once I stepped into the cool air conditioning, I was overwhelmed by the bright lights and smells. Too late, I remembered this was the first time I'd been somewhere public since I'd transitioned, and I understood why Liam had hesitated when I got out of the car when everything hit me all at once. The phone behind the glass partition at the counter rang, and it sounded like the volume was up to a hundred. The music on the radio screeched at me, the scent of body odour was making me nauseous, and all the bright lights and colourful items on the shelves made me feel like I needed to curl in a ball with my hands clamped over my ears. I must have looked like a crazy person while I stood frozen at the door, and the attendant at the counter ran her eyes over me. I forced myself to move.

I moved closer to the counter, and the smell from the attendant threatened to overpower me. Amongst all the other noise, I could hear the steady beat of her heart... And a gushing noise that I couldn't place.

With every step, the burning in my throat grew stronger again, and I realised, startlingly, that it was blood I was smelling. Her blood. And it was alluring and intoxicating. I wanted to wrap myself in it.

My gaze drifted to her throat, at the throbbing pulse in her neck, and I finally placed the gushing sound. It was her blood pumping beneath her skin.

I stopped a few steps away from the counter, fearing that if I were to move any closer, the need to leap over the counter and sink my teeth into the sweet spot where her shoulder met her neck would overpower everything else.

"Are you okay?" Her voice wavered a little. The woman looked about forty. She probably thought I was high. It would have been my first thought in her situation.

"Isolde. I've got it." Liam came up behind me, startling me. I'd been so fixated on the woman that I hadn't heard him enter the store. I stayed where I was while Liam paid for the fuel. He returned to me and gently took my hand, unfurling it from the fist that had formed at my side. He pulled me close to him and pressed his lips to my temple, guiding me from the store and back into the morning light.

The burning in my throat eased a fraction, and I allowed myself to relax into his side.

"Just breathe. I should have stopped you from going inside. That would have been too many senses triggered at once. We need to ease you into situations where you're exposed like that." He steered me towards the passenger door, and I slid into my seat. I looked down at my hands and saw that they were shaking from the effort of trying not to tear that poor woman's throat out. I waited until Liam had joined me in the car interior before speaking.

"I just... I wasn't expecting to be a threat to people..."

Liam paused in the motion of putting on his seat belt and shot me a confused look.

"What do you mean? I didn't think you were a threat to her. Did you think that was what I was worried about?"

I studied his face closely, unsure of how to respond.

"I just... All I could focus on was her blood..."

Liam continued to look at me with a furrowed brow.

"You mean the sound of her heart beating and the blood pumping?"

"Yeah..."

"Eventually, you'll get used to it. But you're not a threat to humans, Isolde. Daywalkers don't have the instincts that night-walkers have. I'm not worried about that with you. I didn't want you to become overwhelmed with all of these changes right now, that's all. Let's ease into the outside world bit by bit, okay?"

I nodded absently. Perhaps he had been a vampire for so long that he no longer focused on the smell, the irresistible scent that had me ready to leap over that counter to get a small taste. Liam reached across the centre console and squeezed my hand.

"Let's go and get this over with." He turned the car on, and I watched the store slip away outside the car, wondering what had just happened. And whether I was indeed as safe as Liam believed I was.

CHAPTER THIRTEEN

Ten minutes later, we stood in front of the manor again, and I struggled to keep my anger in check. I didn't want to talk to Patrice and especially didn't want anything to do with Damon, but we had too many questions that needed answers. Unfortunately, they were the ones who would be able to provide them.

Gerard was the first person we encountered again, having been waiting for us. He alerted Barbara, and she joined us while we headed into the conference room. Patrice was sitting at the table waiting for us. Gerard must have given her a heads up we were coming. I was glad that Damon seemed to have the sense to stay away. However, his cowardice, leaving Patrice alone to deal with the mess, further cemented my disgust with him.

"Gerard told me you had a run-in with Aurora and Will last night."

I raised an eyebrow at having our interaction with my dead sister and fiance be called a run-in.

"Yes," Liam stated, and we both remained standing whilst the others all took seats at the table. Other Order members came into the room and took seats as well, and I started to get an uneasy feeling. It looked like a full meeting had been called. I froze when Daniel entered the room, noting the wound and the bandage around his throat. I could feel the anger simmering off of him, though if it was directed towards me or the elders, I wasn't sure. I turned back to Patrice, unable to deal with Celeste's death yet.

"And Gerard also tells me that you have requested that the Order cloak the homes of your family members?" I crossed my arms, sensing that this wouldn't go smoothly.

"It wasn't a request." The anger I'd been fighting to suppress was racing to the surface, and I had the strangest sensation of my eyes flickering. Some of the Protectors gasped. I had no idea why, and at this point, I didn't care. Patrice, for her part, continued to regard me coolly.

"You've made it quite clear that you want nothing more to do with us, Isolde. Why should we help you now?" She sat back in her seat, crossing her arms, and I noticed that a few others raised their eyebrows and looked at her.

"Is that how the elders are going to play this? Seriously?"

Watching the other Order Members look back and forth between us, it would have been almost comical if I wasn't ready to jump across the table and strangle Patrice. Liam moved closer, resting a hand on my shoulder and squeezing it lightly.

"You came here and threatened us, and now you expect us to help you?"

How had I ever felt a connection to this woman? I watched her closely, sensing that behind her bravado was a very healthy dose of fear.

I allowed a slow, dangerous smile to pass over my face.

"Oh, believe me, Patrice. I still have every intention of bringing the Order to its knees. That wasn't an idle threat," I said, snapping the fingers on my right hand, and everyone gasped as a ball of fire appeared in the palm of my hand. A few of the Protectors scrambled out of their seats, and Liam moved with lightning speed to stand before me, his hands on my shoulders and his eyes wide. I shook my head at him and indicated that he should move. He reluctantly did so, moving to stand behind me, his body pressed close, keeping his hands on my shoulders. While he had known about my fire ability, this was the first time he'd seen me summon it without a candle, and I could tell he was a little shaken at this revelation.

"I started working on this a few weeks ago. Some of my amazing powers that you were all promising would arrive. I have a few secrets up my sleeve. Wanna see mine, Patrice?" I let my lips curl up into a sneer, and Patrice had the sense to look alarmed. "I'll show you mine if you show me yours." I waved the flame around in the air, enjoying myself while those closest to me recoiled further. "If you expect me to stop whatever is coming next, the Order will protect my family, and they will jump through whatever hoops I make them jump through. You know why?"

Liam was still tense behind me, but I couldn't worry about him right now, focusing all my attention on the other people in the room. On one woman in particular.

Patrice's eyes widened, but she cleared her throat before answering. "Why?"

"Because you fucking owe me." I glared at her for a moment before snapping my fingers again, extinguishing the flame.

I felt all eyes on me, and I relished the fear I could feel coming off them all in waves. "Besides, you all kept telling me how I was the most powerful amongst the Order... Do you really want to test me?" So many looks were exchanged, and as one, the Protectors turned to look at Patrice. She still hadn't taken her eyes off my face, but she must have felt the weight of all those eyes staring at her, and after a beat, she nodded her head slowly. The others sighed collectively, and Liam relaxed slightly, his grip on my shoulders easing a fraction.

"Now, besides protecting my family, I have another question." I moved to the seat opposite Patrice's, which Damon usually sat in— the two heads of the table. Liam moved to stand beside me, presenting a united front.

"I want to know how the elders managed to keep the details of both prophecies from Liam for all these years." I leaned back in the chair and crossed my arms, continuing to stare at Patrice closely.

"I'm interested to know the answer to this, also?" Gerard spoke up, and Patrice raised an eyebrow when she looked at him. "We are all intrigued to know what other secrets the elders have kept from us." He gestured around at the others at the table, and it was my turn to raise an eyebrow when the others nodded.

"Looks like we aren't the only ones pissed off, Patrice," Liam said from beside me, speaking for the first time since we'd entered the room.

Patrice looked around the room, appearing to realise that the elders may not be as in control as they thought.

"No one in here is required to be here, Patrice. The Order is meant to be a family and focus on protecting people. But this last week, we've realised that that is not necessarily true, and we want answers." Barbara entered the conversation now, and I couldn't resist the smirk that crossed my lips. I may have lost faith in the elders, but the other Order members seemed to be on my side after all. Patrice shot her a stunned look. I knew she and Barbara were close, and she undoubtedly felt her disappointment the most.

Silence descended over the room as everyone continued to look at Patrice, waiting for answers. Finally, she sat back in her seat and sighed.

"Firstly, I have never intentionally worked against anyone in this room. We have always been working towards the same cause – keeping humanity safe from vampires and finding a way to end the war between the bloodlines. Yes, the elders kept the full details of the prophecy from the rest of the Order, but that is because they hoped they had interpreted it wrong and that we wouldn't have to sacrifice Order members and their families to achieve it."

I couldn't hide the snort of derision that escaped from my lips, and Liam once again placed his hand on my shoulder.

"Spare us the line, Patrice." Liam's voice held the same level of scepticism that I felt, and I could tell from the looks on the faces of the others that many of them felt the same way.

"Whilst it isn't a line, I will answer your question. When you came of age, Liam, and joined the Order as a daywalker with the ability to read minds, the elders at the time were wary of where your allegiances might lie. The decision was made to have a spell cast that guarded the elders' minds so that certain thoughts and pieces of information didn't end up in the hands of the daywalkers. We know how they feel about us. They've never made a secret of it." Liam crossed his arms now, and I could tell this was not going down well with him.

"Conveniently, though, those thoughts and pieces of information related to myself and, later, Isolde. And my brother... And her sister." Liam said, nodding towards me before continuing. "Certainly wouldn't want that information getting into the wrong hands, would we? And what of Alana? How the fuck did the Order believe that the prophecy was about her when she wasn't a twin?" I hadn't even thought about that before now. I was interested to see what Patrice said.

"She was. But she and her sister were split up in the foster system after the fire that killed the rest of her family. The elders lost track of her, though," Daniel spoke for the first time, answering instead of Patrice.

I could still feel his anger but noted that it seemed to be directed at Patrice, not Liam or myself.

"More fucking lies?!" Liam glared at Patrice, who looked uncomfortable.

"I didn't make the rules, Liam."

"You didn't push back against them, either! We all trusted you! You. Not the other elders. *You.*" He pointed a finger at her, and she recoiled slightly. "This group has followed *you* from place to place. Because *you* were our family."

The anger and betrayal that Liam had been bottling up for the past week and a half had finally surfaced, and it broke my heart to hear it in his voice. I put my hand up beside me, and he took it without hesitation, lacing our fingers together and resting them on my shoulder.

Patrice's face dropped when she finally realised the true impact of her deceit and the pain it had caused, and I saw her deflate a little more while tears formed in her eyes. She looked around the room again, taking in how hurt everyone was. It wasn't just anger that had everyone lashing out. It was the lack of trust that she'd had in them and the betrayal of the confidence that they had placed in her.

Barbara cleared her throat beside me, and we all looked at her when she spoke up. "I think we all need to process everything. And Patrice, it would be best if you found a way to make this all right again. We all need each other now. Everything is about to go to hell in a handbasket, from what I've been able to decipher of the Gemini Prophecy after reading it this week." She looked at me. "The flood was just the start. We have no idea what else is coming, and I'd rather we all be united once it starts." Around the table, the others exchanged looks, and a few nodded. Liam's eyes found mine, and he squeezed my hand.

"Agreed." I looked back at Patrice, who nodded at me. "But, I can't extend that courtesy towards Damon."

"Damon has already realised that he has lost your trust and won't be an issue. He has left the Manor for the time being." A mixture of relief and disgust washed over me, and I knew I'd been right not to trust him. At least Patrice had remained to face the consequences of her actions.

"I won't be answering to the elders any further. They have lost the right to have a say in any decisions Liam and I make." Patrice nodded again, and I rose to my feet, squeezing Liam's hand when he stepped forward.

"Isolde and I will be back. We won't stay here, and I need time to process all this."

I knew how much it pained Liam to have learned that so many secrets had been purposely kept from him over the past five hundred years, and he no doubt wondered what else he hadn't been told. He looked at me again, and I nodded before allowing him to lead me out of the room.

We drove back to the house in silence, both lost in thought. I followed Liam inside and accepted the glass of blood he handed me wordlessly, having been doing my level best to ignore the burning that had been building in my throat since last night. He watched me drink it, then silently poured me another glass. I watched him closely, becoming concerned at the look on his face and the fact that he hadn't uttered a single word since we walked out of the Manor.

"I feel like there's more going on with you than what you've been telling me, isn't there?"

And there it was. The question I had been so hoping he wouldn't ask. That I'd been avoiding because I didn't want to become another person who kept things from loved ones.

I put the glass down without drinking and looked at him.

"What do you want to know?" I asked while he leaned back against the bench and crossed his arms, his eyes searching mine.

"Whatever it is that you're not telling me." He didn't know what I was keeping from him, and I wondered briefly how much I should tell him.

"Connor spoke to me in a dream the other night." I left out that I also seemed to be seeing Aurora's memories. I figured it was best to keep it to myself until I worked that part out.

"He did what?!" Liam asked loudly, and I felt my stomach flip at the expression on his face.

"Well, I'm pretty sure it *wasn't* a dream. He spoke to me and said he was testing out the connection he'd forged between us." I wrapped my arms around myself while he silently processed what I'd said.

"He told you he'd forged a connection with you... And you didn't tell me?"

"I didn't want to hurt you or say anything more until I knew what it meant." He let out a breath and straightened up.

"I think I need to get some air. I'll be back in a while." He strode back through the door we'd not long entered and left me standing alone in the kitchen.

I wasn't sure how to handle this. We'd never fought before, at least not since we'd been together, and my heart hurt to know I had caused him more distress. I could have returned to the office and his journals, but I didn't want to delve further into his memories. It felt like an invasion of his privacy after the conversations we'd just had. Although I couldn't control the flashes, I didn't need to do anything to cause them to appear unnecessarily.

CHAPTER FOURTEEN

*L*iam eventually returned, but the distance between us remained, even when we fell asleep beside each other. But whilst we slept, we gravitated together, and I awoke in his arms. He didn't speak when he did kiss my forehead before getting up, leaving me with the empty feeling I'd been battling ever since he'd gone for his walk yesterday. When it was time to leave, I silently followed him to the car, and we began the drive to the Manor.

When we were halfway there, Liam finally broke his silence, and I jumped when he cleared his throat. I had been staring out the window, trying to deal with my emotions.

"Once we leave the manor today, we need to pause. You're still going through the transition with the blood memories, and I want to put a little distance between everyone and us until we can fully understand who knows what and the things that are coming."

Relieved that he had finally spoken, I nodded. I didn't have an issue with hiding out at the house together and ignoring all the bull-shit for a little longer. Especially if it meant we could get past this wall that Liam had built up around himself. I'd not experienced any more unwanted visits from Connor, and the less chance of seeing Aurora and Will right now, the better I'd feel. I just needed a time-out before I eventually exploded.

Liam drove into the underground car park for the first time since my transition, a sign that he at least wasn't intending to leave immediately, and I followed him into the elevator.

Once the doors closed, he smacked the emergency stop button before turning to press me back against the wall, bringing his mouth down to mine and kissing me hungrily. A thrill ran through me, and I responded immediately. I pulled him against me while I stroked his tongue with my own. I could feel that he was already hard against my abdomen, and he lifted me off the ground to sit on the handrail. I wrapped my legs around him, pulling him into me. I gasped when he ground himself against my centre. I reached between us and undid his fly as his mouth moved down to my throat, and I moaned with each movement between us. I pushed his boxers down and pumped my hand along his shaft while he groaned into my neck. I felt a shudder run through him when I squeezed lightly and continued guiding my hand up and down. I let my head fall back against the wall while he rubbed my sensitive bundle of nerves through the fabric of my underwear, and both of us began breathing heavily. I was very grateful for my limited wardrobe options, having been left with only the dresses I'd left at the Manor. He lowered his finger to push my underwear aside and inserted two fingers inside me to ensure I was ready for him, crushing his mouth to mine when I moaned loudly.

I used the hand still holding him to guide his tip to my entrance. Once we were aligned, he pushed inside me with one hard thrust of his hips, and I gasped against his lips. With both hands on my hips, he started moving inside me with long, deep strokes while my inner walls clamped around him, my orgasm exploding through me.

"Fuck." He growled into my neck when I began moving with him, the intense pleasure giving way to another wave as my next orgasm quickly grew. I could feel him getting closer to his release, and I reached a hand up to push his head down, guiding his mouth closer to my neck, urging him to bite down, knowing that one bite would send us both over the edge together.

He didn't hesitate. I saw stars when he bit into me and began to suck, intense pleasure rolling over me. His muffled moans mingled with mine when I felt his release run through him. A few more strokes and we collapsed back against the wall together, our breathing heavy.

Removing his mouth from my throat, his forehead met mine.

"Don't keep secrets from me, okay?" He asked, and I nodded as I kept my eyes locked on his. We stayed that way for a moment before I finally let go of his hips and shifted my weight from the handrail. I let my feet fall back to the floor, though his hands gripped my hips until I regained my balance.

With one final kiss, we righted our clothes. Liam looked much calmer when he hit the emergency button again, leaning against the wall beside me and holding my hand while the elevator began moving again.

I couldn't keep the grin from my lips, especially when the door opened to Barbara standing before us, one eyebrow raised and a slight smile on her face. She looked us both up and down, taking in our casual stance, and her gaze lingered on the mostly healed bite mark on my neck before snorting as she turned and walked away. Liam and I exchanged a look and burst out laughing.

Patrice had been busy in the past twenty-four hours, and the spells to cloak each of my family members' homes had been performed. More Order members had begun to arrive from overseas, and I was introduced to them while they sat around the now full conference table, although Damon remained absent. Once again, I was revered by people who had spent years awaiting my birth and subsequent introduction to our mad world.

Ainslie was present, along with a few others who assisted the Order from time to time. I embraced my best friend, still wary about having her mixed up in all of this, but I was selfishly relieved to have someone from my old life to experience this with. She had been brought up to speed on everything that was going on and had volunteered to be on one of the teams that were going to be protecting my family. As someone who was practically a family member anyway, she would be staying with my parents and Briseis for now.

I let Liam do the talking for us today, and once he'd given his orders on how the protection details on my family should run, he waved his hand in my direction.

"Isolde and I are going to step away for a few days. She needs to focus on getting through the transition with the blood memories and harness these new powers before we can face whatever is coming next." I waited for the protests to start, expecting the Order to want us where they could keep an eye on us, to control us. But Patrice simply nodded.

And just like that, I suddenly had no expectations placed upon me. It felt like a weight had been lifted from my shoulders. For the past few months, I had been at the mercy of others' demands on my time. Not having anyone to answer to, even if just for a short amount of time, was something I was not going to say no to.

When we left the Manor, I expected we'd head back to the house and lock ourselves away for a few days or weeks. Instead, Liam began driving us out of the city, and I looked at him expectantly.

"I thought a change of scenery might do us both some good. We might never get a chance at a real vacation together, so this is the best I can offer. I've found us a cottage to stay in at Stanthorpe, no one else around." He raised my hand to his lips when I smiled over at him.

"That sounds amazing. Exactly what we both need right now." I settled myself into my seat, getting comfortable for the few hours it would take us to get there, and closed my eyes, eventually drifting off to sleep.

. . .

I closed the front door and looked down the empty street before me, aware of the sounds of rioting not far away. I was still determining how long we could remain in this house while the common people led an uprising against the aristocracy.

The day before, I had been amongst the crowd when the guillotine had dropped upon the neck of a King, something I wasn't sure I'd ever see. Eve had wisely remained absent, having seen the signs growing and stepping away from the world of the French monarchy. The less attention we brought to ourselves now, the better. But I needed to ensure that the members of the Order were safe and had begun to ready themselves to leave this city behind. I hadn't been staying with them recently, having fallen back into bed with Eve, and it was easier to avoid the Order when these urges came over me.

I shook the image of Eve bent over before me while I pounded into her from my mind, and I began the short walk to the current property that the Order had glamoured to hide their headquarters. They were to start the move to the new world on the next available ship, and I was unsure if I would be joining them or remaining with Eve's family for the time being. Vampiric activity remained strong here, but there had been reports of attacks in the newly established United States of America, so the decision had been made to abandon Paris for the time being to protect those in New York. At least here, more daywalkers were present to control the nightwalkers.

A commotion in the alleyway I had just walked past brought my musings to a halt, and I veered off course, turning back towards it, my hand on the stake strapped to my thigh beneath my long coat.

My eyes immediately fell upon a couple pressed back against the wall, the man thrusting deep with his mouth pressed against the woman's neck. Believing I had stumbled upon a couple amid a lovers tryst or perhaps a man partaking of the company of a woman he had paid for, I turned to leave the alley once more, but a movement nearby caused me to pause and look closer. I grew wary when my brother stepped from the shadows, not having noticed my presence.

"Perhaps don't kill her, Adam. We don't need the fucking Order

beating down our door again." His tone was bored, and the man who was rutting away turned to look over his shoulder, and I noted with resignation it was indeed Adam. He growled at Connor, holding the woman against the wall, her throat already gleaming with blood from where he had begun feeding whilst he thrust into her with hard, powerful motions. She was already close to death, her head lolling to the side and her eyes closed. I was disgusted and reached for the stake again but stopped when Connor stepped forward and punched Adam in the face instead. He reeled backwards, and the woman slid to the ground. He jumped to his feet and launched himself towards my twin. Connor raised a hand, and Adam halted before making contact, his feral features going slack. I stayed hidden in the shadows, watching Connor move closer and glare into Adam's face.

"Get your shit under control. You have been leaving a trail of bodies, and I am tired of cleaning up after you. You have become sloppy, and the coven is becoming far too crowded with all the newborns waking up." His voice was low and deadly, and I noticed how his jaw clenched while he stared down the creature before him. This interaction was so strange, and I didn't understand why my brother was acting this way, but Adam nodded, his mind seemingly under the control of whatever hold Connor held over him. They melted into the darkness, and I approached the woman to check if she was still alive. Finding a faint pulse, I took her in my arms and carried her with me while I continued to the Manor. I handed her over to the healers to ensure she survived the night while trying to make sense of everything I had just witnessed.

The memory dissolved around me, but instead of returning to reality, I stood again in the room where I had last seen Connor.

"Interesting... I wasn't aware that my brother had witnessed that particular exchange." The man himself was sitting in the armchair,

swirling amber liquid that I assumed was whiskey casually around in the thick crystal glass that he held in his hand. I took in his expression, and I could feel the waves of exhaustion rolling off him, which surprised me. I wasn't aware that nightwalkers could feel this way.

"I'm sure there is plenty about Liam you are unaware of, Connor." I moved to the wall opposite him, leaning back with my arms crossed, my eyes fixed on him should he make any sudden moves.

"I'm sure there is, like how he can keep a woman like yourself so satisfied. I can smell him all over you. How are my brother's skills between the sheets? I bet he learned a lot from Eve over the years. I hear she's insatiable." He smirked, and I could tell he was attempting to goad me into a reaction while he took a mouthful of his drink, holding my gaze over the rim of the glass.

"I must thank her for those lessons, then. Because he truly knows how to make me scream." I refused to allow Connor to gain the upper hand, and he laughed, his eyes flashing between the piercing blue and the brown I had noticed so many times.

"Oh, you came to play, didn't you, Isolde? I do like that. You've got spirit. The Order hasn't managed to turn you into one of their mindless drones just yet." He placed the glass on the table beside him and rose, coming closer. I tensed, but he stopped a few feet away and crossed his arms while he looked me over. His eyes moved slowly up my body, his gaze appreciative, before settling to look into my own.

"He truly has done well for himself, that brother of mine. Your sister is also something and knows her way around the bedroom, but you... He's almost outdone himself." I didn't need the image of my sister and Connor together that flashed through my mind, and Connor continued to smirk while I looked at him with disgust. "Didn't you know that your sister likes to be shared? She and Will have been busy since she awoke. Inviting anyone who will join them to share their bed. She is quite the screamer herself."

"What do you want, Connor?" I refused to give him the reaction he wanted, and he laughed again, closing the distance between us. He raised his hand and twirled a lock of my hair around his finger, and I *held myself still, unsure if he could hurt me in this hellscape he had created between our minds. He raised my hair to his nose and inhaled deeply.*

"Do you like to be shared, Isolde?" His eyes held me transfixed, and I inhaled sharply at the unexpected attraction rising within me. I swallowed hard. He began running the fingers of his other hand lightly up my arm. I fought the urge to close my eyes and lose myself to his touch.

"You're not Liam," I said, more as a reminder to my traitorous body, and Connor's eyes flashed again.

"No, I'm not my brother Isolde. I'm something much more." He stepped even closer, and I struggled to keep myself from gasping when the tip of his nose grazed the side of my neck. The hairs on my arms raised at the sensation, and I couldn't bring myself to push him away when his lips settled close to my ear, caging my body in with his hands pressed against the wall on either side of my head. Although no part of him touched me, I could feel my body screaming for more. I willed myself to take control of the situation, but I felt the desire ripping through me.

"You're using your powers," I said, trying to convince myself, and he let out a low chuckle while he leaned in closer.

"No, I'm not... this is all you. You want this. You're craving what you know I can do for you." His words were a low whisper in my ear, and somehow, with a resolve I wasn't aware I was capable of, I placed my hand on his chest and pushed him away from me. He stepped back without resisting and grinned at me while I panted heavily.

"I don't know what your fucked up end goal is here, but Liam is the only brother I want." He cocked his head to the side while he took in my words, so at odds with how my body was still reacting to his closeness.

"For now. We'll see what will happen once you see more of the memories. But until then...." He crossed the distance at super speed and kissed me hungrily, my body yielding immediately, much to my absolute disgust. He ended the kiss and pressed his forehead to mine. "Until then, Isolde, that's just a taste of what we could be together." I was left feeling cold when he disappeared, and the connection dissolved.

• • •

Without waking, I settled into a fitful sleep until I was awoken by the sensation of the car slowing down. I opened my eyes when Liam brought the car to a stop in front of a cute, cosy-looking cottage nestled amongst a lovely little garden at the end of a long driveway. No other buildings were within eyesight, exactly like Liam promised, and I breathed in the smell of the countryside.

"Did you sleep okay? You were mumbling a little over there." Liam surveyed my face, and I shook my head.

"Just another memory. Nothing important, though." There was no way I could tell him what had just occurred between myself and Connor. He didn't need to know that his brother could control my mind and make me do things I *did not* want to do.

Whatever you need to tell yourself, Isolde. Connor's words rang in my mind, and I willed myself to shut out the memory of his mouth on mine and how my body had reacted. To be in this moment with Liam and ignore all the crap for as long as possible. But when I exited the car, my body gave one last involuntary shudder at the memory of Connor's hand on my arm, trailing his fingers so gently up to my neck. It was hard to remind myself that the man was a creature of pure evil in that moment of tenderness.

I pushed the memory from my mind, jumping slightly when Liam's arms wrapped around me from behind before allowing myself to sink back into his embrace. We stood staring out at the paddocks and the herd of cattle spread out before us, munching on grass and utterly ignorant of the world's ways.

"Thank you for bringing me here," I said quietly, and Liam squeezed me before turning me to face him.

"My motives may not have been entirely noble." He lifted my chin and kissed me softly.

"No? What other motives could you possibly have? I thought you were all about pure thoughts and the good of others," I whispered against his lips before shrieking when he grabbed me and threw me over his shoulder.

"Not when you're wearing that dress, Isolde. Then I want to do all sorts of dirty things to you." I felt my heart rate pick up at the change in his tone when he pushed the door open with his foot and carried me inside.

CHAPTER FIFTEEN

oving through the cottage to the bedroom, Liam used the hand that wasn't holding me in place to reach up under my dress, showing me how dirty those thoughts were with his fingers. Moaning, I did nothing to stop him from tossing me on the bed. He leaned over and claimed my lips while he continued working his fingers between my legs, rubbing over the fabric of my underwear, and I writhed under his touch.

"What do you say, Isolde? Should I keep it pure with you right now?" He whispered against my lips while I rocked my hips against his hand.

"No. Definitely no pure thoughts and actions here, please," I said breathlessly, and he chuckled, moving to lie beside me without moving his hand away. He looked down at me, continuing to tease me, and I moaned again. "God, Liam, please. I need more."

"I love it when you beg." His voice had taken on a rough, commanding tone, and I felt it right down to my toes.

"Please, Liam. Make me come."

His eyes lit up while I continued to beg him, rewarding me by shifting the fabric aside and pushing his finger inside of me, his thumb moving to continue what his finger had started. He knew my body so well that I was on the edge almost immediately, and he continued to hold my gaze as my back arched up off the bed and the orgasm crashed through me. He kept going, his hand moving faster, pulling several more from me, while I cried out repeatedly, overwhelmed by the sensations rocking through me and the intense look in his eyes.

When I came down from the latest orgasm, he pulled his hand away finally and began sliding my underwear down my legs, tossing them over his shoulder.

"Get on your knees." He growled, and if I hadn't already come several times, I swore I would have combusted at those words. This was a side that I had never seen in my usually controlled, calm lover. I hadn't realised how much he liked this dress, but after our encounter in the elevator earlier, and now this, I knew I needed to wear it all the time.

Following his command, my heart sped up with anticipation when I heard him undo his belt. Within seconds, he pushed inside me with one quick thrust, and I cried out again. He leaned over me to wrap his arm around my chest and pull me upright against him. With his other hand pressed firmly over my overstimulated bundle of nerves, his thrusts pushed me to rub against his fingers with each movement. The hand he had been using to hold me against his chest slid inside the low neckline of my dress and squeezed my breast, pinching my nipple before moving to my throat, thrusting harder into me. My eyes rolled back, and my head fell back against his shoulder.

"That's it, Isolde. Scream my name."

I gasped as my heightened senses became overwhelmed again, and I did, indeed, scream his name.

"Fuck, Liam. Don't stop!"

"Wasn't planning on it."

I hadn't thought it was possible, but he moved his hips faster, and I raced towards the edge again.

"Fuck, Isolde. You feel so good." He sunk his teeth into my neck and held me tight around the throat while I continued to whimper. He kept going, his lips pressed to my skin while he fucked me hard, and I toppled over into oblivion, finally taking him over the edge with me, our cries mingling together.

He held me firmly against him, my body limp in his arms while I fought to catch my breath. Once we had the energy to untangle from each other, I lay back on the bed, snuggling into his side while he wrapped his arm around me.

"Who was that? This dress seems to bring out a whole different side of you." I trailed my finger over his chin, turning his head to bring his gaze to mine. He studied my face closely, moving to press a tender kiss to my forehead and breathe in my scent.

"I just had a bit of a realisation yesterday when I went for a walk. I was holding back from you, too." He ran his hand up and down my side, holding my gaze.

"What do you mean holding back?"

For a brief moment, I worried about what awful truths were about to come tumbling from his beautiful lips.

"When you were human, I didn't allow myself to unleash that side of my nature fully. I know talking about Eve is a sore spot for both of us, but it was only when I was with her that I could fully let go because I wasn't afraid of breaking her."

I opened my mouth to speak, but he raised his other hand to place a finger over my lips. I bit his finger, and he laughed.

"I realised last night that I no longer have to hold back with you. I don't *want* to hold back with you anymore. Can you handle that?" He asked, and I stared at him for a moment.

"Are you kidding? I fucking loved that. I craved that."

He pulled me in close and kissed me hungrily.

"Good, because I'm not done." He pushed my arms up over my head, using his belt to clasp my hands to the bedhead before kissing his way down my body. I gasped when he showed me just how much he had been holding back before, working my body in ways I didn't know were possible and ruining me for all other men.

Several hours later, I sat in the kitchen and watched Liam make dinner, having gone to get some supplies in town while I took a shower. Seeing him standing before the stove, shirtless in jeans and barefoot, made me painfully aware that this was the most relaxed I'd ever seen him in the eight months we'd known each other. It was as though getting away from Brisbane had flicked a switch within him. I wished we could just stay here, ignoring all responsibilities, and just be Liam and Isolde, the couple, rather than holding the fate of the world in our hands.

"Have I told you lately how much I love you?" I asked, and he looked over his shoulder, shooting me the sexiest smirk I'd ever seen.

"Is this because I'm feeding you?" He asked, and I pretended to think for a moment before answering.

"Maybe that's it. Couldn't be because seeing you this relaxed is doing all sorts of things to my insides right now." He laughed while putting our meals together and bringing me my plate. He placed it on the bench before me and came around to wrap his arms around me, while I stayed sitting on the high bench seat.

"I do feel so much lighter here, you're right. Let's just stay here forever." He said into my hair, his lips brushing my ear.

"Oh yes please, I'm one hundred percent on board with that plan." I hugged him back, before allowing him to step away to go and get his food.

"How about this for a plan? We survive all this bullshit coming our way, and we move out here and just forget about everything else?"

I could tell that only a small part of him was joking, and I studied him closely.

"You're on." We both began eating, enjoying the quiet and this brief pause in reality, almost like we were two regular people in love and not part of some elaborate plan to end a supernatural war.

CHAPTER SIXTEEN

That evening, once my body was entirely spent from all of Liam's attention, the blood memories began flowing in earnest. Memories from Liam and Aurora came flooding through, one after the other, as though all I had needed was to step away from all the stress at home before the floodgates could open. Liam kept busy, ensuring my needs for blood and food were met. But I still couldn't bring myself to tell Liam that I was seeing Aurora's memories along with his own.

He was also more than willing to make sure my needs for him were sufficiently met during any moments of awareness between the memories, and our hunger for one another only grew stronger with each shared moment. By the end of the fourth day, I felt like I had experienced every significant moment in their lives. Thankfully, Liam's dedication to ensuring that I experienced countless orgasms kept me from completely losing grip on myself and my reality outside of the memories belonging to both my twin sister and my vampire lover. I could have done without experiencing every sexual encounter they had both had, finding the ones between Aurora and Will particularly hard to stomach, closely followed by the many interactions between Liam and Eve. The only silver lining was that it was comforting to know that although his number of sexual conquests had been very high over the last five hundred years, none held the intensity and love I knew he had experienced with me.

Although it was summer, the nights were surprisingly cool, and we had a fire in the fireplace. I stared into the flames now while I lay my head on Liam's chest, my bare leg draped across his hips while we enjoyed the quiet contentment that had fallen over us after our latest round of lovemaking. Liam's eyes were closed, his hand running slowly up and down my back.

"How are you handling all of this? I know these past few weeks have been especially hard for you, too." I said, and he let out a breath, opening his eyes to look at me. He brought his hand to a stop at the back of my neck and began massaging it gently.

"It's a lot to take in. To have five hundred years of knowledge ripped out from underneath me and find out it was all just a bunch of convenient half-truths and outright lies will take me some time to deal with." He ran the hand on my leg up my side and cupped my breast. "Thank goodness I have you to keep me distracted." His lips curled into a seductive smile, and he lifted his head to kiss me softly. I opened my mouth to him while we began to explore each other's bodies again, the conversation giving way to moans once more.

Hours later, we finally fell into a deep sleep, the days of dealing with stress, and more recently, the relentless flood of memories and love-making, leaving us exhausted. Thankfully, my dreams remained Connor-free while I lay wrapped in Liam's arms.

We could have slept for days, but we both jerked awake suddenly in the middle of the night when a sense of dread seeped into our dreams. Liam leapt out of bed, throwing on jeans that lay discarded on the floor and tossing me his shirt while I scrambled over the bed to his side. I yanked the shirt over my head, and we both made our way outside, grabbing our stakes from the side of the bed as we went.

But there was nothing untoward that we could see outside, the absence of any artificial light making the sky appear to stretch out endlessly before us. If it weren't for the sense that something was wrong, I would have been in awe of the fantastic array of stars above us. We remained on alert, back to back, while we surveyed the paddocks around us for any sign of the source of the pit of dread in both our bellies.

Just when I began to believe we were experiencing some weird side effect of days of insufficient sleep, the ground beneath our feet began to tremble slightly. Liam grabbed my hand when the shaking increased rapidly, and we both dropped to the ground, unable to remain upright due to the intense rocking and rolling. I'd never experienced an earthquake before, and if I were still human, I imagined its violence would make me feel sick. As it was, my heightened senses were all over the place, and I curled into a ball, Liam's arms coming around me while we waited for it to stop.

After what felt like forever, the shaking stopped as abruptly as it began, and I slowly opened my eyes, looking around. A few trees had toppled over in the distance, and the cows mooed loudly while they ran around in the paddock. I could relate to their terror. Liam checked me over, and we slowly rose to our feet, hesitant, waiting to see if it was truly over or if any aftershocks would follow.

While we stood there, a shooting star streaked across the sky, closely followed by another. Then another.

Star after star shot overhead, and we stared at the sky, gaping at the amazing display. It was breathtaking to behold, and I would have been happy to take in the beauty of it all if not for the internal alarm shrieking inside of my head, warning me that this was all related to the prophecy and a sign of worse things to come.

Liam looked over at me, the concern I felt mirrored in his eyes while the stars continued to fly across the sky. They didn't stop until it was almost dawn, and we finally went inside, deciding that we should spend this one last day in blissful ignorance before we once more headed back into the abyss of the unknown that we'd left behind.

Thankfully, our final day and night were uneventful, and we reluctantly climbed back into the car and drove back to Brisbane. We had managed to avoid any technology while we were away, and I scanned my phone now, responding to concerned messages from my family members and reading the news to see what the so-called experts had to say about the earthquake and sudden, unexpected meteor shower from the night before. There were dozens of astronomers and seismologists across numerous news sites discussing the events, trying to explain away what had happened, each more fantastical than the next. The fact that the Order hadn't been able to keep this from making the global news channels was sign enough that things were spinning out of control, and everything within me knew that this was related to the prophecy.

"We'd better go straight to the Manor. I want to get a feel for what is going on," Liam said when we reached the city outskirts, and I nodded absently while I scrolled through my phone. We remained silent for the rest of the drive - each lost in our thoughts while we tried to grasp everything happening. I couldn't shake the feeling that the earthquake and meteor shower were just the beginning.

Once Liam parked the car, we entered the elevator, and I smirked a little at the memory of the last time we'd been inside. But that smirk disappeared when the doors opened, and we saw who was standing in the lobby of the Manor.

"What the fuck..." Liam's words trailed off when he took in Eve and Ronson's presence. They were standing casually before a very agitated Patrice, and I could tell this visit was unwelcome.

"There you are," Eve said, looking bored while Patrice wrung her hands, biting her lip as she looked to Liam for assistance.

"How the hell are you here?" Liam demanded. Besides Liam and now myself, as far as I was aware, no other vampires, daywalkers included, were meant to be able to find this place.

Eve snorted.

"The Order has never been able to keep me out. I just chose never to enter their precious inner sanctum," she said, and Patrice went still beside her. I could tell that this was news to her. A small part of me took some satisfaction in knowing that there were still things she didn't know.

Liam was glaring at Eve.

"Why are you here now, then?" He asked, his words dangerously low. I tried not to think of all the times he'd been with the woman before me over the last five hundred years, but I could tell from the smirk on Eve's face that she was well aware of the memories I had been privy to over the last week and a half.

"Now that Isolde is up to speed, it's time for our plans to move along. If you refuse to return to our side, we will be wherever she is," she said with a shrug, and I gaped at her.

"Ridiculous. You can't expect to stay here, surely?" Patrice asked shrilly, and Eve turned ever so slowly to look at her, running her eyes over Patrice with a look of pure disdain.

"We'll do whatever the fuck we like," Ronson spoke this time, one of few things I'd heard him say. Even in Liam's memories, he had rarely spoken. Patrice stepped back, perhaps sensing the danger he presented despite being a daywalker. Eve ignored Patrice and moved closer to where Liam and I stood. Liam moved to stand in front of me.

"Back off, Eve."

Eve huffed a laugh. Over Liam's shoulder, I watched her reach up and pat him gently on the cheek with a smirk.

"Oh, Liam... Dear, dear Liam. I find it amusing that you think either of you have any say in what is about to happen. Your only choice right now is if you will return with us or if we will remain here. But from now on, you *will* be with us." Although we'd had no intention of staying at the Manor anyway, I knew there was no way in hell that Liam would want Eve back at the house, and I could tell he was trying to work out what to do. Sensing that things could get ugly, I stepped around him and looked Eve up and down. I refused to let her revel in the power she held over everyone.

"We will come back to the house for now. But you don't call the shots, Eve. If we want to leave, we will be leaving." Over her shoulder, I could see that Patrice was fighting an internal war against the relief she felt that Eve would be leaving, but unhappy that we would also be leaving with her. The Order wanted to maintain control of the situation, but they couldn't win against a vampire who was thousands of years old and apparently could enter the doors of the Manor whenever she chose.

Eve turned her smirk on me now, and I glowered at her.

"Whatever you need to tell yourself, Isolde." She placed a hand on Liam's chest, almost as though staking her claim over him. I fought the urge to smack her hand away, aware that she was toying with me, attempting to goad me. Liam stood still beside me, his hands clenched into fists and his jaw tense.

"See you both at the house. You have one hour."

I didn't want to know what would happen if we didn't comply.

Once Eve and Ronson had swept out the door, we headed into the comms room to work out what the Order had managed to find out about the earthquake and meteor shower we'd witnessed.

"We've had reports of several earthquakes worldwide in areas that don't normally experience movement," Barbara said to Liam while she searched the internet for information.

I continued conversing with Patrice.

"Have there been any other events since I turned? Besides the flood here?" I asked her, trying to bring her out of the distracted state she'd been in since Eve had dropped the bomb that she'd been able to get through the glamours. "Patrice! I need you to focus." Her eyes snapped back to me.

"Sorry. Yes, there have been. The flooding isn't just contained to Brisbane, though it was the epicentre. Flooding events have been occurring in a steady spread outwards. It's already reached out to Sydney, the Queensland and Northern Territory Borders and as far North as Rockhampton. And this morning, we also started to get reports of New Zealand experiencing events. So it's not just Australia now. If we don't work out how to stop all of this, we predict that the entire planet will be affected within several weeks."

I'm sure the shocked look on Liam's face was mirrored on my own. I think I liked it better when Patrice wasn't speaking.

"Okay... So we've got flooding... Like the biblical flood?"

"Not entirely. The flood in the Bible was from constant rain. There's not been any increased rainfall in these instances. The waters are rising on their own."

"That is quite possibly more terrifying." My mind was reeling, but Liam continued to watch Patrice closely.

"There's more, isn't there?" He asked.

Patrice looked reluctant to say what was running through her mind.

"We've got dormant volcanoes worldwide starting to show signs of life. We think that might be the reason for the earthquakes."

Liam swore under his breath, and I just stared at Patrice.

"How long have we got before everything goes to complete shit?" I asked.

Patrice shook her head.

"Honestly, we have no way of knowing, but we need to work out your role in all of this, or the world will explode in a matter of months if not weeks."

Great... No pressure.

CHAPTER SEVENTEEN

When we'd been at Eve's home the last time, I had only crossed paths with Eve and Ronson. I had seen the room I'd been kept in and the way out of the house. But now that we were back, I realised it was an eerily similar set-up to the Manor. But whilst the Manor was glamoured to look like several run-down houses from the outside, Eve's home wasn't hidden. And it was massive. I'd been too out of it when we were here last time to notice it when we left, but I gaped up at it now, wondering how I'd ever missed this place in all my years in Brisbane.

"She certainly likes to make a statement, doesn't she?" I commented to Liam while we climbed out of my car and stared at the three-storey mansion high up on the hill. Even from the driveway, the view out over the city was impressive. However, it was probably much nicer when the river wasn't raging. It had been two weeks, yet the waters were still flowing fast. The water levels had decreased a little, which was how I'd seen my former home, but it was still much higher than usual. Debris flowed by regularly, and I wondered how long it would continue to flow like this.

Probably until I could sort out this whole "end of days" part of the bloody prophecy.

"Yes, Eve has frequented only the most opulent homes in the time I've known her. As you've no doubt seen." It was the first time Liam had come even close to referencing his shared history with the woman who had turned his life upside down, and I had no desire to discuss it any further. Even now, just thinking about it made my insides boil. I'd never been a particularly jealous person in life. But between being turned into a vampire with heightened emotions and learning that my fiance and sister had been having a multiple-year affair behind my back, I guess jealousy was now just another part of my personality I had to get used to. I felt my eyes flash again like they had when I'd become angry at the Manor in front of everyone, and Liam stared hard at me.

"What?" I didn't like the look on his face. He squinted at me like something was seriously wrong with my face.

"Your eyes..." He trailed off, and I raised a hand to my face.

"What about my eyes?"

He shook his head after a moment.

"I must have imagined it... It just looked like they changed colour for a moment. But that's not possible."

I felt my blood run cold, even though Liam was trying to make it sound like it was no big deal.

"What colour did they change to?"

"They looked brown for a moment. But honestly, I was just seeing things. Eyes don't change colour like that." Liam turned towards the house again and reached out to take my hand. I took it automatically and allowed him to lead the way inside.

Inside my head, though, alarm bells were screaming. He was right. Eyes didn't change like that. But I had seen someone else whose eyes had changed from piercing blue to brown once. And I wasn't loving how the jigsaw in my head was starting to put the pieces into place.

Liam led the way inside without bothering to knock. I'm sure he even considered kicking the door out of frustration with our current situation. Neither of us wanted to be here, but we had little choice. As Liam's sire, Eve had a connection to him and could generally sense wherever he was. It was how she had timed her arrival at the Manor with ours. I hadn't been impressed when Liam had divulged that little tidbit of information on the drive over. He'd explained that it was due to the blood memories. It also meant that we were linked in the same way. I wasn't concerned about that, though. I was preoccupied with the idea that a vampire who was thousands of years old and seemed to care little for humans was tied to my vampire lover.

"Well, Eve, you got your way. We're here." Liam yelled from the foyer, my hand still firmly gripped in his. I could tell that he was doing everything possible to contain his anger.

"Jeez, Liam, settle down." A woman I vaguely recognised from some of his memories appeared at the door to our left, leaning against the door frame with a smirk. She was stunning, with long limbs and deep brown skin that caused her piercing blue eyes to stand out even more than any other vampire I'd met. I detected a trace of an American accent in her voice.

"Screw you, Anika," he said, but there was no malice to his words, and he dropped my hand before going over to sweep her up into a hug.

This was a strange new development. I still hadn't seen everything in his life. Five hundred years was a lot to cram into two weeks' worth of memories, and most of the ones I had seen had involved Eve, Connor or members of the Order. Seeing him be friendly with a daywalker was a little bit of a surprise.

"Welcome back, big brother." She hugged him back tightly before stepping back to look him over. Brother?

"I'd say thanks, but given that I don't want to be here, I'm not sure welcome is the right word," Liam said, the frustration returning to his voice.

"Ah yes, Michael mentioned Eve went off on a little retrieval mission." She finally looked at me, running her eyes over me slowly. "So, this is your girl, huh?"

I wasn't entirely sure I liked how she was looking at me. But Liam hadn't taken on his usual protective stance when someone threatened me, so I held her gaze.

"This is Isolde, yes." Liam turned back towards me, and Anika stepped around him to come and stand before me. I tensed slightly. My experiences with the other daywalkers had not been particularly welcoming, and given this woman chose to spend time with Eve, I wasn't prepared to take any chances with her yet.

She continued to inspect me, and I stared right back, refusing to be intimidated. Finally, a big smile appeared on her face, and I was taken aback at the complete change in her attitude when she swept me up into a huge hug and squeezed tightly. I looked over her shoulder at Liam, my eyebrows raised. He shrugged with a smile.

"I like her," Anika said over her shoulder when she finally let go, and I didn't know what to say.

"Um, thanks?" I was suddenly aware of the burning in my throat and remembered it had been several hours since I'd had blood. I truly hoped the intense urge for blood would pass soon because it was incredibly inconvenient. And I was concerned that sometimes humans looked like a tasty snack.

"You need blood. Come on," Anika said.

I had no idea how they all seemed to know when my need for blood overwhelmed me, but I allowed her to take me by the hand and lead me into a large kitchen towards the back of the house. Liam followed close behind.

"Wow." I stopped short at the door. It was the fanciest kitchen I had ever seen, with top-end appliances, including several stoves and ovens. The fridge even had a touch screen, which I'd never seen before.

"Ronson likes to cook," Anika said over her shoulder while she opened the fridge and pulled out a pitcher that I assumed was filled with blood. I turned slowly to look at Liam, unable to imagine the stoic, silent Ronson as a fancy chef who used all the gadgets in this kitchen. Again, Liam shrugged. He seemed unable to do much more than that now that we were back here. I felt there would be many more revelations while we were here. I wasn't sure how I felt about that.

Anika had been chattering while she poured blood into a fancy glass that looked like it was made of crystal. That didn't surprise me in the slightest. From what I knew about Eve, she enjoyed the finer things in life, and her choice of glassware would be no exception. I tuned in to what Anika said while she handed me the glass.

"The others are all starting to arrive," She said to Liam.

I wondered how many *others* she was referring to, but I needed to deal with the burning in my throat before I could focus on anything else. I drained the glass before handing it back wordlessly to Anika. She raised an eyebrow at me before shooting a look at Liam and pouring me a second glass. "Thirsty little thing, aren't ya?" I drained the second glass, trying not to feel self-conscious at her words.

"The transition has been a bit rough. It's only been a couple of weeks, Anika." Liam admonished her, but she just shrugged and took the glass from me again, popping it in the dishwasher behind her. I was relieved that it wasn't the only bloody glass in there.

"So, house rules." Anika clapped her hands, and Liam rolled his eyes with a sigh. "Watch it, Liam. It's been quite a while since you lived with the family."

I found it interesting that they referred to themselves as a family. From what I'd seen of Liam's memories, he didn't consider them family, preferring to stay with the Order instead.

"First rule. Clean the fuck up after yourselves. Quite a few of us are here now, and while we have a housekeeper, if you leave shit around, you will eventually piss off the wrong person." She raised a hand and held up two fingers. "Second rule. Don't piss anyone off." I waited for the rest of the rules, but that seemed to be it. She looked at us both expectantly and didn't seem surprised when Liam huffed a mocking laugh.

"Given that we were summoned here and informed that we had to stay, I don't give a shit who we piss off, Anika."

Someone cleared their throat behind us, and we turned to see a man with pale skin and deep red hair that was cut short enter the room.

He was well built, like every other daywalker I had met so far, and I figured centuries of fighting evil kept everyone in shape. His blue eyes regarded me closely when he came to stand at Anika's side and slung an arm around her shoulders. He towered over her, standing even taller than Liam.

"So, this is the chosen one." He sounded bored, but I could tell it was an act while he ran his eyes over me. Liam growled a little beside me and pulled me close, almost as though he was reminding this man of his claim over me.

"Don't be an asshole, Anthony. It doesn't suit you." Anika smacked him in the chest, and he rolled his eyes at her.

"What? I can't see what all the fuss is about. She doesn't seem any different to any of the rest of us," he said with a shrug.

"I assure you, Anthony, she is more powerful than any of you." Eve's voice rang out behind us, and Liam tensed up again when she entered the room, followed by Ronson and a man I recognised to be Michael from Liam's memories. I felt like this was probably the closest to a compliment I would ever get from her.

She took in Liam's protective stance beside me and rolled her eyes.

"For fuck's sake, Liam, give it a rest."

I detected what I assumed was some jealousy within her aggravation, and I moved closer to Liam, sliding my arm behind his back while I reached around with the other to slide my hand over his chest, coming to rest over his heart, which I could feel beating steadily. He knew what I was doing and chuckled, covering my hand with his own. I was a mouse toying with a hungry cat, but I didn't care. I was tired of dealing with her bullshit.

"I don't know, Eve... I find it hot," I said, my voice low, and she raised an eyebrow, amusement rippling across her features.

"You wanna play Isolde? Be prepared to give it all you've got." Whilst she talked a big game, I could tell the fact that I wasn't intimidated by her mere presence was frustrating her.

"Who's playing? I've already won." I shrugged, and Ronson gave a low warning growl. I flicked my eyes over him. "Careful, Ronson. I'm more powerful than all of you, remember?" I threw Eve's words back at them, and she narrowed her eyes, assessing me closely.

"I didn't say you were more powerful than me, Isolde. Just more powerful than them." Her words were low and dangerous, and Liam squeezed my hand gently, a warning to maybe stop playing with the cat quite so much. Across the kitchen counter, Anthony laughed loudly.

"Oh, this is going to be fun. Eve, I haven't seen someone get under your skin this much in a while. I approve of your woman, Liam." Anthony said, and Anika smacked his chest again. He rubbed the spot, the hit harder than the last one. "What?"

"You know perfectly well *what.*" She shot him a pointed look, and he shot her a cheeky grin, which she answered with a roll of her eyes. They held each other's gaze for a moment longer, and I watched with interest. Could this be the daywalker couple that Liam had mentioned to me once, that were bonded like we had been? If so, their bond appeared to still be intact, unlike ours.

"As fun as all this is, what do you want, Eve? You've forced us here. Now I want to know why." Liam glared at Eve. She finally shifted her gaze from mine to run her eyes slowly over him.

"You can't be surprised that I want all of my family under this roof. Now that you're little Protector lover is one of us, there is no reason for you to remain with them. I've indulged your little rebellion for far longer than I should have."

I gaped at Eve, unable to believe she would even think that a response like that would slide with Liam after everything I'd witnessed of their interactions over the years.

"Fuck you, Eve," Liam's voice came out in a low growl, which sent a shiver of attraction up my spine.

Yep, right on time.

"Liam, darling, watch your tone when you speak to me. I have allowed you to disrespect me over the centuries, but I am growing tired of it. Do I need to remind you of how truly powerful I am?" Her eyes narrowed dangerously while she looked at him, but Liam wasn't backing down.

"I don't give a shit, Eve. You clearly need us here for some reason, so drop the act. What do you want? Never once in all my years have you insisted that I be here, so why now? What's your endgame?" Liam wasn't going to let it go, and rightly so. He wasn't the only one interested in hearing Eve's response. I eyed her coolly, and she once again held my gaze, an aggravating smirk playing across her lips.

"He's right, Eve. Something smells off. What are you planning?" Anika asked, and I was pleased to see that although Eve had a somewhat inflated ego, most of her *family* wasn't afraid to call her out on her bullshit.

"All in good time, my darlings." Eve turned on her heel and walked gracefully towards the door, followed closely by Ronson and Michael. I assumed that these two were the most loyal of her little lapdogs.

"Is that good time before or after the world implodes around us?" I demanded before she reached the door.

"You'll know soon enough." She didn't even look back, and it took every ounce of my little self-control to keep from racing after her and punching her.

"Fucking woman," Anthony said quietly while he and Liam glared at her retreating, and Anika nodded.

Sighing, Liam turned around to look at them both.

"So, what's the deal these days? Do any of you still head out on patrol? I haven't encountered anyone in the last twenty-six years, but surely you aren't all leaving it up to the Order?"

I raised an eyebrow. In all the time I've known him, the involvement of daywalkers in hunting down nightwalker covens had never come up.

Anthony snorted.

"As if we'd leave the fate of the world in the hands of those idiots. Yes, we still patrol. Tonight is our night. Wanna come play?" Anthony grinned, looking between Liam and me.

I looked over at Liam, who nodded. I was interested in watching what the daywalkers did differently and why they felt superior to the Order.

"We'll join you," Liam said, and Anika clapped her hands with a wide smile. She was so bubbly, nothing like I'd expected any daywalkers to act.

"This will be so much fun. And I can't wait to see you in action." She directed this at me, and I wondered what my reputation was amongst the daywalkers. Since transitioning, I hadn't fought any nightwalkers other than the brief exchange with Aurora and Will. I was kind of interested to see what all the fuss was about myself.

"She's not coming just for your enjoyment, Anika," Liam said with a huff, and I patted his chest.

"It's okay. It's only natural that everyone is so interested if that's how Eve talks about me. I hope I can live up to the hype."

Liam's eyebrows were raised, and I shrugged. There was no point denying it, with the constant reminders of my supposed superpowers.

Conversation over, Anika and Anthony left us to our own devices, and Liam gave me a brief tour of the house. He'd spent a week trapped here while I transitioned and had made a point of learning the entire layout whilst skilfully avoiding spending too much time with any of the daywalkers. The house was huge, and I realised there were already quite a few more daywalkers living here than I realised when we'd last been here. All seemed to have varying levels of wariness around Liam and me, which I assumed was due to our connection to the Order. I had known that the daywalkers weren't keen on the Order of the Dragon, but I only saw the full extent of that now. I wondered now why Liam had chosen to remain allied with them, and I voiced this curiosity as we entered the room where I had previously been when I transitioned.

"Honestly, because most daywalkers, whilst nowhere near as bad as nightwalkers, have so little regard for humanity. And I needed the connection with my former self that I felt when I was with the Order." Liam said, closing the door behind him.

We hadn't been assigned a room, so we'd just returned here, figuring this was where we were expected to stay. As long as it was away from Eve, I didn't care.

"And how do you feel now after everything we've learnt the past few weeks?" I went to him and wrapped my arms around his waist while he stood with his back to me, looking out the window. He rubbed my arm before lifting my hand and bringing it to his lips.

"Truthfully? Right now, I feel like the only person I can trust is standing right here with me." I understood how he was feeling, even as I tried to push away the guilt that crept up on me, knowing that even I wasn't being entirely truthful with him. I wasn't ready to deal with the suspicions of what seeing Aurora's memories might mean. Denial was so much easier. So I allowed him to draw the comfort he needed from my embrace and hoped with all my heart that I was wrong.

CHAPTER EIGHTEEN

*L*iam and I accompanied Anika and Anthony later that night, leaving the house on foot after midnight to begin our patrol. Although I'd been a daywalker for nearly two weeks now, I still hadn't put my new abilities to any real test, having focussed instead on the blood memories that were still flooding in, often at the most inopportune times. But now I was a little excited to see what I could do. Before, even though I had been one of the best fighters amongst the humans in the Order, Liam was still faster and stronger than I was. I was interested to see if my advanced skills had continued past the transition. I still had no idea how I was meant to be more powerful than everyone else. And I assumed Eve wouldn't tell me anything until she deemed it the right time. Probably at a time when she could make it as dramatic as possible.

"Hey, newbie. Ready to run?" Anika called back over her shoulder when we were halfway down the street. I knew we were headed down to the large park near Southbank, which was still a bit of a distance away. I had assumed we would be driving, so running there sounded interesting.

"Sure," I responded, but before I'd even finished speaking, Anika and Anthony had become two blurs, moving so fast it was impossible to tell who was who. Liam looked over at me with a grin and took off as well. That left me standing alone. This all occurred in a fraction of a second, and I was stunned. I'd seen Liam move like that before, but to have it happen with so many people at once was a slight shock to the system.

But once that shock wore off, I couldn't wait to try it. I took a deep breath before taking off, running as fast as possible. The world around me turned into nothing more than a blur, and the sensation was exhilarating. It took no effort on my part, and within a minute, I arrived at the park, coming to a halt beside Liam. A distance that would have taken us at least twenty minutes to walk at a regular, human pace, and we'd done it within a minute.

"Why on earth do you ever bother driving anywhere?!" I asked him, and he smirked.

"I only ever drove when you were with me, remember? You were the slow-ass one." I gasped at him in mock outrage and tapped his arm. Anika and Anthony were watching us closely but didn't say anything. They retook the lead, and Liam and I followed while we began moving amongst the shadows of the large trees around the park. This park had had a reputation for years as not being the safest at night, but I'd never lived nearby, so it hadn't been on my radar. But now I could understand where the reputation had come from. There were many homeless people, some in tents, with others sleeping on benches and under trees, all of whom I was sure that the police and general public thought were the problem, refusing to acknowledge the societal issues that had led to these people sleeping here.

But the real problem was the nightwalkers I could now sense prowling nearby. These people were perfect prey, and seeing how vulnerable they were out here was so sad because of how society viewed those down on their luck. Only a few people would have noticed if these people had gone missing. And that was concerning on so many levels. How many people had Connor and Adam recruited to their side just by preying on those so often overlooked by the authorities? And worse, the Order hadn't been focussing on these areas either. I was starting to understand why the daywalkers had such a low opinion of the Order.

"Do you patrol this park every night?" I asked quietly, and Anika nodded.

"Yes, this one and many others. It's not the highly populated areas that are the problem. Some nightwalkers might venture into places like the Valley or the city to pick off drunk revellers when they stumble home, but these are the areas where the nightwalkers truly lurk."

I looked at Liam to see his reaction to this information and his take on it, but he shook his head, indicating that now wasn't the time for this conversation. I nodded and went back to scanning the area. A movement in the corner of my eye caught my attention, and I turned to see a nightwalker that I recognised as one of Adam's followers moving towards a sleeping figure on a nearby park bench. He had been present at the restaurant when I'd first come face to face with Connor and Aurora in her current state. His build alone was enough to put a Rugby player to shame, built like a brick wall but moving with the fluid grace of a vampire.

Anthony was already on him before I'd fully registered his presence, having noticed him whilst Anika was talking to me. He moved with such silent precision that the nightwalker was completely surprised when Anthony leapt onto him from the shadows. He had no time to react before Anthony ripped his head from his shoulders with powerful force, and I was both impressed and disgusted at the same time. Patrolling with the Order had been different from this. They'd had to rely on their weapons, and each interaction with a nightwalker had been almost like a fight to the death. But the daywalkers' powers matched those of the nightwalkers. I wondered why the Order even bothered.

I watched, fascinated, while Anthony hefted the body of the nightwalker onto his shoulders with ease, grabbing the head in his free hand from the ground and wandering casually back over to us. The person sleeping on the bench hadn't even stirred.

"What are you going to do with that?" I indicated towards the body draped across Anthony's rather broad shoulders. He shrugged, and it was almost comical watching the headless body bob up and down behind his head. Almost.

"I figured I'd set it on fire. It's what we usually do. We just need to find somewhere less obvious to do it. I can't have the cops stumbling across a burning body." Anthony said.

Liam looked over at me with a raised eyebrow. I winked at him.

"I think I can help with that," I said with a grin.

Anthony looked confused, but the three of them followed me while I led the way, stopping amongst some low bushes. I indicated that Anthony should put the body on the ground, and he did so, exchanging a look with Anika after he dumped it unceremoniously. Anika just shrugged, having no idea what was about to happen. I hoped that my shielding abilities had survived the transition the same as my fire abilities, as I'd not yet thought to test them, and it would make this rather embarrassing if I couldn't follow through.

The others stayed behind me while I focussed on the body. I'd never had an audience other than Liam when I performed magic. I tried not to feel self-conscious with three pairs of eyes boring a hole into my back when I brought my arms up to waist height and closed my eyes, taking a deep breath while centring myself.

"Hide and protect me," I said aloud and was relieved to feel the power ripple through my body when the air around me began to crackle with magic. I heard all three of them draw sharp breaths behind me, and I knew I'd succeeded in becoming invisible to them. Now for the more complicated part of expanding the protective bubble to include them. With my eyes still closed, I concentrated on the edges of the shield, willing them to grow slowly to extend to where the three of them stood. I knew the moment it had worked when Anthony let out a small whoop of delight behind me, and I tried not to feel cocky. Anything could still go wrong, and the body hadn't been dealt with yet.

Opening my eyes now, I focused on the body on the ground, clicking my fingers and resisting the urge to let out a relieved breath when two small balls of flame appeared, floating above each hand. I could feel the power flowing through me. Seconds later, though, I could feel panic kick in when the flames began to dance before me, the fire growing quickly, unlike when I'd used my abilities in front of the Order the week before. The flames grew so large that I could feel what little control I had slipping away further, almost like my magic had a mind of its own.

"What the fuck..." Anthony said loudly, and Anika shushed him.

Liam stepped close behind me, his chest pressing against my back while he ran his fingers slowly along my arms before cupping my hands with his.

"Just lean into me, Isolde. Use my power to control yours." He whispered in my ear, and the magic began stabilising. The balls of fire were again controlled, and I relaxed a little into Liam's arms. I remembered now that when I'd used my ability at the Manor, Liam's hand had been on my shoulder, and I wondered if that had been the real reason I'd been able to control the flame then.

Both balls of fire were huge now but no longer flickering erratically, and we raised our arms together, merging the flames before us. I inhaled deeply while we guided the ball toward the body and watched it erupt into flames. Nightwalker bodies combusted when set alight, and this one was no different.

"Oh shit!" Anthony suddenly remembered the head still in his hand and threw it into the flames before they disappeared, and I laughed. I never thought I would find death and destruction funny, but there was something so hilarious about watching the head fly through the air, and I wondered if maybe I'd just hit the final point of my sanity and was now completely unhinged. But Anika and Liam also huffed out a laugh, and that made me feel better. At least I wasn't alone in the madness.

Anika and Anthony stepped up beside us, staring silently down at where the body had previously been. All that remained was a scorched patch of grass, with small puffs of smoke drifting upwards.

"That was…" Anika seemed to be searching for the right words.

"Fucking brilliant." Anthony was grinning while he finished her sentence. He looked like a kid who had just unwrapped a shiny new toy at Christmas, although Anika looked slightly more unsure. She looked at Liam.

"Have you always been able to do that?"

I felt Liam shake his head, his hands still cupping mine.

"No, I seem to be able to tap into Isolde's power, but that was mostly her. I just felt the pull towards her then to help her control it."

I turned my hands over and laced my fingers through his, squeezing them while I lowered them to my side.

"Let's go. I wanna see that again!" Anthony was bouncing on his feet. Anika looked at us for a beat longer before nodding, following him out of the bushes. Liam pulled me back when I moved to follow them, turning me to face him before crushing his mouth to mine. He ran his hands into my hair, holding me tight against him and kissing me hungrily.

"I forgot how great that feels," He said, his lips still pressed to mine. I nodded, still feeling the power crackle through us both. The few times he had previously channelled my magic, we'd immediately climbed all over each other. Still, I wasn't interested in having an audience, so we had to make do with another brief kiss. Pulling away reluctantly, I looked up at him, ensuring he knew we would pick this up once we were alone, before following our companions out of the bushes and hunting down another nightwalker to set on fire.

After taking out four more nightwalkers, we returned to the house shortly before dawn. It was the most I'd ever come across in a single night when there wasn't a nest involved, which was both exciting and terrifying. I'd remained relatively quiet on the walk back to the house, not feeling the need to join Anika and Anthony as they ran back in a blur. Liam remained silent at my side, allowing me to mull over my thoughts without interference. It wasn't until we reached our room that I finally started asking the questions forming in my mind.

"Why aren't the Order out there, focussing on where the real problems are? Surely they are aware of the risk posed to those sleeping rough?"

"Honestly, I think it's because they are more focused on keeping the presence of vampires a secret."

I could see my concern mirrored in his eyes, which was a bit of a relief.

"Did you never patrol with them in the past? Surely you understood this world better than the Order?" I was struggling to wrap my head around all of this. Liam ran his hand through his hair as he shrugged his shoulders.

"Although I've sometimes been in the houses that Eve inhabited, it was never longer than a few weeks, and I never went out on patrol. What they have all said is true. I spent more time with the Order, attempting to maintain my hold on the human aspect of myself. I've been so focused on my resentment of Eve that I've avoided them all, yet in one day of being with them alongside you, I'm beginning to realise just how little I was aware of." He had moved closer to the window and stared outside as if the darkness held the answers he desperately sought.

"I don't know that I'd go that far, Liam. I still don't trust the daywalkers entirely. From what I can tell, they only patrol to keep the nightwalkers from growing any larger in number. I don't think saving humanity is particularly concerning to them." I moved to stand beside him, raising my hand to touch him lightly on the cheek. I didn't like what the last few weeks had done to his confidence, even though, at the same time, I questioned why he had allowed himself to be so led astray by the Order. He turned to face me and put his arms around me, pulling me close to bury his face in my hair, and sighed.

"I think we did the right thing after all in coming here." He murmured into my hair, and I nodded.

"Me too. But I still want to know what Eve's plan is. It surely can't just be that she wants us close, to be part of her big happy family."

"Agreed. I think she knows far more about the prophecy than what she has told us, and I want to know what that is. But for now, let's try and get some sleep." He guided me towards the giant bed where I had lain for a week in the transition phase. I resisted at first, not sure I wanted to return to it. But after hours of tapping into my powers, sleep was calling my name, and I eventually gave in, sinking beside him and allowing him to hold me close while we fell asleep, the first of dawn's rays beginning to show around the edges of the curtains.

"I see you and my brother have had a busy night." Once again, just after sleep claimed me, I stood across the room from Connor, where he sat in the same chair, swirling yet another glass of whiskey in his hand.

"Seriously, Connor, what's the go? Why do you keep pulling me in here? Don't you have other people you can annoy the crap out of?" I returned to my usual place, leaning against the wall furthest from him. I'd stopped being afraid of him at this point, knowing he wouldn't hurt me, although I was still unsure why.

"You're so much more fun to talk to than the rest. And watching your sister screw anyone who looks her way is becoming tiresome. Even dear William is growing bored of her and returning to his previous obsession with you."

I knew he was trying to goad me into a reaction, but I refused to rise to the bait, even though the mention of my sister and former fiancé made me feel queasy.

"What's so fun about talking to me, Connor?" I watched his every

move, aware that I lay asleep in his brother's arms while this conversation happened in my mind.

"You fascinate me, Isolde. All these years of waiting for you to arrive, can you blame me for wanting to see the woman foretold to bring about the destruction of my kind?"

"How do you have powers? None of the other nightwalkers seem to have magical abilities, yet here we are, having a conversation in our minds only." I had no idea if he would answer me, but I figured I'd give it a shot.

Connor smirked at me.

"You still have so much to learn, little one. I see Eve is still playing her games." He got up and walked towards me.

I watched him warily, refusing to move. He stopped in front of me, standing so close that I could feel his breath on my face when he looked down at me. I stood completely still while he ran a finger over my neck at where he'd bitten me, the wound long since healed.

"Come and find me again once you work it out." He kissed my forehead while the dream dissolved around us again, and I settled into a dreamless sleep.

CHAPTER NINETEEN

The next few days followed the same pattern as the first. Our days were spent catching up on the few hours of sleep we needed in the mornings, sharing a meal with whoever was around in the afternoons and evenings, and patrolling at night.

I was receiving regular updates from Ainslie about my family and was relieved that, so far, Aurora was keeping her distance. They had decided to tell people that she'd had a psychotic break and was dangerous... I wasn't sure if that would help, but something was better than nothing.

More daywalkers had begun to arrive, and like usual, they were all fascinated by my presence, which was growing old. Eve had been avoiding us for the most part, and I was impressed at her sexual appetite. A seemingly endless stream of daywalkers walking through her bedroom door, a constant rotation of her little band of followers. I'd witnessed this in Liam's memories, but watching it in person was different.

"Is she ever going to tell us what she has planned?" I expressed my frustration to Liam when we walked back into our room after another meal with Anika and Anthony while Eve remained sequestered in her room.

"Eve never does anything without a plan. I have no doubt that this little parade of sex buddies is for our benefit." Liam said, and I could tell he was also over the games.

"Well, it's not working. Other than making me wonder if her lady parts need to be iced."

Liam laughed, turning to pull me towards him.

"Want to give her a run for her money?" He began kissing down my neck, and I leaned into him with a sigh.

"How about we don't worry about competing." I drew his lips to mine, squealing when he reached down and swiftly grabbed the back of my thighs like I weighed nothing, bringing my legs up to wrap around his waist. We continued to kiss hungrily while he pushed me back against the wall, and I allowed all other thoughts to fall from my mind as we explored even more ways to add to the mingled cries that moved through the house.

That evening, we decided to forego patrolling, and once darkness had fallen, I found my way into the library that took up the entire length of the back of the house on the top floor. Liam had gone to get us dinner, and I had downed yet another glass of blood before deciding to settle down with a book. Since everything in my life had exploded, all my reading had been focussed on research, and I was now faced with the daunting task of choosing a book to read for pleasure.

It felt strange to have time out while the world was going to shit, but my anxiety was beginning to spiral, and I would be useless to anyone if I didn't get my emotions under control.

I ran my fingers along the shelves while I read through the titles along the long wall of shelves. Nothing was jumping out at me, and I wondered if I'd lost the ability to read for enjoyment, along with so much else in my former life.

I was pulled from my musings by the sound of a book falling

from the shelf, which made me jump, and I looked over to see a small leather-bound book lying on the floor across the room. There was no one else in the room, and where once this would have freaked me out, I knew without a doubt that someone had used magic to bring this book to my attention. I moved to pick it up, turning it over to read the gold writing embossed on the front. THE PHOENIX PROPHECY.

Oh dear god, not another prophecy book... The last one I read had utterly upended my life, and I wasn't sure I was ready for another one. I cautiously opened the book, worried I'd set off some terrifying chain of events just by lifting the cover. It was only a few pages long, and the paper was delicate.

In a world blemished by darkness and light,
A young woman shall rise with power and might.
Her destiny was foretold in a prophecy of old,
To bring balance to the turmoil untold.
Of seventh son and seventh daughter born,
Her heart will be set to mourn.
There will be trials that she must endure,
Before she reaches the future so pure.
Her power will be unmatched and rare,
Her soul will be pure, her intentions fair.
But to end the apocalypse, she must pay a cost,
To sacrifice what she loves and lost.
A decision she must make with a heavy heart,
For she knows this is where her journey must start.
With tears in her eyes, she'll rise with grace,
To battle the evil she must face.
The fate of the world will rest upon her hand,
As she brings an end to the chaos of the land.
Her journey will end with a triumph so bright,
As she brings balance between the wrong and the right.

. . .

The words triggered a memory of my own for a change, and I flashed back to my dream when Connor and Aurora first kidnapped me. The words had floated in front of me, but with everything that had happened since then, I'd forgotten all about it. Unable to move, I read the words so many times that my eyes started to blur, trying to understand the meaning behind the words. None of it sounded good to me, except that I would triumph... Triumph how, though?

Liam entered the room at the door furthest from where I sat, clearing his throat to get my attention.

"You okay?" He asked as I remained staring at the book. He came to stand behind me and peered over my shoulder to read the words that were now swimming on the page before me.

"I don't know, to be honest," I said, looking up at him and watching his eyes move back and forth while he quickly read each line, his eyes growing wider with each word. "Have you never actually read the prophecy before?"

"No one had ever shown me, but I've been told about it. But they'd never told me the exact wording."

"Out of curiosity, what did you know, Liam?" I tried not to sound judgemental, but I could tell my words had hit a sore spot when he winced. "Sorry." I gently placed a hand on his cheek, and he turned to place a kiss on my palm before straightening up.

"We've established that I knew very little about anything." He led the way back into the kitchen, and I followed behind him, clutching the book to my chest. As far as I was concerned, this was my book now. I watched while he plated up our Thai food, taking the plate he handed me before sitting beside me at the breakfast bar.

"I think it's time we sat down with Eve," I said, taking a mouthful of food. Liam grimaced, taking his own bite of food and chewing slowly before answering.

"I know we need to, but I also know how impossible it is to get that woman to talk when she isn't ready. She's got something planned, I can tell."

"So we just wait until she decides we're allowed to know the truth about ourselves?" I was not on board with this plan.

"You've seen how difficult it is to get Eve to give a straight answer at the best of times. You're welcome to try and discuss it with her. If you can pry her away from her line of men." Liam shook his head while he continued eating.

"Not just men. I've also seen a few women head in there," I said, and Liam nodded.

"Very true. She doesn't particularly have a preference." We continued eating in silence whilst I thought this over.

"Does it bother you at all? Did you ever have feelings for her?" I wasn't sure why I was asking, as I was pretty sure I didn't want to know the answer, but I had to accept that he'd spent centuries on this planet before I was conceived, and no matter how he felt about me, I knew that other women had warmed his bed.

Liam scanned my face before answering.

"In the beginning, I was enamoured with her. I didn't see her for about ten years after she turned me, and I was interested in this life enough to spend time with her. But there was never the connection that I craved. I think she's been separated from humanity for so long that she's lost the ability to connect on an emotional level. And that was something that I needed. I didn't understand that until I met you, though." He took my hand in his, and I squeezed his fingers lightly.

"I think from what I've seen, although she doesn't appear to have any connection to humanity in the same sense we do, there is still something there. She wants you. I know that my presence, whilst necessary apparently, grates on her. The looks I've received from her show that she does *not* love having someone else playing with someone that she believes belongs to her."

"If I belong to anyone, Isolde, it's you." His words were sweet, and yet there was something that struck a chord deep within me.

"I don't think you belong to anyone but yourself, Liam. You've been searching for who you are and your place in the world for so long. I hope you know that I see who you truly are?"

He looked at me, and I could tell he was trying to believe me.

"Who am I? Because you're right, I have been searching without realising it for so long. I thought I was a Protector, different from all the other daywalkers, but now I have no idea where I fit in or my purpose in this world." The sadness in his eyes broke my heart, and I touched his face again.

"Only you can answer that, Liam. I can only tell you who you are to me. You have been my protector and source of comfort through so much, but that is who you are to me. I can't be your sole purpose, nor you mine. We need to work out together what both our paths are, regardless of any bloody prophecies. But the positive thing is, I'm not going anywhere. We are stuck together now through it all. Whatever the next step ends up being." I brought my forehead to his, and he closed his eyes, taking a deep breath.

"For someone who has only been walking this earth for such a short time, I sometimes feel like you know far more than me, my love." He kissed my forehead, and it was my turn to take a deep breath, pushing aside the feeling of deja vu that hit me at the action. It was so close to what Connor had done during our last interaction. The less I compared the two of them, the better. That way would only lead to more pain and confusion, and I wasn't ready to deal with any of that yet. I wasn't sure that I would ever be.

CHAPTER TWENTY

*"*Ugh. *Doesn't it get tiring being so sickeningly in love and stroking each other's egos all the time?"*

Once again, Conor pulled me into the mindscape, and we were in our usual positions. In the real world, Liam and I were wrapped around each other, having fallen asleep after another round of love-making in our room. By now, I could tell Connor seemed to have access to my movements in the real world, and I didn't bother hiding my sneer.

"There's that jealousy again, Connor," I said, my arms crossed while I watched him throw back yet another glass of whiskey.

"Hardly. The two of you exhaust me. All of those pesky feelings and insecurities flying around is enough to drive me to drink." He poured himself another drink before getting a second glass and pouring another one. He walked towards me and held the glass out towards me. "Have a drink with me, Isolde."

I hesitated, eyeing the glass in his outstretched hand.

"You watched me pour it. It's not going to hurt you. And besides, it's a fucking dream. Just take the damn drink."

I glared at him before snatching it from his hand, throwing my head back and allowing the whiskey to burn down my throat.

"Good girl."

I scowled at him while I slammed the glass down. It made a satisfying bang when it met the wooden surface.

"I'm not your good girl, Connor." I refused to play into whatever fantasy he was building up in his mind about us being together, even though his presence now confused my brain. I blamed the dream whiskey for how my body seemed drawn towards him when he stood before me. I watched him throw back his drink, clenching my jaw when my traitorous body reacted at the sight of his throat bobbing while he swallowed.

"You're not Liam," I said once again, as a reminder to myself, but knowing it would piss him off.

"How often do I have to remind you I am far more fun than him?" Connor tossed his glass aside, and it smashed against the wall. He stepped closer to me, holding my gaze while he lifted a lock of my hair and twirled it with his finger.

What was it with these men and my hair?

I was cursing the part of me that was unwilling to fight the control he seemed to have over me, unable to step away even while he gathered my hair around his fist and tipped my head back slightly, forcing my gaze to meet his intense stare.

"What do you want, Connor?" I breathed out a sigh when he lowered his forehead to mine. Why couldn't I control my body around this man? I knew he was evil and meant to be my mortal enemy, and yet I was drawn to him like a fucking moth to a flame. I lowered my gaze to his lips, and he chuckled, aware of my every movement.

"Seems like my baby brother might not be enough for you, little one." He grazed his lips over mine before stepping back with what looked like immense effort, and I felt the loss of his presence, even though I could breathe a little easier now that he was further away.

"He is more than enough for me. I still maintain that you are doing something to me. I love Liam. I hate you." I glared at him, and

he smirked, raking a hand through his hair while his eyes flashed again. "And why the fuck do your eyes keep doing that?"

He raised an eyebrow.

"I think the question you're asking is why have your eyes been doing that?" He stepped closer again and lifted my chin to gaze into my eyes. "You're starting to realise that there are so many differences between yourself and the other daywalkers. Between us and all the other vampires."

I was once again fighting the urge to kiss him and was proud of myself for placing my hand on his chest and pushing him away.

He moved back without resistance, laughing. He was enjoying this far too much.

I was growing more and more annoyed with every moment that passed between us.

"I'm waking up now." I attempted to pull myself out of the connection, but nothing happened, and Connor just watched me with a smirk. "Let me go, Connor."

"But I enjoy talking to you so much more than the others. Let me show you what I'm dealing with right now." The room dissolved around us, and we no longer stood in that god-forsaken house. I had no idea where he had brought me, but judging by the large room we were standing in, it was yet another massive house. In all my twenty-five years before becoming aware of this world, I had never set foot in homes this fancy. These magical and immortal beings loved to surround themselves with wealth.

But it wasn't the room that held my attention. My eyes were drawn to the couple in the corner who were devouring each other. Aurora ground herself against Will, who lay back on a chaise lounge, surrounded by other nightwalkers. Some were partaking in their own sexual experiences, but a few others watched them hungrily. I felt ill at the sight when Connor stepped close behind me and waved his hand around the room, pointing towards the others.

Connor had brought me to see a vampire orgy, and my sister and former fiancé appeared to be the stars of the show.

"Was your sister this much of an exhibitionist in her former life? Because she fucking loves being watched while she's being fucked, and it is growing exhausting watching her ride every member of this coven. She's particularly enamoured with dear William, but I don't think there is anyone left that she hasn't screwed, male or female." Connor ran his hands down my sides while pressing against my back.

I pushed out of his grasp and looked away. I couldn't stomach the look on Aurora's face while she rode Will, staring over his head at the couple standing behind him. The woman ran her hand through my sister's hair.

"Does that mean you've fucked her as well?" I spat the words out as I stormed from the room.

I wanted out of this hellscape now.

Once again, the room around us changed, and we were back in the house. I didn't think I'd ever be grateful to be back here, but anything was better than that. I marched towards the bottle of whiskey and grabbed it by the neck, taking a large drink and slamming it back down, willing the burn to erase the scene from my mind.

"Now who's jealous, Isolde? Don't you like the idea of me buried deep inside your twin sister, fucking her brains out?" He came right after me, grabbing my arm and swinging me around to face him. The smirk on his face was laced with desire, and his chest rose and fell rapidly when he closed the small distance between us. I held myself perfectly still, glaring at him while he held my gaze, gripping my chin to keep me from looking away.

"Yes, you're jealous. You want me, and you hate yourself for it. But you crave my lips on yours." He crushed his mouth to mine, pulling me into his arms and kissing me hungrily before I could react. "You want me to make you scream." His voice was husky while he ran his hands down my sides and yanked my hips into his, forcing me to feel how hard he was against my abdomen. He nipped at my neck between hungry kisses, and I gasped, torn between desire and repulsion at how my body reacted.

"No, I don't." My body was not agreeing with the words coming out of my mouth.

Connor laughed darkly and spun me around, pulling my back flush against his chest while his hands roamed my body. My mind was at war with my body, and I gasped when his lips blazed a path up my neck, stopping at my earlobe, which he took gently between his teeth.

"No, Isolde. You clearly don't want this. You really don't want my hand here," he whispered in my ear while he cupped my breast with his hand, and I arched into his touch.

"And you obviously don't want me to touch you here." He ran his other hand down my abdomen, and my breathing quickened when he traced a circle around my belly button.

"I... don't... want..." I struggled to form words while his hand moved further south, and I gasped when his fingers slipped beneath the band of my yoga pants, inching closer and closer to where I was aching between my legs.

"No. You don't want me to make you come over and over, do you, Isolde?" He began to rub his finger over my sensitive bud, and I groaned. He moved his hand faster, feeling my body tense up while he kissed my neck. My hips began moving of their own accord, and I rode his hand.

"But you shouldn't come, Isolde..."

Just when I was sure my body was about to explode, he ripped his hands away, whispering in my ear while the dream faded.

"Because I'm not Liam."

In reality, I sat up quickly, still panting, and nausea ripped through me. I could feel the sweat covering my body, causing me to feel cold even in the summer heat.

That fucking asshole.

I leapt from the bed and ran into the bathroom connected to our room, hearing Liam stir when I began throwing up. He flew into the room behind me and pulled my hair back out of my face while I retched, rubbing a soothing hand up and down my back. I had been unsure if vampires could throw up, but I was proving it was possible.

Eventually, the retching subsided, and I reached up to flush the toilet before leaning back against the cabinet as I sat on the cold tiles. Liam poured me a glass of water and pressed it into my hands, urging me to drink.

"Are you okay?" He slid down to sit beside me and put an arm around me. I realised I was shaking and fought not to throw up again at the memory of his brother's hands all over me.

"Yeah." I let my head fall to his shoulder and stared at the wall opposite where we sat.

"What happened?" There was no suspicion in Liam's voice, and his complete trust in me felt like a knife was being driven into my heart. I decided to go with a bit of the truth.

"Connor pulled me into his mind again and showed me Aurora screwing the entire coven."

Liam's grip on me tightened, pulling me in closer.

"I'm so sorry, Isolde. I wish I knew how to break his hold over your mind. I'll talk to Eve and see if we can do anything. Maybe the Order knows a spell." I felt his jaw clench against my forehead where I was leaning into his chest, and I nodded.

I had a feeling there was no way to break this. And a small part of me wondered if I even wanted to. Because aside from being forced to watch my sister grind against the former love of my life, a small, treacherous part of me wished Connor had finished what he'd started.

And I hated myself for that.

CHAPTER TWENTY-ONE

The following day, I got up earlier than Liam, unable to sleep properly after the interaction with Connor. Although daywalkers didn't require much sleep, I was pretty sure we needed more than what I'd had last night.

I was exhausted and pissed off.

Very pissed off.

I was done with having no control over these interactions with Connor and my sleeping mind being easily seduced by his crap. I chose to ignore that my waking brain was also confused.

I loved Liam. That was all I was focussing on right now. And Liam deserved better than a girlfriend who was horny for his literal evil twin.

I stumbled into the kitchen, intent on making a giant cup of coffee. Anika was already there, making herself some breakfast. It was so rare to see her without Anthony that I stopped still for a moment, unsure what to do. She smiled over at me, perhaps sensing my confusion.

"Anthony is having a lie-in. But I've never been great at lying around once I'm awake. You can join me if you want?"

Of all the other daywalkers in this house, Anika and Anthony were the only ones who made me feel even slightly welcome. The rest either acted like we didn't exist or watched me warily. We were still waiting to learn how this prophecy was meant to play out and what the whole "she will end the war" part truly meant.

"Thanks. I'd like that," I said, and I was surprised that I meant that. Anika was such a ray of sunshine amongst all of these crabby daywalkers. If it weren't for her, I wasn't sure Anthony would be half as nice as he was. He was only just bearable as it was, constantly throwing sarcastic comments our way and trying to get under Liam's skin. I think seeing us in action had earned his begrudging admiration, but even so, he liked to make pointed remarks about the Order at any chance he could. Liam took it reasonably well, but we had been avoiding too much time around him unless we were patrolling together. He at least respected our abilities and rarely said anything rude when we were setting bodies on fire.

I accepted the bowl of fruit Anika handed me, and we sat at one of the tables near the window. A part of the kitchen had been set up with cafe-style tables and chairs, allowing the option to sit in smaller groups or join others at one of the more oversized tables on the deck.

"I thought I heard you up through the night. No offence, but you look awful." Anika commented before she took a mouthful of food, and I grimaced, taking my own bite before answering.

"It would appear that Liam's brother had set up some psychic connection between us when he attempted to turn me. So he's been taking liberties and entering my dreams unannounced to fuck with me."

Anika paused, her spoon halfway to her mouth as she processed what I said.

"Wait, a nightwalker has psychic abilities? How is that possible?" Her spoon clattered back down to her bowl.

"No idea. Liam seems to think it was because Connor had abilities before he was turned, but that doesn't track with everything we know, right? From what I've been told, Order members have transitioned in the past, and their abilities didn't remain. Honestly, there is so much about Connor that doesn't track with anything I know about nightwalkers. He seems different to the others." I wasn't sure why I was relaying my concerns to Anika, someone I barely knew. Still, I realised that the list of people I could confide in was minimal these days, and Liam wasn't great about discussing anything to do with his brother and his connection with me.

"I've never had the pleasure of meeting Connor, but I've heard the stories. He's one of the worst amongst them, Isolde. Don't let whatever shit he's twisting around up there fool you." She gestured towards my head. "They are all predators, and it sounds like he's toying with his food."

"Oh, I believe you. He's a bastard. He took great pleasure in showing me what my sister and... Actually, you know what, I don't want to talk about that anymore. I don't feel like throwing up again." I slid the bowl away from me, unable to continue eating. Just the thought of seeing Aurora and Will take part in that depraved vampire orgy was enough to turn me off my food.

Anika watched me while she continued eating.

"You know, we've been waiting for the chosen one to come along for a long time, but I don't think anyone ever considered how crap it would be for you. I'm guessing that's also the case within the Order?"

I nodded, and Anika clucked her tongue and screwed up her face.

"Did you know about the Gemini Prophecy as well?" I asked.

Anika shrugged before answering.

"Some of it. I wasn't aware of Liam's involvement. I always put Eve's interest in him down to the fact that she wasn't used to not getting her way. It's been amusing watching him get the upper hand with her over the years."

I tried to smile but didn't enjoy being reminded of Liam's past with Eve. Even though I knew how much she annoyed the crap out of him.

Anika reached across the table and squeezed my hand.

"I know it seems like it, but not all daywalkers are completely devoid of human feelings like the Order would have you believe."

"In my own limited experience, aside from yourself and occasionally Anthony, that has been the case," I said pointedly, and Anika laughed.

"True, most of the ones you've met here haven't been great, but they are all Eve's little lackeys. Liam has spent most of his years avoiding daywalker interactions, but a few have remained quite human. They seem to be the ones who have managed to forge an actual emotional attachment to someone. There is a lot about this world that neither of you understand. Being forced to see the truth behind the Order will be great for you both."

I thought about what she said for a moment.

"I have a question. If it's not rude to ask?" I asked, and Anika nodded.

"Ask away. I'm an open book."

I believed her, too.

"Liam mentioned that he'd met a daywalker couple once who were bonded. Like we were before I transitioned. Is that you and Anthony? I've watched how the two of you move around each other when no one else is around, and it's almost as though you can read each other's thoughts?"

Anika smiled.

"You're very observant. Many others hadn't picked up on that, but with his abilities, Liam picked it right away, of course."

"Our bond hasn't survived the transition, but Liam said you were bonded before your transition. Was there any time when you couldn't hear each other?" I was clutching at straws, hoping that the bond would return and she might have the answers.

She sat back, quiet for a moment before answering.

"I met Anthony when I was a member of the Order, and he had already become a daywalker."

I felt my eyebrows rise, and Anika laughed. That was the furthest from my mind of everything I thought she might say.

"That's right. I knew Liam when I was a human, although we didn't live in the same group. I was in the New York Manor. I had only just learned about this world and was quite young within the Order when I met Anthony on patrol one night. He was intrigued by me, and I him. You know how the Order feels about daywalkers, obviously. So I met him often in secret, and we eventually fell in love. It wasn't long after he first fed off me that the bond formed. I still don't understand what happened, but I suspect my magical abilities did it. I was one of the Order members with psychic abilities, like yourself and Liam, so I think that is part of the reason. But I never had the chance to investigate it further. For obvious reasons, I couldn't tell anyone in the Order about it, and Liam only found out after I became a daywalker." Anika shrugged, seeming content to leave the story there, but I still had many questions. I was unaware that other Order members had become daywalkers other than Liam. There was still so much I didn't know, which was frustrating.

"So your bond survived the transition entirely, then? You didn't have any issues when you first turned?" I was desperate to know if there was any chance of the bond between myself and Liam reforming.

Anika shook her head, and I deflated a little.

"No, we never had a time where the bond was broken. I wish I had that answer for you."

The sadness must have been showing on my face because she reached across the table and squeezed my hand again.

"I keep wondering if I've come through the transition broken...." I hadn't voiced this concern to myself, let alone to anyone else, and saying it now made me feel like crying. I could already feel the tears forming in the corners of my eyes.

Anika got up and pulled her seat around to sit next to me, wrapping her arm around me and giving me a side hug. I was taken aback at such a comforting gesture, and I froze for a moment before allowing her to provide me with what support she could. Since I'd transitioned, aside from the brief interaction with my parents and sisters, I'd had no physical touch from anyone other than Liam, and I realised now how much I needed it.

"I don't think you're broken, Isolde. I think that you've had to deal with a lot, and it's going to take time to work out who you are now," Anika said.

I felt a tear escape, making its way down my cheek.

"It also probably doesn't help that you've got a psychotic asshole whispering to you in your sleep."

I laughed, but it came out as a snort, and we both cracked up laughing – a nice bit of humour amongst all the sadness.

Anika moved her seat back to sit across from me again, and I sat back in my chair, studying her.

"So, you were in the Order? Do they know that you're a daywalker now?"

Anika nodded, a twinkle in her eye.

"Oh, they know. There have actually been a few of us over the years. But I'm guessing they didn't tell you that. I think we're a bit of a dirty little secret amongst the elders. Those of us who chose this life over remaining in the Order aren't something they want widely known. When I transitioned, the head of the New York Manor was not impressed. The fact that they allowed Liam to remain amongst them has always made the rest of us quite curious about why... But now that we know the truth of the prophecy, it makes sense. They wanted to control him."

"So is that why Anthony gives Liam such a hard time about remaining with the Order? Because of how they treated you?" I wondered at what point Anika would grow tired of my questions, but it felt good to have someone who gave me straight answers.

"Well, most daywalkers have a pretty low opinion of the members of the Order. But yeah, he wasn't impressed with how quickly my supposed family cast me aside, especially because I turned to avoid death altogether. I didn't go to Anthony and ask him to change me. I was fighting with a nightwalker and thrown off a bridge. The fact that I didn't die immediately was a miracle, but

Anthony was with me, and I would have died if he hadn't turned me. We were already in love, and the idea of continuing to live without me wasn't something he could handle. I imagine Liam was presented with the same issue when he turned you?" She asked.

"To a degree. I'd made him promise that if there were ever a chance I might return as a nightwalker to ensure that didn't happen. I know he hoped it would never come to that, but it turns out it was always our destiny for him to turn me into a daywalker." I wondered if the bitterness I felt at what we'd been forced into would ever dissipate.

"I know your psychic bond may not have survived the transition, but I can promise you one thing. The love that you have for one another is still there. I don't have Liam's ability to read people's minds, but I've seen how you both are together. You are each other's strength, and I think that is more important than any other bond that exists. Hold onto each other, Isolde. Love like that doesn't come along every day. I get the feeling that what is coming will be particularly difficult. I can sense the change, and I know you have too."

I tried not to shiver at her words, but I knew she was right, and I wondered how long it would be before we were forced to face whatever had been unleashed on the world the night Liam was forced to turn me.

And I wondered if we would be ready.

CHAPTER TWENTY-TWO

That night, Liam and I headed out to patrol once again. This time, we decided to go solo, figuring we could cover more ground if we spread out from the others. And Liam was pissed at Anthony, who had had another dig at him earlier in the day. I hadn't been there, but I'd heard the two of them arguing, and when I'd asked what had happened, Liam had just said not to worry about it. I figured it was probably something to do with the Order, so I let it be.

We'd decided to hit Roma Street Parklands, and not long after midnight, I trailed behind Liam when he led the way along the darkened path amongst the gardens. We'd been here a few nights earlier and noticed more nightwalkers lurking nearby. I was growing very concerned at the alarming number of nightwalkers we were finding and realised that the Order honestly had no idea how many people were being turned.

I was shaken from my dark thoughts when I noticed a movement out of the corner of my eye, and I managed to alert Liam by calling his name before the nightwalker hidden amongst the trees flung itself at him. My ability to sense them in the dark was on high alert, and I knew there were more nearby. I moved forward to assist Liam but was ripped backwards by a second nightwalker and turned to face my attacker. In life, the girl in front of me would have been lucky to have been around seventeen. I pushed that thought aside while I moved to strike her in the chest with my fist. She flew backwards and hit a tree with a grunt, though it barely seemed to stun her before she rushed towards me again.

I could still hear Liam fighting with the other nightwalker, leaving me to continue fighting against her alone. She drew close again, and I leapt into the air, striking her with my foot. She flew back again, landing in a heap on the ground. I moved quickly, tapping into my new vampire speed, and was on top of her before she could rise again. I still wasn't sure I could handle killing a nightwalker with Anthony's preferred method of ripping their heads from their shoulders, so I settled for driving my stake into her heart, moving before she'd even had a chance to blink up at me.

Liam's opponent was more mature than the vampire I'd taken on, and he was giving Liam a bit of a harder time than the one I'd just killed. I rose to assist him while the nightwalker squared off against him. Watching Liam fight constantly reminded me of watching a well-choreographed dance, and it was no different now. He circled the male, skilfully avoiding each punch he unleashed. Reading your opponent's mind was a convenient skill, and I smirked when Liam sidestepped a kick that would have caused great pain to a human. I could tell that Liam had the upper hand, so I just settled myself to watch. I knew it was probably twisted to be turned on by watching your lover in a fight to the death, but it was hard not to be aroused as Liam's muscles rippled with each movement while he played with the nightwalker. Perhaps Liam was using him to burn off some lingering frustrations he felt with being around Eve and her brethren.

Finally deciding to put the creature out of his misery, Liam made a similar move to the one I had earlier, unleashing a kick that sent it flying backwards. I heard its spine snap as it smacked hard into the tree behind him. But a snapped spine wasn't enough to stop a nightwalker. Liam was upon it immediately. He slammed his stake into its chest, watching with a dangerous smile while the light dimmed from its startling blue eyes. He rose slowly before turning to face me while I watched him closely.

"Feel better?" I asked, resisting the urge to move closer and climb him. The spark in Liam's eye told me he had an inkling of where my thoughts had gone, and he smirked a little. He would have started strutting if he was any other man, but Liam didn't need to strut. He was confident enough to know just how good he was.

"A little. We should probably get rid of these before we keep going?" He gestured towards the bodies, and I nodded.

He dragged the body of the vampire he'd killed over to where my former opponent lay before moving towards me. A slight shiver ran through me when he stopped behind me, running both hands down my sides, pressing his chest against my back and covering my hands with his own. Even without raising our hands, I could feel the connection between us grow, and I took a steadying breath while I pushed my arousal aside, trying to concentrate on raising the barrier around us. I felt a rumble in his chest when he chuckled, and I knew he could feel my emotions through the magic that rippled around us.

"You are not helping," I said quietly, and he kissed my neck.

"Sorry." He didn't sound even remotely sorry, but I managed to get myself under control, feeling the power run through us both. I laced my fingers through his, raising his arms with mine.

"Hide and protect us," I whispered, and the air around us began to crackle once again when the barrier raised around us, cloaking us from prying eyes. I willed the flame into being before guiding it towards the bodies, watching with satisfaction when they erupted in flames. Each time we performed the magic together, it became easier. If any members of the Order were to witness this, they would be terrified at the power we could wield together. I knew it could be dangerous and that it could be hard not to get caught up in that power. To become lost in it and set the world ablaze. The flames remained unstable when I channelled them on my own, and I worried that if I were to test it without Liam, it would burn out of control. I could feel Liam tighten his grip on my hands while we worked together to keep the fire under control as the bodies exploded.

Once all traces were gone, I extinguished the flame, and we breathed a collective sigh, the magic still rolling through us both. I could feel the barrier around us continuing to crackle, and I turned slowly in his arms, reaching to loop my arms around his neck when he pulled me in close and lowered his lips to mine. We kissed hungrily, and I was grateful we'd decided to patrol without the others tonight. It had been hard to resist the pull towards each other when we'd patrolled with Anika and Anthony, but with the barrier around us and no one else within its confines, there was no need to deny ourselves tonight.

"I need you," I whispered against his lips, and he groaned, nodding his head while he trailed kisses down my neck. His hands moved their way down to grip my hips. We worked together to remove my leggings before he pushed me back against the tree that was thankfully within the barrier with us. I was already ready for him, and he was buried inside me within seconds, having freed himself of his belt and undoing his jeans. We sighed together when he moved his hips slowly, my legs wrapped tight around his waist, and my head fell back against the tree, giving him access to my throat. He kissed me hungrily before biting down, and I moaned while the pleasure shot through me. His bite alone was enough to take me over the edge, and I cried out when the orgasm rocked through me. He continued to move at a leisurely pace, and I managed to find the sweet spot that allowed him to press against where I needed him most with each movement. He moved his mouth away from my neck and pressed his forehead against mine, our eyes locked while we continued to move together. Feeling his orgasm growing, I pressed my mouth to his neck, knowing that my bite would have the same intense reaction for him. He moaned when I bit down, my teeth growing sharper, and we both found our release while his blood made its way down my throat.

I pulled my mouth back when he slowed his movements against me. We brought our foreheads together again, closing our eyes while the magic continued to flow and the pleasure rolled through us both in waves.

"God, that's addictive," Liam whispered, holding me close.

We were both shaking, and it took a few minutes before I could lower my legs to the ground and support myself while he grabbed my leggings, helping me pull them back on. Somehow, the barrier was still up, and after a few more minutes of holding each other close, we brought it down together, stepping back onto the path and heading off in search of more nightwalkers.

Chasing the rush of the magic and the pleasure that still rocketed through us both.

Two hours and several stabbing and sex sessions later, we decided to call it a night. The adrenaline from all the fighting, magic and fucking made me jittery, and I could tell Liam was feeling the same.

Perhaps we should try not to succumb to the crazed urge to go at it each time. I feel like my heart is about to beat out of my chest. I thought to myself while we walked over the footbridge between the gardens and South Bank.

I looked over at Liam, who nodded as though I'd said the words out loud.

I stared at him when he looked over at where I'd come to a sudden halt in the middle of the bridge.

Why'd she stop? Liam looked around us.

I knew the moment he picked up on my racing thoughts when his eyes snapped back to mine.

Can you hear me? His gaze was intense while he searched my face.

Yes.

I was torn between euphoria and terror, and I knew my head was an incoherent mess, even while he pulled me hard against him and hugged me tightly. I couldn't tell if my heart was racing due to the continued adrenaline or the realisation that our bond had finally returned.

It must have been all the magic we were using tonight. Liam's voice in my head was filled with joy at the knowledge that he could hear my thoughts again. However, the joy faded when he sensed I wasn't as delighted as he was. *What's wrong?*

"I don't know that you're ready to handle how messed up my head is now," I answered out loud. I searched his face, and his expression softened.

I remember how hard it was in the beginning. At least now I can help you sort through the mess. And I can help keep Connor out now.

I refused to let my mind wander to thoughts of Connor right now. No matter what he thought, he was not ready to see what his brother was capable of.

I allowed him to hold me close and pushed all thoughts except my love for him out of my head, determined not to allow this moment to be ruined by evil twins and potentially fucked up girlfriends.

CHAPTER TWENTY-THREE

e arrived back at the house and headed straight for the shower. Because our bond had only truly formed the day before I was turned, we'd never had the opportunity to explore its full potential. And by full potential, I meant during sex. Liam had always been able to hear me when we'd been together while I was a human, but hearing his thoughts while he was buried inside me and had me pressed against the shower wall was a new and addictive experience. But after the night we'd had of giving in to our animalistic needs over and over, we were both exhausted and passed out as soon as we crawled into bed.

This time, instead of being pulled into Connor's mind, a memory began to form the moment my eyes drifted closed.

I entered the large auditorium, intent on getting a glimpse of her. I'd felt the change in the air for months and knew that it meant that the female twins were now activated. They must have turned twenty-five in January, the younger one coming into her powers and about to become part of the aggravating Order of the Dragon. It had taken me this long to find out who she was, and now I knew where she would be with the aid of one of Adam's latest recruits. The internet was still a bit of a mystery to those of us who had been around long enough to remember a time before modern technology ruled the world, so he'd turned a cyber expert a few months ago, and it was proving quite handy. However, said expert spent more time ripping people apart than sitting in front of a computer, which wasn't ideal. I had long grown tired of cleaning up the messes left behind by all the damn young ones Adam was turning left, right and centre. He was paranoid now that we knew the 'Chosen One' was active. He still knew nothing about the Gemini Prophecy, though. I doubted I would have survived this long if he had any inkling of the true power I wielded. How I had managed to keep it from him for all these years felt like a miracle, but I suspected there was more behind it than that, like so much else in my god-forsaken existence. I needed to find a way to bring it to his attention soon, though.

Adam had been trying to get to her for the last few weeks, but Liam was always lurking in the dark, playing the part of a good little protector. I knew they were waiting for her tattoo to form fully. It never ceased to amaze me at how stupid they were, letting their newest members walk around, clueless, until their tattoos were fully formed. They were usually sitting ducks if we got wind of any of them first. But not this one. The protection surrounding her was fucking ridiculous. But they thought she was safe during the day. And I loved the challenge.

I looked around while I moved towards the stairs leading to the back of the lecture theatre. I felt her eyes on me before I could locate her, but once my gaze met hers, I knew it was her instantly. I would have known this was her even if I hadn't seen her social media profiles. It was like she was calling me to her. And I was fucking hooked.

She was gorgeous, even casually dressed, with her long, dark hair tied in a messy bun. And to think, there was another woman as identically stunning out there. How did their poor little human men manage to stand tall in front of such beauties and think they were equal? That boyfriend was a lucky man. Or should I say fiance now, judging by the massive rock on her finger? Good luck actually making it down the aisle.

She watched me intently while I made my way to the back of the room, turning fully in her seat to keep her eyes locked on mine. I wondered if she'd ever seen Liam and was mistaking me for him. The thought aggravated me. I was tired of being reminded that my saintly brother was out there. We'd come face to face a few times over the centuries, and each time, it was a punch to the gut.

She finally realised she was staring at me and blushed before turning back around, busying herself with preparing for the class. I kept my eyes on her the entire time. From how she sat, I knew she was aware of my gaze.

I'd been lurking in shadows for so long I'd forgotten how to be around others and only became aware of how much of a creep I probably looked like to the others around me when the woman next to me cleared her throat loudly. I slowly turned my gaze to hers, and she shrank back in her seat before gathering her belongings and moving a few seats away.

Smart move.

When the lecture drew to a close, I waited until a few of those around me had risen to their feet. Locking onto their minds, I erased any thoughts of my presence and slipped into the shadows once more, moving at speed to leave the room. I'd long ago mastered the ability to disappear. But her presence would remain with me. There was so much connecting us now, and the path we were walking together just became much more interesting...

The memory started to fade around me.

"*Interesting.*" Connor's voice rang out, and I was yanked from his memory into that same room. He wasn't sitting in his usual chair, and I stepped back against the wall, startled by how close he stood before me, looking at me as though trying to peer into my mind.

"What's interesting?" My voice shook slightly, still thrown by the feelings his memory stirred up. I'd had brief glimpses of his mind when I'd seen his interactions with Liam in the blood memories, but this was different.

"I can sense the change in you. Something has finally broken *through that barrier you'd thrown up around your mind." He paused momentarily, and his eyes flashed from blue to dark brown and back. Like Liam had described mine doing. I watched him closely, and his face settled into a scowl.*

"My god, you're as bad as your fucking twin. Mind you, I didn't realise Liam had it in him to go at it like that all night. Good for him." He glared at me, and I rolled my eyes at his jealousy.

"Wow, getting slut shamed by an evil vampire. Although it doesn't surprise me that you're cheering on the male in the scenario. For someone who frequently tries to get into my pants, you are certainly judgemental... Or do you wish that it was you I had been riding all night, Connor?" I could tell from his reaction that I'd hit the nail on the head, and I smirked when he stepped back, his eyes flashing again.

"Don't be ridiculous. No point in being jealous when I know I could have you screaming like that half the time." He walked over to the whiskey and poured himself a glass. The man sure did love his whiskey.

"Just keep telling yourself that, Connor. And what do you mean, the barrier I'd thrown up around my mind?"

He threw back the whiskey and placed the glass on the table before moving to sit in the chair again, watching me closely. I remained where I stood, ensuring to keep a distance between us. I didn't need a repeat of what had happened the night before.

"You have no idea of your true powers, do you, little one?" Connor smirked again, and I glowered at him.

"Enough with the cryptic bullshit, Connor," I snapped, and he sighed, shaking his head.

"Dear, dear Isolde. When will you learn how much I love playing with your beautiful mind? Amongst other parts of you." He laughed when I let out a frustrated growl. "And you make it so easy! As if I'm going to give up the answers without having fun first. It's like you know nothing about me at all."

"I don't know anything about you other than this persona you put on for me and the fact that everyone keeps telling me how evil you are," I said, glaring at him.

"Oh, I am evil. Listen to what everyone is telling you, Isolde. They're right about me." His eyes flashed, and he moved so fast that he stopped before me once again before I even had a chance to blink. "I've done so many awful things you couldn't even imagine," he whispered, and I shivered involuntarily.

"And yet, the glimpses I've had inside your mind tell me that you're not as evil as you want everyone to believe."

He stepped back and looked at me.

"What glimpses inside of my head?"

For once, it seemed he didn't have all the answers.

"The flashes of your memories I've had. Although your memories aren't as strong as Liam's and Aurora's, I've seen some of yours too." His eyes flashed again.

"That's not possible."

"Why not?" I was intrigued that I seemed to have touched on a nerve. He didn't want me inside his head any more than I wanted him inside mine.

"Because I made sure you weren't able to see them." He glared at me like it was somehow my fault.

"Well, I guess you're not as all-powerful as you think, Connor. Cause I've seen through you, and I know you're not the big bad you make yourself out to be." He closed the distance between us again and pressed me back against the wall. His jaw clenched as he placed both hands on the wall on either side of my head.

"Don't talk about things you don't understand, little one." His words were threatening, but I just held his gaze.

"What are you going to do to stop me?"

I was taunting him now, and he knew it. His eyes flashed yet again. I'd never seen him come so close to losing control before, and I could see the cracks starting to show.

"You've had every opportunity to hurt me, yet here we are."

"Do you want me to hurt you, Isolde?" His face was so close to mine that kissing him right now would be so easy, and I could tell he was thinking about it when his gaze drifted to my lips.

"No. I'm not into pain."

"I think you might be. I think you'd be begging me to hurt you."

"What. The. Fuck."

Connor spun around, and we both stared at Liam, who was standing in the middle of the room, watching us. The expression on his face made my stomach drop.

"Liam," I said quietly. I shoved Connor out of the way, moving towards Liam, who was glaring at Connor. Once I was within reach, Liam pulled me behind him. I could feel him shaking.

"Brother." Connor tilted his head in mock greeting towards Liam, and Liam erupted. He raced towards his brother, but Connor vanished, and the room dissolved around us.

I sat up straight in bed, and Liam leapt up to get away from me.

"What the fuck Isolde?" He grabbed his shirt and yanked it over his head, glaring at me. I'd never seen Liam so angry, and knowing I was the cause made me feel sick. "You weren't doing anything to fight him off. What has really been going on when he pulls you into his mind?" He demanded.

"He's been fucking with my head, I told you," I said quietly, still sitting in bed while he began pacing.

"You were almost inviting him to fuck you, from what I just saw!" I could hear his thoughts and knew he'd seen more than I realised. He'd been there long enough to hear me tell Connor I suspected he wasn't as evil as he claimed. This meant he had seen Connor almost kiss me, and I did nothing to push him away.

Liam followed my line of thought and nodded.

"I could tell he'd pulled you in, so I went in to try and pull you out, and I found the pair of pressed up against a fucking wall!"

"It's not what you think, Liam." Yet my mind flashed involuntarily to the night before.

Liam's face dropped. His arms slackened at his sides, and I

watched the fight drain out of him. He grabbed his shoes and flung the door open.

"Where are you going?"

"I can't even look at you right now." His voice shook, and I could feel the bile rise in my throat when he slammed the door behind him. I ran for the bathroom to throw up once again. Once I'd emptied the contents of my stomach, I curled up in a ball on the bathroom floor and let the tears fall, terrified that Liam would never be able to forgive me.

I wasn't even sure that I deserved his forgiveness.

CHAPTER TWENTY-FOUR

I remained in our room for the rest of the day but took a walk when Liam still hadn't returned by the evening. I had had so few moments to myself since I transitioned, and our conversation last night had my emotions on high alert. After walking awhile, I sat on the bench that overlooked the river close to the nearest City Cat terminal and considered the water that continued to rage. There was still so much debris floating by, and I watched in silence when a large boat floated by, having broken free of its moorings. I was powerless to do anything when it slammed into the ferry terminal, and the gangway screeched loudly with the impact. Eventually, the water pushed it further, and the gangway went with it.

I just watched it all silently.

That was a strong symbol of how I was feeling inside right now.

"Interesting to see you here without Liam."

I wasn't surprised to find Eve suddenly sitting beside me, watching the boat go further downstream.

"I was wondering how long it would be before you came to find me." I returned my gaze to the river before me and waited for her to speak. Something told me she had been waiting for me to be alone.

"I wasn't sure if Liam would ever leave your side. He's quite protective of you, you know. In all our years together, I've never seen him like this over anyone."

I knew what she was doing. She needed to remind me how long she'd known him, that he was hers, long before he'd been mine.

"I don't know that I'd call what I've seen between the two you of as being together. More like a very long fuck buddy arrangement." I wouldn't allow her to believe she had any power over me.

She gave a little laugh beside me.

"No, I guess you wouldn't see it that way. He always kept himself that little bit distanced from me. I knew he was waiting for something better to come along. I should have known it would be you."

I turned and looked at her.

"Is there a reason you needed to wait for Liam to be away before we spoke?"

"We have a lot to discuss Isolde. Some of it concerns Liam, but he isn't ready to hear the hard truths just yet. He has always been quite guarded regarding myself and my family. His family, too, not that he ever wanted to admit it. He always saw himself as a member of that ridiculous Order of the Dragon first, attempting to ignore what he truly was." She wrinkled her nose in distaste.

"And what is that, exactly?"

"I'm going to tell you a little story. About how this whole mess started." While she spoke, her voice took on the lilting tones of a storyteller. We didn't look at each other when she continued, staring out at the river but lost in the past.

"This isn't in the Order's history books. Those who know the truth don't like to admit their part in how this endless war began. A few thousand years ago, around the time of the Greeks, an incredibly powerful coven of witches resided in the land now referred to as Ireland. Before there was any talk of the being known as God now and any current religions you'd be aware of.

The coven was led by the most powerful members, Sithech and his wife. Sithech was a cruel man and attempted to rule their people through fear. But his wife was fair and kind. Their people rallied behind her and tolerated Sithech only because of their love for her. And amongst her people was a man who loved her more than any other. He eventually became her lover.

Sithech knew how the rest of the coven felt about him, and he grew incredibly jealous of their loyalty to her. He flew into a rage when he learned of the relationship between his wife and her lover. They eventually overthrew him, and he was cast out of the coven. The marriage was dissolved, and he left, vowing vengeance.

But they forgot how powerful Sithech was. On the night of their marriage, whilst the coven celebrated their union, he brought a powerful curse down on them both. They awoke the night after the celebrations completely changed. Her lover became cruel, a feral creature who could no longer walk in the light and craved the blood of humans. All that remained of his former self was his passionate love for his wife, but it was an obsession now. He became the first nightwalker. And his wife... She became the first daywalker. She retained the memories of their former selves. Her love for him and her magic remained, but she was also cursed with a need for blood. But she found she was able to survive on the blood of animals.

She attempted to find ways to break the curse. But she could no longer overlook these details as he began killing those within the coven and the people in the nearby villages, turning more of them into the same violent creatures by draining them of blood. The remaining adults within the coven rallied behind her and allowed her to turn them into daywalkers as well.

They soon discovered these creatures could not be killed easily. Eventually, they learned they could only be destroyed through a silver stake to the heart, their heads being removed, or burning them. And so began a millennia-long war that has moved across the world in secret. Though their origin has become a legend and the basis of many religions."

I was brought out of my transfixed state as Eve turned to me, her eyes on my face.

"You knew the wife, didn't you?" My voice was barely more than a whisper.

After staring at me for a few moments, she eventually nodded.

"Yes. I was forced to watch the people I had loved and respected my entire life become creatures of the purest evil overnight. They ripped the villages around us apart. Those villagers had relied on us for protection from all magical and supernatural beings. Instead, we caused their demise because we could not bring ourselves to end them all. By the time we were able to, it was too late. The bloodshed had spread far and wide, and the entire cursed land was a war zone for a time. We eventually managed to limit their damage as humankind grew in number and civilisations rose."

For the first time since I had met her, her cool facade had dropped, and I could see the sadness behind her eyes.

"The children of the original coven were the first with dragon tattoos, which appeared the same night that Sithech uttered that goddamn curse. But over time, it changed to only being those within the bloodlines who were the seventh sons and daughters like they are now. They didn't band together until around eight hundred years ago. Before that, they were all random, long-lived individuals with magic in their veins, and sometimes we fought alongside them. But once the Order developed, we stopped working with them when they became so fucking high and mighty. Their histories are hidden from the vast majority, though there are one or two that would know the truth."

At some point in her story, I had twisted in my seat to gape at her, taking in everything she said. When it became apparent that I wouldn't say anything, Eve continued her story.

"As far as the Order and Liam are aware, the daywalkers who were around in the beginning have all been destroyed by the night-walkers, but a few of us remain. We eventually were forced to turn others outside of the coven to become like us. Out of either desperation to increase our numbers or for the few who found mortals they fell in love with. But we were still vastly outnumbered by the nightwalkers. While we have eliminated many of those early nightwalkers, the curse will remain until the original players are reunited."

The point of her story was beginning to dawn on me.

"The prophecy about me, that I'll have the power to end this... It means I can kill him, doesn't it?"

She studied me once again before nodding.

"The Gemini prophecy came about around six hundred years ago. And then the Phoenix prophecy followed around fifty years later. At first, I gave them no real attention, as there had been many prophecies that all proved to be utter bullshit, spewed forth by the Order to give themselves some relevance. But then I became aware of Liam and his brother's existence, and I was intrigued. Twins where one of them was destined to be a member of the Order and males... When I came across Liam that night, I had to turn him. I couldn't risk losing the chance to set the wheels in motion in case there was any truth to it all. It didn't hurt that he was so beautiful, either. And so good between the sheets once he got past that ridiculous obsession with God," she said with a smirk.

I glared at her.

"Oh, come on, Isolde. Lighten up a little."

I felt my temper starting to flare again, and she laughed.

"That rage you have been feeling bubbling away beneath the surface? That is key to all of this. You carry the powers of both blood-lines within you now," she said.

I'm pretty sure time stood still while I tried to comprehend what she'd just revealed.

"I... what?!"

"It's why you see the memories from all of them. You needed to be fed on by all three of them to activate the powers fully during your transition."

I stared at her in shock.

CHAPTER TWENTY-FIVE

"So, I'm what? Some sort of fucked hybrid?!"

She shrugged like she hadn't just dropped a massive revelation in my lap.

I took a deep breath, pushing the shock aside as best I could.

"How did you manage to keep all of this from Liam when he has your blood memories?"

"I can choose which memories are seen by those I turn," she said.

I was reminded of my most recent exchange with Connor.

"I didn't know that was possible," I said, my concern growing.

"Only a few of us have that power," she said with a shrug.

How did Connor have that power?

"Do I have that power?"

"Perhaps. You have already proven your power, even before you were turned. I've heard about your fire abilities whilst you've been out patrolling this last week. The original coven had similar powers, as well as the ability to move objects with their minds, amongst many others." She looked at the river again and nodded towards a tree moving towards where we were sitting.

"Use your telekinesis on that. Liam mentioned that you had

previously been trying to work on it but could only really get things to move slightly. Is that correct?"

I looked at her, wondering what else she and Liam had spoken about. No one seemed to have told her I needed his touch to control my abilities. After a brief hesitation, I nodded, and she waved towards the river.

"Try using it now to stop that tree from continuing down the river."

I hesitated for a few moments before focusing on the tree. In the few months before my transition, the most I'd been able to do was get a vase to shake a little and the occasional accidental door slam, though I had spent many hours trying. It had only been with Liam's assistance that I'd been able to move anything properly.

I took a deep breath and concentrated on the tree, staring at it while it passed us by, expecting it to continue. Instead, it stopped abruptly, the water flowing around it while it floated in place.

At first, it didn't move at all, but gradually, my mind began to fatigue, and it began to move inch by inch. I tried to maintain my concentration, but eventually, I lost focus, and the tree continued on its way once more while I gasped for air, having expended all my energy. I felt my need for blood spike once more, and the burning in my throat returned with force. I felt my eyes water while the hunger consumed me, and Eve raised her wrist to my mouth.

"Feed."

I didn't hesitate and bit into her wrist, beginning to drink hungrily. I realised how intimate our current position was when the hunger started to wane. She had her other arm around me while I sat so close that I might as well be sitting in her lap. Her hand was tangled in my hair, with her lips pressed to my temple. Anyone walking by would have seen two lovers in an embrace.

I pushed her hand away, and she let her arm fall to her lap, the amusement at my reaction evident in her eyes. There was something about this woman's power over those around her, like moths drawn to a flame.

I didn't like it.

"What's going on?"

I ripped my gaze from Eve's to find Liam standing behind her. I knew her blood was still on my lips when he took in how we were both sitting wrapped together. For her part, Eve merely turned to look up at him, her grip holding me to her. My insides churned at being found in yet another compromising position.

"Just getting to know Isolde. And sharing some information." She removed her hand from my hair, but not before she turned to brush her lips against my temple once again, giving the air of comforting a lover. She shifted slightly before standing gracefully, and Liam's gaze fell to her wrist, which had already begun to heal, before returning to look her in the eye.

"And just how did you share this information, Eve?" His words were low and lethal, but Eve merely smiled at him before walking towards him and stroking his arm. She wielded her sexuality like a weapon, and I noted a slight shudder pass through his body that Liam could not hide. She turned to look back at me once more, her hand moving up his neck and pulling his head down to hers so that she could bring their lips together in a demanding kiss that he didn't immediately push away from. Her eyes remained open and held my gaze the entire time while she kissed him hungrily, pressing her body into his before Liam finally had the presence of mind to push her away and step back, his eyes full of warning. She smiled at us both.

"Leave Eve. Now." Liam's voice shook, and she laughed, low and intimate.

"I'll be seeing you both soon. Real soon." She turned and finally walked away, and I felt the weight of her presence begin to lift. I remember her words from a few days ago, telling me she was more powerful than I was. I knew without any doubt that I couldn't trust her.

Liam stalked over to stand before me before dropping to his knees and pulling me roughly to him, crushing my mouth with his own. Like he needed to remove the memory of Eve and that kiss from our minds. I returned the intensity, clinging to him like he was a life raft amongst the insanity I had just been exposed to, but I felt a memory beginning to drag me away, and he held me up when I collapsed forward into him.

I woke to the smell of blood and immediately jumped to my feet. I surveyed the room I was in but saw nothing out of place. I moved into the next room of our shelter, the ample gathering space where, only the night before, Adhamh and I had exchanged our vows before our children, the rest of the coven, and the villagers from nearby. A few bodies still lay around the room where our guests had fallen asleep, having dropped in exhaustion after hours of celebration. We had invited those from the surrounding settlements that we continued to protect from the darkness with our magic.

I tripped over the body of one of those villagers now, their form only just visible in the darkness that blanketed the space. I bent to shake them awake, but they didn't move, and when I touched their arm, there was no warmth to their skin. I swallowed hard while I conjured a small ball of fire in my hand and brought it closer to the still form on the ground. In the light of the flame, I could see that the woman on the floor was dead, her throat having been torn completely open in a way I had never seen before. Her head had been almost completely ripped from her body, and I struggled to keep down the bile that rose from my stomach. There was a strange burning in my throat, but I ignored it as best as possible while I willed the flame to grow larger, allowing me to see more of the gathering space. I turned slowly in place, surveying the room and the rest of the bodies that lay around the room. Every single person had the same sickening wounds.

Frantically, I raced to each body to see if any remained alive, but they were all dead. How had I slept through their screams? Where were my children? And where was Adhamh?

I ran outside and saw that dawn would soon break on the horizon. Other members of the coven emerged, and we all gathered, the horror beginning to dawn on us as we followed the trail of bodies. It seemed as though only those in the main shelter and outside had been attacked. Those within the smaller shelters appeared to have remained unscathed.

"I have never seen anything like this. What could have done this to them?" Siobhan asked tearfully.

I hugged her close, my eyes searching the faces of those around me, and I sagged with relief as I saw my twin daughters, Eireann and Isla, step out of Siobhan's shelter. My son, Daemon, had chosen to leave with his father months ago, and I silently prayed to the mother that he was safe. Adhamh's twin sons, Aden and Chey, stood amongst the young men who had gathered together, taking protective stances around the younger children, ready to protect them against whatever evil had managed to penetrate the protective wards around our homes.

"I don't know. I don't know," I whispered. I couldn't think straight, the burning in my throat becoming unbearable. Over Siobhan's shoulder, my eyes drifted to a rabbit peeking out of the nearby thicket of trees. Moving at a speed I didn't know I possessed, I instantly fell upon it, sinking my teeth into it while it kicked and screamed fruitlessly. I drained it of blood until it stopped shrieking and twitching. Coming back to myself, I dropped it in horror and stared down at my shaking hands before looking up into the eyes of the others while they surveyed my actions, their faces pale.

"What evil is this?" Aoife whispered, and I began to shake uncontrollably when they all gathered together, some raising their hands, ready to protect themselves from whatever I had become.

Maeve saw him first, calling everyone's attention to the path from our home to the village closest to us. As one, we turned to see Adhamh, and I cried out his name, rising to my feet, tears streaming down my face.

"What has happened?" I rushed towards him and threw my arms around his neck. He wrapped his arms around me and held me close, breathing in my scent, and I felt his body relax into mine.

"There now, love. I have returned." I continued clinging to him

while the others watched us closely. Many seemed to grow even more uneasy while they just stared at Adhamh.

I stepped back and took in Adhamh's appearance properly for the first time since he had entered the clearing.

He was coated in blood, and I covered my mouth to stop the scream from escaping when I took in the changed eye colour, a feral gleam to them when he reached for me again. I became aware of the evil presence that drifted off of him. I don't know how I had managed to miss that in my relief at seeing his return, but now it was so strong that I could do nothing but slowly walk backwards from him as he continued holding his arms out to me.

"Aoibh, what is it, my love?" There was something about his voice. Almost like a predator attempting to lure its prey with a false sense of safety.

When he advanced, I used my powers to throw up a shield between us and called my coven to my side. Thankfully, between myself and Adhamh, they saw me as the lesser of two evils and moved to stand behind me, throwing up their shields.

That Adhamh was unable to break through our shields was another shock. Our powers had always been evenly matched, yet he seemed unable to produce even the smallest amount of magic to push back against us.

"What are you?" My words were a whisper in the wind, and I was thrown by the laughter that answered me.

Sithech stepped out of the woods behind Adhamh. We had not seen him for weeks, not since the council had voted him out, and he had left, spitting threats while he passed.

"You should have known better than to believe that I wouldn't find some way to punish you for the humiliation you brought upon me, Aoibh." He gestured towards where Adhamh stood, attempting to find some way around the shields we had cast around ourselves and the children. Adhamh's sons had begun to cry silently from where they stood at my side.

"What have you done, Sithech?" Maeve yelled, and Sithech laughed again.

"I have cursed them both. I replaced Adhamh's magic with a lust for the blood of man. He will know no rest for all eternity. Will never again feel the sun upon his face. But I made sure he still knew his love for you, Aoibh. Love that will consume him, along with his need for blood." He gestured towards where Adhamh watched me hungrily.

"And what of Aoibh?" Siobhan asked, her voice trembling.

"She will be forced to walk the earth for as long as Adhamh does, knowing this is all her fault." He pointed at me, the smile on his face showing the madness within. "Animals may sate your hunger for blood, as you have already noticed, unlike his. But you exist to balance his evil. There always needs to be a balance, as we all know."

Magic did require a balance amongst all aspects of nature, and clearly, the way to balance the pure evil he had inflicted on Adhamh was by placing a curse upon me to keep him from becoming a scourge upon the earth. Sithech shifted his focus onto Adhamh now.

"You took what was mine. This is the consequence of your actions, brother."

Adhamh ignored his words, continuing to watch me and only me.

"Better run along now. The sun is almost up, and you don't want to see what happens if you are caught out in the daylight." His words were like a command, and Adhamh slowly moved back into the woods, disappearing into the darkness that was beginning to make way for the dawn.

"Goodbye, Aoibh. It is now on you to ensure he doesn't destroy everything we built together." He threw his shield up when Maeve flung a ball of flame at him, and he disappeared into the darkness, leaving us all to deal with the fallout of one man's jealousy.

I could only pray to the mother that this would not be the end of Adhamh and me, that I could find some way out of this curse to save the man I loved.

. . .

I shook free of the memory and found myself wrapped in Liam's arms. He sat with me in his lap, stroking my hair while waiting for me to return. I hated how vulnerable these memory flashes were making me, and I was just grateful that they hadn't occurred when I was in mortal danger. I prayed that it would continue.

Liam must have noticed the change in me, reaching down to lift my chin so that I could look him in the eye.

"What did you see?"

I took a deep breath, trying to understand what I had just seen.

"Eve told me to feed off her when my bloodlust set in. Although I suspect now, she set everything up for you to see or force me to see that memory...." My voice trailed off when Liam's expression hardened. He shifted me off his lap to sit beside him.

"What did you see?" His tone was strained as he repeated the question, and I reached up to touch his face. He pulled away from my touch, and I let my hand fall to my side.

I knew what I was about to say would blow everything he'd ever believed apart.

And that Eve hadn't been as honest with me as she'd claimed. I wondered if she'd meant for me to see that memory.

"Did you know Eve was the original daywalker, Liam?" He stared at me, his eyes wide.

"What? No, she isn't... She can't be... I'd know..." His words were pleading, and he shook his head. "I would know, Isolde."

There was no time to ease him into all that I now knew, and I repeated the story that Eve had told me earlier, my heart breaking as yet more of the truths that had been held from him were laid bare. I wondered how much more he could take, but I ploughed on, needing to share what I now knew and had seen in the memory. When I told him about my hybrid vampire status, Liam's face turned pale, and it was a long time before he responded. I watched while he processed everything, taking it all in.

"So, her finding me that night was no coincidence? She knew of the Gemini Prophecy?" I nodded slowly, and he let out a shaky breath. After a moment, he helped me get to my feet, standing beside me while he ran both hands through his hair before leaning his forearms on the walkway railing and staring across the river. The vein in his neck pounded while he gritted his teeth.

"Did she explain what our role in all of this is meant to be? Aside from your powers? Connor and I must play a part in this too, and Aurora... We have to if it was us that activated your powers." He glanced at me when I moved to stand beside him, mirroring his stance. I shook my head, and he exhaled, turning away again.

"We didn't get that far in the conversation. But, from her words as she left, I guess we'll find out soon enough."

"I fucking hate this. I hate all of this. I've spent over five hundred years living with all this knowledge that now turns out to be a lie. I don't even know who the fuck I am." He stared at his hands, the anger and frustration coming off him in waves. If it had been anyone else, I would have wanted to step away, fearing what he might do. But I reached up and placed my hand on his cheek, relieved when he leaned into my touch instead of pulling away, allowing me to give him the small comfort I could.

"I know who you are, Liam. And there is nothing that I turn away from. We face all of this shit together, remember?"

He looked at me again, studying my face for the longest time like he was trying to memorise every feature.

His mind was such a jumble of thoughts that I couldn't catch any of them.

"I don't know if we are together in this anymore, Isolde. I can't just ignore what has been happening with you and Connor and that you've lied to me. With everything we've learned these past few weeks, you had to know that I needed your honesty. And yet you chose to keep the fact that my brother has been seducing you in your dreams... That you allowed him to kiss and touch you in ways that..." He looked down at his hands that were clenched into fists before him. "We've never discussed monogamy, but I assumed it was implied... And for it to be with my twin brother, who I have been at war with for over five hundred years... I don't think I can get past this." I could feel my heart breaking at his words, and the panic inside me started rising when he stepped away from me.

"Please, Liam. You have to understand that when he pulls me into his mind, I lose all control of who I am. I think he can tap into some part of me that I'm unaware exists and use it against me." I was begging now. I moved towards him to touch his face once again, but he stepped away from my hand, and I let it drop to my side.

"You're it for me, Liam." I could feel tears starting to build behind my eyes.

"I need time, Isolde. These past few weeks have been a lot, and now, knowing everything that has been going on... I don't think I can trust anything you do right now. There is obviously so much more happening here than I ever imagined," Liam said, and I could hear his thoughts bouncing from one thing to another. I had wondered how much more he could handle and knew he'd reached his breaking point.

"I love you, Liam. You know that... I know you know that." I wanted to grab him and never let go, terrified of what I knew would happen.

"I don't think that's enough right now." He took one final step back when I reached towards him again. "I just... I'll see you later, Isolde."

My heart shattered when he turned and walked away again.

CHAPTER TWENTY-SIX

I stayed there for hours, praying Liam would eventually return. But I knew in my heart that when he'd said he needed time, he didn't mean a few hours. He meant days, weeks, years... Possibly an eternity.

I struggled to keep myself together and knew that staying here wouldn't make it any better. So I got to my feet and began walking when the sun rose.

I had no idea how long I had been walking for or even where I was going. My mind was a jumbled mess of everything that had happened over the past few weeks. I wish I understood how Connor drew me to him and why I let him do things I would usually never do. This wasn't who I was. I didn't cheat. Liam had my entire heart.

When I finally stopped walking, I wasn't even slightly surprised to find myself standing in front of that abandoned house where Connor and Aurora had held me captive weeks ago and attempted to turn me. Part of me knew why I was there and who would be standing inside waiting for me. And yet, I couldn't stop myself from stepping through the door.

Connor and I studied each other closely when I entered the room and found him sitting exactly where I expected.

In that damn chair.

The fear I had once felt had long been replaced by something else. He didn't say anything at first. He just watched me while I looked at him. It was scary how much he looked like his brother. I fought to control the pain in my heart at the thought of Liam.

"I'm more like my twin than he'd like to admit." I felt my eyebrows rise at his words, and he smirked. "No, I didn't read your thoughts. I could just tell what you were thinking. Seeing into your thoughts outside of our shared dreams is a luxury only my brother has."

"Why do you hate him so much? I know that there is something inside of you that still has access to human emotion," I said, and he crossed his arms when he sat back in the chair again, studying me closely for a few moments.

"So, you've worked me out, have you, Isolde? Is that why you're here? To convince me that I made the wrong choice?" He cocked his head to the side, and I felt my stomach plummet at the expression on his face. Choice. That word confirmed my suspicions about myself for the last few weeks, and I struggled to control my emotions.

"So I'm right? You are like me, a fucked up hybrid of the two bloodlines." He raised a finger to his lips.

"Ssshhh. Correction. I was once like you. But I made my choice, just like you eventually will. It will be interesting which way you decide to go... Take the path of duty and honour... or the path that leads to eternal pleasure." He let the word roll off his tongue in a way that made it clear what sort of pleasure he was alluding to, but I wouldn't allow him to distract me.

"No, you are still like me. I can feel it. You think you've switched that side of you off, but it's still there, just beneath the surface. You try to make out that you're this evil badass... But really... You spend each day fighting a war within yourself." I felt this with absolute certainty.

Connor's eyes flashed before he smirked at me once more. He used his vampire speed to stand before me in a fraction of a second and lifted a strand of my hair, rolling it between his fingers while he gazed at it. I held myself perfectly still, and he eventually looped my hair back behind my ear, his fingers lingering when they brushed my throat.

"You're so convinced that you know me. But I think you have me confused with my gallant younger brother. He was always the moral centre... I was the one who had fun." He took my hand and turned it over, tracing his finger over the different lines. He looked back at me from under his long lashes. "Don't you just want to have fun, Isolde?" He smiled seductively, and I fought to ignore the stirrings of attraction within myself.

He's not Liam, I mentally chastised myself.

Connor laughed. "Oh, Isolde, I have so much fun with you. I can't wait to see how long it takes before you finally give in to me."

"I hate to disappoint you, Connor, but I have no intention of ever being involved with you. I've never been the type to go for the bad boy." I removed my hand from his, growing annoyed with his constant games and innuendo, knowing it was all just a smoke screen. He moved closer to my side and kissed my cheek.

"You say that now. But you forget, Isolde, I know what's happening within you. I remember all too well how the conflict currently warring inside your pretty little head feels." He brought his lips close to my ear, and the feeling of his breath on my neck sent a shiver down my spine that I couldn't suppress.

"And in your heart." He placed his hand on my chest, where I knew he could feel my heart thundering away. I wished his touch repelled me, but the part I had been fighting to suppress was drawn to him and everything he represented.

"Eventually, you'll want to know what living as I do feels like. Without the weight of the world on your shoulders. You have no idea." He started to kiss my neck, and I had to fight to pull myself away. Eventually, I got a hold of myself and stepped out of his reach.

"I know this is all an act, Connor, and I don't buy it for a second. You forget that I know that you also retain the ability to walk in the daylight." I pointed to the window that he currently stood in front of. "You stand in the sun's rays and do not so much as flinch. So you can keep pretending that Liam is the only one still possessing his morality. Just know that I know the truth." I turned and walked away, praying that I was right... And a small part of me wondered what would have happened if I had just given in.

I walked a little further before reaching a park near my parent's house. My sisters and I had played here countless times as children, and I sat down on one of the benches overlooking the playground, lost in thought.

My phone rang in my pocket, and I pulled it out, seeing Mum's name on the screen. I had forgotten I even had it on me and considered ignoring it. But it was the first time she had called me since I'd left them all at Briseis and Dean's house, and something told me this wasn't just a catch-up call.

"Hello?"

"Oh, thank god you answered." Mum's words came out in a jumble. I could hear the emotion in her voice and felt my grip on the phone tighten.

"What's happened?"

"Aurora attempted to attack the house last night. When she didn't get in, she went to one of her friends' places and got an invite." I felt my blood run cold when she started crying.

"Who?" I whispered, lifting my eyes to look up at the sky.

"It was John's place. Jacob was staying there." I knew what she was going to say next.

"She killed Jacob, didn't she?"

"Yes." She said with a loud sob and completely broke down. Dad's voice replaced hers a moment later.

"She killed John and his family as well." His voice was rough, and I tried not to imagine how they were all standing together right now.

"What is Ainslie saying is happening with the Order?"

"She said they will handle it, whatever the fuck that means." Dad never swore, and I wished, for the thousandth time, that I could spare them all from this grief. The same grief that was tearing me apart inside.

"I'll find out what's going on. I'm so sorry, Dad." I managed to say before I hung up and began to cry in earnest.

I shouldn't have been surprised that this exchange and memories of my twin caused the now-familiar sensation of being pulled into a memory.

I kissed Jacob goodbye, more out of habit than anything else. I'd barely been holding it together since my argument with Isolde earlier this morning. I was grateful that Jacob had plans without me so that I could cry without anyone else around.

Ever since Will had died, it was like I was living inside a black pit of despair. And because no one knew of the true nature of our relationship, I couldn't even mourn him openly as Isolde had. Not that she seemed to have done much in the way of mourning. She was already rolling around between the sheets with someone else only months after his death. Sure, Liam was fucking hot, but how do you go from being madly in love with one guy who was murdered in front of you to suddenly jumping into bed with another? And I seriously doubted that this was a new thing. He seemed to know her pretty damn well for someone she's just started talking about. And who the hell were all the other people who had been trekking through the house the past few weeks? I had never heard her mention any of these people before. Something didn't add up.

I went into my cupboard and pulled out the jumper of Will's that I had smuggled out of one of the boxes when Isolde wasn't looking and breathed in the lingering scent of him once again. When would the pain of his death ease?

Tears began running down my face, and I curled into a ball on the floor, sobbing hard. I gripped his jumper to my chest, despairing that this was all I had left of him. How could someone so full of life just be gone? Without having the chance to really live?

Eventually, my sobs eased, and I finally sat up. The smell of burning fabric reached my nose, and I looked down to see a puff of smoke coming from the material still gripped in my fist. I cautiously opened my hand and gasped at the sight of the burnt fabric. How the fuck had that happened? I threw the jumper away from me and stared at it in horror.

Back in my own thoughts, I stared at my right hand, confused at what I had just seen. How had she managed to do that? Aurora didn't have any powers...

I continued walking for the rest of the day, dealing with the latest round of grief that Jacob's death had unleashed and the guilt of being unable to prevent it. I wasn't ready to return to Eve's house and face being there without Liam, and I was still puzzling over the memory from Aurora.

As dusk began to fall, I stopped in front of a park I had been driving past my whole life. It was the same park where Liam had told me the truth about who I was only a few short months ago, although it felt like a lifetime now.

I walked over to the picnic table where we had sat that night, lying on top of the table and staring at the sky when the stars began to appear.

How had everything become so complicated? Life had been simple once. Like many other women in love, I'd been floating through life without any real problems. And then the world exploded, reality hit, and everything became so much worse. Now, I was living out some internal battle within my mind, one half of me wanting to give in to the darkness, to stop feeling everything so deeply. The other half of me was screaming to do the right thing, return to the daywalkers, join forces with the Order, and wage war against an evil army.

"It doesn't have to be this hard, you know?" A voice came out of the darkness, and I jumped up so quickly that I would have been dizzy if I had been human.

It appeared that Connor was able to sneak up on me. I remembered now that he had somehow hidden an entire room full of nightwalkers from me a few weeks ago, but something told me this was different when he stepped out of the shadows. Despite the darkness, I could see him clear as day, the benefits of superhuman vision.

"What doesn't have to be so hard?" I clenched my jaw and willed my body to behave when Connor came to stand beside me. I hated how my body reacted whenever Connor came near me, like something within me hungered for his touch.

He leaned back against the table, crossing his arms and turning to look at me. I focused on my breathing, refusing to give in, and I could tell he was enjoying the effect he was having on me.

Bastard.

"Making the decision. It would be so much easier if you just gave in. That's what I did. And believe me, life, or un-life if you will, has been much simpler. There has been none of the soul-searching nonsense you have been feeling, just simply living for the pleasures and ignoring the crap."

I groaned, throwing my head up to stare up at the stars.

"Stop feeding me the bullshit line that you don't care about anything. You keep forgetting that I've seen your memories. I know full well that this is all an act. You haven't made any damn choice. You just put up the façade of being evil so that you don't have to deal with all the crap you struggle with daily." I went to walk away from him, but he reached out and caught my hand, turning me to face him.

"Alright then. So what emotion am I feeling right now, oh wise one?" There was a dangerous glint in his eye. Like he was daring me to tell him the truth about who he was.

"You're scared."

"I think your radar is a little broken." He scoffed.

"No, it's not. You're scared. You don't know how to deal with what I force you to feel. You've never met another hybrid like you, and now that I've come along, it's forced you to deal with all the crap you've been suppressing for centuries. And it scares the hell out of you." His jaw clenched, and his eyes flashed. His hands balled into fists, the one holding mine squeezing my fingers painfully.

"I'm not the one you want to strike out at, Connor. You're angry at everyone and everything. Life would be easier for you if you were filled with the mindless hunger of a nightwalker, but you have emotions. You do feel, possibly even deeper than a human. It's our curse." I stepped closer to him, his hand still gripping mine, forcing him to look into my eyes. I was tired of him always being the one to talk, to tell me how I was feeling and give in to the hunger, to run away from the pain that the conflict inside caused.

He searched my eyes for a moment, the anger still boiling beneath the surface, though I could feel something else within him stirring. His other hand reached up and worked its way through the hair at the back of my head, and before I knew what was happening, he was kissing me.

My initial response was to pull away, but that thought flew out of my mind when I kissed him back with the same hunger and intensity that drove him. Maybe it was his emotions feeding my own, but I knew that a part of me had wanted to do this since I had woken up to this nightmare. Without knowing how I got there, I was lying back on the table with Connor on top of me, kissing my neck, sending chills down my spine.

"You want to understand why I made my decisions, Isolde? Let me show you." He whispered in my ear before pulling back and looking down at me.

I blinked, stunned by his sudden absence on top of me. It took me a moment to realise what he was offering when he placed his wrist at my mouth.

"Bite."

So I did.

CHAPTER TWENTY-SEVEN

I stared at the beautiful woman before me, sitting across the table in the tavern I frequented nightly to escape the monotonous life of learning to run the family estate I had little care for. I often wished I had been born second, without any expectations of me, like Liam. I had no desire to marry and force some poor woman to start producing an army children, which had been the expectation placed upon my parents.

"I've been watching you, little Lord." She smiled seductively, her black hair coiled high upon her head. A woman like this did not belong in a tavern such as this one. Her finery caused her to stand out amongst the men and women packed inside, avoiding the cold winter night. But then, most women of such apparent wealth did not, in my experience, tend to undress you with their eyes in private, let alone amongst a boisterous crowd of rough men and women.

"Have you now? And why is that?" I reached across the table and took her hand, bringing it to my lips to press a kiss to the back of it slowly. I was well-versed in the ways of the female sex and had danced this dance a few times. But this woman was vastly different from those

I had taken upstairs in the past. I needed to play this little courtship differently. She needed to be wooed and seduced.

"You intrigue me. I wish to get to know you better." Her eyes told me exactly how she wanted me to know her better.

"Should we go somewhere quieter then? Do you have a room upstairs?"

A woman like this surely wasn't travelling alone, so I was surprised when she nodded coyly. Without caring about the looks we received from those around us, she took me by the hand and guided me towards the stairs that led up to the rooms above. Something inside me told me that a woman who cared so little about what society thought of her was dangerous, but I was too intrigued to turn away now.

She led me to her room above the noisy tavern. It was one of the nicer ones. I'd rarely been in this room. The other rooms were better suited for the brief interludes I required them for, and this one was usually occupied by the lesser nobles who had stopped for the night whilst on their travels – the mystery of who this woman was deepened. But I didn't have a chance to think on this more as she turned and pressed me back against the door once it closed behind me. Her lips met mine hungrily, and I kissed her back. I was unaccustomed to women being so forthright, but I was more than happy to allow her to control this situation.

She deftly removed my shirt, and I turned her roughly to begin unlacing the back of her dress. The outfits that noble women wore were so damn hard to remove, and it took far longer than I would have preferred. Eventually, we were both naked and lying on the bed.

"You are so beautiful," she said while she straddled my hips and hungrily kissed my face and neck, rubbing against me. It was more than evident that this woman was no maiden, and I knew I was at risk of losing my heart without even knowing her name. I was already painfully hard, and I groaned when she eased down upon my shaft and began riding me slowly, running her hands over her ample breasts. She moaned as she rolled her hips, holding my gaze the entire time. It was almost a religious experience, and I gripped her hips, urging her to

move faster while I stared up at her. She leaned forward to press her chest to mine and kissed me, slower than before, before running her lips down my throat.

"Who are you?" I whispered breathlessly, feeling my release build as she moved her hips faster, her lips pressed to my neck. She ground herself down, moving her hips in a slow, circular motion, and I felt my eyes roll back in my head. I had never experienced anything like this before, and I knew I was ruined for all other women.

"You'll find out soon enough," she whispered back, and I was too far gone to be concerned about what she meant. Pleasure shot through me just as a sharp pain began radiating up my neck, starting beneath her lips. I was dimly aware that she had bitten me, and her bite somehow drew the euphoria out while she drank from my neck. My brain screamed that this was wrong, but I was powerless to do anything, with the pleasure continuing to rock through me while she sought her own release, prolonging my own never-ending orgasm. She moaned against my neck while she continued to draw the blood from my throat, her orgasm rolling through her and causing her to shake. I began to feel lightheaded, but still, something stopped me from fighting her off, and my eyes gradually closed when she slowed her movements, her lips remaining at my throat.

Distantly, I was aware of the door opening and someone entering the room, and she finally sat up. I couldn't find the energy to open my eyes but vaguely heard a man's voice.

"Aoibh, my love? Did you summon me? But what is this?" I felt her move off me, my mind slipping further into the darkness as she spoke.

"I have a gift for you, Adhamh. A peace offering. Doesn't he remind you of Aden and Chey? He has a twin, too." There was silence now, and I tried to fight off the fall into the whirling black, but another, more intense pain began at my throat, and the darkness claimed me.

. . .

I blinked, and the memory faded. I returned to myself with Connor's wrist still held to my lips. He had sat me up while I was in the memory and now held me against his chest while I sat sideways in his lap.

"Eve? It was Eve and Adam who turned you?" I searched Connor's face for answers, unable to believe what I had just seen. To say that I was shocked by Eve's involvement was an understatement. I'd always assumed Adam was his sire, but knowing that the daywalker involved was Eve was more than I could have ever imagined.

Could a memory from his blood be faked?

"There is far more for you to see, little one. Keep going." He urged me to continue feeding from his wrist, and I bit down again, immediately slipping into another memory.

CHAPTER TWENTY-EIGHT

I genuinely believe that a year ago, I awoke in hell. I was surrounded by the most evil creatures imaginable. Although I appeared to be the same as them, I still clung to the vestiges of humanity that remained inside me. For the last twelve months, I had been expected to follow along with the rest of the coven and was drawn to the man who controlled them all. They were all sadistic killers, and I have watched while many of them fed so brutally that they ripped the heads of their victims off with their ferocity. I hadn't been able to bring myself to kill anyone yet and hid this fact from the others by going into their feeble minds and changing what they thought they had seen. It was a talent I had discovered by accident, but I had used it to my advantage for months.

"Your brother will have his powers within the Order activated soon. Is it not your twenty-fifth birthday tomorrow?" Adhamh asked, watching, bored, while one of the others fed hungrily off the young prostitute he had brought back to the estate Adhamh had claimed. The bodies of the previous owners were rotting away in the unused kitchen, their heads having been torn from their shoulders and now lying in the dry-

store cupboard. I never went in there, having only made that mistake once.

"I have long stopped tracking the days," I replied, my tone bored while I lied through my teeth. I knew what day it was and what that meant for my brother. I had learned much since entering this endless nightmare, including that my brother was fated to become my mortal enemy. I didn't understand why I seemed so different from the other nightwalkers I was surrounded by, but I knew my sheltered younger brother was not ready to face the creatures that stalked the darkness. He had always been so devout in his belief in God, a being that I had long ago come to believe was not as accurate as the priests claimed, and I now knew to be a complete fairytale.

"We will pay him a visit tomorrow night, you and I." I felt my heart stop briefly, something else I had managed to keep hidden from those around me. I was the only one who continued to have a heartbeat and draw breath, but I also used my abilities to hide this from them all.

"Why? Surely the Order will have already drawn him into their circle?"

"I have been watching, and they are still following their usual pattern and waiting for him to be ready before informing him of his destiny. It truly is laughable." I knew there was no arguing and agreed to accompany Adhamh to my former home the following night, wondering how to save my brother from joining me in this living hell.

I kept my arms locked around Liam's upper body, playing my part well while I fought the internal war raging within me as we watched Adhamh tear our mother's throat out. Liam was no match for my strength while I held him tight, though I was impressed at the effort he was putting in nonetheless.

Perhaps having my brother at my side through this nightmare

wouldn't be so bad. With any luck, he will be like me, and together, we could gain control of the coven and bring the madness to an end.

I allowed the daydream to help me escape the reality of my situation while Adhamh turned his attention from our mother to my brother, who had now gone rigid in my arms, the scent of his fear filling the air.

Adhamh stepped forward, his gaze falling upon my brother, who began to whimper in my arms. The sound of glass shattering distracted us both, and I looked over to see Callum pointing a crossbow at me through the window. I swore and let go of Liam, who dropped to the ground and landed in the pool of our mother's blood. Adhamh was already fleeing the room, and I wondered briefly if this many people would be what it took to kill him finally. The villagers behind Callum held torches, and I wasn't interested in seeing what would happen if he managed to use better aim with the next bolt. His eyes were set on me while I watched him reload. I looked down at Liam again before hastily following Adhamh out the door.

Adhamh was already long gone, and I knew he would leave me to make my own way back. I aimed for the trees behind the manor but heard a noise behind me. I turned towards it, seeing Liam racing away from the servant's entrance, covered in blood. I ran after him, although I was unsure of what I would do once I found him. He couldn't know what I had become, or the Order would come after me, and I had managed to avoid them so far. But perhaps I could get him to see what I truly was, and he could help me find a way out of this mess.

I followed Liam, remaining silent, waiting to see where he was going. He stumbled upon the ruined church on the outer edge of our estate, one neither of us had known about in our youth, but I'd discovered in my wanderings when I was older. When he didn't appear after some time, I eased my way inside and came upon a scene I had not expected. There was the woman who had started me on this path to madness, feeding from my brother, who lay upon the altar.

"You!" I yelled, expecting her to look up, but she simply raised a hand toward me, and I flew back against the wall, unable to move

while some invisible force kept me there. I struggled to free myself but was no match for whatever magic she possessed. I heard my brother's heart slow and eventually cease to beat. She finally looked up, wiping the blood from her mouth, and released the magic that had kept me pinned against the wall. I moved quickly and appeared at her side, grabbing her roughly by the hair and pulling her away from Liam's lifeless body.

"Who the fuck are you?"

She looked up at me with such a condescending smile that I considered punching her, but I knew that I was no match for her.

"Why are you doing this to my family?"

"You have much to learn, dear boy. The wheels are now in motion, and it is time you understood your part." She placed a hand on my cheek, and I was stunned by the sadness I saw behind her eyes.

"What do you mean, my part? You're the one who is doing all of this."

"I had to. This has all gone on for far too long. And it needs to end. This is how it has to be. It is all that I can do." And she began to explain some prophecy about twins and ending the nightwalkers once and for all.

"Why are you telling me this? I'm a nightwalker?! Why would I be involved in ending them."

"You know that isn't true, Connor. You are different to them. Have you not worked this out?" She looked at me with pity in her eyes, and I growled.

"Speak plainly, devil woman." I shook her roughly, tired of all these games.

"You are a hybrid. The first of your kind. Created to activate the spell."

"Spell? I thought you said it was a prophecy."

She laughed.

"That's what everyone needs to believe. But it is a spell. Just like this whole mess started because of a spell. And once the second set of twins come along, and the most powerful of you all is turned, becoming a

hybrid like you, the spell will be cast. She will finally end this miserable existence with fire in her heart." Her words meant nothing to me, but she continued to speak regardless of the confusion on my face.

"There needed to be balance, darkness and light. There always needs to be a balance."

It was like coming into the story halfway through without anyone explaining what had occurred in the beginning. And none of it made sense.

"What the fuck are you talking about?!"

"You were never meant to exist!"

I stared at her while she threw her hands up in the air.

"Start from the beginning, woman. You are making absolutely no sense. Clearly, I exist. I'm standing right here."

She took a deep breath and glared at me for a moment. I could almost see the wheels in her brain turning.

"We have been attempting to end the curse of the nightwalkers for a millennium. But we have been unable to stop their spread until now. A spell was cast to bring the pair of you into existence, to ensure that Liam would have the power of a seventh son of a seventh son. But he also needed a twin who possessed the dark side to his light. Who shared a womb with him. To share his power and play his own part in the spell." She gestured towards me, and I fought against the emotions these words stirred.

I had always known that Liam was a better man than me, but to have someone refer to me as his darker side was like a knife to the gut.

"This was the only way to have both men capable of wielding the powers of the original coven. Specifically, from Adhamh's bloodline," she said.

My mind was reeling from all this information, most of which still made no sense to me.

"What about this other set of twins you were rambling about? Where are they?"

"They will not be born for many years yet. It took us centuries to have everything exactly right to create you and Liam."

"Centuries? Surely you can't be serious?"

"Such powerful magic always has a price. In this instance, that price is time. But when the female twins are born, the one with the full powers of the Order will be the one to bring it all to an end. She will be more powerful than any of us combined, with the bloodlines of the strongest members of the original coven running through her veins. She will become a hybrid, like you."

"What of Liam and the other female twin? Are they to be hybrids as well?" I prayed she would say yes, that Liam would somehow be changed like I was, and I wouldn't be alone with this knowledge for centuries.

"Liam will awaken as a daywalker in seven days. I have just started his transition now. The other female will become a nightwalker, so we have a twin on either side."

"Let me guess - so that they balance each other out?" I was starting to hate the word balance.

"You're catching on quick, Connor." She patted my cheek, and I felt my eyes flash.

"Why can't I just kill the nightwalkers, then? Or you, for that matter?" I didn't understand why this all needed to be done in such an elaborate and fucked up way.

"You don't have the power to kill Adhamh on your own. No single nightwalker, daywalker or Order member does. This was the only way I could create beings with the power to do so. You are simply the first step. But you must remain at Adhamh's side to ensure all the pieces are right once the time comes."

"I don't understand why I needed to be the hybrid. Surely it should be Liam if he's got the powers of the Order." There seemed to be so many loopholes in her logic.

"You and Liam are two halves of the same whole. Surely you have worked out that you have powers that no other nightwalker has? The ability to control minds and enter dreams? Liam has similar powers. Yours were activated by the spell when you became a hybrid, and Liam's were activated by his turning twenty-five. I need him within the Order, something that wouldn't have happened if he was activated first as the hybrid. It will be different for the female twins, though. When their time comes, the younger twin needs to have her powers within the order activated before the older twin becomes a nightwalker, so they will both have their powers before turning. But the younger twin, the one with the blood of both a seventh daughter and a seventh son, will become a hybrid like you once she is changed by all three of you."

I stared at her, trying to understand everything she was saying. So much of her plan was being left up to chance.

"Who are you?" I demanded once again.

"In life, Adhamh was my husband. My name is Aoibh. The spell that created the first nightwalker and daywalker started with us. Cast by the leader of the coven that all members of the Order originated from, a man named Sithech." She laughed, though little humour was behind it.

"Adam and Eve?" My mind was reeling.

"That's right, the original Adam and Eve. Cast out of paradise when a snake tempted Eve with an apple. Sithech became Seth, a name often aligned with Satan or Lucifer. At least they cast him correctly in their little story." She smirked a little, but I couldn't see anything funny about any of this. "Adhamh and I must be together when the time comes for this to end. And the steps that I have set in motion now will ensure that will happen. So you will be playing your part, Connor. Because you're tied to all of this now, whether you like it or not." And with those final words, she disappeared in a blur, leaving me standing alone alongside my brother's body, my brain a mess of questions and horror from what I had just learned.

I stayed there for the next seven days until Liam stirred, and then I slipped out into the night again.

How long was I to be expected to play this part? Adhamh could never know of this, or he would just kill me. But Aoibh had said it could be centuries. Something that I prayed was an exaggeration. Because with each moment I was exposed to this evil, it was harder to keep a hold of my human side.

· · ·

I pushed Connor's arm away from me and leapt to my feet, needing to put distance between us while I processed everything I had just seen. I could feel my hands shaking, and I raked them through my hair, staring at him in shock. Connor watched while I began pacing, making no move to offer any further explanation.

"Eve set this all in motion? She told me she'd heard about the prophecy, but that memory...."

"Eve has been lying to so many people for centuries. I have no idea how she keeps track of it all. But she has manipulated this entire charade from the start. We are nothing more than her pawns in all of it." Connor's expression clouded over, and I had to remind myself again that he was not Liam, although that thought made me think of something Eve had revealed to Connor five hundred years ago.

"What the hell did she mean about you being created to be Liam's darker self?"

"Exactly what she said. Aurora and I exist purely so that you and Liam have the powers of the seventh son and daughter flowing through you. But because Aurora and I shared the same wombs, the magic from you guys passed to us. It's certainly been comforting to know that my entire existence came about so that my saintly younger brother gets to be the good guy. If I weren't already evil, that would have been enough to set it off," he said darkly.

"Quit trying to convince me that you are this evil being when you just confirmed that you are like me."

"I'm nothing like you, Isolde. That memory was five hundred years ago. I have spent five hundred years surrounded by creatures of the purest evil and expected to play my part. And I did. I played it well. I have killed. I have destroyed families. I've toyed with my brother countless times out of spite and anger. Do not fool yourself. I am not the tragic hero in all of this." Connor stalked towards me, stopping inches from my face and glaring at me.

"Is that why there is this pull between us? Because we're both hybrids?" I needed all the answers now, and this was the closest I'd come to learning the truth of who I was.

"I don't know. I feel a similar pull towards Aurora, and I imagine Liam has felt something as well, at least before her transition. Who knows, maybe it's because I'm literally Liam's other half." Connor laughed darkly.

I liked this theory. It made me feel marginally better about the fact that I seemed to be so attracted to my boyfriend's twin brother.

"That explains a lot." It also explained my memory of Aurora's inadvertently using fire magic.

"Of course, that's the answer that you cling to. Anything to deny the truth behind what is happening between us." Connor shook his head.

"Nothing is happening between us! I love Liam. Whatever this mess is between you and me, it means nothing!"

"It means everything! There was a connection when I first saw you in that university auditorium. I know you felt it - stop lying to yourself!" He gripped my shoulders and shook me slightly, but I shoved his hands away.

"I thought you were Liam!"

"You hadn't even met Liam yet!"

I didn't know who was angrier, but I stepped away from Connor again, needing to keep the distance between us in case it spiralled into another anger-fuelled kissing session.

"Stop trying to convince me you're the one I should be with, Connor. If I'm forced to choose, you know I will choose Liam."

Connor had been moving to close the space between us once more but came to an abrupt halt at my words. It was like the fight just fell out of him, and his expression closed over once again, the mask of evil settling over his features.

"If that is your decision, Isolde, then so be it. But know this - I have no intention of remaining Eve's puppet through all of this. Whatever her master plan is, I will be playing no part anymore. I chose this path for myself long ago, and I'll be damned if that witch will play me any further. I did what she needed. I made sure Adam was the one to turn your sister. I told him about the prophecy but left out a few important parts. As far as he knows, we failed. I ensured that Aurora and I didn't feed on you until Liam was in the room." His eyes flashed again while he glared at me. His jaw twitched, and I could tell he struggled to control his emotions.

"But I'm done now. So when we meet next, Isolde, all traces of my tortured soul will be gone, and you better believe you won't like what you see instead." With those words, he vanished, leaving me standing alone again after having yet more truths dumped on top of me.

I could feel so many emotions beginning to swirl inside me, the last few weeks of constant chaos threatening to overpower me.

I began to shake uncontrollably and felt something inside me snap. A burning sensation began to form in my chest.

My arms flung out wide, my head snapped back, and my entire body erupted, sending a fountain of flames soaring into the sky like some fiery bat signal.

Everything around me was ablaze, and I lost all control of the power that engulfed me.

A single thought flowed through my mind.

Let it all burn.

EPILOGUE

LIAM

$\mathcal{I}$ had spent the night killing any nightwalkers I found in a failed attempt to work off the pent-up anger and frustration within me. When daylight arrived, and I was no closer to getting past it all, I had walked without a destination. I returned to the home that had once been my sanctuary but now felt empty and cold without Isolde.

I desperately needed a drink, and once I walked through the door, I made a beeline for the whiskey cabinet. I poured myself a glass and took both the bottle and the glass onto the balcony. Night had long since fallen, and I stared out at the view, the lights of the houses across the river in Bulimba twinkling away. Even with all I knew was occurring between Isolde and Connor, I needed to know she was safe. I regretted leaving her the way that I did.

But how was I meant to get past the fact that Isolde was drawn to my brother? The same brother who I had been fighting for the last five hundred years and was a creature of the purest evil? What did this mean of what Isolde had become? She was something different, and I felt sick knowing that it was my fault. I was meant to protect her, yet I had been coerced into turning her into something no one had anticipated. I needed to speak to Eve and force her to explain what Isolde had become.

I threw back my second glass of whiskey and began to pour my third when a flash of light in the distance drew my attention across the river. I could feel a burning sensation in my chest that I knew had nothing to do with the whiskey, and I watched a ball of flame shoot into the sky. I could think of only one thing that was causing that, and coupled with the burning in my chest, I knew immediately that Isolde was in danger.

I jumped to my feet, intent on reaching her as quickly as possible when a noise behind me caused me to turn around.

Damon stepped out of the shadows in front of me, closely followed by another man, and I was surprised that they had been able to keep their presence cloaked from me. That surprise turned to anger when the stranger raised his hand towards me, and my body seized up. Unable to move, I could do nothing to stop him when he came towards me, keeping me in place with his magic. He stopped in front of me and dropped his arm to his side, but whatever he had done kept me from being able to move from where I stood. I had never experienced magic like this before, and genuine fear began to pump through my veins for the first time in a long time.

"What are you doing, Damon?" I demanded, and he smirked at me from behind his companion.

"I thought surely Eve would have told you the truth by now. I shouldn't be surprised, though. She always did like to make things as dramatic as possible." He gestured towards the man beside him, who was surveying me closely.

"This is my father. You can call him Seth. We have a lot to discuss. But first, let me just do one thing." He reached forward and touched my forehead. I felt a sharp pain before falling into darkness.

PHOENIX RISING

BOOK THREE

This one is for all those who wonder
if magic can truly exist amongst the mundane,
if vampires and dragons are real,
and what it would be like to save the world.

SONG LIST

My Legacy – Bradley Walden, Patrick Cunningham
Holy Ground – Sebastian Kenz
American Horror Show – Snow Wife
Ready Or Not – Mischa "Book" Chillak, Esthero
Masquerade – Euphoria, Bolshiee
Leave Me In The Dark – Alexander Stewart
You've Created A Monster – Bohnes
Figure You Out – Voila
Die For You – The Siege
Save Yourself – My Darkest Days
Lifetime – Three Days Grace
Breathing Underwater – Hot Milk
Dangerous Game – Klergy, Beginners
Harder to Breathe – Letdown
Feel Nothing – The Plot In You
Hell and Back – Self Deception
Empty – Letdown
Numb the Pain – Clarx
Runnin' – Adam Lambert

Arcade – Duncan Laurence
Before You Go – Lewis Capaldi
Just Pretend – Bad Omens
The Death Of Peace Of Mind – Bad Omens
Sex And Candy – Alexander Jean
Ceilings – Lizzy McAlpine
Villain – Neoni
Can You Hold Me – NF, Britt Nicole
Paralyzed – NF
Hurtless – Dean Lewis
Where You Belong – Matt Hansen
Little Girl Gone – Chinchilla
Hurts Like Hell – Tommee Profitt, Fleurie
Something To Hide – Grandson
Witness The Masterpiece – Ganyos
Dead Or Alive – Stileto, Madalen Duke
Up – Adelitas Way, New Medicine
I Hate Everything About You – Three Days Grace
Where Do We Go (No Escape) – Klergy, Katie Garfield
Up In Flames – Ruelle
Dial Tone – Catch Your Breath
Drinking With Cupid – VOILA
Middle Of The Night – Rain Paris
Lovely – Lauren Babic, Seraphim

PROLOGUE

What would you do if you'd been turned into a creature that no one had ever heard of and discovered that there was only one other like you in the world?

A man who wore an identical face to the man you loved and stirred up feelings that you couldn't explain. A man who everyone told you was pure evil, yet you had seen into his soul and knew there was more to the story.

What would you do if you discovered you were destined to save the world? With the responsibility of saving millions resting on your shoulders, but you haven't been provided with the manual on how to actually do it.

Would you accept this fate? This duty? This curse?

Or would you give in to desire and let it all burn to the ground?

CHAPTER ONE

The world was on fire. All I could feel was the searing heat of the flames that had erupted out of control from my body as the toll of months of stress and grief overcame me finally.

"Isolde!"

I had no comprehension of time passing or anything that was occurring around me, too tangled within myself to notice anything but the rage that spewed from me.

Let it burn! Let it burn! The words ran through my mind on an endless loop.

"Isolde! Dammit!"

Distantly, I heard someone screaming my name over the roar of the flames and the words being chanted over and over in my head.

"Fuck it! Isolde! Snap out of it!"

A hand reached through the flames and latched onto my wrist, wrenching me out of my own head and back to reality. Immediately, the chanting and the rage that had burned within me ceased. A sense of calm washed over me as the flames disappeared as quickly as they'd appeared. The owner of the hand stepped in front of me, gripping my shoulders and shaking me hard.

"What the fuck was that?! I leave you alone for five minutes and turn around to see a flaming bat signal shooting into the sky!"

I blinked up into his face, disorientated. His features swam into focus finally, and I stumbled forward as my knees gave out beneath me.

"Liam?" I whispered, scanning the face of the man before me.

"No," he replied, his voice deathly quiet as he glared at me.

"Connor..."

"Always the second choice," he muttered, and I shook his hands off me.

"How did that not burn you?" I gestured around me, taking in the circle of scorched earth I stood in the centre of.

Melted steel and charred wood were the only remnants of the picnic table that had previously been beside me.

"Fucked if I know," he said with a shrug, and I squinted at him.

"So you just decided to play hero and reach into flames, knowing full well that if a nightwalker catches fire, they combust immediately?"

"Well, given that I'm not a nightwalker, I guess I'm immune to that little bit of fun," Connor said.

I continued to stare at him.

"Stop looking at me like that," he said gruffly, raking a hand through his hair.

"How am I looking at you?" I asked, refusing to look away.

"Like I'm redeemed or something. Just quit it."

I found it interesting that I could make him this uncomfortable just by looking at him.

"Why did you come back?"

"Are you seriously asking me that? You lit this park up like it was some sort of portal to hell and thought I wouldn't turn around to see what the fuck was going on?" It was his turn to stare at me like I'd grown a second head.

"Well, given that you'd just given me an impassioned speech about how the next time I'd see you, you were going to be all dark side, yes, I'm surprised to see you standing here after reaching through flames to get to me," I said, raising an eyebrow.

He hesitated before answering. "I may have been a little hasty when I said that."

"A little hasty? Seriously, Connor?" I stepped out of the circle of charred ground, holding my hands out before me and inspecting myself for any signs of damage.

There wasn't a single burn on either Connor or me. Even our clothing remained untouched.

"Why aren't we dead?" I looked over at where he remained standing inside the circle.

"I already told you, I have no fucking idea. That would be yet another Eve question, I guess." He rolled his eyes and let out a sigh. "Why'd you decide to set the world on fire?"

"I didn't mean to... I just lost it for a moment, and suddenly, I was on fire." As I finished speaking, I became aware of the sirens getting closer.

Connor looked towards the flashing lights that were coming down the street.

"I'm going to go out on a limb and say that someone has alerted the fire department to your little pyrotechnic display. We should probably get out of here."

I looked at him momentarily, and he gestured to the other side of the park. I hesitated before following him as he disappeared in a blur.

We slowed to a walk a few streets away, and I fell into step beside him while he slid his hands into his pockets, refusing to look at me.

"I'm still waiting for the real reason you came back," I said.

Connor shook his head, chuckling, although there was little humour behind it.

"I see you were really paying attention when I gave my impassioned little speech earlier," he said, his voice dripping with sarcasm.

"You reached through fire to get to me without even knowing if it would kill you or not, Connor." I stopped walking, grabbing his arm to turn him to face me. "I need to hear you say the words. I need your honesty."

He glared at me, and for a moment, I thought he would disappear before answering.

"Because I fucking care. And I'm ready for this whole nightmare to end, but that won't happen if you're dead because you decided to dabble in spontaneous hybrid vampire combustion!"

As I opened my mouth to respond, a searing pain shot through me, and I fell to my knees, gripping my head in my hands.

A burning sensation seared my chest, and I watched a ball of flame shoot into the sky. I could think of only one thing that was causing that, and coupled with the burning in my chest, I knew immediately that Isolde was in danger.

I jumped to my feet, intent on reaching her as quickly as possible, when the sound of footsteps caused me to turn around.

Damon stepped out of the shadows before me, closely followed by another man. I was surprised that they had been able to keep their presence cloaked from me.

My body seized up, and that surprise turned to anger when the stranger raised his hand towards me. I could do nothing to stop him when he came towards me, keeping me in place with his magic. He stopped in front of me and dropped his arm to his side, but whatever he had done kept me from being able to move from where I stood. I had never experienced magic like this before.

Genuine fear began to pump through my veins for the first time in a long time.

"What are you doing, Damon?" I demanded, and he smirked at me from behind his companion.

"I thought surely Eve would have told you the truth by now. I shouldn't be surprised, though. She always did like to make things as dramatic as possible." He gestured towards the man beside him, who was surveying me closely.

"This is my father. You can call him Seth. We have a lot to discuss.

But first, let me just do one thing." He reached forward and touched *my forehead.*

I felt a sharp pain before falling into darkness.

"Isolde?!"

For the second time in five minutes, I was brought back into reality by Connor yelling my name as he shook me.

"What the hell just happened?"

I staggered a little as he pulled me to my feet. "I... I think I just had a flash from Liam."

Connor's face clouded at the mention of his brother, but I ignored it.

"I think something has happened to him."

"What do you mean something has happened to him?" Connor's eyes flashed, and I decided to tuck that little bit of information aside for another time.

"I need to go right now." I pushed him away and took off, leaving him standing there staring after me while I raced to make sure Liam was okay.

CHAPTER TWO

he front door slammed as I raced to the balcony where I had seen Liam, Damon and Seth in my vision, praying that what I'd seen hadn't been real.

It had taken me fifteen minutes to get here, and I cursed the river between where I had been and where I was now. I had tried to see if I could run across the water, but that had been futile. Ignoring the water still sloshing inside my runners, I came to an abrupt halt outside the glass doors. The bottle of whiskey was still there, and the glass Liam had used was in pieces on the ground, but there was no sign of him or anyone else.

I swore under my breath.

Had what I'd seen really happened?

And if it had, what the hell was Damon's plan?

Did the Order know his true identity?

I needed answers, but those answers lay with several different people, and they were all in different locations.

I knew where I needed to go first.

. . .

Fifteen minutes later, I kicked in the front door of Eve's house and screeched to a halt.

"Anika!" I yelled from the foyer, praying that Anika and Anthony were still there and hadn't gone out on patrol.

"Isolde?" Anika appeared before me, entering the room in a blur from the kitchen. Anthony followed behind at a slower pace, his eyebrow raised.

"Thank god," I said, sagging against the hall table in relief.

She let out a small laugh. "Well, that's not usually how people greet me after screaming my name like the sky is falling." She ran her eyes over me. "What's wrong? Where's Liam?"

"That's why I needed you. I need to know about the bond and how it works."

Anika's eyebrows flew up. "What do you mean?" She gave Anthony, who was watching me intently, a wary look.

I began pacing. "Our bond came back two nights ago."

Had it really only been two days since we'd finally been able to hear each other's thoughts again? How had everything gone so wrong in such a short amount of time?

"That's great!" A huge smile spread across her face as she clapped her hands together.

I held her gaze for a brief moment before looking away.

"Not great?" She asked as the smile faded.

"Let's just say there was some stuff Liam wasn't ready to hear rattling around inside my head," I said, still unable to look at her.

"Okay," Anthony said, stretching the word out while exchanging another look with Anika.

I didn't need to be bonded to either of them to know that they were having a telepathic conversation regarding my sanity.

"And then I just had a complete meltdown and turned into the human torch on steroids. Minutes later, I get a flash of what I think was a vision from Liam, and I think he's been taken by one of the elders of the Order and the witch who started the whole daywalker, nightwalker curse." I spoke so fast that I started to trip over all my words. I was amazed that Anika and Anthony could follow anything I said in my word vomit.

"Wait, what?! A witch and a curse?" Anika's eyebrows had now reached the outer stratosphere.

"I'll explain all of that later, but is it possible for me to see visions from Liam through the bond? Not flashes of his memories, but like, what is happening to him right now?" I looked from one to the other frantically.

They exchanged yet another look.

"Yes, it is possible. If one of you is in danger or their emotions are particularly heightened," Anika answered for the both of them.

I let out a long breath.

"Okay then. Fuck, that means Liam's been taken, and I don't know where the hell to start looking... Can I get in his head? Liam did that with me when Connor took me, but I thought that was because of his abilities."

Anika looked over at Anthony again.

"We've never really been in circumstances where we've had to test that, to be honest. Getting kidnapped seems to be something you guys specialise in," Anthony said.

I glared at him, and Anika sighed as she swatted him on the arm.

"This is serious, you lump."

"Is Eve here?" I asked, not entirely sure I was ready to deal with her.

But if anyone were going to have answers, it would be the original daywalker who had been playing with my entire existence for centuries.

Anika shook her head, and I deflated.

"I can't believe I'm going to suggest this, but you might have to go to the Order. Perhaps the seers can help? You said one of the elders took him, right?"

"Yeah, but I get the feeling he isn't quite as loyal to the Order as they all think."

Anthony snorted. "How shocking, an elder of the Order who

isn't who he says he is." He ducked as Anika tried to smack him again. "What? Tell me I'm wrong."

"Just quit the sarcastic remarks. It's not helping," Anika stared him down, and he pretended to zip his lips while she turned back to me.

"Honestly, the Order needs to be where you start. As soon as Eve swans back through those doors, I'll tell her you need her."

I considered how much to tell them about what I'd found out tonight but realised there wasn't enough time for that bombshell to be dropped right now.

"Tell her that her son and ex-husband have taken Liam. That should light a fucking fire under her ass."

This information was met with silence as they both stared at me.

"I'm sorry, her what and her what?!" Anthony demanded, and I shrugged.

"See how much she's ready to tell you. But you can also tell her I've had a good chat with Connor tonight, and I know everything."

I turned and walked back out the door, leaving them both standing there with their mouths hanging open.

I could kind of understand now why Eve enjoyed the dramatics so much.

The door to the Manor slammed against the wall with a loud thud that shook the entire building as I kicked in a front door for the third time in an hour.

"Isolde?! What the hell?!" Barbara came tearing in from the library, a heavy book raised over her head.

"What exactly were you planning to do with that?" Gerard asked when he entered the room behind her, eyeing the book as she slowly brought it down to her chest and hugged it close.

"Whatever," she huffed at him before turning back to me. "Isolde, what on earth is going on?"

They both looked at me expectantly.

"Where's Patrice?"

Gerard let out a sigh. "God, what's she done now?"

Barbara glared at him.

"It wasn't her this time," I replied.

"But someone has done something? Wait, where's Liam?" Barbara asked, looking behind me.

I guess we're just a package deal now. I hoped that was still the case and that once I got Liam back, he could forgive me for all the crap with Connor.

"That would be the something that I need to talk to Patrice about."

Patrice appeared at the kitchen door as if summoned by the sound of her name.

"Isolde? What's wrong? Where's Liam?"

"Damon fucking took him," I said, stalking towards her.

Barbara moved swiftly to Patrice's side, her expression unreadable as she positioned herself between us.

"What?!" Patrice looked taken aback. "What do you mean Damon took him?"

"He literally knocked him out with magic and took him."

"Damon doesn't have powers like that," Patrice said, shaking her head as she raised a hand to her mouth.

"There is a lot you don't know Patrice. Can you contact the seers to see if they can trace where they've taken him?"

"Who's they? I thought you said it was Damon who'd taken him?"

I was starting to grow frustrated with having to explain everything constantly.

"Yeah, Damon took him. Along with his father."

"His father?" Patrice asked slowly.

I could hear the disbelief in her tone. Letting out another sigh, I rubbed my temple, attempting to soothe the nagging pain that was starting to develop.

"It's a lot to explain, but Damon isn't who we think he is. Please,

Patrice, just get the seers on to finding Liam, and I'll explain everything," I pleaded, and Patrice hesitated before nodding and disappearing towards her office.

I returned my attention to Gerard and Barbara as they stared at me, their mouths open, much like I'd left Anika and Anthony.

"Isolde, what is going on?" Barbara asked, her voice shaking a little.

I took pity on them and gestured towards the conference room.

"We should probably all go in there. I have a lot of information, and I'd rather just do it with everyone at once than have to go over it continuously," I said, giving Gerard a pleading look.

He nodded and moved towards the stairs while Barbara followed me into the other room.

Moments after we took our seats, we were joined by everyone else who was in the house. Daniel slid into the seat beside me, and I reached over to squeeze his hand. I still hadn't had a chance to talk to him since Celeste's death. I was relieved when he squeezed back.

Patrice was the last to join us, taking her usual seat.

"I've asked the seers to try and get a read on where Liam is."

The fact that she didn't say 'where Damon took Liam' gave me the impression that she still wasn't entirely sure if she believed me.

"Okay."

"What is going on, Isolde?" Patrice asked, and I let out another long breath, unsure where to start.

"The prophecies are bullshit. I'm not a daywalker."

The silence was deafening.

"What do you mean?" Gerard was the first to speak up, but it was Patrice that I looked at as I went on to explain.

"The prophecies were made up by Eve. It was all a front for a spell that she set in motion. It started with Connor being turned, and my transition was the final step. It had to be Liam, Connor and Aurora who turned me, ensuring that I became something different. A hybrid of both bloodlines. You guys were spoon-fed only the basic information to ensure I was in the right place at the right time."

"I don't understand." Patrice shook her head, her eyes wide as she stared at me.

I noticed a few others shifting in their seats and could sense their unease.

"Eve is the original daywalker. She was a part of the coven from which the entire Order descends, as was Adam. She pissed off the wrong person, and he placed the curse on both of them that started this whole thing. But here's the kicker... Damon is her son."

A collective gasp echoed through the room as everyone looked at me in disbelief.

"How is that possible?" Christian asked from where he sat next to Barbara, who seemed to be struggling to process everything I'd said so far, her face pale.

"I don't know the exact logistics of that part. While Liam and I were apart tonight, I had a vision of Damon and his father, the witch who started the initial curse, showing up at Liam's house. Damon knocked Liam out using powers that, apparently, no one knew he was capable of. But not before he divulged who he truly was."

"I don't even know where to begin with all of this," Patrice said quietly, and I nodded.

"I get it, believe me. There is still a lot that I don't know, but right now, all I want is to get Liam back."

"So do I." Eve's voice rang out from behind me, and we all turned towards the doorway where she stood, leaning against the door frame.

CHAPTER THREE

Within seconds, I was on my feet and standing in front of Eve, our faces so close that our noses were almost touching while I glared into her eyes.

She didn't even flinch.

"You have a lot of explaining to do, Eve," I said in a deathly low tone.

"Yes. I heard that Connor divulged his version of events tonight," she replied in a bored tone, maintaining her casual stance.

But when she shifted slightly, I could sense her unease.

"He didn't *tell* me anything. He *showed* me everything. I saw his memories of what you did to him and what you told him the night that you turned Liam."

"Connor barely knows the full extent of it all. He only knows the information I chose to impart that night. I'll admit, I never expected him to be the one to tell you, though. He was meant to keep his distance."

Frustration rose within me as she continued with the vague responses. I felt the burning in my chest start, and Eve's nostrils flared. The only sign of emotion she had shown since she walked in the door.

"Keep it under control, Isolde. You need to learn to keep your emotions in check, or you'll destroy those you care about," she said softly, nodding towards the Order members behind me.

Once again, that sense of unease rolled off her as her eyes flickered between them and me.

"I didn't think you cared about anyone in this room, Eve."

"I don't, particularly. But we need all those with magical abilities to be in one piece if we're going to win this."

"What's that supposed to mean?" Barbara spoke up behind me.

I glanced over my shoulder to see they had all risen to their feet.

"It means that you all have a role to play in what's coming. Which is why we need to get Liam back," Eve said, her gaze fixed on me.

"I want Liam back because it's Liam, not because he's some pawn in your fucked up game manipulating all our lives," I said, barely able to contain the rage that had started whirling through me.

"Oh, how sweet. How ridiculously co-dependant of you."

I clenched and unclenched my fists at my sides. "Fuck you, Eve." The burning in my chest started again, and my eyes flashed.

Eve smirked, and the burning intensified. A flame shot from my right hand, and I heard someone yell behind me.

"Now, now, Isolde. It's not time for that yet. You don't want to burn the precious Manor down."

Patrice had finally had enough. "The pair of you - sit down and stop snipping at each other," she said in a tone that did not allow room for argument.

Eve looked at her with a raised eyebrow, the smirk still playing across her lips.

"I really do find it so entertaining when you Order members think you control anything," she said, but she moved to sit at the table.

I returned to my seat beside Daniel, managing to get my emotions under some level of control.

At least enough not to burn the house down.

"Right. I want answers," I said, and Eve sat back in her chair, crossing her arms over her chest.

"Of course you do."

"Start from the beginning, and save the bullshit this time."

She regarded me coolly for a moment before letting out a theatrical sigh. "Fine. Yes, it's a spell. It's not a prophecy."

Across the table from me, Patrice watched Eve closely. "Explain," she said, her voice low and even.

Eve remained silent for a few moments, inspecting us all slowly. Almost as though she was considering how much truth she needed to tell.

It took every drop of my limited self-control to keep myself from launching at her. But just as I was reconsidering setting her on fire, she finally spoke.

"For over three thousand years, I have done everything in my power to destroy the nightwalkers and find a way to end this damned curse. Believe me, I've tried to end myself on countless occasions because I cannot stand another minute on this wretched planet. However, Sithech, who eventually became known as Seth in all the myths and legends, tied up every possible loose end. But six hundred years ago, I finally found a way." She nodded towards me.

I tried not to react as every set of eyes turned towards me.

"But why go to all the effort of creating two very elaborate prophecies?" I couldn't wrap my head around all of the deception.

"Those prophecies were the words of the spell. But to ensure that the Order of the Dragon would protect both sets of twins, the spell's words were passed off as a prophecy. And, I couldn't risk Seth finding out about it and therefore putting a stop to the whole thing."

"So you knew Seth was still alive?"

"I suspected it, yes."

"Did you know about Damon?" I asked, crossing my arms, mirroring Eve.

For the first time since I had met her, I saw a crack in the armour that Eve had built around herself as her face dropped slightly.

"No. I had no idea that my son was still alive until Anika and Anthony confronted me about twenty minutes ago. How long has he been a member of the Order?" Her voice wavered as she turned to Patrice.

"I..." Patrice's voice drifted off, and she appeared to struggle to answer.

Eve raised an eyebrow.

"You've been bewitched," she stated, and the rest of us exchanged confused looks.

"What do you mean, bewitched?" Gerard asked, looking ready to jump out of his seat as Eve stood and moved towards Patrice.

Patrice flinched and stared, wide-eyed, while Eve reached forward and touched her forehead. Patrice went rigid, and her eyes lost focus.

"Hey! What are you doing?!" Barbara leapt from her chair, moving to stop her.

Eve raised her other hand, halting Barbara in her tracks with the same magic I had seen her use on Connor in his memory.

"I'm helping her, you stupid woman."

"Eve," I said, my voice low. She flicked an annoyed look my way but didn't remove her hand from Patrice's head.

After a few moments, Patrice slumped down in her seat, and Eve released her hold. She returned to her seat, and Patrice looked at us all, momentarily disorientated.

"What did you just do?" Barbara asked Eve, her voice shaking as she moved to Patrice's side.

"She was under an enchantment. I have no idea how long it has been in place, though." Eve shrugged.

"Do you think it was related to Damon?" Gerard asked as he followed Barbara.

"I can almost guarantee that it was," Eve said, continuing to watch Patrice.

Patrice let out a shaky breath and shook her head as though she was trying to get her thoughts back in place. She blinked a few times, and her gaze drifted towards me.

"Isolde?" Her voice wavered, and her brows knitted together. The look of confusion was alarming, and I looked at Eve with a raised eyebrow.

"Did you do something to her memory?"

"Yes. I gave it back to her."

Gerard crouched down beside Patrice's chair and looked her in the eye.

"Patrice? Do you remember where you are?"

"Gerard... I... just give me a minute." Patrice closed her eyes and rested her head against the back of her chair.

We all waited quietly until she opened her eyes again and looked directly at me. I was relieved to see her eyes had lost that glassy look.

"I am so sorry, Isolde," Patrice said, her eyes welling up, and it was my turn to be confused.

"What for?"

"I had no control over any of it."

"Any of what?" I asked, trying not to sound as impatient as I felt.

"Damon... He wasn't an elder..."

We all stared at her in silence for a few moments.

"What?" Barbara was the first to speak.

"Damon appeared after we discovered we were wrong about Alana and learned of Isolde's birth. He said he was an elder from the English Manor, and he put an enchantment on all those who were in the Los Angeles Manor at the time. He planted false memories in our minds."

Similar to the magic I'd learned that Connor wielded.

"He was the one pushing for you to be turned, insisting that Liam needed to be the one to do it. He knew Aurora would become a nightwalker and said it was necessary." Patrice looked pale.

"He must have known about the spell," Eve said, her voice shaking.

It was all starting to fall into place.

"Did you know about Aurora needing to be a vampire before Damon came along, Patrice?" I asked.

"No. I swear." She shook her head adamantly. "All I ever knew before he appeared was that the Chosen One was meant to have powers stronger than all of us. Liam came to me and told me he'd had a vision of you becoming a nightwalker and kissing Will. I spoke to Damon about it, and that's when he told me about the Gemini Prophecy and that it would have been Aurora that Liam saw in the vision."

This all explained why the memories of Liam talking to Patrice about me turning seemed so at odds with the version of Patrice I knew when I first arrived.

"But... I read the Gemini Prophecy here. It was in this library that I first read it. How had none of you come across it beforehand?"

"Because I was the one who placed it in your path that night, Isolde," Eve said, and I turned slowly to look at her.

"What?" I asked quietly.

"It was the beginning of the activation of the spell. When you read the Gemini Prophecy and then later saw the vision of the Phoenix Prophecy, that set the final part of the spell in motion, readying you for the transition once Connor, Aurora, and Liam turned you."

I felt like I was going to be sick. "You mean to tell me that I unknowingly cast this fucking spell on myself?"

"Funny how that works, isn't it?" She said with a smirk.

Something inside of me finally snapped. Before anyone else could react, I raised a hand, and Eve flew across the room, smacking hard into the wall. I used my telekinesis to hold her in place as I stalked towards her, producing a ball of flame in my other hand and getting ready to launch it at her.

"I'm betting that you're wishing you hadn't taught me how to focus my powers last night," I said, my voice low and lethal.

A brief look of panic flashed across her face, though she managed to hide it quickly, her face again taking on the familiar expression of indifference.

"Isolde, stop," a voice said from behind me.

Eve's eyes flicked towards the door while I continued staring at her, my hand raised above me with the flames still burning.

A hand wrapped around my wrist, and I felt the rage drain away as my mental hold on Eve broke and the flame in my hand extinguished.

"Oh, Liam, thank god you're okay!" I heard Barbara call out, and I turned slowly to face the person still holding my wrist. Although I suspected who I would see, my eyes widened as I heard Eve's feet hit the floor.

"Good to see you again, Connor," Eve said from behind me.

Connor and I held each other's gazes, and for a brief moment, I forgot about everyone else as he slid his hand up to weave his fingers through mine.

Then, the room erupted into chaos.

CHAPTER FOUR

The distinct sound of chairs being pushed back in a hurry rang out behind me as everyone leapt to their feet.

But my eyes remained locked on Connor's.

He stepped closer, ignoring everyone around us while he held my gaze.

I heard someone start running, and I turned in time to see Daniel moving towards us with his stake raised high.

"Daniel, No!" I moved to stop him, breaking free of Connor's grip, but Eve raised a hand, and Daniel flew across the room, hitting the wall hard with his right shoulder.

"Seriously? You could have just let me stop him without hurting him," I said, exasperated.

Eve just shrugged and inspected her fingernails.

I loathe this woman with every fibre of my being.

"Why can't I kill the asshole that is responsible for the death of my wife?" Daniel asked, his voice shaking as he rose, his eyes locked on the man behind me.

"Well, I mean, sure, you could blame me for that. Or, you and your wife could have let us take Isolde," Connor said with a shrug.

I closed my eyes briefly and took a few deep breaths, resisting the urge to punch Connor. Seeing the rage growing stronger in Daniel's eyes, I turned to face Connor again.

"Don't be a dick. This isn't going to go well if you keep insisting on playing the villain role that you and I know is complete bullshit." Connor opened his mouth to retort, but I raised a hand to silence him. "And don't try the whole 'I'm not the hero of the story blah blah blah' attitude again. You know I can see right through that facade, and precious time is ticking by while we all sit here bickering amongst ourselves."

Connor glared at me but kept his mouth shut while I answered Daniel finally.

"You can't kill him because we need him, apparently, to destroy Adam and end this all finally. I don't know the specifics. Eve still hasn't divulged that information." I shot her an accusing look before turning back to look at the other Order members, who were all watching this exchange with wide eyes.

"Isolde? What is going on? I have begrudgingly accepted that she can get through our wards." Patrice gestured towards a bored-looking Eve. "but how on Earth can a nightwalker have found this place and managed to walk through the door?"

I felt the little energy I had left drain out of me. It had been two days since I had slept, and I was pushing the limits on how much sleep a vampire needed.

"Because he's like me," I replied.

Patrice stared at me, and the silence that filled the room felt like it was closing in on me. I wondered how many more bombshells we could drop before they all became catatonic.

But I hadn't been given the option to ease into any of this either, so I might as well rip the bandaid right off.

"You mean, he's a hybrid as well?" Barbara asked quietly from Patrice's side, and I nodded.

"But... He's fucking evil!" Gerard looked Connor up and down, making no attempt to hide the disgust on his face.

Connor's response to this was to give a slight bow with a smirk. "Evil asshole at your service. See, he believes me," he said, looking at me as he jerked his head towards Gerard.

This time, I did punch him.

Watching him fly backward was pretty satisfying, but I would have preferred it if he hadn't laughed as he leaned back against the wall and crossed his arms.

"You're definitely an asshole. That much is true."

He bowed again. I turned away from him, rolling my eyes.

"Isolde, if what you are saying is true, then Gerard is right. He is evil. The amount of death and destruction on his shoulders is staggering," Barbara said, eyeing Connor warily as he ran an appreciative gaze over her slowly.

She let out a little squeal, stepping closer to Patrice. I'd been on the receiving end of that smoulder before and knew how she felt.

"Look, I know what he's done, but I also know the remorse he has felt when he's done what is necessary to survive for the past five hundred years," I said, turning towards Connor again as I finished speaking.

He glared at me.

"I'd still really like to know how you've managed to see those memories." He cast a look at Eve, who shrugged at him.

"Perhaps you're not as skilled as you think you are, Connor."

Connor's eyes flashed, and he stepped closer to her, his mouth twisted into a sneer.

"Wait, so you're seeing his blood memories and Liam's?" Patrice interrupted, ignoring the exchange.

I nodded. "Yes, and Aurora's as well. It's all part of the fun hybrid package."

"So that's how you found her here?" She directed the question to Connor.

He seemed momentarily surprised that someone was speaking to him without yelling. "Yes. But I've always known where the Manor was - if that's what you're asking?"

"It wasn't, but that's also the last thing I wanted to hear. If you were able to track Isolde due to the bond formed by your blood memories, then Eve, as Liam's sire, will be able to do the same for him."

Everyone turned to look at Eve as one.

"Of course I can. That's the whole reason I came here. You all just insisted on this ridiculous need for the truth before I could discuss it with you," she said, shrugging again.

I growled in frustration. "Enough with your fucking games, Eve. Where have Seth and Damon taken Liam?"

"Here," she replied.

As if it was the most obvious thing in the world.

"What do you mean, here? He's not here," Gerard said loudly.

"This is where the bond led me. My guess is he's in a pocket realm that Damon has created within the Manor."

"What the hell is a pocket realm?" Gerard asked.

Eve rolled her eyes. "See, this is why the Order is completely useless. You've all lost the magic of the original coven and must rely on histories written by people who don't know anything," She said, looking impatient while the rest of the Order members exchanged confused looks.

Eve continued with her story. "There were once far more dangerous creatures that walked amongst us than the vampires you have become so obsessed with. Creatures from other realms who could pass into ours without resistance. Covens like ours were responsible for stopping as many of them as we could. And we could create our own hidden pocket realms."

I had no idea where to even begin to unpack all of this information.

Daniel was the first to speak. "What other creatures? And where did they all go?"

"Creatures you couldn't even fathom. Banshees, Faeries, and Leprechauns are a few. As for where they all went, I have yet to find the answer to that. But I have not seen any of them since the night

Seth cursed Adam and me. I have long suspected he found a way to close the realms when he cursed us, but I've not worked out how."

"Wow, so you don't have the answers for once? Something that you can't control. That must really frustrate you, Eve," Connor said with a slight smirk.

She didn't rise to his taunts, though, as she levelled that bored gaze on him once again. "The only thing frustrating me right now is this conversation. We need to find Liam and start setting everything into motion to end all of this with Adam." Eve turned to Patrice. "Take me to Damon's quarters."

Scowling, Patrice moved towards the door, and I looked over at Connor, who gestured for me to walk in front of him.

"After you," he said, and I gritted my teeth as I followed behind Eve and Patrice.

The other Order members remained in the conference room.

"Do not check out my ass," I said while we made our way up the stairs, and he laughed.

"No promises."

"Just remember who owns this ass, Connor. Nothing has changed." I reminded him over my shoulder, and his eyes flashed briefly as he clenched his jaw, and all traces of humour disappeared from his face.

"Believe me, Isolde - I am fully aware that you are another person who chose Liam over me. It's something that I am more than accustomed to after five hundred years of being the second choice and knowing I'm literally his evil twin."

If we all made it through this alive, I was going to be arranging therapy for this man.

CHAPTER FIVE

We followed Patrice to Damon's room, which was in a different wing of the Manor to mine and Liam's rooms.

Eve opened the door and walked to the centre of the room, looking around. For the second time in twenty minutes, the mask of indifference had shifted, and I could see that being inside her son's bedroom for the first time in three thousand years was affecting her.

"You truly had no idea he had survived all these years?" I asked, empathy for her situation overriding my usual dislike.

"No. My daughters died after three hundred years, longer than most of the other coven members. I refused to allow them to become daywalkers, although they both begged for it. They wanted to remain with me until the end of all of this. But as a mother, I couldn't allow them to become a part of this cursed life. As much as I have missed them every minute and hour since."

"How charming. You actually have a heart buried underneath the layers of ice. Who would have thought?" Connor's sarcastic words broke the spell that had allowed Eve to open up properly, and she looked at him with that now familiar, infuriating smirk.

"Don't worry, Connor, there's far more ice than heart."

"Good, I was getting worried for a moment."

I sighed. "Can you feel anything indicating that the pocket realm is in this room?" I asked, diverting Eve's attention from Connor as she eyed him with amusement.

She closed her eyes, going completely still. I could feel a crackle of magic in the air as she used her abilities to reach out around her.

After a few minutes, the magic faded, and she opened her eyes, shaking her head.

"I can't feel it in here. This might take a while. You need to go and sleep because once I find it, I will need you at your full strength to help me get into it and release Liam from any enchantments Damon and Seth have placed upon him. If they've worked together to do it, I suspect I won't be strong enough on my own."

This was the first time I had ever seen her admit to any weakness in her powers or act in any way caring towards me, and I wasn't sure I liked it.

Connor certainly didn't seem to agree. "You expect her to sleep with everything going on?" He asked, shaking his head.

"I expect the pair of you to get some rest. Now that you've joined us, Connor, I require your full involvement in all of this. Once I find the pocket realm, I'll send one of the little Order minions to come and find you both." Eve ignored Patrice's affronted expression while she smirked at Connor. "Though I suspect, with the little puppy dog eyes you have been casting towards Isolde, I'll find you together. What a dilemma for you to be in Isolde, both handsome O'Brien brothers in love with you. It must be so difficult to decide which one to be with. Or you could try both. I've ridden both those stallions, and it's quite a ride."

Connor growled and stepped towards her. I just shook my head in disgust and gripped his arm.

"Don't. She's just being Eve and trying to get a reaction. You can sleep in Liam's room." I led the way out into the hall without giving Eve a second glance.

"That is the last place I will get any sleep," he said, and I shrugged.

"Well, you're not sleeping with me, and there are no spare rooms in this place right now, so it's either Liam's room or you go back to Adam."

I could tell that neither of those options sounded appealing to him. But when we reached my and Liam's rooms across the hall from each other, he begrudgingly opened the door to Liam's room when I pointed at it. He shut the door behind him while I opened my own.

The last time I was in this room, I thought I'd never see it again, and it felt strange to see it still looking the same, albeit with fewer of my belongings in it. I stood in the doorway momentarily, jumping slightly when Patrice touched my shoulder. I hadn't realised she had followed us.

"I hope you know what you're doing, Isolde," she said quietly before heading back the way we'd come.

I watched her leave, feeling a tightening in my chest, before stepping inside the room, shutting myself in with all the memories.

I moved towards the bed and sunk into the incredibly comfortable mattress. The fear I had been pushing aside for hours started to creep in, and I had no idea how I'd sleep while worrying about Liam and knowing that Connor was across the hall in Liam's room. I knew Liam would be incredibly unhappy with this turn of events.

Surprisingly, sleep did manage to claim me, and within minutes, I was out like a light.

I stared at the face of the woman in front of me, identical to the one I had been obsessing over for the past eight months. Aurora was the spitting image of Isolde, and seeing the familiar nightwalker hunger behind those eyes was difficult to stomach.

She'd just awoken from her transition. After ripping apart the homeless woman Adam had presented her with, she had mounted

William and had her way with him for several hours in front of everyone.

I was pretty sure her sister would be horrified by everything about this scenario. Still, now that Aurora had shifted that hungry gaze towards me, I struggled to push aside the knowledge that it wasn't Isolde standing before me.

"I can tell you want me, Connor. Why fight it?" Aurora asked, walking towards me, naked and confident in her sexual appeal.

"Who said I was fighting anything? Perhaps I just don't want anything to do with you?" I asked, ensuring that my tone of voice remained bored.

"I've seen how you look at me. I've seen in Adam's memories how you've obsessed over my sister. You want her and want to see if being with me would satisfy that craving."

The simple fact that she could glean that information from Adam's blood memories was concerning. Not the wanting Isolde part, but that Adam had noticed my interest in her. I would need to get inside his head and remove that information. The last thing I needed was for Adam to work out that there was something more to this interest than me trying to end her before the prophecy came to pass.

"I don't know what you think you saw in those memories, Aurora, but my interest in your sister is entirely based on ensuring that her existence doesn't cause the end of us all."

"You can tell yourself that all you want, Connor, but I can see it in your eyes. The lust... the wanting..." She took a final step towards me and pressed her naked chest against my own. Having just walked out of the shower, the towel around my waist did nothing to hide my arousal at her presence. I clenched my jaw as she kissed my neck while she pulled the towel away and guided her hand up and down my shaft.

I groaned, and my self-restraint nearly snapped when she dropped to her knees and moved to take me in her mouth.

I was no monk. I'd been with thousands of women over the years, but never a nightwalker, and not once within the walls of the houses where the coven resided.

But Aurora was right; a part of me wondered if giving in to this attraction to her would rid me of the need for her sister.

Revulsion at my weakness crashed through me, and I gritted my teeth as I slipped into her mind.

I grimaced, attempting to push away the guilt as I envisioned her wrapping her lips around me, planting a false memory of me fucking her mouth with abandon before stepping away, knowing I needed to keep up the charade.

No one could ever know the truth.

I awoke as Connor opened my bedroom door, the light from the hall spilling in behind him. I sat up, trying not to replay the memory that had infiltrated my dreams. The last thing I wanted was to see him fucking my sister's mouth while she pleasured herself, even if it was a false memory. There was so much about this fucked up situation we were in that I wasn't ready to deal with, and I just wanted to get Liam back and hold him close.

"What's wrong?" I asked as Connor remained in the doorway, his expression unreadable as his eyes drifted over me.

"Eve's found the pocket realm. It's in Liam's room."

CHAPTER SIX

I followed Connor as he led the way back across the hall. Being in here without Liam felt strange, even more so when the space was filled with Eve and Connor's presence, two of Liam's least favourite people. I felt like I was betraying Liam by allowing them into his private space, but like it or not, I needed their help to get him back from Damon and Seth.

God, it had only been a day, and I already felt like I'd lost a limb without him. I hadn't realised how dependent I'd become on him, and I wasn't sure how to feel about it. Were we co-dependent, like Eve had said, or was it the bond that tied us together?

"I can feel the entrance of the pocket realm over here," Eve said when I came to stand next to her.

She stood in the corner of the room that Liam used for meditation and mind-clearing. She held both hands before her, and the magic in the air made everything around us static, and our hair rippled around us as though lifted by a breeze.

"What exactly is a pocket realm, anyway?" He asked, watching Eve closely as he sat at Liam's desk.

"It's a pocket of space in a realm we create ourselves. My coven used them to hold any creatures we couldn't kill easily until we could send them back to their own realms. Often, we didn't know where they had come from originally, and we didn't want to inflict these monsters onto other unsuspecting realms. This was the best way to keep them contained. But, once we no longer needed to contain those creatures, the magic was lost, and now I'm one of only a few with the knowledge of how to create them." Her voice wavered, but her hold on the magic remained despite the emotions she struggled to keep hidden from us.

"So you can just open any realm that someone else created?" I asked.

Eve shook her head. "Not easily. I will need to work out how to unlock this, and it will take time." She looked over at Connor. "I need you to try and get into Liam's head for me, and best to take Isolde with you."

He looked surprised before his expression closed over. "I can't get into his head. And even if I could, I highly doubt that will help the situation."

"Of course you can get into his head. You're bonded to him."

My eyebrows flew up as I gaped at her. "What do you mean, they're bonded?"

"They are essentially two halves of the same whole. It is the same for you and Aurora," she said dismissively.

I looked at Connor, who shook his head, his eyebrows raised high. We both turned to look at Eve, silently requesting further explanation.

Eve let the magic around her drop with a sigh.

"Look, I know you both have many questions, but right now, we need to focus on contacting Liam while I figure out how to get into this pocket realm. So stop asking all these pointless questions, and Connor, you will teach Isolde how to get into Liam's head. Her bond to Liam also exists at present, and he will most likely respond better to her than you."

Connor and I exchanged a brief look before he shrugged. He sat back in this chair, crossed his arms, and fixed his tense gaze on Eve.

"Don't think you're going to get out of explaining all that shit in detail. Given the last time we crossed paths, you dropped a bunch of nonsense on me and then disappeared for five hundred years - I am not letting you out of my sight until you tell me everything."

The pair commenced a silent battle of wills, staring at each other without blinking until I'd finally had enough.

"Connor, let's go and work this out." I tapped my head. "While Eve works that out." I waved my hand towards the corner where Eve still stood. "And then once we have Liam back, we will sit down with Eve and get the answers we need."

Connor turned his haughty glare on me, and I crossed my arms.

"Fine," he spat out, and Eve smirked, turning back to the corner and raising her hands again.

I moved to sit in the seat on the other side of Liam's desk, and Connor swivelled his chair before resting his forearms on the desk as he faced me.

"Ready to be in my head again?" He asked with a seductive smirk.

I glared at him. "This is serious, Connor."

"Oh, I'm well aware that this is serious, Isolde."

"Well, quit it with the 'fuck-me' eyes and just help me work out how to get into Liam's head."

"So you admit it? You do want to fuck me."

I leaned across the table slowly, and he moved closer, his eyes focused on my lips. "Let me be clear, Connor. I will never fuck you. Not if you were the last hybrid vampire on Earth."

He smirked. "If you say so. I look forward to the day you eat those words. While I eat something else."

I suppressed a shudder at the heat in his eyes as he held my gaze.

I sighed as I rubbed my temples. "Seriously, Connor. Enough."

He held my gaze a moment longer before nodding and sitting back again.

"Fine. For now." His tone made it clear that he wouldn't let this go, no matter how much I wished he would.

"So what do I need to do?" I asked.

He closed his eyes and pinched the top of his nose. He looked exhausted, and I wondered if he'd managed to get any rest in the last few days. After a moment, he opened his eyes and looked at me again.

"It'll be easier if I just show you rather than trying to talk you through it. I'll pull you into my mind like I've been doing the past few weeks. And then we can try to go into Liam's mind together."

I looked over at where Eve was still working on the pocket realm before eyeing him warily. "I feel like this is a bad idea. The two of you don't exactly get along."

That was the biggest understatement in the history of all understatements.

"I can keep myself out of sight if necessary. But we don't really have time on our side, and this isn't something I've ever taught anyone how to do before. I just sort of stumbled across it all," he said with a shrug, and I continued to study him closely.

I wasn't entirely sure that I believed his motives were pure, but I had to go with it for now.

I nodded and watched as Connor closed his eyes and let out a long, slow breath, appearing to use tactics similar to those Liam taught me when I was learning how to clear my mind. He stilled, and I felt the now familiar mental tug of being pulled into his mind.

CHAPTER SEVEN

"*And here we are again, alone at last,*" *Connor drawled, sitting in the chair in that godforsaken house once again. Usually, I was leaning against the wall opposite, but this time, I was straddling his lap.*

"I knew I shouldn't have trusted you," I said, feeling my eyes flash while I tried to pull away, even though my body was already responding to his nearness. He trailed his fingers lightly up my back before gripping my neck and holding me still.

"Did you ever think that maybe I didn't put you here?" He narrowed his eyes while he studied my face closely before shaking his head. "Of course you didn't. You're still in denial."

He lifted me roughly and set me on my feet so that he could stand up and put some distance between us while I pondered if there was any truth to what he'd said. I didn't think I'd put myself in his lap, but with all the conflicting emotions rolling through me, I couldn't say with certainty that it hadn't been my doing.

"As much as I'd love to continue this very tiring merry-go-round of Isolde lying to herself, let's just work on getting into my perfect twin's mind, shall we?" His tone was clipped.

I nodded and ignored the subtle dig. "What do I need to do?"

He hesitated, running his eyes over me, and I knew he was annoyed that I was refusing to discuss our issues further.

"Look, once this is all sorted out, we can talk about feelings, but right now, I can't focus on anything except getting Liam back and doing the whole 'save the world' thing, okay?" I threw my hands up, letting my frustration get the better of me.

Connor continued to watch me closely until he finally nodded.

"Fine. But don't think for one moment that I don't know that you're just deflecting to put off admitting to yourself that there is more between us than just sharing a similar origin story."

I glared at him. "I'm not going to dignify that with a response right now. What do I need to do?" I asked again.

Connor closed his eyes as he sighed and pinched the bridge of his nose again. "We need to try and reach out and find the bond that Eve claims is between us all. I've never felt it with Liam, but then, I've never tried to look for it, so for all I know, it's been there all along."

"Why haven't you tried to look for it?" I asked, and Connor laughed.

"Are you serious? Why would I have looked for it? We're mortal enemies, remember?"

"No, what I know is that when you were forced to watch while Adam killed your mother and attempted to turn Liam, you were hoping you wouldn't be alone anymore. And when Eve told you the truth, you sat with your brother's body for an entire week to make sure nothing happened to him. Every encounter you had with Liam over the years was laced with your feelings of loss and missing your brother. Why didn't you ever try to tell him the truth?" I asked.

Connor shook his head and clenched his jaw. "Pass. If you don't have to talk about how you truly feel, I don't have to answer that question either." He held my gaze, the challenge more than evident in his eyes.

I decided I didn't want to poke that wound right now. "Okay, so how do we feel the bond?" I asked.

"It's like the mind-clearing you do. You need to block out the physical world, or in this case, this mental space we're in, and reach out with your subconscious, searching for any threads in the air around you."

I took a deep breath and closed my eyes, attempting to block out everything but my own breathing. I'd yet to succeed at clearing my mind without having a flame to focus on, and I was struggling now. I felt Connor move to stand behind me, pressing his chest to my back.

"Focus on my breaths," he said quietly, his breath caressing my ear, and I willed my body not to react as desire rippled through me.

"How is this meant to help me focus?" I whispered.

He didn't answer, just continued breathing in and out at a steady pace, and I forced myself to focus on each time his chest rose and fell behind me. Surprisingly, my thoughts slowly cleared until all I was aware of was each inhale and exhale, our breathing now in perfect sync with one another. A sense of calm washed over me, and the familiar sensation of magic filling the air began to flow through me. I heard a strange humming sound, and I realised it was familiar. I'd heard it often when Liam and I were bound together by magic. I reached out in my mind, searching for the source of the humming, following it into the deepest reaches of my psyche, and found a golden thread weaving its way through the darkness.

"Got it," Connor whispered, and together we reached out mentally and clamped down on the thread, yanking it towards us.

The strangest sensation rippled through me as though I was hovering on the edge of a cliff. I felt Connor's hands grip my hips tightly, holding me close, and together, we fell into the void.

I felt my feet hit something solid after what could have been hours or mere seconds, and I opened my eyes.

The room we were in was familiar, and I felt my chest tighten when I realised we were in Connor and Liam's childhood home.

"Fuck," Connor said quietly behind me.

"Why are we here? Did we do something wrong?" I asked him.

He continued to hold me close to his chest, and I felt him shake his head. "No. This is where Liam's subconscious has brought us. But I have no idea why we would be here. I thought it would take us some-where important to you both, to be honest. I never in a million years thought it would bring us home." His voice cracked on the word 'home'.

Despite everything going on between us, I reached down to cover the hand on my right hip and squeezed gently. He let out a ragged breath that brushed against the shell of my ear, and I leant into him a little more.

I looked around the room, and my gaze fell upon a chair with its high back turned towards us. I saw the occupant's leg and knew it had to be Liam. I went to step forward, but Connor pulled me back.

"Wait," he said quietly and stepped around me. He squeezed my hand gently before moving slowly towards his brother. "Liam?"

I had never heard Connor sound so unsure, and I fought against the sudden wave of fear.

Connor edged closer to Liam, and although I knew I should be concerned that he may attempt to hurt Liam, a part of me knew I could trust him. I wasn't ready to give that instinct too much thought, though.

"Connor?" Liam leapt out of his chair and spun to face us both, joy written all over his face. He looked so different to the Liam that I knew now, and I realised that his mind had taken him back to when he was human. The hair that he had always kept short was now past his shoul-ders, pulled back with a ribbon, and there was no trace of his usually muscular physique behind the long-sleeved white tunic.

Connor seemed to be at a loss for words as he stared at him.

"Liam, are you okay? What did Damon and Seth do to you?" I asked.

Liam's gaze moved to meet mine, and he looked confused before looking back at Connor.

"I'm sorry, I didn't realise you had someone with you. I was just so glad to see you. Father said they have been looking for you for weeks. He called me back from the monastery. Where have you been?"

He didn't recognise me. He'd completely disregarded my presence, his attention focused on his brother. The brother that he hated and was his mortal enemy. Well, immortal enemy, if we were being technical.

"I... only weeks?" Connor asked, and Liam nodded.

"Yes. He and Mother have been frantic. They've sent men out all over to try and find you. Where have you been?"

Connor glanced at me, his eyes wide. He opened his mouth before promptly closing it again and shaking his head.

"Liam, don't you know who I am?" I stepped closer, but Connor signalled for me to stop moving.

"Are you the reason my brother has been gone for so long?" Liam's tone was accusing, and I took a sharp breath when I saw the anger on his face.

"No, Liam. This is Isolde. She had nothing to do with where I've been," Connor said, stepping in front of me to shield me from Liam's glare.

"Then answer me, for goodness sake! Father has all but given up and insists that I return for good and run the Estate." Liam's voice began to rise, and I could see the panic in his eyes.

Looks aside, the man before me was so unlike the Liam that I knew. Where my Liam was confident and commanding, this version was a shadow of that man. The idea of running the Estate in his brother's place terrified him, and the fact that he could barely look at me made it evident that he had no experience with women.

"I'm so sorry I worried you all. I'm back now. I'll take care of every-thing with Father, I promise." Connor reached towards his brother, his tone soothing as though calming a small child.

I watched this interaction in shock, unable to recognise the man I loved or the tenderness Connor showed him.

Liam allowed Connor to hug him, and Connor managed to get him to sit back down before returning to my side.

"What the hell is going on?" I whispered, and Connor shook his head as he gave me a look I couldn't understand.

"Liam, I'm just going to go and talk to Father," he called back to his brother and pulled me from the room.

CHAPTER EIGHT

he O'Brien Estate dissolved around us, and we returned to Liam's room in the Manor.

Connor stared at me momentarily, his eyes searching mine while I tried to reconcile the version of Liam I had just met with the one I knew. He touched my cheek briefly before looking towards where Eve stood in the corner, her focus still on the pocket realm.

"Eve, we have a problem," he said, jumping up from his seat.

Eve looked over her shoulder while magic continued to ripple around her. "What's going on?" She asked, her narrowed eyes flitting between our faces.

"It seems as though Damon and Seth have wiped Liam's memories," Connor said.

Eve's eyes widened.

"What happened?" Eve asked, letting the magic drop around her as she turned to face us fully.

"We managed to get into his subconscious, and he was in our family home. He had no idea who Isolde was, and in his mind, it was only a few weeks after I disappeared." Connor looked over at me. "It was like talking to a ghost. He was exactly as he was before he transitioned. I had forgotten so much about that version of him..."

"Fabulous. One more fucking thing to try and fix once we find him," Eve said, sounding exhausted.

I noticed a brief flicker of something else behind her eyes, but it was gone before I could get a read on what it was.

"But we can fix him, right?" I asked, my heart beginning to race as panic set in.

Surprisingly, Connor reached over and took my hand, squeezing it. His touch was like a balm, and my heart slowed once again.

Eve watched this exchange with interest before answering. "I hope so. Because we need Liam, and that version of Liam was completely useless. It took me decades to knock all that religious nonsense out of him." She closed her eyes as her hands balled into fists at her side.

"What about you? Are you any closer to getting into the pocket realm?" Connor asked, nodding towards the corner of the room.

"Well, now that I know that it's been created in the image of your childhood home, that will make this slightly easier. Just keep yourselves busy a bit longer." She dismissed us both and moved back to the corner, conjuring the magic back effortlessly.

I looked at Connor, and he moved over to the couch at the end of Liam's bed, flinging himself down wearily.

"Did you manage to get any rest at all before?" I asked, standing in front of him.

I moved to run my hand through his hair. He jerked away from my touch and stared up at me. I dropped my hand to my side, swallowing hard. It had been such an automatic movement and had taken us both by surprise.

"Forget which brother you were talking to for a minute there, Isolde?" He asked with a raised eyebrow, frowning as his eyes flashed from blue to dark brown and back instantly.

"Sorry," I murmured, feeling terrible.

No matter what was happening between us, he didn't deserve to feel like he and his brother were interchangeable in my life. But I wasn't entirely sure if that had been why I'd reached out to him. I had wanted to comfort Connor, and Liam hadn't been on my mind for that brief moment.

"To answer your question before your very interesting lapse in judgment, no, I didn't get any rest. I was starting to drift off when Eve came in and found the pocket realm. And the past few weeks have been particularly exhausting dealing with your transition and keeping everything from Adam and your sister." He closed his eyes and let his head drop back to rest on the top of the couch.

I reached down to take his hand, and his eyes flew open again.

"Come on." I pulled him up and led him across the hall to my room. "You need to get some sleep. You can use my bed, and I'll come and get you once Eve gets in." I gestured towards my bed, and he hesitated for a moment.

"Will you stay?"

I knew it took a lot for him to ask me that, and I weighed up my options. If I stayed, it would encourage him to continue pursuing me. But if I left, it would hurt him, and I didn't want to deal with that fallout when he inevitably grew frustrated again, like earlier when he'd threatened to walk away from everything.

I nodded slowly. "Yes, I'll stay."

We moved to the bed and lay down beside each other. We didn't touch, but Connor's eyes slowly drifted closed, and his breathing evened out as he finally fell asleep. I lay awake a little longer, trying to push away the fear that we wouldn't be able to get Liam back, both physically and mentally. I wasn't ready to imagine a world in which Liam didn't know who I was.

Yet, even as I worried about Liam, my gaze kept moving to the man beside me. Why was I so drawn to him? Was it as simple as him being the other half of Liam, like I'd said to Connor? Or was I lying to myself to try and justify the feelings that I couldn't control?

⁂

I was ripped from my dreamless sleep as someone banged the door open, and Connor and I both leapt to our feet, our fists raised, ready to fend off an attack.

Instead, we found Daniel watching us from the door. His expression was stern, and he ran his eyes over Connor first before falling on me with a glare.

"Sorry to interrupt whatever the fuck this is, but the witch sent me to fetch you both. She's found a way in." He turned abruptly on one heel and marched across the hall.

Feeling a stab of guilt, I looked across at Connor, who shrugged as he got up.

Why hadn't I simply told Connor no when he asked me to stay?

I sighed and returned across the hall with Connor close behind. Patrice, Barbara and Daniel were all in Liam's room, along with Eve. She looked annoyed, but I couldn't tell who with, and I also didn't really care.

"So what now?" Connor asked, and Eve pointed towards the corner. I gasped as I saw a door suspended a foot above the ground, shimmering slightly.

"Connor, given that Liam apparently has no idea who the rest of us are, I think it's best you go and get him out," Eve said, and everyone, including myself and Connor, turned to look at her with varying levels of surprise.

"You can't be serious? We can't send him in. He'll just kill Liam. If he's as vulnerable as you said, he won't be at full strength and be able to fight him off." Patrice waved a hand towards Connor, who glared back at her, his expression growing darker with each word.

"He's not going to do anything to Liam," I said.

Patrice looked at me with narrowed eyes. "He's clearly done something to you, Isolde. You have no idea who you're dealing with. We can't trust a word that he says."

"Enough! It will be Connor, and that's final," Eve said, and there was no use arguing with her.

Patrice glared at Connor again, and he smirked back before turning to look at me.

"See, I keep telling you I am the villain. Everyone else can see it – might as well accept it, Isolde."

"Shut up. Go and get your brother." I pointed at the door.

Connor turned to Eve. "Is it just Liam in there, or am I walking into an ambush?" He asked, and Eve shook her head.

"I didn't sense either Damon or Seth in there, but that's not to say they couldn't cloak themselves, so be careful."

I was still thrown at this caring side of her, and judging by how he looked at her, Connor didn't know what to make of it either.

"So, do I just open the door? Do I need to do anything special?" He turned to eye the door warily.

"It's solid. You just reach out and turn the handle."

Connor took a deep breath, looking like a man about to go into battle. He moved towards the door and slowly grasped the handle before turning it. Hesitating, he turned to look back at me before stepping through the door. It closed behind him.

"This is a bad idea, Eve," Patrice said, unable to keep quiet any longer.

Eve levelled her with a glare. "You have no idea what you are talking about. Connor is bound to his brother. Regardless of everything you think you know, this is the only way we will get Liam out of there without a fight."

"Every time Liam and Connor have come face to face in the last five hundred years, Connor has done his best to kill Liam," Barbara said incredulously, and Eve sighed.

"Look, there is obviously a lot between the pair of them, but I can assure you, Connor would not have killed his brother. Although they are evenly matched in power and ability, even if Connor had ever managed to get the upper hand, he has never wanted to kill his brother."

"Why was it so important that Liam never knew the truth about Connor?" I asked, and Eve turned to look at me.

"Because Connor needed to be as believable in the role as possible. He would never have been able to keep Adam's trust if he'd maintained any relationship with Liam. He needed to play the part perfectly. And he has. You've seen only a fraction of what he has done and what he has had to do over the years to survive. Not only to survive but to be Adam's second amongst his followers. It has sometimes given Connor the power to control Adam. It has all been necessary." She spoke with conviction, and I knew she truly believed everything she said.

"But at the cost of everything else," I said, and she raised an eyebrow.

"He's really gotten under your skin, hasn't he? Falling for the other brother now, too, are we?" She smirked at me.

"If you didn't want me to sympathise with him, you probably shouldn't have had the spell bond us all together, Eve. One of the fun side effects of being bound to them is that I feel everything they feel. You have no idea how much you have fucked us all up with this spell. Or you do, and you just don't fucking care."

Patrice, Barbara, and Daniel were all watching us with interest.

"Interesting that you don't deny you have feelings for them both, though. How long are you going to lie to yourself, Isolde?"

"I'm not lying to myself, Eve. I'm just trying to get us all out of this mess alive," I said, and Patrice laughed flatly.

I looked over to see her exchanging looks with Barbara and Daniel. She met my gaze, and her lips pressed together in a thin line. I could see the judgment behind her eyes while Eve continued speaking.

"We've got a few weeks, Isolde. Why deny yourself in that time? Like I said, I've ridden both those men hard, and you have no idea what you're missing out on."

Daniel coughed loudly, and the three Order members looked very uncomfortable but maintained their silence.

"You really love reminding me how you've fucked them both,

don't you? Is it because you're jealous that they no longer want you? Connor hasn't wanted you since you started him on this path. Is that why you're so obsessed with Liam? Or is it because they remind you so much of Adam? I know the family resemblance is strong, but they aren't him, Eve."

She glared at me, and I knew I'd struck a nerve.

"Did you set out to fall in love with them both, or was that a happy accident?" I continued. "Or unhappy, as is the case, because neither returned your feelings? I know you certainly didn't intend for me to end up with Liam, and it kills you that you can't control that."

Eve stepped towards me, her hands balled into fists at her side.

"Let me be very clear, Isolde. The only man I have ever loved is Adam. Everything I have ever done has been to save him from the thousands of years of evil he has been forced to inflict on the world."

We stood toe to toe, and the hairs on my arm stood on end while the magic in the air rippled around us.

"Then why do you care what is happening between myself and Connor, or that Liam chose me? Or are you just so bitter about the hand you were dealt that you can't stand seeing your little magic experiments making their own choices?" I wasn't allowing her to intimidate me.

"You haven't made a choice, though, Isolde." She opened her mouth to continue speaking but was interrupted by the sound of someone clearing their throat behind her.

She turned around, and we watched Connor walk through the door with Liam behind him. Thankfully, Liam's appearance had returned to normal.

"I see we've missed something important," Connor said, and I swallowed hard at the look on his face while Liam looked around, his eyes wide.

"What is this place? Connor, what evil is this?"

I realised then that bringing Liam out of the pocket realm while his memories were still wiped probably wasn't the best idea when

Liam flung himself to the ground and began praying on his knees. The others stared down at him with wide eyes while Connor and I exchanged a resigned look.

CHAPTER NINE

"What were you and Eve arguing about when we came back through the door?" Connor asked me half an hour later.

Liam had started to lose it, unable to handle all the strangers around him in this apparent hellscape that was so different from everything the fifteenth-century version of himself knew. Connor was the only person he would let within ten feet of him, and the irony was not lost on any of us. Eve had insisted we all leave to see if she could break through the enchantment used to wipe his memories. The others had gone to try and do some research to see if they could find anything as well, leaving Connor and me alone in the hall.

"Nothing important," I replied, and he raised an eyebrow.

"Given that it was about you making choices, sounded pretty fucking important to me," he said, and I glowered at him.

"Seriously? You want to get into this again while your brother is in there thinking he's been dragged to hell?"

Connor shrugged.

"He's not wrong, this may as well be fucking hell," he said darkly.

I had to agree with him on that statement.

"Be that as it may, we are not getting into the same discussion about all of this while Liam is broken, so just let it go." I slid down the wall next to my door and stared at the door to Liam's room.

Connor joined me on the floor, his shoulder touching mine. Regardless of my outburst, I couldn't bring myself to move away.

"What are we going to do if we can't work out how to get his memory back?" Connor asked.

"I'm not ready to consider that possibility yet. He has to remember me," I whispered.

Connor let his head fall back against the wall and stared at the ceiling. "I gotta admit, it's a lot easier for me if he doesn't remember anything about the last five hundred years. Or you."

I hugged my knees close and rested my forehead on them.

"Well, given that it's not about what's easiest for you, you can just push that thought right out of your head," I said, my words muffled by my legs.

Connor placed a hand on my back, and I raised my head. He reached around and cupped my chin with his hand, turning my face to look at him.

"If there was no Liam, would you be fighting this so hard?" He asked sincerely, and I could feel my emotions swirling at the vulnerability behind his question.

I wasn't sure how to handle this side of Connor, swallowing hard as I searched his face. "I can't answer that, Connor. Because there is a Liam," I whispered.

His expression darkened again as the door across the hall opened, and Eve joined us.

"I see I'm interrupting yet another moment between you two," she said, and I let my head fall back against the wall.

"Any progress?" Connor asked, ignoring her jibe.

"Not really. I think it's going to be down to you two and the bond. Whatever magic they've used, his mind is locked up tight," she said, and I sat up straighter again.

"What do you mean it's up to us? Neither of us knows that sort of magic."

"You have your link to his mind, and Connor can get into people's heads. I'm confident you can work this out between the two of you. I need to go and start working on the rest of the plan to get everyone in the right place at the right time. This has all been an inconvenient distraction." She eyed us both like this was somehow our fault. "Where does he keep all his journals? I remember he used to keep them diligently," she said, looking at me.

"He's got a house. He showed me some of them to help trigger the blood memories," I replied, and she nodded.

"Good. Take him there."

"Um... I don't think it's a good idea for Connor to go there... When Liam gets his memories back, he will flip out," I said, refusing to look at Connor.

"I don't give a shit. This is important. Take him there, and get his memories back." She didn't stick around, and once again, Connor and I were left in the hallway in awkward silence.

"Um... how are you meant to get into the house? If Liam's like this, how will we get him to invite you in when he doesn't even know it's his house?" I asked, and Connor shook his head.

"As a hybrid, that rule doesn't apply to either of us. It's how I was able to get in here."

I cocked my head to the side. "You mean to tell me that you could have gotten into any house I was in all this time?"

Connor smiled a little as he shrugged. "Well, I guess we'd better work out how to get the religious zealot into a car and to this house you speak of," he said warily, avoiding answering my question as he rose gracefully to his feet and extended his hand towards me.

I hesitated before taking it. He pulled me up quickly, causing me to stumble into him as I righted myself. I tried not to let the contact affect me, but he smirked when he noticed the shiver that ran through me before I stepped back out of his arms.

"No, Isolde, there's no attraction there at all," he said quietly while he crossed the hallway and entered Liam's room, leaving me standing alone, wishing I had a clue how to handle any of this.

An hour later, I led the way across the threshold of Liam's house.

"Where should I put him?" Connor asked, gesturing towards Liam, who followed behind him, his eyes glassy and his face slackened.

We'd had no choice but to have Connor jump into Liam's mind and attempt to take control because Liam had immediately lost it when we took him to the car and started claiming we were all demons, which was fair but frustrating. There was no sign of the confident man that I knew. While I was aware that people change with time, the human version of Liam felt like a completely different person, one who was content to spend all his time hidden away from the world and denying the harsh truth of the reality we lived in.

"I don't know why, but I can't seem to plant a false memory like I've done with others. It's not sticking, so I have to keep going back and planting it over and over," Connor said, looking fatigued when he walked through the door from the garage. "Where should we set up?"

"Take him through there into the library," I pointed to the door on the other side of the kitchen, and Connor nodded, leading Liam through while I pondered what the issue was with Connor's abilities.

I crossed to the fridge and poured myself a glass of blood from the pitcher Liam had in the fridge.

"It must be something to do with whatever Damon did to his mind. That's the only explanation I can think of right now," Connor said, walking back into the kitchen.

He came to a stop next to me, screwing his nose up when he saw what I was doing.

"I don't understand how you can drink that," he said, doing nothing to hide the disgust in his voice.

"Well, since I don't intend to give in to my nightwalker side and start ripping people's heads off while feeding, animal blood in a glass is the best I can do," I replied, draining the last of the blood from the glass and putting it in the dishwasher.

"You know that there are more options than that, right?" He asked, crossing his arms.

I sighed as I turned to look at him again.

"Let me guess, you'll tell me I need to feed from humans? Or worse, start feeding on poor, defenceless animals?" I mirrored his stance.

Connor shrugged. "Would it be so bad to feed off of a human who was willing?"

It was my turn to screw up my nose. "Yes!"

"Why? Liam fed off you, didn't he?" Connor asked, and I didn't know how to respond to that.

Yes, Liam had fed off me when I was still human, but it had only ever been during sex.

I also didn't feel comfortable talking about our sex life with his twin brother, who clearly wanted in my pants himself.

Connor took the silence as my answer. "Why is it different for you then?"

"There was an..." I hesitated before clearing my throat. "There was an intimate element to it. He wasn't doing it to satisfy his hunger."

"Wasn't he? Are you sure about that? How often did you see him drink animal blood before you turned?" Connor asked, and I opened my mouth to respond before clamping it shut.

I didn't want to get into this with him and admit that until I'd transitioned, I'd never seen Liam drink blood other than my own.

But once again, my silence gave me away.

Connor stepped forward, leaving barely any space between our bodies, as he cupped my face with his hands. "Aside from the murdering and being controlled by Adam, which you are more than capable of avoiding, there isn't that much of a difference between the nightwalkers and daywalkers. It's time to stop denying that side of your nature."

I cleared my throat, trying not to get lost in his gaze as he held my face. I slowly reached up to wrap my hands around his wrists and lowered his hands from my face.

"Being a murderer who's controlled by possibly the most evil person in the world is a pretty big difference to overlook... We should go and start working on getting Liam's memories back," I said, my voice barely louder than a whisper.

His expression hardened before he nodded.

"Of course. Can't get distracted from the mission." His tone was dripping with sarcasm while I brushed past him and entered the library.

He followed behind me, and we both stopped in front of Liam, who was staring off into space.

"Any ideas on how to get in there and break through this enchantment?" I asked, and Connor grimaced.

"As much as I don't want to admit it, I think I'm going to have to be the one who gets in there," he said with a sigh.

I looked at him, raising an eyebrow.

He shot me a look full of challenge. "What's wrong? Don't you trust me to unlock my twin brother's mind, thus returning him to his previous state of hating me and loving you?"

"Not particularly, no." I ignored the last part of his question.

"Well, I guess you're just going to have to see how I go because I'm not sure if you have the power to manipulate minds like I do," Connor said, and I crossed my arms.

"Just... don't be a dick about it, okay? We need Liam, as much as you don't want to admit it. And whether you accept it or not, the Liam we need is the one that hates you and loves me."

"Oh, don't worry, Isolde. I have no intention of making this decision of yours any easier."

"What the hell is that supposed to mean?" I hurled at him, and he shrugged.

"It means that you need to be honest with yourself, and I won't be making that easier on you because of Liam not remembering who you are. When you make your choice and finally accept that there is something between us, it won't be because Liam isn't a factor."

"I've already made my decision, Connor. You just don't want to accept it," I said, shaking my head.

"You forget, Isolde, that we're bound together. I've been inside your subconscious mind... and you are no closer to deciding than you were when I had my fingers buried inside you," Connor said, his words coming out in a low, husky voice.

"Fuck you, Connor." I was barely controlling my emotions now, and he laughed.

"Not yet, Isolde. But soon, you'll be begging me to."

I threw my hands up in the air. "Just... fucking fix your brother! I'm going somewhere else." I stormed out of the room, away from the laughter that followed behind me.

I found my way into the bedroom Liam and I shared and sank onto the mattress, grabbed a pillow and shoved my face into it to muffle my frustrated scream. I knew Connor probably still heard it, but I didn't care.

I felt my eyes flash while I held the pillow against my face, and that just made me angrier, so I screamed again for good measure. When that didn't make me feel any better, I grabbed the first thing I could find, which happened to be the TV remote, and threw it against the wall. The TV turned on, and when the picture appeared, the early morning news came on. I stared at the screen as the news reporter began listing all the things going wrong with the world right now.

"I don't know what to tell you, Jo, but it's getting crazy out here. Aside from last week's earthquake and the floods occurring in the desert, we now have toads falling from the sky here in Sydney. While scientists are saying this is a perfectly normal phenomenon, I'm not going to lie, it's starting to feel like there's more going on," the reporter on the TV said as she stood under a giant umbrella, surrounded by a sea of dead toads on the ground. More were still falling from the sky, and I stared at the television in a daze.

"Um... yes, thank you, Lisa," replied the news anchor back in the studio in a shaky voice, pausing for the longest time before continuing. "And next, we have Brian in Townsville, where, if you can believe it, it's snowing!"

They cut to a man standing in a massive winter coat, surrounded by snow, as he addressed the camera. I barely heard a word he said as I gaped at the TV. It did not snow that far north. It rarely went below fifteen degrees in winter up there, yet they were trying to tell us that the temperature had dropped as low as minus ten degrees in the past twenty-four hours. In the middle of summer.

Most people in that part of the country wouldn't even own a jumper, let alone snow gear. The news was flashing to emergency centres being set up to help the citizens of North Queensland get access to clothing and blankets to ensure no one died from exposure.

I watched in silence as the news went on and on, each story more alarming than the next. In New Zealand, long dormant volcanoes were starting to rumble, a tsunami had wiped out some Fijian islands, and now reports of flooding were coming in from South America. The other side of Australia was also currently experiencing the flooding that had started here the day I was turned.

My heart began to race once again, and I tried to get it together before I slipped into a full-blown panic attack.

If we couldn't get Liam back to normal and work out what to do next, the world would go to complete shit, and I couldn't help but think it would be all my fault.

CHAPTER TEN

By midday the following day, Connor had still had no luck with breaking through the enchantment and was starting to get super cranky.

"This is ridiculous. I don't know why Eve thought we'd be the ones to get through!" He flung himself on the couch across from Liam, who was still staring off into space.

Although Eve had told us to use Liam's journals to see if it triggered his memories, we'd been unable to even attempt it. Every time Connor stopped planting false memories in Liam's head, he'd start ranting about demons again.

"Maybe it's time to accept that you need my help?" I asked from where I stood, leaning against the doorframe with my arms crossed.

I cradled a glass of whiskey against the crook of my arm. Everything about this situation called for day drinking right now.

"Where's mine?" Connor asked, his tone short, eyeing the glass in my hand while ignoring what I'd just said.

"This *is* yours. I've already had about four," I said.

He moved in a blur, stopping before me as he snatched the glass from my hand and immediately drank it in one gulp, holding my gaze the entire time.

"That was a bit dramatic," I said, taking the glass back before he could throw it against the wall like I'd seen him do in the mindscape.

"Well, I'm shitty and needed to take the edge off." He ran his eyes over me. "I could think of other ways to take the edge off that don't include alcohol, though."

"Not going to happen," I responded over my shoulder while I headed back into the kitchen to pour him another glass.

He followed behind me. "What makes you think you'll be able to do something I can't?" He asked, finally acknowledging what I'd said earlier.

"Well, given he is one of the ones who turned me, and we have our bond, I feel like I have more of a connection than you guys do outside of your powers."

Connor's eyes flashed. "And how is that bond going right now? Heard his thoughts at all since we brought him out of the realm?" The challenge in his tone was more than evident as his gaze bore into mine.

"No. But I can feel it. Ever since we used the bond to find him, I've felt that tug, and it gets stronger each time I'm in the room with him. I'm sure that part of the enchantment that Damon and Seth did is stopping me from hearing him." It was the only explanation I'd been able to come up with.

"Or maybe, before they enchanted him, he'd put a block on it," Connor said, crossing his arms.

"He doesn't know how to do that; he was never able to tune my thoughts out fully in the past. And besides, why would he block me out? If he did have that ability, I mean?" I asked.

"Oh, I don't know. Maybe because he saw your obvious attraction to the twin brother he fucking hates and stopped trusting you?"

"Regardless of what you would do in that situation, that is not Liam. Yes, he was angry and needed time to process what I'd allowed you to do to me, but he also wouldn't shut down the bond without knowing I was okay," I said with a conviction that I didn't really feel.

Connor scoffed. "One, don't act like you weren't willingly partaking in what I was offering." He held a finger up as he moved closer before raising a second. "And two, you're giving him far more credit than he deserves."

"Liam is the only honourable one out of the three of us at this point, Connor," I said, lifting my chin as I held his gaze.

"Is that why you're so hung up on this? You feel guilty for how you feel about me and feel like you owe him more?" His voice was low, his eyes drifting to my lips.

"I don't feel anything for you," I whispered back, once again unable to pull away from him when we were this close.

"Liar." He pulled me to him, and his lips hovered over mine.

I could tell he was waiting for me to close the distance. To give in to the attraction between us and be the one to initiate it finally.

My emotions swirled inside me as I stared into his eyes. The air around us felt heavy, like an unseen force was holding its breath, waiting to see what I'd do next. I could feel myself leaning in closer, our lips almost touching.

"No, Connor." I placed my hand on his chest and pushed him back a step.

"You can deny this all you want, but you want this just as much as I do," he said, a nerve in his jaw twitching as he stared at me.

"I can't," I said through clenched teeth as I tried to get my traitorous body under control. "Liam is in the next room! I love Liam, and I don't cheat! I don't know what this is, but it has to stop." I pushed away from the fridge and left the room, Connor hot on my heels.

"You need to be honest with yourself!" He argued, not letting it drop.

"Connor, seriously! Stop pushing this. I am barely holding on as it is, and I can't deal with whatever the hell this is when the literal fate of the world is on my shoulders, and my boyfriend's brain is fucking broken right when we need him!" I could feel the burning in my chest begin to build, and sparks started flying from the ends of my fingers.

Connor was on me instantly, gripping my shoulders tightly as he pulled me close.

"Isolde, we are inside a house. Get it the fuck together," he said in my ear. His proximity just made it even harder to control the flames. "Seriously, you will burn the whole fucking house down."

"Then get me outside," I rasped out, the control slipping further as the sparks grew into flames.

We were both outside in the blink of an eye. Connor held me against him, and I screamed as my head snapped back. My arms flung wide open, and once again, flames shot out of me and up into the sky. I could hear Connor yelling something in my ear, but I couldn't focus on anything other than the burning sensation that churned through me. My entire body, along with Connor's, was engulfed in fire.

"Fuck... your eyes," he said, his words barely discernible over the roaring flames.

His hands slid along my jaw, his fingers tangling in my hair as he pressed his forehead to mine.

Slowly, I started to get the flames under control, reeling myself back in, and the fire began to shrink towards us.

"Come on, come back to me," Connor demanded, his grip tight on both sides of my head.

Finally, I managed to extinguish the flames entirely and pulled in a ragged breath. Connor stepped back, keeping his hold on my face as he stared at me.

"You good?" He asked, and I searched his face for a moment before slowly nodding.

The tension in his shoulders eased slightly. He stepped closer again, sliding his hand to my chin and tilting my face as he brought his lips closer to hover over mine. The air around us began to crackle, although I wasn't sure if that was real or if it was simply inside my head. It would be so easy to close that gap. To allow our lips to meet and see if the world would explode from the fire burning between us.

"Well... this is nice and cosy."

Together, we quickly turned our faces towards the door to find Liam standing a few feet away, his arms crossed. His jaw was clenched, and I knew instantly that whatever enchantment had been in place had been lifted.

"So nice of you to finally join us, Liam," Connor said, letting my face go and casually putting his hands in his pockets as he stepped back.

"Fuck you, Connor," Liam said, not bothering to look at his brother as his eyes bored into mine.

"Liam," I whispered, stepping forward.

He shook his head at me. "Don't, Isolde. I can't... whatever this is... whatever that was..." He waved towards the charred ground around where we stood. "Whatever is going on, just don't try and say it's nothing."

I could feel something inside of me break at the hardness in his voice. No matter how frustrated I'd made him, he had never spoken to me like this.

"It's not nothing," Connor said beside me, and I turned to glare at him.

"Don't even get me started on you, brother," Liam said, his voice shaking as he finally looked at Connor.

And then his eyes flashed.

"What the..." Connor stepped back beside me as I gaped at Liam.

"Liam," I said, my voice stronger as I stepped forward again, and Liam turned his glare back to me. "Liam, your eyes..."

The rage that showed in his eyes was chilling, and I knew that he was struggling to keep his anger under control. As I moved closer, he bawled his hands into fists at his sides, the control slowly slipping.

"Get the fuck away from me, Isolde," he said, stepping back.

I pushed aside the pain his words caused because there were more important things to worry about right now than what was happening between us.

"Liam, stop," I said, my voice commanding as I reached to grab his face, forcing him to look me in the eye.

His eyes flashed again, and I gasped, looking back over my shoulder at Connor, who was watching his brother with a wary expression.

"Take your hands off me." Liam's voice was cold as he pushed my hands away.

I turned back to him. "What happened just now? What snapped you back to yourself?"

He stared at me, his brows knitted together, and his body shook slightly. "Are you seriously asking me this?" He asked.

"Answer the question!" I yelled, needing him to push past his anger so we could get to the bottom of what was happening.

"Fine!" He spat back. "I felt the burning in my chest, like before Damon and Seth showed up. I'm assuming that it was you who sent that beacon of flame into the sky?"

I nodded.

"Well, this time, it burned so much I felt like I was about to catch on fire, and that snapped me back, I guess." He raked a hand through his hair, his anger seeming to simmer down a little.

"How's the need for blood going?" Connor asked, remaining where he stood.

Liam looked at him through narrowed eyes. "Why the hell are you asking me that? And how are you out in the sun right now? What the fuck is going on?" I could see the rage starting to fight its way to the surface again.

"We have a lot to explain," I said, and Liam shook his head, his eyes flashing again.

"We? There's a fucking 'we' now?"

"Get your shit under control, Liam," Connor said, appearing at my side. "This is bigger than your feelings right now."

"Fuck you," Liam said, his hands balling into fists at his sides again.

In the months I had known Liam, I had never seen him lose control like this, even with Eve.

Connor stepped into Liam's space. "Hit me. Just let it out," he said, spreading his arms wide as he brought his face close to Liam's.

Liam unleashed, and Connor flew across the yard, hitting the fence with a thud. Liam launched himself after him and began taking every ounce of his rage out on his brother, who didn't even attempt to fight back.

I moved forward, but Connor shot a look at me as Liam took another swing.

"Let him work it out, Isolde."

Liam's fist connected with Connor's cheek, snapping his head back and causing blood to spray out of his mouth.

Eventually, Liam's punches slowed, and he stepped back, wiping the blood from Connor's already healing wounds on his jeans.

"Now that you've gotten that out, let's focus on what's important, shall we?" Connor got to his feet, showing no sign of pain after the pummelling he'd just taken.

But he stepped back quickly when Liam pulled the stake out of his pocket.

"Whoa, Liam!" I leapt into action and grabbed the stake from his hand. "We need him."

"No one needs him," Liam said, and I could see the words hit Connor briefly before his face closed over.

"Yes, we do. Let us explain what's going on."

Liam turned to look at me for a few moments, searching my face before nodding stiffly.

"Fine." He marched back inside, and Connor and I exchanged a tense look before following him.

Liam headed straight for the fridge. Instead of pouring himself a glass of blood, he drank it directly from the pitcher, and I could see the alarm I felt mirrored in Connor's eyes. Once he'd drained the entire pitcher, he slammed it back onto the counter and crossed his arms, staring at us both.

"Well? Get on with it."

I took a deep breath. "Connor is a hybrid... Like me."

Liam's expression remained closed.

"And... I think you might be one now, too?" I continued, looking over at Connor, who watched his brother closely.

"He's got you under some sort of mind control, Isolde. There is nothing good in him," Liam said, holding Connor's gaze.

"Everything we thought about the prophecies... was all a lie."

Liam's eyes moved to mine. "What do you mean?"

Taking another deep breath, I launched into the explanation about the spell Eve had cast, the fact that Connor and I were both hybrids and how Aurora and Connor were created to be the darker versions of us both. Seeing Connor outside in the sunlight just moments ago was proof enough that he wasn't the full-blown nightwalker Liam believed, but I could tell he wasn't sure what to think.

Liam continued to stare at me as I spoke, and he cocked his head a little when I finished talking. Connor had remained silent while I spoke, standing to the side with his arms crossed as he watched his brother through narrowed eyes.

"Why do you think I'm a hybrid now too?"

"Well, for one, the rage you just exhibited. No matter how angry I've seen you in the past, you have never lost control like that," I said, and he snorted.

"Hardly proof, you've never been in my brother's arms in front of me before. You have no idea how much that causes someone to snap."

"Not you, Liam. And you know it. Maybe if it was just your anger alone, but add in the fact that your eyes just flashed several times, and you drained that pitcher of blood like it was water, and you were dying in the desert – I think whatever happened with my flames earlier has turned you."

He stared at me, his expression unreadable.

It finally dawned on me that I still couldn't hear his thoughts. The bond was gone once again.

"What's happened to the bond? Why can't I hear you?"

"The last thing you want is to hear what I'm thinking right now, trust me, but I don't know why we can't hear each other." He nodded towards the door. "I need time to process all of this. I'd like you both to leave now."

CHAPTER ELEVEN

A moment passed before I looked at Connor, blinking back tears while he nodded and turned back to Liam.

"Fine. But we don't have much time. You need to get yourself sorted and onboard, or everything is about to go to complete shit," Connor said, and Liam gave a sharp nod before pointing towards the door.

Connor started towards the door, but I hesitated, still watching Liam.

"I know you hate me right now, but this is all bigger than us and our relationship. I don't think you should be alone while you deal with this. If you won't let me stay, please at least go and see Patrice or Gerard?"

Liam's expression remained cold as he looked at me. "I'll go and see Eve. She'll be able to offer all the help I need."

The double meaning behind his words felt like a punch to the stomach, and I did my best not to show any reaction, even while my heart fractured apart.

"Good." I moved towards the door.

"Try not to spend all the time you're meant to be preparing for the end of the world fucking my twin brother instead."

I stopped at the threshold and took a deep breath but didn't turn around. "Maybe once you speak to Eve, you'll understand that I'm drawn to him because he's the literal other half of you."

"Guess I better go and fuck Aurora then? Call it even?"

I spun around and glared at him. "I haven't fucked Connor."

"Looked pretty damn close to it, though. Tell me, if I hadn't snapped out of the enchantment when I did, would you have started riding him right there in the backyard?"

"I'm done with this conversation, Liam. I'll see you at Eve's house once you've gotten all this out of your system."

"Pretty sure I've got you out of my system. I'm done with you, with us. Once this is all finished, I never want to see either of you again." His expression was resolute as he turned and walked out of the room without looking back, leaving me standing in the doorway feeling like my heart had been ripped from my chest.

Connor met me at the end of the street and gave me a questioning look.

"I don't want to talk about it," I said, putting my hand up.

He nodded, and I was relieved he didn't push it further. I wasn't ready to process what had just happened. That the man who had become the centre of my world had just told me he never wanted to see me again.

"So what do we do now?" He asked.

I sighed, throwing my arms up. "I don't know... I guess we need to go back to Eve. Although, isn't Adam going to wonder where you've been?"

Connor shook his head. "I've often gone days or even weeks without returning to them. And I've been able to alter his memories in the past when I've needed to," he replied.

I wasn't sure how to feel about that bit of information.

"So you can just go into Adam's mind and control him?"

"No. But I can plant false memories of myself, similar to what I've been doing with Liam for the last day. At least, some of the time."

We started walking towards the river.

"So, is that how you've managed to keep up the pretence of being a ruthless killer all these years?" I asked, casting a look over at him.

He continued to look ahead, avoiding looking at me. "Not entirely. It's a skill I've had to work on over the years, and whenever I've noticed any suspicion forming and can't control it... I have had to show my loyalty."

I was pretty sure I didn't want to know what he meant by that.

When I stayed silent, his shoulders tensed up, and he finally looked over at me.

"What's the matter, Isolde? Doesn't quite fit with the tragic hero you've cast me as in your mind?" He taunted, and I shook my head.

"Actually, Connor, it makes me empathise with you and hate Eve even more for the shit she's forced us all to deal with. Especially what you've had to deal with."

Connor scoffed. "Well, just try to keep your rage under control because I don't think we need to draw more attention by you turning into a literal ball of fire."

"About that... Do you really think Liam is a hybrid now? And if so, was it because of my fire abilities, or did Damon and Seth do something to him?" I asked.

He shrugged. "Something was definitely different, and the flashing eyes led me to believe he's a hybrid now, but honestly, we're not going to know until we get to Eve. So let's save the questions for her, shall we?"

I couldn't let it go that easily. There were too many questions swirling around in my head.

"I just... that rage in him... I have never seen him lose control like that. It seemed like the only emotion he was capable of was anger. If he hadn't been outside, I honestly would have thought..."

"That he was a nightwalker." Connor finished for me.

"Yeah... but that's not possible, right?"

"No. But he did see us pretty damn close to kissing, Isolde. I think you're just looking for any excuse so that you don't have to think about the fact that you need to make a choice," Connor said, sliding his hands into his pockets as he walked.

I groaned as I threw my head back and looked at the sky. "You really like to push for the hard conversations, don't you? Remember what happened last time you pushed me on this? I turned into the human torch. Let's maybe table the conversation on my feelings for a while. Because I honestly don't know anymore. And, if I was to turn to you right now and say, 'I want you, Connor', wouldn't you always wonder if it was just because Liam rejected me and I was settling for you?" I asked.

Connor stopped abruptly, grabbing my hand and pulling me flush against his chest.

"I am very aware of how difficult this all is for you. Do you think I like having these feelings for you when I know it will ruin even the slightest chance that Liam will forgive me for the last five hundred years of deception? All I've ever wanted was to get through Eve's fucked up games with some small shred of humanity left and have my brother back." He slid his hand to the back of my neck, forcing me to hold his gaze. "But then you came along and consumed my entire being. Even now, with the literal end of the world occurring, all I can think about is you. And I know he had your heart first, but that's because he's the safe option. Between Will and then Liam, neither of them challenged you." He searched my face, and my chest tightened.

"I..." I didn't know how to respond.

In all our interactions, I had never thought about what he was giving up by pursuing me. I'd believed it was a mixture of wanting to stick it to Liam and the connection that ran through us all. But seeing the look on his face now and the utter devastation in his voice had me questioning all that.

He shook his head as I continued to stare at him.

"Just know I won't make this easy on you, Isolde. I want you. All of you. Not just the idea of who I believe you should be."

"And you think that is how Liam sees me?" I whispered.

"I can't answer for my brother, but all I know is this - If I were in his place right now, I wouldn't be forcing you away from me. I'd hold on for dear life and fight like hell to show you what you were missing." He slowly pulled his hand away and stepped back.

I stayed where I was, refusing to acknowledge the hold he had over me and the tightness in my chest that formed when he turned away and began walking.

I eventually followed, my mind drifting, and I tried to forget what Liam had just said to me while ignoring the tension between myself and Connor.

While distracted, I felt a pulling sensation at the back of my mind. Like an invisible thread was being yanked hard.

"What the hell?" I stopped and shook my head as though this would stop the feeling.

Isolde. I looked around, sure I'd heard my name being whispered. The only person around was Connor, who had stopped a few feet in front of me and was looking at me curiously.

"What's going on?" He asked.

I didn't respond immediately, continuing to look around for the source of the voice, but the street was empty. The sensation in my head disappeared.

"It's nothing..." I whispered.

Connor looked at me a little longer before shrugging and turning away.

Maybe I was just finally losing it.

CHAPTER TWELVE

We arrived at Eve's house after a tense hour of silence, the daylight forcing us to walk at a human pace. Connor hesitated as we stood at the front door.

"I don't know that I'm ready to walk into Eve's web," he said, his tone laced with bitterness while he stared at the door.

I shrugged and pushed the door open, leaving it up to him whether he would follow me inside or stay out the front. I heard voices and headed for the kitchen.

"Oh, Isolde, you're back!" Anika smiled before her gaze flicked past me. "And I see you found Liam."

I guessed Connor had decided to come inside after all.

"Um... not exactly." I wasn't quite sure how to explain his presence.

Anthony saved me from that by letting out a growl and leaping over the kitchen bench, moving so quickly that I barely had time to step in front of him to keep him from using his preferred method for killing nightwalkers. As much as Connor frustrated me, the last thing we needed was for Anthony to rip his head from his shoulders.

"Down, big guy. I come in peace," Connor said dryly.

Anika let out a squeak, seeing the sparks flying from my fingertips as I held my hands up in front of Anthony.

"What is he doing here, Isolde?" Anthony asked, his voice taking on a low, deadly tone.

His hands were balled into fists at his sides while he kept his eyes trained on Connor behind me.

"So, we have a lot to catch you up on... But Connor isn't a nightwalker," I said.

Anthony snorted. "He is not only a nightwalker. He's right up there with Adam in terms of who's running the show."

"See, you really need to listen to all these people, Isolde. Everyone keeps reminding you how evil I am, but you refuse to believe them. Is it my charming personality?" Connor taunted me.

I closed my eyes and breathed heavily through my nose to try and keep myself from erupting out of pure frustration.

"You are not helping, idiot. And believe me, if I were going off your personality, I would have taken you out myself. You're not as charming as you think," I said over my shoulder while watching Anthony.

Anika moved tentatively to Anthony's side, but he flung his arm out to keep her from getting too close.

She pushed his arm out of the way. "Hey, quit that. I'm not some damsel in distress."

Anthony's face twisted into a frustrated grimace.

"Where is Liam?" Anika asked, looking between Connor and me with wide eyes.

"He is having a minor identity crisis. I'm sure he'll be along once he stops sulking," Connor said.

"What do you mean, identity crisis? Have you two still not managed to get his memories back?" Eve demanded as she entered the room.

"Oh, he got his memories back alright... right after Isolde went all fire-happy again and turned him into a hybrid," Connor said.

Eve froze. "Explain?"

If it had been anyone else, I would have shifted uncomfortably under the glare she directed at me. But as it was Eve, I raised my chin and crossed my arms.

"I thought you knew everything, Eve? Do you expect me to believe that you didn't know that the bond between Liam and I allowed me to turn him into a hybrid, too?"

Eve stared at me as if expecting that to be enough to make me answer.

I stared right back, refusing to give in.

Connor coughed behind me, covering a chuckle. "I doubt she's going to give in, Eve."

I have no idea how long we stood staring each other down before Ronson strolled into the room with an annoyed look.

"For fuck's sake, Eve. Just answer the girl." He stopped at her side, and she rolled her eyes.

"Fine," she spat out, throwing her arms up in defeat. "I have no idea what you are talking about. Explain what happened."

I raised an eyebrow.

"Please?" She added through gritted teeth.

Anthony spluttered behind her. "Jesus Christ... I don't think I've ever heard you use that word, Eve," he said, gaping at her before turning to shoot an admiring glance at me.

Connor laughed behind me. "Guess you're losing your touch there, Eve. Knocked down off your high horse by a child." I turned slowly and glared at him. He put his hands up. "Sorry, very obviously not a child. A strong, powerful woman." He corrected himself with a smirk.

I rolled my eyes before finally putting Eve out of her misery. "Connor was having no luck trying to get through whatever enchantment Damon and Seth had placed on Liam's mind. I had another moment where I lost control of my powers, and flames shot out of me into the sky again. Afterwards, Liam came out and had his memories back. But, he seemed different, and his eyes flashed, like ours do," I said, waving my hand between myself and Connor. "He seemed to be having trouble keeping his anger under control. I've never seen Liam like that. And he drank about a litre of blood like he was dying of thirst."

"And you think it had something to do with you losing control of your powers?" Ronson asked after exchanging a look with Eve, who looked pale.

"Well, he said he'd felt a burning in his chest like he'd felt just before Damon and Seth took him. That was when I lost control of my powers last time. He seemed to think that was what brought his memories back," I said, looking at Connor, who nodded.

"But... that's not possible..." Eve whispered, and I exchanged an alarmed look with Connor.

"What, so this wasn't you?" I demanded, and Eve shook her head, closing her eyes and dropping her head into her hands.

"Wait, so does this mean it's fucked up the spell?" Connor asked, stepping toward her.

"I don't know." Her response was muffled as she covered her face with her hands.

"What do you mean you don't know?!"

"Exactly that! The spell relied on Liam remaining a daywalker and Aurora being a nightwalker, with the pair of you straddling the line between the two. Now I have no fucking idea. And I can't exactly talk to the witches who helped me cast the spell because they are all fucking dead!" She threw her head back and stared at the ceiling. "Fuck!"

Ronson stepped close beside her and ran his hand up and down her back. "We'll work this out. We have come too far now," he said quietly to her.

These were the most words I'd ever heard him utter.

Anthony and Anika had remained silent throughout the entire exchange, and Anika cleared her throat before finally speaking up.

"I'm sorry, but can someone please explain why Connor is here? And what do you mean by hybrids?" She was looking between Connor and me with an uneasy look.

"Eve will have to explain it properly, but in a nutshell, the prophecies were complete bullshit. She orchestrated it all and ensured that Connor and I were created as hybrids by involving daywalkers and nightwalkers in our transitions. Connor has been pretending to be a nightwalker for the past five hundred years because Eve made him do it."

"Well, now, let's not give Eve all the credit. I haven't exactly been sitting around feeling sorry for myself for the past five hundred years." Connor crossed his arms and eyed Anthony and Anika closely.

I whirled to face Connor. "Would you just fucking stop?! You've been doing that ever since you admitted the truth last night. You're one person with me and another around everyone else, and it's getting really damn old."

"Perhaps he is simply manipulating you, Isolde. I hear that is one of his specialties," Anthony said, and Anika nodded beside him.

"Maybe he is. I don't even fucking care anymore. I want to get this all over and done with so I never have to think about any of this shit ever again." I turned my back on Connor, who had refused to look at me after Anthony's comment. I focused my attention on Eve. "How much longer do we have?"

Eve's throat bobbed as she swallowed hard and looked at Ronson before returning her gaze to mine.

"We have two weeks... Until the next full moon. And if it doesn't work, the entire world will be utterly devastated and ruined."

"Great, we have two weeks to work out if the spell will still work with three hybrids and a nightwalker. Otherwise, the entire planet will be wiped out. No fucking pressure," I muttered, starting to feel sick.

CHAPTER THIRTEEN

By the time darkness fell, I had begun to feel stifled within the walls of Eve's house. After Connor had disappeared, I'd hidden myself in the room Liam and I had occupied while we stayed here. I had no idea where Connor had gone.

It felt good to finally have space between us after two days together. Being in his constant presence was doing nothing to help all the conflicting emotions whirling inside me.

But now that it had been a few hours, something inside me was calling out for him, and I was doing my best to push it aside. I wasn't even close to being ready to unpack what that meant.

I had been sitting in the window seat for hours, staring out at the view of the city and the river that still flowed fast. I closed my eyes and pressed my forehead against the cold glass. Between the tears fighting their way to the surface since Liam had told me he never wanted to see me again and the intense urge to find Connor, I knew I needed to leave this house.

The restless feeling finally got the better of me. I could feel the control over my powers slipping, and I didn't want to be responsible for burning the house down.

I pushed myself to my feet and crossed the room to the door, pausing to breathe before leaving my sanctuary and facing the others again.

"Hey," Anika said quietly when I walked past her on my way through the library.

She was sitting on one of the couches with her legs curled up beneath her, cradling a steaming cup of what I assumed was tea.

"Hey," I replied, stopping to stand awkwardly a few feet away.

I wasn't sure where we stood after all the declarations made earlier.

"Are you heading out?" She asked, and I nodded. "Want some company?"

I hesitated for a moment before answering. "Just you, right?"

"Yeah. I'll leave the aggravating sidekick at home," she said with a small smile, and I laughed, surprised.

"It's not that I don't like Anthony... I just..."

"I get it. The last thing you need now is to deal with snarky comments, and he is incapable of stopping himself from making them. As much as I love him, I know that sometimes others need a break from the commentary."

She entered the kitchen to get rid of her cup before joining me in the foyer.

"So, where are we going?"

"Honestly, I don't have anywhere in particular in mind. I just need to get out of this house," I said.

Anika nodded before following me silently down the front steps and onto the footpath. We walked for a while in companionable silence before she finally broke and asked the question that had clearly been weighing on her mind for the last few hours.

"So... about Connor? Is it really true that he's a hybrid like you?"

I stayed quiet for a moment before answering. "You saw him yourself earlier. Did he look like a nightwalker to you?" I asked, trying not to sound defensive or angry.

Given everything she'd heard about Connor over the last century, I could understand her reluctance to believe the truth.

"I just don't understand why. If he could choose between living a life like ours and being stuck with Adam all these years, why did he decide to stay? Why didn't he just kill Adam himself?"

"From what I've seen of his memories, Eve didn't give him a choice. He had to keep up the facade until I came along and had to try not to give in entirely to the urge to give up on his final links to humanity. Apparently, the only person who can kill Adam is me," I said, hearing the bitterness in my voice as I said it.

"What does Liam have to say about all of this?"

"We haven't really had much of a chance to talk since all of this came out, and I don't know if we're ever going to get to talk about it, to be honest. Liam doesn't want anything to do with me right now."

"Because of how you feel about Connor?" Anika asked.

I turned to look at her, and she gave me a small, sad smile. "I could see it as plain as day between you today. I've always been pretty good at reading people. I could see the connection between you, even though you are clearly trying to deny it."

I groaned before turning to start walking again. "Do you know how frustrating this all is? I'm meant to be focussing on ending all of this insanity, and instead, I'm caught up in all of these feelings that I may or may not be having for my boyfriend's evil twin."

"The more you ignore it all, the worse it will get. If you don't face it all head-on, it will just keep distracting you."

"What should I do, Anika? I can't give in to any temptation with Connor without destroying my relationship with Liam, but also, a part of me wonders if I truly belong with Liam. I love him more than I ever loved Will, but we are so dependent on each other. That can't be healthy."

Anika was quiet for a moment before answering. "After watching the pair of you over the past few weeks, I wondered that myself. You seemed to go everywhere together. I think that was a habit that Liam had left over from when he was protecting you from the shadows for all those years. But still, if I spent as much time with Anthony as you did with Liam, there is a good chance I would have killed him. But… Liam loves you, Isolde. And you're treading a dangerous path with Connor. You need to be honest with yourself and with Liam about how you're truly feeling. Because deep down, you know who you're going to choose."

Anika's words echoed my thoughts. But knowing someone else thought the same thing made denying it so much harder.

"Ugh, I think I need to go and kill some nightwalkers and just ignore this all a bit longer."

Anika smiled again and waved her hand, indicating for me to go first.

"After you, then."

As I stepped around her, the tugging sensation I'd felt earlier returned to the back of my mind, and I stopped moving.

"Isolde?" Anika said, watching me with her head cocked to the side.

Isolde! Hear me! The voice I'd heard earlier rang out, but I could tell from Anika's curious expression that she'd not heard anything.

The sensation disappeared again.

I let out a shaky breath as I looked around me.

I recognised that voice. It belonged to Damon.

I saw no sign of the man around me and was seriously considering if I had imagined it. It wasn't impossible, given how crazy the past few weeks were.

"What's going on?" Anika asked, an eyebrow raised as she looked around as well.

"Sorry, I thought I'd heard something."

She looked around once more before returning her gaze to mine. "I don't see anything."

"Must have just been the wind," I whispered.

CHAPTER FOURTEEN

Several hours later, the adrenaline of fighting multiple nightwalkers helped me clear my head a little. I'd even managed to use my fire abilities alone without Liam's assistance in controlling the flames, which I was immensely proud of, even though it backed up my fears that I had allowed myself to become reliant on Liam in too many ways.

It was after midnight, and Anika had decided to head back to Eve's house. I wasn't quite ready to turn back, not wanting to return to that room and be alone with my thoughts again. At least out here, I could work out my frustrations by kicking some nightwalker ass.

I made my way to New Farm Park, not far from the Manor. This was the first time since I had been pulled into this madness that I had patrolled alone, and as I walked through the dark park, I was surprised that I wasn't afraid.

I guess I had become more used to this world than I had realised.

I stopped near the children's playground, waiting to feel the presence of any nightwalkers lurking nearby. The giant trees that stood amongst the play equipment were the perfect hiding places, with their open trunks that created little caves and hidden walkways. The trees I had loved hiding amongst as a child were now a stark reminder of all the places where the horrors in the dark could hide.

"Is this a private moment, or can anyone join?" A voice said from the shadows, pulling me from my morbid musings.

I looked to my right, and Connor stepped from the shadows. Of course, the one vampire that showed up was the one I couldn't sense.

"That depends. Which version of Connor will be joining me? The asshole hellbent on convincing me how evil he is, or the other one?" I continued walking while he fell into step beside me.

"How about a delightful mixture of both?" His voice had a teasing tone, and I rolled my eyes.

"Then no, you can't join me," I replied, walking ahead of him, tired of his games.

He quickly reached for my hand, lacing our fingers together while he pulled me around to face him. "I'm sorry, okay? After five hundred years of being the bad guy, it's going to take a while before the walls come down." He slipped his hand free, and I ignored the tingle I felt at losing his touch.

"Where did you go?" I asked, and he grimaced.

"I figured it was time to make an appearance back at the coven. I slipped back in not long after the sun went down. Also, figured we needed a little distance from one another," he added, avoiding looking me in the eye.

It seemed I wasn't the only one feeling the strain under the constant tension between us.

"And did Adam ask where you'd been?" I asked quietly.

"I don't think he'd even noticed I hadn't been around, with all the excitement around your sister and the trouble she is causing."

"What do you mean? What has she done now?" I asked, feeling the anxiety kicking in at the mention of Aurora.

The last I'd heard, she'd killed her ex-boyfriend Jacob and the friends he'd been staying with.

Connor slid his hands into his pockets. "It seems she has been testing her limits. Running off and killing her boyfriend wasn't exactly a sanctioned excursion. Adam doesn't like it when his minions step out of line, and she's been yanking at the leash a little more than he's prepared to put up with. I stepped in to keep him from snapping and killing her. We need her alive, after all."

"This spell is beginning to drive me mad," I said, unsure how to feel about the idea of my sister pissing off the oldest nightwalker on the planet and still avoiding processing the fact that she had killed Jacob.

"Agreed. But only a few more weeks. Either way, this will all be over." He looked exhausted while he ran a hand through his hair.

"What are we going to do if Liam's transition has fucked it all up, and I can't kill Adam?" I asked, finally voicing the words plaguing me since the exchange with Eve earlier.

"We just have to believe that it's going to work... I won't accept that the last five hundred years will have been a complete waste. Enduring everything I have can't have been for nothing." His expression was hard, but I could hear the desperation in his voice.

"What would you have done differently? If you hadn't been royally screwed by this spell, I mean?"

He huffed out a small laugh, the familiar bitterness laced through it. "Pretty much everything. I certainly wouldn't have spent centuries hiding my true nature and blending into the dark... And hopefully, I wouldn't have become enamoured with a woman who was involved with my identical twin brother. But here we are, and I can't change any of it. I'm trying to come to terms with the fact that after all these years, Liam and I will never reconcile." He looked away. "It was a fantasy anyway," he added quietly.

"There is still a chance that Liam will realise that none of this was your choice, Connor," I said quietly, unable to stop myself from reaching up to touch his face.

Moving slowly, he covered my hand with his own and held it while gazing intently into my eyes. His look seared into my soul.

"No matter what has happened in our past, he will never forgive me for what he has seen the past few days, and you know it," he said, his voice husky.

"Not if he doesn't lose me," I whispered.

His eyes flashed. "He's already lost you," he said, moving closer to me.

I couldn't bring myself to step back.

"I haven't made any choices," I replied, and he gave me a slow smile while he moved his hand to grasp the back of my neck.

"Well, I guess I'd better help you make one then."

His gaze turned feral, and he crushed his lips to mine in a bruising kiss, tangling his fingers through my hair while he devoured my lips. I didn't even try to resist when he wrapped his other arm around me to pull me flush against his chest. I could feel every muscle in his body tense up when I ran my hands up his back beneath his shirt and dug my fingernails in.

"Fuck, Isolde," he said against my lips while I dragged one hand down his back, no doubt leaving a mark.

He pushed me back against the nearest tree before grabbing the back of my thighs and lifting me so that I could wrap both legs around his waist. My arms were around his neck, and I moaned when he thrust his hips against me, allowing me to feel how hard he was when he rubbed against my centre, and I ground myself against him, panting.

"God, I want you," he whispered, and he began to lick and suck his way down my neck.

"You have me," I moaned back, moving my head to the side to give him better access.

"Well, this is an interesting development."

We both froze, and I slowly became aware of the presence of nightwalkers when Will and Aurora stepped from the darkness with matching predatory smiles on their faces. Connor tightened his grip on me when my feet hit the ground.

"Something you want to share with the group, Connor?" Will

asked while Aurora clapped her hands, the terrifying grin stretching further across her face.

Connor still hadn't moved, and he gave me a stern look before finally turning, keeping me behind him as he faced them.

"I have no idea what you're talking about. Isolde and I were just having a little chat." He moved slowly, positioning himself so he was placed firmly between them and where I stood, pressed against the tree.

"Hm, interesting. Your little chat looked like it was about two seconds from becoming a porno," Aurora said, looking at me over Connor's shoulder. "Both brothers? Are you that much of a slut, Isolde? I guess we're more alike than I thought."

Will growled while he glared at Connor.

Connor snorted. "Seriously, William? Do you honestly think she is even slightly interested in you anymore? And do either of you really think you could take us both on and survive?"

"Let's find out." Will launched himself at us with Aurora a step behind, and Connor stepped forward to meet them both.

CHAPTER FIFTEEN

*A*lthough Will and Aurora both had vampire strength on their side, Connor had five hundred years on all of us.

He quickly caught Will's fist before it connected with his face. Aurora moved to step around Connor to get to me, but he brought his leg up and kicked her in the stomach, sending her flying backwards.

"Gonna need you to get your head in the game here, Chosen One," Connor said over his shoulder before moving into a spinning kick and propelling Will backward.

"Why, you seem to be doing fine on your own," I snapped back, but I stepped up to his side, ready to take on Aurora as she approached me again.

I turned slightly to miss her right fist when it sailed towards my head, taking the chance to step behind her and yank her backwards into my chest, pinning her to me.

"You need to do your mind control thing here, Connor. We can't kill her, and they can't know what's going on," I called over my shoulder while my sister struggled to free herself from my grasp.

"I can't do them both at the same time, so you're going to have to pick one to deal with," he said with a grunt when Will finally managed to make contact.

"Fine, take Aurora." I shoved my sister at him and spun to face Will, bringing my foot to his stomach and launching him backwards again.

He snarled and threw himself at me. "You have no idea what you're doing, letting him touch you. Neither of them deserve to even look at you. You belong to me," Will hissed, attempting to grab me, but I spun out of his grasp.

Over his shoulder, I could see that Connor had managed to get into Aurora's head, and she stood with her arms hanging at her side, staring off into space.

"I don't belong to anyone, and the Will I loved would know that. You're nothing but a demon wearing his skin."

"Wrong! I'm free of all the burdens humanity laid upon me, and I'm more alive than ever. You could have joined us, but you insisted on playing the hero, like the self-righteous bitch you always were," he taunted while we circled one another.

"So one minute I belong to you and am the love of your life, and now I'm a self-righteous bitch? Pick one, Will. You were nothing more than a little boy playing at being a man, trying to have the best of both worlds with Aurora and me."

I knew that there was no point unloading my hurt and anger at their cheating on this version of Will, but I'd yet to fully let myself deal with that revelation. I stepped towards him, and all my rage raced to the surface. I didn't hold back, using all my strength to punch him in the chest, the impact so forceful that he flew through the air and landed several feet away. I didn't allow him the chance to gather himself together, advancing on him and pinning him to the ground with my knees while I began to take my rage out on him with my fists.

"I trusted you with my heart, and all that time you claimed to love me, you were screwing my identical twin sister! How often did you jump into her bed in the house we bought together? Did you even care about either of us or was it all just a game? You knew it would destroy us, destroy our entire family, but you didn't care." I was breathing heavily by the time I finished speaking, having spent the entire time punching him repeatedly, holding nothing back.

"Perhaps it's time to stop playing with him, Isolde," Connor called out, and I glared back at him over my shoulder while I reached into my pocket and yanked out the stake I'd stashed there.

Connor held his hands up. "Apologies, by all means, continue dealing with your issues." He waved towards where Will lay beneath me, gathering himself together again and attempting to buck me off him.

"You will fail. You will never kill Adam. You don't have the ability to follow through on anything. You are nothing!" Will had apparently decided to lean fully into the supervillain character.

I shook my head in disgust. "You won't be around to find out, either way. Goodbye, Will." I slammed the stake down into his chest.

I felt something inside of me snap as the life drained from him, and my hands fell to my thighs as the gravity of what I'd just done sunk in. I looked down at the body of my first love, and I began to shake. The stake fell from my grasp, and I started to heave great, wracking sobs while I continued to stare down at Will's lifeless face.

I had no idea how long I sat there, but eventually, I felt arms gather me up and lift me off Will's body. Connor held me to his chest, even as he somehow managed to keep his control over Aurora's mind.

"You had no other choice, Isolde. We couldn't risk either of them going back to Adam."

I wasn't the slightest bit comforted by his words, even though I knew he was right.

Eventually, I managed to control my emotions and stepped back from Connor's embrace, staring down at my now completely dead former fiance.

"I'm going to have to get rid of the body... And then, we need to work out what to do about Aurora." I looked back at Connor, and he shook his head.

"I'm having the same problem I was facing in Liam's head. Something is different. I was able to plant that false memory for her the night she awoke, but it's not working now. The false memories aren't sticking for long. I've got her on a constant loop right now. I was a little distracted by what was happening with you, but we should work out what we're going to do together."

"What about when you were getting into my head? Did you have the same problem?"

"I have never tried to manipulate your mind in any way, Isolde, so I don't know if it would be the same with you. All I ever did was use the connection I'd established in your mind when I returned your memories to you. Every word you uttered and action you took within the mindscape... That was all you acting on your own free will," he said, holding my gaze.

I knew he wasn't lying and wasn't ready to deal with what that meant right now.

I looked around to ensure no one else was watching us from the darkness before raising a protection spell around us.

"What are you doing?" Connor asked warily.

"Putting up a barrier so that no one can see me setting a body on fire," I replied, and he raised an eyebrow.

"Is that a good idea? You don't seem to have the best control over your fire abilities."

"I've been using them perfectly fine all night, actually," I replied.

I raised my hands, and sparks started to fly from my fingertips. Magic began to course through me, and I forced myself to focus my energy on the balls of flame that appeared over each hand.

"Shit! We have a prob-"

I didn't hear the rest of what he said when a fist connected with the side of my head. I lost the connection to the magic, and the flames were extinguished when Aurora launched herself on top of me.

"What the fuck?" I yelled, trying to hold her fists away from me.

Connor moved to rip her off me, but she managed to throw a punch back over her shoulder, knocking him backwards before returning her concentration to me.

"The magic must have cancelled out the hold I had on her mind," Connor said, moving towards us again, and Aurora finally managed to punch me in the face.

He grabbed her arm when she pulled it back to hit me a third time, lifting her off me.

"You killed Will! You will pay for this, you bitch," Aurora shrieked, struggling against Connor's grip.

"Can't you get her into her head again?" I demanded.

Connor grunted when Aurora elbowed him in the stomach, and he doubled over while she wrenched herself free and launched herself at me again. I flipped myself upright before she reached me and connected with her chest before she could punch me again.

"I don't know what the fuck you did with that spell, but I can't get into her mind again," he said, moving to my side, and we prepared ourselves for another attack.

"Well, what do we do now?" I asked.

Aurora threw herself towards me again, and I stepped out of her path. Her anger was making her sloppy.

"I don't fucking know!" Connor snapped back. "Normally, I would say just stake her, but we can't kill her."

Aurora stopped abruptly and looked at us both with her head cocked to her side. I realised too late that we'd made a fatal error in admitting this where she could hear us when she spun on her heel and ran.

"Fuck! We can't let her get back to Adam." Connor raced after her, and I followed close behind.

Surging past Connor, I grabbed my sister's wrist, halting her in her tracks. I made a split-second decision and hoped to God I was right. Gathering all my strength, I concentrated my power into the hand wrapped around Aurora's wrist.

"Isolde, what the fuck are you doing?!" Connor bellowed when Aurora was engulfed in flames, her screams echoing through the park.

Usually, nightwalkers combusted once set alight, but for some reason, Aurora remained intact, standing still while the flames surrounded her. I managed to keep them under control while holding Aurora in place. Her screams were ear-splitting, and she dropped to her knees. Although the fire engulfed her, she seemed to be untouched physically.

"Look at her, Connor!" I snapped when he moved to stop me, and he looked back down at her while she began whimpering.

I extinguished the flame, letting her go, and she remained where she was, rocking back and forth while she held her head in her hands. Connor and I stood back for a moment, exchanging an uncertain look.

Taking a deep breath, I stepped hesitantly towards her again. "Aura?"

She lifted her head slowly to look up at me.

"Isolde? What... where am I?" She whispered, her eyes glistening with tears as she blinked.

I heard Connor take a sharp breath behind me.

"You're safe..." I dropped to my knees beside her.

"I don't understand... I -" She stopped speaking, and her eyes began moving erratically.

Her face crumpled, and she began sobbing into her hands while she curled into a ball again and began screaming "No" over and over.

"Fuck..." Connor said quietly, and I wrapped my arms around my sister and held her close.

"What have you done to me?" Aurora whispered against my chest, and I stared at the sky, blinking back tears.

"You're a hybrid. A combination of both daywalker and night-walker. Like me... Like Connor..."

She pulled back and looked at me, the anger and grief shining through her tears. "You should have just killed me," she spat at me, shoving me away before returning to her little ball and crying silently.

Connor moved to stand beside me when I rose to my feet and looked down at my sister with tears streaming down my face.

"How did you know that would work?" He asked quietly.

I shook my head and let out an exhausted sigh. "I didn't. I just prayed it would."

"Well, what the hell do we do now?" He asked while I wrapped my arms around myself, looking between Aurora and back at Will's body.

"I guess... Let's take her back to the Manor. It's closer than Eve's, and I don't think she should be near Eve right now. Not until we can work out what this means for the spell."

Connor looked unhappy but nodded before looking back at Will's body.

"I'll deal with that. Just make sure she doesn't see. I have no idea if she's now got your flame abilities, and I don't fancy finding out right now."

I winced but made no move to stop him when he crouched down to lift Will's body and carry him out of sight. I continued watching my sister heave sobs on the ground for a long time before he finally returned.

CHAPTER SIXTEEN

Connor lifted Aurora into his arms, and I was relieved when she didn't put up a fight when we began to walk towards the Manor. I was grateful that we didn't have far to go. After a few minutes, we stopped out the front, staring up at the crumbling ruins. Even though we were both aware of what lay beneath the glamour, it still appeared to be a row of run-down Queenslanders charmed to hide an opulent manor from unsuspecting eyes.

"I think I should take her in alone," I said, and Connor nodded stiffly before carefully transferring my sister into my arms.

"I'll see you back at Eve's," he said before disappearing in a blur, leaving me standing with Aurora, who continued to sob quietly in my arms.

At this stage, it didn't seem like she was even aware of where she was, let alone who was holding her. I carried my sister up the stairs and kicked the door a few times, hoping someone was still up and heard me because I wasn't brave enough to put Aurora down.

The door creaked open, and I blinked when the light from the foyer hit my eyes.

I froze when I saw who had opened the door.

Liam looked surprised before his expression closed over while he stared at me.

"Um…" I didn't know what to say, and a range of emotions flitted across his face.

I shifted Aurora in my arms, and he looked down, stepping back when he saw who I was holding.

"What the hell?" He asked when I pushed past him.

"Yeah, there's a bit of a story to this, but I need to get her settled," I said, moving towards the stairs.

"What do you mean, get her settled?! She can't stay here!" He followed behind me, and I glared back over my shoulder.

"She has nowhere else to go right now. I can't exactly leave her with my parents or sisters."

"Why do you need to leave her anywhere? She's a nightwalker, Isolde!" Liam's voice was raised.

Doors began opening as we entered the hall where our rooms led off.

"Not anymore," I called back while I pushed the door to my bedroom open with my foot.

"What's going on?" Barbara asked, rubbing her eyes when she stepped into the hall.

"Isolde's just collecting nightwalkers now, it seems," Liam said, his voice dripping with sarcasm while he stood in the middle of the hall with his arms crossed.

"Fuck you, Liam," I said.

There was a collective gasp behind me, and I turned to see that we had more of an audience than I first thought when Gerard and Christian had joined Barbara in the hall. I moved further into my room, gently placing Aurora onto the bed. She instantly curled into a ball, hugging a pillow, and refused to look at me. I remained where I stood for a moment, unsure if I should leave her, but I knew I needed to deal with the Order members currently gathering in the hall.

Sighing, I returned to the hall to find that Patrice had joined everyone else staring back at me. Liam remained further down the hall, his expression unreadable.

"Isolde, what is going on?" Patrice asked, looking between Liam and I.

I couldn't bring myself to look at him, keeping my attention on Patrice. "So, to add to all the other interesting things we've learned in the past three or four days, it would now seem that the flames I wield do more than just burn things," I said.

I noticed Liam's stance change out of the corner of my eye. I looked over at him, and he flashed me a warning look.

"What do you mean?" Barbara asked, and everyone kept their attention on me.

"Isolde, don't," Liam said, and the others shifted their gazes from me to him.

"What is going on?!" Patrice said again, her voice rising with each word while Liam stared me down.

"Fuck it. Liam and Aurora are both now hybrids," I said, and Liam's eyes flashed, causing the others to step back.

"Liam?" Patrice's voice wavered.

He sighed, looking at her finally.

"It would appear that something happened when my memories returned, yes," he confirmed, and Barbara gasped, raising a hand to her mouth.

"And what did this have to do with your abilities?" Patrice asked, turning her attention back to me.

"I'd lost control of my abilities when we were trying to get Liam's memories back, and it appears that this caused something to happen through the bond because Liam said he felt an extreme burning sensation. His memories came back, and his eyes were flashing... Not to mention he seemed... different."

Liam glowered at me. "Seemed to have missed a few details there, Isolde, but if that's the story you want to go with, fine."

"What details?" Gerard asked, speaking up for the first time.

"Should I tell them, or would you like to do the honours of

telling them that you were wrapped around Connor at the time?" Liam asked.

I felt the weight of everyone's gazes when they all snapped their heads around to look at me.

I looked up at the ceiling and sighed, exhaustion and grief suddenly overwhelming me.

Christian cleared his throat. "I think we should give these guys a minute."

After exchanging looks, the rest followed him down the hall. Patrice stopped, waving the others ahead, and they rounded the corner.

"Whatever is going on between you two, you need to work it out because everything that is going on right now is more important than whatever melodrama is happening in your relationship, understand?" She fixed a stern look on Liam.

He nodded, and she shifted her gaze to mine. I did the same, and she gave her own nod back before following the others downstairs.

Alone now, we both remained silent. I leaned against the wall beside my door and slid to the floor, putting my head in my hands.

I heard Liam move to sit opposite me, and I looked up when he rested his forearms against his knees and finally looked at me.

"How did we get here?" I asked quietly.

He sighed, his head dropping back against the wall. "I know I want to blame it all on you, but I think my reaction probably also had something to do with it. Maybe if I hadn't walked away the other night and talked to you instead, you wouldn't have sought comfort in his arms," he said, looking up at the ceiling.

It seemed we were back to the no-eye-contact part of the conversation again.

I looked down at my hands. "I'm so sorry I hurt you, Liam. You know it was something I never intended to happen," I said, feeling my eyes well up.

"I don't think I'm ready for this conversation yet, Isolde," he said, his voice thick, and I nodded.

"Okay. I respect that. But I do have some things I need to tell you. About the spell, I mean." I looked up and waited until he slowly brought his gaze to mine and nodded. "We've only got two weeks until the full moon. Once that happens, if I don't manage to kill Adam that night, the whole world is going to end. And we don't know if it will even work anymore because of your transition... and now Aurora's."

I paused when Liam let out a long breath, waiting to see if he would say anything, but he remained silent while he watched me.

"And... Will is dead," I whispered, struggling to keep my emotions in check when I recalled that I had just slain my former fiancee.

Liam swallowed hard. "Did Connor..." His words trailed off when I shook my head.

"No, it was me. I killed him just before I used my abilities on Aurora."

Liam watched me closely, and I struggled to hold back the tears when he tilted his head to the side.

"Are you okay?"

The fact that he could even ask me that proved that the Liam I loved was still in there, even though he was incredibly angry with me.

"Not even close. But I can't think about that until this is finally over... If I'm alive afterwards. Eve hasn't been clear about what will happen once I've played my part. I don't know if I can handle any more revelations at this point, so I'm just going to pretend that there is a happily ever after for all of us," I said.

Liam shook his head. "I see we're going with denial, then?"

"Correct. Denial is my happy place right now."

"It does seem to be where you are most comfortable," he said.

I ignored the obvious dig he was making at how I was handling everything.

I was too tired.

We stayed silent a while longer before I finally stood up and headed towards my room to check on Aurora.

"Perhaps you should let me keep an eye on Aurora?" Liam asked.

I turned back to face him. "Do you think that's wise?" I asked, and he shrugged.

"Honestly, I have no idea. But with everything that happened tonight and knowing how she felt about Will, I'm not sure you're the best person to help her right now."

He had a point, as much as I was reluctant to admit it.

"Okay. But maybe we should have Barbara or Patrice help, too? She wasn't exactly your biggest fan, either."

He gave a small laugh, and rose to his feet. "I think that is a rather large understatement."

"She killed Jacob," I said quietly.

Liam froze, looking stunned. "Fuck... when?"

I knew that he'd liked Jacob, and this revelation had to hurt.

"The night Seth and Damon took you. My parents called me just before I lost control of my powers. I don't know if she remembers that yet, but she will be pretty fragile. Please help her," I begged, and Liam nodded.

"Of course I will. It's what I do, right? I help and protect people." The bitterness in his voice was palpable, and my heart grew heavy.

"When this is all over, Liam..."

"Forget about it, Isolde. Just get through the next few days, and we'll worry about everything else once we come out the other side, alright?"

I looked at him for a moment before nodding slowly.

"Right. Hopefully, the madness will end in just a few more days."

"I have a feeling that the madness will never be over," he said darkly, and I ignored the shiver that ran through me.

I turned to walk down the hall, stopping when he cleared his throat. "Be careful, Isolde," he said, and I nodded before walking away from him again.

. . .

Once I made it downstairs, I headed for the front door, but Patrice stepped out of the library, and I stopped walking when she spoke.

"I hope you know what you're doing, Isolde?" She asked, and although a part of me bristled at her words, I knew from her tone that she wasn't judging me.

"Honestly, I don't know anymore," I replied, shaking my head.

"I figured as much." She nodded her head towards the kitchen, and I followed behind her.

She moved towards the fridge while I sat on one of the stools behind the bench. A sense of deja vu overtook me, and I was transported back a few months to when I would sit here, and she'd feed me massive breakfasts while clucking over me.

How had we even gotten to this point? I would give anything to go back to those moments now. When I thought my biggest problem was dealing with the fact that vampires existed and I was meant to end some imaginary war between them. If I'd known then how much more complicated my life would become, maybe I'd appreciate those moments more.

I was pulled from my musings to find Patrice pouring two large glasses of white wine.

"So... Your sister?" She asked, handing me one of the glasses before taking a generous mouthful from her own.

"Liam's going to try and help her. We agreed I wasn't the right person for that job right now. Although... She hated him too, so maybe you and Barbara could help?" I asked, and she nodded.

I let out a breath and stared at the glass in my hand.

"And things between you and Liam?" She asked quietly.

I couldn't bring myself to meet her gaze, so I shrugged. "About as bad as they could be. Our relationship is over. With everything that's happened with Connor..." I didn't know how to end that sentence without sounding like a complete asshole.

But then, I was one hundred percent the bad guy in this, and I needed to admit that to myself.

I brought the glass to my lips and drank it all in one go. Patrice's expression was unreadable while she refilled my glass.

"While I don't understand the full details of what has happened, the glimpse I got of Connor while he was here tells me that what we've all believed about him over the centuries isn't the full version of the story. That being said, you had to know that spending time with him would cut Liam deeply," Patrice admonished with a shake of her head.

I fought the urge to defend myself because I knew there was nothing I could say to defend myself at that point. So, I went with honesty instead.

"When Connor first started appearing in my dreams, I thought he was using his powers to seduce me. It was the only explanation I could come up with because I love Liam, and I have never been one to cheat. It was never something that I could understand when others have done it. Because if you love someone, you don't develop feelings for anyone else." I paused, feeling a lump of emotion start to form in my throat.

Patrice remained silent, allowing me to gather myself before I continued speaking.

"But Connor is connected to me. I can't explain it. I don't even really understand it. But I'm drawn to him in a way I've never experienced before. And it's not just a physical attraction. What he's endured for the last five hundred years... While Liam has struggled with what he is, he has at least had the Order to fall back on for support, to a degree. Connor has had no one. And the fact that he's managed to avoid completely giving in to the dark side of his nature is honestly a miracle." I had another mouthful of wine, finishing the second glass. I waited for the alcohol to numb some of the emotions I was feeling, but it sadly didn't seem to do anything. "Do you know what kept him from just giving up? The idea that once it was all done, he might be able to have his brother back." I shook my head and huffed a bitter laugh.

Patrice blinked, her stunned silence making the room feel even larger.

Barbara entered the kitchen, pausing when she looked at Patrice, her eyes wary when she glanced at me. "I take it I've missed something shocking?" She asked.

Patrice nodded slowly, and Barbara took the wine bottle from Patrice and poured her own generous glass until there was none left.

"I assume I missed the lecture portion of the conversation, and now we've moved on to discussing what is going on with Connor?" She asked, sliding an arm around Patrice's back and hugging her briefly before stepping away.

"Correct. But I think I'm going to leave Patrice to fill you in. I need to get back to the others and work out if Aurora's transformation will completely undo the spell." I stood and put my empty glass in the dishwasher while they watched me closely.

"Isolde."

I stopped at the doorway, turning back to look at Patrice.

"Be careful. I know your powers far exceed everyone else's, but... I'm worried about this path you're starting down. I can see the connection between yourself and Connor is real, but... don't destroy everything else you have because of it. I will always be here for you, regardless of what occurred in the lead-up to your transition and the Order's unknowing involvement," she said, swallowing hard.

"You will always be part of the Order, Isolde - we are a family. But so is Liam, so please... tread carefully," Barbara added.

I looked between them both before nodding slowly. "I will. The last thing I want is to hurt anyone," I said, hoping that was enough for now.

"Stay in touch," Patrice said.

I gave them a final nod before turning and walking out, emotions swirling through me while I steeled myself for whatever reception I would receive once I returned to Eve's house.

I felt a heaviness wash over me when I walked out the front door. Something about the exchange with Liam had felt final. Like I had let go of some vital piece of myself, and I wasn't sure how to handle it. Even though we'd not said it in so many words, I knew a line had been drawn, and our relationship was over.

I had never experienced a break-up before, and the fact that it was with Liam, the person I had believed was my forever person, was something I couldn't wrap my head around.

Connor was waiting for me outside Eve's home, but I couldn't meet his gaze when I walked past him.

"Hey, what happened?" He asked, grabbing my hand before I could climb the stairs.

"I just... Liam was there." I knew I didn't need to explain further, and he let my hand drop, allowing me to walk ahead of him.

I could tell he had questions, but I was relieved that, once again, he didn't push me to talk about it. I was ready to curl into a ball and sleep for a year but knew I needed to fill Eve in on the latest development.

I was pretty sure she was going to flip out.

With Connor still following me, I walked through the house, checking each of the main rooms before stopping outside Eve's room. I could hear noises behind the door, and I cringed. I was pretty sure I was about to interrupt one of her and Ronson's epic sex sessions.

I wasn't in the mood to be exposed to that. Neither of them had any issues with public nudity. Or inviting people to join them.

"Not going to knock?" Connor asked behind me, and I shot him a glare over my shoulder.

"I think we can wait until the morning," I said, turning away and heading towards my room.

Connor chuckled, following close behind. "What's wrong, Isolde? Don't want to join them?"

"Not particularly, no. But off you go if that's what you're into," I said, pausing at my door to look back at him.

He arched an eyebrow. "Do you want me to join them?"

"Do whatever you want. I don't care what you do," I said, and he moved closer.

"Are you sure about that, Isolde? Cause that's not the impression I got earlier when you were grinding yourself against me and moaning my name." His tone was low and dangerous, and I suppressed the shiver that ran through me.

"I don't know what you're talking about," I whispered.

He chuckled again, gripping my chin and forcing me to look him in the eye. "Just keep lying to yourself. You seem to be very talented at that."

"Go and find another room, Connor," I said, placing my hand on his chest and pushing him away.

"Don't worry, Isolde. I have no intention of our first tumble between the sheets being in the room that you and Liam were fucking in only days ago," he said with a smirk before turning and walking to one of the other rooms further down the hall.

"Asshole," I muttered under my breath, ignoring the laugh that followed me into the room before I had a chance to slam the door closed.

But it was a long time before I fell asleep, knowing that he was only a few rooms away, while my traitorous body wondered what would have happened earlier if we hadn't been interrupted.

CHAPTER SEVENTEEN

Sometime around midday, I emerged from my room in a dark mood.

"How lovely of you to finally join us, Isolde. I hope the coming apocalypse didn't keep you from sleeping," Eve said sarcastically when I entered the kitchen.

Connor was loitering in the corner while Ronson busied himself behind the stove, banging around using various pots and pans.

I slumped down into a chair at the table. "Bite me, Eve," I muttered while I rested my head on my arms.

"Connor tells me that you had an eventful evening. Care to explain why you went completely rogue?" She asked.

I groaned before lifting my head to look at her. "I didn't have much choice in the matter, Eve. It was either turn her or have her run off to Adam and tell him everything, so I went with my gut."

"If this doesn't work now, I will be laying the blame squarely with you," she said.

I leapt to my feet, the burning sensation in my chest returning while I glared at her. Connor stepped towards me, touching my arm, and the sensation eased.

I shook his hand off. "If anyone is to blame for all of this shit, Eve, it's you!"

"Easy, Isolde," Ronson said, looking at my hands when sparks appeared at my fingertips. I balled my hands into fists at my sides, fighting to push the burning in my chest aside.

"Yes, Isolde, do try to keep your emotions under control," Eve continued to goad me.

Ronson gave her a warning look while Connor moved to stand in front of me and held my face in his hands, forcing me to look him in the eye instead of glaring at the woman I was ready to kill.

"Get it under control," he said quietly, and I swallowed hard, working to get my emotions under control.

The sparks settled, and the burning in my chest disappeared. I exhaled while I kept my eyes focused on his.

"Oh, would the two of you just fuck it out already?" Eve snapped.

Connor turned sharply to glare at her, continuing to hold my face. "I bet you'd love to watch that, wouldn't you, Eve," he said.

"I would, actually. The tension rolling off of the pair of you gives me the impression that by the time you finally give in to the inevitable, it will be explosive," she said with far too much glee for my liking.

I tentatively reached up and wrapped my hands around Connor's wrists, and he turned back to look at me again. I nodded and slowly moved his hands away from my face.

"Can we please focus on what's important right now?" Ronson said, looking annoyed.

I was happy to oblige, sitting back down. "Yes, let's do that," I said, dropping my head back onto my arms and closing my eyes.

I felt Connor take a seat beside me.

"It gets worse," Eve said.

I felt the hairs on the back of my neck stand on end, and I began to feel sick. "How could it possibly get worse?" I asked, looking back up at her.

"Now that Aurora has been changed, and I'm assuming is a complete basket case, you'll need to get close to Adam physically and mentally. You'll have to go right into the heart of the coven," Eve said.

Ronson slowly turned his head to look at her, a look I couldn't place crossing his features, and he narrowed his eyes.

I stared at Eve while the nausea rolling through me grew stronger.

"You cannot be fucking serious. He will kill her the second he sees her," Connor said, his voice shaking slightly.

"Well, you're just going to have to work out how to keep her alive then, aren't you, Connor?"

"Why does she need to go in there?" Connor gripped the bench, the muscles in his arms tense while he stared Eve down.

"Because that's the final step of the spell. It required you and Aurora to be physically and mentally close to him in the week leading up to the full moon for the spell to come to fruition."

"Seriously, who came up with all these fucking hoops to jump through with this spell?! It just keeps getting harder and harder," I said.

"It is an intricate spell. Every possible scenario needed to be accounted for," Eve shrugged.

I crossed my arms. "At this point, Eve, I feel like you're just making this all up as you go along."

"Agreed," Connor said roughly beside me.

"I don't have to explain myself to either of you," Eve said.

Ronson interrupted her before she could continue speaking. "Actually, Eve, if you need to explain yourself to anyone, it's to them," he said.

I looked at him, my eyebrows raised high. Of all the people to stand up to her, he was the last person I thought would do it. Eve certainly seemed to feel the same way, judging by the stunned look on her face.

"Why?" Connor asked, his arms crossed, mirroring my posture.

"Because the spell relies on the pair of you not fucking up. And

Eve should remember that when she expects you to walk into the lion's den." Ronson kept his eyes on his lover.

She glowered back at him before finally turning back to us, screwing up her face before sighing. "From now on, I will be transparent with you both. The spell requires one of each of the twins to be mentally and physically close to Adam in the days leading up to the full moon. And you two are it."

"You keep saying that, but what do you mean by mentally close to him?" I asked.

"She means you need to open up your mind to Adam's influence," Connor answered for Eve, his tone flat.

I swallowed hard. "You mean... do I have to kill people?" I whispered.

"I will do everything I can to stop that from happening."

I almost believed him.

"How will we convince him he can trust me?" I asked Eve, who shook her head.

"That part I'm not sure of. It's why we must devise a foolproof plan and hope Adam doesn't work it out before the full moon."

A very stupid idea started to form in my mind.

"Actually, despite your misgivings, Eve, Aurora's transformation has opened up the perfect way for me to get into the coven," I said.

She raised an eyebrow. Out of the corner of my eye, I could see Connor turn to look at me and begin to shake his head slowly.

"No," he said, his eyes flashing.

"We have no other choice, Connor," I said.

Eve's eyes narrowed. "You're going to pretend to be Aurora."

I nodded.

"You might be on to something for once, Isolde."

"And once again, fuck you," I said, unable to keep myself from reacting each time she insulted me.

"For fuck's sake, would the pair of you just get the fuck over it?!" Ronson snapped, flinging the knife in his hand so that it spun through the air at such speed that it lodged itself up to the hilt once it hit the wall between Eve and me.

Eve looked at the knife, then back to her lover with a bored look. "That was an interesting little tantrum, Ronson."

Ronson growled at her before returning to the stove and rigorously stirring whatever was in the large pot.

"This is all becoming truly exhausting," Connor said, staring at the ceiling.

"There, there, Connor," Eve drawled.

I ground my teeth together to keep myself from exploding.

Anika and Anthony entered the kitchen and stopped in the doorway, taking in the scene before them.

"I see we're all playing nicely together," Anthony said, and I looked up at the ceiling, wishing I could disappear.

"Shut it, Anthony," Ronson said, not bothering to look at him.

"What's going on now?" Anika asked, sounding exasperated.

I opened my mouth to answer but stopped when Liam entered the room behind them. Connor tensed beside me, and Liam refused to look at either of us.

"Oh, Liam, how nice of you to join us finally. I expected you here over an hour ago," Eve said, using the same tone she'd greeted me.

"Where's Aurora?" I asked, ignoring Eve.

"She's upstairs, resting," Patrice answered, coming through the door after Liam. Barbara, Gerard and Daniel followed close behind.

"What's going on?" Connor asked, staring at the Order members who were currently looking around the kitchen.

"It's time we all joined forces," Eve replied, and Connor, Anika, Anthony and I turned to stare at her simultaneously.

Ronson made a low growling sound in his throat while he marched past our unexpected guests, wrenching his knife out of the wall and glaring at Eve before returning to the stove and continuing cooking.

"Well, you've got us all here now, Eve. So, time to tell us everything," Liam said, crossing his arms and keeping his eyes on her while avoiding looking at Connor or me.

Eve looked over at me, and Liam reluctantly followed her gaze.

"The final part of the spell requires me to spend the next week or so near Adam." I raised my hand when he opened his mouth to speak. "Eve has made it clear that is non-negotiable. We aren't sure if this will even work now that you and Aurora have become hybrids. Which means we can't risk any further changes. So I need to go and somehow stay alive."

"How are you going to manage to convince Adam not to kill you the second you walk through those doors?" He asked, a crease appearing between his brows while he watched me intently.

"Having Aurora change has given me the solution to that issue."

"You're going to pretend to be Aurora?"

I nodded slowly.

His shoulders dropped, and the animosity I'd seen on his face disappeared. "Fuck... Isolde, that is a massive risk. How are you going to convince Adam that you're Aurora?"

I looked at Connor for a moment before looking back at Liam.

Liam's expression darkened once again when he looked between us both. "Fucking perfect." He spun on his heel and marched back out.

I groaned, dropping my head back to my arms and cursing under my breath.

"There, there, Isolde." Eve's tone was far too gleeful.

I really wished I could punch her.

CHAPTER EIGHTEEN

Unable to remain in the house with both O'Brien brothers glowering at each other, I took myself for a walk.

I had been putting off calling my parents, but I knew I needed to update them on what was happening with Aurora.

I reluctantly pulled my phone out of my pocket, turning it over and over while trying to figure out what to say. I wasn't entirely sure how to do that - they weren't aware of my hybrid status or magical abilities.

"Fuck it," I said to myself before pressing the call button under my mother's details.

"Isolde?" She answered on the first ring.

"Hi, Mum."

"Is everything okay?" Her voice shook slightly, and I wondered if we'd ever be able to have a normal conversation again.

"Well... Look, there's no easy way to say this. Aurora is no longer a threat." There was a sharp intake of breath on the other end of the phone. "Wait, sorry, it's not because she's been killed... well, again."

My god, I suck at this.

"What do you mean?"

"Well… I can't really explain it without going into more detail than you need, but she's not a nightwalker anymore."

"So she's… she's human again?" I could hear the confusion in her voice.

"Uh… No?"

"But…" The silence was heavy with questions my mother didn't know how to ask.

"She's like me now."

"A daywalker? But how?"

I let out a long breath. "Do you really want details?" I asked.

Mum hesitated. "I get the sense that there is far more going on than what you think we should know?"

"Correct."

She paused again, then asked the question I hoped she wouldn't. "What about Will?"

"He's… he's no longer an issue… Or around…" I still couldn't bring myself to say the words.

I could still remember the grief I'd experienced in the week before I knew about all this madness nine months ago when I thought Will was dead, but it felt more final now than it did back then. I hadn't realised until now that some part of me still held onto the fact that he was still around.

More silence, then. "How is Aurora taking all of this?"

The way she asked the question told me that she was aware of Aurora and Will's relationship before his death, and I wondered who had told her.

"She's a bit of a mess," I answered, unable to muster up the sympathy to care about that part of Aurora's mental state.

"Does she remember anything?"

"Yeah…"

Talking about Aurora stirred up many emotions I still hadn't dealt with.

I really needed to end this conversation now.

"Just… Just tell her we love her, okay?" Mum's voice was thick on the other end of the phone, and I nodded before remembering she couldn't see me.

"I will... I love you, Mum."

"I love you too, baby. So much."

We hung up, and I continued walking.

I had no idea how to process everything that happened since I turned twenty-five. This time last year, I was preparing for my engagement party. And here I was, twelve months later, a hybrid vampire with magical powers, a twice-dead fiance, an apparent ex-boyfriend for whom I still had confusing feelings and a... whatever the hell Connor was to me. And on top of that, the world's fate was on my shoulders.

I wasn't the least bit surprised when Connor joined me when I sat down in the park a few streets away.

"Guess I'd better get used to spending all my time with you. You know, now I have to spend a week inside the coven without Adam killing me," I said, attempting to sound like it was no big deal.

"That is not happening. We will have to come up with another plan because there is no way in hell I am letting you walk through those doors," Connor responded, his tone rough.

"Eve didn't seem to think it was something we could avoid, Connor. So we're just going to have to work out a way," I said, and he shook his head.

"I just told you I'm not letting you walk through those doors."

"Well, what do you suggest then? It seems as though we have no choice. I need to be near him for the final requirements of the spell to be met, and I don't know how we'll manage that without me entering the coven."

"You won't last an hour in those walls, let alone a fucking week," Connor said, his eyes flashing.

"You're just going to have to do your mind control thing then."

"I'm good, Isolde, but I'm not that good. I've barely survived being near him over the years. I'm not putting you through that."

"What does that even mean?" I asked, and he sighed.

"When I'm near Adam, it's like being in a hive mind. His blood memories create a bond between him and all those who become nightwalkers, regardless of who is responsible for their transition. It's like an infection in their minds. Their ties to humanity are completely gone, and all that remains is their obsessions and a need to kill."

"But, you've managed to avoid being under his control."

"Most of the time. But the longer I'm near him, the harder it is. I usually manage to slip away every couple of days, and that seems to keep me from losing myself, but there have been times that it wasn't possible... and those are the times that have earned me the reputation that you've heard of." He looked away.

I was quiet for a moment while I processed the fact that he had been forced to give in to the darker side of his nature.

"And you think that's what will happen to me if I manage to somehow fool him into believing I'm Aurora?"

"I know it will. Not to mention, you will have to do something about your heart and breathing. That will be a dead giveaway if you don't learn how to switch those off," Connor said.

I hadn't even considered that, and I swallowed hard.

"A week will be more than enough for you to lose yourself completely." He ran a hand through his hair and grimaced.

"Not if you're with me."

He turned to look back at me again. "I think your faith in my abilities is far too high," he said quietly.

"I trust you to protect me," I said.

His breath hitched a little. "Since when do you trust me?" His voice wavered.

I turned to him, touching his cheek to keep him from looking away again. "On this, I trust you completely. You want this all to end just as much - if not more - than I do. And the only way that will happen is if I succeed, so I trust that you will do everything in your power to ensure that I don't fail so that I can kill Adam once and for all."

He cleared his throat while continuing to hold my gaze. "That's not the only reason I want this all to end."

I knew I was playing with fire now, but I couldn't stop myself. "And what's the other reason?"

His gaze sharpened while he smirked slightly. "You know the other reason."

"I'm going to need you to spell it out for me."

He pulled me into his lap, moving me so that I was straddling his lap before skimming his nose up my neck and burying his face into my hair.

"Because once this is all done, you won't have any more excuses to avoid this pull between us. And I look forward to watching you come undone," he growled in my ear, and I couldn't suppress the shiver that ran through me.

I hated how my body reacted to him, as though even the slightest touch was going to cause me to come completely undone.

"Why are you so sure that you'll get to see that?" I whispered, making no move to get up, even though I knew I should.

He grasped my chin so that I had no choice but to look into the piercing blue eyes that burned with lust. I couldn't have looked away even if I wanted to.

"Because you want this just as badly as I do," he said before yanking my face to his and kissing me hungrily.

I wrapped my arms around his neck, kissing him back, knowing this couldn't continue. But I was growing tired of denying myself what my body so clearly craved.

Against my better judgment, I rocked my hips against his, and he groaned while devouring my lips.

"Fuck, Isolde. You have no idea what you're doing to me," he said, kissing his way down my neck while his hands gripped my hips tightly and forced me to continue to rock against him.

I could feel him growing harder beneath the fly of his jeans. If we didn't stop, I would explode right out here.

While sitting in a park.

In broad daylight.

Thank goodness there was no one else around.

"We have to stop, Connor," I whispered, although my body had very different ideas, and my hips sped up, pushing me closer to release.

"I know." His words were barely audible when he buried his face into my neck.

We were both breathing heavily while he continued to guide me back and forth against him.

I couldn't hold back the moan that escaped my lips when an orgasm began to build, and he pulled back to look at my face while I came undone.

"That's it, Isolde. Come for me." Reaching up to grip the back of my head, he slammed my mouth down onto his again, smothering my cry with his lips while pleasure ripped through me in waves.

He kept rocking me with his other hand, prolonging the euphoria, and stars exploded behind my closed eyelids. Slowly, my movements stilled, and he held me to him while I gasped for breath, burying his face into my hair once again. I felt him swallow hard while he struggled to get himself under control.

"The next time we do that, Chosen One, I will be buried deep inside you. That is a promise," he said hoarsely.

And even though I knew it would lead down a dangerous path, a part of me couldn't wait to hold him to it.

CHAPTER NINETEEN

*L*ater that evening, I sat amongst a group of people I never thought I'd see in the same room.

We were gathered in the biggest room in Eve's home, the library. The entire Brisbane contingent of the Order of the Dragon sat at the long table by the window, and I could tell they were all uncomfortable. Given the glares they received from the daywalkers seated on the couches dispersed throughout the room, I couldn't blame them.

I sat on the floor, my back against the wall between two bookshelves. Connor sat opposite me against the wall near the door, his long legs bent with his forearms resting against them. I wished I could melt into the shadows and avoid the occasional glare from Liam, who was leaning against a window. When he wasn't staring at the ground, he would glance between Connor and me. Aurora was in her own corner, glowering at anyone who came near her.

"Well, this is uncomfortable," Anika muttered, and Anthony snorted a laugh, pulling her close to his side on their couch, pressing his lips to her hair and whispering in her ear.

"Yes, indeed. Everyone, do cheer up. We're on the home stretch, and then we can finally all be done with each other," Eve said, clapping her hands together.

She sat on one of the large couches with Ronson beside her, his arm slung across the couch behind her. Patrice shot her a pissed-off look from the head of the long table.

"I'm pretty sure I speak for at least ninety-five percent of the people in this room when I say 'fuck off, Eve'," Connor said while he stared up at the ceiling, giving the impression of boredom, but I could see the tension running through his body when he flexed his hands slowly.

Liam snorted. "You don't speak for me, Connor."

Connor looked over at him, annoyance rippling across his face. "Fine, asshole. You can be part of the five percent on team Eve," he retorted, and Liam's eyes flashed.

I didn't think I'd ever get used to that.

"Fuck you," Liam spat, and I rolled my eyes.

"The pair of you need to shut it," Ronson said before I had the chance to.

That was probably for the best because I would only make things worse if I stepped in the middle of their argument.

"Yes, Dad," Connor muttered, earning him a growl from Ronson.

Anthony struggled to contain a laugh, and I knew he was trying his best to hate Connor but was failing dismally.

"Why are we all here, Eve?" Anika spoke up, sounding exasperated.

"Yes, Eve. Do explain why we are being forced to endure being in a room with 'those people'," Tabitha, one of the daywalkers I had barely engaged with, asked from where she sat in a single armchair.

She was looking directly at the table full of Order members.

"*These people* have been cleaning up the messes of your damn kind for the past several centuries, you pompous bitch," Barbara spat back.

"Okay. How about we all stay on topic?" I asked, using my voice for the first time.

I had the distinct impression that we were all about to descend into one long round of name-calling – or worse – if someone didn't take control of the conversation.

"I agree with Isolde. Let's just accept that we all hate each other and move on, shall we?" Anika said, and I gave her a weak smile.

"For once, I, too, agree with Isolde," Eve said, and I did my best not to rise to her bait. "We are here because we must all be on the same page. Next Saturday is the full moon, which means Connor and Isolde must enter the coven soon to ensure they are near Adam for at least seven days before the spell is completed. And Liam and Aurora will need to remain close to me," Eve said.

Aurora did not look even slightly impressed about that.

I shifted a little while I took in the hungry look in Eve's eyes when she looked at Liam. I knew I had no right to feel jealous, given that we were no longer together and what had happened between Connor and me earlier, but the idea of Liam falling back into bed with Eve made me feel ill.

Liam glanced at Eve briefly before raising an eyebrow at me and jerking his head towards his brother. Connor straightened up and glared right back.

"Why can't I go instead of Isolde?" Liam asked.

Eve arched an eyebrow. "As much as I find it interesting that you want to go in her place, it needs to be one of the girls because we need one of each set of twins in both places," Eve replied.

Beside her, Ronson looked like he was about to say something but was cut off by Liam.

"Fine, I'll go, and Connor can stay here then."

Connor huffed a laugh. "You wouldn't last five minutes. Adam would be able to sniff out your holier-than-thou bullshit and know you weren't me, and then we'd all be fucked. Don't pretend this is about anything other than the fact that you don't want me to be alone with Isolde," Connor said, rising to his feet.

Liam was in front of him in a fraction of a second, breathing heavily. They stood nose to nose, staring each other down.

Eve fanned herself dramatically. "My, my, Isolde. How ever will you choose between these two?" She asked with a sadistic grin.

I squirmed when a number of the others turned to look at me. I had no idea what I was supposed to do, but I certainly wasn't going to get caught in the middle of their pissing contest.

"You're just bitter that they aren't doing that over you," Aurora spoke up, and I choked on a laugh.

Anthony roared with laughter, slapping a hand on his knee. "Oh, I like her too! Can we keep her?"

Anika elbowed him sharply. "Shut up, idiot."

Aurora smiled a little, the first sign that she wasn't entirely broken. I felt a small glimmer of hope that she might be okay after all. I wasn't stupid enough to think that our relationship would ever be what it was, but I didn't want her to suffer for what she'd done when she was a nightwalker.

The whole sleeping with my fiance part might be a struggle to get past, though.

"Boys, you can take them out and measure later. But you are identical, so..." Eve said.

They glared at her briefly before Connor shoved Liam out of his face.

Liam shoved him back.

"For fuck's sake," I said, jumping to my feet and moving towards them in a blur, pushing them apart and holding my hands on both their chests.

"It's like a soap opera," Tabitha said with a smirk.

I ignored her while I glared from one brother to the other. "This is neither the time nor the place for this shit. Get it together, the pair of you," I said quietly.

Neither of them held my gaze for long.

Liam finally stepped back, and Connor covered my hand on his chest. I snatched my hand away and gave him a warning look. He smirked at me and shrugged.

"Asshole," I muttered under my breath while Liam and I both returned to our previous positions, and Connor chuckled.

"Now, before that fantastic display of testosterone, I was informing you all of what needs to happen. Once the sun sets next Saturday, we all need to be ready to move in on Adam's location. Everyone in this room has a part to play, though the twins, particularly Isolde, obviously have the most vital roles."

"What exactly is it that I'm supposed to do?" I asked.

"You're going to use your flames. On both myself and Adam. That's how you'll end it all." She answered matter of factly.

Everyone turned to stare at her.

"So... I'm not just killing Adam? I'm killing you, too?" I asked quietly.

"Perhaps." She showed absolutely no concern at the prospect of her imminent demise.

"What?" Michael asked from where he sat on the other side of her, looking stunned.

I knew he was one of the daywalkers who frequented Eve's bed and wondered if his feelings for her went deeper than the physical relationship I'd assumed it was.

Ronson watched her closely, and his brows knit together while he considered this latest revelation.

I had mixed feelings about this turn of events.

"What are we going to do about Damon and Seth? Or have we forgotten about them?" Liam asked.

I remembered the little whispers I'd heard and wondered again if Damon had been trying to get into my mind or if I was imagining it.

"I will deal with my errant ex-husband and child if they dare to show up. I need all four of you focused on Adam and me," Eve said with a grimace, her tone firm.

I exchanged glances with Liam and Connor before looking at my sister. Aurora just shrugged before looking away. She was still yet to look at me properly, and I knew we'd need to talk soon before I trotted off to take her place within the coven.

Something about all of this felt off. I had the distinct impression that there was more to this all than what we were being told.

Eve had become restless. "Look, I've told you everything now and am bored with this. This meeting is over," Eve said, rising to her feet and sweeping out of the room.

We all watched her leave in stunned silence. Ronson rose swiftly to follow her, his frown still firmly in place.

Slowly, we all rose to our feet, and everyone else left the room until finally, Liam, Connor, Aurora, and I were all that remained.

"Well... absolutely nothing about that made me feel any better," Aurora said. "I'm going back upstairs."

"Aura... wait," I said, and she shook her head at me while she stepped further away from the hand I reached towards her.

"I can't, Isolde. Good luck with what you need to do, but I can't talk to you right now."

"Fine... but at least reach out to Mum and Dad. They need to know you're okay," I said, letting my hand drop back to my side.

There was little humour in her laugh. "I'm not fucking okay, Isolde. Not even close."

With that parting shot, she left the room, and I was once again alone with the two men in my life.

I looked down at the ground, not sure who to look at.

Liam cleared his throat. "You better fucking make sure she comes out of this all alive, Connor," he said.

I closed my eyes, preparing myself for Connor's sarcastic response.

"I will. You have my word," Connor said quietly.

Liam scoffed. "Your word means nothing to me, brother. Make your actions count," he said, stepping towards me and lifting my chin so I looked into his eyes. "Good luck, Isolde." He pressed a kiss to my forehead and walked out.

I stared after him, a lump in my throat that I couldn't make go away, no matter how hard I swallowed.

Connor watched me for a moment, giving me the chance to pull myself back together. "Well... ready to step into the breach?"

I shook my head. "Nope."

"That's the spirit," he said with a smirk.

I followed him when he led the way out of the room. No matter how many times I went over the conversation with Eve in my head, the unease in the pit of my stomach told me we couldn't trust her.

CHAPTER TWENTY

Two days later, I struggled to focus on Connor's words when he tried to instruct me on controlling my humanity around Adam. While Connor had long mastered the ability to switch his breathing and heartbeat off at will, I'd never been put in a position to have to try it, and so far, I was failing miserably.

"If you can't work this out, Isolde, you'll be dead within seconds," Connor said, his eyes flashing while his frustration grew.

My heart continued to beat loudly in my ears.

"It's not simple, and you know it," I replied through gritted teeth.

I was sitting cross-legged on the floor in his room while he paced back and forth near the window. I tried to focus on each breath, willing them to stop. It wasn't as simple as holding my breath, I had discovered.

I was starting to wonder if it was even possible for me. I only had three days before we had to enter the coven. To spend the next seven days locked in a house with the most evil creature on the planet.

Reminding myself of this was not helping my ability to focus.

"I had to work it out pretty fucking quick, Isolde. When I woke up to this life, I was in a room full of nightwalkers, and Eve's voice was screaming in my head to switch it off. My only saving grace was that they had several humans they were keeping alive in that house. I didn't have the luxury of practising for days on end."

"No, but you could go into their damn minds while you worked it out," I snapped and jumped to my feet, choosing to ignore the part about the humans being kept alive in a house full of nightwalkers.

I aimed for the door, but Connor was in front of me instantly, blocking my escape.

He grasped my chin in one hand. "You are not leaving this room until you have mastered this," he said.

I pulled my face out of his grip. "I can't focus with you breathing down my neck!"

Connor stayed where he was, and I refused to step back, not wanting to give him the satisfaction of knowing how much his presence affected me.

"This is nothing compared to what Adam will put you through! You need to learn how to tap into the nightwalker side of yourself. To switch off your heart and embrace the chaos," he said, his tone growing seductive when his gaze dropped to my lips. "Without killing anyone, of course."

I ran my tongue over my lower lip.

We'd not had a repeat performance of our moment in the park in the days since everyone had descended upon the house, but I'd felt the tension mounting. I had successfully avoided situations where Liam and Connor were in the same room. Liam had moved to a room in a different wing of the house.

"You've been pushing me to unleash ever since you first went into my head, Connor. But that's not who I am. I don't have a darker side," I said, and he smirked.

"That's bullshit, and you know it. You're just scared to let that side of you out because you're afraid you'll like her more."

"You think that side of me will be more fun?" I asked, feeling my own eyes flash.

Connor's smirk grew, and he closed the distance between our bodies. My breasts brushed his chest, my body reacting to the electricity running between us when he slid his hand to the back of my neck and began caressing it gently.

"It's possible to tap into the side of yourself that allows you to give in to your desires without crossing over into complete madness, Isolde."

"And what is it you think I desire, Connor?" I asked, attempting to ignore the arousal I could feel rising within me.

"You know exactly what you desire. You're just not ready to accept the inevitable." He brought his lips to my ear. "Don't worry, I'm a patient man. I've waited five hundred years for this madness to end. I can wait however long it takes for you to stop denying what you truly want." He ran his fingers ever so lightly down my back, though I was very aware of the path they followed when he rested his hand on the small of my back, pulling my body flush against his. "Or what you need. But until then," he whispered, lowering his head to brush his lips lightly against mine, "you need to get it the fuck together and play dead." He stepped back, continuing to smirk while he leaned casually against the door.

"Asshole." I was struggling to get myself together while my heart beat wildly in my chest.

"Yes, I am. Now sit your ass back down and try again."

I spun on my heel, marched back over to my spot on the floor, and took a deep breath, attempting to try again.

The following day, I was still no closer to working it out, and I was starting to panic. Connor had moved past flirting to anger, and his frustration made it even harder. I knew his anger wasn't directed at me, and I didn't blame him for erupting at Eve when she enquired how it was going.

Anika and I sat together in the library while I took a break from watching Connor pace back and forth in his room. Anika watched me quietly while I downed several glasses of whiskey. I was pretty sure I'd be classed as an alcoholic soon.

"Maybe this whole thing is useless because the spell won't fucking work anymore anyway, and the whole planet is about to go to hell," I said.

Anika raised her glass to tap it against mine. "We can always hope," she said, a small smile on her lips.

"Yes. What's life without the excitement of an apocalypse anyway, right?" I asked with a laugh.

"Right. Why would you ever want to live a life without the literal fate of the world on your shoulders?" Anika said, getting into the swing of it.

"I know, your life must just be so boring."

She tapped her glass to mine again. "Let's drink to you having a nice, normal, boring life once this is over."

"Amen to that."

"Isolde?"

I looked towards the door to find Patrice and Barbara hovering there. Patrice was eyeing Anika warily, and my friend nodded at her.

"You can join us if you'd like," Anika said.

The two Order members came to sit across from us on one of the overstuffed couches. They sat close together and appeared to be drawing comfort from each other's presence. Barbara's hand hovered over Patrice's thigh briefly before moving it back to her own lap. Patrice's eyes fell first to the bottle of whiskey on the table beside me, then to the glass in my hand.

"I take it there is still no progress with switching off your senses?"

"Not yet. I'm beginning to wonder if it's a skill that is unique to Connor only."

Patrice pursed her lips a little at the mention of Connor, and I could feel her disapproval loud and clear, although she chose not to voice it, much to my relief.

"Perhaps you need to try meditating?" Barbara suggested, and I cocked my head to the side, considering her words.

"I guess it can't hurt to try."

Patrice cleared her throat. "We just wanted to come and check on you. Although we've known for a long time the responsibilities that would fall on your shoulders at some point, I just... I've come to care about you greatly since you became a part of our family, and I don't think anyone has really checked on how you're handling everything after all of the latest revelations," Patrice said.

Barbara nodded silently, her eyes falling to the glass in my hand.

"Honestly... I'm trying not to think about it all too much. Because if I focus on the fact that the fate of the world is literally in my hands, there is a very good chance I'm going to end up rocking in a corner, crying," I said, refusing to acknowledge the fear that kept trying to break it's way through the box I'd mentally shoved it into.

Patrice studied me closely, her eyes warm when she smiled. "I understand that. Just remember, I will always be here for you. Regardless of what happens, we will find a way through this all. You aren't in this alone."

I felt a tightness in my chest, and I nodded at her, swallowing the lump that had formed in my throat.

"Thank you," I said quietly.

"We should leave you ladies to it. Please, if you need help with working out switching it off, come and find me. I will help you any way that I can."

They got up, and Patrice moved to squeeze my shoulder before they left the room together. Barbara slid her hand into Patrice's when they reached the door and looked back over her shoulder, giving me a sad smile before they disappeared down the hallway.

CHAPTER TWENTY-ONE

I returned to my room a little later and lay on the bed, staring at the ceiling while I recalled the conversation with Patrice. I hadn't even considered trying meditation before now, but it had worked when I was learning how to control my fire abilities.

It certainly couldn't hurt to give it a try. I'd exhausted every other avenue before now, and unless I got this sorted out now, we were completely screwed.

Closing my eyes, I focused on the ticking sound from the ceiling fan while it spun lazily above me. With each click, I felt the tension in my shoulders ease and began to feel weightless, like I was floating.

I imagined myself frozen in time, my body no longer dependent on the air filling my lungs nor my heart pumping blood through my veins.

My breathing slowed after what may have been only a few seconds or an eternity.

In my mind, the instinctual movements of all creatures that drew breath no longer held me captive.

I opened my eyes when I felt a change wash over me. The

rhythmic sensation of my breaths no longer forced my chest to rise and fall.

Placing a hand on my chest, I searched for the feel of my heartbeat. I couldn't find it.

Moving slowly from my bed, I placed one foot tentatively on the ground, scared that if I moved too fast, I would undo whatever I had managed to do. Until now, I'd never realised how reliant I was on using my sense of smell. While I'd not noticed any scents in my room before, now that there was no smell, it was disorientating, and I had to fight the urge to start breathing again simply to have it back.

Placing one cautious step in front of the other, I went down the hall to the room Connor had claimed when he was here.

He had been slipping away at sunset each night to briefly return to the coven and plant false memories of Aurora and Will within the minds of each nightwalker to avoid any suspicions being raised. But he returned only a few hours later each time, the exhaustion radiating from him. He had been keeping to himself, aside from when I spent time with him or if Eve was pestering him.

I knocked on the door and waited silently. The door opened, and he looked at me curiously for a few seconds before he became aware of the change.

"You did it," he whispered, his shoulders sagging slightly when he ran his eyes over me.

"Yes... I think we should go tonight. It was hard enough getting this to work. If I stay here much longer, I think my hold over this will slip away," I said, and he nodded slowly.

"If you're sure? It means an extra day?"

"It's now or never," I said, with a resolve I didn't quite feel.

"As you wish." Connor didn't look particularly enthused.

"I just need to do one thing first."

"Let me guess - you need to go and say a dramatic goodbye to my brother," he said, leaning against the door frame and crossing his arms.

"Don't be a jerk, Connor. Yes, I need to go and say goodbye to Liam. Be ready to leave just before sunset, okay?"

"Whatever you want to do, Isolde. You're in charge, after all."

I ignored the bite in his words and turned away, leaving him glowering in the doorway while he watched me walk away in search of his brother.

While I moved through the house, I briefly wondered if I'd slipped and begun breathing again when the overwhelming metallic smell of blood hit me. Looking to my right, I noted that I was in the section of the house that the Order Members had set themselves up in while they were here, and I realised with a start that it was their blood that I was smelling... That it was the only thing that I was smelling.

Pushing the thought aside, I continued on to the room where I knew Liam had made his own after vacating the one we'd shared.

Hesitating briefly, I steeled myself and knocked, hearing a rustling noise inside before he answered the door, shirtless.

I swallowed and tried not to admire the body that was no longer mine to look at.

His expression slowly hardened when he ran his eyes over me.

"I see you succeeded," he asked, crossing his arms over his chest.

"Yeah. I just wanted to come and say goodbye."

"Okay. You've done your duty then."

I didn't think the hurt would ever fade at how dismissive he had become towards me.

"I know that things between us are... strained... but this might be the last time we see each other. I have no idea if this will work, and I wanted to see you before I go."

He sighed and tipped his head back, swallowing hard momentarily before looking at me again.

"I'm sorry," he said, stepping towards me and pulling me into his arms.

Closing my eyes, I wrapped my arms around him. I buried my

head into his chest, fighting to keep from breathing in his scent and undoing what had taken me days to accomplish.

"I'm the one who's sorry, Liam. So fucking sorry."

He shushed me, continuing to hold me close and resting his cheek on top of my head.

"I know you are, Isolde. I know," he whispered into my hair, and I struggled to hold back the tears threatening to break free.

I eventually stepped back and wiped away the single tear that had escaped.

"Be careful, okay? Not just with Adam. I don't trust Connor, no matter how much any of you try to convince me he's been faking the evil side all these years."

I didn't want to argue with him again, so I simply nodded.

"I promise to be careful. Please look out for Aurora. I know she's being difficult, but if you can somehow get her to see our parents or even just talk to them, I think that will help a little," I asked quietly, and Liam nodded.

"I'll do my best."

"And maybe... I know this is asking a lot, but can you try to work on the bond? I need to be able to contact you guys, and getting into your mind would be helpful... Even if it's just while we're asleep."

"Like Connor did with you, you mean?" He asked, his features hardening again.

"Like you've also done in the past when you came to save me in that house."

He surveyed me quietly. "I'll see what I can do."

He continued to scan my face, and I waited for him to speak again, not wanting to push my luck with this tenuous truce we'd reached.

"It's really over, isn't it? You and me, I mean."

Those words hit me like a punch to the stomach... or, more accurately, to the heart.

He waited for me to answer, the expression on his face doing nothing to make my answer any easier to say out loud.

"I..." I knew what I needed to say, but I took the coward's way out. "I thought, when you said we were done, that was you drawing the line?"

His eyes narrowed. "You're going to force me to be the one to end it, once and for all, aren't you?"

I began to stammer a meaningless response, but he cut me off. "You're right, Isolde. There is no going back for us, not when we both know what you refuse to admit to yourself."

Another verbal punch landed in my chest, and the small amount of control I'd had over my emotions cracked open, my eyes welling up with tears. I was definitely going to hell for being such a scummy person.

He shook his head. "Be safe, Isolde."

"Bye, Liam," I said quietly, watching him turn and walk back into the room, shutting the door firmly in front of me.

CHAPTER TWENTY-TWO

The sun slowly slipped below the horizon, and the closer we got to the enormous mansion Adam had claimed for the coven, high on the hill in Teneriffe, the quieter I became.

I tried to ignore the nausea rolling through me but failed miserably, and I stopped to hurl in a bush.

Connor had been a step ahead of me and turned back at the sound. "Hey, it's going to be okay. I won't let anything happen to you," he said, turning me to face him once I straightened up.

He pulled me to his chest, and I allowed myself to draw some comfort from him before stepping back, resisting the urge to take a deep breath. We were still a few streets away, and I knew I needed to get myself under control.

"How will we explain why we're coming in just after sunset?" I asked when we began walking again.

"If he sees us coming in, we got caught in a building and had to wait until the sun went down. I'm going to tell him about Will and that I've been comforting you in his absence," he said, and I shot him a look.

"And when you say 'comforting', you really mean…"

"That we've been at it like rabbits all day, yes," Connor smirked, and I glowered at him. "It's what he is going to expect, Isolde. Aurora's sexual appetite whilst she was with the coven was insatiable. When I said she'd fucked everyone, I meant everyone. Including Adam."

"And including you?" I asked, not sure I wanted to know.

Connor stopped again, and I reluctantly halted beside him. I couldn't look at him when he turned my body to face his and ran his hands up my arms.

"I have never taken advantage of your sister, Isolde. And that's what it would have been. Taking advantage of a woman who had no control over her actions. I might be an evil mastermind, but I draw the line at fucking someone who no longer has access to free will." He lifted my chin gently, and I met his piercing blue eyes with my own.

I nodded slowly.

"I saw you plant the memory of her going down on you in her mind," I said quietly, and the muscle in his jaw tensed.

"A necessary evil. And something that took every ounce of my self-restraint because god help me, I was weak that night. I wanted to give in, to fuck her into oblivion and forget about you. But I couldn't. I couldn't do that to either of you." His eyes searched mine, almost like he was begging me to understand.

And I did. I'd felt his despair that night.

"Do you mean... In all the years you've been with the coven... You've never slept with any of the nightwalkers?"

Connor shook his head slowly. "No. Obviously, I was no monk, but... Something about the idea of fucking someone who was under Adam's control never sat well with me. No matter how much many of them tried over the centuries. I learnt early on how to plant those memories so that no one suspected anything, but that's all it has ever been."

"I feel bad that I *don't* feel bad about the fact that I may have to have to kill Eve along with Adam. I hate her for everything she's put me and the others through, but I think I hate her even more for what she's forced you to endure over the last five centuries," I said, reaching up and touching his face.

He didn't have a smart-ass reply but leaned into my touch and closed his eyes.

"Let's just get through these next few days, and then we can work on making me feel like the last five hundred years were worth it," he said, taking my hand and kissing the inside of my palm before lowering it back to my side.

"Okay," I said quietly.

He swallowed hard, looking at me for another few seconds.

Then he nodded. "Let's go."

When we finally arrived at the house, I followed Connor through the front door and tried to ignore the overwhelming sensation that hit me with so many nightwalkers in one place. I hadn't thought about how this would feel, which wasn't pleasant. It was like a thousand bugs were crawling over my skin.

I shook my head instinctively, trying to shake off the feeling.

"Connor? Where have you been?" Adam's voice rang through the foyer, and I froze behind Connor.

I heard footsteps drawing closer, and I could see the muscles in Connor's back tense underneath his shirt. Being so close to the creature who had brutally murdered my fiance filled me with a mixture of rage and dread.

But with each step that rang out across the foyer, the strangest sensation grew within me. I felt like I was being pulled in multiple directions, and the sound of a million whispers grew louder in my ears. Connor had tried to describe how it would feel when I was affected by the hive mind, but nothing could have prepared me for this. Despite my feelings about Adam, I could feel something inside of me trying to move closer to the owner of that cold, hard voice.

"We lost track of time this morning and had to take sanctuary in a building to await the sunset." Connor's voice had changed tone, and I recognised it from when I had last come face to face with Adam, just before my transition.

This was the Connor I had thought was just as evil as Adam, who I had believed was responsible for my sister's transition. His voice was cold and devoid of emotion, just like Adam's.

Swallowing hard, I pushed aside the alarm at seeing this side of him once again.

"What caused you to lose track of the time?" Adam had stopped directly in front of Connor, and I peered over his shoulder to meet Adam's terrifying gaze.

His eyes bored into mine, and the whispers grew louder. The urge to move closer grew more intense, and I balled my hands in fists at my side. I twisted my face into the bored expression Connor I imagined wore in front of me while I forced myself to hold his gaze.

This was the longest I'd ever looked at him, and I could see now that there was a striking resemblance between him and the two most important men in my life. There was no denying how attractive he was, with his muscular body and short brown hair.

Still, all I felt was the evil beneath the surface, obscuring any attraction I may have felt for him.

"We had a run-in with Isolde. She killed William." Connor's tone remained flat and bored.

Adam lifted one eyebrow slowly when he looked at me. "I see... and how is our girl handling this?" He asked, his eyes never leaving my face.

A strange sense of revulsion and attraction ran through me while my body reacted to the hunger in his gaze. The whispers in my head grew louder still.

I was relieved that Connor stood before me while I fought against that pull towards Adam.

"I've been helping her overcome her pain," Connor said.

Although I still couldn't see his face, I knew without a doubt that he was wearing his trademark smirk.

"I'll just bet you have." Adam's lips curled up into a sneer.

I forced my lips to lift into a coy smile, staring into those piercing blue eyes that were cold and deadly.

"Would you like to join us, Adam?" I rasped out while fighting an internal struggle between the side of me wanting to get closer to him and the logical part of my mind that knew I needed to get as far away as possible.

Adam was too busy surveying me to notice when Connor froze for a fraction of a second, the muscles in his back tensing up.

"I'm sure Connor can handle you all alone for now. We both know his aversion to sharing. Maybe later, though, if he isn't able to satiate your hunger," Adam said, giving me a terrifying smile.

A low growl rumbled through Connor. "Oh, don't worry, Adam. By the time I'm done with her, she won't be able to walk straight. If I'm ever done with her." He reached behind his back, pulling me around to stand before him, my back flush against his chest while he reached up and gripped my throat, pinning me to him.

My eyes widened, and I leaned into my instinctual reaction, playing up my arousal. Not that I needed to do much. It was almost impossible for me not to be turned on when he stood this close.

Adam nodded, his eyes running over my body. "Don't forget to fuck that pretty little mouth while you're at it, Connor. Put it to good use," he said, grasping my chin and forcing me to look into his eyes.

He leered at me for a little longer before sauntering off. Connor kept me close while he began moving through the house. I tried to ignore the smell of blood that followed us towards the back of the house, hoping I wouldn't come across the source of it when my mouth began to water and my predatory senses began to kick in. I realised too late that we hadn't thought about what I would do about blood while we were here.

Connor pulled me into the room I recognised as his bedroom from his memories. He turned and pushed the door closed behind me, pressing his hand flat against the door next to my ear, and glared down at me.

"What the fuck was that?" He asked, his voice barely louder than a whisper.

"You told me I needed to act like Aurora," I replied, matching his volume.

"I didn't mean to proposition Adam the first chance you got! What the hell would you have done if he took you up on your offer?" He pushed me back against the door, and I gasped when the arousal I felt earlier came rushing to the surface.

Connor's scowl took on a hungry gleam, and his gaze dropped to my lips.

"That would have been when you jumped into his mind and planted the image of him fucking my pretty little mouth," I said, and he placed his hand on my throat again.

"I don't think you realise how much effort goes into jumping into the mind of a sadistic killer and altering his memories, Isolde, but if I have to spend the next week constantly fucking around in his head, the less I'm going to be able to protect you in here," he said in a low growl beside my ear.

I prayed we were quiet enough to avoid being heard by the nightwalkers with their enhanced hearing.

"You seem to forget I don't need protection," I hissed back, and he glowered at me.

"What are you going to do, kill them all? You're meant to be blending in. You can't kill them until the full moon, at the very least. So yes, you'll need my protection here. Do *not* draw unnecessary attention to yourself." His eyes flashed.

"Which is it, act like Aurora or a meek little mouse?"

Connor stepped back, pinched his nose's bridge between two fingers, and closed his eyes. I seemed to be very good at bringing this reaction out of him.

My body screamed out for his touch again, and I shook it off. "Where is my room?" I asked, suddenly needing to put some space between us.

Connor's eyes snapped open, and he shook his head. "You are

not going anywhere in this house alone. What the fuck is wrong with you?"

That was an excellent question. I knew, logically, that the safest place for me was by Connor's side. However, I felt white, hot rage shoot through me at the command in his tone. "I am not some little damsel in distress, Connor."

"Oh, I'm fucking aware." His eyes flashed again in response, and he glared at me for a long time, his jaw clenched while he ground his teeth.

"Fine," he spat out, wrenching the door open. "Two doors down, across the hall. Knock yourself the fuck out."

We stared each other down for a few moments before I stepped out the door. He remained silent while I walked down the hall and opened the door he'd pointed towards. I looked back briefly, seeing his eyes narrow, before I stepped inside and slammed the door.

I heard him do the same seconds later, and the walls shook.

CHAPTER TWENTY-THREE

As soon as I was in the room, I regretted letting my pride get the better of me, and I knew I'd made a grave error.

Not only was I now alone in a house full of evil vampires, but I'd set myself up in the bedroom of my ex-fiancé and twin sister, where they had taken part in all sorts of shenanigans, judging by the array of extreme sex toys scattered around the room.

What the hell had I been thinking? I'd been so caught up in trying to prove I could take care of myself and didn't need Connor's help that I'd entered my own personal nightmare instead. And what was I going to do with myself now? At least Connor's room had a bookshelf. There wasn't a single book in this room.

Was this defiance I was feeling part of the hive mind, forcing me to put myself into a potentially dangerous situation to ensure I couldn't be kept from Adam? Or was I just once again running away from my attraction to Connor?

Resigning myself to making the best of this situation that I could, I started to tidy the mess up, using a pillowcase as a garbage bag and throwing all of Will's and Aurora's crap into it before shoving it into the cupboard. I spied a spare set of sheets on the top shelf and set about stripping and remaking the bed, doing what little I could to remove any trace of them within these walls while trying not to wonder who was responsible for doing the laundry around here.

Once I was done, I flopped down on the bed and stared at the ceiling, feeling like the walls were closing in on me.

How the hell am I going to make it through the next eight days?

I'd needed space from Connor, but I felt the loss of his presence the second I had it.

I refused to acknowledge the reason why.

Somehow, I managed to drift off to sleep, pretending I wasn't trapped in a house full of soulless creatures led by the most evil man in the world, even while the whispers continued to wrap their way through my thoughts.

The sound of the door opening ripped me from sleep, and I sat up quickly. A nightwalker I didn't recognise stood in the doorway, staring at me. His piercing blue eyes glowed in the darkness.

If my heart were still beating, it would be thundering in my ears, but now I couldn't even hold my breath.

"Adam tells me that Will is no longer with us. I thought I should come and offer my condolences," he said, his voice low and husky.

A ripple of disgust ran through me.

"I'm fine. Connor has been a great comfort," I replied, leaning into the act that Connor had used earlier.

"Pfft, Connor. He won't be enough for you. You know he hates to share." He entered the room fully, and I stiffened when he closed the door behind him.

"He doesn't need to share." I kept my voice steady, a flirtatious smile playing across my lips, even while I was screaming inside my head.

"Yeah? He's so good that you aren't craving the touch of others?

He must be magic then, to be able to keep you satisfied... But he's not here now..." He continued moving closer, like a predator stalking its prey.

I wasn't going to be his victim, though. "I'm not interested. You can leave now." I stood up and nodded towards the door.

He wasn't going to leave easily, though. "Just a quick fuck, Aurora. Connor will never even know," he whispered, leaning in and trying to kiss me.

I wrenched my head away. "I said I wasn't interested."

"You heard her, Bastien. You can leave now," Connor said, leaning casually against the door frame with his arms crossed.

I resisted the urge to sag with relief.

"I was just offering my services to Aurora to manage her grief."

"Already got it covered, Bastien," Connor replied.

Seeing the tension running through him, I wasn't fooled by his relaxed tone.

"Come on, Connor. You know one man isn't enough for our girl. We can share." Bastien just wasn't getting the hint, keeping his eyes on me.

Connor moved in a blur and appeared between Bastien and me. "You know I don't like to share, Bastien. And it turns out she just hadn't ridden the right man yet. Because she is more than satisfied now." Connors's voice was low, and there was no mistaking the warning in his tone.

I suppressed a smirk when Bastien shrank back, leaving me unprepared when Connor spun to face me and kissed me hungrily. I moaned involuntarily, moving to pull him closer when the headiness of his kiss pushed away the whispers that had started growing again, but he stepped back and faced Bastien again.

"Whatever, man," Bastien replied and slunk out of the room, off to find someone else to fuck.

Connor stayed perfectly still with his back to me for the longest time.

That was fine. I needed a minute to get my libido back under control.

A slight shudder ran through him, and he turned very slowly, flashing me a look of warning before heading back out into the hall. I hesitated before following him.

He held his bedroom door open until I crossed the threshold, closing the door behind me.

"Was that a fun little experiment, Isolde?" He whispered.

I glowered at him. "I was handling that just fine."

"Bullshit."

We glared at each other for the longest time, neither wanting to be the first to give in.

"Just... Stay near me at all times. And try not to piss anyone off," he said finally before turning towards his bed and flopping backwards on it to stare up at the ceiling.

"Does that include you too?" I said, keeping my voice low.

He propped himself up on both elbows to look at me again.

"Since when do you give a shit about pissing me off?"

"Oh, I don't. I just wasn't sure if you were expecting some sort of special treatment now that you're my self-appointed bodyguard." I moved towards the armchair in the corner and picked up the book he had left sitting on the small table beside it.

"Seriously? The Iliad? Are you trying to be a cliche?" I asked, flicking through a few pages.

"You're telling me you're familiar with Ancient Greek Literature?" He asked, raising an eyebrow while he watched me closely.

"I was a history major, remember?"

"How could I forget? That lecture I sat in on was definitely interesting. I had forgotten about the joys of the Spanish Inquisition and their manic need to eradicate the world of witchcraft."

I put the book down and returned his interested gaze. "What was it like? Living through all of that whilst being surrounded by actual evil?"

Connor shrugged. "To be honest, it didn't affect me much. It wasn't like I couldn't control their weak little minds if they had actually been intelligent enough to go after the real creatures of darkness. But they were too busy attacking women who were wise before their time. Or listening to the idle gossip of small-minded people making up stories to make themselves relevant."

"I still struggle to wrap my head around the fact that you have all lived through these time periods that seem so foreign to me."

"I never imagined being alive this long. How I've survived all these years still seems surreal to me. When I was human, I spent all my time bedding women and avoiding the responsibility of taking on running the estate. If I'd known what was going to happen, I don't know." He shrugged. "Maybe I'd have done things differently."

"The joys of hindsight, huh? I keep thinking of what I would have done differently before all this happened, but honestly, I don't know what I would have done... Maybe not agree to marry a man who was fucking my sister," I said sarcastically.

Connor snorted. "I don't know what you saw in William. He was never worthy of either of you. But especially not you."

I cocked my head while I studied him. "I think this is the most normal conversation we've ever had," I said.

He cocked an eyebrow, and his lips quirked up into a smirk. "True. I'm losing my edge. It's been a long week. Don't get used to it."

"Oh, I know better than to think this would last. I'm sure you'll be back to your regular flirty, asshole self in no time."

"Just give me ten minutes, and I'll be back to seducing you, don't worry."

I refused to admit to myself that I was looking forward to it.

"By the way, I took the liberty of sending one of the minions out to obtain blood bags," Connor said, waving his hand towards a small fridge beside his bed that I'd not noticed previously.

"Um... since when do nightwalkers use blood bags?"

"Well, obviously, I controlled his mind to send him on the errand

and wiped his memory afterwards," he said, his tone indicating that he thought that was the stupidest question I'd ever asked.

"And yet... you have a fridge... So this isn't the first time you've done that. Has no one wondered why you even have a fridge?" I continued to push, and Connor glared at me.

"Do you want the fucking blood or not, Isolde?"

"Is it human or animal blood?"

"Human," he said, and I crossed my arms in response to the challenge in his eyes.

"And what if I refuse to drink human blood?"

"Then you better get ready for the bloodlust to set in because I'm not getting you animal blood. They will sniff that shit out in an instant, and then I'll be spending all my time in their heads when they keep coming in here, wondering why the fuck I have animal blood in this house."

I cocked my head to the side. "So that's the only reason? It's not because you take delight in forcing me to ingest human blood?"

"No, Isolde. Regardless of my stellar personality, I'm not actively trying to force you to do something you don't want to do," Connor said, pinching the bridge of his nose yet again.

"Fine," I said, moving towards the fridge.

He didn't move from the bed, watching while I reached inside and pulled one of the bags out, staring down at it.

"How the hell am I meant to get the blood out?"

Connor rolled his eyes before getting up. He crossed to his cupboard and grabbed a glass from under a pile of clothes. I felt my chest tighten when I realised how much of his life he had been forced to keep hidden. Taking the bag from me, he ripped it open with his teeth and poured the contents into the glass before pressing it into my hand.

I stared at the glass of crimson liquid. My mouth started to water now when the scent grew stronger. I turned my back to him, unable to drink while he stared at me so intently. It felt like he'd set me a test, and I wasn't sure if drinking it would mean I passed or failed.

My hand shook slightly when I raised the glass to my lips. Connor stepped up behind me, sliding an arm around my waist.

"I've got you," he whispered in my ear.

I nodded slightly and finally took my first taste.

The difference between animal blood and human blood was almost indescribable. I could feel every molecule coat inside my mouth while every tastebud screamed alive. At first, it seemed hot and thick and nearly cloying when the taste of pure human life force rocketed through my senses.

I swallowed, letting it slide down my throat. It was strangely cooling when it finally fully quenched that burning feeling I'd had in the back of my throat ever since I had been turned. If blood were whiskey, animal blood would be a Johnnie Walker, and human blood would be a Glenfiddich, aged for twenty-six years.

I tipped the glass up faster and began gulping the contents down. I felt Connor shift slightly behind me, and my hands tightened on the glass, a low growl starting in the back of my throat.

"Easy, Isolde, easy," he breathed, not moving a single muscle.

Slowly, the bloodlust faded, and I came back to myself. When the realisation of what I'd just done washed over me, I hated what I'd become even more.

CHAPTER TWENTY-FOUR

Thirty-six hours in this god-forsaken house, and I was ready to climb the walls.

The whispering in my head came and went, driving me slowly crazy. It seemed to be whenever Adam was near Connor's end of the house. The closer he got, the more I felt like I was about to jump straight through the wall to be near him.

After begrudgingly accepting that I needed to remain close to Connor, we'd stayed in his room, catching up on some sleep while taking turns watching the door.

We were rationing the blood bags. I'd tried not to drink too much, not wanting to develop a taste for human blood any more than necessary, and I knew my reaction to it was stopping Connor from drinking it as much as he usually would.

We'd fallen into a somewhat comfortable arrangement until a knock had come an hour ago, commanding us to join everyone in the large formal room downstairs. Connor had squeezed my hand before leading me out of the relative safety of his room to join the largest group of nightwalkers I'd ever witnessed.

I'd seen this room before, in a memory that Connor had dragged me into when Aurora and Will were taking part in a vampire orgy. And now it seemed that I was to get my own front-row seat.

I was wearing some of Aurora's clothes that I'd smuggled out of her room when I was brave enough to leave Connor's room. Now, I was sitting on his lap in one of the large-overstuffed armchairs, wearing little more than a corset and a flimsy skirt. It appeared that the nightwalker version of my sister preferred to wear very little clothing. I struggled against the urge to cover myself, and Connor squeezed my hip gently.

We'd been sitting here for almost an hour, both maintaining our masks of boredom, while Connor ran a hand lazily up and down my thigh. I was busily singing children's nursery rhymes in my head so as not to give in to the growing arousal. Adam sat across the room from us, receiving a blow job from one of his many minions. It was the second we'd been forced to watch since we'd sat here.

I couldn't even look away, as I knew that nightwalker Aurora would have been more than happy to partake in the activities.

Hybrid Isolde was fighting the urge to throw up, although the whispers grew louder every time Adam climaxed, and it had taken every ounce of my self-control not to move closer.

Multiple couples were in various stages of undress, and the constant chorus of moans echoed through the room.

"Try to relax." Connor's words were barely louder than a whisper, and he ran his lips up my neck.

"This is fucking torture," I whispered back while I turned my face towards him and nuzzled into his neck.

"You think it's torture for you? I'm fighting a raging hard-on right now, and every time you move, it's making it even harder."

I smirked at him and wriggled my butt. He groaned before glaring at me.

"Is there a reason you two aren't participating? I'm surprised, Aurora. Why aren't you lining up to take your place before Adam?" A female nightwalker sidled up beside us, looking down at Connor's hand on my thigh with a sneer.

"Fuck off, Sabine. I won't be sharing tonight, so you can just run along now," Connor said in a cool tone, fixing her with a stare that would have sent an average person running.

Sabine just snorted before rejoining the couple she'd been with previously, falling to her knees between the male's legs and taking him in her mouth while the couple continued kissing each other hungrily.

"Connor, if you aren't going to share, then at least do more than tease our girl. I haven't heard the sweet sounds of her coming for days now, and that just won't do," Adam said while he guided the head of the male in front of him roughly up and down along his shaft, fucking his mouth furiously even while he watched us with suspicion.

Connor's grip on my hip tightened, and I felt him tense beneath me. His lips were pressed to my neck again, close to my ear.

"I'll go into their minds and make them think they are seeing us together," he whispered, and I shook my head.

I turned my head so that it looked like I was kissing his neck to everyone else. "That will take too long and too much effort to do that with this many people," I whispered.

I pulled back slightly, reaching down and slowly guiding his hand further up my thigh. His eyes widened before he remembered to look bored. I leaned closer again, my lips grazing his ear, and I felt a shiver run through him.

"Make me come."

Thankfully, no one could see his face and neck clearly when he searched my face and swallowed hard. Using his other hand, he held my head in place and turned his face to run his lips up my neck to whisper in my ear. "Are you sure?"

"Yes," I said breathily, and his fingers worked their way beneath the sorry excuse for a skirt and slipped beneath the tiny g-sting I was wearing. He hissed when he ran a finger through my arousal.

"Didn't take you for a voyeur," he whispered, and I moaned

quietly when he slowly moved his finger up to the bundle of nerves that was screaming for his touch.

He moved his finger in a slow circle, eliciting another moan.

The whispers in my mind grew louder, and I attempted to block them out, knowing Adam was watching us intently.

"It's not from what is happening around us." My voice was so low I was surprised he could hear me.

"Oh yeah? What's it from then?" He applied more pressure while he continued circling, and I struggled to maintain control, focusing on keeping my heart from beating or accidentally drawing breath.

The second part was the hardest because all I wanted to do was gasp at the sensations running through my body.

"You know what it's from."

"Gonna need to hear the words," he replied, moving his finger down and sliding it inside, his thumb taking over and applying pressure to where I still needed the friction.

He used his finger in a come hither action, finding my g-spot and working me inside and out.

"Say it," he growled, and my hips began to move of their own accord.

"Fuck," I said, the word coming out in a slow moan. "You, it's all for you."

He yanked my head down to crush his lips to mine while he moved his hand faster, and my orgasm continued to build. I rode his hand, feeling how hard he was against my butt with each thrust of my hips.

"God damn it, woman, I promised you the next time you came, it would be on my cock."

I cried out, the orgasm exploding through me. I heard Adam's appreciative laugh, the whispers the loudest they'd ever been.

I tried to ignore the fact that I'd just come in front of an audience. Somehow, I managed to keep my lungs and heart from moving, but it was a struggle.

I stayed where I was, slumped into Connor's neck, while the orgasm slowly faded.

"I want you," I whispered, and I felt Connor jerk underneath me.

He lifted me off him and was on his feet in a flash.

"I see you still prefer fucking without an audience, Connor." Adam's voice rang out behind us when Connor swept me up in his arms and moved at lightning speed, taking us to his room once again.

He set me down when he kicked the door shut behind him.

"How much of this is the hive mind talking?" He asked, inspecting me closely.

I looked up at him through lowered lashes.

The whispers had once again subsided to a dull hum now that we'd left Adam on the floor below.

"I'm one hundred percent in control of my mind, Connor. I have been ever since we walked away from Adam the first night we walked through those doors. And I need you to fuck me right now."

Connor reached to tangle his hand in my hair, tugging my head back, his eyes boring into mine.

"Put the protection spell up," he said, his words low.

My eyes widened. "Why?"

"Because I plan on fucking you so hard that you lose all control, and when your heart is beating so fast it echoes in your ears, I don't want to be worrying about who can fucking hear it while you scream my name." He stepped back, and I swallowed hard before raising my arms.

"Hide and protect us," I said shakily.

The magic began to crackle around us.

"Good girl," Connor said.

I felt his words shoot straight to my core, even while I distantly noted the absence of the whispers.

He advanced towards me and pushed me back against the door, kissing me roughly, and I moaned against his lips.

He chuckled. "Already so eager."

He began to kiss his way down my body, yanking the corset down to expose my breasts before bending to suck one peak, then the other, into his mouth. I arched my back, fingers weaving through his hair, and the control I'd held over my breathing finally snapped.

I moaned, and my heart began to beat wildly in my chest. "Good call on the spell."

Instead of answering, he flicked his tongue before moving further down my body. Dropping to his knees, he ripped my skirt and underwear down in one swift motion, and I stepped out of them. He looked up at me while his finger began circling the swollen bundle of nerves again before he lowered his head and sucked it between his lips.

I cried out, and he chuckled when I wove my fingers through his hair, gripping so tightly it had to cause him pain.

"That's it," he said, continuing to suck.

I felt the vibrations of his voice run through me, and he slipped one finger inside me, pumping in and out slowly a few times before inserting a second. I could already feel another orgasm building, and he hummed against my clit while he crooked his fingers to hit right where I needed it.

"Oh god, I'm coming!" Pleasure rocketed through me when I came, and I moaned, throwing my head back.

He continued to suck even while I writhed against him, unsure if I wanted to get away or pull him closer.

"That was fucking beautiful," he said, looking up at me while I struggled to get my breath back.

He rose quickly to his feet and spun me so my back was to him, guiding us both towards the edge of the bed while he continued playing with my clit. I gasped when he pushed me forward so that my hands hit the bed and my butt met his crotch.

He had his clothes off at record speed. I turned to watch when his hand slid up and down his shaft a few times before lining up with my entrance, holding my gaze while he worked his way inside.

We moaned together when he began moving slowly, getting

deeper with each thrust. Once he worked his way in fully, he reached forward and yanked me upright so that my back was against his chest. He wrapped his hand around my throat and turned my head to the side so our eyes met in the mirror on the built-in wardrobe.

The sight of him fucking me in the mirror was almost enough to have me coming once more.

He reached around with the other hand, returning his finger to the same spot that had me screaming moments before while he thrust hard into me, and I cried out again.

"That's it. Scream my name, Isolde. Remember who it is that's fucking you senseless right now."

His whispered words burned like fire through my body.

"Fuck, Connor! Don't stop."

My words sent him into action, and he began fucking me harder until I came again, tightening around him.

"I'm not even close to done, Isolde."

He pulled out of me before tossing me onto my back on the bed, throwing both my ankles over his shoulders and folding me in half before thrusting into me again. He hit a whole range of new places at this angle, and I moaned again when I started seeing stars.

"God, Connor." I was incapable of coherent thought now, unable to think of anything except how he had my body singing.

He reached between us, stroking me until I came again, screaming his name, and he smiled.

"That's right."

He slowed, easing both my legs down. Although it hadn't hurt, it felt good to change positions, and I wrapped my legs around his waist while he bent forward to kiss me, far gentler than I expected when he kept his weight off me, resting on his forearms.

"I've thought about this so often since I saw you in that lecture hall, Isolde. But this," he whispered, rolling his hips at a leisurely pace while I gripped his arms and pulled him in close with my legs. "This is better than I ever imagined. You own every part of me."

His voice was rough, and I returned his kiss while he moved his hips faster, pushing us towards finding our release together.

"Connor," I moaned.

My eyes rolled back in my head when he hit just the right spot, and I tumbled over the edge, taking him with me this time, our cries mingling together.

"God, you're beautiful." He buried his face in my neck, and I hugged him close.

I knew we'd just crossed a line, and now there was no going back.

CHAPTER TWENTY-FIVE

Several hours later, I lay beside Connor, breathing heavily after our latest tumble between the sheets. After weeks of sexual tension, we had more than made up for it, but now the guilt was starting to set in, and I tried not to think about the fact that I had done precisely what Liam had predicted.

"I can hear you thinking from over here," Connor said, his arm slung over his eyes.

I turned to look at him, admiring his naked body while he stretched out beside me. Every inch of his perfect body was on display and threatened to derail me from my maudlin thoughts.

"I just... I can't help but feel like we've just crossed a line we shouldn't have. With everything going on, the literal fate of the world is on my shoulders, and I've just given in to my lust without a second thought about anyone else." I could feel myself starting to spiral down into a mood.

Connor lifted his arm and turned his head to look at me. "And that's exactly why I told you it was much easier giving in to the night-walker side. Putting aside the murdering part, which definitely sucks, the fact that they just do what they want without having to worry about what is right or wrong has its advantages."

I groaned, and I rolled my eyes.

He moved towards me before grasping my chin to force me to look at him. "Let me ask you, did you enjoy everything we just did?"

"It's not that simple."

"Yes, it is. Answer the question. And remember that I was there for every single moan, scream and orgasm, so I already know the answer. I just want you to be honest with yourself for a change," he said, staring at me intently.

I swallowed, unable to look away from his eyes. "Yes," I whispered, swallowing when he flashed me his trademark smirk.

"There's my girl," he said, leaning down to whisper the words in my ear.

I shivered at the feel of his breath on my skin. "But that just makes me selfish," I said breathily when he began kissing his way down my neck slowly.

"Good. With all the shit we've had dumped on us, we deserve the chance to be selfish," he said, trailing his lips down over my collarbone. "There is still plenty of time for the hero shit over the next week. But I refuse to feel bad for attempting to grasp the fleeting moments where I get to do this to you."

He moved further down my body, and he began tracing his tongue around one sensitive peak while he looked up at my face.

I sighed and arched my back, urging him on. He chuckled, sucking it into his mouth and moving his hand down my body, finding the bundle of nerves he had become more than a little acquainted with over the past few hours.

"That's it, Chosen One. Just let me help you relax a little longer."

There was no more talking for a while after that.

After another round, I dragged myself into the bathroom connected to Connor's bedroom and showered. Connor had suggested joining me, but I had smiled coyly at him and told him I needed a moment.

Turning on the shower, I stepped under the rainwater shower head and closed my eyes, letting the water run over me while I slipped into a meditative state and slowly turned my breathing and heartbeat off again. It had become easier now, after having spent three days without taking a breath or hearing my heartbeat pounding in my ears, despite the most stressful situation I've ever been in.

What I needed was a moment to gather my thoughts. Being this close to Connor constantly was intoxicating, and while I'd enjoyed every second of his attention in the last several hours, I knew I needed to get myself back on task.

Because no matter how much he said I deserved to be selfish, I couldn't push past the guilt. Liam and I weren't together anymore, and yet I couldn't help feeling like I was being unfaithful to him, especially when it had only been a little over a week since everything spiralled so spectacularly out of control. If I was honest with myself, I'd been struggling with these confusing feelings towards Connor ever since I'd transitioned.

Although I knew I shouldn't compare, the sex I'd just experienced with Connor was like nothing I'd ever had before. In each of my previous relationships, I had thought the sex at the time was amazing, but this had just blown it all out of the water.

Will and I had learned everything together.

Liam had worshipped me.

But Connor had challenged everything I thought I knew about myself. And not just in bed. Ever since he had given me back the memories stolen from me and pushed me to see the truth behind so many lies, he had been on a mission to force me to focus on what I wanted for a change. While that went against everything I'd ever believed before, the reality was I needed that push.

I looked down at the inside of my right wrist, where the make-up I'd applied had come off, revealing the rising sun tattoo. I'd become so used to it over the past eight months that I often forgot it was even there, but staring at it now, I felt anger rising.

I never would have chosen this life for myself. Ever since my twenty-fifth birthday, my life had been nothing but a series of traumatic events, forcing me into a world I had never wanted any part of. I'd accepted this all, following the predestined paths laid out for me with minimal argument. But right now, a small part of me wondered why I had let others tell me what I had to do without considering what I wanted or needed.

I understood the allure of giving in to the nightwalker side, switching off from the agony of being human, and dealing with all the emotions that came with it.

It was exhausting.

I spent an eternity in the shower before finally drying myself off and stepping back into the bedroom. Connor was sitting on the end of the bed, having finally pulled his pants back on. He watched me closely while I walked to the chest of drawers where he'd stashed Aurora's clothes. I dug around, trying to find something to wear that was a little less pornographic, pausing when I felt him press up against me.

"Do I need to help you switch your brain off again?" He asked quietly, his lips close to my ear.

I'd had to let the protection spell drop, so we were back to whispering.

"No... Given that the thoughts running through my head are agreeing with you for a change," I replied, leaning back into him when he circled his arms around my waist.

"Wow... I feel like this is a momentous occasion. And which of my amazing words of wisdom do you agree with?"

"About how I should take what I want into account more." I closed my eyes when he bent slightly to kiss my neck.

"And what is it that you want?" Despite his relaxed tone, I could feel the tension running through him while he waited for me to reply.

"The right to choose how I live my life. To not have to consider the world's fate when I make decisions constantly," I said before turning and putting my arms around his neck and holding his gaze. "To be able to want you without feeling like I need to justify that to anyone."

Although he smirked a little, I didn't miss how his body reacted to my words. I raised myself to my tiptoes and kissed the spot on his jaw that always gave away his frustration and anger.

"When this is all over, I want to be able to just walk away from all of the bullshit and live my life how I choose. Without the expectations of others weighing upon me," I continued, placing light kisses along his jawline.

His arms tightened around me. "Yeah? Need someone to teach you how to do that?"

"You already are teaching me how to do that," I said, drawing closer to his lips while he held himself perfectly still. "Teach me some more?" I whispered.

He moved his lips to mine, kissing me deeply while I slid my fingers into his hair. "I can think of a million things I want to teach you, Isolde. And none of them will fit into the perfectly ordered life you were living before," he said, his words low and rough, and he gripped my hips, closing all space between our bodies.

"Teach me them all."

"Whatever you ask for, Chosen One. I'm at your mercy."

I smiled and pressed my lips to his again. "Good boy."

"Put that spell back up, and I'll show you just how much of a good boy I can be."

CHAPTER TWENTY-SIX

When the sunset the following evening, a pounding at the door startled me from the book I read while Connor slept. He jerked awake and immediately moved towards the door, not bothering to put any clothes on before he flung the door open. Thankfully, I'd already switched my breathing and heartbeat off again after our last round of sex when I'd lowered the shield around the room. Immediately, the whispers had returned, and now I rolled my head, trying to shake off the pulling sensation that threatened to overwhelm me.

"What?" Connor demanded, and Sabine smirked at him from the doorway.

She ran her eyes over his naked body first before looking at me with a raised eyebrow, taking in my dishevelled appearance. I had pulled the sheet up before Connor had opened the door, but I was very clearly naked as well.

"So sorry to interrupt," she said, sounding anything but sorry. "We are going hunting. Get dressed." She turned on her heel and flounced away.

Connor slammed the door and spun back around. He avoided

looking me in the eye when he moved back towards the bed, scooping his jeans up from the floor.

I threw back the sheet and headed back for the drawers, resuming my earlier search for an outfit amongst Aurora's clothes.

"If we didn't need to stay so close to Adam, I'd be chaining you to the bed right now."

I straightened and turned back to look at him. He was sitting on the bed, fully clothed, looking down at his hands.

"Because you want me all to yourself?"

"Because I don't want you to endure what's about to happen." He was still refusing to look at me.

"Hey." I stood in front of him and placed my hand beneath his chin, lifting his head so our eyes met. The pain that I saw behind his piercing blue eyes was heartbreaking.

"You don't need to protect me," I said.

He ran his hands up the back of my thighs, and I steadied myself against his shoulders when he pulled me forward to straddle his lap.

"I'm not worried about protecting you. I know you're more than capable of holding your own." He buried his head in my neck. "It's what you're about to witness that I'm worried about. You're going to have to fight against all your basic instincts while you watch the most evil creatures that walk the earth rip people apart in front of you."

His words were muffled while he kept his face against my neck, and I began stroking his hair, trying to ignore the dread that was creeping up on me.

"You've shouldered this burden alone for over five hundred years, Connor. Let me share it with you for one night," I whispered, and I felt him shudder beneath me.

His grip on my hips tightened, but he still wouldn't look at me. I continued stroking his hair while he got himself under control.

Finally, he pulled back, and his usual smirky asshole mask slipped back over his features.

"You should get dressed. This view is for my eyes only from now on." He reached up and pinched my right nipple between his fingers, and I gasped at the unexpected pain mixed with pleasure.

I swatted his arm and tried to get up, but he held me on his lap while he leaned in to suck the peak of my left breast into his mouth, running his tongue over it and continuing to roll the other between his fingers.

"Hm, on second thought, let's make them wait a little longer." His hand drifted down between my legs, and his finger circled the bundle of nerves that was already aching for his attention while his mouth returned to my breast.

"Fuck," I breathed out, raising my hands quickly. "Hide and protect us."

Connor huffed a laugh against my nipple and slipped a finger inside me, thrusting it in and out slowly while his thumb applied pressure to where I needed him most.

"I'm impressed you could do that while coming undone, Isolde."

"I was motivated," I ground out while I began riding his hand, wrenching his head away from my breast so that I could crush my mouth to his.

He raised his other hand to clasp the back of my neck, his fingers winding their way through my hair.

"I'm going to be playing the image of you riding my hand like this through my head all night. Or perhaps the one where I was fucking you from behind while you screamed my name... I can't decide which one I like more." He began kissing his way down my neck.

I moaned, rolling my hips, the pleasure starting to build slowly.

"I need you to bite me," I said, and he pulled back suddenly to look at me, his eyes wide.

I nodded and tilted my head to the side, moaning again when his finger hit the right spot. He needed no further invitation, his mouth returning to my neck and kissing me softly.

"That's it, Isolde, come for me," he whispered, and I cried out when I felt his now sharp teeth sink into the spot where my neck met my shoulder.

My body began to shake when pleasure shot through me. My orgasm went on forever while he sucked, and his hand continued to move between my legs. I slumped against his shoulder, unable to hold myself up any longer.

After what could have been an eternity or only a few seconds, he pulled his mouth away and ran a gentle finger over the bite that began healing immediately. I stayed with my head pressed to his shoulder for a few more breaths before sitting back to look at him, my vision blurred.

"The freshly fucked expression on your face right now is the most beautiful thing I've ever seen," he said before bringing his mouth to mine and kissing me deeply again.

I kissed him back, pulling him as close as possible. When we finally broke apart, he rested his forehead against mine, and we both just breathed together with our eyes closed.

The peace that had fallen over us was shattered seconds later when the pounding at the door resumed. Connor growled, depositing me back onto the bed and moved to the door in a blur, barely giving me time to drop the spell. This time, he kept the door from opening completely, guarding me from the view of the person at the door while I focused on my heartbeat and breath, willing them to stop quickly. When the protection spell was lowered again, I gritted my teeth, battling against the whispers that seemed to have grown louder.

"Do not fucking interrupt us again. The next person who bangs on this door will soon be missing a head, understand? Tell Adam we will be there when we're good and ready." His tone was low and lethal, and despite everything we had just experienced, a part of me trembled at the sound.

Whoever was at the door obviously decided it was a good idea to heed his words, leaving without uttering a sound, and Connor shut the door again.

I swallowed hard and stood up, my legs shaking slightly from the powerful orgasm I'd just experienced, along with a small amount of fear.

He eyed me closely when I moved back to the chest of drawers. Once I was finally dressed, I brushed past him without meeting his gaze, and he tugged me back to his chest, his lips at my ear once more.

"I didn't mean to scare you," he whispered, snaking an arm around my waist to hold me firmly against him.

I closed my eyes, nodding slowly.

"It's okay," I whispered back, turning in his arms to face him. "Have you noticed the distinct lack of whispers when I have the protection spell up? I wasn't expecting that."

"It's definitely made the last few days more bearable than I expected... although, I hope it doesn't affect the requirement for us to be closer to Adam..." Connor's voice trailed off, and I swallowed hard.

We've been so caught up in our activities between the sheets that we hadn't considered just how badly this could fuck everything up.

Let's just get this over with." He held me in place for a few more seconds, the tension rolling through his body.

Finally, after pressing a kiss to my neck once more, he let me go. I stepped forward, rolling my shoulders and letting my face fall into the cool facade I'd been using when around the rest of the night-walkers.

"Once more into the breach we go," Connor said from behind me, and I nodded before opening the door and leading the way out of the room.

CHAPTER TWENTY-SEVEN

No matter how much Connor had tried to warn me about what to expect, nothing could have prepared me for the experience of hunting with Adam and the other nightwalkers.

I hung back from the group, hoping that if I stayed out of sight, I'd remain off Adam's radar. But no matter how far I stayed back, the pull towards Adam remained like an invisible tether. The whispers in my mind had become overwhelming, and I barely had control over my actions. I was on autopilot, forced to follow the group while they stalked through the night. I didn't know if it was because the group of them had gone into full predator mode, but I was powerless to do anything when they fell upon their first victim.

Adam sent one of his minions, Sarah, to knock on the door of a nearby home. She would have been no older than sixteen in life, and she wielded her youthful appearance like a weapon. She begged the woman at the door to let her in, tears pouring down her face while she screamed that someone was chasing her.

The woman immediately ushered her into the house, looking outside wide-eyed before shutting the door. Within seconds, her screams rang through the night, and Sarah reemerged, dragging the bleeding woman outside where the rest of the group was waiting. While they fell upon the woman, Sarah returned to the house and slowly began dragging the rest of the woman's family out, one after the other.

I swallowed hard and blinked back tears, fighting back a mixture of bloodlust and revulsion while I stared at the scene before me.

The smell of blood in the air was both intoxicating and nauseating, and I could feel my vampire nature warring with the humanity within me. I felt like I was on the verge of a mental breakdown.

The whispers had grown to screams in my head until I was no longer in control of any of my own actions, and I began to inch slowly closer to the group.

Before I could react further, I was pulled out of my physical surroundings when a familiar sensation washed over me.

Blinking, I found myself within the mindscape with Connor, back in the house where it had all begun.

He had me pressed against the wall. "You need to fight it. You can't give in, Isolde," he said urgently, weaving his fingers through my hair to hold my head steady while he skimmed his nose along my jawline.

I swallowed, already feeling the difference now that I was safe within the mindscape.

"I'll try..."

"Try harder."

The mindscape was already fading.

Back in reality, I swayed on my feet while struggling to distance myself from the screams in my head and was relieved when they finally dulled back to whispers again.

I looked at Connor and nodded subtly.

He nodded back before returning his attention to the scene before us.

He remained nearby, not participating but watching everything closely while the rest of the group continued to tear the family apart. But their victims seemed to almost be in a trance, as they had all remained silent aside from the woman's initial screams.

As the night grew later, the group began stalking through local parks frequented by the homeless. The poor people had no chance of escaping, with nowhere to hide.

I watched while they were ripped apart, one after the other, continuing to push back against the whispers with varying degrees of success. Connor was there each time I seemed like I might slip, pulling me back into the mindscape for brief reprieves.

After each kill, the bodies were carted off by some of Adam's followers, and I realised that this wasn't just purely about satiating their hunger.

Adam was building an army.

Nightwalkers were usually so brutal in their attacks that they often ripped the heads from their victims when they fed. When this happened, it stopped their victims from transitioning. But tonight, not a single one of their victims was beheaded.

The knowledge that nightwalkers were capable of such calculated attacks went against everything I'd been taught, and it scared the absolute shit out of me.

By the time dawn was approaching and we headed back to the house, they had killed at least twenty people.

Not once had anyone commented on the fact that neither Connor nor myself had participated in any of the attacks, and no one paid us any attention when we immediately headed for Connor's room once we were through the door.

Connor barely looked at me when I closed the door behind us.

"You were in their heads, weren't you?" I whispered.

I had seen the lines of fatigue on his face growing more pronounced throughout the night while he maintained his silent vigil.

He nodded slightly and peeled his clothes off before heading straight for the bathroom.

My heart sank further still, knowing that he had spent the entire night going into the minds of the nightwalkers, feeding them false memories of us contributing to the bloodshed while also trying to keep me from joining them.

I followed silently, watching while he turned the shower on with the hot water up as high as it would go and stepped into the steaming water. He stood with his back to me, letting the water run over his head and down his body while he placed his hands on the wall before bowing his head.

It felt intrusive to be witnessing his silent grief like this while another layer of his villain facade was chipped away, leaving a broken man standing in his place.

Unable to find the right words, I slipped out of my clothes and stepped into the shower behind him. He didn't react when I closed the door behind me and pressed myself against his back, sliding my arms around him. I pressed a light kiss to his back and held him close, offering what comfort I could whilst hoping that the burning water would help me strip away the memories of this awful night.

I felt a shudder run through him while I continued to hold him silently.

I had no idea how long we stood like that before he spun quickly, so fast that I barely had any time to react, and kissed me hungrily.

I kissed him back, allowing him to push me back against the wall, pinning me in place while he crushed his lips to mine. I could feel his emotions through that kiss, his despair and frustration rolling off him in waves.

He lifted me, and I wrapped my legs around his waist.

"Use me, Connor. Chase the demons away. I'm right here," I whispered against his lips, and I felt his breath hitch.

Realising he'd lost control over his breathing and feeling his heart beating frantically against my chest, I raised the protection spell around us once more. Shielding us again from the creatures that stalked the halls outside and allowing the broken man to seek solace in my arms without being forced to control the humanity that raged inside him.

Without uttering a word, he thrust inside me, and we began moving frantically together, doing our damnedest to rid ourselves of the memory of all we'd been forced to endure tonight.

Attempting to return to the people we were before we'd walked out that door.

But even the release that followed wasn't enough to forget the lives we had been unable to save.

Once we'd climbed out of the shower, I ushered Connor towards the bed, the lines of fatigue so heavily etched into his face now that it was like he'd aged forty years in one night. Knowing that this had been his life for five centuries was utterly devastating, and I curled myself around him when he fell into a fitful sleep.

We'd fallen into a pattern the last few days where one of us slept while the other watched the door in case one of our sadistic housemates decided to come and play. While I was exhausted, there was no way I was falling asleep while he was this vulnerable.

So I forced myself to ease away from his sleeping form and got dressed before sitting in the armchair once more.

All the while wondering how he had managed to endure nights like this repeatedly and not completely break apart. He had been putting on this act for so long that it would have been so easy for him to become the creature he pretended to be.

But the sarcasm and snark were simply a mask. And I knew without a doubt that, if I let myself, I could fall for the man who hid behind it.

I tried to lose myself in the words of Mary Shelly while I flicked through Connor's original copy of *Frankenstein*, but that now familiar tugging sensation at the back of my mind was stronger than ever.

Isolde! You must hear me! I need to speak with you. Eve is not who she appears to be.

Damon's voice rang in my ears, and although I automatically looked around, I knew that words were coming from inside my head.

The tugging disappeared again, no matter how hard I tried to keep a grip on it, and I sagged back in my chair.

I knew for sure now that I wasn't imagining it.

CHAPTER TWENTY-EIGHT

Once Connor awoke, he urged me to get some sleep. He was subdued still, seemingly unable to bring himself to look at me while he sat on the edge of the bed with his back to me.

If I hadn't been so utterly wrecked, I would have tried to coax him to talk about it, but I also sensed that wasn't how to handle this. So I nodded and slid between the sheets, quickly giving myself over to what I hoped would be a dreamless sleep.

But that wasn't meant to be, and I was once again pulled into one of Connor's blood memories.

I had been looking for Adam for several hours, cursing the damned one-way bond that meant he could find me, but I could never fucking find him.

He'd left the coven just after sunset while I'd still slept, and I had no idea how many people he would have ripped apart before I could get out there. Sabine had said offhandedly that he was off looking for that bloody Order bitch, and it had taken me a moment to realise who she was talking about. And then the dread sunk in. He would try and get to Isolde before her powers fully kicked in.

I'd forced the hacker genius to yank his dick out of one of the newest members of the coven and fire up the dreaded computer, manipulating his weak mind to hack into both Isolde's phone records and that of her philandering fiance to see where they were. And now I was moving at full speed towards a restaurant in Fortitude Valley.

I had to keep him from killing her. These last five hundred years could not have been for nothing. While I knew that Liam was most likely lurking in the dark like her permanent shadow, I was the only one who could even come close to controlling Adam. And we needed Liam just as much as we needed Isolde.

Once I'd worked out where the restaurant was, I finally stopped to work out what my next move was. Panic had overtaken all common sense, and it was only now that I realised I didn't even have a fucking plan.

A scream ripped through the night from the alley behind the restaurant, and every fibre of my being told me that Adam had already found them. I tore around the back and saw Isolde fly backwards. Adam was ripping into the fiance, who was lying on the ground, and Isolde was scrambling to her feet once again. I could already tell that the fiance was a lost cause, but there was no way I could let Adam near Isolde.

Where the fuck was Liam?

When Adam began to move away from the body on the ground towards Isolde, I threw myself between them and punched him in the face when I flashed past, giving myself the split second I needed to get into his head. I commanded him to leave, attempting to convince him that Isolde had gotten away. I could feel his subconscious fighting against me, stronger than ever before, and I began to fear that this would be one of those times when it failed.

I was distantly aware that Isolde had flung herself towards her fiance, and it was at that moment, Liam finally arrived and began pummelling Adam.

I jumped out of Adam's head and stepped back, wondering how I would get around this now. I'd never been able to manipulate Liam's memories before, but perhaps I could keep his focus on Adam only. I melted back into the darkness, watching Adam and Liam trade blows before forcing myself back into Adam's mind. I couldn't risk my brother seeing me, but I wasn't about to sit back and watch him get ripped apart by Adam either. I knew that the Order had no real idea of Adam's invincibility, and Liam was in a fight that would lead to his own death if I didn't do something now.

This time, entering Adam's mind was like it usually was, although I was still fighting against the black fog that was there every time.

When I slipped into the subconscious of others, it was usually like I was diving into water before appearing in a dream where I could direct the person to say and do things. Or even pluck whole memories out of their mind.

But with Adam, it had always been a black fog that I had to push through. I knew that only true evil lurked behind those eyes, and even after five hundred years, it never became any easier.

I finally gained control and forced Adam to retreat, convincing him that Isolde had escaped.

He immediately disappeared, off to find her, even though she was only metres away from him, screaming for her fiance to open his eyes. From my hiding place within the shadows, I watched Liam turn hesitantly towards her, taking a few cautious steps closer while she looked up at him and pleaded for help.

A flash of jealousy ripped through me, and I knew it was because I wished that it was me who would be considered her saviour.

But that wasn't how this was meant to go.

I was never meant to be the one to save people.

That crown had been bestowed upon my twin whilst I had been handed the keys to the dungeon and forced to lock myself in with the devil in the dark.

Doing my best to push the maudlin thoughts aside, I moved further into the shadows, grateful that my brother seemed to have missed my presence in the darkness.

Once the police tore into the alley, I cast a look at the body on the ground before moving at lightning speed. I knew that I wouldn't have a chance to do anything about stopping her fiance from transitioning now that the police had arrived. A middle-class white male in his mid-twenties being brutally murdered in an alley in front of his beautiful fiancee meant that there was no way that body was going to be left unattended long enough for me to remove his head.

As I left the scene, I cursed Adam silently for constantly making things so much more complicated.

And I once again wished death upon that witch who had started this all.

The memory faded around me, but I was pulled somewhere else entirely before I could slip into my own dreams.

Looking around, I was surprised to find myself in the cottage Liam, and I had stayed at while I got a grip on all the blood memories that had rolled through my mind in the days immediately following my transition.

Was that only a few short weeks ago?

I was standing in the single bedroom, the cosy bed rumpled before me, when I heard someone clear their throat behind me.

I spun on the spot, coming face to face with Liam. He was leaning against the doorframe with his arms crossed, looking extremely uncomfortable. I had no idea how much of my current adventures Liam could access. Connor always seemed to be able to see what I was doing in the real world when he pulled me in for these subconscious chit-chats.

"Hi," I said, wrapping my arms around myself, suddenly unsure what to do with my arms. "I see you've worked out how to use the bond to get into my mind?"

"Yeah... kind of wishing I hadn't, though," he replied, his jaw clenched.

I looked down to see that I was still dressed in the outfit of Aurora's that I was wearing in reality. It had been the first thing I'd grabbed, but I regretted the choice now. The lace and leather lingerie left very little to the imagination.

"I don't really know what to say..."

"Not surprising." He turned and walked into the small lounge area of the cottage.

I hesitated before following him, watching him throw himself onto the couch. He sighed loudly and stared at the ceiling.

"How's Aurora?" I asked, figuring I'd go with the least loaded question first.

"About as well as you could expect. She's been refusing to eat or drink or talk to your parents. I spoke to them but didn't tell them where you are right now... I figured the less they know, the better," he said, finally looking at me properly.

"Good call... What did they say?" I eased into the seat across from him, sitting on my hands.

This was possibly the most awkward conversation I'd ever had.

"I don't think they quite knew how to handle it, to be honest. I also think they wished you were the one giving them updates on your sister," he said, and the look he gave me made me feel like a crappy daughter.

"Well, at the moment, saving the world from an apocalypse kind of takes priority over everything else."

"Oh, I'm very aware of where your priorities are at the moment." There was absolutely no way to miss the attitude in his tone this time.

"Look, I get that we have a lot of shit to talk about and that I'm an absolute asshole for everything that has happened in the past few weeks, but I've just had a really terrible night. I don't know how much more I can handle right now, Liam."

Even while I said the words, I knew that I owed him so much more than this. He'd done nothing to deserve the emotional shitstorm I'd put *him through, and yet here I was, acting like he was in the wrong for being pissed.*

I dropped my face into my hands and groaned.

"I'm sorry, Liam. I don't know what's wrong with me..." I let my hands drop to my lap and stared down at them. "I don't know who I am anymore," I whispered.

I heard Liam shift in his seat, and I looked up to see that he'd moved forward to rest his elbows on his knees while he watched me.

"I've been doing a lot of thinking... I haven't really had much else to do... And I realised that I should have known something was going on sooner. I knew that you'd changed when you transitioned, but I was just so relieved that you weren't a nightwalker that I ignored it. I think maybe that's the reason that the bond took so long to come back. Perhaps the bond that formed after your transition was the one that was designed for us all as part of this fucked up spell."

"What are you saying?" I whispered, searching his face.

He shook his head. "I think you were trying to force something that was no longer there," he said, and I swallowed hard.

"But... I do love you, Liam... I wasn't lying any of the times I told you that."

"I know you weren't... But I think once you transitioned, the bond also began forming with Connor... And I think the love you felt for me changed..." The raw emotion in his voice broke my heart.

"I don't know what I feel for Connor, and that's the truth. But knowing who he truly is and what he's had to endure the last five hundred years... The fact that he is still able to... show signs of humanity..." I had no idea how to finish any of these sentences, but Liam nodded.

"I'm starting to understand that. Maybe being in your head now affects that, but I think I need to consider what he's been through... Probably easier said than done..."

Honestly, this conversation had taken a sharper turn to the left than I had ever thought possible.

I could only assume that he hadn't seen everything that had occurred between Connor and me since we'd arrived in the coven, or else he wouldn't be so calm about all of this. Liam was patient, but even patient men had their limits. I was pretty sure seeing the ex you were still in love with have sex multiple times with your twin brother would be enough to break even a saint.

"Where does that leave us, Liam?"

He considered me for the longest time.

"I'd like to say that I forgive you, and we can be friends, Isolde, but... I don't think I'm going to be there any time soon. Let's leave our stuff to the side right now and focus on what's important."

Tears threatened to show themselves, but I willed myself to get it together.

Every conversation with Liam in the past week felt like one long, extended break-up.

"I respect that. And on that note, you should probably know something has been going on." I relayed the details of the flashes I'd been getting from Damon, and Liam's expression grew darker.

"I've not been able to get a read on what he's trying to tell me, but it's enough to make me wary of everything Eve has been telling us," I said.

"This is the same man who left your sister to become a nightwalker and shoved me into a pocket realm after erasing my memories... I don't know if we can trust him, Isolde."

"Well, at this point, it's coming down to who I trust less, not more... And both he and Eve are ranking pretty fucking low," I said, and Liam grunted in response while he considered everything I'd said.

"I'll see what I'm able to pick up here. I can't hear Eve's thoughts, but maybe I can try to talk with Ronson and see what comes up," he said.

I nodded. "Hopefully that leads somewhere." I stood up, and Liam followed suit.

"I'll reach out again once I know more... and Isolde... be safe."

The cottage faded away, and I finally slipped into the dreamless sleep I'd been hoping for all along.

CHAPTER TWENTY-NINE

When I finally awoke, it was to the sight of Connor sitting in the armchair, watching me with a guarded expression. He held the familiar glass of whiskey in his hand that rested on the armrest.

He'd pulled some sweatpants on but remained shirtless, and I had to admit, the view wasn't the worst thing to wake up to.

But the look on his face put me immediately on edge.

"What's wrong?" I asked, sitting up quickly.

He shrugged.

"What could possibly be wrong?" The distant tone told me that the version of Connor I'd seen the past few days was buried deep beneath the facade sitting before me now.

"You tell me? You're the one sitting there looking all pissed off, not me."

"I don't know what you're talking about." His smirk failed to reach his eyes.

"I see... We're back there again, are we? I see the version of yourself that you've kept hidden for five centuries for a fraction of a second, so now you slam the walls back up?" I flung the covers off and marched to the dresser, pulling out the jeans and t-shirt I had worn when we arrived.

I didn't feel like playing pretend in Aurora's clothes right now.

"A moment of weakness doesn't mean you know anything about me, Is-." He cut himself off before he finished saying my name outside the safety of a protection spell.

I glared at him. "Obviously not." I yanked the clothes on and moved to the door.

He was behind me in an instant, his hand holding the door shut while he pressed himself against my back.

"Where are you going?" His breath was warm against my ear, and I suppressed the shiver that ran through me.

"Back to the other room. I'd rather be there and deal with the monsters that come through that door than deal with whatever this bullshit is," I hissed.

I looked down when he snaked his arm around my waist and pulled me back against him.

"You wouldn't last half an hour, and you know it."

I refused to allow myself to melt back into his arms. "Maybe it's you who doesn't know anything about me, Connor."

"Oh, I know everything about you. You're the hero. The good girl. The one who was meant for my perfect brother." The arm around my waist tightened its grip. "You're the chosen one," he whispered, and this time, I couldn't keep my body from reacting when arousal shuddered through me.

"I'm meant for no one," I replied quietly.

"That's not what you've been telling me for weeks. You told me you belonged to Liam." He began to pull me slowly backwards, away from the door and towards the bed.

I allowed him to pull me onto his lap when he sat on the edge, and I turned sideways, reaching to touch his face.

"Unless you have plans to talk to me like a grown-up, this goes no further." I held his gaze, and his jaw clenched.

He let out a long breath and closed his eyes briefly before looking at me with a smirk. "Fine. So, what do you want to talk about? The weather? How cute puppies are?"

I refused to play his games. I just continued to look at him. I could tell this made him uncomfortable, but I didn't care.

Eventually, his cocky expression faded. "I'm not good with emotions - if you haven't worked that out by now," he said quietly.

I smiled a little. "Oh, I'm very, very aware of that. But I'm not playing that game, so it's time to put your big boy panties on."

"I'm sorry, my what?" He looked stunned.

"Your big boy panties," I repeated, enjoying throwing him off for a change. "Instead of deflecting, trying to get me to have sex with you, or giving me some bullshit attitude, you are going to talk to me about what happened last night. That's how a relationship works. Or at least, a healthy one," I said.

He raised an eyebrow slowly while he held my gaze. "A relationship? I wasn't aware I was in one of those."

"I don't really know what to call whatever this is, but it feels like something more than simply scratching an itch, Connor."

He remained quiet for so long that I wasn't sure if he would ever speak.

Finally, his shoulders dropped, and he took a deep breath. "Last night was... I hated that you had to see that. I hated that *I* had to see it. That all I could do was make them believe that we were participating instead of just killing them all like I've always wanted to," he whispered.

I felt a tightness in my chest, taking in the raw despair on his face. "Was what happened last night different to other times?" I asked.

He nodded. "I've never seen them work together like that. There was something different about this. It's almost like Adam knows something is coming... If not for the fact that these nightwalkers will awaken after the full moon, I would assume he was preparing for war."

His words sent a different sort of shiver down my spine now, and I could sense his fear as strongly as my own.

"It was more than convincing them we were participating, wasn't it? Aside from that first woman, none of the victims reacted... You went into their heads as well, didn't you?"

He quirked an eyebrow at me. "You really don't miss a thing, do you?"

"I'm observant like that."

"I've never done that before either. Honestly, this is my first time in a situation like last night. I thought I'd experienced the worst that these creatures were capable of in the past, but this was..." His words trailed off, and I knew he had reached his limit on sharing his feelings when he shifted beneath me and looked away.

I opened my mouth to speak again when a sharp pain ran through me, and I fell back.

Distantly, I felt Connor catch me while I was ripped from reality.

"Finally."

A voice that I'd hoped not to hear again echoed around me when I found myself standing in the middle of a field surrounded by a forest. The green of the grass was like nothing I'd ever seen before, and I knew without a doubt that this mindscape was not set anywhere in Australia. The dense forest was ancient, and I could feel an electric charge in the air.

This was different to the mindscapes that Liam and Connor had pulled me into. While those had felt real, this one hummed with pure magic.

"Damon," I whispered, staring at the man before me.

"That woman had your mind locked up tight against me for a long time, Isolde. I'd begun to despair that I would never get in," he said.

"Let me go," I said through clenched teeth.

"Oh, calm down. I'm not going to do anything to you," he sneered, and I glared at him.

"I'd like to see you try," I said with a bravado I wasn't sure I had any right to feel.

He was in control here. If he wanted to hurt me, there would be no stopping him. And he knew it.

Connor appeared at my side, positioning himself slightly in front of me.

"Took you long enough," Damon said.

Connor stepped towards him but stopped short when Damon raised his hand in warning.

"None of that now. You're not in control here, Connor - I am. And you will both listen to what I have to say."

Another person stepped out from the trees behind him when Damon finished speaking.

I gasped. "Seth..."

"Good to finally speak to you directly, Isolde... Although I must admit, I wasn't expecting to see you with this particular brother." Seth laughed when Connor moved even further in front of me. "What is it with the women in your line and brothers? Does family mean nothing to any of you?"

"That's interesting. Who's Damon's mother again?" Connor spat out, and Seth smirked.

I was still pondering the jab about the women in my line and brothers while they continued to bicker back and forth.

"That family attachment has long since ended. Damon's loyalty to me is well deserved."

"I hardly think so. Your jealousy is the reason we are all here."

Damon's lips turned up into a sneer. "Oh, how little you truly know. That woman has been lying for thousands of years. The memories she has shown you both are false, fed to you to paint herself and Adam as the innocent victims. But we are here to show you the truth."

"How do we know you aren't the ones lying?" Connor demanded.

"As an act of good faith, we will appear in a mindscape you control. You and your brother," Seth said, and Connor physically recoiled.

"Why do you need both of them?" I demanded, unsure I was ready to be pulled into a joint mindscape with both O'Brien twins.

"This connection is weak as it is. We will need the strength of both

of them to be able to relay the truth in full. One that is not powered entirely by magic. There is much for you all to see. So you all need to be present." Damon fixed Connor with a glare.

"What truth?" I asked.

Damon shifted his gaze to me, a slight smile playing across his lips. "Perhaps we will answer those sorts of questions once Liam and Aurora are also present."

Great, he was using our need for more information to bribe us now.

"If we do not hear from you within twenty-four hours, we will not be held responsible for the hell about to be unleashed on this world. That will fall squarely on you two."

The mindscape dissolved around us, and Connor grabbed my hand, pulling me along with him, and we returned to reality.

CHAPTER THIRTY

*B*ack in Connor's room, his arms were wrapped around me, and he held me upright against his chest. His jaw clenched when he looked down at me.

"I don't trust them," I said immediately, and he nodded.

"I don't either. But, if I control the next mindscape, I can tell if they somehow manage to find a way to lie in there, as they said."

"I've never heard that before. I didn't know people couldn't lie when you pull them in there?"

"There's a lot you don't know, Isolde," he muttered, and I raised an eyebrow.

"What the hell is that supposed to mean?"

"Never mind," he said with a sigh, "but if the next mindscape is one that I control, they won't be able to feed us any more bullshit."

I wasn't quite ready to let that last comment go. "What did you mean, Connor?"

He regarded me closely. "It was how I knew how you truly felt in the mindscape. No matter what you were saying, I could feel your true thoughts and feelings. It would be the same in a mindscape I control with Seth and Damon in it."

I decided not to press further, unwilling to accept that I had been lying to myself for weeks.

"You mean if it's one that Liam and you control? They seemed pretty adamant it needs to be both of you."

"That is not going to go well, and you know it," Connor said, shifting me from his lap so that he could begin pacing. "I don't even know if we can both control a mindscape together."

"They seemed to think you can. I know you won't like this, but we need to try to talk to Liam."

Connor stopped pacing and turned to look at me. "You know how he feels about me. He trusts Damon more than me."

"Maybe before Damon knocked him out and took his memories with powers we never knew he had. I think he's probably lost a little trust after that. Not to mention, he wasn't the biggest fan of Damon anyway."

"He's even less of a fan of me," Connor pointed out, and I shrugged.

"I don't think we have much of a choice, Connor. We need to try at least."

"There's that 'we' word again. I don't recall you being able to pull anyone into a mindscape that you controlled?" He said.

I glowered at him. "No need to be a sarcastic bastard, Connor."

"It's my default setting," he said before sitting in the chair again and dropping his head into his hands. "Fuck!"

I watched quietly while he dealt with the struggle internally.

Finally, he sighed and lifted his head, his gaze meeting mine. "Fine."

I don't know what possessed me, but I got up, walked over to him, patted his head, and said, "Good boy."

It was one hundred percent worth it for the look he gave me.

Ten minutes later, we stood in the living room within the abandoned house where Connor had pulled me into all our previous mindscape conversations. Connor nodded at me once I got my bearings before closing his eyes momentarily.

"What the hell?" Liam's voice rang out, and I turned to find him glaring at us from where he stood in the middle of the room.

"Hi."

Liam remained silent, and his eyes narrowed while he focused on his brother.

"We didn't pull you in here to piss you off."

"Why did you pull me in here, then?" He asked, crossing his arms.

"We have some news. And we need your help," I said, and he looked at me silently. "Damon contacted me earlier and insists that Eve has lied to us." Liam's eyes flashed at the mention of Damon. "He said you and Connor need to work together to strengthen the connection so that he and Seth can show us the truth. We'll need to pull Aurora in here as well."

"I'm not sure that's the best idea, Isolde. She's not particularly stable right now," Liam said, and I shook my head.

"They specifically said it needs to be all of us. And I should have included her from the minute I knew about the fucking prophecy."

"We never knew of her involvement before," Liam argued.

Connor cleared his throat. "Well, that's not specifically true for everyone standing here."

Liam scoffed and shook his head. "Oh, I'm well aware you knew what the fuck was going on. It would have been nice to have a heads-up. About five hundred years too late, brother."

"Oh fuck off, Liam. I never had a choice. You don't get to act like you were the wronged party. Who was the one who was forced to spend an eternity amongst the nightwalkers and pretend to be one of them? It sure as fuck wasn't you."

"I refuse to feel sorry for you," Liam said.

Connor let out a bitter laugh. "I don't want or need your pity. But a little bit of understanding wouldn't fucking hurt."

"Not gonna happen."

I'd had enough. "For fuck's sake, the pair of you, shut up," I said, inserting myself into this little testosterone party. Both men turned to look at me with identical pissed-off looks.

"Now, I'm calling the shots because you two can't play nice together. Aurora has a right to be here because, like it or not, she's involved in this, too. So, I am going to attempt to pull her in here. I'm assuming I have some connection with her now due to the whole 'I turned her into a hybrid' thing, so I need you both to shut up so I can concentrate. Got it?" I felt like I was telling off children, but it felt entirely justifiable, given that was how they were both acting.

I took both their silences as acknowledgement and closed my eyes again. I reached out with my mind and began searching for the thread, expecting to find another golden one. But instead, I came across three different ones, red, purple and green. They were fainter than Liam's golden one, making them harder to see. They each emitted a low humming sound the closer I got to them, and I tentatively tugged on the green one.

"Wrong tether," Connor's voice cut through my concentration, and I opened my eyes to look at him.

"How do you know?"

"Because whatever you just did, I felt it," he said, tapping his head.

"That doesn't make sense... I'm not meant to be able to do anything to you, right? I know you both can track me and stuff because you turned me... but I didn't know that went the other way?"

To my surprise, both men exchanged a confused look before giving me matching shrugs.

"Don't know what to tell you, Isolde. One of your many Chosen One talents is that you go against almost every rule in the vampire how-to handbook. Congratulations," Connor replied.

Liam rolled his eyes. "Did you find any other tethers?" He asked, ignoring Connor.

"Yeah, there were three faint ones. They weren't as bright as yours," I said, and Connor's eyes flashed though he remained silent. "Wait... if I need these tethers to get into people's minds, why is it different for you two? Liam was able to get into my dreams for years to ward off night-

mares, but our bond didn't form until after we started using magic together."

"You think the magic we used together formed the bond?" Liam asked, his expression unreadable.

"It makes sense... we never really had an explanation as to why I could suddenly hear your thoughts, but it was only after we'd..." I trailed off, uncomfortable about bringing up our use of magic together that often led to sex.

"Only after the pair of you kept fucking while Liam got high off your magic?" Connor finished my sentence in a far less eloquent way than what I would have put it.

I glared at Connor, and Liam's face paled a little.

Connor shrugged. "What else would have caused it? Your powerful love for each other?" The sarcasm in Connor's tone was more than evident.

I knew we were getting dangerously close to another boxing match when Liam's hands balled into fists at his sides.

"Alright, Connor, you've made your point," I said, ready to throttle him when he smirked again.

Liam cleared his throat. "I don't know why I could get into your dreams. I wasn't ever able to do that with anyone else previously... I assumed it was because I'd spent so many years in tune with your movements."

Connor laughed. "Ah, the constant hero."

"I swear to god, Connor, I am so close to punching you right now," I said.

"That wasn't what you said last night... Or the night before that... Or the entire day before that. You definitely weren't thinking about punching me when I was fucking you in the shower... Or against the wall... Or when you were grinding yourself against me, begging me to bite you."

I couldn't believe he'd gone there.

Liam's eyes flashed, and his gaze locked on mine. "Are you fucking serious?" He whispered, his voice shaking.

"Don't forget, Isolde, he can tell if you lie in here." Connor's self-satisfied grin made my blood boil.

At this point, there was nothing that I could say that would make any of this okay.

"Connor, seriously, shut the fuck up. We don't have time for any of our emotional stuff right now. We can deal with this later, but I need to get Aurora and get her in here right now."

"Don't bother. I'll get her in here with me. Find some way to let Damon know we'll be ready in an hour. I can't be in here right now," Liam said before disappearing.

I stared at the spot he'd been standing for a few moments, trying to get a handle on what had just happened, before I turned slowly to glower at Connor.

"Should we have this out in here or out there, Isolde?" He asked, crossing his arms and leaning against the wall.

"What the hell was that?" I advanced on him. "Some ridiculous pissing match between the two of you? You got your feelings hurt because he wouldn't feel sorry for you, so you just had to keep twisting the knife until you found his weakness?"

He considered me quietly for a moment. "That was pretty much exactly it." He cocked his head to the side as though what I'd said gave him pause to consider his actions just now.

"Why? What possible good could pissing him off do? We need him, Connor. And he has done nothing to deserve any of the shit you just threw at him."

"And I deserve everything he said to me? I deserve to watch him continue to pine after you? To be reminded that he's the hero and I'm the fuck up?" Connor's eyes flashed, and I shook my head.

This whole situation was exhausting.

"You are not a fuck up, Connor. But constantly doing everything possible to cause a fight with Liam... We can't keep going down this same path every time the two of you come face to face. You need to find a way to get past all of this if we have any hope of winning on Saturday.

Otherwise, everything you have endured for the last five hundred years will all have been for nothing," I pleaded.

I was not above begging this man.

He closed his eyes and let his head drop back against the wall behind him, the muscle in his jaw twitching.

"Please, Connor. Just try to get your shit under control," I said, stepping closer to him and wrapping my hand around his forearm.

He opened his eyes and looked at me. His shoulders dropped a little, and he nodded. I let go of his arm and allowed him to pull me into his embrace, and he buried his face in my neck.

"Sorry," he muttered.

"My god... I don't think I have ever heard that word out of your mouth," I said.

His breath brushed against my neck when he growled quietly. "Don't get used to it."

"Oh, I know that was only a once-in-a-decade moment, don't worry."

CHAPTER THIRTY-ONE

"He's not going to come. You pissed him off too much," I said to Connor just over an hour later while we sat against the bedroom door together.

While Connor could function simultaneously within reality and the mindscape, I wasn't so lucky. We'd figured it was the safest place to sit if anyone made an impromptu visit while I was temporarily incapacitated.

"He'll show. It's part of his hero persona. Can't let anyone down, even if he's angry," Connor replied.

I sighed, letting my head bang against the door while I looked up at the ceiling.

"What? It's true. Even now that he's broken up with you for running into my arms, he's still all about protecting you at all costs."

"I did not run into your arms, Connor."

"Fine, now that you've allowed me to corrupt you with my evil dick then."

"Stop it! You promised you would get your inferiority complex under control," I said, frustrated at this endless merry-go-round of Connor's emotional baggage we'd been on for the past three hours.

"I don't have an inferiority complex - I have a god complex. There's a difference." He flashed me what was no doubt meant to be a charming grin.

It wasn't working on me. "Either way, reign it the fuck in," I said, refusing to give in and let him get away with his bullshit.

He sighed. "Fine, I promise to be on my best behaviour."

"Good," I said.

He opened his mouth to respond but paused before tapping his temple. I assumed this meant Liam had made contact.

I sat quietly for a few minutes, watching a range of emotions run across his features, waiting for one of them to pull me into the mindscape. The longer it took, the more I worried that they were locked in some mental battle to the death without me there to play referee.

Finally, after what felt like an eternity, I felt the now familiar tug and closed my eyes while I was pulled in, too.

"What took so long?" I asked once I finally appeared in the mindscape, looking around to try and orientate myself a little.

Nothing looked familiar. We were in the middle of an empty field, but it differed from the one Damon and Seth had been in. I realised it was the paddock beside the cottage Liam had taken me to.

"We just needed to have a little chat," Connor said, his eyes flashing.

I decided I didn't want to know any further details. "Right. Can you two play nice now?" I asked, looking between them both.

They stood a few feet apart, both with their arms crossed, identical pained expressions on their faces.

Liam nodded stiffly. "For now. Let's just get this over with," he said, not looking at me.

"Where's Aurora?" I asked.

"I'm here," she said, and I turned to find her sitting on a rock behind me. "You missed quite the show. These two dickheads were

having yet another pissing contest over you. Nothing unusual. Always about Isolde," she said, her tone flat.

Fabulous. This was all off to a lovely start.

Thankfully, Damon and Seth appeared to my right.

While I pondered what would happen if I set them both on fire inside a mindscape, everyone else sized one another up silently.

"Well, you got our attention. Why are we all here?" Liam spoke first.

While Aurora rose to her feet and came to my side, I felt Liam and Connor move close behind me. Although we were by no means a united front, at least we could present one to the two men who stood before us.

Seth and Damon looked at each other before turning back to us.

"I think it's best we start from the beginning. I'm sure Eve has told her twisted version, but very little of that would be true," Seth said.

I wasn't the slightest bit surprised, having long since known I couldn't trust Eve.

None of us spoke, waiting for one of them to start talking.

"Do they know the real reason for the Dragon Tattoos?" Seth asked, looking over at Damon, who shook his head.

Liam cleared his throat, and we all looked towards him.

"We have always been told it was because mythical dragons were protectors, and as our role is to protect the humans from vampires, that's where the tattoo came from," Liam said, running his finger over the tattoo on the inside of his right wrist.

Seth wrinkled his nose and scoffed. "What a load of nonsense. It is because the coven you all descend from predominantly consisted of dragon shifters, and they accessed dragon magic. The tattoos would appear on the seventh sons and daughters when their magic had come to fruition once they turned twenty-five. It's why the Order has those who control flames and those who can access the minds of others. In dragon form, they communicated telepathically. But the Orders powers now are far more conservative than what the original coven possessed. Whilst not all members of the original coven were dragons, it was the vast majority by the end."

"So Adam and Eve were dragons before they became vampires?" I asked, stunned.

Seth shook his head. "Adam was a dragon. But Eve... Eve was a phoenix."

Silence descended over the mindscape while both men waited for this information to sink in.

"A phoenix?" I asked.

"Yes, a phoenix. A creature with fire abilities that allowed her to catch fire and be reborn from the ashes. Her flames could bring those who had died back from the dead. And she was corrupted by Adam. She had lived hundreds of lives across multiple realms before he came along, each life more beautiful than the last. She was a creature of incredible empathy and love... But once Adam came along and poured his words of violence into her ear, she began to turn on everyone around her. It was no coincidence that the only coven members who survived were those loyal to Adam and Eve. The members of the Order have the dragon tattoos because they are descendants of Adam's line."

"I don't understand... In the five hundred years I've been alive, the only creatures I've encountered are the vampires you created. If those creatures existed back then, where did they all go?" Liam had voiced a question that Eve had been unable to answer.

It was Damon who answered now. "Long ago, this world was linked to thousands of others. We called them realms. Our world was filled with the mortals that you are all familiar with. Often, creatures from those other realms entered this one. Creatures with magical abilities, like the shifters and phoenixes. Some were peaceful and co-existed harmoniously with the humans. Others... did not. Adam fell squarely into the not category, and when he met Eve and began fuelling her power, thus corrupting her... Together, they were incredibly dangerous."

I looked over my shoulder again at Connor. "Are they telling the truth?"

Connor nodded, his expression mirroring mine while a sense of dread started to creep over me. I wasn't sure we were ready to hear what else the men had to say.

CHAPTER THIRTY-TWO

hen we remained silent, Damon continued with his story.

"When my father found a way to bind their powers, he also managed to bind the portals to all other realms to them, keeping them closed. This kept out all other benevolent and dangerous magical creatures, cutting our world off from all other realms. But it also limited the magic of those beings that remained here. It is why the Order members no longer wield the same magic level that covens previously could. And although Eve retained some of her powers, she could no longer access her fire abilities. When she used Adam's essence to create Liam and Connor with the help of another coven, the binding upon her began to weaken, and her powers grew stronger. It took five hundred years for her to become powerful enough to create Aurora and Isolde, using her own essence."

"So... basically, everything Eve told us was a lie?" I asked, my tone flat.

"Most of it will be her twisted version of the truth. I don't know if she truly believes everything she has done has been for some greater

purpose. My father and I only became aware of the weakening of the bindings in the last century. The more I investigated the prophecies, and the closer we came to your birth, we learned that what the Order had believed were prophecies were actually spells, and we realised what Eve had done. Once you joined the Order and your powers began manifesting, I had Patrice push Liam to turn you before your sister became a nightwalker. I had hoped that would halt the spell and keep them from going after Aurora. I had hoped that if you were a daywalker, you wouldn't have access to your full abilities, and it would have meant there would be no need for Aurora to be involved. But with how powerful you were becoming before your transition, I think your phoenix abilities would have come through regardless."

"So... I'm a phoenix," I asked, shaking slightly.

"You were, before your transition, as was Aurora. You were the stronger of the two due to the magic of the seventh son and seventh daughter. But both of your powers were muted by the same binding spell that kept the rest of us from accessing our full strength. If you had become a daywalker like Eve, you would have lost all access to your fire abilities. And if you'd become a nightwalker, you would have lost your powers completely, as we saw with Aurora. By becoming a hybrid, your powers merged with the dragon magic, which made you more powerful than Eve ever was." Damon paused, looking at me.

I nodded, unsure I could form words to respond any further than that.

"From what I've come to understand of the spell Eve cast, she created you within the bloodline of her direct descendants and coordinated everything to ensure you would be born to a seventh daughter so that you were a phoenix with the power the Order behind you. She made sure your mother married a seventh son for even more power, although his bloodline was not tied to the original coven. She did everything possible to boost your abilities and make you stronger than you would have been due to the muted abilities of all magical creatures. And when you became a hybrid, feeding on the bond that ties all four

of you, this brought you as close to full phoenix power as possible. I don't think she anticipated just how powerful you would become as a hybrid, though." Damon said.

Seth stepped up beside him, nodding towards Connor and Liam.

"The two of you were created within Adam's bloodline to amplify Eve's powers. Adam was the most powerful of the dragon shifters who came to this realm, and once his magic started to meld with Eve's, she became more powerful than anyone could have ever imagined. This amplification ability is why she tried to keep Liam close, as he was the more powerful of the two, with the seventh son and seventh daughter bloodline running through him as well. This is why both of you have abilities relating to telepathy, as that is how dragons communicate whilst in their dragon form. And the most powerful dragons had mind control and manipulation abilities, like the ones we've seen with Connor. Liam most likely also has these abilities, but he's never been put in a position where he has needed to use them. But you can't control the minds of other dragons. And because phoenixes are more powerful than dragons, you can't control Isolde or Aurora's minds either."

"But," Damon continued where his father had left off, "Eve had obviously never counted on Isolde becoming romantically entangled with either of the brothers... Or, as it would seem, both of them... Because of this, having your powers constantly amplified, you alone are more powerful than Eve ever was, even though you are still not at your full phoenix status."

My stomach started to churn, and I covered my mouth with my hand. I had no idea how to respond to any of this.

"I guess that explains why she's such a bitch to Isolde while trying to constantly fuck Liam. She must have grown more powerful every time they were together." Connor said.

I glanced back at Liam, who looked like he was also about to throw up. Part of me hoped that was because of his history with Eve and nothing in the last few days, but something about the look on his face told me that this wound was a fresh one.

I turned back to Damon and Seth, unable to look at either of the brothers while I tried to push the image of Liam returning to Eve's bed from my mind. "So that's why you were so against Liam and I being together when I was still human? And why can I control my powers better when Liam or Connor touches me?"

He nodded. "Yes, to both questions. But you have started to gain the ability to control those powers on your own now, correct?"

I nodded slowly, only half listening while I tried to keep up with everything we'd just been told, and realised I'd missed something vital before.

"Wait... Did you say that Liam was the seventh son of a seventh son and seventh daughter as well?" I asked.

Damon nodded.

"But... my mother wasn't a seventh daughter," Liam said, speaking for the first time since Damon and Seth had unravelled everything we'd believed about ourselves.

"She was. It wasn't common knowledge, and no one within the Order knew about the twin sister who died at birth one minute before your mother was born. But Eve did everything she could to ensure she had as much power as possible to boost her own. Connor was turned first to draw you out of the monastery, but she needed him to be available as a backup power source. We believe this is why she created him as the first hybrid. So that he would still have access to his powers but also be able to remain close to Adam. Adam became more powerful once Connor was close by. Every time you went into his mind, Connor, although you managed to manipulate his memories, it also boosted his power."

Connor stepped up beside me now, his expression hard. "Let me make sure I understand all of this," he began, his tone low and dangerous while he looked at them with narrowed eyes. "Adam and Eve were both evil before you bound their powers? These are their less evil versions? And when I used my abilities just to fucking survive, I was providing an energy boost to one of the most evil creatures ever to walk this earth, while Eve was using Liam like her very own sex toy to power up her abilities, making her powerful enough to create Isolde five hundred years later?"

Seth nodded.

Connor looked over at Liam. "I take it back. You've had it worse. At least I only had to fuck her once," he said, and I could almost hear the sympathy in his voice hidden beneath the sarcasm.

Liam opened his mouth to speak, but Connor wasn't finished, turning his anger back to Seth. "Why the fuck didn't you just kill them both back then? Why all of this curse bullshit?"

"My father tried to kill them," Damon snapped, defending Seth, who was scowling at Connor. "He wasn't powerful enough. Phoenixes and dragons are almost unbeatable. The only thing that can kill a phoenix or a dragon is one of their own, and we didn't have many of those around. At least, none that were willing to kill one of their own."

Seth placed a hand on Damon's shoulder, and Damon fell silent as Seth took over the explanation.

"I placed a spell upon their unique abilities, which was meant to make them almost as powerless as humans whilst also ensuring they couldn't be together. If they were kept apart, they wouldn't be able to feed off any existing power they both had and potentially become more powerful again. But I had no idea that this would create the two vampire bloodlines."

"How did that happen?" I asked.

"Adam and Eve are different from the creatures that they created. Adam was already full of darkness, so when he unexpectedly began feeding on the blood of humans, that darkness seeped into them like a virus via the blood memories, and his dragon abilities caused what Connor has referred to as the hive mind. Eve eventually worked out that she could create the daywalkers using similar means, but because she wasn't as inherently evil as Adam, the daywalkers did retain more humanlike personalities. She was truthful with you when she said she was trying to limit the damage caused by the nightwalkers, although I think it was more to protect her and Adam's bloodlines and not necessarily to protect mankind. I'm sure some of the daywalker apathy stems *from the fact that she could easily overlook all the evil Adam did and still believed they were above all others."*

"The guilt that my father felt for creating these creatures is why we spent thousands of years fighting alongside the ones who eventually banded together and created the Order of the Dragon. No one knows who we are. We needed to keep our existence from Eve to ensure she didn't come after my father and find a way to reverse the spell. We kept our direct interactions with the Order to a minimum until Isolde's birth, when I entered the Order, pretending to be one of their own. Although I'm assuming that's not so secret anymore?" Damon asked.

I felt a slight stab of guilt at the knowledge that I was the one who outed him to the Order and let his mother know he was still alive. "In my defence, all I saw was you kidnap Liam in my vision after appearing alongside a man who I had just been informed was the creature that Satan was based on, so I wasn't particularly inclined to protect your secret at the time. Eve didn't know about Damon, but she knew Seth survived."

They exchanged a surprised look.

Liam had moved to my other side now. "Speaking of, why did you kidnap me? You could have told me all this that night instead of knocking me out."

"I tried to. When I touched your forehead, and you crumbled, I was attempting to share my visions. But it seems that Eve had placed a protection spell over your mind, keeping me out. Similar to the one that has kept me from getting into Isolde's mind until now. It's why I needed you two to initiate this mindscape."

"So, you just shoved me into a pocket realm after wiping my memories and hoped no one would find me?" Liam asked, his eyes flashing.

Damon shrugged. "More or less. I didn't take into account the fact that Eve could track you. That was foolish on my part. But the closer we came to the full moon, the more our desperation has caused some important things to be overlooked, which we hope to remedy now, before it's too late."

Liam pressed his lips together while he glared at Damon. "Well, given that I'd still be stuck in there with no memories, I have to say, I'm kind of relieved about that particular oversight."

Damon waved a hand through the air with a sigh. "I would have eventually gotten you out once we managed to avoid what's coming on Saturday night."

"So... When Eve told us Isolde needed to use her powers on her and Adam, what was her actual goal?" Connor asked before Liam could respond to Damon sweeping aside the fact that he had left him alone and defenceless.

"If Eve succeeds, they will return to their former selves. Because of this, the doors to all the realms will be flung open once the spell binding her and Adam's powers have been destroyed, and all manner of creatures will come through," Seth said, his gaze falling on me.

I swallowed hard. This all just kept getting worse.

"This is the true reason for all of the natural disasters occurring. The bonds keeping the portals closed grew even more unstable when you were turned, Isolde. And the closer we get to the full moon, they grow weaker," Damon said.

I took a deep breath, clasping my hands behind the back of my neck and looking up, unable to look at anyone while I tried to work through everything without losing control of my powers... Not that I was even sure if they would work within the mindscape.

"So when Eve said I needed to use my fire abilities on her and Adam to kill him, what she intended to happen was that my flames would destroy the spell that bound their powers. Then they return to their former selves, and we're right back where you started three thousand years ago?"

"Correct. Only a phoenix has the power to destroy the spell that was cast fully. And until twenty-six years ago, Eve was the only phoenix in this realm," Seth said.

"But, won't my flames just kill Eve and not affect Adam? Didn't you say phoenixes and dragons can only be killed by one of their own?"

"Yes, that's true. But if you touch Eve and your powers flow directly into her, your flames won't kill her. It's only if you are using your

powers against her that you will kill her. And you are correct - you can't kill Adam. But that was never her intention."

"Wait, back up a second. If you were both members of the original coven, wouldn't that mean you were both dragon-shifters too? Why couldn't you kill Adam?" Aurora asked. She had remained silent through all this, but now she raised a valid point.

The two men exchanged another look before Damon raised his right wrist, exposing his dragon tattoo. We watched in stunned silence as the tattoo changed slowly, replaced by a wolf's head.

"This was purely a glamour to allow me to infiltrate the Order. My father's real name, Sithech, means Wolf. Before Adam and his brother joined us, our coven's powers were tied to wolves."

"You mean werewolves?" Connor asked.

Seth screwed his face up. "No. Werewolves are a myth."

"So are fucking dragons and phoenixes," Connor muttered.

"In the same way that dragons could take human form, some wolves could do this, too. They became the wolf shifters that the werewolf myth is based upon, but their transition had nothing to do with the full moon," Damon explained.

"So Eve originally was the leader of a coven of witches and wolf shifters, but then levelled up to dragon shifters?" Aurora asked.

Seth shook his head. "I was the leader of the coven and brought Eve in. We were wolf shifters with enhanced magical abilities, the strongest of our kind. And when I met Eve, a Phoenix who had become trapped in our realm, I fell in love with her."

"Well, that was your first of many fucking mistakes," Connor said.

Seth continued speaking as though Connor hadn't interrupted him. "After a few years, her compassion and empathy earned everyone's trust, and we were bound together to protect both our coven and the humans around us... then Adam and his brother came along, followed by the rest of their family. Slowly, the wolves amongst us began dying off. At first, the deaths seemed to be accidents. But over time, I eventually learned who was truly behind them. But I came to that realisation too late, and the dragon shifters had infiltrated the coven entirely, usurping all my followers and placing themselves in positions of power."

"Wait... does this mean that the Order is evil?" Aurora asked, looking over at where Liam and I were processing this new information.

Liam was staring down at the tattoo on his wrist again.

"No. Not all dragon shifters are inherently evil. And from my time within the Order on and off over the years, I've not encountered anyone resembling any of those original dragons."

"What happened to Adam's brother?" I asked.

"You've met him. It's Ronson," Damon said.

I turned slowly to look at Liam. "Did you know this?"

Liam shook his head. "No. I'm as stunned as you are. I've only been able to get limited access to Ronson's thoughts over the years, but I never knew why."

"Was Ronson as evil as Adam?" I asked, turning back to Seth.

"From what little I have been able to tell over the years, Ronson has believed that he and Eve were working towards killing Adam. He was never as bloodthirsty and power-hungry as his brother."

The four of us exchanged wary glances.

"So Ronson is a dragon? I thought he was a daywalker." Aurora asked.

"He was a dragon, but when he lost his ability to shift, he chose to become a daywalker. I have never been able to find out why, but I assume it was because he believed he was helping Eve."

"Did he also love Eve?" Aurora asked.

I looked over at her, curious about her interest.

"I don't know that there was anything more than a physical attraction between them. Once Adam came along, he was the only one she loved. Now it's just them scratching an itch. As you've no doubt noticed, the sex drives of phoenixes and dragons are very high."

That was putting it mildly and explained so much about not just them but all of us.

"So, what must we do to stop everything happening on Saturday?" Connor asked, moving closer behind me.

"We're going to have to do the original spell again. Even without Isolde using her flames on Eve and Adam, the spell binding the realms closed has become so weak that even the slightest push on either side will see them bursting open and potentially rip the bindings from Eve and Adam simultaneously."

CHAPTER THIRTY-THREE

"I don't know that sort of magic," I said, shaking my head.

"You don't need to do it. It will be my father and I who perform the spell. You must keep the rest of them occupied long enough for us to get it all sorted."

"Keep them occupied? How?"

"No idea. You can work that out amongst yourselves." Damon said.

"Just don't set them on fire," Seth added.

I didn't appreciate the look he gave me, as though he didn't trust me not to lose control of my powers.

"What if Isolde and I just simply leave? Will that halt the spell? Or... Was that another one of Eve's lies? Did we not need to be near Adam?" Connor asked

I held my breath as Seth and Damon exchanged a hesitant look.

"Unfortunately, while you didn't need to be there before... If you were to leave now, that would give away the fact that you know something. Remember, Eve is linked to Connor, like Liam. She'll be able to tell the second you leave this house. I have no doubt she would have a backup plan in place. At least this way, we know what to expect."

I felt a sinking feeling in my stomach. Everything we'd been through the last few days and the trauma of last night had all been for nothing? And now that we knew the truth, we couldn't even leave?

"Can we at least remain within the protection spell that Isolde can raise?" Connor asked.

"Perhaps... I assume that you've already been doing that?" Damon asked, looking between us both.

"Yes, although I've been trying not to do it for too long... It seems to keep me from being pulled too far into Adam's thrall," I replied, and Damon nodded.

"And you've noticed this as well?" He asked Connor.

Connor nodded. "Yes, it hasn't been anywhere near as bad as the other times I've been here for longer than a few days."

"In that case, I recommend you keep doing that. Although, I can feel how powerful you are, Isolde, despite how much magic you must be using when raising those protection wards..." Damon said, eyeing me closely.

I shifted uncomfortably under his gaze, understanding now that my increased power was from the boosts I'd had each time I slept with Connor.

Damon raised an eyebrow but didn't comment further.

"Come Saturday, we should only need approximately ten minutes once the sun goes down to rebind the portals... we hope," Seth said.

"A lot can go wrong in ten minutes." I didn't like the uncertainty in his voice.

"Well, you'll just all have to devise a plan to avoid anything bad from happening, won't you? We can't be responsible for everything." Seth seemed to have finally reached the end of his patience.

Neither of them spoke again before disappearing.

The four of us were silent within the mindscape, each taking time to process everything that had been said.

"Is anyone else growing tired of the whiplash from all the reveals that turn out to be complete bullshit?" I asked finally, turning to face the others.

"Well, I lived with the last lie for five centuries, so it's maybe not quite so dramatic for me, but for the record, neither of them was lying," Connor said.

Liam gave a short nod but remained silent, his jaw clenched while he stood with his arms crossed.

I sighed and sat cross-legged in the grass and began absently ripping blades of grass out of the ground while Aurora returned to her rock.

"So what are we meant to do now? We obviously can't let Eve know what we've just found out," Connor said.

"I guess I'll have to find a way to tell Patrice without being overheard within Eve's house," Liam said. "We're going to need to get the Order on board because they are already making plans with the daywalkers regarding Saturday night."

"What plans? Care to clue us in?" I could hear the annoyance in Connor's voice while he moved to sit beside me.

Liam watched him, the animosity on his face growing. "Oh, I'm sorry, did we forget to include you two in the plans? Figured you were too busy fucking to give a shit anyway."

"Oh my god, would the pair of you just shut the fuck up?" Aurora threw her hands up in the air. "We just found out that Isolde and I are mythical creatures that haven't existed in three thousand years, and you two were created as some sort of weird amplifier designed to power up those creatures through sex or mind fucking with them. And yet, the pair of you are still competing to get into Isolde's fucking pants? No. Enough. Just grow the fuck up and get over it." She pointed at Liam. "She has obviously made her choice. You need to accept that and move on." She then turned to glare at Connor. "And you... God only knows why, but she seems to have chosen you. So stop waving your victory flag in Liam's face and be worthy of her."

The two men stared at her, suitably chastened.

My sister turned her gaze back to me.

"You and I have a lot of shit to sort through, but until Saturday night, we need to just focus on what's important. Liam and I will keep *this from Eve while he works out a no-doubt heroic plan with the Order. We'll be in touch once we come up with something." With that, she also vanished, wrenching herself free of the mindscape and leaving me alone with the two men.*

My two men.

"Well... of all the people to take charge of the situation, I would never have believed it would be Aurora." Connor shook his head.

"Agreed," I said quietly, staring at the spot where my sister had previously sat.

Liam cleared his throat. "I'll be in touch." He nodded when I looked over at him before he vanished as well.

"Well... That was fun," Connor's lips curved into a slight half-smile.

"You and I have very different ideas of fun, Connor."

"Maybe so. But I feel better knowing that my suspicions about Eve have been right all these years. She never seemed like the good guy in all of this. I have no doubt that Liam will be beating himself up over every time he fell into bed with her."

I didn't want to think about Eve and Liam together, especially because I strongly suspected he'd fallen into her bed as recently as the last few days.

"I feel a little bad that I gave Damon such a hard time now," I said.

Connor shook his head. "Don't be. He didn't do himself any favours by being such a dick to you and never telling anyone the truth. Certainly could have saved us all a lot of trouble."

"True." I turned to look at him closely. "You don't seem too cut up about the fact that we can't kill them this weekend, though. None of this is going to be over. Not like we thought, anyway."

Connor pulled me into his lap, and I rested my head against his chest.

"I figure once the new spell is cast, Adam can be Seth and Damon's problem. They both can be. I plan on fucking off to somewhere very far away from them all where you and I can spend days, weeks... hell,

months even, getting all of this nonsense out of our systems." He kissed the top of my head.

"That sounds like an excellent plan."

Once we returned to reality, we spent the next day and a half waiting for Liam to make contact again with a plan. The closer we got to the full moon, the more anxiety started to get the better of me.

"What will we do if we haven't heard anything?" I asked Connor as I paced back and forth across his bedroom.

As soon as we'd left the mindscape, I raised the protection spell, keeping it firmly in place.

Connor watched me from the edge of his bed, his expression growing wary when a spark shot out of my fingers when I wrung my hands. He leapt up and moved to stand before me, taking my face in his hands while he held my gaze.

"Get it under control." His tone was commanding.

I forced myself to focus on the burning sensation growing steadily worse in my chest, tamping it down so that I didn't accidentally set the house on fire and possibly free Adam from the binding spell.

"I'm good," I replied after a moment.

He held my gaze briefly before running a hand through his hair. "If we don't hear anything, we'll just leave the house, okay? It can be Damon and Seth's problem."

"Do you honestly think it will be that easy?"

He shook his head. "No, but it's nice to daydream that it might be that easy just to walk away from it all."

Something occurred to me then. "You spent that whole night we were hunting going into Adam's mind, Connor. That's the longest you've ever done that, right?"

Connor cocked his head to the side as he looked at me. "Yes. Why do you ask?"

"Do you think that was why Eve insisted we had to be close to him? So you kept increasing his power by going into his head and hiding my presence from him?"

Connor's face paled slightly. "Fuck." He stretched the word out.

I nodded.

"Nothing we can do about it now. Distract me," he said, reaching for me.

"What is the first thing you'll do once this is over?" I ask, letting him pull me into his chest.

"Sleep... Somewhere other than this bed. I will find somewhere completely mine... or ours... and sleep without worrying about who is on the other side of the door. And I'm going to breathe and let my heart beat without fear that doing so will lead to my death. Or yours."

I pulled back slightly to look into his eyes again. "Wow. That is much more earnest and deep than I expected... Figured you'd go with something along the lines of fucking me senseless."

He flashed me his trademark smirk. "Oh, don't worry, there will be plenty of that too. Neither of us will be wearing any clothes for months."

"Well, that could be awkward if we need food..."

"We'll get it delivered to the front door."

"You've got it all figured out, huh?" I buried my face back into his chest.

"Yep. It'll be our little slice of happily ever after."

I'd rarely given myself a chance to think of what the after part of this all looked like. But Connor's little fantasy sounded pretty close to perfect to me.

I looked out the window to see that the sun was still high in the sky.

"I should try and get some sleep. If Adam decides to go dragging us off on a hunt or making us partake in some fucked up sex shenanigans, I'm going to need more energy to pretend I don't want to rip him apart." I reluctantly left the comfort of his arms and slid into bed while he made himself comfortable with his book in the chair. He'd already had his few hours of sleep earlier while I'd kept watch. Another thing I was looking forward to once this was all over was falling asleep beside him.

"Hey."

Liam's greeting was the first thing I heard when I realised I'd been pulled into a mindscape.

"Hey." I looked around the cottage and found him sitting on the couch again.

"I've spoken to Patrice."

I was relieved we weren't going to try for small talk. I still hadn't dealt with the fact that he'd jumped back into Eve's bed as soon as our relationship was over. Not that I had any right to judge, given my actions with Connor.

"Have you guys come up with a plan?" I asked, taking a seat across from him in the armchair.

"Yeah. We'll stick with the original plan of arriving with the daywalkers when the sun goes down, but we'll keep Eve from getting to you. Just stay out of sight until we give the all-clear that the spell has been recast, okay? Eve's entire plan is contingent on you torching her and Adam once the sun goes down. So we just have to make sure that doesn't happen."

I considered him for a moment. "That all seems far too simple. Just hide until the big bad wolf goes away?"

"Well, it's all we've got. Unless you've got a better idea?" Liam asked, annoyance flicking across his handsome face.

"No... I just worry that we've missed something."

"Look, Adam doesn't know what's coming, right? So it's not like he'll drag you out of the room come sunset. We need to worry about Eve, and she's with us."

I nodded slowly. "Okay... if that's what you guys think will work, then I'll play along."

"Good. We'll see you tomorrow, Isolde."

· · ·

The mindscape dissolved around me, and I fell back into a restless sleep, waking a few hours later to tell Connor the plan. And quietly praying to any gods who were listening that it would actually work.

CHAPTER THIRTY-FOUR

In the early hours of Saturday morning, I lay on my side in bed, staring at the cracks of sunlight that managed to work their way through the heavy block-out curtains above.

"Can't sleep?" Connor asked, looking up from his book.

"No... difficult to sleep when you know that in a matter of hours, the world could end, and it's your job to stop it happening," I replied.

Connor closed his book and crossed to the bed. "Need a distraction?" He asked, sitting beside me.

He slowly traced a path from my shoulder to my hip with his finger, leaving his hand resting there while his gaze met mine.

"What did you have in mind?" I asked huskily.

Connor smirked while he pushed me onto my back and brought his mouth to my ear. "Let me show you."

I was more than happy to let him.

We spent hours exploring each other, keeping ourselves distracted while time ticked away. The idea that each time we came together may be our last seemed to fuel us further, and by the time the sun had slowly begun to sink closer to the horizon, I could feel the magic humming between us.

Someone began bashing on the door just as Connor started working his way down my body for another round, and he shot a glare toward the door.

"Fuck off!" He yelled, returning his lips to my skin and kissing a path down my abdomen.

I arched my back, and he shot me a wicked grin.

"So needy already."

The bashing on the door continued, and Connor growled, jumping up and moving towards the door in a blur. I yanked the sheet up just before he ripped the door open.

"Do that again, and I will rip your dick off," he told Bastien, who stood with his hand raised, ready for another round of bashing on the door.

"Adam wants us all downstairs, now."

"Adam can fuck off, we're busy."

"It is not a request, Connor." Adam's voice echoed up the stairs. "Get down here now."

Connor hesitated, and Bastien peered around him to leer at me.

"Fine. Fuck off, Bastien." He slammed the door in Bastien's face and looked at me.

"It's still an hour til sunset... Can we make it down there and back before all hell breaks lose?" I asked quietly while I got up to find some clothes.

"Not likely. He's probably bored and wants multiple people to suck him off while the rest of us watch." The frustration on his face gave way to concern. "I don't think we should go down there."

"If we don't, he will just come in and make us... Or worse..." I said, hating that we had no choice once again.

We dressed in silence, and I followed Connor down the stairs. I expected to find Adam sitting on his self-appointed throne in the great room, but we followed the sound of voices into the dining room. Connor came to an abrupt halt in the doorway, and I just managed to stop myself from crashing into his back. Peering over his shoulder, I somehow kept myself from reacting when I took in the sight before us.

There were two women – humans – lying naked on the long table. Their arms and legs were bound, with their mouths gagged, and they both looked around, the terror in their eyes evident for all to see.

"What do we have here, Adam?" Connor asked, his voice again taking on the bored tone I'd now come to call his Adam voice in my head.

I could see the tension running through his body, feeling his stress through the magic connecting us.

"We're celebrating, Connor," Adam replied from where he sat at the head of the table.

Something about the way he looked at us both had me even more on edge than I usually was when in his presence.

"What's the occasion?"

"Oh, don't tell me you've forgotten your birthday?" Adam arched a brow and smiled.

There was nothing inviting about that smile.

The stress rolling from Connor into me kicked up another level. "It's not my birthday..." Somehow, Connor managed to keep his voice steady.

"I don't mean the day your human life began. I meant your immortal birthday. I thought we needed to celebrate the day that Eve gifted you to me. Providing me with the son she always promised me she would." There was something more dangerous than usual to his tone.

"And it was such an honour, Adam."

"Was it, Connor? Was it truly?" He was like a predator, playing with his food.

"Have I ever given you a reason to question my loyalty, Adam?" Connor's voice took on its own dangerous tone.

Adam ran his eyes over Connor, a cool, calculating look behind those cold, dead eyes.

And then words I hoped to never hear from his lips rang out through the room. "I know what you are, Connor."

I had to fight against everything inside of me to ignore the voice that started to scream *Run!* in my head.

"And what's that, Adam?"

How the fuck was Connor so calm right now?

"A hybrid." Adam finally shifted his focus from Connor to meet my gaze, the piercing blue eyes boring into mine. "Just like you're little girlfriend behind you. Isn't that right, Isolde?"

Fuck.

Who knew that fancy mansions in Brisbane could have dungeons? I know I certainly didn't, but here I was, sitting in a windowless room resembling a dungeon in the mansion's basement. I didn't even know this place had a basement. Judging from the strong smell of blood around us, this was where they kept the humans they didn't kill right away. Like those poor women that they were tearing the throats out of right now, celebrating Connor's *birthday* while the birthday boy was sitting right next to me.

"Well, they wanted us to stay away from Adam." Connor attempted to make light of our situation while staring at the ceiling.

"Why the fuck didn't he just kill us? Why throw us in here?" I asked, the anxiety bubbling away and causing me to feel sick.

"I get the distinct impression that he knows what's coming."

"What do you mean? Why can't you just go into his head, find out what he knows and get us the fuck out of here?" I wrung my hands.

"Because his mind is locked up tight all of a sudden. I was trying to get in when he dropped that all on us upstairs, and it was like a wall of steel had been built up around his mind."

"Fan-fucking-tastic," I said through gritted teeth.

"Something doesn't feel right, Isolde."

I laughed. "Are you serious? *Nothing* feels right about *any* of this. " I waved my arm, gesturing around our cosy little prison.

"We need to get a message to Liam. Or Damon. The fact that Adam knows what we are and didn't immediately kill us means there is way more going on than any of us suspected," Connor said, his expression darkening.

"Do you think Eve is working with Adam?"

"I honestly can't think of any other explanation."

I hadn't realised it was possible to be any more terrified than I already was, but I guess there was a level higher than I thought.

"Do you think she knows about the stuff with the realms being tied to them?"

Connor eyes narrowed further still. "We really need to tell the others."

A voice rang out from the shadows on the other side of the bars. "Too late for that now, Connor. Not that you would have had much luck. Eve has everyone's minds locked up tight now. She worked out you'd all been communicating with Seth, and we certainly can't risk him getting in the way now." Adam stepped forward, closely followed by Bastien.

We both leapt to our feet, and I conjured a ball of flame in my hand, ready to throw it at him.

Adam laughed. "Remember, Isolde, only a dragon can kill a dragon."

I glared at him, eyes flashing.

Adam smirked in response, crossing his arms. "Try it and find out. I don't think you'll risk it, though. Not when the doors to the other realms are tied to Eve and me. I know you're too much of a hero to risk breaking the bonds ahead of time if there's even a fraction of a chance that they will succeed."

Connor stepped up beside me, and we exchanged a wary look.

"Eve knows all about Seth's plan to do the original spell again, and she filled me in about it all just before you two waltzed through the doors. Imagine my surprise at seeing my lover again after all these years we've been kept apart. Seth's spell made it so that we could not be together, the magic forcing us apart once we were within reach of each other - it just shows how much stronger she is now. The last time we could be in a room together was the night you were turned, Connor. When power rippled through her for the briefest moment." Adam flung open the door, and they both strode inside.

We stepped backwards until our backs collided with the wall, and I looked at Connor, unsure what to do. He shook his head, angling his body between Adam and me, who was watching me with an arrogant smile.

"Do you honestly think either of you are a match for me? Without Isolde's little fire trick, you are both useless. I could snap your necks instantly, and then where would your little plan be? There are two more of you, after all." Adam was upon me in an instant. "Move, you little bitch." He flung me out the door, and I landed in a heap against the wall on the other side of the bars.

He followed behind, reaching down to lift me again, spinning me so that I walked in front of him with my arm wrenched up behind my back. Even though I was strong, I was no match for him, just like he'd said.

CHAPTER THIRTY-FIVE

I knew our time was up when Adam pushed me through the door at the top of the stairs into the dimly lit foyer. I stumbled a little before Adam reached forward and gripped my throat from behind.

The front door crashed open, the wood splintering when it hit the wall. Despite everything, I felt a small wave of relief when I saw Liam leading the way inside along with Anthony.

Liam's gaze fell on me, taking in the way Adam held me before him, and his eyes narrowed.

"What have you done to her?" He growled, moving towards us but stopping short when Adam began squeezing my throat tightly.

Bastien and Connor appeared next to us. Bastien had Connor's arm wrenched up behind his back, similar to how Adam had held me moments earlier.

Connor growled when he saw how Adam was holding me.

"What do you want from us, Adam?" Connor demanded.

I felt Adam turn his head from me to look at Connor.

"You've done your job now, Connor. You've powered our girl up nice and well with all that fucking you two did all day. We've no use for you any more." When the last words left his mouth, Adam dropped me and moved in a blur to appear before Connor.

It felt like it was happening in slow motion as I watched Adam pull a stake from his deep pocket and slam it into Connor's chest.

I screamed when Connor's eyes widened, his mouth opening while he looked at me briefly before looking down at the stake now protruding from his chest.

"No! Connor!" I threw myself down beside him when he crumpled to the ground, ripping the stake out of his chest in a fruitless attempt to keep him alive. He lay utterly still, and I began to sob when the light in his eyes faded.

"Come now, Isolde. You know that once the light fades from their eyes, there's no coming back." Adam's voice cut through the silence while everyone stared down at where I crouched, clinging to Connor's motionless body.

In my mind, I begged him to say something. I'd even take any snarky comments about how he was the villain right now.

But there was nothing.

I finally looked up at Adam, making sure he would see the murder in my eyes. "By the end of this night, I will have ended you. Mark my words."

"Promises, promises," Adam said with a smile.

Liam took a step closer, and I looked up at him, feeling the tears streaming down my face. He looked down at his brother, an expression I couldn't quite discern flitting across his face before he turned back to Adam, his hands forming into fists at his side, and his expression hardened again.

Adam reached down and grabbed me by the throat once again, holding me in front of him so that I was forced to face Liam. I had to remind myself I technically didn't need to breathe when Adam applied more pressure to my throat.

"Now, now, Liam, you wouldn't want me to have to kill your little whore, would you? Or is she Connor's whore now? I'm having trouble keeping track. I don't suppose it matters now that he's lying dead on the floor."

Liam's eyes met mine briefly when Aurora stepped out from behind the group. To my surprise, she produced her own ball of fire in her hand and glared at Adam. Someone had been practising.

Although she didn't seem to be able to conjure the same amount of fire that I could, it was enough that it would do some damage.

"Not yet, Aurora." Eve's voice rang out through the room. She stepped around Liam, closely followed by everyone else.

I felt Adam shift behind me when Eve moved further into the room.

"My love," he said, his tone irreverent.

Eve moved slowly towards him. The others couldn't see her face, but I noticed the smile playing across her lips. It grew wider when she caught my eye.

I pushed aside the grief I could feel threatening to overcome me and focussed my attention on Eve. The large foyer was beginning to feel quite crowded, with so many bodies entering the house and the rest of the nightwalkers coming through various doors from the rest of the house. Out of the corner of my eye, I saw Sabine leap over the railing of the open hall above, landing nimbly in front of Liam and hissing in his face.

Liam's only reaction was to punch her in the face.

For a few seconds, no one moved, like they were waiting for a signal, their bodies tense.

Then all hell broke loose.

Where there had previously been a tense standoff, now there were multiple fights as everyone jumped into the fray.

My eyes remained trained on Eve. She had reached us now, and Adam gripped my throat even tighter.

"You've done well, my love," Eve purred, looking at Adam over my head before returning her eyes to mine. "And you played your part well, too, Isolde. None of this would have been possible without you and dear Connor." She reached forward to run a finger down my cheek, gripping my chin in her hand and forcing me to look down at Connor's lifeless body. "So wonderfully naive."

I wrenched my head from her grasp, feeling my eyes flash while the rage and grief swirled inside me.

To my right, Patrice stopped suddenly, having just slammed a stake into the chest of one of Adam's minions. She turned to look at us, her eyes narrowing, and she moved towards us, sidestepping Bastien, who stumbled into her path, having been kicked across the room by Anthony.

"Patrice, no!" I managed to rasp out, my ability to speak considerably affected by Adam's grip on my throat.

Eve had already noticed Patrice advancing towards her, and she grinned, raising her hand. Patrice froze in place, held motionless by the magic that Eve now wielded so easily.

Bastien reached for Patrice and savagely bit into her neck.

She was unable to move, her eyes widening, and I saw the fear ripple across her face just before Bastien ripped her head right off.

"No!" Barbara screamed from across the room, distracted from her own battle with Sabine.

Daniel managed to stake Sabine before she could take advantage of Barbara's distress.

I could do nothing but stare at Patrice's body before Eve grasped my face once again, looking me in the eye while I fought back tears.

"You can stop this all right now, Isolde. Destroy the bindings on our magic – we will let everyone you care about in this room go. The bindings on the entrances to the other realms are a lost cause now, you know it. Seth doesn't hold the power he once wielded – he won't be able to bind us again, and without us at our full strength, no one on this Earth is safe."

I shook my head and spat in her face.

Adam's grip tightened, lifting me so that my toes were barely touching the ground, and I knew I was moments from having my head ripped clean off.

But I was willing to sacrifice myself if it meant that neither of these monsters returned to their full strength. I knew our time was up. If Seth had succeeded in recasting the spell, it would have happened by now.

Instead, the ground beneath our feet began to rumble.

Aurora appeared at my side, and for a fraction of a second, I thought she'd come to save me.

Instead, she smiled at me—a sad, apologetic smile.

I couldn't utter a word with Adam's grip growing ever tighter. I was scared to use my powers for fear of ripping apart the binding spell.

I couldn't do anything when my sister placed one hand on Eve's arm, moving to do the same with Adam.

And set them aflame.

From the moment her powers spread through them and into me, I knew we had failed, that we'd never had any hope of stopping Eve's plan.

How could we have, having had only days to prepare when she'd had hundreds of years?

While the roaring of the flames grew louder, I distantly heard Liam yell out. When the fire blocked my vision of everything else, Seth and Damon appeared beside him. The last thing I saw was Liam's tortured expression, and then my world was nothing but fire.

CHAPTER THIRTY-SIX

Eve and Adam had begun writhing within the flames, their screams eventually becoming guttural moans while the combination of fire and magic swirled around them.

Although Adam had released his grip on my throat, and my feet hit the ground, I was held immobile by Aurora's flames. They wrapped themselves around me, pulling at me, and I lost all control over my own magic, the fire bursting from me to merge with the ones engulfing us, as though mine and Aurora's powers had become one.

Everything else ceased to exist. My eyes scrunched closed when the pain ripped through me. All I could feel was the flames that felt like they were being torn from my body, the sound of the roaring flames overwhelming me. Every inch of my body felt like it was being stretched to its limit, and a distant thought in the back of my mind wondered if I was about to be torn apart.

Eve's screams and moans now gave way to laughter.

I opened my eyes and saw her fling her arms wide, the flames flickering along her skin, almost like they were trying to pull something from her, testing where to find it. Although my entire body was racked with pain, I was able to focus enough to see that the flames along her skin were gradually changing colour, growing steadily more crimson than those being ripped from me.

"Yes!" She exclaimed, her piercing blue eyes slowly changing until they swirled with red, flickering fire.

She fixed those terrifying eyes on me, and I could see the triumph there when I heard a loud sound over the roar of the flames.

A slow, deep cracking sound, almost like the earth itself was cracking open. It was a sound I'd never heard before, and if I went without hearing it again for the rest of my life, it wouldn't be long enough.

The rumbling beneath our feet grew stronger, and I heard things outside the flames start crashing to the ground.

Adam began laughing. Every hair on my body stood on end, and I felt the last of my magic drain from my body. His head snapped back, and fire erupted from his eyes and mouth while power rippled through his body. For the tiniest moment, I saw a flash of something else, a creature unlike anything I'd ever seen.

I knew I'd just caught a glimpse of his dragon form now that the magic binding him was finally destroyed, and his ability to shift was restored.

Aurora and I slumped to the floor, and the flames abruptly disappeared.

Adam and Eve remained standing, now locked in a passionate embrace. The fighting around us had long since ceased, while everyone – daywalker, nightwalker and Order members alike – gaped at the couple standing within the circle of the scorched floor.

Eve's black hair was now a cascade of crimson-red fire running down her back, and I could feel the power rolling off them both while I took in the flames that shot out behind her, forming into two massive fiery wings. Her skin shimmered with swirls of fire dancing across every exposed surface.

Adam's arms rippled while he gripped her tightly to him, almost as though the muscles beneath his skin were growing right before my eyes.

I felt movement beside me, and I rolled my head to look at Aurora while she reached out to grip my hand.

"What did you do?" I was barely able to utter more than a whisper.

All the energy had been sapped from me, along with my magic, and when I tried to summon a flame, I could not muster even a spark.

"What I had to," she whispered back.

With all eyes still on the couple on fire devouring each other in the middle of the room, no one noticed when Liam and Ronson raced forward, dragging us away from Eve and Adam's feet. Liam gathered me to his chest and swiftly took me into a different room.

The sounds of fighting resumed while the remaining members of the Order and the daywalkers attempted to kill as many nightwalkers as possible before Adam's focus shifted from Eve.

"Are you okay?" Liam whispered in my ear, and I wasn't sure how to respond.

Nothing felt okay. Between losing Connor and having my magic ripped from my body to restore Adam and Eve's powers, I wasn't sure I'd ever be okay again.

"I'm alive. I don't think I can comment any further than that, though." I was struggling to form words and fighting through the lump in my throat.

"I'm going to need you to be as okay as possible because this isn't over yet." His words were urgent in my ear.

Beside me, I could see Ronson holding Aurora upright, her head buried in his chest while his lips moved close to her ear, whispering words I couldn't hear, and her shoulders shook. I couldn't even fathom what was going on there.

"We've lost, Liam," I said, the hoarse words coming out with a sob, and his arms tightened around me.

"Not quite," Seth said.

I hadn't noticed either him or Damon in the room before now, so lost in my grief and exhaustion.

"What do you mean?"

"Liam was able to have a discussion with our friend over there," Seth nodded towards Ronson, who had stepped back to look Aurora in the eye as if checking to ensure she was okay, "and we'd had to devise a new plan. Eve had set everything up so you would be forced to rip the bindings away, regardless of whether we redid the spell."

"But... the gateways to the other realms?" I had no idea how to address the Ronson situation and figured that could wait til later.

If there was a later.

"The gateways are currently open. That was the cracking sound. We didn't have the strength without removing the bonds that were muting our magic. We had no other choice but to destroy them. We've got a tiny window open to us, and we need to act now," Damon said, looking towards Liam, who nodded in response.

Liam turned his attention to me, his grip on my upper arms tightening when I swayed.

"I don't think I have it in me to do anything," I sagged into his chest again.

I was struggling just to keep my head up. Out of the corner of my eye, I could see that Aurora was going through something similar.

"I know. I promise you will get through this," Liam said.

"What do you mean?" My voice shook while I looked up at him.

He smiled at me. "Just trust me." There was something about the look on his face that scared me.

I nodded slowly when Ronson brought Aurora to my side.

Liam looked at Aurora briefly. She was struggling to lift her head, but I could see the determination in her eyes.

"What is going on?" I asked while Aurora stepped into Liam's other side, and he wrapped an arm around her, holding us both firmly to his chest.

"Now," Liam said, looking over at Seth.

Seth nodded before lifting both of his hands beside him. I felt a sudden jolt run through me, and the air around us began to crackle with magic.

But this was different to any other magic that I'd experienced before. I saw the magic weaving through the air and headed straight for Liam. It hit him a fraction of a second later, and he let out an unearthly cry.

I tried to pull back, to scream, "Stop!" but he held me tight against him, rendering me motionless.

Magic flowed through me, my power returning at an alarming rate, and I finally understood what was happening.

Seth had told us that Liam and Connor had been created to amplify our power. And now, with the massive boost from Seth at his full strength, Liam was acting as our charger, replenishing our depleted supplies.

But at this speed, there was no way this wouldn't kill him.

I screamed, attempting once again to pull away, but his arms were like a vice around us.

We would never have been able to recharge in time to be helpful, so Liam was sacrificing himself to give us all a fighting chance.

I began to tremble, the agony of all that I'd lost in the last few months, and especially today, rising inside of me.

I'd already lost Connor. I couldn't watch Liam die, too.

I wouldn't.

Liam was in my head now, the bond that had once been broken firmly in place.

"Just let it happen, Isolde."

"I can't. Too many people have died because of me."

"This was always how it was meant to be. Just trust me. It will all be okay."

"How can you know that?"

"Because I have faith in you, I've always believed in you..." His voice in my head had grown weaker. *"Now..."* I felt his grip finally start to slip. *Give them fucking hell, Isolde."*

And then his arms were gone. Aurora and I remained where we were, but Liam slowly fell to the floor.

Inside my head, something snapped, and my body was flooded

with heat. Power ran through me, unlike anything I'd ever felt. This wasn't just an increase in my powers.

Fire danced around Aurora, the blue-tinged flames trailing behind her like wings. Meanwhile, the fire flickering along my skin was a pale, shimmering purple.

My twin and I stared into each other's eyes, transfixed. The once identical irises were now flickering with blue and purple flames that mirrored each other.

The eyes of phoenixes.

CHAPTER THIRTY-SEVEN

My chest felt tight while I looked down at Liam's body, tears streaming down my face, before turning my gaze to Seth.

"Why?" I demanded, my voice thick.

Seth shook his head. "The only way we have any hope of stopping them is if we reversed the transition you had both gone through. Returning your full phoenix abilities. Liam understood the risk."

"You just took out our strongest fighter." I didn't try to hide the shaking in my voice while I pointed down at Liam, struggling to accept that he had sacrificed himself for this insanity.

"No. I provided our strongest fighter with the powers she needed to fight Eve. Only another phoenix is going to be able to end her finally."

"But if I kill her, what will we do about the doors to the other realms?" I asked, searching the faces of all the others in the room.

"We're going to bind them to someone else," Damon said.

I looked over at him with wide eyes. "I don't understand."

The fighting in the other room grew louder, and I heard Barbara scream again.

"We don't have time to go through this now, Isolde. Just trust us. You must go back in there and end this once and for all. Leave the closing of the realms to us," Seth snapped, and I cast one final look down at Liam before nodding towards my sister, who followed close behind.

I flung the door open and looked out into the mayhem occurring in the foyer.

Adam and Eve were nowhere to be seen.

"I cloaked the house when we walked in. No one can enter or leave, so they will be here somewhere," Seth said in response to the alarmed look I shot him.

I nodded towards Ronson, who had been watching the exchange silently from the corner where he stood with his arms crossed.

"What about him?" I asked, wary of the daywalker whose allegiances I was now questioning.

"We can trust him, Isolde," Aurora said.

I narrowed my eyes and flicked my gaze over each of them.

Although I didn't like it, I had no choice but to have faith that they all knew what they were doing.

With a final nod, we shut the door and began to move through the crowd of fighters.

Anthony and Anika were battling a group of four nightwalkers but seemed to have the upper hand so far. Nearby, Daniel, Christian and Barbara fought with their backs facing inwards, ensuring no one could surprise them from behind while they battled their own group of nightwalkers. Barbara looked up after staking the nightwalker in front of her, and her eyes widened when she saw us.

I gave her a tight smile, hoping once this was all over, she'd still be alive for me to explain what had happened.

Other daywalkers I only knew in passing were locked in various fights, and I was pleased to see that most of the bodies littering the room belonged to Adam's band of followers. But there was no sign of their fearless leader.

"Where would they go? I assume you know this place better than I do," I looked at Aurora while we moved towards the stairs.

She winced, and I mentally kicked myself for reminding her.

"I'm going to hazard a guess that they've gone off to have a romantic reunion, given how much those two love to screw anything that moves and being apart for thousands of years. Adam's room is in the other wing of the house. I only went there once."

I asked no further questions, and we raced up the stairs together.

"Wait," I screeched to a halt before we entered the hall she had pointed to. "Adam is a dragon-shifter now, right?"

Aurora stopped abruptly beside me. "Um... I guess. Why?"

"Well, didn't they say that only a Dragon can kill another Dragon?" I asked, and a flash of understanding crossed her face.

"Fuck..." She said, letting the word stretch out.

"Where the fuck are we going to get a Dragon from?"

A moment later, a solution must have come to her because she took off in a blur of motion back towards the stairs.

"Wait! Where are you going?"

She stopped at the top of the stairs and spun back to face me.

"I have an idea. Go, I'll be there as soon as I can." And then she disappeared.

I blinked, staring at the spot she'd been a fraction of a second beforehand, cursing her name under my breath.

Why was everyone so insistent on leaving me in the dark while expecting me to save the day? If we made it through this alive, I would be enforcing a strict 'fill Isolde in on all plans' rule.

Having checked every other door that led off the hallway, I stopped in front of the one at the very end of the hall, hearing the telltale signs of a couple having sex on the other side.

Of course, it had to be the room furthest away.

Seriously, they had just unleashed hell on earth, and yet their first thing to do was go and have a quick fuck in his room?

Fury began to rise within me, mingling with the grief that I was refusing to acknowledge.

I hated that my sister had been right, and I really didn't want to put myself through seeing what was happening on the other side of that door.

Taking a deep breath, I reached for the handle and flung the door open, wishing I could close my eyes.

Adam had Eve pressed up against the window, fucking her hard against the glass while she screamed his name. Her flames were gone now, appearing human once again.

"Well, this is a sight I could have gone a lifetime without seeing," I said, keeping my voice steady, and they both whirled to face me.

Eve wrenched her dress down over her hips, fixing me with a scowl while Adam growled.

"How are you alive?" She spat, and I raised an eyebrow.

"Probably should have checked to make sure I was dead before the two of you decided to partake in your make-up sex if you intended to kill me."

"A mistake I won't make twice," she said, raising her hands and producing twin balls of fire that she hurled at me. I ducked out of the way, launching my own back at her.

She snarled, sidestepping them, and they hit the window, setting the curtains alight.

"How did you think this was going to go, Isolde?" Eve sent another ball of fire towards me just as someone crashed into the room.

Aurora skidded to a halt at my side, and Eve paused, watching us both uneasily.

"Little worried there, Eve? Weren't expecting to deal with two phoenixes, were you?" Aurora said, and we moved towards her as one, producing flames in each of our hands.

Eve glared at us before clapping her hands above her head, bursting into flames before disappearing entirely.

Adam let out a roar and dove towards us. He reached Aurora first, throwing her through the air. She hit the wall with a thud, but I didn't have a chance to react before he grabbed me by the throat and lifted me off the ground.

"I will rip you apart, you little whore," he screamed, flames erupting from his eyes.

Although apparently, the only thing that could kill a phoenix was another one, it seemed as though Adam was pretty sure he could do some damage, and I struggled against his grip. I wrapped my hands around his wrist, attempting to pull his hand away. He opened his mouth, and fear coursed through me.

Could dragon fire hurt a Phoenix?

My vision began to blur when the pressure on my throat increased, but I became distantly aware that someone else had entered the room.

A split second later, the hand at my throat was gone, and my feet hit the floor again. I stared, my mouth agape, while Adam stood frozen before me, his arms flung wide. He looked down at me, his mouth wide, before our gazes fell to the hand protruding from his chest, having slammed through from his back. The hand disappeared, and Adam slumped to the floor, a giant hole in his chest.

I looked up at the person who had slayed a dragon and blinked. Once. Twice.

My mind was struggling to comprehend what I saw, and I turned in a daze when a scream echoed through the room.

Eve was standing before the door, her crimson flames swirling around her, her long hair alight behind her once again. The fire burned in her eyes while she unleashed a stream of red flames, heading straight for me.

Thinking fast, I sent my own flames to meet hers, feeling the power hit me like a wall when purple met red, and the two flames crashed into each other.

Using every ounce of the power that Liam had poured into me, I began slowly moving closer to her, willing my flames to overpower hers. Eve screamed and tried to do the same, but my flames were stronger, and she pressed herself back against the wall.

Aurora stepped forward, a ball of blue flames raised over her head, her flaming wings outstretched.

"No! This is my fight!" I screamed.

I needed to be the one who ended this woman—the woman who had set us on this path and controlled so much of my past.

It was my destiny.

My purpose.

And I'd be damned if anyone else took that away from me.

"You have destroyed so many lives. You played god." My flames were slowly burning through hers.

I saw genuine fear in her eyes for the first time since I'd met her.

"But you're not a god, Eve." I unleashed one last surge of power, and Eve screamed when purple flames finally exploded through her. She exploded with one last violent scream, red and purple embers flying through the air.

Aurora moved to my side while I stared at the spot where Eve had been standing for the longest time.

Lowering my hands, I glanced at my sister before looking back at the person who had saved me.

Connor stood staring down at his bloody hand, which still held the heart that he had just ripped out of Adam's chest.

He looked at me slowly, his eyes black as night, fire burning in the centre of each one.

The eyes of a dragon.

CHAPTER THIRTY-EIGHT

"How..." I could barely speak. All rational thought had disappeared entirely while I stared at Connor.

Aurora cleared her throat, and I briefly flicked my gaze towards her, scared to look away from Connor for too long in case he disappeared.

"When you mentioned we needed a dragon, I remembered they had said the guys were made from Adam's essence. I also remembered that Seth had told us that phoenixes could bring people back from the dead. I hoped that was right and that if I brought Connor back, he'd return as a dragon rather than his hybrid state. Looks like I was right."

I stared at my sister, trying to process everything she had just said.

"You put all of that together in that short amount of time?" I was very impressed.

"I'm not just a pretty face," Aurora replied, and I could tell she was only half joking.

"No, you're not," I said, reaching to pull her into a hug. She hugged me back briefly, her arms stiff, before stepping back.

"I'll let you guys have a minute. I'm going to see how Damon and Seth are getting on with that spell." She left the room, leaving me standing alone with Connor, who was starting to show signs of life, coming out of the stunned silence he'd been in since he'd ripped Adam's heart from his chest.

"Are you okay?" I stepped cautiously closer to him.

I had no idea if he'd come back as something else entirely, and I was wary of getting too close.

"Isolde?" His eyes travelled over my face, and he finally dropped the heart, moving towards me.

"Yes," I whispered, and he gripped my face with both hands.

I knew that I should care that his hand was covered in blood, but I was too lost in those now burning eyes to give it a second thought.

The intensity in his eyes was incredible, and I knew that if Adam had looked at Eve like this, she would have been powerless against the force behind it.

No one could resist when the person they loved looked at them like this. Like you were the centre of the universe, and they would burn the world down for you.

I'd like to think that if Connor tried to convince me to start murdering people, though, I'd do a better job of saying no.

"This is a new look." He was staring behind me, his eyes trained on my new wings of fire.

Despite everything that had just happened, I laughed, but it came out mixed with a sob.

"Are you okay?" He asked, his gaze returning to mine, and I nodded slowly.

"Yes. I killed Eve."

His lips slowly, oh so slowly, lifted into that trademark smirk. The one that I both loved and loathed in equal measure. The one that I had begged the universe to see once again.

"I noticed. I killed Adam," he replied.

I laughed properly this time. "I saw. I'm very thankful for that. I wasn't ready to test that theory that he couldn't kill me."

He touched his forehead to mine. "Neither was I." He crushed his lips to mine, and I sank into his embrace.

"God, I love you," he whispered against my lips.

I felt tears spring to my eyes. "I love you too," I whispered back, feeling his arms tighten around me.

"I fucking knew it," he replied, and I started to laugh.

"You're such a bastard."

"Yep, but I'm the bastard you love, so I guess you gotta deal with it."

"Gladly."

After losing ourselves in that kiss for a little longer, we reluctantly pulled apart. We knew we needed to make our way downstairs.

The distant sounds of fighting had ceased now, and when we walked down the stairs, I was relieved to see that most of my people were left standing. The bodies of all of Adam's followers were lying in a heap to the side.

Anthony looked excited when he saw me. "Cool wings. Please do your fancy nightwalker bonfire thing," he begged.

I rolled my eyes before turning to inspect the pile. "Perhaps we should take them outside first?"

Anthony pouted. "Fine," he grumbled, moving towards them and beginning to carry the bodies outside with the assistance of Daniel and Christian. Barbara sat on the floor beside Patrice's body, which was now covered by a blanket, and I moved to crouch beside her.

"I'm so sorry, Barbara." I knew that they had been close, and she would take Patrice's death particularly hard.

I wasn't ready to face the idea of the Order existing without Patrice.

"She would have been so proud of you." Barbara's voice wavered.

I moved to hug her, but she pulled back.

"Um... maybe wait until you're not on fire..." Her voice trailed off while she stared over my shoulder.

"I don't actually know how to make them go away," I looked down at the purple flames swirling over my arms.

"What happened? Where's Eve? Did you kill Adam?" Anika asked, appearing at my side when I stood up again.

The others finally noticed Connor, who had remained at the base of the stairs.

"How are you alive?" Anthony asked when he came back inside, looking from Connor to me. "And what the fuck is going on with both of you and the fire?"

I exchanged a look with Connor before answering Anika first. "Adam and Eve are both dead."

My words were met with silence while they all exchanged looks.

"Seriously, what is with the fire?" Anthony wasn't letting this go.

"Eve played us all. This was all an elaborate plan to return her and Adam to their former selves. Adam knew everything and was waiting for us tonight."

"Still not explaining the fire..."

I shot Anthony an exasperated look.

"Eve was never human. She was a phoenix. So am I."

The daywalkers stared at me. But judging by the looks on the faces of the Order members, this wasn't news to them.

"And what about him?" Anthony regained his voice first, nodding towards Connor.

"It would appear that Connor is a Dragon." Tabitha stepped through the door from the kitchen, followed by Michael.

"You knew about the Dragons?" I asked, and Tabitha nodded.

"Eve mentioned once about the fact that dragons had once existed... In a moment of nostalgia, she'd lamented that her former lover had once been a powerful dragon and how much she missed him. She'd described his appearance, though – the burning eyes are exactly like I'd imagined." She was staring at Connor.

"I don't know the full details of everything that happened here tonight. But I think we all need to have a chat with Ronson," I said.

"Where is he?" Michael asked, looking around the room.

"That's what I'd like to know," Aurora said, stepping out of the room where we'd last seen Seth, Damon, Ronson and...

"Liam," I whispered, the man himself following Aurora out the door.

I flung myself at him, briefly noticing that my flames had finally extinguished. He caught me around the waist while I hugged him tight.

"I thought you were dead," I sobbed into his chest.

He squeezed me tight for a moment before stepping back.

My stomach flipped when I saw his eyes had also changed and were identical to his brothers. To how Adam's had been right before he died.

"Nope. I just needed to recharge. I came to when Aurora came back in a few minutes ago. Seth, Damon, and Ronson were gone, though." Liam ran a hand through his hair, looking around at everyone while they silently stared at him.

I looked over at Aurora, who avoided meeting my eyes. It appeared that Liam wasn't aware that he had just been dead and brought back to life as a dragon... by a phoenix. I was not looking forward to dropping that bomb on him.

I slowly became aware that everyone was looking at me now. As though waiting for me to give them direction.

Now that the leaders of the Order and Daywalkers were gone, it seemed like everyone thought I should know what to do next.

Well, they were shit out of luck because I was done.

I looked around, noticing that Connor had disappeared.

"You guys work out what we should do," I said, heading back up the stairs.

I found Connor standing in the doorway of his room, staring inside.

"You okay?" I asked, stopping beside him.

"Yeah... Just..." He swallowed hard and shook his head. "Just processing everything."

I took his hand in mine and squeezed it. "What do you say about getting out of here?"

He squeezed my hand back. "That is the hottest thing you have ever said to me." He turned and pulled me towards him, kissing me hard before leading me back down the hallway and away from the room that had been his prison and sanctuary for so long.

CHAPTER THIRTY-NINE

"*D*oes anyone know if they managed to reseal the entrances to the other realms?"

Once we'd confirmed that the wards Seth had raised around the house had been brought down, everyone had agreed we weren't interested in remaining in the mansion. When Connor had vehemently announced he never wanted to see anything inside ever again, I'd raised a cloaking spell around it and set it on fire.

It was fast becoming my signature move.

Once we brought the remaining daywalkers up to speed on the other realms and the truth regarding Adam and Eve, we'd retreated to the Manor, where we were all gathered around the large conference table. I was avoiding looking at the seat that Patrice usually occupied, not ready to process her death when there was still so much uncertainty around what lay before us.

"Well, the ground stopped shaking... That's got to be a good sign, right?" Christian asked, looking around at everyone else.

No one had the answer.

"I think we all need to get some sleep," Daniel said.

Everyone looked ready to pass out where they sat, and no one disagreed with him. The sound of multiple chairs scraping against the floor echoed through the room.

After a brief discussion in the foyer, the daywalkers agreed to return the following evening. All traces of animosity were gone now. I guess engaging in a battle to the death against a common enemy had brought us all together.

Liam had avoided looking at Connor or me before disappearing after being told he'd not just passed out earlier. I wasn't sure if he'd returned to his house or headed to his room within the Manor. Even though we'd all temporarily put aside our differences earlier, I wasn't sure if there would ever be anything that could bring the brothers together.

Connor followed me into my room without a word. Aurora had also disappeared, and I wasn't sure where we stood either... all things to worry about later, after many, many hours of sleep.

I collapsed onto the bed and felt the mattress dip when Connor lay down behind me. He pulled me close, wrapping himself around me when I pressed my back to his chest, and I felt sleep claim me almost instantly.

"I see you succeeded, Isolde." Damon had pulled me into his mindscape again.

I felt Connor's presence seconds before he appeared beside me while I took in Damon's changed appearance. He seemed to have aged several decades. Whereas before he had appeared as a man in his mid-forties, the person standing before us looked ancient. I would have guessed that he was at least one hundred... Maybe two.

"What happened to you?" I asked, gaping at him.

"The magic that my father had used to keep me alive all these years died with him."

"Seth is dead?" Connor asked.

"His life was tied to Adam and Eve's. Once you destroyed them both, he slipped away as well."

"But... did he manage to close the entrances to the other realms?" I asked, suddenly terrified that everything was about to explode once again.

Damon looked uncertain before nodding. "I think so. He used Ronson as the anchor this time. He volunteered."

"But... how can we trust Ronson? He was by Eve's side all along. Surely he knew what she was planning?"

"According to what Liam discovered when he was talking to him, Ronson had lived for centuries in his brother's shadow before the curse, and the last thing he had ever wanted was a world where Adam was returned to power. He had naively believed that Eve wanted the same thing. She was very good at keeping her true motives to herself. It seems as though, once Isolde transitioned and it was getting closer to the spell coming to fruition, Eve became erratic. Ronson realised there was more to it than he'd been aware of. And then, last week, he followed her and discovered she had met with Adam and told him everything, with the intent of them finally being together again. He blamed himself. I believe volunteering to give up everything and tying himself to the portals was his way of trying to lessen that guilt."

"Do you truly believe this?" Connor asked, his expression unreadable.

"I do. Liam was in his mind when this discussion happened and saw it all. He was also instrumental in getting Aurora ready for what needed to be done tonight. Eve had been whispering in her ear all week, sowing the seeds. Once Liam realised what was going on, Ronson convinced Aurora to do what needed to be done. They seemed to have developed an understanding of one another."

I didn't quite know how to feel about that last bit of information.

"Where is Ronson now?" Connor asked.

Damon shrugged, and the effort behind that simple movement seemed to sap even more energy from him.

"I don't know. I have a feeling he will disappear. He has lost much tonight. It will be a lot to process."

I studied Damon closely. "Why did it all happen this way tonight? Why did you decide to abandon the original plan?"

Damon looked at me sadly for a moment before answering. "When we realised how unstable the portals had become, we knew the only way was to start over again. We couldn't trust that Eve didn't have other plans in place to ensure she succeeded, and this way, we controlled the outcome."

"Why didn't anyone tell us?" Connor asked.

"By the time we'd worked out what was going on, the connection to you both had been blocked by Eve. We had no choice but to hope we succeeded, even without you two knowing what would happen. We hadn't expected to come in and find that Adam knew everything already, though, or that he would kill Connor."

"Yes, that was an unfortunate turn of events," Connor replied, a sarcastic bite to his tone, and his jaw tensed while he crossed his arms.

"What about you? What are you going to do now?" I asked, bringing the conversation back on track before Damon could respond.

"I will be gone soon. I've served my purpose now. I long for this life to be over."

"But... what are we meant to do now? What happens if it turns out creatures managed to get through the portals? Or if something happens to Ronson? None of us possess the knowledge or the magic to fight anything that could get through. With the portals bound again, won't that mean that anyone who may have the magical abilities to close them will have their powers muted?"

Damon smiled at me. It was the first genuine smile I had ever seen on his face. It was laced with sadness and something that looked like pride.

"Surely you've noticed that your powers are stronger now? The four of you are the most powerful creatures on this earth. This time, my father found a way to bind the portals without muting the magic of those who possess the ability to wield it. You will notice this amongst the Order members who were direct descendants of the original coven... Once they start to use their powers, of course. None of them have

attempted much outside of the protective spells and charms. And as for the knowledge, I have hidden spell books in each manor. You just all need to work out where to look." He started coughing.

A deep, rattling cough. It was as though he had aged another decade in the minutes we conversed.

"Wait... does this mean everyone within the Order is a dragon now?" I asked, my eyes widening.

Once the coughing had subsided, he straightened to look us both over, shaking his head. "No. Whilst they are direct descendants, their bloodlines are too diluted now. Connor and Liam are dragons because Eve created them from Adam directly."

He focused his attention on Connor, who shifted slightly beside me.

"I never thought I'd see another dragon again. Or a phoenix. Between you two, Aurora and Liam, you will be unstoppable. Make sure none of you follow down the same path as Adam and Eve."

"So Aurora and I are full phoenixes now?"

"Yes, because Eve created you both directly from her essence, you and Aurora became phoenixes when you turned twenty-five. That is the age when all those with magical abilities come into their powers. But, your powers were muted. Aurora's even more so as she was not dealing with the Order's magic. Your transition to a hybrid made your powers stronger than Eve anticipated. Aurora will eventually be almost as powerful as you, but you have the magic of the seventh son and seventh daughter running through your veins." Another coughing fit began.

"And Liam and I? Are we truly dragons?" Connor asked once Damon had finished coughing.

"If neither of you had transitioned five hundred years ago, you would have been dragon-shifters with muted abilities, much like Isolde and Aurora. Your powers would have appeared around your twenty-fifth birthday, but with the timing of your transitions, that didn't happen. When Aurora brought each of you back, you returned to this world in your true forms."

Damon ran a wary eye over Connor, staring into the eyes blazing with fire.

"You have the ability to do great things, Connor. Don't become twisted like Adam did. He became feared amongst all other dragons due to his intense need to control and conquer all."

He stared Connor down, waiting for him to nod, before he turned to look at me once more, his expression darkening.

"Be wary of this gift. Do not become like Eve. The power to give and take a life is not something that should be taken lightly. It will cause the balance of nature to become unstable. Sometimes, people are meant to die. It is a cruel fact of life. And no one should have the power to pick and choose who lives or dies. Make sure you and your sister don't abuse that power."

Connor wrapped an arm around my waist, pulling me closer, and Damon watched us before he continued to speak.

"My mother was able to be corrupted because of the constant amplification of her powers by being with Adam. Be careful this doesn't happen to you, Isolde. She wasn't always evil."

With those final words of warning, Damon disappeared. Connor and I exchanged a grim look while the mindscape dissolved, and I finally settled into a dreamless sleep.

CHAPTER FORTY

I slept later than I thought was possible, awakening around midday.

Rolling over, I was surprised to find the bed empty next to me, and I sat up, looking around the room for any sign of Connor. Noticing the open bathroom door, I slid from between the sheets and walked silently towards it, stopping in the doorway.

Connor was shirtless, staring at his reflection while he leaned close to the mirror, staring into his own eyes. Although it had been hours since his resurrection, I still wasn't used to the flames that had replaced the startling blue.

"Do you feel any different?" I asked quietly once he'd noticed me standing behind him, his dragon-fire eyes meeting my now purple-flamed ones in the mirror.

"I can feel a burning sensation all over my body. It's not unpleasant, but yeah... it's different. It's almost like something is bursting to get out. I guess that would be the dragon..."

His voice sounded different. I hadn't noticed it in my exhaustion last night, but I could hear it now. It was deeper and slightly rough. Something deep inside me reacted to it, like it was being called home.

"I don't think the dragon is a separate part of you..."

"Yeah? Are you ready for me to call you a phoenix instead of a person?" He asked, his tone full of warning.

It was a warning I wasn't going to heed. "Regardless of everything we've learnt about ourselves this last week, you are simply Connor to me," I said, standing behind him. I looked over his shoulder, holding his gaze in the mirror while I ran my hands up his torso. "The man who has claimed every part of me." I pressed a kiss to his shoulder, and I smiled against his skin when I felt him shudder under my touch.

He held himself completely still, his breathing shallow, while I continued to kiss my way up his neck. I slid my hands slowly down his abs, which were even more impressive than before, before undoing his fly and reaching inside to wrap a hand around him. He groaned when I began gliding my hand up and down, his eyes fluttering closed briefly.

"Fuck." He spun around and claimed my lips hungrily.

I moved to take him in my hand again, but he pushed my hand away.

"Not yet." He turned us so that my back pressed against the vanity, continuing to kiss me hard, bruising my lips.

He quickly helped me remove my leggings before lifting me to sit on the vanity, reaching between us to find the bundle of nerves that would be my undoing. Within moments, I was moaning his name, writhing against his hand.

"That's right. I have claimed every fucking part of you, Isolde. Now come undone," he commanded, leaning down to suck the sensitive peak of my right breast into his mouth.

I didn't even try to hold back the scream that ripped through me, coming harder than I ever had before. He straightened to watch me, the fire in his eyes burning even more intensely.

Once I'd come down from the orgasm running through me, he lifted me down swiftly before spinning me to face the mirror, pinning my hips to the vanity when he pushed my legs wider to thrust inside me. He gripped my throat gently, forcing me to hold his gaze in the mirror while he slid in and out.

"I will never stop thinking about how good this feels," he growled in my ear, and I moaned again, already feeling another orgasm building.

If I'd thought that sex with Connor before was amazing, it was nothing compared to what we were feeling now. Pleasure sparked through my entire body, and when I looked in the mirror, I saw that my eyes had begun glowing. I tried to tamp down on the magic that threatened to let loose.

"Let it happen," Connor whispered.

As though his words were the switch for my abilities, every inch of me lit up, surrounding us in purple flames when I came again.

But this was different to all the other times I'd lost control. Whereas previously, everything around me was at risk of catching fire, my flames rippled only around our bodies, touching nothing else.

Connor cried out while he came with me, the magic crackling through both of us and prolonging the sensation, threatening to break us apart entirely.

Slowly, oh so slowly, the flames died down, and I leaned forward to rest my forehead against the cold mirror while I struggled to catch my breath.

"Fuck. Me." His words were muffled, his mouth pressed against my neck while he steadied himself by placing his hand against the mirror.

"That was intense," I rasped out, my throat raw.

"We might need to work out a way to ration your orgasms... Not sure I can survive that every time," he said, wrapping his arms around me and pulling me upright to lean back into his embrace.

"Yeah, maybe just two or three times a day to start with." I grinned at him in the mirror, and he tipped his head back, laughing.

It was the most relaxed I'd ever seen him.

• • •

After showering together, we headed back to bed. Connor rested against the headboard and drew my back to his chest, wrapping his arms around me and brushing his lips against my temple.

"So, I guess we should work out what we're going to do now," he said quietly.

I sighed and nodded. "Your plan to just disappear and leave everyone else to sort out their own shit is a good one, but I think we, or at least I, have to hang around for a bit first. We still need to find out if anything made it through the portals. There are still night-walkers roaming around. We lost the elder we all trust, and now the daywalkers-" Connor placed a finger to my lips before gently kissing me.

"Relax, love. We don't need to work it all out yet. But I am going to have to work out where I'm going to live now... and we are both in dire need of clothes."

"Oh... so you meant that stuff?"

"Yeah. I'm not quite ready to tackle the big shit just yet."

"Well, you're technically a part of the Order, seeing as you are literally the other half of Liam and a descendant of the original coven... We could just stay here?"

Connor screwed up his face. "That is possibly two of the worst things I could have heard right now," he grumbled.

"Like it or not, my love, you are one of us. But we can find some-where else if you don't want to stay here."

"Together?" He asked, his lips brushing lightly against mine.

"Together."

"Then I guess I can begrudgingly accept that, for the time being, I'm a member of the fucking Order of the Dragon." He kissed me harder, and we became lost in one another again.

This joining was different to any other between us.

Everything was soft.

Every caress was gentle.

Each kiss was tender.

Positioning himself over me, my legs wrapped tightly around

him, he slid in slowly, rolling his hips while his lips met mine softly. There was none of our usual hunger here, just love.

"I was wrong before," he whispered, slowly trailing kisses down my throat. "This is the moment that will play over in my mind."

He pulled away to look down at me, watching my face while he continued moving at a leisurely pace, and I felt another orgasm building. "You have burned yourself onto my heart, Isolde. Every single part of me belongs to you."

I reached up to caress his cheek.

"I love you," I whispered before throwing my head back, moaning when the pleasure slowly spread through every part of me, pulling him along with me, his cries mingling with mine while we each found yet another part of ourselves to share with the other.

CHAPTER FORTY-ONE

That evening, the remaining daywalkers and Order members slowly reconvened at the Manor.

"Was there any sign of Ronson at home?" I asked Anika.

She had joined me in the Manor library while waiting for everyone else to arrive. Anthony was in the control centre with Daniel, learning about all the various systems. The fact that Anthony could even stand being in the Manor, much less have a civil conversation with one of the Order members, was impressive.

"No. All his stuff was gone, along with Eve's. It's almost like they never existed. Tabitha was gone when we got up... the house is pretty much empty now, aside from us and Michael," Anika said, looking down at her hands.

"There are other daywalkers, though, right?" I asked.

"There are a few of us, but not many. Eve had isolated herself quite a bit over the years, and now that I know what was going on, I understand why most of the original daywalkers distanced themselves from her and Ronson. I just thought it was her prickly personality. But it turns out they all knew her beforehand and didn't trust her."

"You mean... There are others from the original coven who are still alive?" I asked, and Anika raised an eyebrow.

"Maybe. We don't exactly keep track of each other."

I felt my shoulders drop a little.

"Why?" Anika asked.

"Well, it would be good to have a few people around who know about the realms... and can explain a few things for us..."

"Oh, you mean now that you and your sister are phoenixes and the guys are dragons? You mean those things?" Anika asked with a wry smile.

"Yeah. Amongst others," I replied, sitting back and taking a sip of the whiskey I'd been swirling around aimlessly in a glass.

"Well, I don't have any words of wisdom on that particular problem. But maybe we can work with the Order for a way to find them."

"Let's just add that to the very long list of things to do." I sighed.

Barbara appeared at the door. "I think we're all here now."

Anika and I nodded at her.

"Thanks, Barbara. We'll be right there."

She smiled briefly before leaving again. It was a smile that didn't quite reach her eyes. Of everyone, she was feeling Patrice's death the hardest. They had been friends for over a century, and I'd often wondered if there had been a romantic element to their relationship.

"What are you guys going to do now?" I asked Anika, getting to my feet.

"I have no idea," Anika said.

"Maybe you guys could move in here?" I asked, feeling Connor moments before he appeared at my side.

"Are you just trying to convince everyone to move here now?" He asked, and I shrugged.

"Why not? If we're all stuck in this life, we might as well be stuck together."

"That's the spirit," Anika said with a grin. "I don't know that there is enough room for us all here, to be honest. And I don't know that Anthony is quite there yet. But we'll be around."

"That's something, I guess."

We entered the conference room together, and I looked around to see who had joined us. Anika moved to sit next to Anthony, who was still chatting to Daniel. Gerard was talking to Barbara across the table from them, and Christian was watching Michael closely while he looked around the room, his face screwed up. Liam was sitting alone, reading through what looked like reports.

I looked around for Aurora, but I couldn't see her.

"We'll find Aurora later," Connor said quietly, and I turned to look at him.

"A problem for another day, right?"

"You're learning."

Gerard cleared his throat, and we took our seats across from him.

"So, we've been gathering some information. Reports have started coming from the other Manors, and the waters are receding in the areas with flooding. There hasn't been anything about volcanic activity today, but it will probably take more time before we can be certain. But there have been no reports of toads falling from the sky today, and judging by the return of the summer heat outside, I think it's safe to say things are calming down," he said, still looking exhausted.

"That's good. What about the other nightwalker nests? Have we tracked all of those down?" I asked, looking at Connor.

"I've given Gerard the locations of all the ones I was aware of. Hopefully, we'll be able to track down which ones they were taking all those bodies to, or we'll have quite a few new nightwalkers to deal with in the coming days."

"No thanks to you," Liam muttered under his breath.

I turned to glare at him. "No. We are not going to do this now. We couldn't stop what was happening, and you know it."

Liam held my gaze momentarily before looking back at the reports before him.

A few others shifted in their seats before Gerard spoke up again.

"The London Manor has been in touch as well. There have been reports of some... interesting creatures attacking people in the last twenty-four hours."

"So some things managed to get through before Seth could rebind the entrances to the other realms?" I asked, feeling dread begin to coil low in my belly.

"It would seem so. We've had multiple reports in different countries."

"What about here?" Connor asked.

Gerard was quiet for a moment. "We went back to the house earlier to ensure everything was safe. There were traces of magic in the air that I'd never detected before. It almost felt... I think other-worldly is the closest I could come to describing it." He exchanged a look with Barbara, who shuddered in response.

"Well... that doesn't sound great," Anika piped up, and a few of us nodded.

"So basically, instead of just dealing with nightwalkers, we now have an army of nightwalkers and a bunch of other creatures that none of us know how to kill, which are stuck here with no way to get back to where they've come from. And magic is no longer muted, so we potentially have thousands of humans who have woken up today with abilities they never knew existed," Anthony said, listing every-thing off on his fingers.

"That about sums it all up, yes," Christian said.

Anthony sat back in his chair and held both thumbs up. "Fucking fantastic."

"And here I was hoping we could just take a really fucking long holiday," Connor said, ignoring the look that Liam shot him.

"I think, aside from dealing with the nightwalker situation, which we are all more than equipped to do, all we can do with the other issues is wait and see what happens," Daniel said, speaking for the first time since we'd entered the room.

"We need to get the seers involved. We need to track down any original daywalkers that might still be alive. And try to get a read on where Ronson went. We'll need them if we have creatures from other realms wandering around," I said, and Barbara made a note on her notepad.

I still found it amusing that they took minutes during these meetings.

"Well... this has been a great meeting," Anthony said sarcastically.

Anika lay a hand on his arm.

"Are we going to have another elder here soon?" I looked over at Gerard.

He and Barbara were now the most senior Order members for the Brisbane chapter.

"I've spoken to the elders today, and they've agreed that, for the time being, Barbara and I will run things. We are stretched too thin all over the world, and honestly, after what happened with Damon infiltrating our ranks, I doubt we'll warm to anyone new coming in... at least for the time being."

The remaining Order members nodded, exchanging relieved glances. I noticed that Daniel was eyeing Connor warily. I'd been so caught up in the animosity between the brothers that I'd temporarily forgotten that Daniel held Connor responsible for Celeste's death. The allegiances in this room were on pretty shaky ground.

"Well... I guess that's it then," I said, looking around the table to see if anyone else had anything to add.

Everyone rose to their feet and started to head off in various directions.

"Isolde?" I stopped at the door, looking back to see Liam still sitting at the table.

I waited until everyone else had left, including Connor, who hesitated at my side for a moment before following Anika and Anthony out of the room.

I stayed near the door, unsure of how this conversation would go.

"What are you planning to do now?" Liam asked quietly.

I knew he wasn't just asking about me.

"I don't know. Given that my house was flooded and things with us..." I waved my hand between us half-heartedly. "I don't really have anywhere else to go... and neither does Connor."

Liam scowled.

"Is this going to be too hard for you? I don't want to make things uncomfortable for anyone, least of all you. And this place is as much your home as mine. Maybe even more so." He had been with them for hundreds of years, after all.

Liam let out a long exhale while he stared at his hands. "I don't think I can stay in the same house, knowing how things are between you."

I nodded, expecting as much.

"I'll go back to my place," he said, and I shook my head.

"I don't think you should be alone, Liam."

"Well, I don't have much other choice, Isolde," he replied, saying my name with a bite in his tone.

I looked at him for a moment while I mulled over our options. "We'll go back to Eve's place. Anika was saying how empty it was. That way, you can be here with the others and won't have to deal with... us."

He regarded me for a moment. "You'd do that? You hated it there."

"I hated Eve. Now that she's gone... it would be nice to make it somewhere I'd want to be. But I'll still have to be here. We all need to work together now with all this other stuff."

He nodded stiffly.

"Do you have any idea where Aurora went?" I asked.

"Possibly to your parents. She didn't really check in with me when she disappeared last night."

I nodded. It was about time I went and saw my family anyway.

"I'll try my best not to be a dick to Connor," Liam said, getting to his feet.

I shot him a weak smile. "That would be nice... but I'm not

expecting any miracles. I know it will be a long time before you two manage to sort out your differences."

Liam scoffed. "I think it will be a very long time, Isolde."

"Well... it's a good thing we're all immortal now, isn't it."

CHAPTER FORTY-TWO

Connor and I stood in the hallway on the second floor of Eve's house, staring at all the closed doors.

"Well, we obviously can't take that room," Connor said, glaring at the door to the bedroom I'd been using.

"Why not?" I asked, surprised.

He turned to look at me with an incredulous look. "Just stop and think about it for a second, Isolde."

It took me far too long to realise he meant because Liam and I had shared the room. "Oh."

"Yes. Oh," he replied with a raised eyebrow and crossed his arms.

"Well... what about the room you were using?"

"It's too small," he said, and I laughed at his grumpy tone.

"Why don't you guys just take Eve and Ronson's old room?" Anthony called out from further down the hall.

"No!" We shot back, and Anthony cackled.

I smiled when I heard the sound of a hand smacking flesh and Anthony's responding grunt when Anika said, "Shut up."

"I guess we could check the other rooms," Connor said, giving me a wary glance.

"Lead on," I said, waving him ahead of me.

"Don't check out my ass," he said with a smirk when he walked in front of me.

"I promise nothing," I said, loving hearing his responding laugh.

After we finally settled on one of the rooms on the third floor, I got into my car for the first time in weeks and prayed it would start. Although I was incredibly grateful that my transition to a full phoenix meant that I no longer needed to drink blood, I was a little sad to have lost some of my other vampire senses, such as being able to run all over the city in the blink of an eye.

Connor had grumbled that he needed to learn to drive now, which I had found far more humorous than he thought I should.

On the drive to Briseis' house, I tried to work out what I should say to my family, hoping that Aurora was there. After pulling up in the driveway, I sat in the car for a few minutes, staring at the garage door while I worked up the nerve to go inside.

A tap on the driver's side window made me jump, and I placed my hand over my racing heart while I looked up to see my father smiling at me through the glass. He didn't seem at all surprised by the change in my eyes.

"Hey, you. I was wondering when you were going to show up."

"Sorry... It's been an interesting few weeks." I said, climbing out of the car and letting him pull me into a hug.

"So I've heard."

"About that... what do you know?" I asked, stepping out of his arms and falling into step beside him while we walked to the front door.

"Your sister arrived early this morning with the most fascinating story, with eyes that appeared to be made of blue flames. But she has also been a complete mess, so we're trying to piece everything together."

I nodded grimly and let him lead the way inside.

We found Mum and Briseis in the lounge room, where Briseis' children were staring at the TV, transfixed by the cartoon blue cattle dog dancing around on the screen.

Briseis looked up when we entered the room and ran to hug me, holding me tightly while she sniffled over my shoulder.

"What's all this about?" I asked.

She shook her head and stepped back, wiping away a tear. "I'm just so glad you're both okay."

"Where's Aurora?" I asked after I'd hugged Mum and ruffled the hair on each kid's head.

Neither of them looked up, too caught up in their show. I couldn't blame them; I'd watched this show with them a few times over the years and loved it. Maybe I needed to babysit to catch up on it with them. Just do everyday, boring, human things for a while.

"She's upstairs sleeping. We might need you to fill us in on everything that happened. I know you rang me to explain that Aurora was no longer a -" Mum cut herself off, looking down at the little people lying on the floor, and indicated we should all head into the kitchen away from prying ears.

"Yeah... honestly, I'm not sure how much of the story you all want to hear, but yes – Aurora is no longer a threat. At least, not to anyone but herself," I said, sighing.

I sat at the dining table while Briseis started busying herself, making tea, and my parents joined me.

"What about William?" Dad asked, an over-protective look on his face.

I glanced at Mum, and she shook her head. She mustn't have shared the news of Will's last death with Dad.

"Will is... he's no longer an issue."

"Ah..." Dad looked away, and I knew he'd worked it out.

"And what about your vampire status?" Mum asked, watching me closely.

"I'm no longer a vampire..." I said, not sure how to tell them what I had become.

"Aurora mentioned something about a phoenix... honestly, her story was so all over the place, but I looked it up. Is that what you are? Some mythical creature that is basically a ball of fire and can never die?" Briseis asked, her eyes wide.

I looked between the three of them and sighed again.

"That's a pretty accurate assessment of what I am... What Aurora and I both are."

"But... how..." Mum was struggling to form the right questions and coming up short.

"Honestly, this may all fall under the banner of 'you don't really want to know', but we were created to have these abilities. It was all part of some elaborate spell to get a phoenix and a dragon's powers back."

My words were met with complete silence and astonished looks.

"Yeah... probably best that we just leave that all alone," Briseis said finally, and I couldn't help but laugh.

"But... it's all over now, right? You guys won?" She continued, and I paused before responding, working out how much they needed to know.

"For now... we're not sure if more bad stuff is going to happen, but the stuff I've been dealing with for the past year is done with at least."

"Okay." She nodded.

We talked about mundane family things a little longer until I finished my tea and got to my feet.

"I should go and speak to Aurora before I leave."

"Just... go easy on her, Isolde. I know she messed up before all of this happened, but after losing her once... I can't bear to see this family fall apart again," Mum said, and I looked at her for a moment, contemplating her words.

"Mum... I think you're going to have to accept the fact that some things can never be mended. I'm glad she's alive, but we have a long way to go before I can forgive her for what she did with Will. And she's got a long way to go to deal with everything that has happened since." I didn't wait for her to respond, heading upstairs to the room Briseis had told me Aurora was sleeping in.

I knocked lightly on the door before opening it, finding my twin sitting in the middle of the bed, staring at her hands.

"Hi," I said, stepping into the room and closing the door quietly behind me.

Aurora looked up at me and nodded. Neither of us spoke for the longest time.

"Are you okay?" I asked finally, not sure what else I could say at this point.

Aurora raised an eyebrow. "What do you think?"

"I think you've been through a lot of shit and are going to need help getting through it."

"And let me guess... You're going to be the one to do it? To rescue your poor, broken sister."

"Nope," I replied, and she blinked at me. I could tell that wasn't the response she'd been expecting. "I wouldn't have the first clue on how to help you, and we've got too much shit between us for me to be of any help to you. But I think you should speak to the people in the Order. It's not like you can just start seeing a regular therapist with everything you've been through."

Aurora regarded me thoughtfully, and I didn't attempt to speak again. Once upon a time, I would have felt the need to fill these silent pauses, but now, I just needed her to take control of her life.

"I'll think about it," she said finally, and I nodded, returning to the door.

"I am sorry, you know." I just barely heard the words, and I swung back to see her staring at her hands again. "About Will... about all of it."

I closed my eyes for a moment, working to keep the mixture of grief and anger in check. I didn't want to produce those flaming wings in my sister's house until I could control when they disappeared.

"Maybe one day we'll be able to put it all behind us... We have an eternity ahead of us, I guess. But today isn't that day, Aura. I'm glad you're alive and that you were able to help with everything the other night... But... I'm not there yet."

"Neither am I." Her features hardened, and I shook my head.

"Just... go and speak to someone at the Order. And soon. Mum and Dad don't know how to help you, and honestly, I don't want any of them tied up in this life."

She didn't bother responding again, and I left, unsure if the conversation had even been worth having.

I arrived back at Eve's house and stared up at it. I would need to stop referring to it as Eve's if it was ever to feel like it was my home.

Knowing that Connor was waiting inside for me helped, though. Wherever he was, that was home now.

However cheesy that sounded.

But I also knew that the Manor was still a haven for me. And that was because of Liam. Even though we weren't together anymore, I needed him. I needed Connor to be okay with that, and I needed Liam to be okay with Connor.

So much of all our lives were up in the air, but for now, I planned to take each day slowly and deal with whatever came along without focusing on being the Chosen One anymore.

I figured I could live with that for now.

EPILOGUE

LIAM

I didn't know if I would ever get used to the change in my eyes. I'd been staring at myself in the mirror for a good twenty minutes when someone pounded on my bedroom door.

At least I didn't have to worry about drinking blood anymore, but that was at least easier to hide, and I'd perfected that lifestyle over five hundred years. Adjusting to this new normal was going to take a while.

I strode to the door, pulling on a shirt before opening it. I'd made the mistake of opening the door shirtless to find Isolde there an hour ago, and neither of us had been particularly comfortable during the exchange when she'd asked if I'd seen Aurora. I was growing tired of constantly watching over others, and babysitting a reluctant phoenix wasn't how I wanted to spend the rest of eternity.

"What's up?" I asked, looking at Gerard while he stood outside my door.

"We've managed to find Aurora," he replied with a frown.

I fought back a sigh. "Where is she?"

"Christian managed to track her down in a bar in the Valley. She's very drunk and refusing to leave. Of the three of you, we figured you were the least likely to have trouble getting her out of there without drawing too much attention to the situation."

"Of course. If Isolde showed up, Aurora would throw a tantrum, and Connor would just throw her out the door without giving a shit who sees. Got it," I said, hearing the bitterness in my tone.

Gerard nodded with an apologetic smile.

"No worries, I'll go get her. How's Barbara going with figuring out that charm to hide these?" I asked, pointing at my flaming eyes.

"She's almost got it, but you'll need these again for now," Gerard said, handing me the sunglasses that had become a permanent part of my attire for the past month.

I nodded.

It wasn't anyone else's fault that the four of us were now stuck wearing sunglasses in public, regardless of the time of day. But the sooner Barbara came up with the right spell to hide all our new unique abilities from non-magical eyes, the better. In theory, it should be the same as the magic used to conceal the Manors, but it was proving difficult when applied to a living creature instead of a building.

"I think she's still struggling with using her magic while grieving Patrice. Her abilities don't seem as pronounced as the rest of us yet," Gerard said, his face softening.

"They were together for eighty years... I think it's going to take more than a few months to deal with what was lost."

When Barbara finally admitted that she and Patrice had been more than friends for all these years, we were not surprised. Their connection had long been noted, but they had chosen to keep it between themselves for their own reasons, and none of us had ever pushed them to discuss it. Most Order members sought their sexual releases outside of the Manors. The strain between myself and Isolde was more than enough reason for me to avoid ever being with anyone else who lived this life ever again.

I pushed aside the usual wave of anger that rose within me when I had to endure seeing Isolde and Connor together. The fact that we all worked for the Order and had to share space during the day when they were in Manor was enough to drive me to drink.

Perhaps I should simply join Aurora while she pissed her immortal life away rather than drag her out of yet another fucking bar.

I made the short walk to the Valley from the Manor and found the bar Gerard had told me Aurora was holed up in. Christian met me at the door, looking pissed.

"She is refusing to leave. I'm worried about her losing control of her powers and torching the whole fucking place," he said, raking a hand through his hard.

"Do Isolde and Connor know we've found her yet?" I asked, their names leaving a bitter taste in my mouth.

"Yeah, they are on their way. They'll take over dealing with her once you get her out of there."

I nodded and made my way inside. She'd picked one of the grimiest bars to drown her sorrows, which didn't surprise me. I'd found her in worse places over the past few weeks, and I knew we needed to get her help as soon as possible. Amongst everything else, it really wasn't a great idea to have a drunk and depressed phoenix doing the rounds of Brisbane's seediest bars. Although she was more than capable of holding her own, the sweet and innocent appearance had brought her attention of the lecherous kind, and I'd had to knock more than a few assholes out before she could set them on fire.

"Oh, look. They've sent the hero to come and save me again," Aurora said, her words slightly slurred. She drained the glass in her hand before slamming it back down on the bar. "Another one," she said, glaring at the bartender.

He shook his head and looked at me. "Get her out of here, mate. She's had more than enough," he said.

"Hey! Don't talk to him. I'm right here," she said, smacking her hand on the bar.

He glared at her. "Fine. Get out before I get security to kick your ass out."

Aurora's hands flexed, and I saw a tell-tale blue spark shoot from her fingers at her side, out of the bartender's view. I cleared the distance between us in two steps and grabbed her hand.

"Don't even fucking try it. We. Are. Leaving," I said, glaring down at her.

"Sure thing, Dad," she replied, making no move to follow me.

I growled, having had enough. I grabbed her and threw her over my shoulder.

"Good call, mate." The bartender's words followed me out the door while Aurora shrieked at me, pounding her fists against my back.

I set her down in the alley outside and turned her to face Isolde and Connor, who both looked as pissed as I was.

"Oh yay, the whole family is here," Aurora said.

I closed my eyes and breathed heavily through my nose, trying to shake off the desire to smother her.

"Seriously, Aurora. What the fuck?" Connor said, his jaw clenched. "As if we don't have enough shit to deal with, having to remove you from bars constantly is getting fucking old."

"Agreed," Isolde said, avoiding looking at me just as much as I was avoiding looking at her.

"So just leave me alone, then." Aurora shrugged.

"I would fucking love to, however, you are a liability until you get your shit sorted. So quit drinking and acting like a fucking child." Connor's voice shook, and I saw the flames in his eyes through his sunglasses.

"Well, well. What do we have here?" A voice said from behind him and Isolde, and they spun so that all four of us were staring into the darkness together.

A woman stepped out of the shadows and ran her gaze over us.

"Yeah, lady, you really don't want to get involved with this," Connor said.

The woman's lips split into a wide, unnatural smile, her sharp teeth glistening in the darkness.

This was no ordinary woman.

"What the hell..." Isolde whispered, stepping back slightly.

The woman moved towards her, and Connor jumped between them, kicking the woman back into the darkness.

I shoved Aurora behind me while Isolde let her powers out, her purple flames wrapping around her and into the flowing wings of fire that I would never get used to seeing.

"Ooohh... a phoenix," the creature said, stepping back out of the shadows.

Isolde raised her hand, a ball of flame forming, ready to be launched. But the sound of metal scrapping against metal from behind the creature made it turn around.

It let out a short scream before it was cut off by a sword, appearing as if from nowhere and slicing its head off.

None of us moved when another woman, dressed in black leather pants and a jacket, stepped into the light.

"So... this is the famous team of phoenixes and dragons I've been hearing about," she said, sliding her sword back into its sheath at her side while she surveyed us all.

"Hardly a team," Aurora said with a scoff.

I glared at her before returning my gaze to the woman before us.

Isolde was still surrounded by her purple flames, and Connor was poised, ready to strike beside her.

"Who are you?" I asked.

She took her time answering, running her eyes over each one of us slowly. She didn't look impressed.

"They call me Imogen."

"Okay, Imogen. What was that, and how did you know how to kill it?" Isolde asked, her flames dimming until all that was left was the ball of purple fire in her hand.

"That was a faerie. And I know how to kill it because that's my job."

"A fairy? Like Tinkerbell?" Aurora asked.

"I don't know what the fuck a Tinkerbell is, but that sounds far too sweet of a name to apply to any of those creatures." Imogen sighed.

"You're not from our world, are you?" Isolde asked, letting the fire die.

"No. And I need your help. Although I must admit, I was expecting a lot more." She looked at Connor and me in succession. "You two don't even know how to shift, do you?"

Connor shot me a questioning look, and I shrugged. She'd obviously heard about us from somewhere, but I had no clue what was happening.

"God, you're all just babies. This is going to be so much harder than I thought."

"Hey, I'm over five hundred years old. Watch who you're calling a baby," Connor said while I bristled at her words.

"How nice for you. When you're over a thousand, perhaps you'll work out how to actually access your powers."

"Hey, for someone who says they need our help, you're not really winning our trust right now," Isolde said.

Imogen sighed again.

"Seriously, who are you?" Aurora asked.

"I am from another realm. And I need your help to get home. After we hunt down all the creatures coming through from my world."

The four of us froze and then looked at each other.

"What do you mean, coming through? The portals are closed," Connor said, his eyes narrowed.

"Well, you missed one. Because I watched her come through one not far from here about three hours ago and was hunting her ever since."

"Fuck," Connor said, looking at me quickly before turning to look at Isolde.

"Yes... Fuck indeed," Imogen said. "I think we need to go and speak to your people, don't you?"

She pushed through our little group and marched out of the alley, leaving us staring at each other, wondering what the fuck had just happened.

I guess this wasn't as over as we'd hoped.

IF YOU HAVE A MOMENT

Please take a moment to leave a rating or review on the platform you purchased from or Goodreads. Every review helps in an incredible way.

ACKNOWLEDGMENTS

This book could not have been written without the love and support of my husband, Andrew. Having you by my side and cheering me on while I've navigated my way through the many phases of sharing my work with the world has made it far less daunting. Olives you!

To my daughter, Evelyn, thank you for being my biggest fan even though you haven't read a single word in these books. Having you tell everyone we meet that Mummy writes books makes my heart swell a million times bigger.

To my sister, Melinda, thank you for being as invested in this journey as I am and for teaching me how to actually talk to people about my books without completely freezing up!

To Jammi-Lee and Shannon, thank you for your honest feedback and love of these characters. I couldn't have asked for two more dedicated beta readers and proofreaders!

To my amazing editor and one of my oldest friends, Krystal, thank you for your dedication to ensuring that my words make sense. If it hadn't been for all our late-night/early-morning Facetime chats from opposite sides of the world talking about our love of books, I don't think I ever would have been brave enough to start sharing my stories with others.

To the Writing Friday gals, Lauren, Mel, Kaitlyn and Demi, thank you for all the pep talks and unhinged chat sessions. You have all helped me to understand the author space in ways I never thought possible. Every time we meet, I learn something new!

To Charmi-Lee, thank you for being my super fan and introducing me to the Brisbane Book Club group! Having readers like you makes this whole author journey so rewarding.

And finally, to all the members of the Bookstagram community that I have had the absolute pleasure of interacting with, thank you for creating a safe space for Indie Authors and being our biggest supporters.